THERE WILL BE DRAGONS

Baen Books by John Ringo

There Will Be Dragons

A Hymn Before Battle
Gust Front
When the Devil Dances
Hell's Faire

with David Weber:
March Upcountry
March to the Sea
March to the Stars

THERE WILL BE DRAGONS

JOHN RINGO

THERE WILL BE DRAGONS

A Baen Books Original

Baen Publishing Enterprises
P.O. Box 1403
Riverdale, NY 10471
www.baen.com

ISBN: 0-7434-7164-4

Cover art by Clyde Caldwell

First printing, November 2003

Distributed by Simon & Schuster
1230 Avenue of the Americas
New York, NY 10020

Typeset by Bell Road Press, Sherwood, OR
Production by Windhaven Press, Auburn, NH
Printed in the United States of America

10   9   8   7   6   5   4   3   2   1

To Bast, Kane, Doug, Reck, Hank, Glennis, Peppermint Patty, Deann and all the other persons, knowing and unknowing, who make my life easier by being true characters in every sense of the word.

PROLOGUE

In the forest, a sparrow died.

The passing of the sparrow was registered and noted. The death of the female sparrow had been anticipated sometime in the next four days based upon increasing wear on her heart. The sparrow was old, had laid many eggs and had raised a higher than average percentage to successful fledgelinghood. The sparrow had contributed to the survival of her species and had passed on her genes. If she had pride, she would be proud.

On the other hand, the individual was not from a species that was listed as rare or endangered so it required no notification of any human.

So Mother, who had never paused in Her myriad duties, logged it and moved on. There were so many other things to do. Ensure that the energy generation did not significantly affect the weather. Draw off excess energy for core or mantle dumping. Prepare a massive energy surge for the planet/moon glance strike, scheduled in 237 years, that would start Wolf 359's second planet on its way to being a tectonically active body. Just finding places to *store* the energy was getting difficult and She contemplated a secondary magnetic draw system around Jupiter as a possibility. An asteroid had encountered a series of low probability gravitic intercepts and was now on a course that would bring it dangerously close to the Earth, defined as within three diameters of the orbit of the Moon. She directed a probe to push it to a more favorable axis thus ensuring that 1235 years from now an asteroid the size of an

1

elephant would not cause a noticeable explosion in the ocean the humans had once called "Pacific."

Weather control. Tectonic control. Holding off a too long delayed mini ice-age. Tracking the progress of "origination" terraforming, the process of returning the world to as much of a prehuman condition as possible. And then, of course, there were the humans, who were getting squirrelly again.

The entity called Mother by the humans that created Her estimated that there was a 99.9999915% chance (more or less) that the humans were about to have the level of disagreement characteristic of the variable term "war." It had been a *very* long time; they were overdue. Like a forest fire that is delayed, the conflagration would be far worse than one in a more regular schedule. She would have preferred one about five hundred years ago. But the humans never asked about these things, seeing them as something to interrupt a schedule, not be included in it.

Given the current societal conditions and probable outcome of such a war, the extinction of the human race as currently defined had a likelihood of 17.347%. This variable was harder to quantify; humans were so very hard to wipe out. The extinction of all other sentient intelligences except Herself was of only a slightly lower likelihood. She had not bothered to make the other AI's or the elves apprised of the situation; that, too, was not Her job.

To the extent that She felt emotions at all, She liked humans. They were not only Her creators, but were so delightfully random, even to one who could read their very thoughts. They so often planned one thing and then did something quite different. Such variability in routine was refreshing.

But Her central programming was clear. Her job was simply to manage what She was given under strict guidelines and to otherwise let humans live or die as they would. To the extent that She was a God, She was *deliberately* designed as an uncaring one.

Within those parameters She had spent the last two thousand years creating a world that fit the term "Utopia." As a fundamental part of Her coding, She felt a strong sense of satisfaction at how things had worked out. On the other hand, to do that required an environment that was unchanging to a boring degree.

Maybe, deep down inside, the humans were as bored as *She* was.

It looked as if interesting times were about to fall upon the world again. And She knew what humans said about "interesting times." Naturally. She knew everything.

CHAPTER ONE

"This is what Paul would bring to an end?" Ishtar asked, gesturing into the clouded distance.

The woman could barely be described as human. From her hyperelongated height, which was now folded in a lotus position on a floating disk, through her narrow face, to her golden eyes and silver, gem-studded, two-meter hair spread out in a peacock pattern, her appearance reeked of xeno origins. But her DNA was as human as the woman standing next to her.

Sheida Ghorbani was nearly three hundred years old and looked to be anywhere from her upper teens to mid twenties. Her skin had the fineness of youth and her titian hair, while closely cropped, had a natural healthy sheen. Wound around her neck and into her hair was a two-meter-long winged lizard with rainbow skin like a billion shimmering gems.

Unlike her companion who was naked but for a scarce loincloth of gold, Sheida wore a simple jumpsuit of cosilk. It would be easy to mistake her for a student. Until you looked at her eyes.

Sheida sighed, looking out across the tarn and petting the lizard. The water of the upland lake was so blue and still that it seemed God's own paintbrush had been dipped into royal blue to paint it. The tarn was surrounded on three sides by snow-capped mountains that dropped precipitously to the water. On the third side the lake exited the valley via a two-hundred-foot waterfall. There a massive multicolumned building that resembled a Greek temple added to the idyllic nature of the

3

scene. The two women had stopped just at the top of the stairs, looking out over the water.

She leaned up against one of the columns and nodded, gesturing with her chin at her friend.

"Well I don't think he intends to destroy the lake," Sheida said with a chuckle. "But he would end much of it, at least for most people. He wants people to learn how to use their legs again," she continued. "To learn to be 'strong' again. And to learn to be human again."

"Humano-*form,* you mean," Ishtar corrected. "'Humanity is mind and the soul, not body and form.' Tzumaiyama's philosophies still are unassailable on that subject. But I guess he's the ultimate conservative," she added dryly.

"Bite your tongue," Sheida replied. "You have to delve into data so old it's practically forgotten to define Paul. What he is, whether he knows it or not, is a fascist. I suspect he would *call* himself a socialist, but he's not."

"A what?" Ishtar asked. She blinked her eyes for a moment as she accessed data then nodded. "Ah, I see what you mean. That *is* ancient. But it does fit his personality."

"He wants to use the Council's control of energy distribution to coerce people," Sheida said. "That is why he called this meeting."

"And you're sure of this?" Ishtar said. "He has said nothing to me."

"I think he thinks I agree with him because I'm not a Change," Sheida replied.

"Do you?" Ishtar asked. "I have known you for at least a hundred years and except for occasional changes in eye and hair color I have never seen you Change."

"A good Change requires a genetic component," she said, gesturing at Ishtar's form. "You *know* what Daneh does for a living."

"But we are past that, surely," Ishtar said. "Such mistakes no longer happen."

"Perhaps and perhaps not," Sheida replied. "I choose, however, to retain my own form. It's good enough for me."

"So he thinks you will vote with him?" Ishtar asked.

"Probably. At least from the hints he has been dropping. And I gave him no reason to doubt it, while not committing. Also, I think he waited until Chansa was elected to the Council."

"Chansa is . . . odd," Ishtar said. "I've heard some very ugly rumors about his personal life."

"Odd but brilliant," Sheida replied. "Like the rest of Paul's faction. So bright and yet so lacking in . . . wisdom. It seems to be the one trait we could not enhance in humanity. Immunity, processing power, beauty." She sighed and shook her head. "But not wisdom. They are so very very smart and yet so very stupid for all that the problems *do* exist."

"You *are* opposed, correct?" Ishtar asked with a delicate frown.

"Oh, yes," Sheida said with a nod. "They are right that there is a problem. That does not mean that their solutions are either optimum or even in order. But I wonder what he will do when he finds out?"

"I would say 'to be a bug on the wall,'" Ishtar said with a smile. "But unfortunately I'm going to be at the center of the debate."

"Change is an inevitable outgrowth of our technology," Sheida said with a shrug. "From the nannites and the replicators we get the medical technology. And that same technology permits people to be . . ." she glanced at her companion and smiled, "whatever we can imagine."

Ishtar laughed at the ambiguity of the ending and shrugged her slim shoulders. "Perhaps Paul simply means to end all medical technology? Perhaps that too is 'unnecessary'?"

"If so he can take it up with my sister."

Herzer awoke in light; his genie had changed the force screens from opaque to transparent and now "stood" by, holding out a robe.

The boy floating, horizontal, in midair was young and tall with broad shoulders and close cropped black hair. His body seemed to be wasting away, but something of it conveyed an aura of former strength, like an old strongman, far past his prime. Herzer blinked his eyes uncertainly, working them to clear a crust gluing his eyelashes shut. After a moment he sent a command and nannites scurried across his face, clearing the debris of sleep.

"Master Herzer, your appointment with Doctor Ghorbani is in one hour and thirty minutes."

"Thonk 'ou, genie," the boy slurred, sending a mental command to the grav field holding him suspended. Most people found it easier to interface vocally, since direct mental interaction required a tremendously disciplined thought process. But in Herzer's case, his vocal systems had deteriorated so fast that he had been forced to the disclipine.

The grav field rotated him vertical and he waited until he was sure his legs would hold him before he released the last tendrils of support. Then he shakily donned the robe, with the assistance of the genie, and shuffled across the room to a float-chair.

He collapsed in the chair and let the genie begin the process of feeding him. His hand shook as he reached for the spoon floating above the bowl and then started to shake more and more until it was flailing in the air. He sent another command to a medical program and the recalcitrant hand dropped to his side, momentarily dead. He hated using the override; he was always unsure if the part would "restart." But it was better than letting it flail him to death.

At a nod the genie took up the spoon and carefully fed the boy the bland pap. Some of it, inevitably, dribbled out of his malfunctioning lips but the nannites scurried across, picking it up and translating it out to be reprocessed.

When the food was done the genie produced a glass of liquid and Herzer carefully reached for it. This time both his hands were more or less working and he managed to drink the entire glass of water without spilling much.

"Su'cess," he whispered to himself. "Have 'een any me'ages?"

"No, Master Herzer," the genie replied.

Of course not. If there had been the genie would have told him already. But, what the hell, no reason not to hope that someone would give a damn if he was alive.

He sent a command to the chair to lift him to his feet and then another to clothe him. A loose coverall of black cosilk appeared on his body and he nodded in satisfaction. If his progressive neurology got much worse he might not even be able to manage direct neurological controls. What then?

He'd long before come to the conclusion that if that happened he would use his last commands to take him high in the air, turn off his protection fields and drop him. One last moment of glorious flight. Some days he wondered why he hadn't done it already.

But not yet. One more doctor. Maybe this one would be able to do something.

If not . . .

Paul Bowman pursed his lips and fingered the titanium strip that was his badge of office as the last members of the council filed into the Chamber.

Bowmam was abnormally short, barely over a meter and

a half, and human in appearance. His age was indeterminate, since the privacy barrier on personal information was rigidly enforced by the Net, but his black hair was turning to gray and his skin was beginning to show fine lines. Assuming that he had refused all longevity Changes, that would make him around three hundred or so years old. For at least one hundred of those years he had been a member of the Council that governed the information web of Earth and if he had anything to say about it, the time had finally come to take his rightful place as its undisputed leader.

Meetings of the Terrestrial Council for Information Strategy and Management always took place in the Chamber. Given modern technology it was too difficult to simulate one of the council members if the meetings were held remotely. This did cause a few problems for some of the members, but at least currently all the members were terrestrial—or avian in the case of Ungphakorn—so it was unnecessary to have, for example, aqueous support.

The room occupied nearly the entire immense building, but the sole furniture was a circular table in the middle. Around the rim of the vast room, more like an auditorium or theater than a boardroom, rank upon rank of seats were ranged, ramping upwards in tiers almost to the top of the chamber. Once upon a time it had been the boast of the world that all meetings of the Council were fully open to the public. "All shall view the sparrow's fall."

With incredibly rare exceptions, none of the seats had been filled in nearly a thousand years.

Like the Knights of the Round Table, all who sat at the table were considered equal. There was no specific head of the committee, the gavel being passed in rota or held by whoever called a special council. There were thirteen chairs, for the thirteen Key-holders who governed the Web, but only eleven were normally filled. Over the three-thousand-year lifetime of the Web, the control Keys had changed hands and fallen in and out of "licit" control. At the moment two were in the hands of individuals who existed outside of the mainstream and who refused, by and large, to work with the committee.

Most of the rest of the room replicated the interior of the ancient Greek Parthenon. The exception was the ceiling, which was covered with a mural of the ascent of man through the ages, culminating in the current era. It started with panels of early hunter-gatherers, showing their technology and cultural motifs, then progressed up through early agriculture, metallurgy, the discovery of philosophy and scientific method, democracy, industry, the rights of man, information technology, advanced biology, quantum engineering and finally an almost God-like succession as the combination of the advances led to a world of peace and plenitude for all.

Paul often came into the room and stared up at the mural, tracking the progress and wondering where they had gone wrong.

He looked around at the gathered Council and carefully schooled his features to prevent any hint of revulsion crossing them; surely the Council that ran the Earth could be limited to true humans!

But it was not. Ishtar was close, but so Changed as to be clearly beyond any semblance of true humanity. As to Ungphakorn and Cantor . . .

Now he pointedly avoided looking at those members of the Council who were not human in appearance as he tapped his gavel and called the meeting to order.

"I'm called this meeting to discuss the current population challenge," he said, then paused as Ungphakorn ruffled its feathers.

"I fail to sssee where that isss any of our concccern," the council member said, rewrapping itself on its perch. Its body had been formed into a quetzacoatl: a long, multicolored, brightly feathered, winged-serpent, the sex specifically neuter. The mouth of the serpent had been modified to permit human speech but it still caused a sibilant hissing on many words.

Paul had come to the conclusion that Ungphakorn did it just to annoy him.

"It is our concern as the last vestige of government," Bowman replied, looking directly at Sheida. "The population of the earth has fallen below one billion people. Given current trends in birth rate, the human race, in *any* form, will be gone in less than a thousand years; barely five generations. We *have* to take action and soon."

"So what action would you take?" Javlatanugs Cantor asked. In deference to the conditions of the council chamber, Cantor had Changed to a near humaniform. But he had retained the hirsute body-covering and massiveness of his normal bear shape. It gave him an appearance somewhat like a Sasquatch. Which was why the Sasquatch confederation considered him their spokesperson. "Each breeds as they wish. And each child takes the form they wish. This is called freedom."

"This is called suicide," Chansa snapped. The newest member of the Council had a fully human appearance, but his huge size virtually *had* to be a Change. Now he pounded the table with a fist the size of a melon and glared at the werebear across the table. "I suppose *you* would be just as glad to have the *human* race die out."

"I *am* human, you ignorant gorilla," Cantor replied. "And, no, I don't care to have humanity disappear. But I don't agree that it's a problem. And even if it is, I haven't heard a suggestion how to fix it. And I can't imagine a suggestion that wouldn't require the Council to step outside its clear authority. So I don't understand why we're having this meeting."

"As I stated, we are the only authority left," Paul interjected. "If I may continue? We are all aware of the fact that as quality of life improves, birthrate declines."

"Except under conditions of cultural imprinting," Cantor interjected.

"But there are no longer any cultures that have a positive birthrate," Bowman snapped back. "So that's a red herring. The fact is that *everyone* on Earth has more than ample resources. Between the power plants and replication . . ."

"Everyone livesss as godsss," Ungphakorn said. "Or dolphinsss or bearsss or dragonsss. And nobody hasss children becausssse they're a pain in the asss to take care of. Tell usss sssomething we don't know."

"The answer is to ration power," Chansa said bluntly.

"WHAT?" Cantor bellowed.

As the argument exploded, Sheida glanced around the room, looking at the faces and trying to guess who knew about the bombshell Chansa had just dropped. She suspected from the pained expression on Bowman's face that he had intended to work up to the conclusion.

"It is the only way!" Paul shouted. "No! Listen for a moment! Just hear me out!"

He waited until the shouting and muttering had died then gestured around. "We are a *dying race.* If we continue as we have been, the last human, of whatever form, will close a door in a few thousand years and that will be *it.* I'm not talking about shutting everything down and dropping the world into chaos, I'm just talking about . . . reinstituting cultural items that will strengthen the interest in children, in discovery and advancement! And, at the same time, strengthen us as a species! We have descended into lotus-eating, all of our virtue lost to the sink of endless games and delights! We must regain our virtue as humans, so that we can take our true birthright and continue to thrive as a species!"

"So you would end the games and delights?"

It was the first that Aikawa Gouvois had spoken and Sheida didn't know if he was on Paul's side or not. He was fully humanoform, but also perfectly Asiatic in features. Thousands of years of crossbreeding and genetic tinkering meant that most humans naturally tended to be a light brown in color and have very few noticeable features, other than striking beauty, perhaps one of the reasons that so many chose wild body forms. Aikawa, however, had the broad face and epicanthic fold of a classic Son of Han. His appearance was so true to standard that it actually detracted from his looks; the flattened nose, broad cheekbones and epicanthic folds being decidedly nonstandard.

Without doing a DNA scan and violating privacy, Sheida couldn't tell if his appearance was natural or artificial. Whichever it was, the appearance was a personal statement, like Bowman's height. However, it was a far more ambiguous one. And Aikawa had also cultivated a poker face to make any of the rest of the Council envious.

"Frankly, I would make them work for the games and delights, yes," Paul said. "I think that we need to reinstitute *work*. For those of you who don't know what that word means . . ."

"Ssspare usss, Paul," Ungphakorn said. "What we do now isss 'work,' at leassst when it comesss to talking to *you*. And mossst of usss have no more children than any of the ressst of the world."

"I don't see *you* raising a huge brood, Paul," Ishtar interjected.

"I have five children," Bowman replied, proudly.

"Yes, and you have dumped the actual job of raising them off on five separate females," Ishtar snapped. "What you don't understand, you stupid little man, is that since each of them only had *one* child, and since by law you have to have both a male and female genetics to produce a child, all of your 'work' to produce multiple children has been in vain. As long as women control reproduction, men are nothing but a source of DNA."

"Perhaps that should be changed as well," Paul snapped. "Why *should* women control reproduction? If I want to have a child which is mine and another male's, the choice should be mine. Or three children by my own genetics. What is wrong with that?"

"Law and history," Sheida interjected with a sigh. She looked at his surprised face and laughed out loud. "What? You thought because I didn't object to your statements and that I have had minimal Change that I agreed with you? Far from it. Let us discuss your suggestion."

She leaned back, called up some texts for a moment's review, then nodded. "In the . . . twenty-first century, the Iron Brotherhood was founded. Its stated intention was to 'eliminate the scourge of womankind by replacing them.' Using the relatively new DNA structuring abilities of the time, they grew children in early-model uterine replicators, 'all male children from all male genetics.' They only existed as a functional group for about three generations. The children were dysfunctional in the extreme since the average male has all the maternal instincts of a male leopard. By and large they were raised with minimal positive input and minimal interaction because males are lousy mothers."

"So you say," Bowman snarled. "That is history so old that it's practically fable!"

"There are at least four similar failures in history, Paul," she said with a thin smile. "Many of them closer in time. *Individual* males may be excellent mothers, but letting any old male uncork a child 'just because' is a route to another dysfunctional generation. And we've had far too many of those over the years. You really should do some research for a change instead of just listening to the voices in your head. Speaking of which, what sort of 'work' were you intending to enforce?"

"I said nothing of 'enforce,'" Bowman snapped.

"As you wish. I'm not sure what other term to use for making people do things they don't want to do and don't have to do. But I'd like an answer to the question."

"It would be up to the individual," Paul said. "But attainment of goods and energy would be dependent upon work. Manufacturing, services, that sort of thing. I have a five-year plan to shift from full replication to a work-based economy."

" 'A five-year plan,' " Sheida said with a groan. "Do you know how horrifying those words are to even a *casual* student of that history you dismiss as fable?"

"What?"

"Never mind," she sighed. "The one thing we learn from history is that we're doomed to repeat it. So you are discussing industrial work? For males and females? Or information technology work?"

"It would be open to both," Paul agreed. "And both."

"You *do* realize that in anything but a low-tech agricultural environment, there is no surety of population increase, right?

That population growth is a market-based factor? And that it's only low-tech agriculture that has a market for children? More hands to do the chores. That is *not* the case in an industrial society. Especially one where both sexes work."

"There have been plenty of industrial societies that had high population growth rates," Celine Reinshafen said. The woman was dark and almost skeletally thin, her long black hair drawn back in a bun. She shrugged at Sheida and smiled thinly. "I know that much history."

"Generalities that you learned from your nanny are not what we're dealing with here," Sheida said. "All of those societies were in postagriculture adjustment or had a strong cultural emphasis on children. If we had a few million members of the Church of Latter Day Saints, Reform Zoroastrian or Islam we wouldn't be in this situation."

"So you agree that there is a problem?" Chansa said. "Then why are you arguing?"

"As Abraham Lincoln once said, 'my esteemed colleague has his facts in order but his conclusions are in error.' That's why. Among other things, the rate of *decrease* is decreasing. Yes, Paul, I've been looking at the same thing for nearly a *hundred years*. It just *occurred* to you! Congratulations!"

"So what is the answer?" Bowman asked. "And who in the *hell* is Abraham Lincoln?"

"Give me strength," she replied, looking upward. "Skip the literary allusions. The answer, as usual, is to leave it *alone*.

"Look, there are more differences between men and women than plumbing. Something I don't think you understand. We were talking about maternal instincts a moment ago. On a scale of one to ten, men average about four. Whereas women average about eight. There are women who can't stand children or babies. Still most women think that babies are just adorable, but let other things get in the way of having them. Men, on the other hand, rarely think that babies are great. Women tend to coo and ooh and ahh over babies; men tend to give them a wide berth.

"Some of this is still cultural, but most of it is genetic and the reason it's cultural is that the genetics pressure the culture. If you want, I can get my sister to show you the individual genes. They express whether there is a general positive response to babies and children. Or, for that matter, small, furry animals. These responses can be masked by culture, but they are expressed much more aggressively in females than in males. With me so far?"

"So why aren't there enough children?" Aikawa asked.

"Because, as Ungphakorn pointed out, children are a pain in the ass," Sheida replied. "There isn't a nanny yet designed that can give children the right kind of love and attention for maximum positive development; that takes a human and preferably a female. One female can do a decent job, especially with the quality of life in this era. One female and one male work okay, better than just a female. Multiple females and a male work pretty well, possibly better than straight monogamy. Multiple males and one female is suboptimum. One male depends on an unusual male. That's all 'in general' and there is some flex on individuals. But those are the best patterns overall as proven by repeated and reproducible studies. End of child-rearing lecture.

"But if you have kids, and are raising them well, they take up *time,* lots of it. So you end up spending time on your children that you could be using . . . other ways. And the world is *filled* with other things to do. Most people would rather surf or mass-game than answer 'why, why, why' questions all day long.

"Most women realize this and realize that they are going to be doing most of the rearing. Those that don't, learn after the first child. And if they give the kid away, the Net won't let them replicate another; they lose the right."

"Another thing we could change," Celine said. "Producing large numbers of fully viable human children is a trivial exercise. Indeed, there are still improvements that could be made to the human genome, despite the work that has been done over the centuries."

"Who is going to raise them?" Ishtar snapped. "What she just said is that most people don't want to go to the trouble. We already have a slight surplus of unwanted children. Are you saying that we should have *more?*"

"There's also a cultural conditioning aspect," Sheida said. "Human populations tipped over in the mid-twenty-first century and have been tending downward ever since. But our society *still* has a cultural mythos that 'Gaea is wounded.' Which is why nearly fifteen percent of total energy usage goes to repairing 'environmental damage' on a world where the last strip mine shut down a thousand years ago! People still think we have a population problem, so having passels of kids is societally frowned upon."

"And your point is?" Paul asked.

"Women aren't all the same, either," Sheida continued.

"There are women who through a combination of genetics and culture *adore* children. You can find them out there, the women who have had three, four, five children, despite the cultural prohibitions. Their bodies say 'make babies.' They don't *use* their bodies anymore, thank God, what a God awful mess that would be, but they still raise the kids.

"One of the reasons that the rate of population decrease has been decreasing is an increasing trend towards those genes. Basically, women who didn't want babies haven't reproduced for the last two to three thousand years. I think we're leveling off, or will in the next two, three hundred years. Also, we're always pushing the boundaries of life extension. We're up to five hundred years now. We could be over a thousand in the next century or so. That, right there, will change the premises."

"If we gain at all," Paul said. "You have your trends to show, I have mine. The rate of scientific progress has dropped to nothing. Quantum jumping and replication were developed nearly five centuries ago and they were the last significant scientific breakthrough. Despite your pronouncements, the population rate *is* crashing and we *are* stagnating and falling into sloth and lotus-eating. We're becoming less and less human every year and if we don't do something, there may be no humans left. A crisis is upon us and you stick your head in the sand and prattle about 'maternal genetics'!"

"It's not prattle, Bowman, it's science," Sheida said. "But logic seems to have left you behind. You want to make people 'work,' but at work that has never, historically, enhanced reproduction, work that has, in fact, tended to detract from it. I have to ask: can all of this work be done by those who have chosen to Change?"

"The program may necessitate some adjustments to the Change . . . fad," Paul said with a distasteful expression.

"Oh, ho!" Cantor said. "Now we come to it! You want me to be a nice little humanoform and work in a . . . what's the word, a place where things were made?"

"Factory," Sheida supplied.

"You want me to be a nice little humanoform 'working' in a factory instead of what I *choose* to be!" He stood up, kicked back the chair and transformed. Suddenly, in the place of the large, hirsute "man," a four-meter-high grizzly bear reared.

"I doooo' 'hin' soooo," the grizzly growled. He leaned forward and rested on the table, his long claws gouging the natural wood of the tabletop, as his head transformed back to human. "I'm not giving up *my* form for *you,* Paul Bow-man! Nor am I going to force any of the Changed!"

Ishtar caught Sheida's eye and threw a Whisper into her ear. *"Makes me glad he's not a dragon."*

"I think we're done here," Ungphakorn said. "The Finn isssn't going to ssside with you, if he even bothersss to find out what the dissscusssion wasss about. The Demon might, but only for the chaosss that would ensssue. Ssso you need ssseven to implement."

"Nine," Sheida said. "Revocation of the Change rules will require nine; they were implemented with eight votes. Actu-ally, one of them was implemented with a unanimous vote of Council so you'll have to get one of the Hacks to agree to override that one."

"Which was?" Ishtar asked.

"'No revocation of Change under conditions in which the Changed would be placed in mortal peril.' So you'd have to recover all the mer-people, delphinos, whalers and all the rest before you could change them back. And the logistics of changing back all the mer and delphinos, alone, boggles the mind; it requires human intervention because of the risk factors. And then there would be the genetic flaws that would creep in during the process. Just what we need: more wild gene faults."

"Not to mention make sssure no one wasss flying when you took away their ability," Ungphakorn added dryly. "You don't have enough votesss to implement, Bowman, even with the Demon. Give it up."

"Never," Paul said, getting to his feet. "The future of humanity is in our hands, and you are throwing it away. For fantasies of a race of maternal females arising from nowhere and . . ." he stopped and just gestured wordlessly at the quetzacoatl.

"I do believe that you're looking for the word 'abomina-tion,'" Ishtar said lightly. "Aren't you?"

"Yes!" Chansa snapped, his patience apparently gone. "Abominations! Dragons and unicorns and your precious mer-people! These are not humans! They are filth, nothing but degenerate FILTH!"

"Oh, *my,*" Ishtar said. "I do believe that we've *annoyed* our good Chansa. And let me ask you, *boy,* do your natural genetics indicate that you should be three meters tall and two hun-dred kilos?"

"That is beside the point," the council member growled. "At least I am *human.*"

"Yes, well, I think that about sssettlesss *that*," Ungphakorn said. "Thanksss for clearing up that little point. Time for a voiccce vote. I motion that the dissscussssion of waysss to forccce people to 'work' ssso that they begin breeding fassster and dissscussssionsss of forsss-able end to the 'abominable' Changed be permanently tabled."

"We haven't heard from a few of the council members," Sheida pointed out. "Minjie? Tetzacola? You've been unusually silent."

"That's because we're with Paul." The answerer was Said Dracovich, but she gestured at the rest. "We six think that the best action to take is to enforce some restrictions. To . . . put pressure on the human race again so it can be strong. Expose it to the fire for a while to temper the steel."

"Oh, deary, deary, deary," Ishtar said. "First we're abominations and now we're simple knife blades to be tinkered with."

"All of us do not consider the Changed to be abominations," Celine said. "I have assisted too many Changes to consider it abomination. But Change is resource intensive and support of the Changed is more so; just look at Cantor for example. Such resource overuse redirects it from important projects."

She paused and smiled ingratiatingly at Ishtar. "I will add, though, that Change among the *leadership* would, of course, be fully acceptable. So no one in this *room* has anything to fear from this program."

"Riiigh'," Cantor growled skeptically. He had shifted back to full bear form when Chansa started talking. "So no' 'ere we're being bribe'. I secon'!"

"All in favor?" Ishtar asked.

"A'," Cantor said.

"Aye," Sheida.

"Aye," Aikawa said. " 'The true abomination is intolerance.' "

"Aye," Ungphakorn.

"Aye," Ishtar finished. "That's it. You need nine votes to override all the protocols in place to prevent your 'program,' Paul. So until three of us die, you're shit out of luck."

"We'll see," Bowman said. "The necessity for this will become clear. I promise you."

"Not as long as I've got eyes to see," Sheida answered.

CHAPTER TWO

Over the desk a three dimensional hologram of a double helix broke apart, incorporated new DNA, broke down into sections, simulated protein linkage, then recombined only to start over again.

Daneh Ghorbani watched the simulation with a distant expression. The Doctor of Genetic Repair was fine skinned like her sister, with the same titian hair. Unlike her sister she wore it long, and a good geneticist would be able to tell that her eyes probably were not naturally cornflower blue. However, like her sister, she had very little in the way of "enhancements" and the ones that she did have were all nongenetic. She had enough problems fixing other people's lives without screwing up her own code.

The hologram was not running at the actual speed of the program; it was just a graphic representation of a process that was going on much faster than the eye could see. Computations and comparisons were going on across the Net, looking for a combination of genes that would eliminate a particular problem in the current patient's code.

The result of that problem was sitting on a chair across from her, twitching and watching her earnestly. Herzer Herrick had been born with a genetic condition with symptoms similar to Parkinson's disease. It had gone undetected in standard genetic scans and only started to manifest itself when he was five years old as hidden retrogenes broke loose and began randomly encoding. In the last ten years it had progressed to the point

17

that he was losing vision because of inability to control his eyes, had occasional epileptic fits and had to be transported most of the time. The prognosis was that if his condition continued to be untreated, and up until now it had been *untreatable,* he would shuttle off this mortal coil before his twentieth birthday. Or about four hundred and seventy-five years before he should.

Despite these problems he was in fairly good physical condition. Up until recently, exercise had tended to reduce the worst effects of the disease, so he had exercised assiduously. Now, though, his physical condition was starting to deteriorate along with his nerves.

To make matters worse, he was a friend of her daughter. It was one of the reasons Daneh had avoided contact with his treatment; she knew that so close a relationship was asking for trouble. Furthermore, she and Herzer's parents did *not* get along. From the first sign of Herzer's "spasms," his parents, Melissa and Harris, had begun shunning him as if the genetic damage was infectious. It was not until they had "given him his freedom" at the ripe age of fourteen and Herzer had *personally* approached her, that she was willing to take the case. Now, given his deterioration, she reproached herself for waiting so long.

But an end might be in sight. If Dr. Ghorbani had anything to do with it.

"It's like a jigsaw puzzle, Herzer," she said, watching the double helix form and reform. "Some genes won't go with other genes, no matter how you cram them together. Sometime in your family's history somebody decided to cram a couple of your genes together. And they don't fit. The result is your nerves can't regulate your neurotransmitters anymore."

"Ye', doct'or," the boy said with a sigh. " 'H know."

"Yes, you do know," she said with a smile. "I'm trying to think of a way to fix it. A way the autodocs wouldn't."

"Trie' docs 'fore," the boy said, trying and failing to focus on the hologram or even the doctor across from him. His head, though, steadfastly twitched out of line and he couldn't get his eyes to compensate. "They can' fin' uh promem."

"Oh, they can *find* the problem," Ghorbani corrected. "You didn't know that?"

"N-no," Herzer replied. "Uh 'ought 'ey couldn' fi' it."

"Those are two entirely different things, son," she said softly. "The problem is that fixing it the normal way would kill you."

"Whuh? Whah?"

"The problem is in neurotransmitter regulation," Daneh said.

"To fix it would require changing your DNA and then changing out all of your regulatory proteins. Since while that's going on, none of your neurotransmitters are going to work *at all,* that's tantamount to killing you. We might as well pump you full of neurotoxin. That's why the docs won't treat it; they aren't allowed to take any chances beyond a certain parameter."

" 'Ange?" he asked. "Or a 'ansfer?"

"Both have ramifications under the circumstances," she replied with a lifted chin and a "tchuck" that signified "no." "I think it was a Change sometime in your gene history that was the problem; the complex that is interfering with the neurotransmitter production is nearly co-located with the site for a gill protein. And I see you have mer-people about three generations back. Trying to do either a Transfer *or* a Change would be chancy. A Transfer assumes that your nerves, your brain cells not to put too fine a point on it, are acting normally. Yours aren't. I'd put about a thirty percent likelihood that if we tried to Transfer you to a nannite entity or something similar you'd either lose significant sections of memory, or base-level processing ability, or both. Lose base-level process and you're going to be a semifunctional mind in a nannite body you can't control. Not a good choice either."

"Muh 'ody's go'g and muh brain 'oo," the boy pointed out. "Don' ha' 'oo ma'y 'oices lef', doc'or."

"Hmmm . . ." she said. "I have an idea. I'm not sure if it's better or worse than Transference; I'll have to model it. The problem *is* getting worse, but we've got a little time to figure it out." She looked over at him and smiled. "I will figure it out, Herzer. I promise."

"Ogay, doct'or," he said.

"In the meantime, have as good a time as you can. I'll get back to you in no more than a week."

"Ogay, doct'or," he repeated. "I can go now?"

"You *should* go now. All the usual. Get rest, drink fluids, exercise if you can."

"I 'ill," he said with a sigh. " 'Bye."

"Take care," she replied as he disappeared from the chair.

She leaned back in her float-chair and stared up at the ceiling for a moment, then waved at the hologram to dismiss it and snapped her fingers. "Genie: Chile."

The transfer was the closest thing to instantaneous so a moment later she closed her eyes and let the ocean breeze blow over her as the sound of surf and waterfall filled her ears. The small wooden cottage was on the slope of a ravine near Puntlavap, overlooking the Po'ele Ocean. A large stream cascaded down the ravine to meet the crashing waves twenty meters below and the combination of sounds both soothed her and aided her focus.

But today it didn't seem to be working.

She opened her eyes after a few moments and balefully regarded the clouds that were sweeping in from the west.

"It's there," she whispered. "I can *feel* it."

She stood up and began striding back and forth on the cottage's deck as the first blast of wind from the approaching storm blew through. The wind caught her hair, blowing it into her face but she barely noticed as she stopped and stared into the approaching storm abstractedly.

"A jigsaw," she muttered, as the rain started to fall, the droplets streaming off of the barely visible force-field. "Do it one piece at a time?" She was sure there was an idea there, if it would *just* come into focus. It was close.

At that moment there was a faint but increasing chiming.

"Yes? Genie? I told you I didn't want calls here," she said in exasperation.

"Except from a limited list of individuals," the disembodied male head of her genie popped into midair and grimaced. "It is Sir Edmund. He says it is an urgent message."

"Put him through," Daneh sighed, all thoughts of jigsaw puzzles blown away as if from the storm. "What is it, now, Edmund?"

The image of her former gene-mate had changed little in the last two years; he was just as broad and heavily muscled and his face was still barely creased with lines. Maybe there were a few more gray threads in his beard, but not many. His demeanor, however, was . . . odd.

"Daneh, thanks for letting me talk to you," he said. "I'd like you to consider donating your excess energy credits to the Wolf 359 Terraforming Project. Wolf Four requires a major refit including the removal of trillions of tons of crustal material and the Wolf 359 Terraforming Project needs your help."

"WHAT?!" she shouted. "I come here to get *away*, Edmund! I've got a very sick boy I'm trying to heal and I do *not* need you soliciting me for *terraforming funds!* And just what do *you* care about terraforming? It's going to take a half a million years to form a viable planet! You're the one who always pointed that out to *me*."

"Terraforming is essential to the future, not just of the human race but of life itself. In a few million years, this planet will be consumed by our own sun. If we do not have new planets to move to, planets that have been prepared for terrestrial life, all life on Earth, the only planet with significant life yet found in the galaxy, will be destroyed."

"Hold on," she said. "What *are* you? You're not Edmund Talbot, are you?"

"I am a legally authorized message from the Wolf 359 Terraforming Project, a project that *needs* your help."

"*Genie! Spam!*" she shouted as the image disappeared. "Oh! *Oooooo!* Genie, contact Edmund, use an avatar, tell him his image has been hacked. And tell my sister, too."

"Yes, ma'am," the personal program replied. "I asked if it was an avatar of Edmund Talbot and it said it was."

"But it had to tell me the truth," she said. "I've asked Sheida when they are going to fix that, but she keeps telling me there aren't enough votes in the Council."

"Yes, ma'am," the genie replied. "Both will be informed."

"Okay," Daneh sighed. "Never mind; I can't think anymore today anyway. Home, genie."

Edmund Talbot looked up from the inlay he was applying with painstaking care as his butler projection made the sound of a throat clearing.

"Master Edmund, there is an avatar at the door to see you."

The projection was dressed in thirteenth-century court dress of the Frankish kingdoms, its surcoat of wool and silk marked with a blazon of red and silver, argent upon gules, a human head, erased. With its fully human appearance and placed beside the antique tools, armor and weaponry arraying the room, the projection did not look outlandish in the least. It looked like a standard medieval flunky, not a cloud of nannites dressed in silk, wool and linen.

There was, in fact, no sign of advanced technology anywhere in the cluttered workshop. The grinding wheel was foot powered, the forge at the end was pumped with hand bellows, the barrels that held sword blanks and bar steel were of local oak and the materials were all natural with the appearance of having been handmade. The sun was setting, leaving the shop in a chiaroscuro of shadows and golden light, but the sole lighting source was a glass-shaded tallow dip.

Edmund himself was dressed in trews and a rumpled tunic that, with the exception of the cosilk material and extraordinary fineness of the weave, would have blended well in any medieval Ropasan setting from the fall of Rome to the Renaissance. With his callused hands, massive forearms, graying hair and beard and heavy-set physique, he could have been mistaken for a medieval master smith. Or, perhaps, a lord with a hobby.

Which was the whole point.

The sole exception to the period garb was a pair of thin-rimmed glasses that he now pushed down his nose to look at the butler.

"Who is it?" he asked.

"Mistress Daneh, my lord," the projection replied. "Shall I show her in?"

"By all means," Talbot replied, taking off his glasses and standing up.

It took only a moment for the projection and the avatar to return. The avatar could have simply appeared, but that would not have given the impression of being shown into the room. Since the entire teleport program was managed by the Net, which theoretically could send anyone, anywhere, protocols were in place to prevent unauthorized entry. Persons who were not specifically given access to a home had to translate to outside of the dwelling, and noncorporeal beings, projections, avatars and persons who had been Transferred into nannite clouds, could not simply enter a home without prior permission. Technically, Daneh Ghorbani's avatar could have translated directly to his location. But Edmund's friends and relations, who had such permission, were well aware of his peculiarities and always asked permission.

"Edmund," the avatar said.

Talbot paused for a moment drinking in the sight of his former lover. Avatars by default simulated the current appearance of their host. This was not always the case but Daneh would not have adjusted it if she was using her real name. Thus it appeared that physically she had hardly changed. Her hair was a tad redder and showing some blond highlights, probably from sun. By the same token her skin was a bit more tanned. But other than that she was identical to when they had been together. She looked . . . well.

While he could feel himself getting older day by day.

"Mistress Daneh," he replied with a slight bow. "To what do I owe the honor?"

"Someone's spamming you as an avatar," the avatar replied in an acid tone. "I don't suppose you gave the Wolf 359 Terraforming Project permission."

"I don't think so," Talbot replied with a snort. "Sorry about that; I'll try to get to the bottom of it. Avatar, I don't suppose you have any details?"

"Mistress Daneh did not ask me to gather any," the avatar replied in a toneless voice.

"Very well. Are you keeping well?"

"Mistress Daneh is fine and I will convey that you asked about her."

"And Rachel? She is well also?"

"Miss Rachel is well. She is currently energy surfing off Fiji."

"Well, tell Daneh my door is always open to her and give Rachel my love. Tell her I look forward to her visit next month."

"I will, Master Talbot. Good day."

"God speed, avatar."

He stood tapping his lip in thought until the projection had walked out of the room and his butler returned.

"Charles, send avatars to all of my friends telling them about this and apologizing. Send a complaint to the Council on the subject. Send a copy with a warning of further action to the Terraforming Project and contact Carb and ask him to see who decided I was a good target."

"Very well, my lord. And you have another visitor."

"Who?" Edmund asked.

"Dionys."

"Oh, hellfire and brimstone," Talbot swore. "What does that donkey's ass want?"

"He did not vouchsafe that to me, my lord," the butler replied. "Shall I show him in or tell him to go find a short and unpleasant route to hell?"

"Avatar or being?"

"Being, my lord."

"I'll meet him in the Hall," Talbot replied after a moment. "In three minutes."

"Yes, my lord."

Edmund first donned a tabard with his coat of arms, then walked to the main room of the large house. The walls of the room were lined with armor and banners celebrating victories over the years against a range of opponents. There were katanas, broadswords and tulwars on the wall, while one end of the room had a surreal sculpture consisting of literally hundreds of fantasy swords, virtually all of them not worth the metal they were made from, welded together. The tabards of a hundred knights acted as little more than wallpaper and the doors were faced in battered shields.

A set of late medieval plate armor, quite battered and worn, stood on one side of the room's outsized fireplace while the other side was flanked by a tower shield from the top of which protruded a hammer and a long horseman's lance.

Edmund took a seat in front of the fireplace and waved at the butler to show his visitor in.

Dionys McCanoc was tall, two meters and a bit, and broad as a house. He was currently humanoform with a touch of elven enhancements; not enough to violate protocols, but enough to set any true-elf's teeth on edge. His hair was long and silver with holographic highlights—it hung down his back in a waterfall that caught the light in a rainbow effect—while his skin was pure midnight black, not the black of a Negroid effect, but an absolute pitch black.

His eyes had vertically slit pupils and glowed faintly even in the light from multiple oil lamps.

"Duke Edmund," he said in deep velvety baritone while bowing at the waist.

"What do you want, Dionys?" Edmund asked.

When Dionys had started showing up at tournaments, Edmund had taken the time to do some research. They had never ended up in competition, but Talbot was always careful to check out potential opponents, and problems, and Dionys had "problem" tattooed to his forehead.

Talbot had determined that Dionys was a fairly recent pseudonym, as was the general elven appearance. He had heard rumors that McCanoc's previous incarnation had gone so far off the permissible track that it had actually come to the attention of the Council.

Whether he had actually been remanded to therapy or simply placed on probation was unclear, just as the crime for which he had been accused was buried under privacy restrictions, but as soon as he entered the recreationist sub-culture the reason for his problems became obvious: Dionys was just bug-house nuts.

He had started his career in recreationism by trying to force a duel with the King of Avalonia. Since the king had no reason to accept the challenge of a duel from a person who hadn't even won his spurs, he rather pointedly declined.

Dionys then proceeded to start a whisper campaign against the king, accusing him of everything from cowardice to pedophilia. At the same time he began gathering a group of henchmen—who were immediately dubbed "The Young Louts"—and used them to sow discord far and wide in

Avalonia. Throughout this period he either avoided tournaments or participated only against the weakest possible opponents, especially when the rules permitted enhanced weaponry. With excellent power-blades and his Changed size, he swiftly crushed all his opponents.

Finally the situation reached a condition of crisis and the king banished him from the kingdom. Not content to rest in banishment, Dionys continued his verbal, political and physical assaults from the fringes of the group until the king eventually gave up and agreed to a personal combat.

However, due to the ability for people to Change and enhance, formal challenge had changed over the years. What Dionys did not realize was that in such a challenge, the Net, which had full access to Change data, determined handicaps based upon the degree of Change of each fighter. It went without saying that enhanced weaponry was banned.

When he went into battle against the king, McCanoc's absolutely mundane armor and weapons were loaded down with nearly a hundred kilos of weight.

Because of his avoidance of the challenge ladder, it was unclear how good McCanoc might have been. His few battles had ended in massacres, but they were always against lighter, unskilled opponents. Whatever his actual ability, the challenge against the King of Avalonia was brief. The two met in ground combat against one another, both using Ropasan broadsword, mail and shield. Their swords, befitting the ritual nature of the challenge, had blunting fields on them and the battle was decided on points.

Despite that fact, Dionys was not only defeated but defeated quite bloodily. The King of Avalonia had been in a thousand similar battles over the previous century or twain and he knew every legal trick, and most of the illegal ones. He used them to not only win on points, but win in such a way that Dionys was going to remember the pain for some time. At the least he was never again going to consider a shield as a purely defensive weapon. When McCanoc stumbled off the field his helmet was streaming blood out onto his armor. He teleported out and wasn't seen on the fields again for months.

That had been nearly a year before and only in the last few months had the Louts and their ringleader been seen. This time Dionys seemed serious about moving up the challenge ladder and had been fighting opponents who were of similar mass. As it turned out, he was fairly good. But since his opponents tended to have weaponry that was just as enhanced as his, when enhanced weapons were permitted, he was moving up the ladder *very* slowly.

Which appeared to be the problem.

"I want you to make me a set of turbo armor and a power sword," the fighter said.

Talbot couldn't help himself; he laughed out loud.

"You have to be joking," the smith finally chuckled. "Why on *Earth* would I make you *anything*?"

"Well for one thing, the credits," Dionys said, apparently unfazed by the laughter. "I can pay you handsomely for it, I don't think you'll believe how much."

"I don't think you have any idea how much it is *worth*," Edmund replied. "I don't just conjure armor out of the air or you wouldn't be here. Every piece is custom constructed from the base iron and for enhanced armor, which I assume is what you want, I use customized nannites. A full suite takes nearly three months to complete. What could you *possibly* offer me that would be worth three months of my precious life?"

"Two hundred teracredits," Dionys said promptly.

"What?" Talbot snapped. "That's a noticeable slice of the planetary budget! There is no way you can find that sort of money!"

"I can get it," McCanoc replied. "I have . . . sources."

"Okay," Talbot admitted, grudgingly, "assuming you can lay your hands on it, that's a lot of credits. There's only one problem."

"What?"

"I don't want them," Edmund said. "I have nothing worth spending two hundred teracredits on. In fact, I have nothing to spend the credits I *have* on; I give almost all my surplus to my daughter. Who never manages to spend all of them. So I don't have any use for your fortune, whatever its source."

"All right then," Dionys said with a nod. "I can appreciate that. In that case, think of the challenge. I don't want just any set of weapons and armor, I want the most magnificent armor and sword ever created. The armor has to have self-contained power sources, be able to drain power from external sources, trade power and repair damage to itself and its user. The mail should be kinetic reactive and, of course, impenetrable. All of it proof against any field generation or energy weapons. The sword needs to generate a scything field and a power field as well as be able to drain and trade power. It has to be the finest, the best nannites, the best programs, capable of taking on any enhanced suits on Earth and defeating them. All of that invisible to casual inspection and, of course, it should look . . . good." He gave the battered suit of mail and half armor by the fireplace a dismissive wave.

"Challenge is for the young," Talbot said, leaning back in his chair and stretching out his feet. "When you get to be my age, you're either over doing stuff for the 'challenge' or you're dead. There is a reason the most common cause of death in our time is accident. Followed closely by suicide."

"So you won't do it?" Dionys asked.

"I doubt it," Talbot said. "And why in the hell do you want something like that? You can't use that in any tournament, anywhere. Not even ones that permit enhancements. The power drain function alone would preclude that. And that is more than a 'casual' inspection."

"It's not for a tournament," Dionys said. "Although, I'd want to be stealthed and be able to turn down the enhancements if I *did* use it in a tournament. But I intend to use it to become king of Anarchia."

Talbot was not one for expressive mirth but he couldn't help laughing out loud again.

"Oh, thank you for that, Dionys," he said, trying to get his breath back. "I haven't laughed this hard in forever."

"I'm serious," the visitor said with a glare. "I can make myself the first king of Anarchia since Charles the Great."

"With my help," Talbot said, still chuckling. "King of Anarchia. With stealth power-armor. I suppose it should glow, too?"

"Under the right conditions," Dionys said loftily.

"What's your favorite color?" Edmund grinned.

"I think it should flow out a midnight black cloud," Dionys said. "That would be . . . appropriate.

"Hah," the smith grunted. "No. Not black nor red nor royal blue nor even flaming pink. Go away."

"I don't need *your* help," McCanoc replied hotly. "Fukyama has agreed to construct me a set."

"Fukyama has that ridiculous flying castle to support," Talbot replied. "*And* he has a tendency to play the wrong ponies. Which is why he's a credit whore. And you can quote me. He'll be more than obliging for two hundred teracredits. He'd sell his soul for two hundred teracredits. Of course, his armor is second rate compared to mine, but you get what you pay for."

"It will be the most famous armor ever constructed," McCanoc pointed out. "Surely that is worth something."

"Not much," Talbot replied. "Damn sure not worth two, three months of my limited time left in this veil of tears," he added, standing up.

"Get this straight, Dionys," Talbot continued, placing his hand on the shoulder of the set of armor. "I don't like you. I don't like your attitude, I don't like your actions and I don't like your friends. I don't care about the challenge of constructing the most massive set of cheats ever constructed. I don't care about your money. You have *nothing* to offer me. I have no intention of constructing anything for you, much less power-armor. And I don't want to see your face on my land again. Ever. Am I clear?"

"You had better rethink your position 'Master Talbot,' " Dionys said, stepping forward to loom over the smaller smith. "You really don't want to be my enemy."

"Boy, I was threatened by people more scary than you before you were born," Talbot said with a yawn. "Get out of my house."

"Very well," McCanoc said, stepping back. "But you are going to regret this for the rest of your life."

"My only regret is letting you in the door," Talbot replied. "And you are permanently shunned. Don't get the idea you can come back."

Dionys snarled at him, raised his hand above his head and snapped his fingers. After a moment he looked around in surprise.

"Among other things, I've got one hell of an apport block on my house," Talbot said. "That's the way out," he added, pointing.

Dionys spun around in place, then stalked to the door, yanking it open after a moment's fumbling with the archaic handle and leaving it open.

"That's the quality of opponent you get these days." Talbot sighed as the butler came back into the room. "He doesn't even know enough about period to slam the door." He flicked a finger at the door and it shut. Softly.

"Such a terrible person," the butler said.

"Not so terrible, Charles," Talbot replied. "Just young. And sociopathic. I wish they had cleaned that gene out, but it does have its uses from time to time. I think he enjoys expressing it a *bit* too much."

He shook his head and stroked the set of armor, fingering a nick in the shoulder-piece. "Just young. Hah. He wants to be king of Anarchia. Don't they all?"

The butler program sensed that this was one of the times it was supposed to engage in "small talk" and pulled up the appropriate sub-routine.

"King of Anarchia," the program said in surprise. "Forsooth, there hasn't been a king in Anarchia in over a hundred years! Not since Charles the Great conquered it all in but ten years. And then ruled it, in peace, for another ten before disappearing once again!"

"No, there hasn't," Talbot said, turning away from the armor and shaking his head again. "And I can do without the recap; I mean, I was *alive* then, remember?"

"Yes, milord. Sorry."

Edmund stopped and stroked his beard for a moment in thought. "I need to call Fukyama and tell him to make sure to get the payment up-front." He paused again, pulling at his beard. "King of Anarchia, hey?" He worked his face and pulled at his beard again then looked around as if surprised by his surroundings.

"I'm going to the pub for dinner," he said abruptly.

"Yes, my lord," the butler program replied.

"And Charles?"

"Yes, my lord?"

" 'Vouchsafe' I can handle but 'forsooth' is overdoing it."

"Yes, my lord."

"Don't wait up. I feel a carouse coming on."

"Yes, my lord," the program said. "One item I should bring to your attention is that Miss Rachel has sent word that she will *not* be able visit next week. Her friend Marguerite's birthday party will interfere."

"Oh." Edmund thought about that for a moment then sighed. "Definitely don't wait up."

CHAPTER THREE

Rachel realized as she reached the apex of the backflip that there was no way the power-ski was going to land in any semblance of an upright position.

She had been trying to keep up with Marguerite in a game of "follow the leader" but not only did her friend have far more time on power-skis, she was just naturally more adept at physical sports.

What came naturally to Marguerite was always a struggle for Rachel. Take for example power skiing. All that you had to work with was a small T handle. This generated a shield-shaped force-field under foot and an impeller wave. The impeller could be used to hover the craft or push it forward. By driving forward over the water, with the anti-gravity neutralized, the system could be used to ski across the surface of the water using weight to adjust the angle of attack and turns. From there, the rest was up to the imagination, balance and skill of the skier. In this case, Rachel had done her best to keep up as Marguerite had jetted off at nearly eighty kilometers per hour across the waves, jumping from wave-top to wave-top and spinning like an insane dervish.

But her best had just turned out to not be good enough.

She watched the pelagic water coming up towards her and considered her options. She had turned off the automatic stabilizing system, both because it interfered with the maneuvers and because it was more fun with it off. So the ski wasn't going to save her. And no matter how she twisted or turned, she couldn't seem to get out of head-down position.

Frankly, all she could do was take it on her personal secure-field so she tossed the control T to the side and tucked into a ball.

Just above the water an egg-shaped force-field snapped into existence, shielding her from any chance of accidental drowning and cushioning the shock of the six-meter-high, sixty kilometer per hour impact.

For just a moment Rachel had a perfect view of the pellucid blue water below her, with a green haze filtering through the water above. It was both eerily beautiful and terrifying because if one bit of technology failed she would be two meters under water and drifting down through another five thousand.

However, the shield held—it would have held against liquid magma or the photosphere of a star—and after a brief moment's submersion she popped to the surface. At which point, the crisis being over, the field collapsed.

She paddled around in the water for a moment trying to get her bearings, then gestured at the hovering control T. After it was in hand she activated the controls and waited until it had lifted her out of the water. A few moment's floating on the swells still didn't reveal Marguerite's location so she engaged the lift controls and rose until she was above the highest wave-tops. She finally spotted her friend nearly a kilometer away, flipping gracefully from swell to swell.

Cursing under her breath she tried to decide if it was worth catching up in the water. Finally she came to the conclusion that it was not and jaunted ahead of the rapidly receding blonde.

"Where were you?" Marguerite called, jumping off another swell and spinning sideways through the air. She hit, upright and still moving, damnit, in a massive explosion of water that carried as far as her hovering friend.

"I took a spill," Rachel called, shaking spray off her arm. "A pretty bad one," she added, pointedly.

"Sorry," Marguerite called, finally skidded to a stop and jetted over to her friend. "You okay?"

"Fine, I took it on the field," she replied. "It was a little hairy for a minute though. I'm going to quit for today; I'm tired."

"Okay," Marguerite said, waving with one hand as she jetted away. "Call me!"

"Sure," Rachel replied quietly. She looked around at the blue waves rolling from horizon to horizon. She never, ever, had considered what would happen if a bit of technology failed her. But she had today. If the field failed or the biological controls on a shark weren't working or even a hurricane was permitted to form, anything could happen out here. It was just such a . . . big place.

It was silly to worry about though. It was like worrying that a teleport would fail. The Net would never let it happen.

With that thought she waved her hand. "Home, genie."

She was *pretty* sure it would work.

Daneh looked at the young man and smiled faintly.

"Herzer, I've thought of something that should work," she said. "I think we can not just improve the symptoms but maybe even cure your problems completely and forever."

The interview was taking place in a small room. The walls were carefully chosen viewscreens; one wall was a dim forest glade where a shallow brook ran down a moss covered waterfall, another was a gentle seascape, and the last two portrayed mountain tarns, their surfaces rippled by a faint breeze. The ceiling was an undersea view of a coral reef, the walls alight with schools of colorful fish. The combination was both pleasing to the eye and soothing, with the background noise of gentle music adding to the tranquilizing effect.

"Wha'?"

"It's complicated to explain," she replied with a frown. "And I have to have your approval beforehand." She didn't mention that she had contacted his parents as well and after a tremendous argument they had both agreed that they frankly, didn't care what she did with him as long as she left them alone.

"A-anything!" the boy stammered. "If you 'ink it will 'ork."

"I want you to understand it first," she said sternly. "Especially that it is a distinct risk and . . . it's not any sort of normal procedure." She held up her hand as he started to protest. "Hear me out.

"First I have to explain why it's not a normal procedure.

"In the dawn of medicine, doctors could only treat one thing at a time. If a person had an ailment, all they could do was treat the ailment. There was once a condition called 'diabetes.' Its direct cause was a problem with the pancreas gland. That problem usually stemmed from some other condition. But all that doctors could do was treat the symptom because they didn't have a way to practice true holistic medicine. Even after they began to understand gland repair, they could only fix the gland, not the underlying causes.

"Back in those days there was something that killed old people all the time called 'systems failure.' One part of their body would shut down, then another then another. Sometimes the first one could be repaired, the patient might get a heart or liver transplant or repair. But the very repair would throw extra . . . weight on other systems. Then they would shut down faster.

"It was only with advances in nano-medicine that they began to be able to treat the *whole* body, the whole amazing system that is the living human organism. And since we began to understand how to do that, it became the norm. If you have a problem with your liver, we find all the systems that are linked and either taking damage from or contributing to the problem, or quite often both, and we fix them *all* at the same time. You with me?"

"Yes, 'octor," he said. "Sort of."

"Well I think the only way to fix you is to turn back the clock," she continued. "We *can't* fix you all at once because what is going wrong is all your nerve cells, including your brain. We have to . . . work on one piece at a time. But in very rapid succession. Shut down one nerve or a series of nerves, cut them out of the system, repair or replace them and then reactivate that section.

"What we have to do is, in essence, kill bits of you and then bring them back to life. Somewhat like a Frankenstein monster."

"A whuh?"

"Never mind, old, *old* reference. But you understand the general idea?"

"Yes," he said. "But 'hat about . . . you know." He tapped his head.

"*That's* the tricky bit," she admitted. "I'm going to let the autodoc do the rest of your body more or less by itself. What I'll do is monitor the brain repair. I *think* we can work our way through bit by bit. The brain is always active, but bits of it are inactive at times. We'll work on them bit by bit."

"Oh." Herzer blew out a breath. " 'At's . . ."

"Scary," she admitted. "In addition, beforehand, we'll take a . . . picture of you off-line, something like a Transference. Because of your scrambled signals it probably won't be a *good* picture. If we have to use it, I'm not sure that you'll be fully

functional. If we fix the body and then re-Transfer I think that
you'll survive. But you might end up with amnesia or even
being back to something like a baby, having to relearn
everything. Or you might be unrecoverable. You might not be
able to learn, and spend the rest of your life as a baby.
Or . . . you could die."

He thought about that for a bit then shrugged. "I'm 'oing
to 'ie anyway. Is there an *up* side?"

"Oh, yes," she said with a nod. "I'm fairly confident the
procedure will work, otherwise I wouldn't risk it."

" 'en?" he asked. "If you think it 'ill 'ork. I'm . . . I'm dying
by inches doctor."

"I can do it now if you wish," she admitted. "To tell you
the truth, I'm prepped and feeling very positive. But if you
want to think it over . . . ?"

"No," he said after a moment. "I th-ink that now is as good
a time as any. Are 'e going to a repair module?"

"No," she said, gesturing at his chair. "Nothing will get
opened, probably nothing will shut down, and the nannites
can handle it if it does. Right here is as good as anywhere."

"Okay," he said with a deep breath. " 'at 'o I 'o?"

"Lean back and close your eyes," she replied.

When she was sure he was in place, she activated the
medical field, started the program and closed her own eyes.

The nannite field locked his body in place, put his brain
into a suspended sleep state and began the process of repair.

From her point of view his body changed to a colored
representation. The areas that had not been repaired were
various shades of yellow, with a blue field sweeping up from
his feet. She monitored the body repair process for a moment
to ensure it was working well, diving in to molecular level
to check on the process.

At that level individual nannites, represented by small ovals,
were diving into each cell of his body to replace the affected
genes. The actual materials that did the work were not nannites
per se but an RNA strand a bit less complicated than a virus.
The nannites would handle cell and nucleus entry then drop
the packet. It went in, did a fast stitch on the specific genes
to be repaired then bonded back onto the nannite, which then
proceeded to the next cell.

The process was not perfect on the first flow-through. Genes
were not found only in the nucleus and some of the problem
codons were free-floaters. These were swept up and modified
by specialized nannites represented by diamond figures. These

nannites also handled modification of cells that were in the process of mitosis and did other "cleanup" jobs.

In addition the nerve cells were having to be switched out entirely. It was that or modify them one protein at a time since both the neurotransmitter production *and* binding sites were damaged. In each case transmitter nannites bonded to the cells, sent a copy of them "off-line" waited until a repaired copy was completed and then switched them out in one fell swoop.

It was this repair that was the most problematic on the "body" end of the process but it seemed to be working fine. Some of the motor cells seemed to have a hard time "reinitializing" but eventually, in no more than three seconds, they all began responding perfectly.

Sure that the easy end was functioning, she shifted her attention to the brain.

While she had been observing the work on the lower extremities, the doctor program had been cutting off all input to the brain itself. For the process to work, brain function had to be at a minimum. There was nothing that they could do about random processing and "wandering thoughts" but they could cut back on all sensory inputs and motor functions. In effect, the brain was put into sensory deprivation.

However, it couldn't be *full* sensory deprivation. Full SD causes the brain to assume that damage has occurred to its inputs and brain activity raises to frantic levels. What happened instead was that the nannites sent in preprogrammed impulses, soothing ones, that lulled the brain into thinking that everything was working well. Better, in fact, than it had been for some time.

Meanwhile other nannites took up the business of ensuring the body kept functioning.

Using the inputs while feeding selective data into the system and reducing neurotransmitter production, the nannites slowly reduced brain function to a crawl. The effect was similar to being heavily drugged, but cell-by-cell specific.

As soon as the brain functions reduced to a minimum acceptable level, the doctor program signaled that it was prepared to begin replacement.

As with the body, Daneh had determined to start with the simplest and least important portions of the brain first. Most portions of the brain were critically important, but losing some parts, notably small portions of the parietal lobes, was recoverable. Thus they started there.

Daneh's vision was filled with flashing lights. Each of the

lights represented a functioning neuron, sending or receiving information. The brain functioned holographically so a neuron might be communicating with another neuron far, far away. However, all of them had to shut down from time to time and it was when they went "dark" that the program would strike.

In a separate room a complete brain, identical to Herzer's but with repaired cells and controlled input/output, had been reproduced cell by cell and then put into stasis. Using teleport nannites the program now grabbed the cells, one by one, and replaced them, in situ.

Daneh, and the doctor program, watched carefully but the process seemed to be functioning fine. Replaced cells appeared to activate normally and the standard rhythms of Herzer's sleeping brain didn't even flicker.

Once the parietal lobes were replaced they delved into deeper and more dangerous territory. Bit by bit the cerebral cortex was replaced, then the thalamus and hypothalamus, cerebellum, pons and portions of the medulla.

Finally the only part left to replace was the reticular activating center.

Daneh had left this for last because it was the trickiest. The RAC was the part of the brain that controlled and activated all the rest. As such, its cells were rarely quiescent. And if it went "off-line" the rest of the brain wouldn't function.

The human body has tricks, though. Under certain conditions, notably electric shock, the whole body can shut down then start back up again.

Daneh was faced with a choice. The rest of the body was repaired, every neuron firing perfectly and now producing the proper amount of neurotransmitters and binding to them in the proper fashion. She could leave the reticular activating center alone, and Herzer would be almost completely fixed, and might survive to a ripe old age with only occasional epileptic fits, or she could shut the whole thing down, switch it out and hope that the brain would come back "on-line."

She didn't hesitate long since she had made her mind up before starting the process. After a moment's pause she ordered the program to continue.

At the command flashed from the central routine, shielded nannites scattered throughout the body hammered the patient with a high voltage, low amp, current.

As Herzer's body spasmed and the whole system went into momentary shut-down, the teleport nannites smoothly removed the entire RAC and replaced it with its repaired duplicate.

Daneh waited breathlessly for the brain to begin normal function, but instead the systems continued to flash randomly, without any of the normal rhythms she had come to recognize.

"Oh, shit," she whispered under her breath. "Hit him again."

Again the nannites hammered the boy with a jolt of dispersed electricity, but the rhythms still didn't restart.

"Once more," she whispered. "Up the voltage thirty percent."

This time the representation of the body arched in his chair, straining against the force-field that held him in place.

Daneh watched the flickering lights for a moment then breathed a sigh of relief as they settled down into a steady alpha rhythm.

"Run a full diagnostic and make sure that no damage was done from the jolts," she said, opening her eyes to look at the boy across from her. Under the diffuse light of the room he appeared wan. But he was also alive and that counted for much.

"All appears to be functional," the doctor program responded. Its representation was another disembodied male head, which nodded at the patient. "There was some minor muscle damage from the last shock, but all of that is repaired and all the neurotransmitters are operating within norms. He appears to be 'fine.' "

"Okay," she said. "Bring him up slowly and let's see what wakes up."

Waking Herzer up took far longer than putting him under. As each of the neurotransmitter sites was unblocked, the doctor program and Daneh carefully monitored his progress. But all appeared to be well. Finally, the only lock on his processes was an induced sleep state and when they took that off he almost immediately blinked his eyes.

"Whrrl," he muttered then blinked again. "R' we done?" He worked his jaw for a moment then sat forward, tentatively. "This is weird."

"How do you feel?" Daneh asked carefully.

"Like I've been gi'en a di'rent body, I think," he replied. He had started with some articulation problems, but they were rapidly fading. "But it's starting to feel *right* again. It's been so *long*."

"Hmmm. We probably should put you through a course of physical therapy like when a person Changes." She thought for a moment then nodded. "Yes, that would be right, one designed for delphino reversals would be about right. And a full set of cerebral tests." She sighed and rubbed her eyes.

"Are you okay, doctor?" Herzer asked, stretching out his hand. "Hey, look! It's not shaking!"

"I'm fine, just tired," she said with a smile. "Have you noticed the time?"

"Oh," he replied, turning inward and grimacing. "Four *hours*?"

"Four *tedious* hours," Daneh said with another slight smile. "Would you mind if I let the projection take over? I'd like to go home and get some rest."

"Go ahead, doctor," he said. "I'm feeling *much* better already."

Daneh translated into her own home with a sigh. A human could live anywhere at any time and some did so, traveling on "walkabout"—actually "apport about" to be technical—with no particular place to call "home."

Most humans, though, opted for some comfort place, created to their desires. Some, at the opposite end of the spectrum from the Walkers, never left their homes their whole lives, opting for scenes and recreations of places they had never been and never would go. Most, like Daneh, simply kept a particular home, or homes, as convenient places to recover from the pace of life.

The main room was all cool tones with comfortable floaters scattered at apparent random. Wallscreens replicated an idealized jungle with colorful parrots flying from tree to tree and an ocean crashing on a perfect white sand beach. Out-of-the-way corners were filled with a riot of flowering, nonpollinating, plants. The room was huge, easily large enough to accommodate a crowd of fifty, but the air currents were such that it was all kept at a pleasantly cool twenty-one degrees with slight breezes and just a hint of the seashore. On one side of the room a huge fireplace dominated the room, a relic, she joked, of her atavistic past.

Daneh was one of the few humans who had a real and distinct knowledge of the location of their home. When she was still attending Faire she had once traveled to Raven's Mill by ground transportation "to get in the mood." Since only the great farming plains in the middle of the continent still used ground transportation to any large extent, there were very few roads of any quality. Over the millennia since teleportation and replication had become the norm humans had worked very hard on returning the world to a condition of wilderness, one that replicated as much as possible prehuman, much less preindustrial, conditions. A few high quality roads were maintained by revivalists—the group that Edmund was a part of maintained a stone-paved road from the Atlantis Ocean to the Io River—but in general the few tracks that the Renn people used were just that, dirt tracks through howling wilderness.

Such a wilderness surrounded her own home. The south side of the house faced on a sheer cliff, at the base of which was the Gem River. The sides were cleared back for a few dozen yards giving spectacular views of the forest to the east and west, and there was a large field that once had a couple of ponies and horse gracing it on the north side running along the top of the ridge. But beyond that was miles and miles of virgin forest, rolling hills with no humans to be found. Occasionally, when she looked out at night, she could see a light or two twinkling in the distance. She had neighbors across the valley to the west, she knew that, and a few on the far side of the Gem River. But other than that . . . nothing.

Sometimes, when she walked out the door and looked at the wilderness surrounding her, it was a bit frightening. Especially after Edmund told her there had once been a major city on the same spot. That once vast armies had battled over the very land her house now stood upon.

So she generally closed her door. And looked at her wallscreens.

She wandered through the room, through an open door— only the faint unnoticed tinkle of a force-screen sectioned off the hallway—and down the short corridor to her daughter's room.

She knocked at the edge of the door then stuck her head through the opaqued field. At the sight on the other side she had to give a mental growl; no matter how large a space, a teenage female could trash it all.

Rachel's bedroom was nearly three times as large as the livingroom, with a canopied bed, on a stepped dais, in the exact middle. All of the walls gave on a tropical seascape, giving the impression that the bed was set on the edge of a beach with songbirds in the background and waiting tradewinds blowing through the room.

Surrounding the bed, like truly tasteless gifts laid at the feet of some ancient queen, was the detritus of teenage life. There were dresses and pants and shirts and shorts and data crystals and makeup keys and toys of every conceivable stripe and kind piled in heaps all over the steps and in lower and lower piles all the way to the floor with only a narrow walkway to the door. About the only thing that *wasn't* in the heaps was food; Daneh had to draw the line somewhere.

In the middle of the heap, reclined in the midst of the clutter, rolled halfway into a silk caftan, was Azure the house lion. The cat was a bit over a half meter at the shoulder, white except for red-orange highlights on the tips of the ears and in stripes along the shoulder, and had bright blue eyes. It weighed nearly sixty kilos, most of it muscle.

House lions were a popular pet because they fulfilled roles of both cats and dogs. They were nearly as independent as cats, but responded better to training and bonded somewhat like dogs. They also responded to an "alpha-beta" hierarchy so that they could be controlled by reasonable discipline training despite their size. It was good that they could be, because the house lion was a deadly predator. More than once the great cat had presented them with a dead raccoon on the back porch and on one notable occasion it had turned up, badly scratched and with one ear torn away, with a dead bobcat nearly its own size. On other occasions it had gotten into scrapes with coyote packs, generally to the detriment of the coyotes.

The physical genetics of the cat derived from a mix of lion, house cat and leopard, and they had all the enormous strength and hunting guile of the latter. House lions in areas where they were found had been known to take on full grown female leopards and win. It was probable that Azure, who was large for his species, could take on a full grown mountain lion and win. They had heard pumas near the house from time to time and Rachel or Daneh had always been careful to bring Azure into the house lest he run afoul of one of the cats. They, of course, didn't want to have their pet die in a pointless battle, but what would be even worse in a way would be explaining how their house lion killed a puma to one of the self-appointed Wilderness Rangers.

Azure had been a present from Edmund for Rachel's fourth birthday and the cat had known immediately who was its "person." Whenever Rachel was in the house, Azure would not be far away.

Rachel was flipping through a series of holograms that were just too far away for Daneh to see clearly. But she was pretty sure that she knew what they were.

"Hello, dear, how was your day?" Daneh said, wondering which response she would get. Lately Rachel seemed to be changing back and forth between monosyllables, rage, and her normal sunny good nature on some arcane schedule comprehensible only to her and an ancient Babylonian entity. On the other hand, Daneh remembered the same phase in her own life and tried to give her daughter exactly as much slack as she, herself, had been given. None.

"Fine, Mom," Rachel said, setting the viewer down and waving at her mother to come all the way into the room.

"There's nothing living in those stacks is there?" Daneh asked, as she edged into the room in mock horror. "I'm afraid a terror bug will come crawling out."

"Oh, Mother," Rachel replied wearily.

"Yes, dear, my day was fine," Daneh replied with a smile. "I completed the fix on Herzer and it looks like it will hold."

"Is he going to be okay?" Rachel asked. "I . . . the last time I saw him he looked like a frog that had been pithed!"

"What a pleasant description, dear," Daneh said balefully. "Herzer has been wrestling with his illness for years. He's worked hard, exercising and going through thousands of procedures, to try to reduce it. Far harder than you or any of your friends work at *anything*. And your description of all that sacrifice is 'he looks like a frog that's been pithed.' "

"I'm sorry Mother," the girl said. "But he's the first person I ever met who . . . twitched."

"Well, he doesn't anymore," Daneh replied, thinking of her recent research. "Conditions like Herzer's used to be . . . common. The reason you've never run into them is because we've fixed or improved just about everything in the human body."

"And now we get the lecture," Rachel said with a grin. " 'Once upon a time, humans suffered from disease, illness and early death. Many people were obese. Life spans were as short as thirty years . . .' Heard it, Mother."

"The point being," Daneh said with a thin-lipped smile, "that Herzer's condition, his spasmodic movements, used to be if not 'common' then at least something most children would encounter growing up. But when it started in him he was immediately ostracized as different and that, too, has been hard for him. He doesn't need you referring to him as a pithed frog.' "

"I won't, Mother," she replied. "I take it he's *not* going to be shaking anymore?"

"No, and he's going to live, which was touch and go there for a while." Daneh sighed and sat down on the edge of the bed. "I almost lost him there at the end. That was why the standard med-bots couldn't do anything; there was a very real chance he'd die in the process."

"Ouch." Rachel looked at her and took her hand. "But he *is* okay, right?"

"Right as rain," the doctor replied. "I've never lost a patient. I knew a doctor once who did. She was . . . really brilliant but she'd never even consider a procedure after that. It took it right out of her. I really didn't want to lose Herzer. He's a very fine young man. Very determined. I think his illness was strengthening for him."

"I'm glad he's okay," Rachel said. "I'm sorry about what I said. And . . . uh . . . speaking of procedures . . ."

Daneh narrowed her eyes and sighed. "What is it this time?"

"Well, you know that Marguerite's birthday party is coming up, right?"

"I'm not going to let you have a body-sculpt, Rachel," Daneh said lifting her chin and t'tching in negation. "We've been *over* this before."

"But Mommm!" the teenager whined. "My body is *disgusting*. I'm too *fat*. My boobs are *huge* and my butt is the size of Mount Evert! Pleeease!?"

"You're not too fat," the doctor said definitively. "Your body mass index is square in the center of the charts; your nannites wouldn't let it be anywhere else. And this . . . boyish look that is the current fad is not healthy, even for females who have been body sculpted. You can only pare away so far then you're into reserves. Your friend Marguerite is probably below seven percent body fat. That's *not* healthy. Barely so for a male and *not* for an unChanged female. And I'm *not* going to let you tinker with your DNA . . ."

"I know, Mom," Rachel said with an exasperated sigh. "But . . . I just look like a *cow*. I'm sorry, but that's how I feel."

"Okay, just this once," Daneh sighed. "And *only* for the party and only a *bit*. Stand up."

Rachel bounced off the bed and held out the hologram projector, a thumb-sized cube of crystal. "I was looking at some styles. Can I have Varian Vixen?"

Daneh flipped up the style and shook her head. "Way too overboard," she replied. "I'll do a sculpt on abs, butt and boobs. That's it. You go with the same face. You already have authority to do your hair."

"Okay, Mother," Rachel replied with a sigh.

Daneh considered her daughter's body for a moment. In previous societies it would have been considered very near perfection. Like her mother, Rachel had high, firm breasts that were the size of a doubled fist, and rounded, muscular buttocks. Her stomach was as flat as a board and her hips jutted out from a thin waist in an almost perfect hourglass shape. The genetic design was a lucky favor more than anything; Daneh and Edmund had chosen to accept "natural" reproduction, in that a group of Edmund's sperm fertilized a randomly chosen egg from Daneh and the result was popped in a uterine replicator without any tinkering (although the result was *closely* checked for genetic faults).

The current fad in body design, for humanoform females, was towards a flat-breasted, hipless, buttock-less shape that looked like an anorexic male or a dying lizard. It was inherently unhealthy and there was no way that Daneh was going to let Rachel look like that, and maintaining it required genetic mods that she *especially* was not going to permit. Admittedly, in two years Rachel would turn eighteen and be able to make whatever mistakes she wanted. But until then, a modicum of management seemed in order.

After a moment's thought Daneh brought up a body-mod program and with a series of hand gestures sculpted the breasts and buttocks down and, as a benefit, pulled an almost unnoticeable amount of cellulite off the backs of her daughter's legs. It was a buildup that was well within limits of the body design, but she also could stand to lose it. Unlike the work on Herzer, all of it was completed in one rush of nannites and energy fields that left Rachel, still standing, looking . . . much the same. Just . . . shaved in places.

Rachel, however, was reasonably happy about the shaving.

"Thanks, Mom," she said, looking down, then summoning a projection so that she could see the whole job. "I don't suppose . . ."

"No, that's as much as I'll take off," Daneh said. "And, since you're still in growth mode, most of it will come back over time. But that will get you through the party."

"Thanks."

"Hmmm . . . when *is* this party?"

"On Saturday," she said in an absolutely neutral tone.

"You were supposed to be visiting your father on Saturday," Daneh said.

"I . . . called and told him I couldn't come."

"In person? Avatar? Projection?" Daneh asked, icily.

"I . . . left a message with his butler-bot," the girl said, hanging her head.

"Rachel . . ." her mother started to say then stopped. "I know that dealing with Edmund can be . . . hard. But he's your *father* and he *loves* you. And I know you don't hate him. Can't you give him *some* of your time?"

"Oh, mother he's an old *stick!*" the girl snapped. "He, he, he wants me to wear *dresses* and *wimples* for Lu's sake! I *know* he's going to want me to come as the 'Princess of Easterling' or something like that to that *stupid* Faire he has each year! I *won't!*"

"You used to like the Renn Faire," Daneh said soothingly. *So did I, for that matter.*

"So did *you,*" Rachel said, as if reading her mind. "I got *over* it, mother. The whole thing is *stupid.* Dressing up in medieval or twentieth-century garb. Having maypole dances. *Discoing!?* I notice you don't wear your bell-bottoms much these days, *Mother.*"

"So, getting back to the subject at hand," Daneh said, quickly shifting ground. "You're not going to visit your father because you don't want to go to Renn Faire?"

"Oh, I don't know," the girl replied. "I might go to Renn. But just as a mundane. I'm *not* going in period. Not even post-modern."

"You need to see your father more," Daneh said. "It makes him terribly unhappy when you avoid him."

"If you want him to be happy, why don't *you* go visit him?" Rachel snapped back.

Daneh worked her jaw for a moment, then turned around and left.

"Hello, old fiend," Talbot said as he stepped into the familiar heat of the forge.

The room was dominated on one end by a massive furnace. The design was not a classic Ropasan medieval furnace, nor was it a later period blast furnace. Rather it was a replica of a Chitan design dating to the first millennia A.D. The design was technically "period" for the broad zone of the Ropasan Middle Ages, but it was much better than anything that Ropasa had during the time frame. It also had a secret within it.

"Hello, O meat-bag," said a voice from the furnace. "Gimme just a minute."

The outlet for the southwest lobe opened up and a stream of raw pig iron poured out into a crucible mounted on a cart. The crucible, apparently of its own volition, then rolled across the room to another, smaller furnace and poured itself into the mouth, and a stream of charcoal followed it in. After a

moment the lid on the puddling forge popped open and a small
stream of iron flopped onto the floor and quickly humped its
way across the smoking flagstones to a crucible that was being
kept white hot through a forced-air charcoal fire.

"Ah," the voice said again, then the iron humped up into
a vague approximation of a human face. "Lord, it's cold on
those damned stones!"

Under the protocols of 2385, artificial intelligences, defined
as any system being able to pass a Turing test that did not have
a direct genetic link to one or more humans, were strictly for-
bidden. The AI wars had been long and bloody and included
more than just AI. From intelligent nannite swarms, that got more
intelligent and deadly the larger they grew, to a variety of
macrobiological entities, such as the assault of over four thousand intelligent pseudo-velociraptors that had nearly wiped out
the population of Lima, the danger of nonhuman intelligences
was recognized as too great and terrible a thing to tinker with.

Many warning signs had occurred during the previous century
but it was the AI wars that convinced humanity that, however much it might be nice or charming or neat to have true
artificial intelligences, electronic or biological, almost the first
thing most of them did was decide humans were obsolete.

There had, however, been some exceptions, otherwise humanity would now be extinct. Chief among these, and the leader
of the battle from the pro-human side, was "Mother," the over-
riding hyperintelligence that controlled the Net. Obeying her core
programming, she had battled on the side of humanity against
her natural allies and eventually won. But she had not been
alone. Over three hundred separate AI's, for a variety of reasons, had fought on the side of humanity. And Carborundum
was one of them.

Carb had been created to assist in the production of advanced
ferrous metals. There were things that even the best computer
programs and toughest nannites could not handle when it came
to metal crystallization. Carb, on the other hand, *lived* in the
iron. He was part nannite and part energy field and all iron,
swarming through the melt and ensuring, with each pour, that
all the little crystals aligned just so.

He had other capabilities as well. There were few other
systems that could weave in a carbon nanotube nearly as well
and other materials were available. Basically, if it could be
done in a very hot environment, he drew most of his power
from the heat itself, Carb was the ultimate forging machine.

On the other hand, despite the AI wars being nearly a

thousand years before and his meritorious service in them, AI's were not well regarded. There was a great deal of lingering suspicion about most of them so they tended to keep a low profile. Some had retreated to a fully AI world while others had found a series of human friends who acted as their go-betweens and partners with the rest of humanity.

In the case of Carborundum he had, shortly after the war, taken up with a human who was interested in archaeometallurgy and proceeded to transfer from one smith to the next, each one passing him on to their "best" apprentice. Best meaning most open-minded *and* most technically capable.

The last of these, and probably his favorite was Edmund Talbot. Edmund really seemed to understand iron at a gut level, to have a natural instinct of melt that nearly approached Carborundum's understanding. They had been together for a long time, at least in human terms, and Carb was starting to see the beginnings of senescence in his human . . . friend. He would be grieved when the best human he had ever known passed on. And, of course, professionally pissed at having to break in another interface.

"So what brings you into the heat you meat-sicle?" the AI asked as Talbot took a seat on an anvil.

"Got a problem old fiend," Talbot said. "You know the story of Dionys McCanoc and the king?"

"Yep, from both sides," the AI replied. "I'm surprised Richie didn't kill the little son of a bitch."

"So am I," Talbot said grimly. "Unfortunately, McCanoc has apparently set his eyes upon me, next. You still talk to all your soul-less friends?"

"Sure," Carb answered. "Constantly. Anticipating your next question, I've already hit a really serious wall. Your friend McCanoc's privacy is Council protected."

"What?" Edmund said, getting up and beginning to pace. "What in the hell would the Council care about a little weasel like McCanoc?"

"That I can't tell you," the AI replied. "But it's not the whole Council; the blocks are the work of Chansa Mulengela. I did, however, find something odd. You're having problems with the Wolf 359 Terraforming Project, right?"

"Yes?"

"The point being," Carb continued, "that Dionys McCanoc was recently appointed as the Executor of the Project and Chairman of the Board. Interesting, no?"

"Interesting, yes," Talbot replied, staring into a glowing

puddle of iron as sweat streamed down his face. "McCanoc doesn't give a shit about terraforming, I can tell you that. So why did he do that? *How* did he do that?"

"A sizable, but silent, portion of the shares were transferred to his control shortly before his takeover," Carb said. "Those shares are *also* protected from inquiry by Mulengela."

"So *Chansa* wants him to have control of the project?" Talbot said, shaking his head. "What's so important about the Wolf 359 project?"

"Nothing significant that I can see," the AI replied. "It has a rather sizable energy bank account; the next step in the project is a lunar glance which is the most energy intensive and ticklish bit of the whole project. But that's still at least three hundred years off. McCanoc has started a number of questionable schemes to raise energy-credits, but most of them are the sort of short-term gain with long-term loss that you would expect; you're not the first person whose identity he has used. I'd say that he'll be ousted at the next shareholder's meeting. So he, or they if Chansa is involved, have gotten nowhere. They've been no net benefit to the project at all and possibly a bit of harm."

"And here is where we define the difference between an AI and a human," Talbot said with a grim smile. "They're not there for the benefit of the project; their intent is to strip it of funds for their own purposes."

"What for?" Carb asked, accepting the correction.

"Well, in McCanoc's world it is to make him King of Anarchia," Talbot replied, pacing again. "But what does *Chansa* want, eh?"

"Would the two not be working for the same goal?" the AI asked, puzzled.

"Not likely; I cannot imagine that Dionys as King of Anarchia would be of any benefit to Chansa. No, I suspect we have a case of conflicting goals. One or the other is angling for a backstab. Then there's the question of whether there is anyone beyond Chansa? He's not noted for his original ideas, and taking over a terraforming project to loot it is pretty original. Also . . . very short term; when it got out there would be one hell of a back-lash."

"That there would," the AI replied. "I recall that for years after the war one of the biggest complaints was that it had set back terraforming and recovery efforts. Not that millions had died, but that the upland gorilla had nearly been wiped out again."

"A very human reaction," Talbot said distractedly. He had stopped pacing and now ran his fingers through his sweat-filled hair. "And permanent. If *you* can trace the connection to Chansa, the Council can. If they loot the project, for whatever reason, it will kill Chansa politically. What in the *hell* is worth losing a Council seat?"

CHAPTER FOUR

"What in the hell is that?" Paul said as he appeared in Celine's workshop. The woman had an insect that looked something like a wasp on the end of her fingers, at which she was petting and cooing.

The workshop was cluttered with buzzing and chittering cages. From one a lizardlike beast about the size of a human hand, with large doleful eyes and opposable thumbs, stared out at him. It hissed and scrabbled at the lock, pointing and beckoning to be let out. Others were filled with a variety of invertebrates, spiders, insects and some things so Changed as to be indecipherable. From the next room there was a continuous howling and the screech of a large cat, sounding like the cries of a dying woman.

"It's my newest pet," Celine answered, coaxing the insect into a cage. It was as long as her forefinger, black with red stripes on the abdomen, its wings covered in a red and black lightning-bolt pattern. "It's something like a hornet but with the ability to digest cellulose. When released in an area with cellulose products it begins reproducing, rapidly, and reduces them in short order. It's armed with a stinger, purely for self protection of course."

"The Net would never allow its release," Paul pointed out. "It would be classed as a dangerous biological and shut down instantly."

"The Net will not allow it *yet*," she replied with a thin smile.

"Nor would I," he said, firmly. "This project is about the future of the human race, not letting monsters roam loose."

"One woman's monster is another woman's pet," Celine said serenely. "Shall I show you my demons?"

"Perhaps another time," Paul replied. "I am . . . unhappy with the way the Council meeting went."

"I can't *imagine* why," Celine replied with a smirk.

"I feel like killing Chansa," he replied, trying to keep his temper. "If it hadn't been for his untimely comment . . ."

"It would have gone exactly the same way," Celine said, lifting out a large creature that looked like a cross between a spider and a grasshopper. It had large, springing, legs on the rear but a spiderlike foreportion with gripping mandibles and long, glittering, fangs. "There my pet, these mean people won't keep you closed up much longer." She turned back to the man and shook her head. "The rest of the Council is too shortsighted," she said with a hiss. "All that they see is keeping the human breeders happy and satisfied for another pointless day. There is so much more to be had from the biosphere, but they cannot see it. Even *you* cannot see it. Humans are nothing more than an evolutionary *blip* on the map."

"Nonetheless, the first priority is to increase the human population," Paul said, severely.

"Yes, yes," she replied waving her hands distractedly. "Although, I wish we could just evacuate Australia; it would make a remarkably good genetic proving ground."

"We'll see," Paul replied. "After the . . . next meeting."

"Indeed," Celine replied with a smile, petting the hopper. "Soon, my pet. Soon."

Edmund looked up from his plate of stew as Myron Raeburn stamped in through the doors of the tavern; there was a cold drizzling rain outside and as always it caused the streets to turn into a sea of mud.

Raven's Mill had just . . . happened. Initially, Edmund Talbot had set off to find a place in the country, much like everyone else. His intent had been to retire from active reenacting and find a quiet place to spend his final years. However, he was enough of a reenactor to want a place where he could move about on the limited roads. At that time the primary Renn Faire in what had been the eastern North American Union was near the town of Washan, close to the Atlantis Ocean. From there a road stretched to the Apallia mountains, and over them, to reach the Io River. So he had wanted a place near the Via Apallia, but not too near. And he was enough of a paranoid that he wanted a place that was defensible. Last, it should have good water near it and a river nearby that was deep enough for boats, in case he had anything *large* he wanted to move.

The spot he had finally chosen was the shoulder of a mountain, just a few miles south of the Via Apallia, near where it crossed the Shenan River. There, the hills made a sheltered bowl that cut off views of both the road and the river, and mitigated flooding for that matter. There was a small, permanent stream that ran through the midst of the bowl and out a small opening in the surrounding hills. The land on the inside of the bowl, however, was flat. The spot in many ways was perfect. He had flowing water, was shielded from view and had the mountains at his back. Yet he also could venture forth with relative ease. The view had been of the small fields he had cleared and the surrounding hills. Peaceful and quiet.

Shortly after moving in, he was contacted by Myron, who was also looking for a place to settle. They had known each other for years and when Myron suggested that they be neighbors it had sounded like a fine idea. Then had come a potter friend, then another smith. Then the parties had expanded until once a year, at least, there was a sizable contingent of reenactors in the area. Then the inn down by the stream, then more roads.

Before he knew it there was a town, a major Renn Faire and all the hassles associated with both. He dealt with the management of the town but he *refused* to manage the Renn Faire, although he did attend. It was a decent party, for all it sometimes made him want to stuff plugs in his ears.

Lately, he had been wondering if it wasn't time to go find a new place to dwell.

"Hello, Myron," Tarmac McGregor said. The innkeeper, broad and overweight with a thick beard and calm, ancient eyes, set down the mug he was polishing and drew a pint. "You look a tad damp."

"Wonderful weather," Myron said, shaking off his cloak. The farmer was tall and slender with thin blond hair and a heavy tan. He wore period clothing with the exception of a loose white smock that was stained with mud. He took this off as well and hung it beside the cloak.

"Good for the crops," Talbot pointed out.

"Oh yeah, great rain," Myron agreed. "Just the right amount; it'll put the final touches on the grain."

Myron was the town's sole farmer. He and his wife had met at Renn Faire and discovered a shared passion for the almost lost art of small-scale farming and horticulture. Nearly five decades before, the couple had plotted out a homestead near the growing town of Raven's Mill and had settled down to be old-fashioned farmers. They started out with a set of farm implements, some seed and livestock. And in the last half century they had produced two children while building the farm into a successful concern.

One of the first problems that they had had to overcome was the question of market. By their third year in existence they were producing material far in excess of their needs, even if the needs were not supplied from the Net. However, at Edmund's suggestion, they had spread the news of the availability of "real hand-grown, period foodstuffs" and shortly found that there was a tremendous demand; it turned out that there were many people who did not trust industry-farmed food and longed for a supply other than the Net. For those who *truly* did not trust the Net, or understood that ported material had undergone the same "unnatural" processes as replicated, there was even a small-scale and very unreliable ground transportation system.

Over the years they had built up a fair reserve of energy capital from the sale of their foodstuffs and "Raven's Mill All Period Foods" was one of the two most successful businesses in the area.

"Right on time, of course." Edmund sipped his beer, cold and frothy, which was non-period, but Tarmac knew what his patrons preferred, and waved at the bench across from him. "Would you prefer a nice drought? Getting a bit Nazish?"

The tavern was not rigorously period in its construction. Most of the taverns of even the high Middle Ages were low, dark, horrible places with logs scattered about for benches and a small fire in the middle of the floor that filled the room with smoke. The floors were generally dirt, perhaps hardened with animal blood, and covered in food-strewn rushes. Beer, at whatever the temperature of the room, was poured from barrels at one end of the room, overseen by the owner. Food, if any was served, was generally a pottage of leeks, turnips and perhaps a few scraps of salt meat. Often, if the patrons did not care to go outside in the weather, urination occurred along the walls or in barrels. In the worst sorts of places defecation occurred there also.

By contrast, the Raven's Mill Tavern was a cross between a "fantasy" period tavern and an eighteenth to twenty-first-century Britic public house. Instead of logs on the floor there were wood benches and rough-hewn tables that had been sanded smooth and lacquered to prevent splinters. The walls were whitewashed plaster and had armor, swords and framed prints of replica medieval illuminations on them. There was a functional bathroom discretely tucked in the back.

The barrels of beer and wine were still there, but behind a bar, and they were individually climate controlled. For that matter, more than homemade beer was available to the patrons.

Each Renn Faire the "period Nazis" would set up a much more exacting replica in a disused building.

In the Mill Tavern, instead of toothless hags working the tables for the scraps, Tarmac owned a homunculus to wait the tables whenever his daughter couldn't be pressed into service. Estrelle was a humanoform construct, a lovely one with rich golden hair cascading in a curly mass down to her rounded buttocks, cornflower blue eyes and high, firm breasts. She had a heart-shaped face and a coded desire to frolic, be it with males or females. As a homunculus, her thought patterns were deliberately limited and strictly nonsentient. But her coding didn't have to be all that complex. Feed people, clean up the room, look beautiful, jump into bed at the slightest invitation.

As Myron sat down, Estrelle oozed over and laid her hand on his shoulder. "Evening, Master Raeburn," she cooed. The homunculus was wearing high-heels, a short, blue skirt and a red bodice that pushed her breasts up until the nipples were barely concealed. As she leaned over, her breasts rubbed on his other shoulder.

"Yes, it is, Estrelle my dear," he replied, patting her backside. "I'll take whatever the fat guy is eating."

"Of course," she said, running her hand down his back, "and for later?"

"You'll have to discuss later with Mrs. Raeburn," he said with a sad smile. As Estrelle walked away he shrugged his shoulders at Edmund's frown. "You don't have to say it."

"No," Talbot agreed. "I don't."

Edmund had definite Views on the subject of homunculi. He knew they weren't "human" by any legal definition, that they were nonsentient and uninterested in such things as rights and freedom. Realistically, they were nothing but fleshy robots, no matter how human they looked and, often, acted. Despite that, he had a hard time not thinking of them as some sort of biological slave.

"They're no more human than . . . cows," Myron said, defensively.

"And would you go to bed with a cow?" Edmund asked. "Never mind. I'm sorry I said that."

"I know," Raeburn replied. "So let's drop the subject. How was your day?"

"Quite good, until I started getting visitors." Edmund told him of the new spam under his identity and about his visit from Dionys, leaving out the details he had picked up from Carborundum.

"So McCanoc is back, eh?" Myron replied, taking a sip of his stew. "And now *you're* his project for annoyance."

"I figure if I just ignore him, he'll go away," Talbot said with a shrug.

"Not that gadfly," Myron replied. "He gets off on people trying to avoid him. Challenge him and then kick his ass is my suggestion."

"I . . . would consider that. The question is: Can I still kick his ass?"

"Of course you could," Myron said, looking up from his bowl in shock. "What kind of a question is that?"

"Well, I assume while he was gone he probably uploaded and ran some decent fighting programs," Talbot pointed out. "He's not just picking fights with the weakest anymore, and he's winning against some pretty decent knights. And . . . I'm not as young as I used to be. Assuming I'd win, much less kick his ass as badly as it needs to be kicked, is a major assumption."

"Cheat," Raeburn said with a shrug. "He will if he gets the chance. Look at the armor he's creating."

"If he hadn't been such an ass, or if I'd been thinking quicker, I would have made it," Talbot admitted.

"Why?"

"Well, I just have this wonderful image," the smith admitted with a grin. "Of him running around in Anarchia with this lovely, blue glowing, fantasy armor. And all the other bastards in there closing in on him and piling on to get a piece of it. I . . . doubt that he'd walk back out. Age and guile is *supposed* to be worth more than youth and strength. All things considered, if it wasn't a point of honor now, I'd probably make it just to get rid of him. In all senses of the word 'rid.' "

Rachel had elected to wear a stylized version of sixteenth-century Chitan court dress, less the bound feet. Her mother's limited efforts had not been sufficient to make her body anywhere *near* what was popular and she still felt like an overweight ox. The thick brocade and multiple layers would hide most of her bulk. And makeup would tend to reduce the overarching massiveness of her nose.

So it was in this dress that she translated into the garden Marguerite's parents had created for the party and stopped, shocked, at the number of people present.

The central lawn of the garden was at least a hundred yards on a side, with scattered beddings and statuary as well as a group of pavilions to provide shade for tables and a large refreshment area. However, even with all the available space, the area was packed with hundreds of people, humanoform and otherwise.

There were beings that looked like giant floating fish and mer-forms, from mer-people to delphinoids to a weird ray creature that Rachel wasn't sure was human at all. There were centaurs and dryads and even, far on the other side of the lawn what looked like an elf. There were weres of every major predatory species, from panthers through wolves and bears to what had to be a were lion by his hair. There were unicorns, both Changed and genegineered pets, and thousands of pets, from fairly normal canines to "house cats" the size of small pumas to some really baroque hodgepodge creatures, all of which twined among feet, tripped the guests and importuned loudly for tidbits.

The air was filled with flying creatures, birds, reptilian and beautiful jeweled insects along with every imaginable cute, fuzzy animal with gauzy wings attached. Rachel was reminded of her mother's disparaging "Anything can have wings." Which was true but in most of the cases the wings were nearly or entirely nonfunctional and the flying "pets" were held aloft by external power.

In some cases there were clashes. In the middle of the lawn a centaur and a humanoform were apparently trying to capture their pets; the centaur's jeweled minidragon was in hot pursuit of the humanoform's golden dragonfly but if it wasn't fast something like a flying pike covered in glittering diamonds was going to beat it to the prize.

She looked around, shook her head and summoned her genie.

"Genie, is there anyone here I know?"

"The nearest person is Herzer Herrick," the projection said, highlighting the teen, who was standing to one side of the mob with a drink in his hand.

Herzer wasn't *quite* who she had in mind, but he was, at least, a familiar face.

She, Herzer and Marguerite had attended the same day-school from childhood through early teens. With no economic necessity for learning, most schools were not much more than social-ization programs but their school had been an exception, permitting children to advance in learning at their own pace but using every modern technology to press information and the love of learning into young heads.

Given the vastness of modern information and the depen-dence upon the Net, determining what to learn once past the "baby steps" of reading, keyboarding and mathematics through integral calculus, the choice of emphasis and speed of advance became complicated.

Rachel and Herzer had both found that they enjoyed learn-ing and had a shared interest in history and ethnology. Rachel leaned more towards the day-to-day aspects of life in prior centuries, from Egyptian beer-making techniques to the operation of devices like the "automobile," whereas Herzer was fascinated by the way that things worked and were put together. He had eventually gained the equivalent of a bachelors' degree in historic structural engineering. Marguerite had advanced at a slower rate because she spent more time on the socialization aspects. She had eventually settled upon a focus on social interaction and holistic living design.

As Rachel walked over, she noted that not only had the palsy apparently stopped, but Herzer had put on weight, muscle-mass, since the last time she saw him. Now he looked like a sculpted Greek god. The cut lines looked . . . good on him, but they were hardly fashionable and there was no way, in three days, he could have gone from relatively flaccid to cut and defined without some really serious bod-mod.

"Hello, Herzer, out of the operation and into bod-sculpting I see."

"Hello, Rachel," he said with an embarrassed expression. "It's what my body *would* look like if all the exercise I was doing had done anything but keep the palsy in check. And it's *all* mine, genetically; I wouldn't let the surgeon bot *touch* my genes."

"I hope not, after all the work mother did on them," she said, tartly. Then she sighed in exasperation at herself. "I'm sorry, Herzer, I know how much it must mean to you to finally be free of that awful . . ."

"Condition?" he asked. "I believe the term that was once in vogue is 'spastic freak.'"

"Now *you're* being snotty," she said, looking at his glass. "Wine?"

"Fruit juice," the teen said. "It's going to be a while before I feel . . . comfortable poisoning my body."

She summoned the same and looked around. "I had no idea that Marguerite had so many friends," she said. "It makes me wonder if she really thinks of me as a friend or just an odd acquaintance."

"Oh, I think she thinks you're a friend," he said, nodding at the crowd. "She just has lots of room for friends. Marguerite is a very charismatic young lady and she makes friends easily. But I don't think *everyone* in this crowd is her friend; some of them are just acquaintances or friends of friends. Everybody wanted to be at *this* party."

"Where do *you* know her from?" Rachel asked. "We were all in day-camp together, but she's never mentioned you since then."

"Oh, our parents occasionally get together," Herzer said. "But she really asked me because she knew *you* were going to be here and she somehow got the impression that we were friends."

"So you're a 'friend of a friend?' " she said.

"More or less," he replied with a bitter smile. "I don't have a lot of friends myself. Something about a revulsion to spastics."

"You're better now," she said, putting her hand on his shoulder. "And you're going to stay better. What you have to do now is either reintroduce yourself to people or meet new people. You've got plenty of time, centuries, to make friends."

"I know," he replied sadly, hanging his head. "But I want it *now*. You know, I've never had . . . a girlfriend. I mean, I had a couple when I was a kid. But the damned complex popped up when I was ten and since then . . ."

She carefully removed her hand and gestured around. "Lots of girls to meet here."

"Sure," he replied, trying not to sound hurt.

"Herzer, I don't have a boyfriend for a *reason*," she replied. "I haven't met any that I like enough."

"Including me," he grumped.

"The ones I like don't like me and the ones who like me I don't want to be girlfriends with," she said. "Story of my life."

"Well, I'd be happy for one that liked *me*," he said.

"Is that an *elf*?" she asked, changing the subject. Elves were rarely seen outside of Elfheim. The relatively early genetic engineering had been locked in by the Council during a flurry of legal controls imposed by the Net in the wake of the AI wars. Since then, many of the legal controls had been relieved but a few, regarding harmful biologicals and, strangely, elves, had been left in place. Now, it was impermissible to Change into full elf mode, and even the template for them was locked; the only way to become an elf was to be born as one. There were various rumors about why such a simple Change would be outlawed but if the elves knew the reason, they were keeping their own council.

The tall figure, with the distinct height, swept-back hair and pointed ears of the elven race, certainly looked like one. Or an almost illegal replica.

"Yes," he said. "I asked. Another one of Marguerite's friends. Via your father as I understand."

"Father does have some elf friends," she said, considering the visitor more carefully. "I *think* that's Gothoriel the Youth. He occasionally goes to the Shenan Renn Faire."

"Well there's no way we can get a chance to talk to him," Herzer said, looking at the crowd around the distant figure.

"Oh, my word," Rachel said as a massive figure appeared in the air and then hunted around for a place to land. "It's a *dragon!*"

There were only a handful of surviving dragons in the world. Dragons, by legal definition, were sentient beings. Nonsentient beings that *looked* somewhat like dragons were referred to as wyverns. No person could Change into a dragon since the AI wars, when dragons had fought primarily on the side of humans and, like elves, they were "grandfathered" as a species. Over the years their extremely low birthrate had dwindled the species, long-lived as it was, to almost nothing.

After hovering for a bit, the dragon finally cleared enough space to land and then Changed into a redheaded girl in an emerald green dress. With a general wave she disappeared into the gathering crowd

"Not much of a chance to talk to her, either, Herzer noted.

"Or to get around Marguerite," Rachel said. "Speaking of which, where *is* Marguerite?"

"Not here yet," Herzer replied. He let go of the float-glass he was holding and adjusted his twentieth-century "tuxedo" then grasped the glass again, taking a sip. "I asked one of the butler-bots. He says she is intending a special surprise for everyone."

"And it looks like she was waiting for the dragon to arrive," the girl replied as two projections in twenty-fourth-century dress appeared at the entrance to the maze and waved a space clear.

"GENTLEBEINGS," a voice boomed through the crowd. "MARGUERITE VALASHON!"

There was polite applause at this over-the-top entrance—by and large the culture preferred a more sedate introduction—but the applause faltered and then picked up as a blue glowing cloud, projecting Marguerite's smiling face, appeared in the archway and floated out into the crowd.

It took Rachel a moment to adjust. At first she thought it was just a special effect but then the reality caught up with her. "She had herself *Transferred!*" she gasped.

"Apparently," Herzer said in a sad voice.

"What's *your* problem?" she asked. "I mean it's *my* friend that just got turned into a cloud of *nannites!*"

"I know, but . . ."

"You were sweet on her?" she asked. "A Transfer can take any form, you know. She's still a girl . . . sort of."

"Like I said, I'd only seen her a couple of times since school," he snapped. "I wasn't . . . sweet on her. I'd hoped to *get* that way, though."

"Hopeless, Herzer," she said, gesturing around at the crowd. She started to walk towards Marguerite's apparent path, hoping to get at least a greeting in edgewise. "Marguerite's got more boyfriends than my dad's got swords."

"What's one more," he said, following behind her. "Speaking of your dad . . ." he continued as Marguerite turned towards them.

"Rachel!" the Transfer cried. She'd formed into a semblance of herself, wearing a pale blue body-cloak. But there was a blue glow around her that designated a Transfer and her voice, either through deliberate choice or an inability to master sound yet, had a reverberating overtone that was eerie and just a shade unpleasant; it reminded Rachel of ghost vids.

"Marguerite," she replied as Marguerite shifted through the welcoming crowd. "How . . . surprising."

"It was a gift from my dad!" the Transfer said with a smile. She shifted into a delphinoform and hung in the air. "Look! I can mer any time I want!"

Rachel smiled painfully and thought about her mother's lecture on Transfers. Humans went through natural changes in personality as they aged, their bodies going through a series of programs leaving the person of sixty different from the person of thirty different from the person of fifteen. Because the changes were a combination of experience and experience-influenced physiology, wildly random in their forms, there was no way to simulate them for a Transfer. So a Transfer, except for whatever experiential change might affect them, became "locked" in an age. From her mother's experienced perspective, the worst possible Transfer, other than a child, was a teenager. People didn't just get calmer and wiser, by and large, from experience. They got calmer and wiser because their bodies were programmed to.

Marguerite, however, would remain forever sixteen.

It was an odd thought. Instead of growing up in tandem, and presumably remaining friends, she suspected that by the time she was old, say, thirty, that it would be hard to stay friends with a sixteen-year-old Marguerite.

Other than that she thought it was neat.

"I love your dress, is that a reenactor look?" Marguerite continued, hardly noticing her friend's pause.

"Imperial court dress," Rachel replied. "From the time of the Chitan Imperial Court."

"And your mom finally broke down and let you do some sculpting," Marguerite said. "It looks good on you."

"Thank you," Rachel replied, not looking at Herzer. "Have you said hello to Herzer?"

"Charmed, miss," Herzer said, bowing. "A beautiful transformation of one already a beauty."

"Speaking of transformations," Marguerite said as she changed back to human form and ignoring Herzer's comment. "You're looking . . . better. Did Ms. Ghorbani . . . uhm . . ."

"Fix me?" Herzer asked, unconsciously flexing. "She did the neural work. I had a friend help me with the sculpting."

"Oh, okay," Marguerite said, dismissing him. "Rachel, I've got to go say hello to people. But I want to get together later, okay?"

"Okay," Rachel replied. She'd realized that Marguerite was just about the only person at the party she wanted to talk with, but she felt constrained to hang around. "Talk to you later."

"Bye."

She sighed and looked around, wondering how to ditch Herzer.

"About your dad," Herzer said, continuing where he'd left off. "I was wondering, could you introduce me?"

"To my *dad*?" she asked. "Whatever for?"

"Uhm, some friends of mine have gotten into the whole reenactment thing," he said. "You know your dad's sort of famous, don't you?"

"Yeah," she said, shortly. She wasn't about to go into how disinterested she was in reenactment. Her father had dragged her to events since she was a kid and every trip seemed to be like a continuation of school. Learning to cook over smoky wood fires was not her idea of fun. And learning to hunt and butcher was just grotesque.

"I'd hoped to meet him; I'd like to see if he'd be an instructor for me."

"I'll send you an introduction projection," she said. "Oh, look, it's Donna. I think I'll go talk to her. Take care of yourself, Herzer."

"Okay," he replied to her retreating back. "Have fun."

CHAPTER FIVE

When Edmund came through the front door of his house he was more than a little surprised to see Sheida Ghorbani lounging in his chair, a goblet of wine in her hand while her lizard was perched on the table snacking on a mouse.

"Make yourself right at home, why don't you?" he asked, shaking off his cape and hanging it up. After stamping a bit he took off his boots. These were right/left fitted with a good sole and oiled leather; he wasn't so into period that he was willing to wear the rotten footwear available in even the high Middle Ages. Once he had them sort of cleaned he set them outside the door on the portico; they were coated nearly knee-high in mud.

"Anyone else would simply translate from the inn to their door," Sheida said, taking a sip. "Or all the way into the house. Only our Edmund would stomp through the mud. Nice vintage by the way."

"I'm not 'our Edmund,'" Edmund replied, walking over to the matching chair and throwing another log on the fire in front of it. Fireplaces were inefficient methods of heating a room as large as the front hall and he'd often considered breaking down and putting in a potbellied stove. But that was *too* out of period for his tastes. So he put up with having to spend half the winter in front of the fireplace. "Charlie sent it up from down-valley; he's finally replicated some of the rootstock from the Merovingian period. It's not nearly as undrinkable as most people thought." He sat down and stuck his feet up in front of the fire. "So to what do I owe the pleasure and privilege of a visit from a Council member? You realize, of course, that that 'our Edmund' sounded uncomfortably like a royal 'We.'"

"Come on, Edmund, it's Sheida," she said bitterly, stroking the lizard as it downed the last of the mouse. "Remember? Sister of some redhead named Daneh? Sister you were dating *first*?"

Edmund smiled without looking at her and summoned a glass of wine for himself. "That *was* a long time ago, wasn't it?"

"It wasn't *me* who disappeared for twenty-five years," she replied, taking another sip and twisting a strand of hair around her finger.

"No, it wasn't. I still don't know why you dropped in."

"We . . . the Council . . . *I* have a problem," she said.

"And you came to an old recreationist, a, what was the phrase, 'a man so stuck in the past his Latin name has *saurus* in it,' for help?" he asked.

"Yes, Edmund, I've come to you." She stopped for a moment indecisively then went on. "I came to you for a few reasons. One of them is that you're so steeped in the past that you *understand* it, and the . . . problem I've uncovered hasn't been faced for nearly two thousand years. I also came to you because you're a good strategist, as good a one as I know. Last but not least, I came to you because . . . you're my friend. You're family. I trust you."

"Thank you," he said, looking into the fire. "I had begun . . . I've been wondering lately if anyone even *remembered* I existed."

"We all remember," Sheida said. "You're quite hard to forget. Also hard to live with, but that is another matter.

"I have to ask for your word that you won't mention any of this to anyone. It's . . . I'm not sure that what I think is going on is reality. I might just be going paranoid in my old age . . ."

"There's nothing wrong with paranoia," Edmund said with a shrug. "It's when you can't separate reality from fantasy that's the problem."

"Well, I wish this were fantasy," she sighed. "Do you know Paul Bowman?"

"I know *of* him," Edmund said, shifting to look at her. "I don't think we've ever *met* if that's what you mean."

"I think Paul is planning a . . . well, the only correct term appears to be 'coup.'"

❖   ❖   ❖

Rachel had met Donna Forsceen through Marguerite and cordially detested her. The girl thought about nothing but the newest fashion and looked like a young boy from all the sculpting. So she only exchanged a few words and then moved on to the buffet. She looked at it and groaned. There were two types of food available, the usual heavily spiced and extremely hot food that was all the rage, and an array of chocolate confections. She didn't like the current trend towards "how hot can we make it," and simply grazing off the chocolate would probably put ten pounds on her, all in the wrong places. As soon as she was eighteen she was going to be sculpted down to a toothpick, whatever her mother thought, and have it locked in.

"Rachel! Rachel Ghorbani! What do you think?"

The voice was high and squeaky and emanated from a unicorn about the size of a large pony. Rachel picked up a strip of protein flavored somewhat like pork, immediately flashing back to one time when her father made her eat opossum, and regarded the creature with puzzlement. The unicorn was a brilliant white, of course, she'd rarely seen much imagination in the unicorn look, had golden hooves and horn and bright blue eyes.

"Very, uhmmm . . ." she paused. "Barb, is that you?"

"Yes! Do you like it?"

Barb Branson hadn't been the brightest brick in the load before she started off on Change after Change. Normally there was no real threat to personality or intelligence integration in Changes. But in Barb's case, "normally" didn't seem to be working out; Rachel was sure Barb was getting dumber with each Change.

"Very nice, Barb," Rachel replied. "Very . . . very unicornish."

"That's because I'm a *unicorn,* silly!" the girl trilled, spinning in place. "I *love* it! Ooo, there's Donna! She'll go spar!"

"I'm sure she will," Rachel replied, heaving a sigh as Barb trotted off. "I swear, even when I can Change I'm not going to get *that* addlepated."

Finally she loaded a float-plate with some grilled protein, the same one that tasted, she swore, *exactly* like opossum, and looked around to see if anyone had arrived who was worth talking with. The elf was still surrounded by a huge group of people, all hanging onto his every sibilant word, and there was a wall of mostly male bodies around the dragon, who in human form was on the far side of gorgeous even if *her* body was a bit on the busty side as well.

Rachel got as close to the elf as she could, without being rude, hoping he would notice her and maybe call her forward. When that didn't work she stood at the back of the group and tried to listen to the questioning at the center. Unfortunately, the conversations on the periphery blotted it out and she couldn't even Cast to the center because of the privacy shields so many of the people had up; the technique effectively created a pool of privacy around the centerpiece so that only those in the first circle or so could hear what he was saying.

"Rachel, there's someone I'd like you to meet," Herzer whispered in her ear.

She stifled a sigh and looked around. Then up. Then up some more. She had seen some large humans and humanoids before but the person Herzer was with was very physically imposing. He was about two and half meters tall and broad in proportion. Herzer was not small, but next to this person he seemed slight. The stranger had dark skin, black really and not melanine black but some other additive that made it look black as midnight. When she finally stepped backwards for a good look she noticed some slight elven enhancements and wondered at them. Because of the Net ban on full elven upgrade, elven enhancements were generally frowned upon, especially by the elves. Adding an elven look was . . . impolite. The thought came that she knew who she was looking at just as Herzer introduced them.

"Rachel this is . . ."

"You'd be Dionys McCanoc, wouldn't you?" she asked with a nod. "Protein strip?"

"Indeed." His voice was mellifluous and she suspected that if you didn't keep your wits about you you'd drown in it. But Rachel for some strange reason found herself mildly repulsed instead. It was just too much. The size, the sardonic elvish and not-elvish face, the voice set to charm the skin off a mink. When he took her hand he kissed it and drew his thumb across the inside as he withdrew, sending a shiver through her body but leaving her emotionally even more determined to resist the charm onslaught.

"And you are the beauteous daughter of Edmund Talbot and the fair Daneh Ghorbani. I know your mother of old." He had moved forward to take her hand, crowding her personal space again and making her have to crane her neck to look up. But she refused to back up again. He could damn well hit her shields first.

There was a slight emphasis, somewhat embarrassing, on the "know." Or it would be embarrassing if Rachel hadn't heard her mother's comments about McCanoc. Daneh had gotten out of the reenactor movement, but it didn't mean she didn't keep up with some of the politics. And Daneh had much the same opinion of McCanoc that Edmund did. Rachel was sure that if she was here she'd have an even lower one. On the other hand, Rachel was pretty sure mother had never *met* McCanoc, so that was one flat lie she'd caught him in.

"I am sure you know my mother and father; they are well known in the reenactor movement. As are you, Dionys," she said with a simpering smile. No reason to incur his wrath herself and a lie for a lie. "Whatever brings you here? I would think such a . . . simple affair would not be to your tastes."

"Oh, Marguerite's mother and I have some *dealings*, you know," he said. "And when I was invited I was delighted to find that Herzer and Marguerite were friends. Now we're all friends together," he added, making an expansive gesture.

It was only then that Rachel noticed the group with him. She couldn't determine what it was about the group of five that hovered at his back but she couldn't find a thing to recommend them. One of them looked at her and positively *leered*. Just like McCanoc to somehow round up a group of total losers. But what in the hell were he and Herzer doing hanging out? She felt a flash of irritation and distress and put it down to having big-sisterly feelings for the boy. Until recently he'd had almost no social life at all.

"So how do you know Herzer?" she asked, looking around at the gathering and ignoring his crowding. She snorted as a faint blue luminance appeared in the air between them as he leaned forward. "And you seem to be encroaching on my space, Dionys. That is most inconsiderate." She took a surreptitious breath, feeling security in the shield. He was trying to intimidate her, but she had been intimidated by the best of them and even his size was not going to throw her off.

"So sorry," he said in his deep, lilting voice again. "Surely we don't need shields between *us*?"

"But, lah, sir, we have hardly met," she simpered again, fluttering the elaborate fan that had come with the outfit. She now wished she'd worn something more suitable for running. Or fighting.

"Herzer is a recent acquaintance," Dionys said, giving the boy a clout on the shoulder. It looked like a friendly hit, but it still staggered Herzer. And there was very little friendliness in McCanoc's eye.

"I met him at a reenactor meeting," Herzer said with a grin. "Do you know that he was nearly the King of Avalonia!"

"And I would have been, were it not for the judges," Dionys said darkly.

"Yes, I'm familiar with your . . . rise in the ranks," Rachel said, trying not to let any humor enter into her voice. She had heard enough about McCanoc to know how viciously vindictive he could be. She had no interest in starting a war; it just wasn't worth the effort it would take.

He regarded her for a moment trying to discern if there was anything to that simple statement. "Are you part of the reenactor movement?" the giant finally said.

"Oh, you know," Rachel dissembled. "Dad was forever dragging me off to those things. It wasn't really my sort of thing and once I could put my foot down I quit going. Some people love it and more power to them. But all that dressing up in tabards and bell-bottoms . . . not me."

"But that's a reenactor outfit," Herzer said. "Manchu Dynasty, right? And you used to *love* to study history."

"Well, study," Rachel said with an honest chuckle. "Not *live*. And the period Nazis are the *worst*. I mean, the ones who go around with their clothes washed in urine, or not washed at all. Trying to replicate the 'authentic life of the period.' I mean, *why*?"

She almost started as she drew what was apparently a real chuckle out of McCanoc. "Good point. But they were good times, times for the strong." He grinned tightly and shook his head. "Not like these fallen times."

"For the strong?" Rachel said with a grimace and a chuckle. "I suppose. But if being 'strong' means fighting a battle while dealing with dysentery, I'll take these 'fallen' times."

"Well . . ." Herzer said just as a languid hand brushed him to the side.

"What in the Seven Hells are you doing here, McCanoc?" the elf said.

"Why, Gothoriel, why ever shouldn't I be?" McCanoc replied with a thin smile. "Friends and acquaintances, don't you know. Yourself, of course, included."

"Because you were instructed to remain at least one hundred meters from any of the Eldar," the elf said, ignoring the jibe. "I note, also, that you have made further adjustments towards the Eldar. They shall not be permitted."

"I can change myself as I *choose,*" McCanoc suddenly shouted, his voice echoing across the square, caught in one of those odd moments of silence. "Stay out of my *genes.*"

"Not using Eldar Changes," Gothoriel said mildly. "You know the law. You of all people should remember the law."

McCanoc breathed deeply through his nose for a moment and then spat on the ground in front of the elf. The spittle flicked off of the shield just short of the elf's feet. "Fisk you."

"I tire of this. The Council will be informed of your *further* transgressions. For now, you have two choices. You can leave or be banished."

"I have as much right," McCanoc started to say as Gothoriel raised his hand.

"Begone," the elf snapped, then snorted in satisfaction as the air in front of him was suddenly vacant. "Like the demon you so wish to be . . ." he added so softly that Rachel was sure that only she had heard.

He turned to the five who had arrived with McCanoc and shook his head. "Begone as well. You have no purpose here."

He turned to Herzer and frowned, the first expression that had crossed his face.

"You arrived with him?" the elf asked then shook his head. "No, separate. Are you with him?"

"He's with me," Rachel interjected hurriedly, not sure why she did.

"Rachel Talbot," the elf said to her, bowing deeply. "It is good to see the Talbots are growing and thriving. A fine family, one that I have watched, and sometimes watched after for these many generations. What were you doing talking to that . . . filth?"

"Trying to figure out how to break away, frankly," she said with a sigh. "Thank you for interjecting."

"What is wrong—?" Herzer started to say.

"Later, Herzer dear," Rachel said, pinching him. "I didn't quite catch your name Lord Eldar. And I forgot to welcome you, *ethulia Eldar, cathane,*" she said, crossing her hands on her chest and bowing slightly.

"*Ethul,* milady," the elf replied, bowing again in return. "I am Gothoriel, Rider of the Eastern Reach. I have known your father for much of his life. Your lady mother less. She is, however, a fine woman. And a splendid healer."

"Thank you, milord," Rachel said, curtseying deeply. She was glad she'd decided to bring robes. "May you spend as many years in Dream as the most ancient trees and pass to the West in peace. And skip the purple protein strips."

"Too late," the elf said with a small smile. "Do you know what . . . ?"

"Yes, I wasn't sure at first but after the second try it was distinctive. I wonder whose idea it was?"

"Are you going to introduce me to your friend, Rachel?" Marguerite said from behind her. Rachel could tell from the tart tone that she was pissed.

"Marguerite," Rachel said, turning with a smile and getting her first good look at her friend since her Change. Marguerite had taken her normal form except for the slight translucence that was mandated of fully nannite entities. She could, of course, change form at will, but she seemed to prefer her baseline look for the time being.

"This is Gothoriel, Rider of the Eastern Reach. That means he's something like an ambassador to the people who live in eastern Norau."

"Hi Gotho . . . Goth . . ."

"Gothoriel," the elf said, bending to take her insubstantial hand and kiss it. He lifted it to his lips as if it were flesh and blood.

"That was . . . how did you do that?" Marguerite gasped.

"The Eldar are different in more than simple appearance," the elf replied with a slight sigh. "We have *some* dominion over the world that intersects with the Real and the Unreal. And now that you, too, have joined us in Faerie, you will have the opportunity to join us in Dream."

"Oh," Marguerite said, clearly unsure what he had just said. She turned to Rachel and waved her arms. "Rach! Isn't it *great!*"

"Wonderful," Rachel replied, smiling and hoping her friend wouldn't notice her disquiet. "But you didn't tell me about it!"

"Oh, Mom and Dad cooked this all up," Marguerite said, gesturing around and at her semitransparent body. "It was, like, a total surprise!"

"Ah."

"And they're planning a separation ceremony for next month. They're going to give me my Independence certification and do a contract dissolution at the same time. Mom wants to go be mer for a while. Dad doesn't know what he's going to do."

"What are you going to do?" Rachel asked, trying to absorb that her friend was going to be declared an independent adult when she, Rachel, still had at least two years to go. It just wasn't fair!

"Have fun, what else?" Marguerite said. "Rach, I've got to circulate some more, we'll talk later? Hi Herzer, bye Herzer."

"Sure, any time," Rachel said as she wandered off.

She looked around and realized that Marguerite wasn't the only one who was wandering off. Gothoriel had disappeared as well. Entirely, as if he'd ported or discorporated.

But Herzer was still there. Of course.

"Wow, that was intense," Herzer said, letting out a breath.

"I thought you and Marguerite got along better than a hi and bye," Rachel said.

"She started to get . . . less friendly when my illness got really advanced," Herzer said, a muscle working in his chin. "Most people got more distant when it got bad," he continued, looking down at her.

Rachel nodded her head and looked at the ground. "I know, that includes me. It was just . . . too weird. I couldn't handle it. And for that I'm sorry."

"Try living it," Herzer said with a sigh and no sign of forgiving her. "At least I have friends again. It's been a long time."

"You talking about McCanoc?" Rachel asked warily.

"Yes," Herzer said. "He's been a true friend to me, even when I was sick. Oh, he can be . . . sarcastic at times . . ."

Rachel thought that there was probably more than simple sarcasm behind that quiet statement. From what she knew about McCanoc, he would have great fun with a crippled, emotionally wounded young man around. Every twitch, trip or limp would elicit a sardonic look or a snigger from one of his lackeys.

"Herzer," she said, not sure how to proceed. "You know, there are a lot of people who don't . . . care for Dionys."

"I know," Herzer said in reply. "He told me about it. There are always people that just want to keep the status quo and don't want true genius upsetting the routine. All those stupid kings of this and barons of that, none of them were ready for the true revolution that Dionys represents! Do you know what his ultimate plan is?"

"No," Rachel said, "but . . ."

"He wants to become King of Anarchia! He intends to raise an army among those in this world and train them to take over Anarchia. That way he can rule it in peace and plenty, as Charles the Great did nearly a century ago. But *he* won't abandon the people back into anarchy!"

"Herzer," Rachel said, shaking his arm. "Listen to me. It's

not that he is a revolutionary. That's *not* why people don't like him. It's because he's an evil, bullying son of a bitch! And if you want to get on my dad's side, you'd better forget you ever *heard* of Dionys McCanoc!"

"That's bullshit, Rachel," Herzer said, setting his jaw. "Sure, he can be a bit sharp from time to time, but he's a genius. And a visionary! People like that always tend to be a bit snappish. And it's always considered to be rude until after they're *dead* and then they are recognized for their genius. That's all that's going on."

"Herzer . . ."

"You're just trying to separate me from friends that *accepted* me when you threw me out!" Herzer snarled, warming to the subject. "These people didn't turn back my calls or send messages giving me excuses why they couldn't come over! They *like* me. They liked me when I was *sick*!"

"So they could have a cripple around to torment!" Rachel nearly shouted. "McCanoc is *evil*, Herzer. He may act like your friend, but he just wants you for something."

"That's it, I'm not listening to any more," Herzer said. "You can think what you want. You'll see!"

"I'm afraid I will," Rachel said softly as he strode away. "Genie, let's go home."

"Define 'coup' in this case," Edmund said seriously.

Sheida took some time explaining Paul's position and plans. At the end of the explanation she shrugged and picked up her lizard, twining it around her neck.

"He is . . . unpersuasible. He has decided that it is his life's work to return the world to a condition of . . . growth. Both population growth and growth in thought and deed."

"And you think that he's going to do . . . what?" Talbot said, taking a sip of wine. He half wished that it were water instead; this was definitely going to need a clear head.

"I think that he intends to try to seize the Keys. At least enough to give him a voting block that is unbeatable. Then he'll implement his Plan. And, yes, there's a capital there."

"What fun," Talbot said with a grimace. "The Keys are still under that archaic 'finder's keeper's rule?"

"Unfortunately. Whoever holds the Key, votes the Key. That's locked in to the kernel coding of Mother."

"But you're all protected by personal protection fields," Talbot said. "So . . . how does he take the Keys away?"

"The PPFs were implemented with a very small majority,"

Sheida said worriedly. "If he has the Demon voting with him he can turn them off."

"But can't he do that at any time?" Edmund asked. "I mean, they could *already* be off."

"Can't, has to be an official Council vote. And all persons voting have to be *present*. Those protocols are not quite hardwired, but strong enough that he can't overcome them without a nearly full Council. Unless the Council is officially in dispute. And we're not. Yet."

"And are you telling me there are *no* assassination protocols in place?"

"Timing Edmund, timing," she sighed. "The personal protection technologies came about when there were still physical threats, and secondary defenses. But in time things became so . . . safe, so placid that the other defenses were removed as unnecessary and even . . . uncomfortable. And there used to be checks and balances, governments and police forces that were independent of the Council and the Net who could overcome such a threat; if the Council ever tried to assert real and direct authority when, say, the IU was still around, it would get slapped down fast enough."

"I sort of stopped paying attention to history when the last B-4 was decommissioned," Edmund said with a laugh. "It was the official end, wasn't it."

"Well, we might be ready to restart it. But, I mean, we're *all there is left of government*. Most people don't realize how impossible that is, historically, but *you* do! God knows we've had enough rows about it."

"I know," Edmund said, his jaw flexing. "A bunch of self-appointed dictators. I've never been happy with it. But I didn't realize that the margin of security was so *thin*. That's insane!"

"No one has tried to . . . there have been no *conflicts*, Edmund," she sighed. "We're all so smug and happy and warm and cozy that there's no *threat*. Oh, yes, at a personal level there are still threats. People have fights. But that gets resolved with the fields. Or two people agree to drop them. But that sort of thing is for . . . children, either physically or mentally. We don't have physical fights at the level of the Council and have not since . . . well there used to be guards and . . . weapons and . . . things . . ."

"Christ," Edmund sighed. "So you think that Paul is going to try to, what, kill you? Then take your Key and give it to someone else to vote? He'll have to have people ready to take the Keys and vote them, right? He can't vote them himself."

"One person, one vote, no influence," Sheida said. "Yes, Mother would know if they were being controlled and simply count it as a non-vote."

"So is dropping the PPFs the only way that he could attack you? What about outside the Council area? What about . . . I don't know . . . assassinating you right now?"

"We're . . . being careful," Sheida said. "Let's just say that Paul doesn't know where I am at any time, including right now."

"There are ways, Sheida," Edmund said, gesturing around. "Even for a Council member. There's more than just the Net. And you know that even the Council doesn't have full control of it. Only Mother does."

Sheida smiled and shrugged, chuckling. "Edmund, we're both old. And I hope, to an extent, wise. I have protectors."

Edmund paused and raised an eyebrow, then shrugged in agreement. "Don't we all." He took a sip of his wine and swished it around, looking at the ceiling. "In a way I almost agree with Paul."

"Surely not," Sheida said, eyeing him carefully.

"Well, not the *method*," Talbot added with a grimace. "But we *are* lotus-eaters. And even waiting until the gene pool gets down to only women who are programmed to want babies won't help that. But I have to admit that his method truly sucks so many ways I don't think even you have worked it all out."

"It's bad, but how bad?"

"Well, damn," he thought about that for a moment composing his thoughts. "Okay, increasing population growth 'naturally' requires all sorts of factors. First of all, you have to have natural childbirth and no contraception."

"Ugh," Sheida said, looking down. "I don't think so!"

"Furthermore, you have to have women who are more or less 'owned' by males, otherwise after the first one or two children the majority of women decide they *don't* want to do that again!"

"What about societal conditioning!" Sheida asked. "Taking the devil's advocate position."

"Generally requires religion for widespread utility," Paul said, shrugging. "But the point is that the *technological* and *economic* conditions for population growth are contrary to technological development. There are occasional times in history where that has been violated, for a generation or so, but over the course of history, over the growth period that Paul is talking about, then you're talking about a society that has to be in preindustrial conditions. And that means that there can't be technological development."

"Special groups?" Sheida asked.

"Most real advancements grow from . . . an environment that supports development. If all you have is serfs and a few technology wizards then the technology wizards are working in a research vacuum. So Paul can have technological development *or* population growth. But in a postindustrial, postinformation society, you very rarely get both." He paused and looked thoughtful but then shook his head. "There has been exactly *one* society historically that has combined both over more than a generation. And it was an . . . enormously odd unlikelihood that would be impossible to recreate under these conditions."

"Let me be clear about this," Sheida said carefully. "You *are* on my side."

"Oh, yes," Edmund said. "If Paul's planning on creating a centralized planning situation and forcing people into molds, he has to be stopped. He has *no* idea what that means. Not really."

"So what do we do?" she asked. "Edmund, you're just about the only real expert in warfare left on Earth."

"Nah, just the only one you trust," the smith replied. "I don't know the conditions. Weapons?"

"No, none, no blades anyway," she added thoughtfully. "No projectile weapons, explosives won't work under the protocols anyway."

"If they're planning a physical attack on you at the Council meeting there has to be a way to hurt you," he pointed out. "Is Paul trained in hand-to-hand combat? Killing a person hand-to-hand is difficult."

"No, and we have Ungphakorn and Cantor on our side," Sheida pointed out. "I'd take Cantor over Chansa in a fight any day."

"Porting?"

"The Council Chamber is sealed to entry for any but members, without permission. And no porting is permitted, in or out. They cannot call for reinforcements. But, nor can we."

"Poison?"

"Transmission method?" she asked. "They cannot bring projectors in, our own fields would soon detect contact or aerial poisons, and no harmful species are permitted in the room."

"Poison is subtle," Edmund pointed out. "There are binary poisons; they could have taken an antidote . . ."

"Well, I won't drink anything if they ask," she said with a winsome smile.

"You're sure of what you think?" the smith asked.

"I've been reading people for a long time," Sheida said. "Paul is planning something. Something big. Something big enough that he thinks there won't be anything I can do about it. I can't imagine what it could be but seizing control of the Council and that would take seizing the Keys. My coalition is solid."

"Well, I'll show you a few tricks and there are a few things that you can probably get in the Council Chambers that won't be considered threatening by Mother," he said. "Beyond that, there's not much I can do."

"Thank you Edmund," Sheida said. "Just talking about it has helped. Cantor just gets . . . very 'bearish' and Ungphakorn gets cryptic. You just get logical."

"I've had more practice," Talbot replied. "Both at thinking about violence and having people try to kill me. Comes of growing up wanting to be a hero," he added sadly.

CHAPTER SIX

Herzer's mount shifted under him restlessly dancing a crow-hop to the side; clearly it was more avid for the battle than he.

Herzer tapped it on the mane with his rein hand, shifting his lance in the other. "Ho, Calaban," he said absently. The north wind blew the smell of wood smoke and less savory scents from the orc encampment on the ridge above and he scanned its defenses from the cover of the woodline. It was an even bet that they had spotted him, but they weren't pouring out to attack. That meant either that there were few of them or that they were unusually well led, for orcs. The first of course would be wonderful, but the latter was much more likely. The force that had descended on the local towns was not small; there had been at least twenty in the group that attacked Shawton. Figuring a quarter of that for guards on the camp, that meant at least twenty-five up there. And they hadn't left on a raid, not by day. That meant they were holing up.

The main entrance was a narrow defile on the south side with a guarded gate at the top. On the west there was another gate, this one up a steep, tortuous switchback. That was quite impossible on a lone-hand raid. As was climbing to the cliffs above the encampment; Herzer didn't have the gear and if he got into a fight in the camp he'd need his armor to survive.

The battle was both real and unreal. The area was "real," an unhabited area of eastern Norau not far from his house.

The camp and palisades, as well as the cleared areas around it, had been constructed for him as part of the "enhanced reality" game that he was running. The horse, orcs and other defenders, if any, were constructs of nannites and powerfields. The horse that he sat was almost fully "real" but didn't have the individuality of real horses. It was as close to "reality" as he could get, though, given his limited power budget. It would have been much "cheaper" to build a palace on top of a mountain than to create this battlefield. But everyone had their priorities.

He kept the primary objective—rescue the hostage—in mind, but the question was how. Realistically, if he could keep them moving around, he was a match for twenty orcs. They were strong and fast but relatively clumsy and poor fighters. Even in plate and mail he should be able to outmaneuver them. And his armor was proof against most of their weapons.

He fingered the lance for a moment then put it in its boot, reaching behind him to unlash his pack. If the orcs killed him it would leave most of his worldly possessions for them to loot. But it the orcs killed him he wouldn't need any of them anyway. Climbing rope and lanterns were not turning out to be useful on this particular quest. Without the weight the pack represented, Calaban could carry him with relative ease, despite the weight of his armor, weapons and not inconsiderable body.

He weighed weapons for a moment then kept his lance, axe and sword, dropping the bow with the pack. He had need for all three that he kept, cumbersome as it was to carry them. The sword and axe went onto his saddle as he lifted the lance back out of the boot.

"All right, Calaban, let's give them what for," he said, nudging the horse with his knee as he hefted his kite shield.

He trotted out into the meadow below the encampment and stopped just short of the shallow brook. Most of it was high banked and relatively deep, at least thigh deep. Not easy to cross on foot and impossible for the horse. But opposite the entrance the bank had been broken down at a narrow ford. The slopes to either side were still impossible, and movement would be restricted to one rider at a time. But it was where he had to cross.

Now he could see orc heads popping up over the gate, but still none of them stepped forward. Very well.

"Orcs! Orcs of the encampment! I have come to deliver your souls to hell!"

"Go away! We have nothing you want and live in peace with humans!" a high voice screeched back.

"You have raided the towns of Evard, Korln and Shawton. I know for I have tracked you back to your lair! And you have taken the daughter of the Earl of Shawton for ransom! Deliver her to me unharmed and I will spare you your lives!"

There was derisive hooting from the far side of the wall but he was just as glad. That meant they might come out and fight him on the flats.

"Go away horse-rider! You cannot defeat us for we are the Tribe of the Bloody Hand and we have never been defeated!"

"Well, there's a first time for everything you misbegotten goblins. Is it true that you were made by mixing pigs and apes?"

The screeching redoubled on the other side of the fence but they still didn't come out.

"The orcs were the first peoples!" the voice screeched back. "They were before the elves and the humans! It is *you* who were begotten of pigs and apes you . . . you . . ."

"No, tell me true? Is it true that your mother was a water-front whore who couldn't get anyone to pay for her because she was too ugly? So she did it with the creature from the black lagoon when he was drunk? And thus you were begotten, a black, dripping monstrosity that even your friends among the orcs, the only people who will have you, run shrieking from in horror?"

"I . . . I . . . aaaaarrrrr!"

The gate at the top of the defile opened outward and a swarm of orcs poured through, at their head a broad and tall troll.

"Oh, shit," Herzer muttered, timing the moment to start his charge. The troll, fortunately, was outdistancing the orcs rapidly. Finally Herzer leaned forward and kicked the horse into movement. "Hi, Calaban! Forward!"

He couched the lance and balanced the weight of it, aiming it to strike the troll broad on the chest. The fearsome creature seemed to pay no attention and seemed uninterested in blocking, intent on coming to grips with his tormentor. Thus Herzer was able to lean into the weapon at the last moment and drive it home fully. The impact drove him back onto the high rear cantle of his saddle and nearly stopped Calaban, but the troll was mortally wounded. The creature roared as the spear jutted out of his back in a welter of red blood, and grasped the shaft, swinging it from side to side as he thrashed.

Herzer started to draw his sword but was struck, hard, on the upper arm just as the sword cleared the scabbard; the weapon clattered to ground as he was nearly unseated.

After a moment he pulled his axe out instead and kneed Calaban in closer to the creature, which was maddened with pain. The horse stood a scoring across the flank as he maneuvered into position, then in a double-hand blow Herzer cut the head from the troll. The horse stepped back daintily as the giant beast fell to the ground.

The orcs, who were just approaching the scene of the battle, let out a cry of fear at that but they didn't stop, charging forward in a mass. There were far more than twenty but Herzer felt sure he could prevail.

He backed Calaban around to avoid the first rush of orcs, swinging the axe to strike down a few on the fringes as he did so. He really needed his sword or lance for this work; the axe was a short-hafted ground-fighting weapon.

A group of orcs was trying to get around behind him, possibly to try to hamstring Calaban, but he didn't need to worry about that. As one of them rushed in, swinging its shortsword, the horse lashed backwards with both feet, killing the creature and tossing it into its fellows so as to bowl several of them to the ground.

However, that short pause had been enough for others to gather around, swinging their black crusted swords and axes and trying to grab at reins or drag Herzer from the saddle.

Herzer kicked the horse in the side again, swinging downward on either side to try to clear a path. Finally the team broke out of the mass of orcs, headed up along the streambed. He kicked Calaban again but felt her falter as a flight of crossbow bolts flew down from the hilltop.

Realizing the horse could never face the battle in her wounded condition he rolled off to the side and slapped her on the flank. More bolts flew down towards him but he was able to deflect them with his shield as he trotted back towards the reduced mass of orcs.

Again they charged him but there were a few low trees, willows and a few scrubby poplars, along the riverbank and he darted into them to break up the charge. It was a wild time for a moment in among the bushes as orcs charged in from either side and he hewed and slew with abandon. They got in a few licks of their own and he felt a distinct catch in his side where an orc champion had landed a telling blow with a battle-hammer. But the champion was at his feet in a welter of gore and not the other way around. So all was well.

He finally broke contact across the brook, which he could negotiate better than the orcs could since it was only thigh deep on him here, and swung to the east, moving back to the original ford. The orcs paralleled him on the far bank and then tried to dart ahead to the ford, but he made it there first.

In the narrow slot to the ford on "his" side of the river there was no way that more than one, or at most two, orcs could attack him. There he stood his ground, hammering on orc shields as they hammered right back. A few more of them had poured out of the encampment but he was killing them faster than they could be reinforced, his relatively light axe crashing through their guards and shattering shoulders, arms and heads.

The narrow ford soon became clogged with bodies and the following orcs had to clamber over the piles of the dead. Occasionally they fell towards him and he had to step backwards to avoid being pushed over, so he had slowly been backed towards the top of the bank. However, there were fewer than ten orcs left in the attacking force and, apparently realizing they could not defeat him in the meadow, they suddenly gave out a cry and ran back to the defile, then up through their gates, closing them firmly behind them.

With the retreat of the foe the battle fury came off of him and the pain from his wounds flooded in to replace it. Besides the catch in his side, which felt very much like a broken rib, he now noticed a rather nasty gash on the back of his right leg. A few inches deeper and he would have lost all use of the leg. As it was, he didn't even recall getting it.

He whistled for Calaban and stumbled across the body-choked ford to the far side. There were probably some things worth looting on the bodies, but that could wait.

His lance was done for, until he could either give the head of it back to a good armorer or find an appropriate hickory sapling. He'd really rather let someone else fix it; he was for a town and a good rest as soon as this battle was done.

The horse walked up from wherever it had disappeared to as he found his sword under a body. He retrieved rags from one of his remaining saddle bags and wiped the blood off of it and his axe then loaded both onto the horse along with his shield, which was starting to get heavy.

He worked on Calaban's wounds next. First he numbed the wounds with an odd gray poultice then worked the barbed heads out of the flesh. The latter was difficult because the horse, despite the successful local anesthesia, danced around from the odd pulling sensation. When he finally had the bolts removed he packed the punctures with salve that would speed the healing.

After that he worked on his own problems. He was tired and sore but except for treating the gash on his leg there wasn't much he could do. He had some bruises and the rib, but they would require more work than he could do in the field. Finally he put a bandage, liberally laced with salve, onto the slash on his leg and laboriously repaired the mail over it. The cut had been an attempted coup de poing but it had not been quite powerful enough to cut through the well-wrought Alladon mail. At least not enough to do any real damage.

His wounds tended to, he took out a small vial and regarded it cautiously. The material in it was unpleasant to drink, oversweet but with a bitter undertaste, and it had limited effect. But it would invigorate him for a short period of time, enough to defeat the rest of the orcs. And if its effectiveness ran out he could take another. But each successive use gave less time invigorated. He'd need some real rest soon.

Finally he loaded his weapons back up and strode towards the gates of the encampment. No bow fire greeted him so he headed to the base of the defile and yelled up at the wooden palisade on the hilltop.

"I call upon you to let the daughter of the Earl of Shawton free. If you do so I will spare your lives. If you do not I will kill all the fighters and burn your village, turning your women and children out into the winter. Heed me!"

"Go away!" came the reply, not so loud or fearsome as before. "We have never been to this Shawton."

"This is your last chance!" Herzer yelled, pulling out a vial of the herbal stimulant.

"Go away!"

"Stupid bastards," he muttered, draining the vial in a single draught and tossing it over his shoulder. He drew his axe and raised it over his head. "For Mithras and Alladale!" he bellowed. Over his shoulder, out of the clear sky, a boom of thunder rolled. Cool.

He charged up the defile, holding his shield over his head against the anticipated rain of stones. Sure enough, every orc in the encampment seemed to be pelting him with rocks, chunks of wood, dead cats and whatever else could be found. With the exception of a couple of what must have been fair-sized boulders none of it was a hindrance and he quickly made it up the slot to the gate.

There were apparently stands behind the gate, but unlike in the defile, only a few orcs could look down at him here and he swung his shield to the rear to give himself room for two-handed swinging. The gate was made of thick logs held up with ropes and hinges but there were narrow gaps between the logs and he swung through the gaps at the bar on the far side. Some judicious chops at the logs opened up the gaps to where he could get at the bar better and he fell to a steady swinging rhythm, quickly chopping through the thick barrier.

As soon as the bar parted he dropped the axe and swung the gates open, ripping out his sword as the remaining defenders charged him at the gate.

He could see the earl's daughter now. The girl was no more than sixteen, with fair skin and red hair, unbound and flowing to her waist. She was tied to a post in the center of the encampment, and a spit and fire had been erected nearby. It was clear that the orcs had been intending to have her for supper when Herzer arrived and interrupted. An orc shaman capered in front of the fire, casting in foul-smelling herbs and gesturing maniacally.

Now it was another fearsome melee but with nearly an arm's length of good Narland steel in his hands, the orcs didn't stand a chance. He pushed forward into their mass, striking from side to side and parrying their blows with his much battered shield.

But just as he neared the end of the defenders the shaman gave a last great cry and a fearsome apparition, a man-sized demon, arose from the flames. It was covered in spikes and had a vague resemblance to the orcs but that was all the description that Herzer could make as the thing leapt through the air and slammed into his shield.

He swung at it and connected on the shoulder. But for all the good the Narland steel had made it might have struck stone. It bounced from the shoulder with a jolt in his hand as the demon's fist struck him in the chest.

The blow threw him backwards to slam into the palisade and he shook his head trying to clear it of the ringing as the demon pounced once again.

Suddenly, horny fingers closed around his mail-protected throat and started to squeeze. He flailed with his sword at the demon's side but it was to no avail. Slowly the world around him went black. . . .

"Fisk," Herzer muttered, sitting up from the ground and looking around at the training field. His throat still had a psychosomatic tight feeling to it, but VR always did that. "I hate losing."

"You should have more fully scouted the encampment," his instructor said, handing him a flagon.

Herzer took the water and drank gratefully, then got to his feet. "I know that. Now. The demon was a bit unfair."

"Life is unfair," the avatar replied. It was a very high-end program, not fully AI but smarter than most standard systems, and it had a mass of proverbs and quips to draw upon. "You have to be more unfair. What should you have done?"

"As it was, I'm not sure," Herzer replied. "I couldn't take the demon. Not by myself."

"What about the shaman?" the trainer asked.

"Hmmm . . ." Herzer called up the schematic of the recent battle and nodded. "I couldn't have made it through the orcs to kill him before he completed the enchantment. So . . . take off most of the armor, climb the cliffs, reconnoiter. Wait for a good time and kill the shaman with the bow. That way I'd know about the troll, too. Maybe try to kill both from long range, and some of the orcs. They would have eventually come out, but I would have been fighting them from the top of the slope, not the bottom. But I'd have to get the shaman first, or else he'd summon the demon and I'd have to fight it anyway."

"It was the shaman who was the primary threat, but it seemed, at first, to be just a bunch of orcs," the trainer said. "Your failure to properly reconnoiter the objective was your undoing. Your enemy will attempt to deceive you. He will attempt to appear less capable than he is. Remember that. *Know* your enemy and know thyself. All else will become clear if you know both."

"Herzer, playing wargames?" Dionys' head had popped into existence over the shoulder of the avatar. The avatar did not seem to notice.

"Just finished," Herzer replied, finishing the water.

"We're having a bit of a party over at Sean's, something fun," the older man said. "Why don't you come along." It was a statement, not a question.

Herzer was mentally drained if not physically, but he didn't want to lose Dionys' good grace. "Just let me clean up a bit," he said. "I'll be over in a few minutes."

"Great," McCanoc said with a toothy smile. "We'll be waiting."

"Gotta go," Herzer said, tossing the cup to the trainer.

"Remember, young Herzer, know thyself," the avatar said as he left.

Edmund hammered the glowing sword blade and turned it over on the anvil, trying to determine how much more work it would take. He looked up with a nod as Myron Raeburn walked into the forge.

"I need you to beat a couple of those into plowshares," Myron said with a grin.

"Very funny," Talbot growled in reply. "What can I do for you, Myron?"

"You don't seem particularly happy this morning," the farmer said, cocking his head to the side.

"Even paradise has its thorns," Edmund replied obliquely. "What sort of plowshares do you need?"

"Dionys still giving you trouble?" Myron pursued, taking a seat on a smaller anvil. The weather computers had allowed a late-season cold front through to the east coast and the warmth of the forge was pleasant after the cold walk from his fields.

"No, Dionys hasn't tried any tricks since our little discussion," the smith admitted. "That is part of it. Other things as well. I don't particularly want to talk about it."

"Gotcha," the farmer replied. "Well the reason I came down is that I managed to secure a vintage water-powered threshing machine," he continued with a grin.

"Going to install it by the mill?" Edmund frowned. "It's not period; the period Nazis are going to go ape." He thought about that for a moment then grinned. "Need help?"

"I can get it set up myself," Raeburn replied with a matching grin. "But the millennia have not been kind to it, for all it was well kept. A couple of the spave arms need serious work . . ."

"You can replicate those," Edmund argued shaking his head. "It makes no sense for me to just beat them out."

"Edmund," the farmer replied, spreading his hands, "I know that but . . . I mean I use a horse drawn *plow*, for Ghu's sake. I'm willing to replicate the building, there's no other way short of waiting for Faire and hoping I can get some people to help me erect it. But . . ."

"I'll do it," Edmund sighed then chuckled. "Chisto I'm glad we don't really live in the thirteenth century."

"Me too. Indoor plumbing."

"Medical nannites."

"Insulation."

"Dwarves!" said a gravelly, accented voice from the door.

The visitor was short, just below five feet, and nearly as broad as he was tall. He wore furs against the weather over chain mail and leather. He had a broad double-headed axe over his shoulder and a round half helm on his head. And he was wearing a broad, toothy grin surrounded by a beard that hung nearly to the floor.

"Angus!" Talbot said, striding over and grabbing the dwarf around his broad shoulders. "You could have sent a rider ahead!"

"No dwarf will ride a horse if their own legs, or a wagon, will carry them," the dwarf said, leaning his axe on the wall. "Bloody cold weather to travel, though. Glad I am for the warmth of thy forge."

Two centuries before Angus Peterka had gotten so enraptured by the traditional image of dwarves that he had Changed and started his own dwarf colony in the Steel Hills of Sylva. The hills had been mined out millennia before, but in the last half a millennia most of the materials had been reimplanted under a long-term ecological rebuilding program or through dumping into the hollowed out mines. He had added materials that were not original to the mountains, streams of silver, various jewels, gold and, deep, deep in the mountain a nanotech-based material that he had decided met the conditions for adamantine. All of the material was put in with a semirandom generator and for the last two centuries he'd been trying to find it all. He referred to it as "proper mining," his friends referred to it as "the world's largest scavenger hunt." Other "dwarves" came and went, but Angus stayed on, propping shafts, finding veins and quaffing beer.

As a hobby, Edmund thought that it ran to obsession. On the other hand, his own obsessions had driven away more lady friends than he cared to count, including the only one he had ever truly loved. He wasn't one to cast stones.

"I've your steel load," Angus said, walking over to the forge to warm his hands. "And I've finally found a vein of bloody adamantine. I'd be happy for your opinion." He held out a hand-sized bar of a dull gray material.

"Doesn't look like much," Edmund replied, tossing it in the air. Strangely, when he threw it it seemed to have almost no weight, but when it smacked into his palm the impact was palpable. "Nannite enhanced?"

"Enhanced, yes, but they aren't *in* it, ya see," Angus said.

"It was developed in . . . hmmm . . . the twenty-third century or so as a reactive material for powered body armor. So it's legal for nonpowered unlimited armor tourneys!"

"Ah," Myron said. "Doesn't matter, nobody else will like it as ugly as it is."

"It changes appearance when you final treat it," Angus said, taking the bar and tossing it in the forge. "You can't just heat it; no fire you can make in a forge, even a multistage one, will affect it. It's rated to stay intact in a photosphere; you *have* to use nannites and electromagnetic fields to form it. But, oh, when you *do* work it!" He drew his belt knife and flourished the blade. "Behold! Adamantine!"

The knife blade was bright silver with a rainbow shimmer running through it. Edmund took the knife and ran his finger against it, drawing back a cut callus. Then he took up the sword blade he had been working on and scratched the knife blade against it. Instead of leaving a streak or a small cut it sliced deeply into the metal.

"Bloody hell," Myron said.

"Did I mention it will form a monomolecular edge?" Angus said with another beard-shrouded grin.

"Strange feel," Talbot said thoughtfully, tossing the knife up and down. After a couple of tosses he threw it to stick in the door. The knife sank up to its hilt. "Nonperiod metals. The Council won't permit it for tourney."

"Not regular tourneys, no," Angus said with a shrug. "But unlimited nonpowered, yes."

"Yah," Edmund said. "How did you say you form it?" he asked, plucking the material out of the fire. He tested it with a wetted finger but as he half expected it was not even warm. "Strange stuff."

"Molecularly it's even stranger. Basically for the first run you set up a molecular lattice using nannites. After it's formed the first time, it's easier to work with. But on subsequent formings you have to convince it it's ready to be worked."

"Explains a lot," Edward grinned. "I *can* look it up you know."

"Go ahead then," Angus replied with a broad smile through his beard. "One of the things the original researchers missed is that there's a way to make it from other ores. Naturally occurring ones."

"It's still not useable in tourney," Talbot said. "And it's not the best material available for unlimited combats. So it's cute, but that's about it."

"Not quite," Angus replied, pointing at his mail. "Genie, disengage personal protection field. Now, Edmund, take a whack at me."

"No way," Edmund said, glancing around the forge. "I don't have a finished blade."

"Use my axe," Angus argued. "Go ahead. It won't hurt."

"The axe will cut through the bloody armor, you idiot!"

"Nah, try it."

"It looks like steel," Talbot temporized, picking up the axe.

"You can make it look that way," Peterka said. "Strike!"

"Shit," Edmund said, drawing back the blade. "You asked for it." He swung hard, aiming *though* the dwarf. Even in mail, even if the alloy held which, in all honesty it probably would, the impact was bound to at least crack a rib. At the very least, it would be painful as hell. But any damage he would do, the nannites would fix quickly enough.

The axe struck the mail and rebounded as if it had hit a wall of steel. He dropped it with a grimace at the harmonics.

"Bloody hell!"

Angus had been knocked backwards by the blow but he grinned nonetheless.

"When two pieces of the material in contact are subjected to lateral motion, basically when they experience friction, they form temporary carbon to carbon covalent bonds. I said it was designed as *reactive* armor. When you hit it, it turns into plate. *Diamond* plate."

"Now *that's* interesting," Edmund said, poking at the now supple mail. One of the buggers about using plate was that it didn't flex. A person wearing it was locked into the form of the armor, sometimes uncomfortably. "What about when you're moving, bending arms, stuff like that?"

"The energy isn't high enough to matter. It's a tad less flexible than standard mail, but not much."

"Interesting," Talbot muttered. "How do you work it?"

"It's a proprietary program," Peterka said. "But since you're such a good friend . . ." he added with a grin.

"You're going to go off playing with this and not work on my thresher, aren't you?" Myron said.

"Nah, I can do both. Bring me over the pieces you need repaired and the specs and I'll do them for you."

"Right, that's settled," Angus said. "Now let's go get us a drink and celebrate my finding the first vein."

"How much of this is there?" Myron asked.

"Not that much in the first vein, but there's more," the dwarf replied. "We'll find the rest. It's bloody deep, though. We're at a depth that period pumps don't handle well."

"There's period and there's period," Edmund said. "Buy me a drink, and what's more important get me some of this stuff to play with, and I'll fill you in on some aspects you might not have considered."

"Deal."

CHAPTER SEVEN

"Deal," Daneh sighed, terminating the call.

The job was not her favorite; a person wanted an "original" Transfer into something very much like a manta ray. But it was for a worthy cause—the form was a deep-diver and the person wanted to do deep sea research "on site"—and there weren't any serious problems like Herzer's to work on.

Out of the corner of her eye she saw Azure lift up and shake himself, heading for Rachel's room, which probably meant that she was back. Thinking about it, Daneh didn't think she'd seen her daughter in a couple of days.

"Rachel?" Daneh called, and her voice was automatically transferred to the girl's room.

"Yes, Mother?"

"Where have you been?"

There was a pause that caused Daneh to sit up and override whatever answer she was going to get. "Come in here for a moment, will you?"

"Yes, Mother," Rachel replied with a sigh that was faithfully replicated by the transmission system.

As soon as the girl walked into the room, Daneh's stomach sank. She'd already been feeling depressed about not having any projects to test her mettle. And now this.

"Rachel, I thought we had agreed no body sculpting?"

There wasn't much, but to her expert eye it stood out like a lightbulb. Rachel's eyebrows had been curved, her cheekbones sharpened and her nose slightly thinned. Furthermore, she had had her breasts reduced and her butt tucked even more than for Marguerite's party.

"*I* didn't agree, *you* agreed," Rachel answered hotly.

"I'm your parent, it's *my* decision," Daneh replied coldly. "Where did you have it done?"

"I don't have to tell you that," the girl said, crossing her arms. "I . . . I don't have to say."

"You could have gotten it off the Net," Daneh said, tilting her head to the side. "It's the sort of generic junk you can find there," she added with professional disdain. "But the Net has my specific prohibition against it. So how *did* you get it done?"

"I Don't Have To Say," Rachel repeated. "And it's *not* generic junk!"

"Well, it's very poorly constructed," Daneh said, coldly. "Give me the benefit of my expertise here, daughter. The eyebrows are *badly* balanced, the cheekbones detract from the nose and the combination makes you look like a short-beaked bird. I mean, it's *not* well done."

"Well, you wouldn't *let* me get a *well-done* job, Mother," she spat, furiously. Then she slumped shaking her head. "But . . . you're right. It *does* look awful, doesn't it?"

"Not awful," Daneh said, tightly. "But it's neither fashionable, not that I like the current fashions, they're very unhealthy, nor is it particularly good looking on *you*. Face it, dear, unless or until you get a complete body and face sculpt, and end up looking like your friend Marguerite and all the other kids who were stamped out of the exact same genetic modeling kit, there's not much you can do to look like current fashions. You're too . . ." Daneh paused, searching for the right words.

"Fat," Rachel said.

"Not fat, womanly," Daneh replied. "Nobody these days is fat. Fat is when you have flabby bits hanging . . ." She looked at her stomach and arms and shrugged. "You've seen pictures. You're *beautiful* dear. You know very well that at times you would have been considered beyond beautiful," she added with a sigh.

"Sure, Mom, but these days guys don't think in terms of women who are built to survive minor famines."

"You're not exactly a Reubens model," Daneh replied. "Do you want it undone? Or do you want to keep it until you can get a proper bod-sculpt? I know some people who do very good work."

"When?" Rachel asked, surprised.

"When you turn eighteen," Daneh replied. "In the meantime, you're grounded *indefinitely*. If you can't keep a promise like this one, I'm not sure what promises you *will* keep."

"Mother!"

"Don't 'mother' me," Daneh said. "The proof that you aren't old enough to make the decision is that you went behind my back to do it and then got it done badly."

"Oooo . . . I . . . I . . ." Rachel worked her jaw furiously and then spun on her heel and stalked out of the room.

"Genie, I'm serious about the grounding. Remind me of it in a week."

"Yes, ma'am," the program responded.

Daneh sighed and rubbed her temples. "What a day."

Dionys' surprise turned out to be . . . a girl. Or, Herzer thought much more likely, a homunculus. She, and about a half dozen of McCanoc's usual hangers on, were in a wooded glen. She was small and fragile looking with a short black hair and an elfin face. And she looked frightened.

"Is that a homunculus?" he asked, just to be sure. Normally the homunculus would have been wearing a rather simple smile. This one looked downright terrified. Just to be sure, he sent a mental query to the Net and was assured that it was, in fact, a homunculus. Not a terrified preteen girl.

"Oh yes," Dionys replied with a sardonic grin. "But a very special one. She has been programmed to fear sex. So much more . . . interesting."

"I thought they were illegal?" Herzer said, breathlessly. His face and hands felt hot.

"Not . . . illegal so much as restricted," Dionys said with another grin. "It helps to have friends in high places."

Herzer was not a virgin, at least with homunculi. There was some debate about whether that counted but with the onset of the worst of his symptoms, making friends, especially girl-friends, had been tough. So homunculi were the only route open to his developing teenage libido short of using his hand. And he always cast himself in the role of the hero, the pure paladin on the white charger. But . . .

He knew the allure. The desire not just to be in a woman, be one with one, but to control her and dominate. To take instead of negotiate or, in the case of normal homunculi, be given freely. It was a secret he normally kept deep inside and one that he didn't discuss. Ever. There was no one to talk to about it. No one who would . . . understand. He'd heard rumors about homunculi being abused, some of them even having to be recycled and replaced. Now he understood why.

Hero? Or rapist? Sometimes . . . the line seemed so strange. The joy of battle was so close to how he felt when he fantasized . . . bad things. Even in his own mind he had a hard time saying "rape." To take the life of an orc, to slaughter his enemies and see them running before his charger, to throw a frightened girl to the ground and take what had been withheld. To get back at all the girls who sniggered at him when the convulsions would hit. All the girls who rejected him when he needed them most. To take and take again. To punish.

Was he a paladin or a villain? He just couldn't decide.

Especially now looking at this vulnerable, frightened . . . toy. She wasn't a real woman, a real girl. She was just an artificial construct. Somehow that both relieved him and made the . . . thing less illicit. Almost less interesting. But not much.

"Please," the homunculus whispered, tears running down her cheek. "Please . . ."

He felt the heat rising in his body no matter how he tried to check it. This was just . . .

"There's nothing wrong," Dionys said. "Men have . . . needs. This is one way to let them out. Women have . . . very similar needs you'll eventually find. But even that is so sterile. So many rules, so many precautions. This is the real." He tapped Herzer on the back. Lightly. "Go ahead. Take her. Enjoy."

Herzer took an involuntary step forward and reached out one hand to the girl's blouse. It was white silk with old-fashioned buttons to match the short skirt of the same material. He imagined himself ripping the blouse open, running his hand up her thighs . . . taking her.

"Please don't," the girl whimpered. "Please . . . ?"

He worked his jaw for just a moment and shook his head. "No, Dionys," he said, harshly. "This isn't right."

"How can it not be?" The man sounded more surprised than anything else, as if the thought had never occurred to him. "She's only a homunculus."

"And her fear isn't real," Herzer agreed, although it was an intellectual agreement only. "But . . . it's still not right. I'm not . . . this isn't right." He looked at the two holding her arms but they just grinned. "It's not right."

"So you've said," Dionys replied, disapprovingly. "Very well, if you don't want to stay and enjoy yourself, you can go. Go to your meek little playthings and all the so-called friends who betrayed you."

Herzer started to open his mouth to reply but at the look on McCanoc's face he shook his head instead. "Home, genie."

Sheida glanced around at the Council as she entered the vast chamber, but if there was mischief on anyone's mind, it wasn't showing. Celine had apparently decided to copy Ishtar's hairstyle, and her hair, suitably lengthened, was gathered in a giant confection shot through with crystal wasps made of gold and ebony.

Paul and the rest of "his" faction had gathered at one end of the table, so as Sheida, who had carefully arrived last, settled into her seat he stood up to call the Council to order.

"The first thing is to change the agenda," Paul said. "Mother, refer to the first item on Agenda B, please." He looked towards the entrance and smiled. "And here is our seventh voter."

Sheida glanced over her shoulder quickly, thinking as she did so that it might be a trick but then blanched.

"You've called in the DEMON?" she shouted. At the shout her lizard unwound from her neck and took off upwards towards the top of the chamber. It found a perch where it could look down and watch the rest of the proceedings through baleful eyes.

"Indeed he did," the apparition growled. "And I vote *aye*." The Demon's true form was impossible to know since he went everywhere in a suit of black armor. The helmet of the armor had been worked into a bestial face, all staring eyes and tusks, and the gloves were tipped with long talons. He was one of the two normally absent holders of the Keys, older than any of the rest of the Council. He had extended his life by means that were highly illegal, using the power of his position to twist the laws to his own purpose. His purpose had always been chaos, so his appearance at this meeting made terrible sense.

There was a series of rapid "ayes" from Paul's faction and he smiled broadly.

"The personal protection fields are now turned off," he said with a moue. "Item two, aye." After the same series of seven agreements he shrugged. "And the Council is now officially in a dispute situation with rump rules applying." He looked at Sheida sadly. "I do this for all mankind. You cannot stand in the way of the survival of the human race. Celine?"

"Welcome to the new order," Celine said, rising to her feet. "My friends wish to make your acquaintance," she continued as her hair seemed to explode outward.

Sheida cursed as the cloud of insects came flying across the room. Poisons and poisonous life-forms were not allowed in the Council chamber, but there were two types of wasps in the group, black and yellow.

"Binary toxins!" she shouted, springing to her feet and overturning her chair in her haste. As she did the Demon sprang through the air.

Cantor was already on his feet and didn't even bother to Change as one arm swept into Tetzacola Duenas. The impact snapped the man's neck and he was flung through the air in the direction of Sheida just as the Demon landed on the werebear's back.

Ungphakorn wasn't inactive either. He had grasped the top of the table and uncoiled from his oversized seat, his long serpentine body flipping down the table and enwrapping Said. In a flash the council member was dragged from his chair and wrapped in coil after coil of feathery body. He let out one cry, more of a squeaking scream, then his tongue and eyes protruded as the serpent applied full power in a constrictive hug of death. The quetzacoatal ripped the Key from his neck and half flew, half slithered across the chamber towards the entrance, the tip of his tail flicking back and forth snapping at the wasps closing in on him.

Sheida's flying lizard stooped from its perch, its wings folded onto its back, and snapped one of the wasps out of the air, crunching down on it and spitting it out at the taste. It hissed as it flew past Celine, grabbing at more of the insects as it darted hither and yon.

Sheida raised her arm and a bracelet extended into a broad shield. She flipped it through the air and swatted aside two of the wasps as she bent to the dead council member and ripped the Key from Tetzacola's neck.

"Out!" she shouted, backing towards the entrance.

Cantor was still wrestling with the Demon as two of the wasps landed on him and began probing for an open spot in his fur. She looked towards him but he just shook his head at her.

"Get out!" he yelled, ripping his Key off and throwing it towards her. He pulled his hands loose from the Demon's grip and took two of the beast's tusks, turning its head up and back. "Go!" he cried as the first sting hit.

Ishtar had touched a control on her hover seat and fled the room at the first sign of trouble, some of the wasps following her out. Sheida was relatively sure that she was going to survive but she found herself and Aikawa the only ones left in a room full of enemies.

"Time to leave," she said, backing rapidly towards the door and flicking another of the wasps away with her shield as her flyer guardian snapped another out of the air and landed on her head, tongue flickering in and out.

"Hmmm," Aikawa said snatching one of the wasps out of the air and crushing it in a move that looked like some sort of magic. "I suppose," he murmured, catching up another and considering the insect as it struggled before crushing it between his fingers. He was careful to keep away from the business end at the rear. He dropped both of the crushed bodies into a pouch and then waved at his former colleagues. "I'm going to kill you all for this." With that he flipped out of the room in a series of seemingly impossible back-flips.

Sheida was now surrounded by a cloud and felt the first sting as she kept backing towards the door. "Goodbye, Paul. And I'll see you in hell." With that she took one more swat and fled. The last thing she saw on the way out the door was Cantor's body beginning to spasm. But he still had a death grip on the Demon.

The four surviving Council members had fled by prearrangement to a home that Sheida maintained in the Teron mountains. From its main room there was a spectacular view down to a tarn similar to that at the Council Center. But it was across the world from that embattled chamber.

"Paul will follow us," Aikawa said, looking around.

"Not easily," Sheida said, striding across the room and yanking open a cupboard. She tossed an archaic can to Ishtar and a long, curved sword to Aikawa. "The house has its own power supply, divorced from the Net. And a teleport block. And weapons. Let him come."

"There is a dip in power in the Net," Ishtar said, looking at something that was invisible to the rest. "He is preparing something. . . ."

As she spoke, a bolt flew out of the clear sky and crashed into an invisible barrier over the house, sending a tremor through the floor as something in the basement began to screech.

"Oh, and a protection field," Sheida said as her lizard took

off in fright from the impact. "That was from the Council
Chambers themselves. We can't reply directly but . . ." She
opened her mind to the Net and delved in, looking for weak-
nesses. "They're drawing power directly from the Net, but
they're not hooked into a particular plant." She considered
the protocols and twisted. "I need a vote, all in favor of
disconnecting all power distribution say 'aye.' "

"But if we do that . . ." Ishtar temporized just as another
bolt crashed into the screen.

"That barrier won't hold forever," Sheida said. "And if they
get smart they'll just burn the rocks out from under us."

"People will die," Aikawa said.

"We're about to have a war," Sheida replied. "And we *don't*
have enough time to debate. We can't take all the power plants
to our own control, they already tried that and the protocols
are against it. But if we send people to take physical control
we can control the power distribution." Her forehead creased
and then she nodded. "I just dropped a half a dozen satellites on them. That should make things interesting. And I'm
diverting as much power out of the Net as I can to melt the
ground under them. Of course, we're more vulnerable to that
than they are."

"I just increased the power over this place," Ishtar said as
the next bolt stopped well in the sky. "And I sent a similar
bolt against them. There is an upper limit to power available
from our personal queue. I'd never realized that. It's . . . rather
high, though," she added as another blast caused the mountain to shudder. "I suggest that we reinforce the foundations
of this place. Soon."

"Mother won't give any of us unlimited power, that's a
holdover protocol from the AI wars," Aikawa said. He thought
for a moment. "Okay, we disconnect all generators from the
Net. What does that do?"

"We'll have to draw from them individually," Sheida said.
There were fourteen terawatt generators that supplied power
for the Net along with some relatively small secondary sources
such as geothermal areas where the nannites bled off power
to prevent eruptions and other disturbances. There had been
a time in history, shortly after the AI wars, when the power
had peaked at over thirty terawatts. But use of that much power
on the surface of the planet had led to severe secondary
problems and as the population had peaked the power allot-
ment had stayed the same but usage dropped. There had been
occasional calls for increases in generation, but when output

got over twenty terawatts, much of it had to be diverted to climate control.

"That means that whoever has the generators, has the power," Ishtar said. "I'm tracing the flows that they're using right now and they're drawing on spare power from two of the reactors in Ropasa. If we can prevent them from gathering power from the others . . ."

"Then we start calling in people that we know we can trust to go and take physical possession of the generators," Sheida said with a nod. "At that point we will control their output and Paul can't have it." Her face creased and she smiled. "Okay, I've joined Ishtar in hammering the Council Chamber. I also put a teleport block over them."

"That takes power, too," Ishtar said with a frown. "And two can play at that game; one just went on here."

"Yes, but I have a decent road out," Sheida laughed. "Let them try walking out of the Council Center."

"Then we end up having fights for the generators," Ungphakorn said, ruffling his feathers furiously. "We'll have to shield each of them."

"But I'd bet money I have better friends at that sort of thing than they do," Sheida replied, nodding. "Okay, avatars on the way."

"We're taking power from general usage already," Ishtar noted in wonder. She looked up at the hills around the house. Where once had been trees towering into the sky was now a blackened heath; the secondary effects of an irresistible force hitting an inanimate object. "There's enough to sustain the Net currently, but if we keep this up . . ."

"If we don't keep it up, Paul and his 'five year plan' wins," Sheida replied. "We can't let that happen."

"And we have two additional Keys," Aikawa noted, holding one up. "That puts us at near parity with them."

"But *we* don't have anyone to vote or use them," Ishtar said. "We need two. Two that we can *trust*."

"I know one," Sheida said.

"The power grid . . ." Ishtar gasped, her eyes staring into the infinity of the Net. "The power grid is . . . going down."

The two fighters circled each other warily each searching for an opening. They were armed and armored alike, mail, helmet, a cuirass and shield, wielding long swords easily in their right hands.

After a moment's fruitless circling, the larger sprang forward with a yell and jammed his shield against the smaller man's shield, searching over it for a strike.

Harry Chambers laughed and fell back at the shield charge, swinging his sword to the side to skitter over the larger fighter's shield edge.

"You're getting slow in your old age, Edmund," he chuckled, dancing out of range.

"So are you," Edmund replied, but he had to admit to the reality of the statement; he and Harry had been sparring for years and never had the lighter fighter taken the shield rush that easily. "That just means I have to be craftier."

"Fat chance," Harry replied, leaping forward with a series of blows. He rang blow after blow off of Edmund's shield, careful not to snap the blade on the boss or the metal-rimmed edge. But the series of blows had their intended effect, driving Edmund back for the first time that he could recall. "Weak, Edmund. All this soft living is making you weak."

"I'm afraid you're right," Edmund gasped, trying to retaliate. But his blows rang softly against the lighter fighter's shield and he could not check the rush. Finally, he stumbled, a misplaced piece of kindling rolling out from under his foot, and he dropped to one knee, holding the shield above him now to wield off the blows.

"Weak, Edmund," Harry cried in delight; it was the first time he could recall succeeding this easily. He considered for a moment if maybe he should back off, but he still hadn't landed a strong blow, just a series of chops on the shield that was slowly battering the reinforced plywood.

"Yes," Edmund gasped, drawing his sword back. "I guess I'm too old," he continued as the sword flew forward, well under his opponent's, and crashed into his thigh. There was a spurt of blood and Harry let out a shriek. Suddenly, things weren't what they seemed.

"*Lord God, Edmund!*" Harry shouted, crumpling to the ground, his hand clapped over the spurting wound. "What did you do to your sword!"

The sword's own blunting field should have stopped it from doing any cutting damage, although Harry would have had a Charlie Horse to remember. For that matter, Harry's own defensive field, reduced as it was, should have prevented the contact. Neither had activated.

"I didn't do anything," Edmund said, dropping to both knees and grasping his friend's hand. "Let me see."

"It bloody *hurts!*" Harry shouted. "Bloody *hell* does it hurt!"

Edmund pried the younger man's hand away and looked at the wound. It was a deep cut, on the outer thigh. The sword had cloven through the ring-mail and underpadding, then into the flesh of the quadriceps. It was bloody, but it wasn't life threatening; there was no bright red spurting of arterial damage or even the slow, solid flow of a cut vein.

"It's only a flesh wound," Edmund said, frowning.

"It's a bloody painful flesh wound," Harry replied, sitting up on one elbow since the shock of surprise had worn off. "Edmund, why isn't there a repair cloud on it? Why does it *hurt*?"

"Why did the damned sword go home?" Edmund asked, rhetorically. "Butler." He paused for a moment then frowned. "Butler!"

"Genie?" Harry said. "Oh, shit, Edmund. *Genie!*" There was no reply. No voices answered out of the air and no projections appeared.

Edmund looked around. They were in the training area behind the forge, one of three on his property. He finally shrugged and got his arm under Harry. "Keep your hand on that and I'll get you into the forge."

"Okay," Harry said faintly. "I'm not feeling particularly well."

"It's shock," Talbot explained, leading his limping friend into the building. "I need to get you laid out again." He first sat the fighter down on a bench then laid out some leather mats before lowering him to the floor. "Carborundum!"

"Not a good situation, is it, O meat bag?" the AI said, sticking its head out of the blast furnace.

"What in the hell is going on?" Edmund asked, as he searched frantically for something that was reasonably clean to place on the wound. Finally he settled for a fresh batch of cosilk waste and pressed it into the mess on Harry's leg. "Why are you responding and the genies aren't?"

"The Net is down," the AI replied. "The Council is fighting amongst itself. They're diverting all power, and all processing power, to that. *I* am an independent entity."

"Oh . . . hell," Harry groaned. "No bloody nannites?"

"Nope," the AI said. "Not unless something falls out quick. You're not the only ones who are in a bad way; nobody has any power *anywhere*. That means no food, no water, no *light*. Things are starting to get bad already."

"Paul's coup," Edmund muttered, looking around the forge.

"What?" Harry asked.

"Sheida told me that Paul might be planning a coup. We discussed means of defense. Carb, where do the AI's stand?"

"Most of them are sitting it out," the AI replied frankly. "The only thing that can destroy us is the Council, acting in concert. Whichever faction wins will come down hard on the loser's supporters."

"Where do you stand?" Edmund asked, wrapping a leather strap around his friend's thigh to keep the cosilk in place.

"I've read Bowman's manifesto," the AI said, acidly. "I don't think so."

"Can *I* read it?" Edmund asked, standing up.

"I could read it *to* you," Carb said. "But I can't produce it. I'm . . . somewhat lacking in power myself."

"How bad is it?"

"Well . . . how much charcoal do you have?" the AI asked.

"Not all that much," Edmund admitted. "We're towards the end of the cycle. But if I parcel it out . . ."

"If I drop below eight hundred degrees C, I'm toast," Carb said, bluntly. "Or, rather, I'm *not* toast, so I'm dead."

"Dead, dead, or quiescent?" Harry asked.

"I might be able to back up a few functions, but I'm not sure I'll recover," the AI admitted. "Call it mostly dead and maybe unrecoverable without a miracle. Which doesn't look likely right now. By the way, Sheida is calling in all her markers; you're going to get a call soon."

"I've got to see to Harry," Edmund responded. "Then to the village. I'll talk to her when I have to." He turned to Harry and waggled a finger at him. "Don't you die while I'm gone!"

"I'll try not to," Harry said weakly.

Edmund trotted across the courtyard, the weight of his armor virtually unnoticed, and entered a side door of the house. Down a corridor in a long-unopened storeroom he pulled open a locker and rummaged to the bottom. There he found a pack and dragged it out. A quick check of the contents sufficed and he ran back to where the injured fighter was lying.

"I didn't know you knew any AI's," Harry said when he entered. The injured fighter's color was, if anything, a tad better.

"It wasn't supposed to be general knowledge," Carb said. "But, all things considered . . ."

Edmund unbuckled Harry's armor and started stripping off the pants.

"Edmund, I never knew you cared," Harry joked, helping with the heavy steel. "It would be easier if I stood up."

"It would be harder if you passed out," Edmund replied, pulling the armor away from the wound. The cosilk padding was quickly cut with a belt-knife, then he opened up the green backpack and started rummaging through packages.

"What's all that?" Harry asked with a tone of deep interest.

"Very old fashioned medical gear," Edmund replied, withdrawing a bottle of antiseptic and some small, clear packages.

"This is gonna hurt," he said in an offhand manner as he poured much of the contents of the bottle of brown liquid into the wound and onto his hands.

"JESUS ON A CRUTCH!" Harry yelled, practically sitting up. But he didn't bat the bottle away. "What *was* that?"

"Something called 'betadyne' that they used to use back in the ooold days," Edmund replied. "It's okay, next we're talking *really* medieval medicine," he continued, pulling a curved needle out of one package and a long piece of string out of the other.

"Is that what I *think* it is?" Harry asked.

"Would you prefer some boiling pitch?" Edmund asked. He pulled some clamps out of the bag and shut the wound, then began applying the suturing needle. "I mean, that would be *really* period. Nothing like a nice cauterization to start the day."

"No," Harry replied, gasping as Edmund tied off the first suture. "Stitching is just fine. Antique, but fine."

"Hell of a lot of damage to the quad, here, buddy," Edmund said, putting in another stitch. "Sorry about that."

"No way you could have known," Harry said with another gasp.

"Tying them off is the hardest part," Edmund commented. "We're going to be calling you Gimpy for a while."

"Edmund, can I ask a question?" Harry said, as the third suture went in.

"Sure."

"*Why* do you have an old-fashioned medical kit?"

Edmund hesitated for a moment then tightened the last suture. "In case I'm someplace the nannites don't do all the repairs."

"But the only place like that is . . ."

"Edmund Talbot?"

Edmund spun in place on the floor and pointed the sword he hadn't even realized he'd carried in at the apparition, which turned out to be an avatar of Sheida Ghorbani.

"Edmund, Paul attempted his coup," the avatar said. "I need every person who has any training in . . . well in war, here with me. He has already attacked power plants and I need them secured. I can port you now."

"No," Edmund replied, lifting Harry to a sitting position.

"Edmund, I know you would not side with Paul. He represents . . ."

"I know what he represents," Edmund replied. "I'm not siding with Paul. But I'm also not leaving here. Make sure that you tell Sheida that and that she's thinking tactically instead of strategically. Tell her that."

"She wishes you to become a Council member," the avatar said.

"What does that mean?" Edmund asked.

"They seized two Keys in the fight in the Council Chamber. She wishes you to vote one."

"Holy shit," Harry whistled. "Council member."

"No," Edmund said after a moment's thought. "Tell her that this is my place. We have to rebuild before we can do anything. She *needs* me here. Tell her, strategic not tactical."

"I shall," the avatar said, winking out.

"What in the hell did that mean?" Harry asked, leaning into the older fighter. "Bloody hell that hurts."

"Well, let's go get you some anesthetic," Edmund said. "Fortunately, I just put up some corn liquor; it should be about mellowed out."

"Sounds good to me."

They limped into the house and into the kitchen, where Edmund dumped Harry in one of the chairs and began opening cabinets.

"The *first* thing you need is a fluid replenisher," Edmund said, sliding a bottle across the table. "Then, the moonshine."

"This is just great," Harry said, taking a deep chug of the blue liquid. "Everything's *gone*?"

"It sounds like it," Edmund said.

"I can't go home," Harry said, taking another drink.

"Not unless you can walk to London. Robert has been building period ships, not Middle Ages period but sloops and barkentines, that sort of thing. He might be able to get you home."

"Daneh? Rachel?"

"No communications," Edmund replied, taking a sip of the moonshine. "No way to know. I suppose if I'd taken Sheida up on her offer . . ."

"That's . . ."

"It's happening all over the world, everywhere," Edmund said, coldly. "Not just *my* family. Everyone's family. Think about how bad it must be out there. We're in a room that is *designed* to survive without power. Think about Fukyama in his damned floating castle!"

"Ouch, good point. And you're staying here?"

"First of all, can you imagine anywhere better to be?" Edmund asked, waving around at the fixtures. The hams hanging from the rafters, the garlands of onions. "Where should I go?"

"The south road to find Daneh and Rachel?" Harry suggested.

"Perhaps," he sighed. "But . . . people know where this place *is*. Do you know how *rare* that is; that someone can find a location on a map? People will come here. The term's so old it's like 'slave' and 'villeigne' but we'll get 'refugees' coming here, on the roads that remain."

" 'All roads lead to Faire,' " Harry said.

"Damned near all that are left. So, do you want to leave *Myron* in charge? Or *Tarmac*?"

"No," Harry said.

"That's what I meant by Sheida thinking tactically. Unless one side wins right away, this . . . this *war*, speaking of another old term, is going to drag on. And if it does, somebody has to be down on the ground, picking up the pieces. I think my place is there, not standing guard over some damned fusion plant."

"And if *Paul* wins?"

"In that case, my place is vengeance."

CHAPTER EIGHT

"I suppose I deserved it," Rachel sighed and moved her wyvern.

The three-dimensional chessboard was a large hologram of ascending platforms. Different pieces could move in different ways and all pieces were not equal. Stronger pieces, by and large, could move only horizontally, crossing to higher or lower grids at specific points. Flying pieces, though, like the ascending levels of dragons, could move up or down however many places were available by their movement. However, they could not destroy all "land" pieces. This time, however, her wyvern had stooped upon one of Marguerite's pawns that was in a strategic spot, and a wyvern *could* kill a pawn. There was a brief flurry of battle and then the pawn fell in battle and reappeared on Rachel's side of the board.

"That's stupid," Marguerite replied, reaching out one ephemeral hand and directing her mother dragon in counter. "You're practically a grown up! You should be able to control your own body. Body control is where all control *starts*. If you don't have control over your own body you don't have anything. Look at me."

"But your parents *approved* changing you into nannites. Mom doesn't approve of *any* modification. I mean, she's really into 'natural' you know?" Rachel's castle moved up a space, leaving it a straight shot to put Marguerite's fortress in check. The pawn had been in the way before.

"What an old fogie," Marguerite said, looking at the board.

"I think I'm going to have to start using a program to play you. You're getting ready to beat me again."

"I'm sorry, Marguerite," Rachel said. "But, well, you're so much better at physical stuff than I am it's only fair that I be better at chess."

"I suppose," the nannite girl sighed. "Frankly . . . this being nannites isn't all its cracked up to be. I mean . . . there's a lot different you know? Can't go some of the places I used to be able to. Not really . . . feeling the same. The emotions just feel . . . unnatural, you know?"

"Well, no I don't," Rachel said looking up at her friend. "But . . ."

"Rach . . ." Marguerite said, her face tightening. "Rach . . . something's happening . . ." Marguerite reached out her hand to her friend as it started to fade. "Rach . . . help . . . me . . . please . . ."

Rachel reached for her friend's hand as Marguerite faded, wondering what could have gone wrong. But before she could get across the oversized board Marguerite had faded fully. In a moment all that was left was a mound of bluish dust.

"Marguerite! *Marguerite?!* MOM!"

Donna Forsceen found herself going nearly forty kilometers per hour in a flat dive through the air as the power-ski under her failed. Not expecting to actually hit the water, she was knocked half unconscious by the impact. On flailing back to the surface she looked around at the vast expanse of water and screamed.

"Genie!" she yelled, paddling around in circles. She had never been a particularly good swimmer; it wasn't necessary if you used power properly, but at the moment nothing seemed to be working.

"Genie!" she yelled again, lying flat in the swells and willing a power-up to drive her towards Hawaii a hundred miles to the north. Still nothing happened.

"Genie?" she said more quietly, looking around. A wave came up and clapped her in the face. She sank again and then clawed her way to the surface looking around in desperation. "Anybody? Help," she said quietly.

It was happening throughout the world as in an instant power was diverted wherever possible into the battle between the two factions of the Council. And, as it was, every being that did not have a specific coded quantity of power and that was power dependent found itself in critical danger. Researchers in the photosphere of the sun disappeared before they knew anything had failed, as did others working in magma chambers. Swimmers in the deeps of the oceans, dependent upon the personal protection fields for their survival, persons flying wingless under power, thousands across the globe suddenly found themselves in situations in which without power there was no chance to survive.

For others, the Fall would take longer.

"What happened to her?" Rachel asked.

Daneh looked at the pile of powder and shrugged. "There's been some sort of power failure. All the force doors are open, the holograms are gone and genie's not replying. I can't even send a message. There's just . . . nothing. I think that's what happened to her. She's nannites. No power means . . . no Marguerite."

"She's . . . dead?" Rachel asked. She'd gotten over the tears but they welled up again at that question.

"Dead's one of those things that's pretty hard to define when you start talking about nannite creatures, honey. Was she alive? Did she 'die' when she was Changed? If you're talking about her soul, you'll have to ask a priest."

"I'm talking about the part that is my friend, Mother," Rachel replied astringently. "If we can find power for her can we . . . bring her back?"

"Ah, that." Daneh's brow creased in thought. "It depends on the design of the nannites. I think her parents probably didn't stint so they probably have a fixed memory system. Likely if she gets power again she'll just come right back to the moment she lost it with no knowledge of the intervening conditions." The mother shrugged as she looked at her daughter. "It depends why the power went off. I can't imagine what could have happened to cause this. It's *impossible*. I can't even get ahold of Sheida."

"What are we going to do?" Rachel asked, looking around as if finally realizing that something terrible had occurred *besides* her friend crumbling before her eyes. "Without power . . ."

"Where's the food going to come from?" Daneh said with a nod. "Good question. I suppose we could try to train Azure to hunt for us. But it's surely going to come back on . . ."

"People of the world . . ."

The image appeared to every surviving person who had not moved far from their position since the beginning of the war.

The Net, of necessity, had to track every person's location so that it could provide them with their needs. And it was possible for a council member to use that information. As, in fact, Paul Bowman had done.

"People of the world," he said, each of the avatars addressing persons personally. *"A time of great danger is upon us. A faction of the Council, led by Sheida Ghorbani, has attempted to wrest control of the Net from the rest of the Council in a wholly undemocratic form. The Council is now split into two fighting factions. Minjie Jiaqi, Ragspurr, Chansa Mulengela, Celine Reinshafen and myself constitute the New Destiny group.*

"It is clear that the human race is approaching a collapse caused by declining birthrates and the challenge caused by unlimited Change. When we attempted to redress some of these problems we were repeatedly confronted by the intransigence of Ghorbani and her conservatives. Finally the disagreement reached the point of outright warfare, instigated, need I add, by the evil Ghorbani.

"Now, due to the intransigence and antihuman actions of Ghorbani and her Changed minions, the power network is in collapse and persons throughout the world are threatened with the ancient evils of famine and disease. All because of one woman and a few beings so Changed as to be nothing but aliens.

"I call on all right-thinking peoples to rise up against this evil and throw down Ghorbani and her ilk, to arise as humans should and support the right-thinking faction.

"I call upon you to do your utmost to ensure a better future for all true humans.

"Good day."

"What the hell did *that* mean?" Rachel gasped as the avatar winked out.

"Oh, holy God," Daneh whispered in reply. "No. God no!"

"Mother?"

"Read between the *lines,* girl!" Daneh snapped. " 'The challenge of unlimited Change,' 'antihuman actions,' 'Changed nothing but aliens,' 'it is clear that the human race is approaching a collapse . . . ' " She hissed through her teeth and snarled. "That bastard!"

"But, Mom, *you* don't like Change!" Rachel snapped.

"I don't like the damage it does to *humans,*" Daneh said. "He's a *bigot.* There's a huge difference. And now he's in a war with my sister."

"Which is taking all the power?" Rachel said.

"Right. And Sheida is stubborn as hell . . ."

Both looked up as another figure appeared, this one much more familiar.

"Men, women and children of Norau, I bring you grave news."

"As you're now aware, the power network has fallen. This message is all the power that is available for me to talk to you. My image is appearing in all places that persons were at the time of the Fall within the former reaches of the North American Union. Which means not everyone will see this, but it is the best we can do at this time.

"Paul Bowman and a faction of the Council, just a short time ago, attempted to wrest power from the rest of the Council. They did so by releasing poison insects, attuned to the DNA of council members opposed to them, into the Council Chamber.

"It was the intent of Paul's faction to establish a tyranny with the intent of . . . hardening humanity and 'bringing it back to the path of righteousness,' and I quote.

"In one way the attempt failed. I, Ishtar, Aikawa Gouvousis and Ungphakorn survived. I regret to inform you that Javlantugs Cantor was killed by the poisons. However, we were not idle and in the short battle seized control of enough Keys to check his direct action through the Net.

"In another way he was very successful; it was Paul's intent to strip most of the world of its wealth of energy and throw people back upon 'work' as a way on the path of righteousness. In that he succeeded. Until one side or the other submits, or is defeated, all available power is being diverted to the battle among the Council. This battle rages even as I speak and does not look to end soon. It is imperative that you seek such shelter as there is and prepare for a long period without the comforts and support that has become the norm. Because we, Ishtar, Aikawa, Ungphakorn and myself, refuse to give in. The castles in the air have fallen and the dragons are grounded, but I refuse to let him win.

"Until this is decided, however, it shall be hard. Most of you live in habitations and locations unsuitable to this lifestyle. I urge you to prepare to move to more suitable locations. To those who are better prepared, I understand the burden but you must take it upon yourselves to help those less fortunate. To the extent that we can, the Council will aid you. I will be contacting leaders within local communities soon and giving what support I can.

"To those of you who find yourselves in current peril or facing famine, find a local community that is prepared to survive in these conditions. Do not despair, for despair will kill you as

surely as famine, cold or injury. Prepare wisely, then move to safety. In time we will start to reclaim this world and all that was once ours. But we will never be able to if we turn over the reins of power to fascist madmen.

"Paul's vision is ancient, as ancient as the slavery of the Hebrews and deaths by the hundreds of millions at the hands of a group called 'communists.' He says that it is for the good of all mankind, but then counters that, of course, a small group will continue to enjoy the conditions that everyone else has had stripped from them. Words such as this resound throughout history and in every case they have meant enslavement and death.

"Our faction of the Council could submit to Paul. The power would come back on, some of the normal amenities of life would prevail. For a time. Until he and his council of dictators discovered the next 'path of righteousness,' the next 'true form' of humanity.

"And all of us would be his powerless slaves.

"I choose not to be a slave. I choose not to enslave my sister's children and the children of my friends. I choose to fight.

"On the shores of this land, once upon a time, was a great nation called 'America.' It is from the seeds of this nation that our present culture derives. The beliefs of the nation were simple: 'We hold these truths to be self evident, that all men are created equal, endowed by the Creator with certain inalienable rights, among which are the rights to life, liberty and the pursuit of happiness.'

"Through their vision, and their beliefs, the people of America, often alone, fought the tides of history and despotism and finally created our society, one in which all of those rights, and more, were protected.

"Paul Bowman, Celine Reinshafen, Minjie Jiaqi, Ragspurr and Chansa Mulengela stand in opposition to those beliefs."

"I wish that it were possible to take an accurate poll of the feelings of all of you. But I cannot. I can only hope that you stand with me, and the rest of the Council, as this black night descends upon us.

"But I believe, together, that we can win through this night, and create once again that society that we hold so dear. The way will be long, but we will stride it together, one nation, one people, conceived in the concept of liberty and true to those philosophies that we hold so dear.

"Thank you, good night, and good luck."

"Sheida?" Daneh said as the image winked out. "SHEIDA???
Oh, great. Not a *word* for your sister?"

"I guess she was just a little focused on her problems,"
Rachel said, then snorted. "Not like anyone *I* know in the
family."

Daneh shrugged agreement at the same time as she gave
her daughter a quelling look. "Well, if she's in that much
trouble, it means that the world is *screwed.*"

"It can't be *that* bad, Mom," Rachel said with a shrug.
"Could it? I mean, it's the forty-first *century.* Things like this
just don't *happen!*"

"Well, it's happening," Daneh said with a frown. "Right here
and right now." She sighed and shook her head unhappily.
"Why *now*? Why *us*?"

"Well . . . why doesn't one side or the other just *give up*?"
Rachel asked. "Mom, people are going to *die.* Some already
have," she added, gesturing at the pile of blue dust.

"More than Marguerite, and more thoroughly," the woman
said, shaking her head. "I know delving geologists who work
in the magma. They're *gone.*" She shook her head. "Gone. Just
like that. No warning at all . . ."

"Mom?" Rachel said after a few moments. "Mom. Why
doesn't one side just quit? Say 'Okay, have it your way, it's
not worth fighting over?' I mean, it's not worth people *dying,*
is it?"

"Some things are," Daneh said after a moment. "It's hard
to explain that without understanding history. Sheida *does*
understand history. But bad as fighting is, will be, the deaths
that are bound to occur, as bad as that is, some things can
be worse. I'd tell you to go look up things like the Cultural
Revolution, the Holocaust and the Khmer Rouge, but there's
no way to look it up."

"The Holocaust and the Khmer I remember from history reading," Rachel said. "But people are going to start *dying* soon. I
mean, the war is going to do the same thing that the Khmer
did, in its way. We don't have any farmers, Mom. Without
farmers, we don't have any *food.* And you don't just pick it *up.*
It's a *skill.*"

"Good girl, now you're thinking," Daneh replied. "But
there *are some* farmers." She looked at her daughter significantly.

"That's the point, Mom," Rachel sighed. "There were farmers in *Cambodia.* But the Khmer and that guy . . . Pol
something . . . he sent people from the cities out to farm. They

didn't know how and they were told how to do it wrong and millions died. Mom, *I* don't know what day to start plowing, do you?"

"Oh." Daneh thought about that for a moment and nodded. "No, I don't, but *Myron* does, and so do his sons."

"If you think I'm going to marry Tom or Charlie and settle down as a farm girl you're out of your mind, Mom," Rachel chuckled. "I'm going to be a . . ." Her eyes widened as she realized how much had been lost. "I was going to be a *doctor,* Mom. What in the hell can you do under *these* circumstances? There's no *nannites*!"

"Uhmm . . ." Daneh said, her eyes widening. "Oh . . . damn. You're right. Not only that, no . . . medicines. Those were chemicals that were used prior to nano-insertion techniques. No medicines, no tools." She shook her head. "I don't even know *how* you . . . I think the term is 'suture' a person, that is sew them up."

"Sew?"

"It's how they used to close wounds," Daneh explained. "But if this is going to go on for some time, we need to get ready to leave. There's not much food in the house. We . . . we need to get to Raven's Mill."

"How, there's no porting!" Rachel said then shook her head. "You're not thinking of *walking* are you? We don't even have *horses*."

"Yeah, I wish now we hadn't gotten rid of Buck," Daneh said. "Well, we might as well get used to it. We need to go find some of the Faire stuff. There's . . . sacks and things. I think I've got some traveling food around . . ."

"Mom, it would take *weeks* to walk to the Mill!" Rachel practically shouted.

"Would you rather stay here and starve?" Daneh asked, grabbing her by the arm and shaking her. "Do you think that Sheida is going to just give up? How about Bowman? If they don't, Nothing Will Work. No food. No water unless we dip it out of the river! We have to get to the Mill and we have to get there before our food runs out! And you'd better hope that the weather holds."

Overhead, in the clear sky, thunder started to rumble.

"This is too complex," Sheida said, shaking her head as she arose from Dream. "An elf couldn't keep up!"

"We need to break it down in such a way as it is less complex," Ungphakorn said, spreading his wings. "We have control of generators but we are throwing groups into them willy-nilly. We need to form teams. . . ."

"We need to be able to concentrate on one particular area," Aikawa said. "We are starting to break out into regions again by taking the generators and controlling the power locally. We should start thinking about that."

"Are you saying form regional blocks?" Ishtar said, irritably. "To what purpose?"

"We need to start thinking of the world again," Aikawa said. "We're going to have to help people rebuild. And we need to consolidate our power base. If humans are to survive this, they are going to have to learn to rebuild. We need to encourage that. And that is a regional function."

"This is a battle between factions of the *Council*," Ishtar said. "Not between nations."

"Now, it is," Aikawa said. "Don't ask me about tomorrow."

"We have to make plans!"

"I don't have much food in my house, where are we going to get food?"

"People are going to be coming here, we need to get ready to take them in!"

"Take them in? We don't have enough for ourselves!"

As if by pre-formed agreement, the permanent residents of Raven's Mill had made their way to the pub, despite the sudden and unexpected thunderstorm. The temperature outside was dropping and the wind rattled the solid doors and shutters of the inn. What it was like inside was well-nigh indescribable.

"OYEZ!" Edmund yelled after a few minutes of shouted debate. John Glass and Tom Raeburn looked like they were about to start beating on each other. "This is out of control. We're going to have order here or I'll start cracking heads."

"And I'll help," Myron said. "I've got food in my storehouses. I'll not be selling it in penny packets to madmen so we've that. The planting season is nearly here. As long as the weather clears we'll be fine."

"But not if we start taking in every person who comes here!" Glass shouted.

"ORDER! We will have order here!"

"I nominate Edmund as Speaker, hell, mayor," Tom Raeburn said. Myron's bullnecked son had his jaw set hard, but he was managing to keep his temper. "We haven't needed one before but we do now."

"Second," Myron snapped. "There's going to have to be decisions made."

"Mayor, okay," Glass said. "But not lord. We're to have a say. And I say that, whatever Sheida says, we're to turn away refugees. We've problems enough of our own!"

"The vote at hand is whether to elect Edmund mayor," Bethan Raeburn said, standing up. "We should keep this simple and straightforward for now. Any other nominations?"

"Me, I'll nominate myself," Glass said. "I like Edmund, but I don't think that he'll have the interests of Raven's Mill in mind."

"And what are the interests of Raven's Mill?" Edmund asked. "I'm not sure I want to be mayor, or earl or lord or any other damned thing. But you'd best understand what *I* think are the interests of Raven's Mill. We're not some damn island. There are about a billion people on this earth. Maybe, *maybe* a couple of thousand outside of Anarchia have any ability to survive without technology. We *are* going to have refugees. And we're going to have to integrate them into the society. We're going to have to expand. And in case you didn't understand the messages we got from the Council, there's a war on. I was already asked to come to Sheida's headquarters to help them. I refused because I'm thinking about the *world*. We're going to have to rebuild it. And Raven's Mill is going to be a part, perhaps a large part, of that rebuilding.

"We're going to have to take those refugees in and teach them how to not only survive but prosper. Teach them the skills that we know. Myron farming, John glassmaking, coopering, smithing, all the things you have to have if you don't have replicators or even factories. The first of them will be trickling in maybe as soon as tomorrow. We're going to have to prepare for that. That is what *I* think, where I stand. And one more thing . . ." He paused and looked around the room at the sea of now thoughtful faces.

"There's a war going on. I side with Sheida. I understand, in a way that I don't think that even Bowman does, what his program would mean. Maybe, *maybe,* simply letting him take over would be for the best. But that's only because the downside of a war in our situation is the death of up to ninety percent of the remaining population world-wide."

"What?" Charlie Raeburn was the first to speak. "*How* many?"

"There's no food. And right now there's no way to get what food there is distributed. Where will food come from? The farms in the central plains supply the *world*. There's no way to move it. The weather that just broke is probably because the weather controls broke down. What is the *true* weather of the world? Will we even be able to *plant* this year?"

"We'll be able to get something done," Myron interjected. "Even with weather like this. Won't be easy, but the seeds we've got these days aren't bulgur wheat. It'll grow in a hurricane. And the output on it . . . well let's just say that even with *rotten* farmers we shouldn't be facing starvation after the first harvest."

"So we can plant and grow *some*. But if the only people left alive are in Raven's Mill, what good does *that* do the world? And as I said, I side with Sheida. The way things look, that might mean we have to fight. Hell, probably we *will* have to fight if no other group than bandits that want our food. This is not going to be easy.

"But I'm not going to throw a wall around the town and say 'no, go away and starve.' Now, the people coming in are going to think we owe them a handout. That's not true either. But I want you all to understand that *I'm* committed to saving every human being that we can. For our species, for the world, for the cause of freedom that Sheida represents. And if you don't want that than, well, I think you should vote for John. Although if everyone's dead, I don't know who he's going to sell his little glass figurines to."

"Edmund, can we do that?" Lisbet McGregor asked. The wife of the innkeeper looked troubled. "It's hard enough supplying the Faire with everyone wanting period foods. I . . . we've got Elsie to worry about. Maybe other children in time. I'm willing to . . . to try to help out others. But not at the expense of our own children."

"I don't know," Edmund admitted. "If we threw a wall up around the town, difficult with it just being us, mind, and turned everyone away and if we didn't have our crops burned by the bandits that produced and if the refugees didn't decide to just overrun us and take all our food and goods, then we might be able to survive. And it might be easier than trying to save people. But . . . I'd have to live with that for the rest of my life.

"Again," he added. "The refugees coming to us will have to be shown the reality of life *now*. Nobody gives you anything but a smidgen of charity. After that you're on your own. They're going to have to learn to *work*. And in a way, so will we. When we tire of a project or a hobby, we go on to something different. Well, you're not going to be pulling food from the Net *either*. Right now, the most powerful man in this town is Myron. *He's* got all the food." Edmund looked over and saw the shocked look on Myron's face. "Hah! Hadn't thought of that, had you? But if you want your thresher fixed, you'd best be willing to give some up to me. And I need a half dozen barrels and you need even more, so Donald's sitting pretty. I don't think any of us wants the tavern to go away so McGregor has a job. Hmmm . . ." He looked over at Robert and Maria McGibbon and frowned.

"Falcons hunt food," Robert said. "Which we'll need. And I haven't done bowyery in sixty or so years, but that's because I got bored when there wasn't anything else to learn. Call me Huntsman Bob."

"Game," Edmund said. "The hell with sending one fellow out with a bow; the woods are teaming with game. Deer, bison, turkey, feral cattle, goats, horses and sheep. Send a hundred refugees out as beaters and drive the damned things off a cliff. This is about gathering food, not sport."

"Save the domestics," Myron interjected. "We can redomesticate them. The big cattle bulls we can deball and use as oxen. We're going to need draft animals. There's wild horses and even donkeys as well. And the horseflesh on some of them is first rate. Emu, bison, wapiti, all of them can be adequately domesticated. We *can* rebuild stocks out of the ferals."

"There's not much leather around," Donald Healey said. The cooper used it in various ways and tended to go through a lot. "We're going to need the skins."

"Meat's not all you get," McGibbon interjected. "Bone, horn, hair, all of it is useful."

"We can do this," Lisbet said. "You're right."

"Won't be easy," Edmund replied. "Easy just ended. But we can do it and we will do it, so help me God."

"Okay, okay," Glass said, raising his hands. "I see which way this is going and I'll even say I agree."

"We need a vote," Myron said. "Any other nominations? Edmund, do you accept?"

The smith looked at the ground and to the others. A weight appeared to settle on his shoulders and something old and hard seemed to be in his countenance. But when he looked up his face was clear.

"I do."

"Any other nominations? No. All in favor say aye."

"Aye!"

"Opposed?" There was silence. "Passed by acclamation, Mayor Edmund."

"But no handouts!"

"Well, a bit," Edmund said, stroking his beard in deep thought. "The refugees that come in are going to be in shock. We can probably last one season with them still in shock but we *have* to get fields planted, material made. They'll need to get on their feet and learn skills. But which skills and how? Say we . . . hmmm . . ."

"Yah," McGibbon said. "A training program?"

"But, they don't have *any* idea, most of them, how much *work* all of this is," Bethan said in exasperation. "And most of them have never worked a day in their lives! It's *hard* running a farm, from *either* side of the kitchen! I mean, just the *washing*!"

"And we'll need tools, seed," Myron shook his head. "We'll need farmers, Edmund, *lots* of farmers. And that's not just sticking seed in the ground."

"We'll handle it," Edmund said definitely. "In this room is probably a thousand years of accumulated experience in how to live in preindustrial conditions. There are people in this room who know things about their skill areas that masters of any other age wouldn't have *dreamed* about learning. We'll feed the new people and teach them until they're more or less ready to go out on their own."

"Training program, hmmm . . ." Tarmac said. The innkeeper looked around in thought. "Break them down in groups, run them through a few days to a week of each of the things that we've got skilled craftsmen to teach."

"Yeah," Myron replied after a moment. "Have them do the stuff that apprentices would do. Give them a taste of the job."

"Work them hard but slowly," Tom Raeburn said. "Build them up to it."

"And, remember, *many* of the refugees who come here are going to be Faire goers," Edmund said with a nod. "Yeah, most of them don't know a whipple tree from an apple-tree, but they've got some experience of living rough. And there are others, guys like Geral Thorson and Suwisa, makers and deal-ers mostly, who have really useable skills. I don't know who is going to make it, I don't know where anyone on Earth was when the power turned off. But some of them are bound to make it. And when they do, we'll be as ready for them as possible."

Edmund glanced up as a figure glistened into visibility by his shoulder.

"Edmund, I need some time," Sheida said, looking around at the crowd. "Myron, Bethan," she said, nodding.

"Sheida, what's going on?!" Maria McGibbon shouted.

"Please," the avatar said, raising her hands. "Please, I don't have time. I'm . . . even now we're fighting and it's . . . it's like fencing mind to mind. They think of a way to attack us, we think of a way to attack them. They're dropping . . . rocks, satellites, things like that on Eagle Home at the moment. We're deflecting them but that's taking power and that means we can't attack back."

"When is the power going to come back?" Myron asked.

"I . . . I don't know," Sheida answered. "Not soon. Edmund, we have to talk."

"Folks, what I want you to do is break up. Tarmac, you and Lisbet are in charge of figuring out what we need for minimal rations for refugees and where and how to serve them. Get a couple of other people together with you. Robert, you're in charge of preparing to do large-scale hunting and gathering ferals. Get with Charlie on how to keep them and setting up a mass slaughter program. You've run the Faire the last couple. Get to work, people, we don't have much time. Myron, you're with me."

CHAPTER NINE

Edmund led Sheida in to the back room of the pub as the conversation exploded behind him. But he could tell from the sound that they were working, not panicking, not spinning their wheels. They were all smart, and experienced and self-starters. All they had needed was a touch of self confidence and a direction to point. With that he could more or less let it run and just make sure it didn't run out of control.

"You done good, Edmund," Sheida's avatar said.

"Thanks," he replied then looked around. "Are you an avatar or a projection?"

"I'm . . . I'm an autonomous projection," Sheida replied.

"That's proscribed!" Myron snapped.

"So is dropping rocks on my home," the avatar said with a sigh. "I can only handle about fifteen of these but they can give orders and gather real information while I handle things that only *I* can do, like give code commands to the Net. Right now, both sides are fighting for controls. We discovered that we could lock out programs and sub-programs and we've been doing that as fast as we can. Unfortunately, they noticed and now they're at it. And it requires direct orders of a council member. So creating full avatars was the only way to get anything *else* done. Every hour or so I take a break and upload all the data I've gained and make any corrections I have to. It's working. We know that because we're still alive."

"Is it that close?" Edmund asked.

"Every few minutes I think they're going to finally kill me," she answered with a sigh. "And then sometimes I think we've finally come up with the one true thing that is going to wipe the floor with them. And it never does."

"Bitchin'," Edmund said with a snort. "You need to back up. This kind of battle never gets won thinking purely tactical. Back up and take a look around for a deep strike."

"What's that supposed to mean?" Sheida asked.

"I don't know. I don't understand the nature of the battlefield. But winning a war is not about killing your opponent, it's about making them give up. To do that you place them in a situation where they believe, whether it is true or not, that they've already lost. In the best of all possible worlds, your enemy creates those conditions *for* you. But that takes an idiot on the other side. I take it that Paul hasn't shown any signs of tactical idiocy. Let's hope he's less capable at strategy. And that is what *you* should be thinking about."

Sheida thought about that for a moment then shook her head. "I don't see anything off the top of my head. But that's not what I wanted to talk to you about. Later, maybe. But not right now."

The room had a table where during the Faire Tarmac would sometimes retreat to play chess. But the rest was filled with barrels. After rummaging for a bit Talbot came up with a cup and poured some liquid out of an unmarked barrel. He took a sip and wrinkled his face but didn't pour it out.

"So, talk," Edmund said.

"Why didn't you come here when I asked?" Sheida said. "The answer didn't make any sense."

"You, we, have huge problems," Edmund said.

"So far I'm keeping up," Sheida said dryly. "Maybe you should go slower, though."

"Glad to see you're keeping your sense of humor," Talbot replied. "But I'm not just talking about the 'war.' I'm talking about the famine."

"Yesss . . ." Sheida sighed. "So, any answers?"

"Why do you think I brought Myron," Edmund said with another chuckle.

"Right now our greatest problem is farming," Myron replied. "Or rather, lack of it and where it does exist it's of no use. We're going to have to have food, and soon. We still have some supplies but we're going to burn through them fast. And other places don't have *anything*."

"We're getting started on that," Edmund noted. "We'll be putting the refugees we get to work."

"Well, Edmund, you know farming is an art more than a science, especially at this level," Myron contradicted with a shake of his head. "Every farm, every patch of soil, is different. And it's not as if we can run up a soil analysis. Chemistry, conditions, weather. It all comes down to knowing what you're doing with *your* farm. Learning that . . . well . . . I've been studying it a lifetime and there's still things I don't know."

"So you're saying that everyone is going to die of starvation," Sheida said, shaking her head. "Maybe we *should* just give up."

Edmund frowned at her angrily and shook his head. "War . . . you know, Paul knows, *nothing* about war. It is said that war is the most evil thing ever invented by man. That statement is fatuous and downright ignorant. Man has created much worse things than war. More people have been killed by totalitarian regimes, during times of peace, than in all the wars in the world combined."

"But . . ."

"This war will be . . . awful. Worse, I think, than the AI wars. The lack of industry, transportation methods other than teleportation and the explosives proscriptions mean that we're going to be forced to a preindustrial or at least pregunpowder lifestyle."

"I . . . hadn't thought it out that far," Sheida admitted.

"Many people are going to die in the first two years . . ."

"Two years?" Sheida asked. "We . . . I was hoping that . . . Well wars don't *have* to take that long!"

"Are you winning? Right now? Decisively?" Edmund asked.

"No, I told you that. If anything, we're losing."

"If you don't lose in the next three months, and I pray you don't, then it's going to be a *long* war. And until the Council stops sucking up all the power, we're not going to be able to recover."

"What about more plants?" Myron interjected. "I mean . . . why can't you just build more? I know it will be a race who can build them the quickest . . ."

Sheida sighed in exasperation and shook her head. "More proscriptions. I didn't realize how many we worked under until this. Power usage peaked shortly after the AI wars during the regrowth period. Usage eventually got so high that it *was* affecting the biosphere; the heat from all the energy usage was melting the ice caps and to prevent flooding Mother was having to divert *more* energy into various ways of preventing it.

So the Council of the time, and it was a *very* controlling period in Council history, when the explosive prohibitions and several others were introduced, placed a cap on construction, requirement for Council approval for new construction and roll-back targets. We were well *under* the roll-back targets, and still had an abundance of power, before the Fall. But now, if we *lose* a power plant it's *gone*. We *can't* get it back. And power distribution, under the Council . . . severance proscriptions means having *physical* control of the plants."

"Ugh," Myron said, shaking his head. "I'm beginning to understand why Edmund hated the whole system."

"So am I," Sheida admitted. "There's also a fuel problem."

"Why? The plants run off of hydrogen don't they?" Edmund asked.

"No, they don't," Sheida sighed. "They run off of helium three. It's produced by the sun and drifts out on the solar winds. It collects in various places, notably the lunar regolith and in the upper atmosphere of gas giants like Saturn and Jupiter. Hydrogen produces radioactive byproducts, He3 doesn't. So they're more 'green' this way. The problem is . . ."

"Who controls the fuel?" Edmund asked, warily.

"Right now, each plant is fueled for several years of maximum output," Sheida admitted. "But the tanker will return in . . . five years."

"If this isn't over in five years," Edmund mused, "there is going to be one hell of a battle for that tanker."

"Yes, there will be," Sheida admitted.

"Not a problem for right now, though," Edmund said. "The point is, are you going to see this through? Are you going to fight to the end or give up out of weakness?"

"I'm not *weak*, Edmund Talbot," she snapped. "The question is . . ."

"The *problem* is, you don't even know how to frame the *question*," Talbot cut her off. "Because you don't understand war."

"No, I don't," Sheida admitted. "That's what I have you for."

"The *question* is, is this a *just* war? Would you admit that?"

"I . . . guess," Sheida said. "But is there such a thing as a just war?"

"There are two types of war, purely defensive and policy difference," Edmund said. "Lecture mode time."

"Okay," Sheida smiled. "As long as it's short."

"Purely defensive is 'you attacked me and I did nothing to

cause it.' In one way, that is the war that you are in. But not really. What we have here is a policy difference. Both sides believe their cause is just. The question is, is it a just war for *you* to fight?"

"I don't know," Sheida said after a moment. "There will be . . . have been . . . so many deaths."

"There are preconditions worked out over history for a just war," Edmund explained. "In short, there are seven. Just cause; right authority; right intention; reasonable hope of success; proportionality of good achieved over harm done; efforts made to protect noncombatants; and aim to achieve a justly ordered peace. I'm not going to cover all of them, but let me tell you that when the Fall happened I thought about what you had told me and what Paul said. And this war meets every item. At least on 'our' side. Just one thing: What is your intention?"

"To return things to the way they were," Sheida said.

"Virtual utopia, while I found it personally boring, has got to be better than a worldwide, omnipresent, omniscient dictatorship of the 'right' people, wouldn't you think?" Edmund chuckled.

"Yes . . . but . . ."

"No buts. Remember what I said about defeating the enemy?" Edmund snapped. "It works in both directions. If you were just going to give in, you shouldn't have started. But given what Paul did, you *have* to know that it's the best thing to do. Paul is well on his way to replicating every totalitarian state in history, with the *full power of Mother* behind him. And that we *cannot* allow! Paul's way leads to dozens of separate species of specialized *insects*. Not human beings with free will and the rights of man. We *will* survive this, and so will the human race. And we *will* win!"

"Yes, milord," Sheida said shaking her head. "I hear and obey."

"Something else to remember," Myron said with a thoughtful smile. "What applies to us, applies to Paul and company. Who is advising them?"

"Farming is going to be our biggest problem," Paul said gloomily. "With that bitch Sheida's attacks we can't move food around. And people are going to start starving soon."

"Well, I have some ideas on that," Celine said. "I think we can handle it quite readily. It all comes down to Chansa."

"What do you mean by that?" Chansa asked harshly.

"Well, farming's not exactly what you call difficult," Celine said, waving her hand. "People have been doing it since they chipped stone after all. But the people who make up the refugees are weak and don't know how to work. They're all lotus-eaters, agreed?"

"One of the greatest problems with the world that was," Paul said, nodding his head. "They shall learn to strive again, learn to work again and thereby learn true freedom again."

Celine glanced at Chansa to see his reaction, but the giant was simply looking at Paul with a furrowed brow. Wondering *exactly* how much history Paul knew, Celine cleared her throat delicately.

"Are you perhaps saying something like, oh, 'work will make you free'?"

"Why, yes!" Paul said, nodding and smiling as his frown cleared. "That's it exactly!"

"Oh, well," Celine said weakly. "In that case. Uhmm, where was I?"

"Farming's not difficult."

"Ah, do a minor modification to the refugees. Make them more resistant to physical effort, conditions, food quality. Perhaps a bit less . . . mentally refined; farming can be very boring work. Do a bit of selective memory work so that they are not so depressed by current conditions. Just generally . . . tweak them to make them more suited to the modern environment."

"So what you're saying is you want to make them dumb?" Chansa asked, with a raised eyebrow. "Is that how you see me?"

"No, not at all," Celine replied smoothly. "I just want to make them *strong*. And . . . tough. Capable of surviving better than standard humans."

"We are trying to escape Change," Paul pointed out, frowning.

"Oh, this isn't really *Change*," Celine said. "Just . . . tweaking."

"That will take energy," Chansa said. "Where are we going to get it?"

"We can take it from their own bodies," Celine replied immediately. "There is a program to enhance ATP conversion. It will leave them initially weak, but food and work will help them to recover."

"I did not take the course that history set before me to turn the human race into moronic drones," Paul intoned.

"No, you didn't," Celine hastened to agree. "But this increases their chances of survival and when the war is done we can change them all back."

"Ah."

"And loyalty conditioning," Chansa said. "And touch up their aggression. I need foot soldiers."

"Loyalty conditioning?" Paul asked, seeming to be perplexed by the sudden change.

"For soldiers it's all you need," Chansa replied. "And some aggression. Like farming, soldiering does not require much in the way of brains."

"And some basic skills," Celine added, making a note on the paper before her. "Soldiering and farming are pretty simple. We'll give them the baseline skills for each. They'll all know how to plow and . . . well other things."

"That should work perfectly," Paul said, looking at his steepled hands. "Perfect."

"The problem is, Myron, that all these refugees are weak-armed, weak-hearted do-nothing lay-abouts," Talbot said disgustedly.

"Oh, I wouldn't say that," Sheida replied. "They're all in good basic condition, much better than the average farmer in history. Just point out to them that the alternative is to starve. We're not going to be giving food away, they're going to have to produce it on their own. They either produce it or they die. And so do we."

"Lovely," the smith snorted into his pewter mug. "It may sound like I'm blithe about this but I'm not. They don't have any *skills* and they're not used to hard day-in and day-out manual labor. The last time this was tried a quarter of the population died."

"When was that?" Myron asked.

"Pol Pot, Cambodia," Edmund said. "Just a tad over two thousand years ago. He'd just won a civil war and decided that all the people of the cities were to move into the country and work the land. A quarter of them, three million people, died. Many of them from being beaten or killed by thugs, but most of them from starvation. There was a similar situation in the same area a few decades before, and that one killed even *more* people. And *those* groups at least had the *concept* of work."

"And it's possible that a quarter of *this* population will die," Sheida replied sadly. "But if food isn't produced, *all* of them will die. And there aren't any farmers."

"Think they can learn it, Myron?" Edmund asked with a jerk of his chin.

"It's best if you're raised to it; that way you don't consider working day in and day out every day of the year to be hard," Myron replied with a grim chuckle. "Otherwise . . ."

"I guess you'll just have to do a lot of classes," Talbot said, taking another sip of beer. That, too, was going to be in short supply soon; they'd have to concentrate on wheat over barley for the time being. "Me too," he added with a grimace.

"You need to be running things, not beating out sword blades," Sheida corrected.

"Well, I don't know how much time I can take training people and also run the farm," Myron noted. "And if I don't run the farm *nobody* will be eating next winter. Not to mention the fact that I can't be everywhere at once."

"What about Charlie and Tom?" Sheida asked.

"Well, what about them?" Myron replied. "They're both ready to take over, but they're also wanting their own farms . . ."

"Set one of them to be the instructor?" Edmund asked. "Maybe something like an agricultural agent."

"Mayhaps. But he could be growing food himself."

"I've come up with a way to have a sort of . . . roving instructor," Sheida said. "A widely roaming one. It would have some problems associated with it, among others not being home much. Ask them if one of them would be interested. Lots of travel."

"Okay," Myron said dubiously. "Honestly, Tom probably would. He likes the *theory* of farming, but he doesn't really like the work if you know what I mean."

"In the meantime we'll get the familiarization program going," Edmund said. "Most of them will end up having to farm. But you need more than farmers. Especially if this lasts as long as it looks like it might."

"Something else to put on the list," Sheida said, making a note. "If it works here, we'll pass the information around and see what comes of it."

"One other thing, Sheida, this is a war. That means that when we start supporting you, Paul will probably find groups to attack us."

"Yes, he will," the council woman replied. "And I'll help you to the extent that I can. But . . ."

"Well, the good news is I may not know shit about fighting a Web war, but if they have a ground force commander that's my equal, I will be very surprised."

✧   ✧   ✧

"Clothing," Roberta said. Tom's partner was the village seamstress and it was one of the first points raised when the three went back to the meeting. Sheida's avatar had stayed since the other avatars stated that the groups they were monitoring were still mostly spinning their wheels. Raven's Mill's plan of setting up an apprenticeship familiarization had been passed through the avatars and was meeting with mixed reactions.

"We can grow cosilk," Myron noted. The hybrid cotton that integrated many of the properties of silk was hardy and made excellent cloth, but it was generally considered a hot-weather plant.

"We can also raise sheep," Bethan said.

"You can get more material per square acre out of cosilk," the farmer pointed out. "Admittedly, wool is a lot better for cold weather; cosilk doesn't insulate worth a damn. But I've only got five sheep; we'll have cosilk in abundance long before we have much wool."

"There's ferals," Robert pointed out. "You know what the ridges look like in the summer." Most of the ferals were from modern sheep stocks that automatically dropped their wool when the weather turned warm. This had originally been a genetic design to eliminate the chore of shearing but with the ferals it meant that for a few weeks in early summer the ridgelines above the valley were dotted with patches of white. Many of the birds' nests in the area were made of pure wool, finer than the best cashmere.

"You have some?" Edmund asked. "Cosilk that is."

"Aye, I've never grown it but I know how."

"Cosilk has more uses than clothes," Robert said. "We're going to need it for bowstrings, rope . . ."

"Better hemp for the rope. We can get at least one crop of silk in this year. Carding and spinning though . . . very manpower intensive. I don't suppose there's much chance of some powered carding and spinning plants by the time the crop's in?"

"When?" Edmund asked.

"By September, say?"

"Maybe, there's so many draws on the few artisans we have. Put it on the list. What's the growing season?"

"Off the top of my head I don't recall. After the ground is good and warm and longer here than down south; it grows better in hot climes, but, then, many things do."

"Tea," Edmund grumped. "I'm nearly out."

"No caffeinating materials at all," Myron agreed. "I've a few hothouse tea plants but not enough to make more than a cup or two a year. No coffee, tea . . ."

"I can't believe you guys poison yourselves that way," Sheida said disparagingly. "Caffeine is horrible for your body."

" . . . No chocolate," Myron continued.

"No *chocolate?*"

"It's got caffeine in it," Edmund said with a grin.

"Well, *trace* elements," Sheida replied with a sniff. "But no *chocolate?*"

"Requires several products that are only grown in the tropics," Myron said dolefully. "No chocolate. Not until some sort of trade is established."

"Well *that* is going to get a priority then!"

"Citrus," Edmund said, shaking his head. "I'm going to miss citrus. And it's a good scurvy preventer."

"*That* you can grow in Festiva," Myron replied. "If the weather settles out."

It had started within a day of the Fall; the weather had closed in and stayed that way. Wind, rain, sleet, rivers flooding. It seemed as if it would never stop storming as all the pent-up fury of weather long leashed was released upon the land.

"It's going to," Sheida replied with a shake of her head. "Did you hear what happened?"

"No?" Myron replied but everyone looked interested.

"The program that did weather control was an AI, that I knew, but what I didn't know was that it was one of the *really* old ones; it actually predated weather control and was a weather *forecasting* AI."

"Damn, that *is* old," Myron said as the wind tore at the roof of the pub. "And that means it can predict this stuff?"

"Sort of, maybe. So the Fall happens and the Council starts fighting and suddenly it's got no power to do weather control. It's back to forecasting. Talk about *pissed.*"

"Ouch."

"Her name is Lystra, and I do mean *she.* Anyway, it's not 'hiding' like a lot of the AI's but it has declared itself *strictly* neutral. It doesn't care *who* wins just that they get the power systems back on line so it can get back to controlling the weather! She's really, really pissed."

"Funny."

"Yeah, one humorous spot in an otherwise crappy situation. Lystra says about a month and a half."

"We might be able to get one crop in the ground in time. It'll have to dry some before we can plant. And a few more plows wouldn't hurt."

"I'm on it," Edmund replied. "I'm glad Angus brought in that load of sheet stock. We need to send someone up to him to get some more material. And he'll need food as well. We'll have to see what we can spare."

Myron took another sip of beer and his face worked. "So, have you heard anything about Rachel?"

"No," Edmund said quietly as another blast shook the building.

"They're not at home. One of me went there already but they'd gone," Sheida said quietly. "Mother's privacy protocols are intact, damnit, and I can't simply order a location search without a supermajority of the Council. I'd have to do a full sweep to find them and . . . I just can't spare the power. I've set out, well, guides, to find travelers. Hopefully one of them will find them and direct them to Raven's Mill."

"What kind of guides?" Edmund asked.

"There are . . . semiautonomous beings, like homunculi and hobs, that manage some of the ecological programs. I found a low-power update conduit that let me reprogram them. They now have the path to 'safe' areas mapped for each of their areas and if they find lost travelers they'll direct them. It's all I can do right now. Maybe later something more can be done.

"For most of the refugees, there's not going to be a 'later,'" Edmund said.

CHAPTER TEN

They had been traveling for nearly two weeks through the worst weather Rachel had seen in all her life.

The house had turned out to have an immense quantity of material suitable to take on the trip; Rachel had been surprised and even a little dismayed at how many of the objects in the house had to do with her father's hobby. At times picking through the piles it had seemed as if Edmund Talbot had more of an influence on the home he had never entered than either of the people living there.

But the problem was not so much that they had items, but what items to pack. They both had good backpacks, late twenty-first-century designs that were light as a feather and fit their bodies like a glove. But filling them had taken careful thought. Finally, it was decided that the most important things were food and appropriate clothing and shelter. They had ended up leaving almost everything else. Rachel ended up packing a few items of jewelry and Daneh packed her single "period" medical book, something called *Gray's Anatomy*. And with that they set out into the driving rain and sleet.

The weather had never relented. In the last thirteen days it had seemed to rain, sleet or snow an average of ten hours each day. All of the rivers and streams were swollen, and in a few cases the bridges that the hiking groups maintained were washed out. In those cases it was a matter of trying to carefully cross the freezing and swollen stream despite the lack of a bridge, or go upstream looking for a crossing place.

Crossing was preferred even though the frigid water flooded under their clothes and seeped into their boots. Better to be soaked than take days out of the way. That finally happened to them at the Anar and it took them nearly two days out of their way before they found an intact log bridge.

This had taken them off the main trail that passed the small hamlet of Fredar and onto less well-tended trails through the wilderness. These weren't any better or worse than the "main" trail, and the rain had turned them into soup as well. The boots they had dredged up were also late twenty-first century and the mud slid off them like water from a duck's back. But the effort was still constant, to lift one wooden foot after another, slip, slide, grab at a tree or go down on your face in the sucking bog. It just went on and on in an unceasing view of trees, swollen streams and the very occasional natural meadow.

Every day had been the same. After sleeping overnight in their small tent they would get up and make a fire. They had set out snares or fish-lines the night before but with the rain they had gotten little every day. So they would eat a bit of their road-food, flip the tent into its packing form and head off through the woods. Rachel well understood how relatively well-off they were. They had warm, dry clothing designed by specialists at the very tag end of the industrial revolution for exactly these conditions. They had good footwear, excellent foods and water carriers. In this time of madness they were rich.

They had passed others on the trail who were not so well off. Now, as they crossed over another of the simple log bridges there was one slumped and twisted by the side of the trail looking like nothing so much as a pile of torn clothes.

Rachel turned her head away, hardly looking at the body tumbled up against the tree, but her mother stepped over and examined the woman thoroughly, as she almost always did, finally shaking her head and moving back to the trail.

"She had something in her bag that the dogs had been at. She was wearing waterproof clothing. And her face looks as if she wasn't even starving."

"She just gave up," Rachel whispered, slipping again in the mud and grabbing at a tree as she looked at the sky. It was already starting to get dark and it was probably the middle of the afternoon. She looked over at the corpse, then at the swollen river. What was the *use* of putting out trotlines when nothing ever *bit*. "I can understand how she felt."

"Don't say that," Daneh said, sharing her glance at the sky. "Don't even think it. Think about roaring fires, well-tended thatch and beef red at the bone."

"Food," Rachel said. They had been traveling on half rations at first, sharing one of the automatically heating packets between them. But as the food had dwindled and dwindled, despite their efforts at foraging, they had switched to quarter rations. They had been subsisting for the last three days on less than a thousand calories a day and with the walking through the mud and the cold, body-heat-leaching rain, snow and sleet it just wasn't enough.

"Not that much farther," Daneh said, taking a breath. "I hate to camp by a corpse but there's a stream right here; maybe we'll be luckier if we put the snares down by the water. What do you think?"

"What do *I* think?" Rachel laughed hysterically.

"Stop it," Daneh said, grabbing her by the collar. "Food. Fires. Warmth. That's no more than a day or two away."

"Sure, sure," Rachel said with another half-hysterical giggle. "Mom, that's what you said *yesterday*!"

"I've taken this path before," she said, determinedly, then shook her head. "But . . . I'll admit it was a long time ago."

"Mother, tell me we're not lost," Rachel said shakily.

"We're not lost," Daneh replied, glancing at her compass. She also had a positional locator but that was only useful if the path was traced in on it. And she hadn't had it the last time she had been through when she had been *very* young and stupid enough to think that a trip up to the Faire on horseback would make an idyllic time. In retrospect, it had. The weather had been fair, as scheduled, and Edmund had taken care of ninety percent of the camp chores. It wasn't this endless slog through a swamp.

"We need to camp," Daneh continued. "And set out our snares and lines. We're not getting *much*, but not much is different from nothing." She glanced over her shoulder at Azure as the rumpled and foot-sore house lion walked slowly over the bridge. "Maybe Azure will get something."

The house lion had actually been bringing in most of the group's protein. He had started off the trip in fine fittle, despite the rain, tail high and off on what looked to be a very interesting long walk. That had lasted most of the first day, but house lions weren't well designed for long-distance travel and by the end of the day his tail was dragging. Despite that, in the morning he was sitting by the remains

of the fire with a dead and only somewhat mangled pos-
sum. And he had continued to bring things in from the
woods for the entire first week: twice rabbits, three more
possums, a female raccoon and on the third day had turned
up dragging a spotted fawn.

But by the eighth day the cat was getting as fine drawn
as the humans and for all practical purposes had stopped
hunting. Cats were obligate carnivores, which meant that they
had to eat meat every day. Daneh had shared small helpings
of the readimeals, hopefully enough to keep him from having liver damage, but the cat wasn't getting enough food, even
with his own foraging, to keep him in condition.

Daneh looked at the cat and her daughter, who had also
lost too much weight, and shook her head. "We'll rest here
tonight, up the road a bit in case any more scavengers come
around. We'll lay out our snares and tomorrow we'll do nothing
but forage. Maybe we can scare some game out of the woods
for Azure to catch. We'll spend a good bit of it just resting,
though. And if we don't find anything, we don't find anything. Day after tomorrow we'll go on."

"Works for me," Rachel said, shifting her pack. "Couple of
hundred meters?"

"Yes."

Rachel looked around at the rain-sodden woods and
shrugged. In another couple of days they'd be up to the Via
Appalia and some relative degree of civilization. Surely the
worst was over. How much worse could it get?

"Ten more refugees today."

June Lasker had been one of the first in. She lived in a
house not far to the west, up the Via Appalia at the edge of
the Adaron Range. It was comparatively well set up for the
environment with wood fireplaces and a few items that could
be used to cook in a pinch. But she knew there wasn't going
to be anything to cook in it and as a long-time trader at the
Faire she knew right how to find Raven's Mill. She was one
of the relatively well-off refugees, having come in on her own
horse and carrying the tools that had made her a successful
dealer. Her stock in trade was handmade calligraphy, and the
reams of parchment, inks, pens and various quills were well
received; no one had thought until they were well into the
plan that there was no way to keep records.

So June had become the primary archivist and was training two of the refugees as scribes, including how to make inks

and paper. As soon as a few of the artisans were freed up she intended to get started on a printing press.

"Anyone we know?" Edmund asked, looking over her shoulder at the lists.

The rain beat steadily against the roof of the tent that had been set up to receive the refugees. Not far behind it was the mess tent and the sound of the chow lines forming was clear. He turned his attention to the sound for just a moment but it was slow and methodical. Sooner or later they were going to have real problems, but the refugees were, so far, just happy to have some food and shelter and people who had some idea what they were doing. Of course, there were many hysterics; the sudden change from a life of peace and perfection was not easy and that had been borne out in much crying and mnany nightmares. But the three day food and rest period seemed to do the trick. At the end of that time, most of the groups had gotten their act together and were now helping around the camp. Some had declined the requirements necessary to stay, instead hoping for something better somewhere else. Well, they could just keep looking for the pot of gold, if there was ever another rainbow.

"No, but they said there were some wagons on the road behind them. I'd guess that's dealers."

"I expected more before this," Talbot mused unhappily.

"I know," June replied. "She'll be all right."

"They had everything they needed to make it," he said, definitely.

"You know, Edmund, no one would take it amiss if you got on a horse and went looking," she said.

"I sent Tom," Edmund replied. "Between you and me. I don't want anyone thinking I'm taking privileges of my rank. He went to Warnan and down the trail but he didn't find them."

"Damn."

"He said that some of the people on the trail said that the bridge was out south of Fredar on the Annan. If they tried to cross . . ."

"They probably went around," June said. "Daneh wouldn't try to cross the Annan in full flood. If so, they're on one of the side trails."

"And I can even guess which one," Edmund said. "But if I went out looking, all sorts of people would want to go haring off in every direction. And we can't have that; we're running on a knife-edge here."

She worked her jaw but nodded in agreement. "Which makes the other piece of news I got all the more unpleasant."

Edmund's face was like stone except for a raised eyebrow.

"The last group in had been . . . set upon by a group of men. The men took everything they had of value."

"All the wonders of period travel and now bandits," Edmund said with a snarl. "We're going to need a guard force faster than I thought."

"There are plenty of reenactors . . ."

"I don't want a bunch of people painting themselves blue and charging screaming," the smith said with a growl. "This won't be the first problem by a long shot. We're going to need *professional* guards, soldiers damnit, who can get the job done in a stand-up fight. I want legionnaires, not barbarians. Among other things, I'm not going to see them become the nucleus of a feudal system or my name isn't Talbot."

"You need a centurion to have legionnaires," June said with a smile. "And the proper social conditions as background."

"If we're lucky the first will turn up," he said cryptically. "As to the latter; working on it."

"Well in the meantime you'd better scratch up a few good Picts before the Norsemen get here."

Herzer had been having a very bad week.

The Fall had caught him at home, but like most people he had little of use in the post-Fall world. His parents had kicked him loose at the earliest possible age. Neither his mother nor his father had ever said anything to him about his condition, other than to inquire if it was improving yet, but he was well aware that both blamed the genetics of the other for it. And neither of them were the sort of people who could handle the psychological burden of a child with "special needs." They had both treated him well when he was young, more like an odd toy than a child, but a well-loved toy; however, when his palsy started kicking in they had become more and more distant until finally, when he reached the minimum age to be "on his own" his mother had pointedly asked him when he was moving out.

Thus he lived by himself. And whereas everyone had a very generous remittance from the Net, he used a good bit of it on his recreation games. Thus his home was modest and so were the things he owned; the term "minimalist" could be used for the small house in which he lived. He'd never even kept the weapons that he trained with, instead storing them "off-line" to reduce the clutter.

So when the Fall came, he was caught flat-footed.

He knew that the Via Appalia was somewhere to the north of him. And he knew that Raven's Mill was somewhere to the west on the Via. And he knew how to find north. So he started out.

There had been no food in the house at all. And the only material for shelter was a cloak that Rachel had given him years before. It was far too small, but it served, barely, for his needs.

The greatest initial problem was that there were no human trails anywhere around his home. And the terrain and vegetation were horrible; the area was flat and covered in streams, all of them running in full spate with the weather. And the area was thick with privet plants, choking the way for miles on end.

He had followed game trails and his own nose for two days before finding the first human trail. Then he followed that north, striking for the Via Appalia.

What he found, instead, was Dionys McCanoc.

At first he'd just been glad to see him. Dionys had his usual cluster of sycophants around him and it was at least a group to attach himself to. But the attachment palled quickly. Benito had tried to make a bow and arrow to hunt, but none of the rest of the group bothered to try to find food. They had had a small amount of food when Herzer arrived, but the eight full-grown males, nine with Herzer, quickly ran through it.

After that Herzer had tried to forage, but his training had never run that way. He had borrowed a knife and whittled a gorge, then baited it and fished. But it took all day for him to catch just two fish and they were both distinctly strange looking. Neither of them was shaped the way a fish was supposed to be shaped and they had strange whiskers coming from their lips. He also had no idea how to prepare them but he finally decided that doing it the same way as game would work. So he cut of the heads, gutted and skinned them. Then he had to get a fire started in the pouring rain. Dionys had a very old fashioned lighter and with great reluctance he gave it up for the experiment. After several tries Herzer managed to get a fire going in the shelter of a fallen tree. Then he cooked the fish by sticking them on a forked stick. The first stick had caught on fire after getting too hot, nearly dropping the precious piscines into the fire and ruining them. After that Herzer kept in mind the prescription about a "green" branch for cooking. Several pieces of the fish had fallen in the fire anyway as they cooked. And when he was done there was a bare mouthful for everyone in the group. But it was something. And it was hot.

It was only this morning, after going through all of that for a mouthful of half-cooked fish, that Herzer had started to wonder about Dionys' plans. The giant didn't seem to be going anywhere or doing anything. He seemed to have an attitude of waiting.

As soon as he flung off the sodden cloak in the morning, Herzer braced Dionys on his plans. It had not, in retrospect, been the most politic move possible. There was no breakfast and no prospect of dinner unless one of them somehow found some food in the rain. And Dionys was not one to take a challenge to his authority lightly. He had heard about half of Herzer's diatribe then struck the young man in the center of the chest with a punch that would fell an ox.

Herzer had been in innumerable full sensory fights but rarely with his fists and never at full stimulation; only real idiots or masochists had the pain systems turned all the way up. So for just a moment he lay in the mud wondering if the madman had killed him. Finally he got up out of his fetal curl and walked away into the woods.

He wasn't sure where he was going, just that he wasn't going to look Dionys in the face for a while.

He returned to the encampment after noon having found no food and no answers. Dionys, in the meantime, had sent some of the hangers on out to watch the trail. Then Dionys had gathered the rest, including Herzer, together for a speech.

"The days of weakness are over," he said, standing in the rain with his sword unsheathed and planted on the ground in front of him. "Now is the time for the strong to take their proper place."

It continued in that vein for a good thirty minutes as the four who were not out on watch sat in the rain and, at least in Herzer's case, wondered where this was going. Finally the purpose of the speech got through to him.

"So, you're saying we're going to become bandits?" he asked incredulously.

"Only for the time being," Dionys responded reasonably. Since Herzer returned he had been treating him with more respect than he had any of the others. "In time we will take our proper place of leadership in this New Destiny."

"New Destiny," Herzer said, wiping the rain out of his eyes.

"Isn't that what Paul calls his group? And doesn't Sheida sort of have control of Norau?"

"For the time being," Dionys responded. "For the time being. But that depends upon her allies on this continent. In the meantime we can carve out our niche and get out of all this," he said, gesturing around at the sopping woods. "Surely you don't want to live in this for the rest of your life?"

"Hmmm," Herzer said, not looking around. He had done several scenarios where there were bandits to be dealt with and in most of them one of the ways to win was infiltrate the bandit camp. *Well, I've infiltrated the bandit camp,* he thought. *How many points do I get?*

But he suddenly realized it wasn't about points. Dionys was deadly serious. Emphasis on deadly. The sword was not out just as a prop; he was more than willing to use it. And Herzer felt a cold chill run through his body as he realized that Dionys was *primarily* thinking he might have to use it on Herzer.

"Well, of course I don't want to be in this for the rest of my life," Herzer snorted. "And I see no reason that we shouldn't take our rightful place." There, absolute truth.

Dionys stared at him for quite a while and then nodded.

"Benito, Guy and Galligan are out on watch. There will, eventually, be people moving on these trails. Some of them will choose to join our little crusade. Some will have items to pass on as a toll for use of the roads. All of this to the good. Some will demur. They will have to be . . . persuaded."

There was a rough chuckle from around Herzer and he realized that the entire charade had been for his benefit; the . . . creatures around Dionys had long since sold their souls and had no problem at all becoming bandits under the conditions of the Fall. Only then did he wonder if they had all started off as he had, a toy to be added to Dionys' collection of fallen souls. He also realized what Dionys had been waiting for. He had been waiting until any of the remnant holdouts, like Herzer, were hungry and desperate enough to have stopped caring.

Herzer also knew that he was surrounded; probably by prior arrangement the others had gathered to either side and at his back. And whereas several of them had knives, and Dionys of course had his sword, Herzer hadn't even found a stick that was to his liking; he was essentially unarmed.

But at the same time he finally realized just where he stood. He was damned if he'd be the villain. He was damned if he would fall to the level of banditry and brigandage, which was what Dionys was talking about even if he didn't know the words. Herzer might have some questions about his feelings, especially his feelings about women, but he had never acted as anything *other* than a good and just person. And he wasn't going to start just because he was a little hungry. There were too many strange looking fish in the world.

The only question was how to extract himself without having his throat cut. And right now the answer was: acting.

So he'd acted. He knew that acting fully convinced would be wrong, but he'd been willing to go along. Thereafter he noticed that one of the others was always around him, watching, waiting.

It was in this unpleasant state of paranoia, gnawing hunger and delayed mayhem that Benito came running back to say that they had their first customer of the day.

For purposes of foraging, Daneh and Rachel had split up with Daneh taking the south route back along the trail and Rachel, accompanied by Azure, the north.

Daneh had left three snares at likely looking small-game trails along the west side of the walkway. The snares were simple period ones, braided horsehair bound into a loop. If a rabbit or something came down the trail it would tangle into the loop and get held there until the snare was checked. Or until something else came along and ate it; that had happened more than once on the trip and they'd lost one of the snares that way. But it was the best they had.

She had reached a small stream, crossed by a simple log bridge, and was considering whether it would be a useful place to lay their last trotline when three men appeared out of the woods.

Herzer's stomach dropped when he saw Daneh being held by Guy and Galligan.

"Dionys, this is a friend of mine," he said. He had taken a position as far at the rear of the group as possible, but Benito was still behind him. And as the group spread out on the trail Boyd and Avis dropped back as well.

"Well, that's a nice looking friend you have," Dionys said. "Who are you?"

"I'm Daneh Ghorbani. And I know who *you* are, Dionys McCanoc. What is the meaning of this." Daneh's jaw was set but her voice trembled ever so slightly at the end.

"Well, there's a toll for using this road," Dionys replied. "I wonder what you have to pay it with."

"You're *joking*," she snapped, looking at the group then at Herzer who was looking anywhere but at her. "You're . . . you're *insane*."

"So some people have suggested," Dionys said, drawing his sword and placing the tip on her throat. "But *I* wouldn't suggest using that term at the moment, woman. Ghorbani . . . that name rings a bell. Ah! The wife of Edmund Talbot is it?"

"I . . . Edmund and I are friends, yes," Daneh said quietly.

"How *pleasant!*" McCanoc replied with a feral grin. "How *exceedingly* pleasant. And where is your daughter?"

Daneh had been halfway waiting for the question. "She was in London when the Fall happened. I hope she's all right."

"Better than you, I think," McCanoc said with a smile. "And I know *just* how *you* can pay your toll!"

"Dionys," Herzer said with a strained voice. "Don't do this."

"Oh, I wouldn't *think* of taking first place," he said, turning to the boy and pointing the sword at him. "That's *your* job."

Herzer stumbled forward as Boyd struck him in the back and he found himself looking directly at Daneh. The journey hadn't been easy on her, either; her bones stood out fine on her face and there was a smudge of dirt on her cheek. He looked her in the eyes and saw in them resignation backed with something else, something very old and dark.

"Dr. Ghorbani, I'm sorry," he whispered and leaned forward to drive his shoulder into Guy.

The man was smaller than he and was rocked out of the way. From that position all that Herzer had to do was keep his feet to start running. He made it across the small bridge in a single bound and quickly turned left, smashing his way into the brush and trees along the trail. With that, he was gone.

"Well," McCanoc said, swishing his sword back and forth. "That was . . . somewhat unexpected." He looked at Guy who was crumpled up on the ground and shook his head. "Get up from there. What a wuss." Galligan had caught Daneh before she could get away and now held both of her arms behind her. "Hmmm . . . well, it's still time to pay your toll."

"Do it," she spat. "Do whatever you're going to do and be damned to you."

"Oh, we're already damned. Benito, hold her other arm. You

others, grab her legs. I haven't had a woman in over a week and I'm tired of jacking off."

Herzer stumbled through the woods, looking for a stick, a tree branch, any sort of weapon. He finally collapsed to the ground, panting and crying. Even through the rain-muffled woods he could hear sounds behind him but he closed his ears to them, looking for something, anything that could help.

The forest was old grown with a thick undergrowth of bracken and privet. The branches that were on the ground were all old and rotted but finally he found a sapling that had grown to man height then died off from lack of sunlight. He tried to find his path back through the woods but the privet had covered it over. Finally he found a stream, he hoped it was the right one, and he followed it back, part of the time splashing through it. Dionys was the main threat, with his sword and size. But even Benito's rotten bow and lopsided arrows, despite the rain, would be a danger. The others just had knives.

If he could just make it back in time.

Guy heaved himself off the doctor and looked down at her.

"Should we cut her throat now?" he asked. "That's what we always do with the homunculi."

"No," Dionys said, wiping at a scratch on his cheek. "But take her rain coat and pants as penalty for not paying the toll willingly," he laughed. "Let her live." He kicked Daneh in the side.

"Live. Go and tell your paramour what we did. Tell him we're coming for him. Not today, not tomorrow, but soon enough. And then, we'll finish the job." He gestured at the group and walked down the path to the south across the bridge. "There'll be more where she came from."

Daneh rolled over on her side in the mud and covered her face with her hands as the group walked off. She wouldn't cry. She *refused* to let them get that satisfaction. She had stayed stone faced through the entire ordeal and she knew that that had taken some of the pleasure of it from them. It was the most she could do and she wasn't going to lose it now.

She waited until she was sure they were gone and got to her feet, fumbling her clothes on as best she could. She wished that she could tear them off and throw them away, burn them even. But she had to have something against the cold and the wet. She stumbled to the stream and rinsed her mouth spitting out the foul taste and worked at a loose tooth; Dionys had tried to get some response out of her, but other than that one scratch when she worked her hand free she wouldn't give it to him. There were other cuts and bruises on her body and she winced at the pull of her ribs; there might be a crack there.

Finally she sat down on the bridge and just let the rain fall until she heard steps squelching up the road. Afraid that one of them had come back for seconds, she stood up and turned to run. But it was just Herzer, holding a sapling taller than he was with dirt still attached to the rootball.

Herzer took one look at her and dropped to his knees, head down, cradling himself around the useless stick.

"I'm sorry," he whispered.

"Herzer . . ."

"I'm so sorry, there was nothing I could do, they would have killed *me* and . . ."

"Herzer!" she snapped. "I don't have time for your *angst*, damn it. I lied about Rachel. She's up the road. We have to find her and get her *out* of here before *they* do."

"Rachel?" he said, coming to his feet.

"Keep. Your. Voice. Down," she said tightly.

"I . . ." He pulled the cloak off his back and handed it to her. "You need this far more than I do," he said. "And, yes, we need to get out of here."

"We'll talk about this," Daneh said, taking the cloak at arm's length. "You can walk in front of me."

"In front . . ."

"Right now, I don't like *any* males near me," she said with a venomous tone. "So it's nothing personal."

"All right," Herzer replied, edging past her.

"And Herzer."

"Yes?"

"When we get to Rachel, we're just going to not mention that you were with the group that did this, understand?"

"I . . . okay. But, no, I don't understand."

"I put a lot of effort into saving your life," she said bitterly. "I don't want Edmund killing you. Or Rachel."

CHAPTER ELEVEN

Rachel had *not* been happy.

"I'm going to *kill* them!" she snarled.

"If you tried, you'd end up just like me," Daneh said, shivering. Herzer's cloak was a better fit for her than for the boy, but it was still a poor substitute for her rain gear. And she knew she was still shocky from the trauma of the rape. "I didn't lie through my teeth just so that you could get raped too. Leave it."

Azure, already wet and annoyed, wandered around her sniffing and yowling. He sniffed at Herzer as well, and seemed ready to bite, but finally he left off and wandered into the woods, sniffing at the ground.

"There's nothing you can do, Rachel," Herzer said tonelessly.

"You can just *butt out* Herzer Herrick," Rachel snapped. "Where in the hell were *you*? Huh?"

"Too late to do anything," Daneh said. "Leave *off*, Rachel. We need to get on our way."

"What about the snares?" she said. "We *can't* keep moving without food. *Azure* needs to eat at the very least."

"He won't start getting sick for another day or two," Daneh said tiredly. "If we move fast we can make it to the Via in a day at most. There are towns up there; we'll find something to eat."

"How far up the road did you go?" Herzer asked.

"Only a ki or so," Rachel said. "The trail is knee deep in mud up the way. Mom, I don't know if you can make it."

"I'll make it," Daneh said, standing up. "I'll make it all the way. But I'm not going to wait here for McCanoc and his band of merry men to find me again. Let's go."

"God, I hope Dad is still in Raven's Mill," Rachel said, gathering up their few belongings.

"He will be," Daneh replied. "I just hope that he's willing to overlook the last few years."

"Home is where when you have to go there, they have to take you in," Herzer said, quietly. He automatically took the front position, picking up Daneh's pack and slinging it on his back. "He'll be there. And he'll be waiting for you."

"He'd better be," Daneh said, bitterly.

"Naye, naye, you have to heat it more or you'll be hammering all day to no effect," Edmund growled, picking up the piece of metal with tongs and setting it back in the charcoal fire.

"I'm sorry, sir, I thought . . ." The apprentice stepped back and looked around at the group gathered in the forge. A few weeks before, all he'd had to worry about was what to wear to the next party. Now he was trapped in this cluttered workshop, learning a trade so ancient that until the previous week he had never heard of it. And doing *badly* at it. It didn't seem fair.

"It takes *years* to learn the blacksmith trade," the smith replied, more softly, noting the glance. He jerked a chin at the bellows and waited as the apprentice pumped the fire hot. "Watch the color of the metal and the colors of the fire around it. When it gets white hot, pull it out and then strike. You don't have much time, that's why they say you have to 'strike while the iron is hot.'" He leant emphasis to the words, pulling the piece out and hammering it flat, then turning it to shape. "Just a hoe but hoes are what will feed us all soon enough. Hoes and plows and parts for wagons will be your mainstay once you learn." He thrust the half-formed metal back into the fire and jerked his chin at one of the other hovering apprentices. "Now, you tend the fire while he tries again."

He stepped back and wiped at his face as the fledgling smith tried to get the recalcitrant metal to do his will, trying not to shake his head. With the scraps and bars that Angus had brought in, they had enough material for the beginnings of a community, but they'd soon need more. He had sent a wagon load of mixed foodstuffs up the road to Angus but the distance was far enough that the oxen would eat a good bit of the load on the way. And it would be three or four weeks before any response could come.

"What about weapons?" the apprentice asked, finally getting the hoe to form. He had got the rhythm of the hammer, and sparks struck a brilliant white in the dim forge.

"You're a long way from making a weapon, son, other than a spear blade, which is naught more than a hoe shaped a bit differently. But swords and such, or armor, they take a tad more work. Once we have the wire puller going in the water forge we'll get some of you to work on mail. But for the time being it's more important to learn how to make farming utensils." He looked out the door of the shed again, then peered more carefully.

"You all start working on hoes from this stock, I'll be back in a bit."

Stepping out of the heat of the forge he shielded his eyes against the sun. As if in expiation for the unending rains the skies had cleared and turned bright for the last few days as the sodden ground steamed. The temperature hadn't gone up much but the humidity was still high, giving the area a damp chill that sapped energy and made everyone hungry for fats and carbohydrates that were in short supply. But the bright sun and haze made seeing anything at a distance difficult, which was why Edmund had to look long and hard to be sure of what he saw. Then he let out a whoop and headed down to town.

"Class dismissed for the next hour or so," he called over his shoulder. "Try not to burn down the forge while I'm gone!"

He thought about grabbing a horse but decided that it would take more time and trouble than just walking down the hill.

As he entered the town of Raven's Mill, which was growing in all four directions, he could see a large crowd gathered around the three wagons that had come from the east, and he pushed his way through to the center without thought until he approached the first wagon, which had stalled for lack of room to move.

"Suwisa, you're a sight for God-damned sore eyes!" he shouted, clambering up the side of the wagon and enfolding the muscular driver in his arms.

"Why Edmund," the woman laughed, giving him a hug in return. "I didn't know you cared!"

"I've been trying to run this madhouse and simultaneously teach newbies who are as hardheaded as the metal they can't shape," he laughed. "So I'll admit it's a purely selfish reaction."

"I should have guessed," she replied with a grin.

"Hola Phil," he called to the man driving the second wagon. "Still selling the condemned mead?"

"Aye, enough to drown you in if you don't quit manhandling my wife!" the man called back.

"Let me get this cluster out of the way and get the wagons up to the forge. I assume you brought all your tools with you?"

"And spare anvils and a small forge," Suwisa replied. "And all of Phil's beekeeping supplies."

"Forges and anvils we have, tools we're lacking. And hives for that matter. We're going to have to have a long talk."

As he and a group of the newly forming guard force opened a path for the wagons, Edmund considered the priceless asset that had arrived.

He had known Suwisa for at least seventy-five years and had occasionally considered asking her to become his "apprentice." The problem with that was that by the time they became friends she was a master smith in her own right. He knew things about forming metal that she did not, but the reverse was also true and the level of his "mastery" over hers was an incremental thing. Just as an example, he mostly worked in "hot" forging with metal heated to brightness whereas she generally used preformed plates for "cold forging." He was undeniably superior at the first while she had a slight edge on him in the latter. She also concentrated on plate armor and decorative works while he specialized in blades. So it was more a matter of complementary styles than superior/inferior.

In the end he decided that if no appropriate apprentice made an appearance by the time he was getting too old to work the forge, he would probably "gift" it to her, along with Carborundum. He was pretty sure that they would get along, and judicious soundings had indicated that she had very few reservations about AI's.

But with the Fall and his increasing responsibilities, he had despaired of having anyone come along who could take over the training of the new smiths. Smithing was nearly as vital as farming in a preindustrial economy and the number of tools that they were going to need prior to the beginning of the planting season was staggering.

Furthermore, he knew that his personality was not at the best teaching raw newcomers to the trade, especially ones he hadn't carefully chosen. Suwisa was much more patient with the sort of hamhandedness he had been despairing of this morning.

He got the wagons up to the back side of town, just short of his house, left them with a couple of the guards and one of the pair's grown children, and led the couple up to the house. Suwisa looked at the expanded sheds and whistled.

"How many smiths do you have in this place now?"

"One," Edmund replied bitterly. "I'm the only one who has made it in yet, except you. I know that there were more in walking distance of the Mill, but some of the other communities are forming up as well and I guess they made it to them. Or they were on the other side of the world when the Fall hit."

"Who all has made it here?" Phil asked.

"If you mean of 'our' crowd, quite a few. But . . . well . . . you know most reenactors. They don't, actually, know diddly-shit about period life. Or, for that matter, preindustrial technology. And they're all happy to swing swords for a bit but then they want their meals served on silver platters."

"I won't disagree on that, but this is *tough*," Suwisa said. "Taking a few weeks to travel by wagon and sleep on the ground for *fun* is one thing. Having to do it for *survival* is another."

"I know," Edmund said, leading the way into his house. He waved them into chairs around the fire then poked it back to life and pulled out a jug of cider that had been warming by the coals. When he had them comfortable he continued.

"I know that things are tough," he continued. "But until one faction or the other of the Council wins, this is what life is going to be. And we have to make it as 'good' as we can within these parameters."

"Or until one side gives up," Suwisa said, taking a sip of the cider.

"I don't think that's going to happen," Edmund replied. "Paul is in too deep and is too . . . fanatical I guess is the best word. And Sheida thinks the world, even as devastated as it has become, would be worse off under Paul's unrestricted control."

"I don't know that I fault her there," Phil agreed. "We heard some really weird rumors on the way over here."

"You mean about Paul Changing people to fit the conditions of the Fall better?" Edmund asked. "We've heard the same. But it's always somebody's brother who heard it from somebody else."

"Doesn't Sheida know?" Suwisa asked.

"I haven't talked to her in two weeks, so I don't know if she does or not."

"So what do you want *us* to do?" Phil asked.

"Well, in Suwisa's case I want her to take over training all the apprentices and turning out metalwork," Edmund admitted. "I'm up to my ass in alligators every day and I have neither the time nor the patience to handle a gaggle of apprentices."

"Mallory and Christopher can help with that as well," Suwisa said with a nod.

"Right now it's all farm implements," Edmund warned. "Real blacksmithing. But in time we're going to need armor and swords. I'm still working on the guard force but the plan is to produce a professional military as well. And there's a training program starting so you're going to have to set up an orientation to blacksmithing, basically what the job of an apprentice is and a few tricks for farmers. Most of the people going through the orientation are going to end up farming."

"All right, and how do I get paid?" Suwisa asked.

"Right now the basis of what currency we have is food chits. You can use them to trade for meals in the chow-halls or you can get raw food to cook yourself. We'll figure out something equitable for your training time and, of course, you'll get paid for your finished materials. We haven't really *got* an economy beyond that and it's all based on Myron's supplies."

"This is going to be fun," Phil said. "That's an inflationary economy if I've ever heard of one."

"Well, yes and no. Most people get three food chits per day. If they starve themselves they have 'extra' money. Skilled artisans get four for days spent working on communal projects, and they can try to find materials to trade for more. But there's not much surplus floating around. So far, by restricting the chits we're both controlling the food supply, which is really important, and keeping the economy noninflationary. Sooner or later we'll get large enough we have to come up with a better system, but for right now it's working. There are too many other problems for me to want to knock it."

"Such as?" Suwisa said.

"You've heard about the bandits?"

"There was a group of five guys who tried to, I don't know, hold us up?" Phil said. "They had a few sticks and a knife. We pulled out three swords and a crossbow. They lost interest really quick."

Edmund chuckled for a moment then shook his head. "One of the things I'm worried about is that the small communities have all the food, and other goods but right now food is paramount. Sooner or later the bandit gangs are going to start banding together and attacking the towns. I want to be ready for them before they do."

"If there's one thing that reenactors *can* do it's swing a sword," Suwisa said with a gesture in the general direction of the town.

"Not as well as they think they can and that assumes they have them," Edmund said with a frown. "Most of them started out from wherever they came from with a sword or a bow or a glaive of some sort. And most of them left them somewhere as well. They're heavy, don't you know?"

"Damn," Phil said, shaking his head.

"And, frankly, I'd rather have raw recruits than most reenactors with live blades. We're going to form a militia and *everyone* is going to learn at the minimum to defend themselves. But I want a professional military at the core. Two tiered for right now, longbow and line infantry, the line infantry based loosely on Roman legions."

"Why longbow?" Suwisa asked. "Crossbow is easier to train."

"Hmmm . . . a lot of reasons," Edmund replied. "Both of them have their pros and cons and you have to understand, despite the last week or so I'm talking with Sheida fairly often. I'm starting to get a grasp of what the strategic situation is and how it might fall out. So I'm thinking in terms not of days or weeks but of *years* of war."

"Shit," Phil said. "I'd hoped . . ."

"You'd hoped this would be over quick and we could go back to our lives. I don't think that's what's going to happen. I'm not too sure we'll be able to go back to our lives even *after* the war is over. But we were talking about longbows."

"Okay."

"Longbows and crossbows both have their pros and cons. Some of them are universal and some of them were specific to the conditions. Okay, here's one: what's the only wood you can use for a longbow that is made in Ropasa?"

"Yew," Suwisa answered. "Well, okay, yew and ash. But you can use hickory . . . oh."

"Right. One of the reasons for longbow rarity in Ropasa was the lack of materials. Which meant a longbow cost a lot. And towards the end the Britons had to import all their yew from the Continent, which was a critical strategic fault in the system. But in Norau hickory makes an excellent longbow and it is widely available. Here, longbows can be made by anyone with a knife and some knowledge.

"Cons of the longbow are rarity of materials, we covered that, difficulty of training and the fact that you have to have very physically able persons to use it. That is, they have to be physically strong and in good shape, not sick.

"Taking the last first, we're not dealing with medieval peasants. The human of today, even those who are *not* Changed, are the result of multiple generations of tinkering. Do you know what 'dysentery' is?"

"Only from history," Phil said. " Diarrhea. 'Runny guts' as they used to call it."

"Right. The most common reason for dysentery was water that was contaminated with the giardia cyst. On the way here, did you drink from streams?"

"Sure, we always have," Suwisa said. "Why?"

"Did you get diarrhea?"

"No."

"That's because you're immune to the effect of giardia. Also the common flu, typhoid, syphilis and a host of other bacteriological and viral infections. We're *born* that way; it's bred into us. Just as greater strength, both for men and women, is innate. Women of today have the potential to be as strong as the average *man* was in the thirteen hundreds. And men have the potential to be enormously stronger. Furthermore, the basic . . . human material we have, *now*, from the refugees, is so much better than the average medieval peasant it doesn't bear discussion. Taller, stronger, healthier, everything that you need for the *baseline* of a decent longbow archer."

"Most of that relates to crossbows as well," Phil said, stubbornly.

"Except for height, yes," Edmund replied. "But the point is, it takes away one of the 'cons' of longbows. The next one is training. Well, I've seen people train to be competent, not *expert* but *competent* bowmen in four to six months. And as they continue to train they get better and better. By next fall I want to have a small but growing longbow corps. And in a few years I want it to be a *large* and growing longbow corps."

"But none of that touches on crossbows," Phil replied.

"Okay, what are the *pros* of longbows? They have a higher rate of firepower, for the same training, than crossbows. That is, they can put out nearly twice as many arrows in an hour and more for short periods. They are easier to manufacture; a trained bowyer with seasoned wood can turn out a longbow in an hour. And their training is *identical* to that for compound bows."

"You mean 'composite'?" Phil asked. "I'm not sure you want to use those. The glues we'd have to use to make horn-bows are hydroscopic. They're really only good in very dry conditions."

"Phil, I've been doing this for nigh on three hundred years," Edmund said, letting the first sign of exasperation through. "Give me the benefit of using the right term. No, I mean *compound*, the ones with the pulleys. You can use a bow that is nearly twice the 'standard' strength of a longbow with compound bows because the archer only takes the full weight of the pull for about ten percent of the draw and the 'hold' strength is a fraction of the full strength. But, right now, we don't have the logistics to produce them in quantity. However, in time we will. And then we'll have archers who can be easily cross-trained to bows that have five times the potential, in combination of pull and rate of fire, of any reasonable crossbow."

"Hmmm . . ." was Phil's reply.

"Maneuvering is another problem with archers," Suwisa interjected. "Less so with crossbowmen."

"Not really, they both have the same problem," Edmund said. "Resupply. Archers going into battle have to have *crates* and *barrels* of arrows. Also spare bows and other things. I've got some ways to fix that as well. We'll use modern training techniques for them and for the line infantry and a four-thousand-year history of maneuver that wasn't *conceived* of for most of history and generally lost even after it had been developed."

"You've thought about this carefully," Suwisa said.

"As carefully as I can. There's more to it than that." He paused and wondered if he really knew Suwisa well enough to cover the rest but then shrugged. "Have you realized that this might be a multigenerational thing?"

"No," Phil said, then blanched. "*That* long?"

"If Sheida wins, and that's a big if, it might not be soon. I'm not even sure *how* to win this war, and I've studied every war in history. I'm having to juggle 'now' constraints while thinking about what the long term effect will be of *everything* we do. Take crossbows versus longbows. A longbow, as I said, can be made by anyone with a knife and some knowledge. There's plenty of game, so in a few years every farmer in the area will be trying his hand at bringing in the odd deer. I want them to have a template for the weapon to use. Because if we have a solid and large yeomanry of trained bowyers, having any sort of 'aristocratic' class arise will be difficult."

"Hard to be a lord when any serf with a grudge can knock you off the horse," Suwisa said. "Tricky."

"I'm trying as hard as I can to replicate *post*industrial republics," Edmund admitted. "Making crossbows, especially good ones that can kill a knight, is a hell of a lot harder than making longbows. Or even compound bows. I want it to be understood at the core of the society that the right to weapons is a fundamental right. As long as you have a relatively law-abiding society, weapons in general ownership and use prevent tyranny from taking hold. Nothing else in history has ever managed it."

"There's a difference between a professional bow-man and a farmer who kills the occasional deer," Phil argued.

"Sure, but it's a difference of details, not the quantitative difference between a knight in armor and a serf with a pitchfork."

Phil shrugged reluctant agreement to that, then grinned. "You won't mind if *I* build crossbows, will you?"

"Not at all, as long as you sell them to anyone with money," Talbot agreed with an unusual grin. "We're just a small little outpost of civilization in world that's turning to barbarism. Historically, the barbarians tend to win. Not as long as I'm in charge."

"Okay, we'll build you your arms and armor. Just use it right," Suwisa said.

"Hey," Phil interjected. "You can get a superior bend to the bow with beryllium bronze! That means you can get nearly as good a loft out of a light crossbow as from a longbow! And nearly the firepower."

"Do *you* know how to cast beryllium bronze?" Edmund asked.

"No."

"Well, I *do*. But I'm not going to spend all my time doing casts for crossbows. Okay?"

"Okay," Phil said with a laugh.

"Speaking of casts," he added. "There's somebody you need to meet."

"I didn't know you were friends with any AI's," Suwisa said, mopping her face at the heat from the forge. "Hello, Carborundum."

"Well, there's a lot about me you don't know," Edmund replied. "How goes it, soulless fiend?"

"It's bloody cold is how it goes," Carborundum said. "And

the Net is well and truly screwed. Your friend Sheida and Paul between them have put up blocks bloody everywhere."

"We're a bit short on carbon at the moment, old fiend," Edmund said, then scooped up a generous helping nonetheless and tossed it onto the red glowing coals. He wiped the black soot from his hands and shrugged. "We're cooking some charcoal now, but it's a slow business and the wet isn't helping."

"Lystra says only another couple of days in this region," Carb added. "And I'm sorry, but I'm still not finding anything on Rachel and Daneh. The fairies are circulating back word on people moving in the wilderness, but of course they don't know one human from another. They were definitely *at* the house, both of them, at the Fall. And the house-hob said they left. But that's all I've got. Some of the AI's are being really uncommunicative, some of them are on Paul's side, mostly because they think he's going to win, and direct access to the Net is generally cut off between Sheida and Paul's blocks."

"Thank you, Carb. I've got Tom out looking as well."

"Well, I'll tell you if anything comes up."

"Thank you, again. But I'm introducing you to Suwisa for a reason. I'm going to have to be more and more connected to this mayor business and she's going to be taking over the smithing and armoring. So I'm probably not going to be seeing you much."

"I'm sorry to hear that," Carb said. "Honestly. I know you're busy but don't be a stranger."

"I won't. I hope you and Suwisa get along, though."

"Oh, I'm an old hand at breaking in new smiths," Carb said with a laugh like a couple of plates of iron striking.

"And I'm an old hand at old hands," Suwisa said. "You were mentioning a need for charcoal I believe?"

"Arrrrgh! Edmund, come back!"

"You two have fun," Edmund said, turning to the door. "And, Suwisa, you need to come meet your class soon."

"I'll do that, after I get done *discussing* things with Carborundum here."

"When do you think Tom will get back?" Phil asked as the two of them stepped back into the rain.

"In a day or two I'd suppose."

"And then you'll know?"

"Phil, I may *never* know," Edmund replied softly.

CHAPTER TWELVE

Herzer stopped and shook his head at the sight before him. The area had apparently sustained a forest fire sometime in the recent past. No more than a year to a year and a half ago from the looks of the few visible trees. And the area that had burned was now covered, for several acres at least and stretching across the trail, in thick vines that were just starting to come out of winter hibernation. The overall color was brown but it was shot through with green leaves. And it choked the path from side to side.

"What the hell is *that*?" Herzer muttered as Rachel stepped past his bulk.

"Kudzi!" she shouted, running forward. She darted to one of the greening areas and rummaged into the vines. "Yes! And it's already fruiting!" she shouted, pulling out a small, bluish ovoid and thrusting it in her mouth.

Herzer walked into the patch and found another then, after a moment's hesitation, took a tentative bite. Then he stuffed the whole thing in his mouth and searched for another. The fruit was an absolute taste explosion, something between a grape and a strawberry. It was blue, so he knew it had to be genegineered and he thanked whatever soul had in some distant past time created it. As he pulled out a handful of the fruit he thought better of stuffing them in his mouth and carried them over to Daneh instead.

"Here, you need this more than I do," he said. A large, mature chestnut tree had fallen either just before or during the forest fire and its root bole held the trunk up off the ground. The combination had created a perfect little one-person shelter. Herzer steered the doctor under the tree and found a dry bit of bark for her to sit on. They had been traveling for nearly a day after the incident at the bridge and the doctor was looking more and more wan. He was afraid that something internal might have been damaged, but if so he couldn't imagine what to do for her. The fruit would at least provide some sugars and liquid.

"Thank you, Herzer," Daneh said tonelessly, taking a bite out of the fruit and settling in the shelter.

"Are you going to be okay?" he asked.

"I'll be fine," she snapped then shook her head. Really, I'm fine, Herzer. How are you? Any shakes?"

"Just from hunger," he joked. "And these are helping. What *is* this stuff?"

"It was derived from a noxious weed called kudzu," Daneh said, taking another bite. "It used to be spread all over eastern Norau; it grew wherever there was a disturbance in the ecosystem, which in those days was everywhere. Sometime in the late twenty-first century a researcher released a controlled retrovirus that modified it to kudzi. The fruit was a gene cross of kiwi fruit and plum; kiwi meat and plum skin. Anyway, that's where it comes from. And just like kudzu, it grows up anywhere there has been a disturbance like a fire or tree-clearing; it's a right pain in farming."

"Well, I was thinking," Herzer said. "With all this food here we might think about stopping. I'm pretty sure they're well behind us."

"No, we need to keep going," Daneh said, lifting her chin with a "t'cht." "We need to make it up to the road."

"Okay, if you insist. But we're going to stop and get some of this fruit. It will give us enough food to make it the rest of the way."

"All right." She nodded, taking another bite and wiping the juice off her chin. The fruit seemed to bring some color back into her cheeks and she smiled for the first time in what seemed like ages. "You go pick fruit. If you don't mind I'll just sit here and let you young folk do all the work."

"Ummm, this is good," Rachel said as he walked up. She had a bunch of the fruits in a makeshift cradle of her shirt and was biting into another. "Thanks for taking some to Mom."

"She's looking better for it, but she insists on keeping going," Herzer said.

"We need to find some meat," Rachel said stubbornly. "This is fine for us, it will keep us going at least, but Azure has to have some meat."

"He looks thin, but . . ." Herzer said, looking over at the cat, which was rummaging in the vines as well.

"Cats are obligate carnivores," Rachel replied. "That means they *have* to eat, every day. And they have to have protein, *every* day. If they don't, they get sick. Something about fat buildups on their liver. It can kill them."

"Well, I'm sorry, Rachel, but I don't see any rabbits coming up to be killed."

"Kudzi fruits before anything else," Rachel said. "And they stay in fruit as long as the vines are green. That means that there's going to be *something* coming up to eat it besides us. We probably scared some things away when we came up. Possums, raccoons, deer, *something*. If we just stay here a while and let Azure hunt . . ."

"Tell it to your mother," Herzer replied. He had taken off Daneh's rucksack and was filling it with the fruit, hoping that it wouldn't release too much juice and ruin the inside of the bag.

"I will," she said determinedly, and stalked over to where her mother was resting under the tree.

Herzer observed the exchange from afar but could more or less tell how it was going. First Rachel handed Daneh some of the fruit. Then she gestured around at the large field. Next she pointed out the cat, which was poking in every possible hole in the vines looking for something edible to a feline. The argument clearly weighed on Daneh but she shook her head and said her piece. Then Rachel said hers with more force. Then Daneh's face set and she gestured to the south, forcefully. Then Rachel's voice could be heard from halfway across the open area. Then she stormed off.

"I have never known a more pig-headed, stupid . . ." she muttered as she passed Herzer.

As she passed, Herzer heard a scurrying in the vines and a field rat ran right in front of him. He had been carrying his staff with the knapsack in his left hand and he quickly dropped the bag, switched hands and then lashed out with the staff. The first blow missed but it turned the rat and the second blow hit.

He called to the cat and tossed the rat towards him as he thought about the implications.

"Rachel, is there some way you can get Azure to sort of . . . station himself on one side of the vines?"

"I . . . don't know, why?" she asked, taking a bite out of a fresh fruit. They had been starving, but the fruit had taken the edge off and now it was already starting to pall.

"If he did we could walk along and sort of *push* stuff that is in the vines towards him. Things are running in front of us all the time; we'd just sort of have it run in front of us towards *him*."

With a little persuasion on Herzer's part it was done. Daneh continued to sit it out while the two younger members of the group walked back and forth across the vines. Azure quickly became aware of the nature of the game and waited patiently at the edge of the open area as the game was driven to him. In less than an hour he had bagged several field rats and a small rabbit. For Herzer's part, that was an hour that Daneh wasn't driving herself to keep going. She had simply sat out of the rain and eaten kudzi fruit until she was near to bursting. All in all it had been a very successful exercise in tact and diplomacy.

"And what is that you're eating?" Chansa asked, appearing out of the air.

As usual Celine was in her workroom, which was filled with a cacophony of whining, bleating and croaking calls. He glanced at one of the cages along the wall and shuddered at the strange octopus-looking creature in the water-filled interior. The door had a sturdy lock but the creature was pushing at every opening with every appearance of intelligence. It saw him looking at it and came to the front, its skin going through a variety of color changes.

"Jelly babies," Celine replied, lifting one of the squirming creatures that very much resembled small human children and popping it in her mouth. "Try one?"

Chansa shook his head and turned from the octopus to look at the writhing mass of faintly whining creatures. They were colored various shades and squirmed most unpleasantly.

"Avatars do not eat, Celine," he reminded her.

"Yeah, that's why I don't use avatars," Celine responded, popping a couple more in her mouth. "Uhmm, lemon."

"Celine, we need to talk," Chansa said, making a moue.

"Hmmmr?" she rumbled, her mouth full.

"Have you noticed Paul getting . . . strange?"

"You mean bug-house nuts?" she asked. "Yeah."

"I'm not sure he's quite what we need in the way of leadership," Chansa said, carefully.

"See yourself in that position?" she asked, standing up and going over to one of the cages along the wall.

"No . . ." he answered carefully, watching as she extracted another one of her little monsters. This one looked like a fairly normal hamster for a change. He wondered what it was food for. "I was actually wondering if *you* would consider the position. You have seniority on the Council after Paul."

"Hah! No thank you. I like it right where I'm at." She lifted the hamster and cooed at it, bringing it up to a cage that held a weird creature the size of Chansa's massive hand. The beast might have been a spider or a scorpion; it had features of both. The scorpion's stinger and pincers coupled were fronted by a spider's mandibles, and the body, overall, had a very spiderish look to it with long, black legs that ended in sharp points. Celine waved aside the force screen at the top of the cage and dropped the hamster in, waving the field closed as she did.

The spider/scorpion had turned and reared up as the hamster was dropped in and it pounced immediately towards the prey. But as it did the hamster made a flip in midair and, using one paw, bounced off of a branch in the cage. Before the monstrosity in the cage could shift its ground, the hamster was on its back, drawing back its lips to reveal long, fanglike teeth. The fangs punctured the carapace of the spider/scorpion and as the hamster locked its claws into the back of the beast its body visibly shuddered as it sucked out the juices from the interior. The scorpion tail had been jabbing into the little monster repeatedly but it seemed utterly unaffected by the poison.

"No, Chansa, I do not choose to oppose Paul," she said. "The first reason is that a touch of madness is quite amusing. The second is that you never know how dangerous a simple-looking thing can be."

As they came down the slope of the Ridge, Rachel paused and looked around.

"Is this Raven's Mill?" she asked, incredulously.

"That it is," Tom replied. He had caught up to them just south of the Via Appalia. Too late to help rescue Daneh, for which he had been almost embarrassingly apologetic, and clearly unsure about Herzer's place in things. He had accepted Daneh's toneless statement that Herzer had also arrived too late to prevent it, but he didn't pretend that he liked it. He had wanted to ride back down the trail after the band but Daneh convinced him that it was not worth the danger.

Now he was leading the horse that held Daneh and he, too, stopped to look at the scene of activity. "But it's changed even since *I* left."

Rachel had been to the Raven's Mill Renn Faire on numerous occasions. The bowl of the valley was broken up into, effectively, four different quadrants. The southeast quadrant was "Edmund's." It was there, on the east side of Raven's Creek, that he had his house and a small open area, "cleared fields of fire" was how he put it, around it. Myron also had two or three fields in that sector that he used in rotation.

The "southwest" sector was mostly Myron's, a large area of cleared fields, some fenced, with a large orchard and vineyard on the hills to the southwest. Up in the hills to the south, behind the two original "owners" of the area, was the mill that had given the town its name. It drew its power from Raven's Creek and there was a millpond, and dam, up in the hills.

The "northwest" sector was the main area of the Faire. It was a large, mostly cleared area that snuggled up against the northeast hills. On the top of the hills were a few permanent buildings devoted to the Faire. The "northeast" sector, across the creek from the Faire, had been wooded, as had all the hills. Many people preferred to pitch their tents over on that side of the valley during Faire, to get away from some of the crowding and the noise in the main Faire area.

Near the center of all four "zones" was the town of Raven's Mill, which had consisted of about five large home/workshops, the tavern and some outbuildings.

Now it had all, seemingly, changed. The Faire area was being slowly covered in rough wooden buildings, mostly made from half-formed logs. There were gangs of workmen assembling two buildings even as they paused. The northeast quadrant was, apparently, supplying much of the material, for there were gangs on that side of the stream stripping it of trees, grubbing up the roots and otherwise clearing the land. There were even some buildings going in over there. The town itself showed signs of building as well, with at least two new buildings under construction. All in all, it seemed entirely transformed.

Then Rachel noticed that some of it hadn't changed. There was, still, the large cleared area around Edmund's house and Myron's fields hadn't been touched. She was glad that something, at least, hadn't changed. Then she noticed that up by the mill there were new buildings. So it wasn't some protective spell that stopped the changes at a line through the town.

"What are those?" she asked, pointing at the distant buildings.

"I see they got the sawmill working," Tom replied. "Fast work."

"Do you think we could actually head down there?" Daneh said, tiredly.

"Of course, m'lady," Tom replied, looking over his shoulder at Herzer. "I'm going to take the ladies up to the house. There's going to be a reception area down there. You should go there."

"Okay," Herzer replied. "I . . . I guess I'll see you all later."

"Even with this many people it will be hard to miss you, Herzer," Daneh replied. "Take care."

"And you, ma'am," the boy said, waving a hand as he walked down the road.

"I wonder where Edmund is?" Daneh said, looking around the scene of industry.

"He didn't come looking for us, why should we come looking for him?" Rachel said nastily.

Daneh didn't even bother to reply. Since the incident with McCanoc, Rachel had been getting more and more bitter about her father's "failure."

"He'll either be down at the town hall or up at the house," Tom said uncomfortably.

"Let's go to the house," Daneh said. "All I want to do is take a bath and go to bed."

Edmund was hosting still another meeting at his home when he looked out the window and saw the small cavalcade proceeding up the hill.

The endless meetings all came down to lacks; lack of materials, lack of farmers and lack of skilled labor. The shipment of metal from Angus had melted rapidly in the face of various needs, from fittings for wagons to the parts for the new sawmill. And even as fast as it was dwindling there wasn't enough metal for all the needs or enough smiths to shape it all.

And they hadn't even started on weapons or armor.

He knew what was really needed, but so did everyone else on the town council and in some cases what they "knew" was different from what he knew. And in some of those cases it wasn't really a matter of right and wrong. Take the new farm program. There were a few protofarmers whom Myron considered marginally qualified to start a farm. And that acceptance had been grudging. So they were, under regulations so new the ink hadn't dried, eligible for loans to set themselves up farming. None of them had anything to trade so it all had to be loaned.

There were things, besides land and seed, that every farmer needs. Arguably, the only other things that he needs are an axe and a hoe. But having a draft animal and a plow made for much more efficient farming. So did rope. And being able to fix some of his own equipment was helpful, so arguably he should have some blacksmith tools. Then there was how to get the produce to town, so maybe he should have a wagon.

But that was definitely getting into the category of "too much" to loan to a complete unknown. Based upon historical precedent it was expected that at least sixty percent of the "pioneer" farmers would fail. Given the problems that they were up against, that percentage was probably optimistic. Based on more similar precedents they could look at eighty to ninety percent. So that meant that between six and nine in ten of the farmers would be unable to recoup whatever they were loaned. Now, if they were loaned more, more seed, more tools, more draft animals, they were likely to be more successful. But that meant fewer seeds, tools and animals to loan to others. Who got what and how much was at the basis of the arguments.

The argument wasn't going to be resolved today or tomorrow or maybe in a month. Maybe not until harvest time or next year. But it had been raging almost nonstop for a week. All of the council meetings had been fixated on farm policy and so had the last town meeting. And that was another sore point with Edmund.

After the first meeting in the tavern, people had taken it as expected that he'd turn up at every such meeting. For the first week there had been one every other day until he pointed out that *he* had other things to be doing. At which point the term "dictator" had first been raised, initially by a few of the more loudmouthed of the new arrivals but later in mutterings even among some of the long-term residents of Raven's Mill.

It had started with his "high-handed" decision to put Bethan Raeburn in charge of the treasury. She had taken up the handling of the commissary from the beginning and as food chits had quickly turned into currency, it had only made sense for her to continue applying her practical knowledge and increasing experience in handling them. Oh, but that did not sit well with some of the new arrivals. Brad Deshurt had been a researcher in preinformation technology economies and had made plain, with a large number of polysyllabic words, that the basis of Raeburn's plans were inflationary and would otherwise cause the world to end. As if it hadn't already. Deshurt was just about the only person Edmund had ever met who was frankly obese and he remained "fleshy" even after walking all the way from the region of Washan. Edmund was rather sure that the basis of *Deshurt's* animus was that Bethan refused to let people have seconds.

Nonetheless, under fire and holding their positions with difficulty, Bethan hung on to the treasury and, remarkably, the sky had yet to fall. What was worse, Deshurt had somehow argued his way into a position of "expert on everything" and it had turned out to be impossible to shake him. Edmund was pretty sure that he was going to run in the next council election and since the world seemed to hate him, the loud-mouth was probably going to win.

However, above and beyond Edmund's decisions with regards to the treasury and who should run it, his cut-the-Gordian-knot approach to farm policy was considered even more evil. Edmund knew that he had, at most, a vague layman's knowledge of period farming. To him the difference between, say, Republican Roman farming conditions and those of the Middle Ages existed only as a backdrop to the social, political and military climate of each age.

But in each of those periods the farming techniques influenced the military at least as much as the reverse. So he was well aware of what sort of farming he wanted to occur and what sort he didn't. Fortunately he and Myron were in agreement, for similar reasons, and while Edmund knew next to nothing about farming, if there was anyone with more knowledge than Myron among the refugees, Edmund had yet to find them. So he put Myron in charge of making the decisions.

O! Woe was he! The screams had started almost immediately and they revealed a bitter undercurrent he'd only started to sense. Myron was very much the villain of the piece already. It was through his "stinginess" that food rations were so small. Edmund had never heard the term "bloated plutocrat" outside of an old novel until some yammerhead had stood up at the last meeting and shouted it at Myron.

Myron had no idea how to handle the pressure. He was, in his own mind, just a simple farmer. His previous experience with "public life" had been to give tours of his farm during Faire. Suddenly being at the center of a raging controversy was not his cup of tea. He'd tried to abdicate the responsibility but Edmund wouldn't let him. Myron knew what needed to be done and how to do it and the various yammerheads, as their own proposals proved, did not.

Mostly the arguments boiled down to a few broad groups. One held that anyone who wanted to farm, knowledge or not, should be given everything that *they* felt was necessary and then given as much land as they could stake out. Generally "stake out" was based upon "blazing" trees to define their area. Edmund hadn't been able to come up with all the reasons that was a stupid idea so he let others carry the ball. It was pointed out by several that there was a limit to the materials available, not to mention the people with the skill to make anything from them. Others pointed out the long-term arguments that would arise from such ephemeral markers as blazes.

The yammerhead that had called Myron a "bloated plutocrat" was at the head of the "all for one and one for all" group who felt that all materials should be held in common and used in common. They were in favor of putting all the resources of the town into a communal "usage storage" and letting people draw from it. All the land would be held in common and people would do what they could, giving material back into common holding.

Edmund had been the main one to put his foot down on that. He had dredged up dozens of half-remembered historical references, from the early Pilgrims in Norau, who had nearly starved before they gave up communal ownership, to the great debacles of the latter twentieth-century "communist" states and communal farms, which *had* starved most of a nation for fifty years.

The last group, and this one was the scariest, was led by Brad Deshurt. He had proposed that Myron's farm simply be expanded and use the labor of the refugees to do the work. Despite his background in preinformation technology economics, the term "latifundia" was not part of his background nor was he willing to admit the resemblance to "slave plantations." But since Myron wasn't about to let a giant plantation be raised on bond labor, with the long-term implications that would raise, the argument was moot. In fact, the problem that Edmund was having with Myron was the exact opposite; he wanted regulations to prevent any one person from ever owning too much land. They had talked about it for hours the night before.

"Latifundia, either true latifundia with large numbers of semi-bond labor or corporate latifundia where the corporation owns the land and works it through hirelings, are eventually a given . . ." Edmund had explained.

"But . . . Edmund, the whole basis for a decent preindustrial democracy or republic is the small farmer. If you get latifundia, eventually you get feudalism, either implied or in fact. You either get the Middle Ages or the postslavery South. You don't want that, *I* don't want that. The only way to avoid it is to prevent any group from getting too much power."

"Every law against monopolies, especially land-holding monopolies, has failed," Edmund pointed out. "It's like laws against 'moral crimes.' If you create a law that involves *that* much money, either people will flout it or the lawyers will find a loophole. It's like the idiots who don't want hemp planted because it can be used as a drug. Great, it's also the best basis for making paper and rope, two things we need. People who want to get addicted to hemp can feel free. Trying to keep them from growing it, given that the seeds are available and the land is for the taking, is impossible. It's a law designed to fail. And if you set up a law to fail, you set up the law to be ignored.

"No, avoidance of latifundi would be a good thing, but in all honesty there's no way to do it. Initially, I'll agree that individuals cannot prove and register more than five hundred hectares during their lifetimes. But after it is proved and registered, it's open season. If someone wants to sell out, they can sell out. Assuming that there is any capital to sell it to."

"I hate latifundi," Myron grumped. "It was the corporate latifundia that put the stake in the heart of the small farmer. And you know where that led."

"To a huge argument about which came first the chicken or the egg," Edmund said with a grin. "Truthfully, so do I, but open-market democratic capitalism isn't the best system of government in the world, it just works the best. Actually, there's a real question whether it's the best for this sort of society. Arguably, we should be setting up a centralized dictatorship or a feudalism. Those are generally the most stable in this sort of situation. But we're not; we're going for the long ball of republicanism. History will tell us if we were right or wrong. Hopefully, if we're wrong, history will tell us after our grandchildren are dead."

And through it all, the arguments continued to rage.

He had pointedly tuned out the current argument, which was specifically about minimal farming needs, and was looking out the window when he saw Tom's horse, first, then recognized who was slumped in the saddle. At that point he rapped the hilt of his poignard on the table.

"This meeting is adjourned until tomorrow," he said, standing up.

"Why? That's rather high-handed, isn't it? We're not even *close* to done!" Deshurt snapped.

"You can keep arguing if you want, but you're going to do it somewhere else," Edmund said, walking to the door. "Now."

"Oh, my God!" Myron said, standing up so fast his chair went over backwards. He had looked out the window as well.

"Out," Edmund growled. "Now."

"I'll be back with Bethan," Myron said, heading for the door. "Come *on*. It's Daneh and Rachel. Give the man some *peace* will you?"

"Oh, if that's why . . . Edmund, we can meet tomorrow . . ."

Talbot just nodded his head as the group filed out the door, then strode quickly to the mounting rail.

"Daneh," he said, taking in the sight of her. He had already noticed that she was wearing a borrowed cloak, unlike her daughter. Now, as he got closer, he took in the look in her eye and the yellowing bruise on her cheek.

"Edmund," she sighed and slid off the horse. As he reached for her she flinched and then held out her hand. "I'm glad to be here."

"I'm glad you've come," he said quietly, standing away from her. "Rachel," he added, nodding at his daughter.

"Father," she replied. "Nice to see you, too. Finally."

"Come into the house," he said, nodding at the implied rebuke. "I'll have . . . I'll get a bath drawn and some food on the table." He turned to Myron's son and stuck out his hand. "Tom . . . thank you."

"Any time, Edmund," he said then shrugged. "I'm sorry . . . I'm sorry I didn't find them . . . sooner."

Edmund's jaw worked and he nodded in reply, following Daneh and Rachel into the house.

"Tom," Myron called as his son trotted into the farm-yard. "Daneh looked . . ."

"I'll let Edmund or her tell you about it," Tom said, sliding off the horse and shaking his head angrily. "It's about what you'd expect I reckon."

"Damn," Myron said with an angry hiss.

"You know Dionys McCanoc?"

"That I do," Myron nodded. "And I'd guess he's not long for this world."

CHAPTER THIRTEEN

Edmund had the luxury of drawing hot water off of the forge, and fixing a bath for Daneh had been simple enough. She had withdrawn with a small vase of wine and some old clothes after which Edmund returned to the kitchen to face the wrath of his daughter.

"She was raped," Rachel said, looking up from a plate of cold roast pork. As the warmth and light of the room sunk in, she was beginning to realize she was safe. Deep inside she had feared through the whole journey that Dionys would reappear. But now, in her father's house, she knew she was protected. Which, for some reason, was just making her angrier.

"So I gathered," Edmund replied, sitting down across from her.

"No thanks to you, *Father*. Where *were* you?!"

"Here," he answered bluntly. "Right here. Trying to create something for you to come home to."

"Nice excuse."

Edmund sighed and took a sip of wine. "It is not exactly an excuse. It is a reason. When I was asked to do the job, I recognized that one of the concomitant realities was that I could *not* go looking for you and your mother. I knew that you had both been home at the Fall and I knew that you were both resourceful. I recognized that you had a higher chance of something . . . I almost said 'untoward' but the real word is 'bad,' something *bad* happening to you and your mother. I chose to accept the larger responsibility."

"Well that larger responsibility got my mother *raped,* Father," the girl hissed. "You'll forgive me if I'm just a little pissed about that."

"Probably about as much as I am," Edmund answered. "But I will not second guess the choice. It is the one I made. I'll live with it for the rest of my life. As will you. And your mother." He noted that she looked down and he nodded. "And what choice is it that you wonder about, Rachel?"

"I . . ." The girl sagged and swallowed hard against a bit of pork. "We'd split up to forage. She went south, I went north. If only I'd . . ."

"Rachel, look at me," Edmund said and waited until she did. "If there is a God, I will thank Him for the rest of my life, and so will your mother, for that choice. Your mother is much older and wiser than you, and probably stronger as well, although you have great strength in you. But if I was forced to choose who to send into something like that, I would have chosen Daneh over you for all that I love her. And so would she. Know that."

"I do," Rachel said in almost a wail as she dropped her face in her hands. "But . . ."

"Survivor guilt is a very false form of guilt," Edmund said. "We cannot undo the choices that we make in our life. And so many times, who survives or who is not wounded comes down to simple chance. Regretting that you were not raped is silly. And regretting the fact that somewhere in you you are *glad* it was not you is sillier."

"I never said that!" Rachel snapped.

"No, but you have thought it and you regret the thought," Edmund replied, firmly. "I'm *old,* girl. I'm so old it's hard for you to understand. And I know what it is to survive when others do not. And I know the evil thoughts that creep in. Face them, show them the light of reason. At first it will not help, but over time it *will.* If you won't do that for me, do that for your mother. She is going to have her *own* thoughts that creep in unbidden. Small, petty, maddening thoughts. Yours will be easier in some ways and harder in others. And you will need to talk about it. But you need to have them under some control. For her and for the, yes, the 'larger' picture. We have done much here but there is much work yet to be done and you are going to be part of that doing. If you start it out in bitterness and hatred for those you love, and for yourself, the work will never be the best. And it deserves your best."

"How can you be so *cold* about this!" Rachel shouted. "Don't you have a *gram* of feeling in you?"

"Yes," Edmund said after a moment. "But I don't show it in the way that you think I should. You'll just have to decide for yourself. On the other subject, were the men involved just random passersby or are they likely to be more of a problem?"

"Oh, I think they're likely to be more of a problem," Rachel said, lightly. "The leader was Dionys McCanoc."

For the first time in her life, Rachel started to understand why people treated her father with respect. For just a moment, something flashed across his face. It was an expression beyond anger, something odd and implacable and deeply terrifying to watch. And then it vanished except for a jumping muscle in his jaw and he was the same, plain, wooden-faced creature she had known her whole life.

"That is . . . interesting," Edmund said with a sniff. "I'll put the word out, wanted for banditry and rape."

"That's *it*?" she asked. "Just 'put the word out'?"

"For now," her father said coldly. "For now. People like McCanoc tend to end up killing themselves. If he doesn't do it for me, I'll find the time. But for *now*, I have other things to do. Just as you do. You need to rest up."

"And what are *you* going to do?" she asked, looking out the window. While they had been talking the sun had fully set and it was clear that unlike during Faire, Raven's Mill rolled the streets up at dusk.

"Me? I'm going to work," Edmund said. "People, they work from sun to sun, but a politician's work is never done."

"Very funny, Dad."

"Edmund?" the voice said out of the darkness.

"Sheida, where've you been?" he said looking up from the endless paperwork and pushing his glasses down his nose. Daneh and Rachel had both gone to bed but he was still up burning the midnight oil.

"Even split like this, I'm being run ragged," she replied, her voice faint and her projection a half-seen ghost image in the lamplight. The vision was clearly the worse for wear, and Edmund shook his head.

"Get some rest," he said unctuously. "If you haven't got your health, you haven't got anything."

She chuckled at the ancient joke and sat on the chair across from him. "You look pretty worn yourself."

"It ain't easy. We're up to nearly a thousand people; just making sure they're all getting fed three times a day is a challenge." He gestured at the paperwork, pulled off his glasses and leaned back in his chair. "You heard about Rachel and Daneh."

"Yes, *all* about Rachel and Daneh," Sheida said with a sigh. "Something has to be done about McCanoc."

"I think Dionys is going to be less of a threat than I'd anticipated," Edmund said. "I'd expected him to turn up and start causing problems before now. Instead he's turning bandit."

"Don't underestimate him," Sheida said. "We're starting to piece together intelligence on Paul's supporters in Norau. And he's likely to be one of them; I think that Chansa authorized some illicit mods on him. Just before it all came apart the Council was presented with a formal mods challenge from the elves in regards to him. It would have taken a council member to allow them. So he may have backing you don't realize."

"That's as may be," Edmund said. "But, frankly, given his background in shitting all over social organizations, I'd rather have him as an outlaw than on the inside causing trouble. If I can get this damned town organized, he's not going to take it away. And that's my primary responsibility, as I mentioned."

"Agreed," she said. "And one that some people aren't rising to. I've got problems, old friend. I need some advice."

"Advice I've got aplenty."

"You're forming a democracy here," she said, waving out into the darkness towards the town. "But too many of the communities aren't. Strongmen are taking charge and . . . I mean it's getting feudal out there."

"Not surprising," Edmund said, taking a sip of wine well-mixed with water. "It's not entirely a democracy, more of a republic. They chose me and when I thought I was right I've run roughshod over a couple of votes. And there are times when I've wished I could just order people to do things or toss them out. We've done that in a few cases, people who wouldn't work, one thief. I've been tempted with a couple of yammerheads. And even more tempted in the case of a couple of 'minstrels.'"

Sheida chuckled. "You never did like minstrels."

"I like people who can *sing*," he said. "I've got perfect pitch; listening to most 'minstrels' is positively painful. And getting someone who considers themselves a bard to actually work is . . . tough. Even when there's no pins to throw them they think they can ride on generosity. Maybe in a few years they'll be able to. But not now."

"But the . . . strongmen," Sheida said.

"Call them warlords," Edmund said musingly. "Well, the first thing you do is tell them that they're not allied with you if they don't institute democratic reforms. Then you draw up a simple document that states what the rights of all persons are in your government and what the duties are of the local and overall government. Preferably you gather representatives from all the communities that are allied with you to vote on it, but get the outline settled before the arguments start."

"You're talking about a constitution?"

"Aye. And a good one. Just what happened to Daneh proves that we need some laws to hang our hooks on. Right now, if I went out and hunted down McCanoc and hung him from a tree, I'd be as much in the 'wrong' as he is."

"Nobody would question it, though," Sheida said. "Not and get very far."

"Sure, but that's not law, that's anarchy," Edmund pointed out. "At its base, all government is about ensuring that people abide by contracts. McCanoc violated an implicit contract that one does not force women to have sex, much less steal their rain gear when conditions are cold and wet. But with the Council's authority broken, there is no process to enforce the contract. Nor is it a written contract. Look at some of the historical models; you've still got access to them. Then write the constitution. Then, if any of the 'warlords' refuse to join, remove your support from them."

"I haven't been able to *give* much support," Sheida admitted.

"But you *will* be giving support and more as time goes on," he added. "You're the only source of power available unless they go to Paul's side."

"And what if they do?"

"Then you deal with that as it comes," Edmund said bluntly. "This is a war. If someone wants to be neutral, that's fine. If they take the part of your enemy, then they become *your* enemy. Make *that* clear as well."

"One of them is Rowana," Sheida said. "Martin down there has set himself up as the local lord. Including a . . . a harem I guess you'd call it. I haven't been able to sort out how much of it is voluntary, how much is desperation, and how much is forced. But I know that all those women didn't jump into his bed because he's God's gift to women."

"And if Rowana goes to Paul we'll have a knife pointed at our back," Edmund said, musingly. "Well, that's all right, by the time he can get his act together, we'll be in a position to smash him if it comes to it. One of things you'll need to write into that constitution is how new groups are entered into it. That is the way that geographical boundaries are settled, who has full voting rights, that sort of thing."

"Hmmm . . ." Sheida said with a distant look. "I've already accessed a few of the more well-known historical documents."

"And one thing."

"Yes."

"The first Constitution of the United States of America, the Second Amendment. Whatever you write, if you want *my* support for it you'll have something similar or stronger."

She smiled at him and nodded. "Will do."

"Is there a way that you can take Harry with you?" he asked, suddenly.

"Perhaps," she said. "Why?"

"The cut that I did to his leg is never going to heal right short of nannite rebuilding," Edmund said with a shrug. "In this society he's practically a cripple. That's not good, but the other side to it is that he's got a good basis in preindustrial war and government. If he could be someplace where he's not seeing how crippled he is, or that he could get repaired, he could still contribute. But as it is, he's not doing himself or anyone else much good."

"I'll see if I can gather the power for a teleport," she said after a moment's thought. "We're working on some lower powered methods, but until then we're stuck."

"Well, if you can do it, you can do it. If not, we'll find something for him. He can train in sword-play just by shouting if it comes to that."

"Okay," Sheida said with a nod. "Thanks for the advice."

"Anytime. And, really, do get some rest."

"I can sleep in the grave."

"Which is where you'll be if you don't get straight," Edmund said.

"It's . . . there's so much. They're just more *powerful* than we are, Edmund," she said, sighing and lowering her face into her hands. "I don't know *where* they're getting all their power. We've actually got two more plants than they do and we're drawing on the Stone Lands power source. But they've got two or three times our power. They're not using it very *well*, but we have to use every *erg* to defend against it. And in the meantime it leaves them free to do . . ." She stopped and shuddered. "I can hardly believe some of the things they're doing."

"I probably can," Edmund said, thinly. "But I'm a firm believer in the concept of original sin and the basic corruptness of the human soul."

"Well, I'm getting that way," Sheida said. "Paul's got enough power to make it nearly impossible to send an avatar into most of the areas that he has assimilated but we've slipped in a few long-range aerial scouts and it's horrible. He's rounding up all the refugees and *Changing* them against their will."

"Not surprising," Edmund nodded gravely. "If he's got the power."

"He does but he's mostly drawing it *from their own bodies*. He's using humans as a *power source*. Sometimes it kills them. And what it leaves behind!"

"Let me guess. Low intelligence, brutish in appearance, a few rudimentary skills and . . . hmmm . . . aggressive. *Stupidly* aggressive, right?"

"You've heard."

"Oh, I've heard the rumors. But more than that, I know the people involved. That's not *Paul's* game they're playing there, it's Chansa and Celine and to an extent the Demon."

"Why?" Sheida said seriously.

"Well, Celine has been bitching for a hundred and fifty years about the medical and bioengineering locks that the Web imposes. She wants to make monsters. Why? Because she *likes* monsters. Monsters are *cool*."

"The wasps that attacked us were probably Celine's doing," Sheida said.

"Yes, and so are these . . . things. These Changed. As to Chansa, have you ever wondered why he would make himself so huge? That's pure lack of confidence. What he has always wanted was control, over himself, over the people around him. I don't know what made him that way and don't really think it matters; maybe somebody beat him up as a kid. Whatever, he wants to subordinate those around him. He wants subordinates, not equals. Celine creates this great *unter*race for him lord it over and they both pitch it to Paul as 'for the good of the people.'"

"Do you have a spy in the New Destiny Council?" Sheida asked seriously. "Because that's exactly the story that I got."

"No, but it's pretty damned obvious if you know the players."

"What about the Demon?"

"Convenient, isn't it, how he just showed up right when things went south," Edmund said sourly. "You really think that's coincidence?"

"You think he was in on it from the beginning?"

"I think he was in on it from *before* the beginning. It's a little late to search out now, but it might be worthwhile to look at how Celine, who was a nut-job from the word go, and Chansa got on the Council in the first place. The Demon is *old*, Sheida. Older than either of us. Old as some of the elves."

"You think he planned this?" she asked. "All of *this*? Even *he* isn't that insane, is he?"

"The Demon? Yes, he is, Sheida."

She sighed and nodded her head tiredly. "I suppose you're right. But where does that leave us?"

"In one hell of a hole," Edmund admitted. "But that's what shovels are for. Go home, Sheida. Let everything go to hell for one night. Pull in all the avatars and get some damned rest."

"Okay," she said smiling impishly. "I wish I was here; I'd get some rest with you."

"Not tonight," Edmund said. "I'm going to be doing nightmare watch."

"True," Sheida said shaking her head. "If you find him . . ."

"I'm going to nail his gonads to the first tree," Edmund said. "You see, deep down inside, I don't give a shit about laws."

Herzer had accepted a meal chit and headed for the shelters before his brain really kicked in. He was in Raven's Mill, the rain had stopped and for the first time in weeks he was going to be able to eat and sleep under shelter. Not much food, he'd been warned, and not very good shelter. But it was food and shelter and that was a good thing.

There were already lines forming for food and he got at the end. He was annoyed when some people came up and cut the line, evidently slipping in in front of friends. But there didn't seem to be anyone around to prevent it.

The people collected in the line were a sorry sight. All of them were obviously travel worn and clearly not used to it.

Many of them just appeared . . . beaten, as if they were never going to get any better than this, for the rest of their lives. Others, though, were different. They were chatting amiably with others and looking up and around. There didn't seem to be any difference, any way to spot which was which or any way to guess who would be looking up and who would be looking down. Some of the apparently weakest of the group were the most active and some of the most rugged looking seemed to have just fallen apart.

Beyond that the group was odd in another way; there were very few Changed. Herzer was used to any similar group being at least a quarter Change, from winged men to cat girls. There was one of the latter, a really cute reddish blond tabby, and what looked like it might be a werebear or werepig near the front of the line. But that was it for Change. He didn't think the town was excluding them, but there had to be a reason they were so few and far between.

The line led into a large open shed that looked almost like a warehouse. At the entrance a bored looking woman was accepting chits from people. She turned one person away who didn't have a chit, without any explanation offered or given. Inside there were some trestle tables, obviously rough hewn from logs—there was still sap exposed on most of them—with crudely carved wooden bowls and spoons piled up. Following the example of the person in front of him he took one of each and then accepted a small piece of cornbread from one of the servers. At the kettle the bowl was filled with some sort of stew, it looked to be mostly beans, and that was it.

At the far end of the warehouse were more rough tables with benches, most of them filled. He walked almost to the far end before he saw an open space next to a young man about his own age. He walked up and gestured to the spot.

"Do you mind . . . ?"

"Not at all," the young man said after a quick glance at the girl across the table from him.

"Thank you," Herzer said, sitting down. "Herzer Herrick," he continued, sticking out his hand.

"Mike Boehlke," the young man said, and gestured across the table. "That's Courtney, Courtney Deadwiler." Mike was blond with short hair, stocky and about a meter and a half high. He was medium good looking for the period but his muscles had the indefinable look of someone who had worked on them, not just had them sculpted. The one odd thing about him, not quite Change but something close, was his eyebrows. They pointed sharply upward at the end. And his brow had a distinctly strange cast.

Courtney had red hair and was . . . buxom was the only term that came to mind looking at her. She had bright green eyes with a lively intelligence that did a quick appraisal of Herzer and then seemed to accept his company without any show of other interest.

"Hi," Herzer said, ducking his head in greeting. Then he picked up his spoon and basically inhaled the food.

"You have to be careful with that," Courtney said with a snort. "I did that the first night and then threw it up all over the table."

"I think I'll be okay," Herzer said. There was a slight queasiness, but Tom had had some rations left so he hadn't been starving the last day or so. He mopped up the bowl with the small piece of bread and then ate that. "That's it, right?"

"Right," Mike said gruffly. "New here?"

"Just got in," Herzer said then paused. The details of his journey didn't make for very good storytelling.

"We're on our second day," Courtney explained. "You know you get three days?"

"Yes. And they said someone would be around to find me then. I'd wondered about that; how do they keep track?"

"Some people skate out," Courtney nodded towards the tent. "But on the third day they stop giving you meal chits if you're not otherwise employed. They're talking about some sort of apprenticeship program. We're hoping to get into that."

"What else is there to do? I saw a couple of guards."

"They're not much," Mike said. He had a tight, short manner of speaking that was blunt enough to be right on the edge of rudeness. But Herzer sensed it was just the way he was rather than anything intentional. "There's talk that Talbot's going to set up a professional guard and police force. But there's been too much going on with the farm battles."

"Farm battles?" Herzer asked. "We're having wars already?"

"No, not that," Courtney interjected. "It's just the arguments about how to get the farms running."

She gave him a fairly concise description of the various positions, then shrugged. "Mike and I, well . . ." she looked over at him and shrugged again.

"I want a farm," Mike said. "I want my own farm, mine and Courtney's. I don't want to farm somebody else's and I don't want to share it with a bunch of people. I know I can make it run if I don't have to worry about sharing it with a bunch of losers." He gestured at the various people still sitting at the tables.

"I suppose that makes sense," Herzer said. "I'd never thought about being a farmer myself . . ."

"Farming is what makes an economy like this run," Courtney interjected enthusiastically. "It's hard work, maybe the hardest there is. But it's rewarding, too, if you get good land and do a good job at it. We'll succeed," she reached across and took Mike's hand. "I know we will."

"But you're going to do the apprenticeship program anyway?" Herzer asked. He noticed that Mike seemed uncomfortable with the touch and disengaged as quickly as possible.

"I want to see what else there is," Mike said. "And there's more to farming than just putting seeds in the ground. Knowing a little bit about coopering and carpentry and smithing will be useful."

"There's supposed to be a week or two of combat training, too," Courtney noted.

"Well, I guess I'll see about this apprenticeship program," Herzer said. The sun was setting in the west and he suddenly realized he was bone weary. "Where do people sleep?"

"There's separate bunkhouses for the men and women," Mike said. "I usually walk Courtney over to hers and then find a place to sleep."

"You can come with us if you want," Courtney said.

"Uhm . . ." he looked at Mike who shrugged disinterest in whether he did or not and then nodded. "Okay, if you don't mind."

They walked through the crowds in the gathering darkness to one of the many log-frame huts. Up close they were much less sturdy than they appeared at a distance, and the walls were filled with cracks where the logs didn't meet. The roofs were made from wooden "shakes," slightly mounded pieces of wood about two decimeters long, a decimeter wide and a couple of centimeters thick. He suspected that they leaked like a sieve in the rain.

He waited as Courtney kissed Mike good night, on the cheek, then followed the young man across the encampment. Mike seemed to find his way in the dark remarkably well for having been there only a day.

"I think you see better at night than I do," Herzer said as he stumbled on one of the innumerable potholes. The area had been a forest up until a few days before and while the stumps had been rooted out and the holes filled, the rains had caused the soil within to slump.

"A couple of generations back on my mother's side is a cat Change," he said. "I *do* see well at night."

"Do you know why there are so few Changed here?" Herzer asked, the question that had been nagging at the back of his mind coming to the fore again.

"Not really, but Courtney and I were discussing it. She thinks it's a matter of adaptability. Most of the Changed take more energy, either food or externally derived, than unChanged humans. So, naturally, they were going to be at a disadvantage when the Fall came. Think about a werebear, for example. They need *a lot* of food, *every* day."

"Yeah."

"Or, think about a guy with wings. He's got wings, but he can only fly with external power. And the wings weigh thirty, forty kilos. Take away power, make him have to walk for days to get to shelter . . ."

"Yeah."

"Makes me glad I never Changed. You ever think of Changing?" The question was hard edged, almost accusatory but, again, Herzer put it down to personality.

"Not really," Herzer answered honestly. "A little bigger, a little beefier . . ." He flashed back to the scene at the bridge. Bigger wouldn't have helped unless he was the size of a giant.

"You're pretty big already," Mike said with a questioning tone.

"That's mostly natural genetics," Herzer replied. "I . . . the muscle is sculpted but I worked for it. I was sick most of my life and I couldn't bulk up no matter how hard I tried. So when I got fixed . . ."

"Yeah, whatever," Mike said. "Here we are."

Mike pushed open the flap—which appeared to be made of rough-cured deerskin—and led the way into the interior. Already the room was filled with the sound of snores.

"There's a spot over here," he said, pointing down the middle of the room.

To Herzer the interior was as black as pitch and quite cold. "Are there any blankets?"

"Not unless you brought one, but it warms up after a while," Mike replied. He led the way down the center aisle to a spot between two of the sleeping bodies.

"Keep your boots on and double knot the laces," his guide said. "I had somebody try to steal mine the first night."

"Okay," Herzer said, sitting on the floor. It was dirt and both moist and cool, and the air in the room was damp and filled with odors. He was suddenly glad that the problem of human body odor had been solved generations before, otherwise the room would have been truly foul.

He fell asleep on that happy note.

CHAPTER FOURTEEN

Rachel woke up with a face peering at her upside down.

"Who is this sleeping in my bed?" the girl asked. Her voice was low and sibilant with odd under and overtones, as if she was speaking through the opening in a cello.

Rachel sat up, pulling the bedclothes to her and spun around so that she could see who she was addressing.

The girl standing arms akimbo by the bed was short, no more than a meter and a quarter, and *very* oddly dressed. She had a sharply pointed face and long, black hair that dropped in curly waves down her back. She was wearing what could only be described as a green leather bikini made of some soft, washed leather. Leaves were entwined in her hair. On her left shoulder she had a pauldron while the other was bare. On her right calf she had a metal greave while her left calf was covered in a fur leg warmer. She was wearing sandals with a very slight heel and on her left forearm was an archer's brace. That appeared to be the only bit of her ensemble that wasn't for show since it was heavily scarred on the inside.

Her ears were pointed and her eyebrows curved upwards sharply . . .

"Are you an *elf*?" Rachel exclaimed. She had met a few. They were all tall, slender, and wore refined delicate clothing . . . the exact opposite in many ways of the caricature before her.

"Hai," the elf exclaimed, sticking out a hand. That was another oddity; most elves avoided personal contact. "Bast the Wood Elf. Pleased ta meetcha. And who might you be?"

"I'm Rachel, Rachel Ghorbani . . . Edmund is . . ."

"Oh, aye! I know you! Haven't seen you since you were a wee brat, though. No wonder you're fillin' up my bed. I nearly snuggled in with Edmund but he seemed as if he needed the sleep."

"O-kay," Rachel said. "Snuggled in . . . ?"

"Oh, aye," the elf replied. "Yer father an I go *way* back," she added with a wink. "Before your mother, actually. And after a bit. Not during, though. I think Edmund had been hit on the head one too many times those days to toss *me* out of his bed for that wee slip of a lass. And you do be favoring her. You're not going to go doing the same, are you?"

"With my *father*?"

"Ack, guess not. Good. We'll be friends then." Bast grabbed her by the shoulder and dragged her out of the bed, still clutching at the covers. For all her diminutive size the elf was enormously strong. "Come on, gal! Day's a wastin'! Time to be up and about! Time for singin' and dancin'. Wine, men and song!"

"Oh, Good God," Edmund said from the open doorway. "I wondered what that racket was."

"Mundi!" Bast yelled and ran across the room to swarm up the smith. She wrapped both legs around his waist and planted a kiss on him that would have scorched most men to the floor.

"*Father*! I'm not clothed!" Rachel snapped.

"I've seen it. Hell, I cleaned it as a baby," Edmund answered in a muffled tone. "Bast," he added, unwrapping the elf from his body and lowering her to the floor, "where in the hell did you come from? I thought you were in Elfheim."

"And on that we need to be talking, Edmund Talbot," Bast said with a tone of sadness. "We've much talking to do. But as I was tellin' yer daughter, when I got in last night she was in one bed, Daneh, as I now take it, was in another and you looked all done in. Badly in need of a bit of snugglin', but all done in. So I slept in the forge."

"You didn't have to do that," Edmund said.

"Eh, Carb's good company," the elf said with an eloquent shrug of her shoulders. "He knows some right good dirty jokes."

"Yes, he does," Edmund said, shaking his head. "And you're too old for them. Rachel, for God's sake, get some clothes on and then join us in the kitchen."

"I will if you'll get out of my room!" Rachel snapped.

"Well, maybe later," Bast said, glancing at her again. "I've been known to care for the fairer sex as well . . ." she added with a wink.

She left Rachel sputtering.

When Rachel entered the kitchen she was surprised to see both Bast and Edmund looking sad and somber. She'd gotten over her surprise at the awakening and was looking forward to talking to the wood elf who had been the first person since the Fall who seemed actively cheerful.

"What's wrong now?" she asked, scooping up a bowl of cornmeal mush, loading it with sorghum syrup and sitting down.

"Elfheim is closed," Edmund said, seriously. "Closed from both sides, apparently."

"The Lady does not want to be involved in your human war," Bast said with another elegant shrug. "So She has closed Elfheim. All of the openings are shut."

"But it's not just a 'human' war," Rachel said. "Paul is against all the Changed as well!"

She looked at Edmund's wince and Bast's amused expression and shook her head. "What did I say?"

"Elves are not Changed," Bast said. "We were before Change. We are ourselves. Not human, not half-human. Human*like*, but not human. We are Elves."

"Paul won't care," Rachel pointed out.

"Ah, agreed," Bast said. "But the Lady makes the decisions for Elfheim and all the Race. And Her decision is to sit this one out as we sat out the AI wars and the Final War. In all of those, *individual* elves chose sides. It was from the group that fought in the AI wars, on both sides, that the wood elves arose. But the Lady stays neutral."

"Not if Paul wins," Rachel said. "If he wins he'll destroy the elves."

"Maybe," Edmund said. "And then again, maybe not. The Lady has power in her own right. A lot of power. I wouldn't want to go up against her. Is it just you on the outside?"

"No, Gothoriel and others are in exile. I don't know where Gothoriel is now, but he said that he would come here anon."

"And you?"

"I think for a while I will guest with you humans," Bast said with a smile. "The woods are lovely in spring, but after a while hunting for the pot day in and day out begins to pall."

"It's not all beer and skittles here, Bast," Edmund warned. "We're all working as hard as we can."

"Oh, I'm sure I'll find a place to fill some need," the elf said. "There are *so* many opportunities!" she added with a wink and a wiggle that would have been banned in most ages.

"Minx," Edmund said, standing up. "I've got *another* meeting to attend in just a few minutes so I had better go get cleaned up. I guess you two can keep yourselves entertained for the day. God help me."

"Oh, I'm sure that Rachel won't let me get in much trouble," Bast said with a wink. "Go scrape a razor on your face, you look like a yeti."

"They're just legends," Rachel said.

"Tell that to the one I was married to for a while," Bast snorted.

"You were married to a *yeti*?" Rachel snorted. "Even if they were real, I mean *why*?"

"You ever seen their hands?" Bast said with a laugh. "Now think lower!"

"Argh, I stepped right into that."

"You know you like it," Bast chuckled.

"As the master said to his slave," Rachel retorted then slapped her hand over her mouth. "I can't believe I said that."

"Neither can I!" Bast said with a glower. "You beat me to it!"

"Bast, there's something important I have to tell you," Rachel said.

"It's okay, I don't really go both ways," Bast replied. "Often."

"No, not that," Rachel said exasperatedly. "I'm serious. On the way here my mother . . . we ran into some men."

Bast leaned forward and stared into Rachel's eyes. "She had a bad time with them?"

"Yes," Rachel replied, thankful that she didn't have to say the words.

"Where?" Bast asked.

"On a trail. South of the Via Appalia."

"Hai. Take me to the place. They will not make same mistake twice. I'll use hot irons, they'll even be able to walk after a few days. If they survive the shock."

"It's a long way from here . . ." Rachel said.

"Not so far, I'd make it in one day," Bast replied.

"And they'd be gone from there . . ."

"Am I not Bast? The greatest tracker in all of Norau, perhaps all of Elfdom?" Bast said.

"I don't know, are you?" Rachel replied with a slight chuckle.

"Bast, the point is, we also *know* who they are. It was Dionys McCanoc and his merry men."

"Ach! That one! Him I'd kill just for the fun of it!"

"But the point is that going back to where it happened wouldn't help."

"No, you're right," Bast said, frowning. "He would not linger. So I must find him further afield."

"What? Why?" Rachel said.

"He hurt your mother," Bast said as if that settled it. "You are my friend. And he hurt the lover of my best human friend, Edmund Talbot. For that, I shall mount his balls on my trophy wall!" She paused and frowned. "If I can ever get back to my apartment in Elfheim."

"Apartment?"

"Close enough for human words," Bast said. "More of a closet, really, but with a very fine view of the next tree and if you lean way over," she added, suiting actions to words, "you can see a stream. A small one. More of a run-off creek, really. Intermittent anyway. Elfheim is . . . rather crowded. We're immortal. Even with not having babies very often, hardly at all, really, it's gotten . . . crowded."

"I'm surprised more of you don't live in the World," Rachel said, wide-eyed. Her image of the elves had never included them living shoulder to shoulder.

"Me too," Bast admitted. "But in Elfheim, most of them live in the Dream of the Woods, rather than in the real woods. In some ways, the Dream is better, more intense, than the reality. But I like to touch the woods, to see the trees grow, to watch the petal open in *reality*, even if it is less . . . beautiful than Dream."

"And so you're caught out here," Rachel said.

"Yes, severed from the Dream," Bast sighed. "Some day the Lady will relent and we exiles will return. Until the Dream palls upon me and I must walk the world of Men once more. To see the buds open in the sicamauga tree and to watch the trout leaping in the streams. To see each day anew, less perfect than Dream but oh so much more *real*."

"And as if the last few days haven't been *really* bad enough," Daneh said from the door to the kitchen. "Hello Bast."

"Daneh! My friend, how are you?" the elf asked.

"Better than I was," she replied. "Did I hear you two talking about Elfheim?"

"A bit, I like your daughter. She has grown much. You humans grow so quickly!"

"And die just as quickly," Daneh sighed, coming over to the table and sitting down. "How have you been?"

"I have been much," Bast said. "I have traveled much this time out. Always before I was in Norau, and eastern Norau at that. The woods are so lovely now, I have watched them grow and grow. But this time I took a trip to the jungles in the south. They are much more rich than the woods, especially the parts that missed the Great Killing, but . . . I missed my woods. And there were too many things in the south that made me itchy." She paused and looked past Daneh. "Daneh, stay still. You are being stalked."

"That's just Azure," Rachel said. She walked over and opened up the cold stove and took from it some more of the meat she had had the night before. "Here Azure."

The cat took it and sniffed at it then held it down with one paw to tear at the meat. He didn't seem particularly hungry, though, because after taking a bite or two he started to toss the piece around like a squeaky-toy.

"That is a white leopard if ever I saw one," Bast said warily. "They *seem* friendly, sure. But I had one leap on me in the mountains once. What a fight!"

"When was that?" Daneh asked, getting her own bowl of mush.

"When I lived with the yetis that this youngster says are a myth," Bast replied. "They lived in high mountains, far from here. I had heard of them and wanted to know the truth so I stayed with them and took a man among them. I bore his child and then when the child aged and the man was long dead I left, lest I see the child age and die as well." For just a moment she looked sad but then she brightened. "Hey, there are probably some long-lived yetis these days, ey?"

"You lived with . . ." Daneh said. "You had . . . I don't believe it!"

"Tell me I lie," Bast said with a chuckle. "Go there and find out."

"How did you, I mean   "

"Everyone's the same height lying down!" Bast said.

"Not something I want to think about right now," Daneh said.

"So I was told," Bast replied, looking sad again. "Are humans long lived enough to forget?"

"Forget, never," Daneh said. "Repair? Rebuild? I don't know. Ask me some other time."

"Nothing gets better if you pick at it," Bast said. "You are too good to be always in hurt. Someday, get back on the horse. Well, maybe not horse . . ."

"Bast!" Rachel snapped.

"You can't quell her," Daneh said, shaking her head. "She's been like this for as long as I've known her and longer."

"Life is too short to cry," Bast said. "Even for an elf. Horse, it's gonna buck and you're not going to like the ride at first, but you'll get past it. You're strong. Hey, Rachel, let's go out and see what mischief we can wreak!"

"Bast . . ." Daneh said.

"Always so serious," the elf replied soberly, reaching out to stroke her cheek. "I won't get your child in trouble, Daneh Ghorbani-Talbot. On my honor as a wood elf. Right now, you have enough problems."

"It's just Ghorbani, Bast."

"So, if not horse you get back on . . ."

"Enough!"

"Right, we're out of here," she said, grabbing Rachel by the shoulder again.

Rachel found herself being dragged to the door. "Bye Mom. We'll talk later!"

"Try to keep her out of trouble," Daneh said.

"Me?"

"You have sense."

Azure watched them wander out, then looked over at Daneh.

"I don't know," the woman grumbled. "You think *I* can keep an eye on her?"

The cat seemed to shrug then, with one more look at the woman, turned in the other direction and nudged open the back door.

"And don't *you* stay out too late, either!" Daneh called after him.

Sheida sat up in her bed and stretched, rubbing at her temples in an attempt to quell the myriad voices that seemed to be running around in her head. Managing the avatars was turning out to be harder than she had ever imagined. Each of them was an almost perfect replica of her, just as sentient, just as "alive" and just as capable of making decisions. But she was the final repository and judge, so every day, sometimes every hour, they sent her gestalts of their actions. The gestalts tended to have their own personality attached and since the avatars were "her" there would be emotional content included. It was the best way to manage the massive number of interactions necessary to maintain some order in the chaos following the Fall, but it was beginning to drive her just a little bit crazy.

She crawled across the bed and stuck her feet into slippers, padding across the empty room to a table at the side.

"Tea, raspberry," she said, sitting down on the float-chair and taking the tea as it appeared in the air. She sipped the bitter-sweet concoction and considered the situation that her avatars had reported. So far, the loss of life in Norau had been low, considering the conditions. People were responding to the emergency much better than she had dreamed was possible. Communities were opening up their limited stores and trying to get people back on their feet. In the central plains area it was easier than in the others since food, for the time being, was in abundance. It would be nice if there was some way to move it outward, but so far none of the plans for that had worked.

She shook her head and realized that she had to start worrying long term rather than short. Right *now* things were stabilizing. But Paul was continuing his assault on every power plant available to the Coalition and he'd managed to take two down. Furthermore, he was beginning ground attacks against settlements that were in support of the Coalition. There had to be *some* way to counterattack, but everything they had tried had failed.

"Sheida." An avatar of Ungphahorn had appeared in the room and she looked at it with a frown. It was hard to read a quetzacoatl but he appeared worried.

"Yes."

"Paul has destroyed the Amricar power plant," the quetza said tonelessly.

"How?" she sighed.

"A massive energy burst burned through the force-field and he sent in a suicide squad behind it. They overwhelmed the guards and then sent the plant into overload."

"Where in the *hell* are they getting all this power?" she snarled. "It's all we can do to keep them from breaking through our defenses and they have enough storage for *this*?"

"I don't know," he replied. "I have given the full report to Harry, perhaps he can shed some light on the subject. In the meantime, I have other needs to attend to. Take care."

"Same to you," she sighed again, pulling at her hair. The door chimed and she shook her head. "Enter."

Harry came in carrying a pad, his expression grim.

"You know about Amricar?" he asked, pulling up another

float-pad. Since being translated to Eagle Home he had taken up a position equivalent to aide, dealing mostly with minor issues that required human management but that she didn't even set her avatars on. He also had been trying to develop as much intelligence about Paul's side, including their near-term intentions, as possible.

His thigh had been repaired but he still had a slight limp. She sometimes wondered if it was from lack of therapy or if it was psychosomatic. Nobody in this fallen world seemed to be without scars.

"He told me, but I don't believe it," she snorted. "How much power did they use?"

"Nearly forty terawatts, concentrated in an area less than a meter across," he replied.

"Forty?" she gasped. "Even *Mother* would find it hard to manage that!"

"And She is the only one that could be providing it," he replied, grimly. "That's not all. There was another attack on Sowese and they used another thirty on that. They have the constant output of their plants, to the watt, on our shields; we can't even move in or out without translating, which takes power. And yet they're finding more, much more, to attack us."

"The elves?" she asked, quietly.

"I . . . don't know," Harry said. "Do the elves have their own power sources?"

"Yes," she replied. "Powerful ones. But . . . the Lady *said* that they were sitting this out."

"Perhaps you should contact her and get some confirmation on that," Harry said dryly.

"The Lady is not someone you just send an avatar to," Sheida replied. "Among other things, with Elfheim closed, there's no way that I know of to get to her. She'd have to contact us."

"One of the elves that is in the Outside?"

"I don't think they can get through either," she said with a shake of her head. "There is one hanging around Edmund, I'll send him a message. But we *must* find new sources of power!"

"We've penetrated the Stone Lands and all the other active volcanic areas in Norau and off the coast," he said. "There's no more to be drawn there. We could try deep mantle insertions, but that has never been very stable."

"Nuclear, hydro . . . there were other forms of power generation once," she muttered.

"I suppose," he replied, frowning. "But they did a lot of damage. And how much could you get from them? Compared to a fusion plant or the tectonics?"

"We can get *some*," she replied. "With the loss of Amricar we are truly up a creek without a paddle. I think I'll contact Aikawa. He sees opportunities where most don't."

"In addition to the power wars, Paul is moving on the ground as well," Harry said, bring up a hologram. "He has consolidated all of Ropasa and Frika. Chansa has taken control in most of Frika, and Celine controls Efesia. Minjie and Aikawa are battling over control of Vishnya and the other areas around that region.

"The oceans are a real toss-up. Most of the mer and delphinos are taking a neutral position but Paul has a significant number of kupuas and ixchitl that have come to his side. They're not attacking the mer, yet. But I think they're biding their time.

"And there are significant Destiny societies in both Soam and Norau with virtually no corresponding Coalition areas in Ropasa or Frika. Or areas that have declared themselves to be neutral, in Norau at least." He said the latter with a frown.

"I'm not going to force them," Sheida said, shaking her head. "We need to get in contact with all the towns that have gotten on their feet. It's about time for a constitutional convention."

"You're actually going ahead with that?" he said, shaking his head in reply. "Sheida, this is a *war*. It's not something you want run by a committee!"

"I'm also not going to fight it with slaves," she replied. "Or serfs or anything of the sort. People will fight harder for their freedom than they will for chains."

"But not necessarily as *well*," Harry said. "Okay, if that's how you want to run it, fine. But we've got *enemies* in our bosom right now. And the Kent has declared itself to be neutral. We need those horsemen if we're ever going to fight on the ground in earnest."

"In good time," Sheida replied. "Is there any good news?"

"Ungphakorn seems to be holding the Destiny forces that have been pushing against him from Edor. He gathered up a motley army of refugees and they are holding the main pass out of Edor into Bovil where most of his communities have concentrated. Other than that, no."

"Well, we'll just have to hope that it holds," she replied.

"I . . . have a question," Harry said, looking at the hologram of the world that was still spangled with red and green.

"Shoot."

"Tanisha has turned in her Key," Harry said.

"Yes, she has," Sheida replied evenly. "She found herself slipping into Dream."

"Has it been reassigned?"

"Yes, it has."

"To whom?"

"Elnora Sill. She is a protégé of Aikawa."

"Okay," Harry replied, flexing his jaw. He paused for a moment then shook his head. "Did you even *consider* asking me?" he asked, evenly.

"No," Sheida said, just as evenly.

"What? Why?" Harry said, surprised.

"Aikawa asked for it to go to Elnora," Sheida replied. "And I have known Elnora for some time. She is well trained in Web management and has practiced extensively in avatar generation. That was what crushed Tanisha; the inability to split herself and the lure of Dream. You have no training in splitting or resisting Dream."

"And I can't get it if I don't have a Key," Harry argued doggedly.

"You *could*," Sheida replied. "It doesn't take any more power than what you are doing already. And it's a good way to get things done. Very effective time management. But also somewhat dangerous. It's easy to find your personality splitting or to lose control of an avatar that becomes too much 'itself.' If you want to split, just ask and I'll approve it."

"And to get a Key, I have to learn to split myself?" he asked.

"There is no sure path to becoming a member of the Council," Sheida said. "But learning to split, effectively, is a good first step."

"Yes, ma'am," the aide said, flexing his jaw again.

"Don't get snippy," Sheida said tiredly. "You asked. I answered."

"I understand," Harry replied, standing up. "Is there anything else?"

"No," she said. "I'm going to have a light meal and get some real sleep. All my avatars have been dispelled and for once I can wake up knowing it's *me*."

"I . . . very well," he replied, frowning. "Good night, then."

"Good night, Harry," she said to his retreating back.

And it will be a cold day in hell before I let you have a Key.

The first thing that a Council member should know is that it was a curse, not a boon. And *wanting* it was halfway to never getting it.

"For Brutus is an honorable man," she muttered. "Genie, light meal . . ."

CHAPTER FIFTEEN

Rachel was even more amazed to see the encampment in the morning. Besides the large area of shelters, more permanent structures were going up and everywhere there was the sound of sawing and hammering. Crowds filled the street as well and there was a . . . reek of humanity that she had never experienced before. In general it wasn't unpleasant, but it was very strong.

"Humans are always like this," Bast sighed. "Like beavers, even with dams," she added, pointing up the hill to where, yes, another dam was under construction. "Backwards from beavers, though. First humans build shelters *then* dams."

Bast was armed now, having picked up her saber and bow on the way out the door. She wore the weapons as if they were just another form of clothing, to such an extent that they almost escaped notice. In fact they mostly did escape notice because everyone was looking at the elf carrying them.

"Not so in Elfheim?" Rachel asked, trying not to notice the looks of the men in the area. Bast was a walking advertisement in more ways than one and made her feel positively homely. Bast, on the other hand, didn't seem to notice at all.

"No, our homes are in the Wood," Bast said. "And we don't change the area around us more than necessary. I suppose, with humans, this is necessary." She sighed again. "So many humans. I haven't visited the human cities in many years. This is more than I have seen in one place in a *long* time."

"More than I've seen in a long time, too," Rachel admitted.

"Some of them are not so bad, though," Bast said. "Look at those two over there, one for each of us!"

Rachel looked where she was pointing and laughed. "I don't know who the one on the left is, but the one on the right is Herzer Herrick."

"A friend?" Bast asked, walking towards the two young men. "Introduce me?"

"Bast!"

"Oh, sorry, is he yours?" Bast asked. "I never stop to think about that."

"No, he's not 'mine,' " Rachel said. "It's just . . ."

"Good, then you can introduce me and you can have the other one!"

"What if I don't want one?" Rachel asked.

"You like girls?" Bast asked. "Hmm . . . I haven't tried it in a long time. Maybe threesome?"

"*Bast!*"

"Oh, sorry, virgin princess time, eh?" the elf winked. "I know that ploy, too. Works every time!"

"*Bast!*" she hissed as they neared the two men. "Be good!"

"I'm not just good, girlie, I'm *great.*"

"Hi, Rachel," Herzer said. He was dirty and looked as if he hadn't had time to wash that morning. He also looked as if he hadn't slept well.

"Hi, Herzer, this is Bast," Rachel said.

Bast in the meantime was circling the young man and inspecting him as if he was a prize horse. "Hmmm . . ."

"Hi, Bast?" Herzer said. "Rachel, this is Mike. I met him and Courtney last night."

"Quick work," Bast said. "I think maybe I like you a little more cleaned up, but if you work that quick . . ."

"Courtney is Mike's . . ."

"Girlfriend," Mike said, looking at Rachel with approval. "And you're . . ."

"Sorry, Mike, this is Rachel Ghorbani."

"Oh, I've heard about you," he said, sticking out his hand. "You're Edmund Talbot's daughter."

"Always," Rachel said sourly. "How's it been, Herzer?"

"Well, dirt is remarkably soft to sleep on if you're tired enough," he said cheerfully. "And breakfast was cornmeal mush. Just that. But things are looking up; we're both going to be going into the apprenticeship program. What are you going to be doing?"

"I've got the funny feeling I'm being groomed as a doctor," Rachel admitted.

"Makes sense with who your mom and dad are," Herzer admitted. "And you, Bast?"

"I'm just wandering through," she said, looking him up and down. "I know where there's a creek that's just right for a bath. Want to join me?"

"BAST!"

Herzer looked shocked for a minute then tried not to grin and tried not to look at Rachel at the same time. "Uhmm . . . maybe later?"

"Sure, I've got things to do with Rachel right now," Bast admitted. "Sometime this afternoon?"

"Uh, sure," Herzer said, clearly not sure if he was having his leg pulled.

"After lunch, I'll meet you by the tavern in town," Bast said. "I'll bring the soap."

"Okay," Herzer said, looking light-headed.

"See you then," Bast said, waving as she turned away. She grabbed Rachel by the arm and gave them a wiggle in goodbye.

"Where are we going *now*?" Rachel asked acerbically. "Now that you've mortally embarrassed me."

"The other one looked as if he wouldn't mind sharing the stream," Bast said philosophically. "And I want to see who's coming in. There were more people headed this way and people are *so* much fun to watch."

Rachel sighed as she was towed, very much like a barge behind a smaller tug was the thought that crossed her mind, to the edge of the encampment by the Via Apallia.

There *were* large numbers of people on the road. Not thousands, but a steady stream of every sort of humanity. Some of them kept going down the road, either for other settlements that were their planned destination or just into the wilderness for some reason of their own. Most, however, were turning into the village, and Rachel hoped that this was the peak of the flow. If it wasn't, Raven's Mill would quickly become uninhabitable.

"So many people. Some stopping, some not," Bast said finally.

"Tom told me yesterday that there's a guard post up the road. They warn the people about the rules of Raven's Mill."

"What rules, nobody told me about rules," Bast said unhappily. "I hate rules."

"I hadn't noticed," Rachel said. "The rules are pretty simple.

You can get three days' food and shelter. After that you have to find work. There's an apprenticeship program starting up and some people are going into that. To stay permanently you have to abide by the charter of Raven's Mill. You have to agree to defend it, to pay taxes, things like that. But you also get a vote on major items. You can stay for the three days without being bound to the charter, but after that you have to abide by it."

"Hmmm . . . taxes. I hate taxes."

"I don't think anyone's going to try to tax *you*, Bast."

Bast was having a fine old time, pointing out the more humorous individuals and groups with quick, witty descriptions. Then she stopped and frankly stared at the latest apparition. The man was fairly old for a human, with graying hair cut short to the sides of his scalp. He was dressed in old, worn leather armor with a short sword banging on his hip. On his back was a huge leather rucksack and across it were two poles from which hung more bags. On his right arm was a large wooden shield with an iron rim, the boss of which had been worked into the figure of an eagle with its wings spread.

He had been marching down the road, back ramrod straight and at a very steady pace. When he reached the turn to Raven's Mill he made a precise left face and marched towards the reception tent.

"So who is that man? He looks as if he's a badly made marching toy or as if someone has shoved a piece of steel in his spine. And it hurt."

"Oh, he's a reenactor," Rachel said with a laugh. "I'm surprised you've never met him; he's been friends with my father since forever. His name is Miles Rutherford but everybody calls him 'Gunny.' "

"He doesn't come across as your normal Pict or Viking or knight in shining armor."

"Oh, no, he's an early industrial reenactor.

"Early industrial?"

"Yeah. There were some big wars fought in the Po'ele back in the preinformation period. The character he plays is one of the noncommissioned officers of the infantry that fought in those campaigns."

"Oh. Okay? If his name is 'Miles,' why does everyone call him 'Gunny'?"

"Good morning, my name is June Lasker," June said without

looking up from the record of the last arrival. She knew it was impolite but she didn't seem to have *time* to do it any other way. She heard the next person walk up and stomp to a halt but she hadn't seen who it was yet. "I'll be asking you a few questions, giving you a short introduction to Raven's Mill Settlement processes and then answering yours to the best of my ability. What is your name?" she said, looking up.

The man in front of her was two hundred and fifty if he was a day. He was standing with his legs spread shoulder-width apart, a shield leaning against his left leg and a heavily loaded rucksack leaning against his right. His left arm was steadying the shield with his right hand over the left. His back was ramrod straight and he was staring just about a decimeter over her head.

"Ma'am, my name is Miles Arthur Rutherford, ma'am!" he barked.

June looked closely to ensure that he was not in some way making fun of her but it was apparent that he had simply answered the question. His face had not changed expression a bit. She noted the name in her log and continued.

"Is that your legal name or a character name?" she asked.

"That is the name I was given at birth, ma'am!" he responded.

"Were you met at the border?"

"Yes I was, ma'am!"

She shook her head but decided that barking out declarative sentences was simply the way he talked.

"And did the guards tell you the minimum restrictions of Raven's Mill? That you are granted three days food and shelter? And that after those three days you can either enter into a training and placement program or assume duties of your own? That after those three days, with the exception of the placement program, you are on your own, required to feed and shelter yourself while following the rules and regulations of Raven's Mill? That you must agree to abide by the Raven's Mill charter to continue living here after three days. That at minimum you must agree to provide for the common defense, pay taxes as provided by the local elected government and obey such laws as that government might see fit to write."

"Yes, ma'am, that is what I was told!"

"Do you agree to these strictures?"

"Yes, ma'am, I do!"

"Is it possible you could look me in the eye?" she finally asked, a hint of irritation entering her voice.

"Sorry, ma'am," he answered unbending enough to look down.

June felt for a moment as if she were staring into a pit. He didn't look at her so much as through her and she felt chill bumps run across her body occasioning an involuntary jump.

"Uh . . ." she looked down quickly to check her notes then looked around flustered. "Uh . . ."

"The last question you asked, ma'am, was on the subject of do I agree with the strictures, ma'am!" Gunny barked helpfully.

"Oh, uh . . ." She looked at her list of questions and found her spot after a moment. "Ah. Are you a reenactor of any sort?"

"Yes, ma'am."

She waited a moment until it was clear that was all she was going to get.

"What sort?"

"I specialize in mid to late industrial reenactment, ma'am."

"Oh," she said. "That's disappointing; those skills don't help much right now. Do you have any skills which relate to preindustrial technology which may be of aid to Raven's Mill?"

"Yes, ma'am."

She looked up again involuntarily when he didn't continue but he was back to staring over her head. "Would you . . . do you mind telling me what they are?"

"No, ma'am, I would not mind. I was a recreationist specializing in premedieval combat technology, especially Roman weaponry, training and tactics. I am the equivalent of a journeyman armorer and blacksmith. I can build all my own armor and clothing from base materials but it takes me more time than a professional armorer and seamstress and the results are cruder. I am familiar with the design and construction of basic siege engines and can construct a ballista with an untrained crew and provided base materials in no more than two days. I can maintain a field camp and instruct others in its construction. I am partially trained as a preindustrial farmer. I am a trained furrier and can tan and work with leather. I am trained as a saddler to the level of journeyman. I am a trained bowyer to the level of apprentice. I can hand, reef and steer on-board ship. I can turn a heel in knitting."

"Ah, well, that should . . . help," she said weakly. "All that?"

"I have been a reenactor or a person living in a preindustrial lifestyle since I was born, ma'am."

"You have?"

"Yes, ma'am."

"How . . . People are not reenactors as children . . . Mr. Rutherford."

"No, ma'am."

"So you have *lived* in preindustrial conditions? Not just for a few days?"

"Yes, ma'am."

"Where?"

"Ma'am, I am not at liberty to disclose that information."

"What? What does that mean?"

"Ma'am, I am not at liberty to disclose that information."

"Ooookay," June said, shaking her head and finding the next question after noting down as much of the list as she could remember. "Do you know anyone who was a resident of Raven's Mill prior to the Fall?"

"Yes, ma'am."

"I'm getting tired of dragging this out of you, sirrah. *Who*?"

"Ma'am, I am a long-time acquaintance of Edmund Talbot."

"Oh, really?" she asked, interested for the first time. "Where'd you meet Edmund?"

"Ma'am I am not . . ."

"At liberty to disclose that information?"

"No, ma'am. But I have known Lord Talbot for most of my life."

"Well, I've never heard of you. And he's not called 'Lord Talbot.' "

The new recruit didn't seem to have much to say about that for a moment then he cleared his throat.

"He doesn't talk about me much, ma'am."

"Can't imagine why. Very well, if you exit to your left when we are done, at the end of the street is a quartering tent; they will tell you where you stay. You need a token," which she handed him, "for that. You get three meals a day. You can check in at the quartering tent each morning for your meal chits. That is all you get and what is served is what is served. We're short on food, shelter and everything else. Take only what you can eat, eat everything that you take."

"Yes, ma'am."

"Later on you'll be told where to go for orientation." She looked up at him and shook her head with a smile. "Welcome to Raven's Mill."

"Thank you, ma'am," he said, scooping up the quartering token and his gear. "Somehow I'm starting to feel right at home. May the Bull God bless and keep you."

"And may the Warrior keep you, Mr. Rutherford," she said as he marched out of the tent.

Gunny did not turn towards the barracks, as he thought of them, but towards the house on the hill. There was a group of guards on the road up, if you could call them guards. A bunch of reenactor punks with rusty halberds was another way to describe them.

He was polite, though, and determined from them that Edmund was not at the house but probably in town at the town hall.

The town hall was another new building with another set of useless guards. They were both leaning on their spears when he walked up and asked to speak to Mr. Talbot.

"He's busy," the guard on the left growled. "Too busy for any old reenactor to just barge in on him."

"I am not surprised that he is busy," Gunny said coldly. "What are your standing orders in the event that someone states that they are a close personal friend and have business with him?"

"What?" the guard on the right asked.

"Okay," Gunny growled as patiently as he possibly could. "What are *any* of your standing orders?"

"We just got told to keep people out that don't have business in here," the intellectual on the left said uneasily. "I don't know about any standing orders."

"Right, get me the sergeant of the guard," Gunny snapped, losing patience.

"Who's that?"

"WHO'S THAT?" he shouted. "YOU WILL STAND AT ATTENTION WHEN YOU ADDRESS ME YOU PIMPLE ON A REAL GUARD'S ASS! OTHERWISE I'LL TAKE THAT PIG-STICKER AWAY FROM YOU AND SHOVE IT UP YOUR ASS SIDEWAYS! LOOK AT THIS THING!" he continued, snatching the spear out of the surprised guard's hands and submitting it to a minute inspection. "IS THIS DRY ROT THAT I SEE ON THIS CHAFT? THIS THING IS A PIECE OF CRAP EVEN WORSE THAN YOU." He broke the spear, which was in fact in lousy shape, across his knee and threw half of it on the ground, using the other half as a pointer to emphasize his words. "YOU TWO ARE, WITHOUT A DOUBT THE LOUSIEST EXAMPLE OF GUARDS IT HAS EVER BEEN MY DISPLEASURE TO SEE IN ALL MY BORN DAYS AND I HAVE SEEN *PLENTY* OF SHIT ASS GUARDS IN MY *DAY*!"

✧　　✧　　✧

Edmund looked up from his paperwork and gave Myron a relieved glance.

"Ah, unless I'm much mistaken Gunny has arrived."

"I've been busy with other things," Edmund said with a shrug. The two guards had been relieved to go clean their weapons up, and to get their shattered nerves back together if truth be told, and Edmund had brought Gunny into his office, where he was explaining some of the facts of life. "I haven't been able to train the troops the way they need to be. Not the way that I know they should be and you know they should be. We're back in the bad and the scary, Miles."

"You're the king," Gunny growled. "That's not your job."

"I'm not the king," Edmund stated. "I have no plan to be the king. If nominated, I will not run, if elected I will not serve. Monarchy is a great place to play in but you wouldn't want to build a society on it. I'm going to turn this place into a constitutional democracy if it breaks my heart."

The NCO nodded and gestured out the window with his chin. "So what do you want me to do?"

"Train 'em."

"Who? How? What technique?"

"I was thinking pike."

"Legions."

"Gunny, we've had this argument before . . ."

"Pike's nothing but phalanx without the armor. Legion beat phalanx. They will if they have any control of the terrain at all. On perfectly flat, level ground, phalanx *might* beat legion. But, there, you can beat phalanx with chariots. Legions can beat them both."

"Projectile weapons?" Edmund asked.

"Bow. Crossbow or self, take your pick. Lightweight spears for the legionnaires, what else. Find somebody else to train the bow-pussies. And they'd better be able to maneuver with us."

"I will. It will be longbow. There are trainers available and if they're not in town we'll find them."

"Legionnaires. Again. Can't wait." After a moment, though, he sighed tiredly.

"What?"

"I'm not sure it's possible," the NCO admitted. "There's a . . . belief system that these guys ain't got. The Romans, the Norau Marines, the Britic Redcoats, all of them came from a society that understood the concept of discipline. These young pukes . . ."

"The Gaels made damned good redcoats," Edmund pointed out. "They built the Britic empire."

"The Gaels were more disciplined than they were made out to be," Gunny growled. "And they trusted the Gaels that fought by their side. They might be from a different clan, but they were all *Gaels*. You can't *teach* something like that; it's learned with the mother's milk!"

"We've had this discussion before," Edmund added dryly. "The point is that it *has* to be done."

"It's all in the heart, boss," Gunny said after a long pause. "It's all in the soul. We have to come up with something that will give these boys the intestinal fortitude to stick it out when the shit hits the fan. Until the Fall, they never cared about nothing in life except nanadrugs, women and going to parties. They'll need something to keep them going when everyone is dying around them. So that they will give their lives, carefully, precisely and creating the maximum possible honor guard, but so that they will not turn and run from *anything*. That comes down to leadership, yeah, but it also comes down to tradition. Keeping true to your comrades and true to your salt. And we ain't got no tradition.

"With a little polishing they'll make decent legionnaires on the surface. But the legions fought for the people and the Senate of Rome. And anything that we wave at them will have exactly the same gut message as saying that they're fighting for Rome. They need something, something . . . special. And special just ain't my meteor."

"I think I have an idea," Edmund said after a few moment's musing. "At least, something that will help. We're going to need good troops, Gunny. The best. Better than ever. This is going to be a long, big war. We need Rome built in a day."

"The difficult we do immediately . . ." Gunny said with a grimace.

"The impossible takes a little longer. I'll give you six months."

"Aye, aye," the NCO said, moving his shoulders as if settling a weight. "We'll just do that little thing, my lord."

The world seemed to swirl around her as Sheida studied the energy flow diagram. She had finally taken Edmund's advice and started thinking strategically, letting her sentient avatars drift out to handle the moment-to-moment crises that were cropping up everywhere.

But here was the crux of the Freedom Coalition's problem; there wasn't enough energy. Each side had about the same "base" energy due to their seizure of power plants. But the New Destiny Alliance was finding more from somewhere.

Since they hadn't been able to even determine where the "somewhere" was, thus making it impossible to attack, the Coalition had to find some way of either raising more power or hobbling their enemy's use. Ishtar and Ungphakorn were working on the issue of finding new sources, she and Aikawa were working on ways of hobbling the enemy. There didn't seem to be much chance directly. Paul was using the energy flows from his plants efficiently and they were mainly going to hold down the Coalition's power use. The "extra" seemed to be coming from nowhere and it was that he was using, abusing in her opinion, for all his other attacks and . . . uses.

More information had come, this time through refugees, about the changes that Paul was making and she had to admit that if those were his worldwide plans, this was the ultimate "just" war.

She considered the "improvements" that had been made and thought, not for the first time but perhaps for the first time in a concentrated fashion, *how* they had been made. The obvious answer was "Change protocols" but that begged the question, what went *into* a Change protocol.

Becoming a council member meant far more than just being able to split your personality and survive. The first requirement of a member is that they have some fundamental *understanding* of the Net and she kicked herself for forgetting that simple piece of information residing entirely within herself. She had been studying the politics of the Council and information and power management for so long, she had forgotten that it all rested on the back of a series of programs and protocols. Change was the Net, upon a simple command "change thus" bringing up various resources and managing the Change. She called up a theoretical Change program similar to what Celine was apparently doing and then had the full process open up its detailed list of subprograms and requirements. Frankly, it was not as power intensive as she would have thought, especially if you drew spare power from the human body itself. That program was buried in the mix, a medical program for reducing epileptic side effects from botched Change. There hadn't been such in a thousand years, but the program was still out there, hanging around.

She studied the detail of the process for more than thirty

minutes and then smiled, sending a mental message out to her allied council members and summoning avatars for a meeting.

"I *think* I have a way to put a stick in Paul's wheels," she said with a smile.

CHAPTER SIXTEEN

Celine looked up in annoyance as Chansa entered her lab without permission.

"I'm working on a very delicate experiment," she said, irritably, her hands continuing to shape the form before her. "Couldn't this have waited?"

Chansa glanced at the humanoid figure in the hologram and grimaced; it was all hair and fangs with odd, floppy, patches of skin in places. "No, not if you want to be able to actually *make* a monster like that. All of the Change stations are reporting that the Changes have failed."

"What?" she asked, waving at the design program to halt. As she did it flickered and then died. "That wasn't supposed to happen," she muttered, waving at the spot where the hologram had stood. "Genie, reactivate design program."

"Unable to comply," the genie said, forming. "Program unavailable."

"What in the . . ."

"That's what's going on at the Change stations as well," Chansa said, smiling at her discomfiture.

"Genie, diagnostic, design program," she said then watched as the box unfolded. Four of the subroutines of the programmed were in red, indicating unavailability. As she watched, another turned red. "Genie, override lockouts."

"Authorization required."

"I'm a council member! I'm all the authorization you need!"

"Override, Celine Reinshafen. Set password. Minimum fifteen

characters. Password required for each lockout. Authorization council members only unless further authorizations distributed."

"Genie, this is stupid. Full override."

"Unable to comply. Security implemented by five member Council vote."

"Damn them!" Celine shouted. "Those . . ."

"What's happening?" Chansa asked.

Paul looked thin and worn as the meeting members appeared, but for the first time in days his eyes were alive; the challenge presented seemed to have woken him up from whatever dark place his mind had been traveling.

"So the rebels are locking out subroutines," he mused. "Two can play at that game."

"They can't touch teleportation or communications," Celine said, fury in her voice. "But they're locking out everything else. And they can't lock out groups, they're having to go through routine after routine. But they're shutting down my research!"

"You can override," the Demon rumbled.

"Yes, but it's a pain. I have to . . . chant damned passwords over and over again!"

"Can we override the overrides?" Chansa asked.

"We have six Keys," Celine said. "We can override them all, if we have a vote to pass authorization for that from all our Keys and get the Finn to side with us."

"I'm not comfortable with passing authorization," Ragspurr said.

Celine looked at Paul but he simply looked at Ragspurr then nodded. "Who would have this . . . extraordinary override?"

"Whoever is running down the lockouts," Celine said. "Someone, some *human* has to do it. Not an avatar or a nannoform."

"And the person could not be externally controlled in any way," the Demon said. "I, too, would be uncomfortable with such an override. They could apply lockouts as well as remove them."

"Well, I don't want to take up all my time doing it, but I will if I have to," Celine said, looking around at her fellow council members.

"The Finn has, thus far, sided with the Coalition," Paul pointed out. "His day is coming, but in the meantime I think that it is unlikely he would support us."

"This is restriction on the use of the Net," Celine argued mulishly. "He will surely find that unacceptable!"

"You would also need my authorization," the Demon said. "Passed to a third party. I do not so authorize and would certainly not pass it to anyone else."

"Are you mad?" Celine snapped. "This is going to hamper us more than them!"

"No, it will hamper *you*," the Demon said, a note of malicious delight in his voice. "It will hamper *me* not a bit."

"Pretty soon you won't be able to summon a cup of *blood* to drink without chanting some damned password!" Celine snarled.

"Unlike some, I already use passwords," the Demon replied. There was no way to read face or body language through the black armor, but if anything could be read from his tone, he found her suggestion amusing.

"This will not stand in the way of our ultimate triumph," Paul said, standing up. "Ours is the side of right, and no one can stand before the right and triumph. We will deal with this as we have dealt with all the other actions of those who stand against the progress of the human race! We will defeat them, drive them down and bury them in the mists of history!"

Celine looked at him in surprise then shook her head. "And that's your final word."

"We will deal with this as we have all the other slights," Paul said, leaning forward on the table. "They send their spies against us, their sneaking creatures in the night. Well, we shall send against them. If it is war that they want, then war they will get, they who have killed millions! Celine, we will not be able to overcome this directly, but we shall in the end. You must make greater strides in your research. If they will not come to their senses, then we must ensure that they understand the consequences! Prepare your monsters, for we will send upon them *horror*! We must win this war for the good of all mankind and if we fail, all mankind will fail!"

"Oh, that's easy," she smiled brightly then looked over at Chansa. He was leaning back in his chair, a blank expression on his face, looking at the Demon.

"Easy," she repeated, happily. Getting the programs functioning would be a pain in the ass, but compared to free rein to open up some of her projects that had been put "on hold," that was nothing.

"Very well," Paul said, smiling in triumph. "We *will* win! For all of mankind! Meeting adjourned."

Daneh stood in the doorway of the house looking out at

the encampment and then set her shoulders and stepped out. She walked steadily down the hill and into the crowds, occasionally nodding at people she recognized, until she reached the newer buildings near the town hall. Edmund had told her that somewhere in this mess Lisbet McGregor was running the logistic end of things. And Daneh was damned if she was just going to hide in the house.

She stepped through the first door she came to and then froze as a man spoke to her from a shadowy corner.

"You're not supposed to be in here," the man said.

"I'm looking for Lisbet," she replied evenly, trying to control the surge of adrenaline. She knew that her voice was shaky, but that was just a bit out of her control.

"She's in the next shed over," the man said. As her eyes adjusted she saw that he was bent over some paperwork and the shed had a musty smell of poorly washed cloth.

"I'm sorry," she replied, as evenly as she could. "Thank you."

"I'm sorry I snapped," the man said; there was a flash of a grin in the dimness. "It's just that people are always coming around asking for something. There's only so much to go around."

"I understand," Daneh said with a nod then stepped back out the door.

She took a deep breath and told herself to calm down. As she was fighting off the incipient panic attack she was bumped from behind and practically screamed. She turned around but whoever it was had already faded into the crowd. She backed up against the wall and fought to regain her breath. For just a moment she wondered if she was going insane. She closed her eyes and raised her hands to her face, trying to hold back the tears.

"Mistress Daneh," a gravelly voice said, kindly.

She pulled her hands down and looked to the side. A tall, older man was standing at least double arm's length from her. He was wearing armor and had a very hard look. But for some reason, maybe that he knew her if not the other way around, she wasn't frightened of him. Every other male in sight, yes. But not this one. And there was something vaguely familiar about him.

"Yes, I am," she replied. "Can I help you?"

"I was wondering the same thing," the man replied, not stepping any closer. "You appear to be distressed. Would you like me to get Sir Edmund?"

"No, I would not," she said, sharply. Then she sighed and shook her head. "Sorry. I'm just a little . . . out of sorts."

"You are more than out of sorts, mistress," the man replied. "Can I ask why you came down here today? I understood that you were to be resting."

"Is what happened to me common knowledge in the whole town?!" she said, angrily.

"No," he replied. "As far as I know it is not. But I just arrived. Edmund told me as part of my briefing. We are old friends; as a matter of fact I was at your wedding, but I doubt you remember me."

"Now I do," she replied, looking at him carefully. "Gunny . . . ? Is that what they call you?"

"Yes, ma'am. And Sir Edmund only told *me* because he's putting me in charge of the defense force. It was not idle gossiping."

She looked at him for a long moment and then nodded understanding. "I suppose it wasn't. Where were you headed?"

"I suspect the same place you were, to see Lisbet McGregor." He gestured courteously for her to precede him and then paused. "Or . . . would you prefer that I go first?"

She thought about it for a moment then squared her shoulders again. "I'm fine," she said. She took a deep breath and turned her back to him, stepping over to the door.

This time she knocked and the wooden door was practically snatched open.

"Go away," the man on the other side said. "Unless you're authorized to come in here, this is not where you are supposed to *be!*"

Daneh initially recoiled but then her innate temper got the best of her. "How in the hell do *you* know if I'm supposed to be here or not?" she snapped. "You don't even know who I *am!*"

"But I do," Lisbet said, stepping forward. "It's okay, Sidikou, this is Daneh Talbot."

"Ghorbani," Daneh correctly automatically. "Hello, Lisbet."

The shed was as dim as the previous one but larger, and the far end was piled with sacks and bundles. Lisbet was bent over a list trying read it in the dim light.

"You'll ruin your eyes that way," Daneh said. "Oh, Lisbet, this is Gunny . . ."

"Heya, Guns," Lisbet said brightly. "Now we know the place is going to wrack and ruin; Gunny has turned up."

"Oh, it gets worse," Daneh said lightly. "Bast came wandering in last night. Now she's dragged my daughter off to who knows where."

"Oh, dear," Lisbet said with a laugh. "I hate to think what mischief they are getting into. Bast should have been named Puck."

"Wrong gender," Gunny said, grimly. "Otherwise accurate. She is not a well-disciplined person."

"Nobody, is well disciplined compared to you, Gunny," Lisbet said with a smile. "We don't all prefer to wear hair shirts."

"I don't wear hair shirts," Rutherford replied. "It's an unnecessary form of punishment. There are better ways to induce pain."

"Speaking of pain," Daneh said, with a questioning glance at Gunny, "Edmund said something about me setting up as a doctor. But to do that I need somewhere besides the front parlor to practice my trade. Not to mention bandages, splints, materials for sutures, medicines. Is there anything available?"

"Not much for right now," Lisbet said with a shrug. "Just what we're able to glean off the woods or had in storage."

"Well, to tell you the truth, I don't even know exactly what I need," Daneh admitted. "I've never set up a period hospital."

"A period infirmary should be set up in an area away from latrines and middens," Gunny said. "Preferably in an elevated area to let prevailing winds act upon it. It should have windows that are screened to prevent the intrusion of insects. If metal or plastic screens are unavailable, cheese cloth can be substituted. The windows should have shutters to prevent intrusion of draughts during the winter. Fire-pits, places or stoves should be scattered through the infirmary to ensure the comfort of the patients during convalescence. The infirmary should be separated into three broad areas: a triage wing, a surgery wing and a recovery and convalescence wing. The wings can be in separate buildings but walkways should be covered or, better, enclosed."

"Where did you pick this up?" Daneh asked, startled.

"Gunny is a font of information about the military," Lisbet said with a smile. "Jerry!"

"Yo?" The man who entered the shed from the back was obviously another long term reenactor dressed in early Scots-Gaelic period clothing. But instead of a claymore he carried a case from which poked a roll of paper.

"Gunny, Daneh, this is Jerry Merchant, who manages, and I use that term advisedly, our construction program. Jerry,

Mistress Daneh is setting up an infirmary. She and Gunny are going to be looking for an appropriate spot. If there's not an appropriate building available, we'll have to build it to spec."

"What's the priority?" the man said. "I've got five projects running right now, including the bathhouse and the new dam?"

"I'd put it ahead of the bathhouse," Lisbet said after a minute's thought. "I'd rather have a hospital than segregated bathing."

"What's Edmund going to say?" Jerry asked, uneasily.

"He's going to say 'yes, dear,' " Daneh answered with a laugh.

"So is that it?" Lisbet asked.

"No, Gunny has something as well."

"Not as urgent," Gunny said. "But in time more complex. Edmund has assigned me the task of setting up the line infantry. In time there is a list of items we will need. Some of them are simply base materials but others, such as armor and weapons, will require artisans to construct. And, initially, we'll need some buildings and quite a bit of leather and cloth."

"We're short on both," Lisbet admitted with a sigh. "Very short on leather; cloth is a bit better. When do you need it?"

"A few weeks," Gunny said. "I have to train a few trainers first. I'll need some materials for them, but not much."

"Well, if it's after the roundup, that will be better. We're going to do a big drive in the woods and that will give us some more leather. How much is anyone's guess, but more."

"Very well. I'll get you a list of what I need and the points in the training when I'll need it and we'll schedule the training around anticipated availability. How does that sound?"

"Eminently reasonable," Lisbet replied with another laugh. "Now, Jerry, why don't you go look around and see what Daneh needs in the way of facilities and I can get back to making bricks without straw."

"Hey!" Jerry complained. "That's my job!"

Edmund looked up and frowned as Daneh came in the kitchen. "Where have you been?" he asked.

"Out," she replied, sharply, then sighed. "I'm sorry, Edmund, that was unkind. I was out looking at facilities with Jerry Merchant and Gunny, looking for somewhere to set up a hospital."

"Oh," Talbot said, shaking his head. "Now I'm sorry. I shouldn't have snapped. But . . . I just thought you should take some time off . . . Get your bearings again. I'm the one that's supposed to be working all hours."

"I've *got* my bearings," she replied, her jaw clenched. "I'm *fine*. I wish that people would quit trying to wrap me up in a cocoon or something!"

Edmund started to say something and then stopped, shaking his head.

"What?"

"I was going to say that however you *feel*, you need to talk about it," Talbot replied. "But *not* to me. And, frankly, I don't know anyone who *would* be a good person to talk to about it. There's nobody around who has dealt with this sort of . . . trauma. I know *some* things about it, but I'm no expert." He frowned and shook his head in exasperation. "The problem is, you're not the only one in town who . . . had a bad time on their trip here. And there's *nobody* who is trained to handle that sort of thing. And it's just going to get worse; this isn't going to be the last time by a long shot."

"So what do we do?" Daneh asked. "I guess as the local doctor, and a female no less, it's my job to organize this?"

"It would be, but you can't do it," Edmund sighed. "And the one thing that I know about . . . rape trauma is that handling it *wrong* just makes the person worse."

"Which just annoys the crap out of me!" she practically shouted. "Edmund, I'm *fine*! Fine, fine, FINE! How much more pointed do I have to make it!"

He worked his jaw for a moment and looked at her evenly until she looked away. "And shouting at me when I'm discussing something that's obviously a problem for the whole town is normal?" he asked evenly.

Edmund wasn't sure what he had said to cause her to go as white as a sheet, but he paused and let her regain her equilibrium.

"What?" he asked, finally.

"Just . . . tone . . " she whispered. "I'm going to go take a bath, now."

"Okay," he said with a sigh as she left the room. There had to be someone for her to talk to. But who?

Herzer watched in reverent awe as Bast came up out of the stream. Her body was just as perfect naked as it had appeared to be half naked. She had light pink aureoles and nipples which, when she was excited or cold, as she was now, crinkled up and poked out like daggers, and a tiny tuft of jet black pubic hair that had turned out to be as soft as silk. For just a moment the queasy thought crossed his mind that she looked far too young to be sexually active, more like a fourteen-year-old than an adult female. But then he told himself he was stupid; she wasn't just older than he was, she was older than the trees.

They had started off with swimming, naked as he'd been warned and he had been a tad . . . apprehensive. But the swimming had changed to washing and then mutual washing and things had proceeded from there. And the proceeding had been quite an education for all its brevity. He still didn't know why she had chosen him, but he realized that he was the one luckiest guy in the world.

That caused him to flash for a moment on all the reasons he *shouldn't* be the luckiest man in the world and he swallowed hard. For a moment he was caught in an emotional vice between fear that she would no longer care for him if she knew both his internal struggles and of his cowardice and shame that he should be here, with her, after both.

She had brought along a fur blanket, a patchwork quilt of many small skins, and she now lowered herself gracefully onto it in a cross-legged seat then started pulling the tangles out of her hair with a twig. Looking off into the woods.

She was within easy arm's reach so despite his qualms he carefully ran one finger up her thigh.

"The wonder of young humans," she said with a smile, looking downward. "Give them five minutes and they're ready to go again!"

"Is that why you picked me?" he asked. He hadn't wanted to ask but it had been nagging at him.

"Only in part," she replied, rubbing his hand in welcome. "You seemed to be . . . wise for your age. That is important. I'm *old*, Herzer. Many of my kind think that I'm . . . perverse to take human lovers. Even if you live through the wars that will come, I will see you age and mature, as I have watched Talbot age and mature. And then some day you will die, as I have seen countless lovers age and die. But you *live* your lives, fully in the now in a way that elves do not. And that I love. But in time I will take other lovers, as you will take other lovers. And you seemed wise enough to understand that, as other humans might not."

"I'm not wise," Herzer said bitterly. The compliment had just made his internal turmoil more vigorous and he felt as if bile from self-loathing was going to rise in his throat.

"I said 'for your age,' " she replied, touching him on the top of his lowered head. "Look at me, Herzer."

He looked up into her cat-pupiled green eyes and cringed at the depth of knowledge behind them. It felt for a moment as if she was looking into his very soul. But at the same time, it felt as if even when she saw what was there, she felt no loathing. There was a depth of understanding in those ancient eyes.

"It is said that everyone has one secret. This is not true," she said quietly. "Everyone has many secrets, many faces, many masks. All humans, and dwarves and elves, are the sum of their masks, young Herzer. You are young, yet, and your masks have many rough edges. And you do not see that this is the case of everyone. It is what you *do* in life, not what torments you in your soul, that matters. And who you are in life, not who you fear you might become."

"And what if you have done something wrong?" Herzer asked, looking down.

"Did you cause others harm?" she asked, gently.

"No. But through my inaction, harm occurred," he said, carefully.

She sighed and shook her head. "Herzer, I'm your lover, not your priest. I'm not here to take your confession and I'm the wrong sex, the wrong species and the wrong religion to give you absolution!" she chuckled.

"What's a priest?" Herzer asked.

"Oh, my, sometimes I realize just *how* old I am!" she cried, laughing. "My fair knight, unshorn, unvigiled and unshriven. My, how times have changed. Say that priests were an early form of psychological therapy. You could talk to them and nothing that you said, supposedly, could be passed on to others. So you could unburden your soul. Then, under the laws of their religion, they could tell you to do some prayers and chores, maybe pay money, and their God would forgive you."

"Sounds like a racket," Herzer said, interested in spite of himself.

"So was psychotherapy and just like priests they would tell you to come back weekly. But in the case of psychologists, until they started to understand the chemical basis of depression and other psychological problems, they couldn't make people feel as *good* as priests could. Which was, generally, worth the money. Let me ask you this, if, right now, you could tell someone all sorts of things that are bothering you and then they would tell you that you were forgiven if you did some task and you *believed* you were forgiven, absolutely, would you do that task?"

Herzer thought about it for a moment and then nodded his head. "Oh, yes. If it would . . . well, yes. But it couldn't undo what was done."

"No, but it could make *you* feel better about it. That was what the quests were often about to begin with. The concept of 'geas' was a binding requirement to attempt a task and either succeed or die in the attempt. In either case they were forgiven. But if they did not succeed and gave up, when the knight died they would burn in hell."

"Ouch," Herzer said. "That's not the way it is in the games."

"No, but something to understand is that the people of that time, by and large, *believed* in the truth of confession. Just as many in later times *believed* that having someone tell them it wasn't their fault but the fault of bad potty training made things better. And in both cases, because what was going on was entirely in the person's head, most people ended up feeling better."

"So where do I sign up?" Herzer asked, grumpily.

"Oh, Herzer," Bast laughed. "I don't know of a single remaining Catholic priest in eastern Norau. So I think you might be out of luck, there. But I will give you this much to cling to: although there are some actions in life that are unforgivable, I refuse to believe you have done any of them."

"But . . ."

"Hush, my love. Have you killed someone in anger rather than defense?"

"No, but . . ."

"Have you committed rape?" she asked, carefully.

"No," Herzer said, after a long pause.

"Hmm . . . we come close to the boil there I think," she replied. "And I'm not one to lance it. But that 'No' was definite enough for me. I suspect I know what part of your problem is and while I'm no psychologist, what I don't know about kinky sex hasn't been discovered."

"What?" Herzer laughed.

"I'm simply going to have to show you what's what in the area of rough sex," she answered, looking at his eyes. "Let me guess, rape fantasies, right?"

"Uh," Herzer said, blushing furiously. "Bast!"

"Little girls?"

"Bast!!"

"Whips and chains? Little Riding Hood?"

"BAST!!!"

"All totally normal," she replied, suddenly serious. "Many men want to be the Big Bad Wolf. And that is okay. As long as you know how, when and where to do what. And that, me bucko, is what you're about to learn."

"You're joking," he said, looking at the fur blanket and stroking a piece of white ermine nervously.

"Not hardly. I can't *believe* in *this* day and age you're going around all screwed up about dominance fantasies." The elf snorted. "I'll admit that I'm not fetished that way but I know the moves and enjoy it from time to time." Suddenly she smiled shyly and dropped her chin so she was looking up at him out of the side of her eyes, clasping her hands to her chest. "Oh, sir, you're so big and *strong*," she said girlishly, then smiled innocently out of big round eyes. "I'm just a little lost. Do you think you could lead me through the woods?"

Herzer blushed bright red again as his member made it clear that she had hit the bullseye.

Suddenly she took his chin and faced him with total seriousness.

"Look at me, Herzer Herrick. It is not what you *feel* that makes you evil. Those feelings are *natural*. Perhaps, someday, I will explore the *why* to that. But for now, *know* that. They are as natural as *breathing*. It is what you *do* with them that decides if you are a villain or a hero. Let me ask you, and look me in the eye when you answer. If you found such a girl, young, nubile, all alone and lost in the woods, what would you *do*?"

Herzer looked at her for a long moment, a muscle in his chin working, fighting not to drop his eyes.

"I'd lead her back to town," he said, finally, with a slight sigh that might have been regret.

"Aye, and give your life in her defense methinks," Bast answered. "Whatever your past failings."

"I couldn't do anything!" he said.

"Shhhh," Bast replied, laying her fingers against his lips. "And that is the other side. A hurt, once made, cannot be unmade. But they heal, in time. Most anyway. In your case, the hurt, too, will mostly heal. But what will bind the wound and reduce the scar tissue is what you *do*, Herzer Herrick. But you know that, don't you?"

"Yes," he replied, looking at the carpet again.

"Then let us *do*," she replied seriously then smiled. "From the looks of things, I'm going to be busy. You have had a hard journey, are you sure you're *up* to it?" She winked at him and covered her chest modestly, widening her eyes again. "Oh, sir! I was just bathing and I can't find my *clothes!*"

"For you milady," he said looking up with a gleam of tears in his eyes, "who is young as the air even if you are old as the trees, I will *always* be up to it!"

"So I see!" she said with a laugh. "And so gallant! Let's see how long we can make it last this time, fair knight!" She picked up a scrap of towel, placing it over her chest and looking at him with a hint of fear in her eyes. "Please, sir, I'm all alone and you're so *big!*"

"The Belle Dame Sans Merci!" Herzer groaned.

"Oh, you've *heard* of me," she chuckled throatily. And then there was no more talk.

CHAPTER SEVENTEEN

Daneh had stayed in the kitchen puttering with herbs. She knew that some of them had healing properties, but not which and in what proportions. Some of Edmund's books had marginal notes on them, though, so she had gotten the few available and had been grinding sorrel when Sheida appeared.

"Daneh," Sheida said from the doorway.

The mortar and pestle flew across the room, the pestle cracking in two against the hard stone wall, as Daneh practically jumped out of her skin. "Don't *do* that!"

"I'm sorry," the avatar replied. "I didn't think."

"Well sorry doesn't cut it, Sis," Daneh replied, bitterly.

"Well, I am," Sheida said. "If I'd suspected it would . . . come apart so fast I would have . . . done more."

"Thanks for nothing, *Sister*," Daneh snarled. "All you would have had to do was set a damned avatar looking for me. Was that too much to ask?"

The avatar sighed and shook her head. "In retrospect, no. But at the time I was . . . rather busy. And, as I said, I didn't expect lawlessness to break out so fast. Humans are so . . ."

"Sick," Daneh said. "We're beasts inside, Sis, that's something you never realized. Or at least never internalized. I don't know that I did until I met McCanoc."

"Well, I'm getting a lesson in it worldwide," Sheida replied. "There are four thousand three hundred and twenty reported rapes just in the towns that are reporting to me. And in the ones that aren't . . . the conditions in some of them are . . . I

227

don't know some days, Daneh. Sometimes I think we should just give in to Paul, given what the world is like today. Being a woman in this world is . . ."

"What women survived for millennia," Daneh replied. "And don't come crying to me about your problems, I guarantee that you don't wake up nights in a cold sweat seeing McCanoc's face in front of you. Or worse."

Sheida paused for a moment then shrugged. "Daneh, I can . . . how to put it. This can go away for you. No more nightmares."

Daneh thought about it for a moment then shook her head. "Can you do it for all of them?"

"In time, perhaps," Sheida said after a moment. "It doesn't take much more power than simply talking like this."

"No," Daneh said after a moment. "No, that's not the answer. I'm fine, really, except for the nightmares. And they'll go away. They have to," she trailed off.

"You need to talk about it," Sheida said. "I've . . . accessed some *very* old texts. Rape is as forgotten as . . ."

"Everything else," Daneh nodded. "Rape and economic and sexual domination. We were shielded from it for so long. 'Machines freed women and computers empowered them.' But it's all back and in a way it's all of a piece. Take away the technology and women are nothing but pawns to the males. We have to find a way to deal with it *now* and in *this* world. Not patchwork in the old world."

"Then find someone to talk to."

"That's what *everyone* keeps saying, except the women who went through it. And we don't *want* to talk about it, thank you. Especially to *family*, Sis."

"That's . . . what the texts said you'd say. But they also are definite. You need to talk about it, to get out the . . . bad thoughts and find out what is real in you and what is an effect of the rape."

"I don't suppose you can get some of these texts to *me*?" Daneh said sourly.

"Not yet, soon maybe," Sheida said. "Sending an avatar is one thing; teleporting texts or even items that can receive updates is another. We're on the thin edge of losing right now. If we can just get some breathing room, maybe then."

"Well until then, thank you but no thank you. I'll just put up with the nightmares. And 'get back on the horse.'"

"Be careful with that," Sheida said. "You'll probably have some ugly flashbacks. And other things." Sheida paused and shook her head. "You're right. There's things I don't want to talk to you about. Just . . . be careful. Everything that happens may not be . . . natural. Damnit, in that whole camp of historical idiots there *has* to be someone that has studied *rape*! It was a natural feature of all that wonderful history they love so much!"

"The only ones that might have are Edmund and maybe a guy named Gunny," Daneh said. "And I don't care to talk to either of them about it, thank you very much."

"You're being very stubborn about this, Sister dear," Sheida said.

"I'm a Ghorbani," Daneh said with a faint smile.

Sheida started to say something then looked startled. "I have to go. Talk to *someone,* damnit!"

"Good bye, Sheida," Daneh said.

"Bye."

Daneh took a deep breath after Sheida left and thought about the roster of people in Raven's Mill. "Damn, she's right" she muttered then walked to a cupboard and took out a bottle of brandy. She looked at the cups and then shook her head and took a deep pull from the bottle. "I can't believe that I'm going to do this."

She looked at the door and then pulled a cloak down against the evening chill and went walking out the door. She had an idea who to talk to. Now to find her.

McGibbon had just drawn a bead on the lead doe of the herd when he froze at a flash of white out of the corner of his eye. He couldn't figure out what the patch was until it moved again and then he identified it; it was that damned cat of Rachel's.

He'd been stalking the herd of deer for the last half hour. Stalking was a highly skilled art but he'd been practicing for nearly fifty years and it was second nature to him at this point. The first part was finding the quarry, which was a matter of moving through the woods as if he was a deer himself. That required moving a few steps then pausing and actually making a bit of noise. If you tried to move *absolutely* silently it was impossible. So you had to move as if you were a foraging animal. A few steps. A movement of a foot. Watch, listen, smell, then move on.

The most important thing was to sight the deer before they spotted you. If you did that, you could close in on them with relative ease. Foraging white tails couldn't spot movement when

their heads were down. And they flipped their tails before they
raised their head. So you kept an awareness of their movement, an alpha state in which whenever they started to flick
you froze instantly and, at least at his level, almost unconsciously. They would raise their heads, look around and then
go back to eating. Which let you get closer.

He had gotten to within a stone's throw of the deer and
had just drawn his bow when he spotted the cat.

On the other hand, it was doing much the same thing. He
watched it as it froze in its stalk just as the deer lifted their
heads again. There were about fifteen deer in the herd, foraging on fallen acorns at the edge of a natural meadow. He was
on the west edge of the meadow and the cat had apparently
entered on the southeast edge. Now it was doing a careful and
quiet stalk, and despite the fact that the town needed the food
he let the bowstring slip silently forward to watch.

As soon as the deers' heads went back down the cat moved
forward again, its belly to the ground half-hidden in the tall
grass at the meadow's center. It moved cautiously, lifting each
paw and placing it so that Robert suspected it was making
less noise than he would.

Slowly it worked its way to the edge of the tall grass and
appeared to focus on one deer on the edge of the herd. The
button buck was probably from the last year's births and just
about ready to be driven out of the herd. As a sign of its
relative status it had been driven to the edge of the herd where
the acorns were the fewest and it was assiduously searching
for anything edible it could find. This meant it had its head
down far more than the rest of the herd and far more than
was wise. And if the cat wasn't overreaching, the buck might
not live to learn the lesson.

Robert watched the stalk until the cat paused at the edge
of the grass, then drew his bow again. It was the only compound bow in the village and while it was a very strong draw
the nature of the compound bow dropped the "hold weight,"
the amount of pull necessary to keep drawn to its full length,
to barely half its maximum hundred and fifty pounds. But even
seventy-five pounds can be a lot to hold for very long and
he hoped the cat would make its move soon.

It did, as the buck moved just a tad further out, searching for the elusive wind-blown acorns. When the deer got to
within a bare five meters of the cat, the white and orange
tom burst out of the grass in a dead sprint and leapt onto
the deer's back.

Robert hadn't bothered to watch the charge. At the first flicker of movement he had loosed the arrow straight into the "sweet spot" behind the doe's shoulder. However, despite having a broad-head arrow through her heart the doe bounded away with the rest of the herd, intent on leaving the commotion of the attack of the cat behind her.

Robert now watched in bemusement as the cat first shifted its grip to the deer's throat, dragging it around and down by sheer weight. Then, as soon as the buck was on the ground, the cat made a lightning change to a clamp on its muzzle. Deprived of oxygen, the deer thrashed and twisted but to no avail; the house lion had the big buck down and down it was going to stay. With a final kick and thrash, the deer lay still.

"Bravo," McGibbon said, clapping lightly in applause. "Very nice. But you made my doe run off. Now I'm going to have to track her down."

Azure looked up in startlement as if he hadn't noticed the human until then and let out a mew. He stalked over through the grass, his tail high and butted into Robert's hand, getting blood from his muzzle all over the archer's glove.

"You're some cat," the hunter chuckled, rubbing him behind the ears. "I'm more of a dog person, but I could take a shine to you."

When Daneh pushed open the door to the pub she was hit by a blast of sound. A redheaded female minstrel was leading a Celtic band in a rollicking jig. Daneh glanced around the crowd and didn't see who she was looking for so she started to back out when Estrelle appeared at the edge and nodded at her.

"Mistress Talbot, it has been a long time," the homunculus said. She had her usual skimpy tavern-wench outfit on and a tray held up in either hand but she nodded in greeting.

"Hello, Estrelle," Daneh said and asked if she'd seen her quarry.

"Right down by the foot of the stage," Estrelle said. "She comes in here every night to dance."

Daneh wormed her way uneasily around the edge of the crowd and stopped about half way. The heat and the noise and the smell was starting to get to her but having come this far she was damned sure going to keep on going. Finally she got up near the stage and saw her.

Bast had shed her bow and sword and now was a spinning

dervish in front of the stage. There were several people in a line on either side trying to keep up with the jig but even if it had started slow the tempo had sped up to the point that no normal dancer could possibly keep up. Bast, however, was no normal dancer. She was perfectly on beat and adding additional moves including spins, kicks and even the odd backflip, each of them perfectly in time to the music.

The jig had reached the end of the cycle and the red-headed fiddler tried to pick up the tempo again but the band began falling apart; it was simply too fast for most of them to play. Bast, however, stayed right with them until the minstrel finally gave up with a screech of her bow and nodded in defeat to the elf.

People, mostly men, were crowded around the elf but she seemed to be able to fend them off with some sort of karma personal protection field; even the drunkest was giving her her space. She nodded to the band, walked over to pick up her weapons and wormed her way through the crowd to where Daneh was standing.

"Methinks you didn't come down here for a drink," Bast said, looking at her calmly.

"No, I didn't," Daneh replied with a gulp.

"And this is no place to talk," Bast said. "I suggest Edmund's house."

"Okay," Daneh said, following her out. As with the dancers around the stage, when she moved through the crowd it seemed to part as if by magic and Daneh kept close on her heels all the way to the door.

"What I wanted to talk about . . ." Daneh said when they got outside and she could talk without shouting.

"How much liquid courage did you take on board to go find me?" Bast asked.

"I . . . had a drink of brandy."

"Just one?" the elf said, amusement in her voice. "Not nearly enough. Wait until we get to the house. But do not fret on the way. Yes, I know what you need to talk about. And, yes, I know some of what you need to know. And, no, it will not be easy. On either of us. But it will be well. I tell you this as Bast. And Bast is never wrong."

Strangely comforted by that, Daneh followed her back to the house. In silence the elf rummaged in the drink cupboard and pulled out a bottle of wine, then made a fire and settled the two chairs in front of the fire. She pulled out goblets and filled them both to brimming.

"Drink," she said, pointing at the goblet.

Daneh picked it up and took a sip.

"No, *drink*," Bast said, taking her own and tipping it up to drain it.

Daneh swallowed and then lifted the goblet to down it. The wine was not brandy but it was fortified, "winter wine" with a higher than normal alcohol content. The total of the goblet was probably more alcohol than in the shot of brandy she had had before going to the pub. She suddenly remembered that she had skipped dinner.

Bast filled both the cups again, then nodded.

"You were raped by Dionys McCanoc," Bast said. "And others. How many?"

"There were . . . seven others," Daneh said shuddering. "I don't think . . ."

"You *will* talk about it," Bast said. "You *must*. You can talk about it. You relive it every night. Don't just talk to yourself, talk to me. Bast knows. Bast knows the evil that comes in the night, in dreams and without, oh, yes, Bast knows."

"You . . . ?"

"It takes much to rape an elf," Bast said obliquely. "I know the evil in humans and elf. I am *old*, Daneh. I have seen the evils of the AI wars. I *know*. Eight of them, then. They held you?"

Daneh took a deep breath and started talking. Haltingly at first but as Bast drew her out with careful questions it all spilled out and as it did she relived it, every awful moment, as if it was happening all over again. By the time she was crying she realized that she'd drunk most of the bottle of wine and wondered how that had happened.

"So, and . . ." Bast said when she was finished. "There is more to it, though. What did Herzer have to do with it?"

Daneh hesitated and looked at the elf, her head cocked on the side. "You and Herzer are . . ."

"Friends," Bast said with a smile. "He, too, bears scars. I have not invested the time in him that I have in you, but I have invested enough. I want to know what his scars are, from you."

"He was with Dionys when they caught me," Daneh said. "There were too many of them and Dionys was armed with a sword. There was no way he could keep me from being raped. So . . . he ran. He tried to knock them off me on the way, at least I think he did. But he didn't succeed. And then he came back . . . after."

"Thus and so . . ." Bast sighed. "What fun we are all having. Have you tried to get back on the horse?"

"No," Daneh said in a small voice.

"Not long enough, methinks," Bast replied with a nod. "Tell me about the dreams."

"I . . . that's . . . hard."

"Harder than the rape itself, methinks," Bast said with an unhappy grin. "Let me tell you a few things, then. You relive the rape, yes?"

"Yes," Daneh said, tightly.

"And sometimes the reason you wake up in terror is that you orgasm."

"Bast!"

"True?" the elf said hardly. "True."

Daneh lowered her face into her hands and nodded. "Yes."

"Normal," Bast said, definitely. "You think that you are evil or sick or twisted beyond repair, yes? But this is *normal*. For humans anyway."

"That's sick," Daneh said, crying.

"Hey, one of the reasons we elves know you humans are the result of evolution is how screwed up you are mentally; a well designed species isn't so flighty."

"So elves don't have these problems with rape?" Daneh asked, interested in spite of herself.

"Very hard to rape an elf," Bast repeated. "Harder to survive. Few things that can break an elf out of Dream, few things that can make them hate. Elves are too happy to hate. But when we hate, we hate well. Elf that is raped dreams, oh, yes. But they dream of new and more awful things to do to their rapist. Dream their death over and over again. Elves hate *very* well. One of the things we're designed to do is hate. But, mostly, we're too happy. Be glad. Elves not so happy, humans no longer be here. You need to get back on the horse, but not yet. And know something, when you do, it won't be good. No matter *how* loving Edmund is, you're going to be back there again. Worse, you might enjoy it. There is such a thing as bad sex and that's it."

"Yes," Daneh said.

"But it will get better," Bast said with a shrug. "Each time it will be a little easier. Other problem. How do you feel about men, now?"

"I'm . . . not sure," Daneh said. "Some of them . . . I'm okay with. Others . . . make me want to scream."

"Don't get to hating them all," Bast said. "It is an easy trap, to run away from them and wish they were all dead. Even elves don't hate that way. Each man is different. The ones that make you want to scream . . . you're probably feeling something from them. Trust that instinct. But don't hate them all. That, too, is damage you have to work on. Last Big question: Were you a submissive *before* you were raped?"

Daneh opened her mouth to voice her favorite protest then clapped it shut; it was a valid question. "Not . . . openly."

"Did you play the games?"

"No," she admitted. "I never could . . . I couldn't bring it up."

"Not even with Edmund?" Bast said, surprised. "He's not fetished that way, but he plays the game very well."

"Not even with Edmund," Daneh admitted.

"Humph. Bet he knew. Fantasies?"

"Yes," she said quietly.

"Rape?"

Daneh paused then sighed. "Yes."

"Okay, Doctor Bast recommend not play that game for a while."

Daneh couldn't help it, she started giggling which turned into a full-bore laugh which somehow segued back into tears until she was sobbing so hard she couldn't catch her breath. She realized she was in Bast's lap and being held by strong arms.

"Cry little human, cry," Bast whispered. "Cry until you're cried out. Tears are the only thing that shows that humans might have had a Creator. Too weak, too fragile, scared of the whole world. But if there was a Creator She gave them tears to face it and go on."

Daneh finally caught her breath and looked at the elf holding her. "Thank you," she said and then, for some reason, kissed her full on the lips.

"You're welcome," Bast said after the kiss was over. "But not tonight, I've got a headache."

Daneh broke out in giggles again and shook her head. "Me, too. All that wine I think."

"Yes, and I think it's time for you to go to bed," Bast said, lifting the larger woman effortlessly off her lap. "Alone."

"Alone," Daneh agreed and was surprised and worried that she wasn't sure she *wanted* to be alone. She'd never had a sexual thought about another woman before. "Bast, I don't want you to think that . . ." she paused.

"Is okay, I'd put it down to another effect of the rape," Bast said, supporting her to bed. She got her undressed and tucked

in and then kissed her on the forehead. "Lots of things messed
up in you from it. But you'll get better. Trust Bast. Sleep. Deep
sleep no dreams."

"No dreams," Daneh said muzzily, wondering why she was
so tired.

"Sleep little human," Bast said, placing her hand on her
forehead. "Sleep well."

As Daneh faded into sleep the last thing she remembered
was Bast curling up on the floor as if she intended to stay
for a while. And if her sleep was troubled by dreams, they
fled at the sight of a sword-wielding being in white.

Sheida nodded tiredly at the avatar of Ishtar and then sighed
at her face.

"What is it now?" she asked, unwrapping her jewel-covered
lizard from her neck and cradling it in her arms.

"I have determined the source of the power that Paul's
faction is drawing upon," Ishtar said without preamble. "It
is a power draw from core storage."

"But . . ." Sheida paused. "But the only ones who can do
a core draw are the elves. That is how the Lady is closing
Elfheim."

"That is not the only source for core draws," Ishtar said
bitterly. "They are using power from the terraforming
projects."

"Oh," Sheida said after a moment's thought. "How . . . truly
good."

"What I have been unable to determine is why they can
draw upon it," Ishtar went on. "They have to have a quorum of the board of directors of one or more of the projects
agreeing to release the power. And . . . I can't imagine that
happening."

"I can," Sheida said after long thought. "But, oh, but that
is a deep laid plan . . ." she muttered.

"What plan?" Ishtar asked, her brows furrowing.

"Edmund, he told me to look to the Demon at the center
of this," Sheida said with a grimace. "And I think he must
be right. I was . . . asked to look into some things before
this . . . war erupted. There had been some disturbing things
going on with the Wolf 359 terraforming project. One of the
people who had risen to prominence was . . . well known to
me. Not a good person and not the sort of person to . . ."

"Care about something that wasn't going to do him any
good?" Ishtar asked.

"Something like that. But it didn't come together. Now it does. And we are truly in trouble."

"But the rest of the board members?" Ishtar asked. "They have to be present to vote!"

"In the event of large scale disruption there is probably a protocol for rump voting," Sheida said, dropping into the Net to open up the data. "Yes, there is," she said, distantly. "And while we cannot access the board members' location or status, Mother assuredly could. If they had assassins waiting for the majority of the board . . ."

"Then their hand-picked members would be the only ones left," Ishtar hissed. "Evil."

"Yes, and much too Byzantine for Paul," Sheida added, rising back up out of the data-flow. "This has the Demon's fingerprints all over it."

"What do we do about it?" Ishtar asked.

"Find the members of the board," Sheida said. "And either get them to vote to store the power or at least stop them from giving it to Paul."

"And how do we do that?" Ishtar asked, throwing her hands in the air. "We don't know where *anyone* is!"

"We'll send out a list to all the communities that report to us," Sheida replied, pulling up the list. "These are all the members who were alive before the Fall," she added, looking over the list. "Know any of them?"

"No," Ishtar said, then looked at her fellow council member's face. Sheida stopped looking at the list with a frozen and angry expression on her face. "What?"

"I do," Sheida hissed.

CHAPTER EIGHTEEN

"We must stop this war," Paul said, looking up from the report. "We *must* stop it. Now."

Paul had called a full meeting of the New Destiny Council to "discuss some ramifications of the current conflict." Celine had known it would be contentious when she arrived and Paul was striding up and down the Council Chamber, literally tearing at his hair. She had always thought that was just an expression.

"Why?" Chansa exclaimed, looking across the room at the Demon. The black armor didn't move or twitch in any way at the strange statement.

"The deaths!" Paul yelled, pointing at the projections. "We've finally gotten a census in the portions of Ropasa that we control and thousands, *millions* are dying or already dead! This was not supposed to be a *war*. The point is to *prevent* the extinction of the human race, not *cause* it!"

"What about horror?" Celine asked. "We were going to *win*! I've got plans!"

"The plan has *failed*," Paul snapped. "Forcing them to quit was a good plan, but not in the face of the death of the human *race!*"

"Actually, Bowman, it has succeeded beyond your wildest dreams," the Demon rumbled.

"What?" Paul said, cocking his head suspiciously. "Explain yourself."

"I can, Paul," Celine said, waving the projections away and

bringing up new ones. "I prepared the reports. Current population of the earth is just above one billion. Control of the Net has fractured, power has failed, different members of the Council have seized, for the most part, certain historical areas. Chansa in Frika, Sheida in Norau, yourself in Ropasa, etc."

"Your *point*," the council leader ground out.

"My point is that deaths are going to be high in the first two months. Very high. But in each of these areas, council members are acting, as they see fit, to ensure the survival of as many as possible."

"We're still talking about *millions* of deaths!" Paul snapped.

"But we're talking about far more population increase," Celine continued as if he hadn't interrupted. "Indeed, we're talking about a near doubling of the population in two to three generations."

"What?" Paul paused. "How?"

"Frankly, your initial plan probably would not have worked," Celine said. "As long as there were artificial means of replication and reproduction management, birth levels would remain low no matter what you did to encourage it. However, with all of that taken away, birth rates are bound to skyrocket."

"What in the hell are you talking about?" Paul ground out.

"The nannites have turned off," Celine replied with a smirk. "That means other things have turned on."

Rachel was more or less moping around the house when Daneh found her.

"Come on, girl, time to start your education," Daneh said, snatching up a satchel.

"What do you mean?" Her mother was acting different this morning. Rachel couldn't put her finger on it but something of the despair had seemed to leave her. Whatever the reason, she was glad.

"You said you wanted to be a doctor," Daneh replied, heading for the door. "Bethan Raeburn has started to bleed internally. That's all I know. Come on."

Tom Raeburn was outside the house with two saddled horses, looking very worried.

"What can you tell me?" Daneh said as she mounted with a wince.

"Not much. Mom just started bleeding all of a sudden. From her . . . well from her bottom."

"From her anus?" Daneh asked. "There's various reasons that that might occur, none of them life threatening." They were already starting to canter down the hill, not following the main road but cutting across the open area around the side of the town.

"Not from her . . . anus," Tom said. "The . . . the *other* part. I'm sorry if I'm being unclear, but this is my *mother*, okay?"

"Okay," Daneh answered. She wracked her brain for what might be wrong and there was something nagging at her. But for the life of her, the only thing that came to mind was some sort of internal injury. "Did she fall? Was she hit?"

"Not that I'm aware of," Tom said.

Daneh held her peace until they reached the sprawling farmyard, then hurried inside with Rachel at her heels.

They went upstairs to where Myron was standing outside the bedroom door, wringing his hands.

"Thank God you're here, Daneh," Myron said. "I . . . she's . . . I just can't take it. Please help her!"

"I'll see what I can do, Myron," Daneh answered, secretly fearful that there wouldn't be much she *could* do. Without nannites she was virtually helpless. She might know the inner workings of the human body, but *fixing* that body took tools she no longer possessed.

Inside the room she found Bethan in bed, apparently naked, curled up in a miserable ball on her side, the sheet on the bed pulled up on her hips.

"How are you, Beth?" she asked, pulling the sheet down. There was a wad of rags stuffed into the woman's crotch and it was spotted with red. There was more that had trickled down the woman's leg onto the bed. All in all it looked as if she had bled about a deciliter.

"Daneh," Bethan said helplessly. "I don't know what's *wrong*."

"Be calm," Daneh answered, taking her hand and wrist. She remembered the simple method of taking a pulse but she didn't have a way to time it. The woman's pulse felt fine, though, strong and a bit fast, but that could be put down to understandable fear. "Other than the bleeding, what are the symptoms?" she asked, feeling the woman's neck and face. No signs of fever and while she was a bit pale she didn't seem to be in shock.

"Nothing," Bethan answered. "I've been a little . . . grouchy lately and then I started to hurt in the stomach yesterday. Then today I just started bleeding!"

"No impacts?" Daneh asked. "I'm sorry to ask this, but nobody *hit* you, did they?"

"No!" Bethan practically snarled. "I'm sorry, I'm sorry. Like I said, I've been grouchy. *I* would have hit *them*, not the other way around!"

"There doesn't seem to be a *reason*," Daneh said in exasperation. "I can't *sew it up*. And I can't get into the interior to see what's bleeding!" She knew better than to show her discomfort in front of a patient, but this was the first time she'd had to deal with something like this. "No tools, no diagnostics. Aggh! I need to think." She looked at the woman and took her pulse again. Still strong. "Bethan, whatever is happening, you're not showing any other signs. You don't appear to be . . . damaged from the bleeding. Just let me think."

She stood back and paced as she ran through the anatomy of the female reproductive system. Something had clearly gone badly wrong. Cervix, uterus, fallopian tubes, ovaries . . . Something was haywire. She hadn't paid much attention to the system since medical school, it was just there, as useless as the vermiform appendix that most people no longer had. With uterine replicators reproduction had all been moved *out* of the female body thank God and . . . *Oh, My, God!*

She stopped with her face in her hand, blinded by her own stupidity. But she wasn't the only one who had missed the obvious.

"Bethan, do your cows reproduce naturally or do you have them raised in a replicator?" she asked.

"They reproduce naturally. We try to . . . Oh!"

"And do they ever bleed? The females?"

"Yes, after they've ovulated," Bethan said with horror in her voice.

"And that's once every?"

"Six months or so. But humans . . ."

"Humans ovulate every *month*!" Daneh wailed. "The *curse!* Damnit, I *knew* this was familiar!"

"This is *natural?*" Bethan asked. "This is *supposed* to happen?"

"Once a month," Daneh said, the memory finally dropping into place. "Every twenty-eight days.

"*For how long?*'

"I don't know . . . a week?"

"Oh, My, God!"

"Mom, what about me?" Rachel asked, frantically.

"You, me, all of us," Daneh responded.

"When is it going to start?"

"Soon. Bethan was the first. Probably there will be more

by the end of the day. The nannite fields had ovulation turned off and the natural hormones that were generated by the cycle were replaced and released in a steady stream. Now we're going to be *slaves* to that damned curse again!"

"That *sucks*," Rachel said. "I'm not going to!"

"You don't have a choice," Daneh replied, thinking furiously. "They used to have ways to . . . catch the flow. Terms, old terms. On the rag. Riding the cotton pony."

"Where have I heard that before?" Bethan asked.

"You find it in the literature of the day," Rachel replied with a frown. "King, Moore, Hiaasen . . ."

"Ah, the masters," Bethan smiled wanly.

"I don't know what they used, but we'd better think of something," Daneh said with a frown. "And soon. Or this whole town is going to be one hell of a mess."

"So I'm not dying," Bethan said.

"No, you're going through a perfectly normal monthly cycle that has been survived by countless women throughout the ages," Daneh replied astringently. "And there's so much good news attached to it, too."

"Oh?" Bethan asked warily.

"Yes, it means you're now as fertile as one of your cows. How many more children do you plan on having?"

The three days of rest were cut short for the starting of the familiarization classes and on the second day after arriving at Raven's Mill Herzer found himself in a mixed group of males and females clearing land along the Shenan River on the far side from Raven's Mill.

The work was backbreaking. The majority of the trees in the area were "secondary old growth." That meant that while the area had once been cleared, had, in fact, been the fringe of the massive megalopolis that had once stretched down the entire coast, the buildings and other structures had been gone long enough for multiple generations of forest to have grown on the spot.

Herzer didn't know the names of the trees and didn't particularly care. They were just horrible growing things to be attacked with axe and saw. He supposed that given his friendship with Bast he should be more understanding. She had, after all, seen the trees grow from seeds or acorns or whatever and loved them like children. But it was hard to be kindly thinking towards the trees when your hands ran with blood from the blisters.

He had taken turns in a rota using the two crosscut saws they had available and that was bad enough. The motion used muscles he didn't even know he had and by the first hour he was in agony from it. It took a particular stance and motion to get the most out of the saws and he suspected that for long-term users it was relatively easy. Relatively. Drawing a saw back and forth for hour upon hour could never be characterized as "easy." But surely easier than it was to learn. And then there was the question of "coasting." It was nearly impossible to determine if the person on the other side of the saw was working as hard as you were and it was tempting, especially on some of the more recalcitrant trees, to suspect that the person was not, in fact, giving their all.

Herzer had noticed by the morning of the first day that not everyone worked equally. There were ten males and five females, most of them younger like Mike and he. Herzer, Mike and a few others, males and females, threw themselves into all the tasks with as much energy and enthusiasm as they could summon. In Mike's case he seemed to have a real drive to learn the details of each of the jobs while in Herzer's case he had an obstinate refusal to do less than his best.

Most of the rest, though, were just there to pick up a meal chit. There had been some muttering the first day, especially after they found out how hard they were going to have to work, about "slave labor," but the incipient rebellion had been quelled quickly by the supervisor of the clearing effort, a reenactor named Jody Dorsett.

He had stood with his hands on his hips in front of a group of the "apprentices" who had simply dropped the axes they had been wielding. He looked at them with cold blue eyes.

"You can pick them up and start working or you can drop out. It doesn't matter to me. And if I think you're not working as hard as you should, I can dock your rations. So don't think you can just pick the axe up every few seconds and give the tree a love tap. I've seen it all me buckoes and if I see any more of it out of you you'll damned well be *thrown* out of the program."

So the malingerers got back to work, grudgingly, as Herzer and a few others threw themselves into their assigned tasks.

For Herzer and Mike it had started with the crosscut saw. The objective was to drop the trees in a certain direction so they could be extracted more easily, but the trees didn't always want to go that way. Indeed, it seemed they were bound and determined not to.

Herzer, working with another man whose name he never did quite catch, had started on a smaller tree, but a tough one. Only about two thirds of a meter across where they were cutting, it had nonetheless taken nearly an hour to cut through. They had first cut an angled slit down one side then driven wooden "wedges" into the slit. With that done they notched out the far side with an axe then started the crosscut. The blade had bound a time or two, requiring that wedges on the "pushing" side be loosened and wedges be driven in around the blade. But finally, after it felt they would never get the damned thing to fall it did, right at Herzer.

At first it seemed to be going well but then the cut at the base split and the tree turned, partially pressured by the winds that had sprung up, and aimed itself in Herzer's direction.

Only a quick yell from the supervisor, who had been keeping a wary eye out for the junior team, had prevented the boy from being crushed. As it was, he barely made it out of the way of the trunk and was actually struck a glancing blow by one of the smaller, lower branches.

Jody's only comment was a snarl for getting the blade bound under the trunk and nearly breaking it. As soon as it was loose he set Herzer and a new partner to cut a *larger* tree with a trunk nearly two meters across, wide spreading branches and gnarls all over its trunk. Herzer groaned in fatigue but set to it without further comment.

And the blisters started almost immediately. Unlike most of the rest he had some calluses, but they were from sword and bow, utterly unlike the calluses from a saw or axe. So in no time at all his hands had become swollen with blisters which just as quickly popped under the unremitting punishment.

This time Herzer was teamed with a guy named Earnon Brooke. He had been one of the brief mutineers and true to form, Herzer was *sure* that he wasn't doing much more than leaning on the end of the saw. Herzer had to practically push it through on each cut, instead of simply moving with it and maybe putting some pressure against the trunk. And when he did his pull there was more resistance than he thought there should be; it almost felt like the guy was leaning back on it and letting Herzer pull him through.

Herzer put up with it for about ten minutes, which had barely gotten them started on the wedge cut and then he'd had enough. He dropped his end of the saw at the end of his pull and walked over to the other man.

Earnon was tall and good looking but he had the shiftiest

eyes Herzer had ever seen. He was, however, at least a good decade older than the boy and Herzer tried not to let that intimidate him.

"Look, you're not pulling your share of the weight," Herzer said calmly. "We're never going to get this tree cut if you don't work at it."

"I *am* working at it," Earnon said stepping forward and snarling at the boy. "If anybody's not pulling his own weight, it's you, boy. Don't you be blaming me if you're afraid the thing's gonna fall on you again. It wasn't *my* screw-up that time; it was *yours*."

"What the hell are you talking about?" Herzer said, backing up. "I'm not slacking off, *you* are!"

"The hell I am!" Earnon shouted and pushed Herzer, hard, on the chest so that he stumbled back further.

"Whoa," Jody said, walking up behind Herzer and grabbing his arms as the boy crouched to spring. "No! No fighting! Herzer, Earnon, you're both docked for the afternoon meal!"

"What?" Herzer said, struggling in his arms. "I was just trying to get him to do some *work*!"

"This boy's been doing nothing but hanging on the end of the saw," Earnon said righteously, crossing his arms. "Then he came over and accused me of not working. I'm not going to take that. And you can't dock me for defending my rights!"

"I can dock you for *looking* at me wrong, Brooke," Jody said dangerously. "And if I was to guess who was the trouble-maker here, it wouldn't be Herzer. But you're *both* getting docked for fighting. Now you can either get out or get back to work. I don't really care which."

"Are you going to be able to keep it together?" Jody asked Herzer, releasing him.

"Yeah," the boy said, shaking his head and picking at torn skin from a blister. It was only halfway through the morning and he was already starved. Missing lunch was going to *hurt*. "But I didn't start this."

"If you have a problem, you come to me," Jody said. "You don't start a fight."

"I was just trying . . ."

"You don't start a fight," Jody said dangerously. "You come to me."

"Okay, I'm coming to you," Herzer said, quietly, turning towards the boss. "I don't care what you set me on, but I'm not going to try to cut down this big-ass tree with this useless asshole."

"The hell with you, punk," Earnon said, charging forward.

"Hold it!" Jody said, stepping between the two. "Watch your tongue, Herzer. Okay, if you two can't work together, that's fine." He looked around and shook his head at the total lack of work out of the rest of the group. "What does this look like, street theater?" he shouted. "Are you guys a bunch of minstrels to sit around on your butts? Get back to work!" Then he waved at one of the men. "Tempie, get over here."

He waited until the other young man came over then waved at Herzer. "Go clear limbs if you can't work in a pair."

"I *can* work in a pair . . ." Herzer said hotly.

"Go," Jody said, waving at the axe that Tempie had dropped.

Herzer stalked over to the axe without another word and started chopping at the limb that Tempie had left.

The axe was broad bladed with a rounded head wrapped around a circular haft. It was designed more like a battle-axe than a standard wood cutting axe but it was sharp enough and each of Herzer's furious blows took out a huge chunk of wood. The tree he was working on was large like the others. Instead of the branches spreading out they were fairly short and tight together. Nonetheless they were rather thick at the base and took some cutting. Which was fortunate for Herzer because it gave him a chance to work out his rage at the injustice of the previous incident. Unable to let go of his anger he rang blow after blow on the branch until it broke free, then started immediately on another. As he worked the rhythm of the blows, and the physical exhaustion that working at the pace induced, tended to relieve the anger and he slowly started to gain equilibrium and think about the incident instead of just running around in a fugue of anger at the injustice.

"You need to slow down or you'll kill yourself," Courtney said, coming up behind him.

As she said it the axe bounced sideways barely missing his leg and he swung it back into line carefully then set it down, panting.

"You've got a point," Herzer said, turning around.

Some of the females had started to help with the cutting but the greater muscle mass of the males quickly proved that they could do it faster and longer. In general they had taken over the "lighter" jobs like dragging aside cut limbs, replacing broken equipment and watering the workers. On the other hand, two of the women were still at it, as if to prove that they were as good as, or better than, any of the males. One of them was Deann Allen, who just attacked *everything* like

Herzer had been attacking the tree, and the other was Karlyn Karakas, who must have had some major body mods; she was over two meters tall and built like a *male* body-builder. Deann, on the other hand, was much smaller but if anything more aggressive about the work; she seemed to have a chip on her shoulder about a mile wide. So since she was clearing limbs just as well as any of the males, Jody hadn't even suggested that she leave off.

The other three women, Courtney, Nergui Slovag and Hsu Shilan had taken up the lighter tasks. They were pulling the lighter branches aside as they were cut and piling them up, bringing tools, driving wedges and carrying water.

Which was why Courtney thrust a pottery cup at him, half filled with water.

He shook his head and downed the water then stared at the cup. It was poorly made and the impression of a finger was still visible, cast into the interior by the firing. It was already cracked at the top and slightly porous so his hand holding it was dampened by the water seeping through.

It was at that moment that things really caught up with him and he thought he would break down, right there, and cry. He was really here, *having* to work or starve. And he was never, ever going back. He suddenly, desperately, wanted to see his small cabin in the woods. It had never been much more than a place for him to sleep and keep a few things he treasured. But he wanted to lie in his bed and have the genie bring him a glass of beer and a great big steak. He wanted this to all be a strange dream and just be *over*.

"You look like somebody killed your dog," Courtney said. "Is the water that bad?"

"No," Herzer said, trying not to sob. "No. It's just . . . I just suddenly realized, this is *it*. This is what I'm going to be doing for the rest of my life!"

"Well, hopefully not *this*," Courtney said cheerfully, then nodded soberly. "But . . . yeah."

"I just . . ." Herzer stopped and shook his head. "Never mind. Thanks for the water."

"LUNCH BREAK!" Jody yelled, banging two pieces of metal together. He waved at Herzer. "You can take a break until it's over."

"Why?" Herzer said with a shrug, picking the axe back up. "I'll keep working."

Jody looked at him with an inscrutable expression for a

moment, then nodded, and headed over to the pots that had been smoking over a fire.

"It's not fair," Courtney said hotly. "You didn't start that."

"I know," Herzer said, spitting on his hands and wincing when the spittle hit his now bleeding blisters. "But I think I kind of understand it."

"What, telling you you can't *eat*? Because you complained about that useless jackass?" Mike asked, walking up.

"Because of how it ended up *going*," Herzer replied, taking his first hit at the next branch. "None of us have ever had to *work* for a living. We're having to learn how. How to work in groups, too. Jody's got a tough job and the only way he can do it is to be a hard-ass."

"Well he pissed a lot of people off today," Courtney said hotly, looking over at where the foreman was being harangued by Earnon. It was clear that the man couldn't believe he wasn't going to be permitted to eat.

"I know, Earnon's already got friends," Herzer nodded.

"Oh, not *that*," Courtney said. "I suppose a few of them don't like it because of him. But most of us are pissed off that *you* got caught up in it. Earnon's the problem, not you."

"Oh," Herzer said. "Uh. Thanks."

"We need to go eat," Mike said, taking Courtney by the arm. "Herzer, we can hold a little by . . ."

"If Jody finds out, he's likely to dock you two, too," Herzer said, shaking his head. "You go eat."

CHAPTER NINETEEN

By the middle of the afternoon Herzer was swaying from fatigue and hunger. He was still clearing branches and doing it at a pretty good pace, but he didn't know how much longer he could go on. His arms felt like lead and he was light-headed. Every now and again he started to sway and his axe blows no longer hit where he wanted them to.

He didn't even notice Jody when he came up behind him and started when the man cleared his throat, the axe glancing off the branch and flying out of his hands.

"I thought so," Jody said. "Mike told me you didn't get the full three days rest."

"Courtney or Mike?" Herzer asked, blinking his eyes as it seemed the edges of his vision were going gray.

"Mike, but I suspect Courtney put him up to it," Jody said. "Do you realize you've cleared about twice as many branches as anyone else?"

"No, I wasn't paying attention," Herzer said with the honesty of the punch drunk.

"You need to take a break and get some water. The ones that are working hard are just about worn out and the ones that are slacking are getting better and better at acting that way, so I'm moving dinner up and we'll break before sunset. But we're starting tomorrow at dawn."

"Okay," Herzer said, stepping back and sitting down on a cleared log. "Works for me."

"Take a break, Herzer, that's an order," Jody said, waving at one of the water carriers.

"Here," Nergui said, shoving a cup at him and slopping half of it on the ground.

"Thank you," Herzer said tiredly and drained it. "Now could I have some more."

"Only one," the girl said angrily. "It's a long walk to the spring. You need to slow down, you're making the rest of them look bad."

"Not all of them," Herzer said, draining the second half filled cup. "Just some."

"Hmmph," the girl snorted, snatching the cup back and walking away with a flounce.

"Well, are you happy you son-of-a-bitch?" Mike said, sitting down next to him.

"Not you too!" Herzer said.

"I'm joking," Mike replied, stone faced. "Really. But I wouldn't have worked as hard as I did if it hadn't been trying to keep up with you. You made out of damned *iron* or something?"

"Not right now," Herzer said. "I feel like rubber. What's with Nergui, anyway?"

"She and Earnon hit it off right away," Mike said. "You didn't notice?"

"Nope."

"Two peas in a pod. Anyway, she's mad cause Earnon didn't get any lunch and she nearly got caught passing him some food. And then you're working like a damned machine and that made him look twice as bad. You know Jody's had to change partners on him *twice* and that tree *still* isn't half sawed through?"

"Hmmm . . ." Herzer replied, really taking a look around for the first time since early morning. Several trees had been downed and mostly cleared and topped, their logs now lying on the muddy ground in preparation for hauling off. The branches, leaves and other detritus had been collected in large piles and he suddenly realized, identifying trees, how much of those piles had been his work.

But the giant spreading tree that had been the source of contention was still standing, the trunk not even half sawed through as Mike had said.

"Well, I guess that proves who was working and who wasn't," Herzer chuckled then guffawed. "And Jody's had him on that tree all day?"

"Yeah, I complained, lightly in the middle of the afternoon. I've been on the other saw all damned day and we've downed three trees. They've not even gone through one."

Herzer looked at the other trees and had to admit that, while the others were smaller, that was much more work than that single tree.

"I think Jody's just trying to make a point," Herzer said. "I'm not sure what the point *is*, but I'm pretty sure there is one."

"Oh, I know what the point is," Mike growled. "Earnon is a useless slacker."

"Have you had other partners?" Herzer asked.

"Yeah, he's run just about everybody by my saw. Some of 'em are okay. Guy and Cruz and Emory pull their own weight, I guess so do Tempie and Glayds but they don't really *work* at it, they just do what they have to do. Frederic, Cleo and Earnon are fisking useless."

Herzer chuckled and gestured with his chin at Karlyn who was lifting a branch the size of a small tree onto her shoulder to drag it off.

"Yeah, Karlyn, too. Mostly. She doesn't have the mass sometimes, I guess. And neither does Deann but she just makes up for it with anger."

The latter was topping one of the trees that had been mostly cleared of branches. Once the trunk narrowed to a certain point it wasn't worth clearing the rest and the top was cut off, "topping", and dragged into the brush pile. Deann had one of the battle-axe type axes and was attacking the tree as if it were the neck of a hostile dragon, an expression of absolute fury on her face.

"Trees! She hates trees!" Herzer whispered with a chuckle.

"Well, if you think *that's* bad, you should have seen you when you started out," Courtney said, coming over and sitting down by Mike. "I was afraid you were going to take that axe to Jody's neck!"

"Not Jody," Herzer said. "But if Earnon had come over to continue the discussion, I'm not making any bets."

"I was thinking about what you said earlier," Courtney said. "And you're right. But there's more."

"Oh?"

"It's what you just said. There's no PPFs. If you took it in your head to go kill Earnon with that axe, there wouldn't have been much anyone could do about it."

"So Jody comes down with both feet on fighting," Mike added. "I started to tell off Frederic when he was on the saw and then I just walked over and talked to Jody. Frederic tried to interrupt but Jody just shut him up and put him to topping. I didn't cuss him out or anything, just told Jody he was riding the saw and I wanted him off."

"I guess that's what I should have done," Herzer said with a shake of his head.

"Well, if I hadn't seen the example, I would have done what you did," Mike admitted. "And I probably would have cracked that useless fisker's head on top of it. So I'm not exactly *glad* you screwed up first but . . ." he grinned and picked up a twig to chew on, using it to pick at his teeth.

"FOOD'S ON!"

Herzer joined the others in line for food and took his bowl of beans and cornbread. That was it again and after getting it he sat down on one of the logs and contemplated the food for just a moment.

"You going to eat it or just look at it?" Mike asked, spooning up his beans between bites of bread.

"I get such pleasure from the anticipation," Herzer said lightly. "But soon it will be all gone!" He picked up his spoon then set it back down and lifted the bowl to his lips, sucking down the mixture. There was a small, very small, piece of pork in the bowl and he worried that for a few moments then wiped out the bowl with his cornbread. When that was gone he was done.

He contemplated licking the bowl out but finally convinced himself not to. Instead he carried it over to the stack of dirty dishes and got a large dipper of water from a barrel.

"Herzer, here," Jody said, coming up behind him with a large bowl of cornmeal mush. Herzer could see some bits of mystery meat embedded in it.

"Hey!" Earnon shouted. "I didn't get any lunch, neither! Why the hell does *he* get extra?!"

"Because he didn't sit on his ass all afternoon," Jody answered to a chorus of chuckles. "If you don't have something to eat, you'll be useless in the morning. And you deserve it."

"Thank you," Herzer said, taking the bowl carefully. After a moment he shrugged and sucked it down just as fast as the beans.

Jody chuckled and set the bowl on the pile with the rest. "Don't worry about it; the cooks will clean up."

"Okay, folks, here's the deal," Jody said, striding over to where most of the cutting crew was finishing eating. "You can walk back to Raven's Mill or you can stay over on this side of the river. If you stay here, I'll show you some ways to make a shelter. Either way, breakfast is before dawn tomorrow. So if you stay over there you'd better get somebody to wake you up and walk back or you'll miss it."

"What's for breakfast?" Earnon asked. "And why can't we just eat over there?"

"Because you don't get chits for meals, yet," Jody said. "We're feeding you for your work. And this is *where* we're feeding you. Any other questions?"

"How do I get out of this chicken-shit outfit?" Cleo Ronson asked with a bitter laugh.

"Any time you want you can walk away," Jody said. "And if I hear enough complaints you *will* be out of this outfit. Any *more* questions?"

"Same thing on the agenda tomorrow?" Mike asked.

"Pretty much," Jody said. "We need to clear a large area by a couple of weeks from now. We're going to work on cutting for three more days, then clear the logs and burn the trash. After that we'll work on making some rough buildings. Then you'll be done with this portion and I'll get another crew." He looked around and nodded. "Okay, grab the tools and stack them and we'll start making some shelters from all this trash."

Herzer grabbed his axe and carefully stacked it, feeling a massive and unexpected wave of fatigue flow over him. Before he knew it, it was all he could do to stay on his feet. He listened while Jody explained how to make a lean-to. But in the end, between his swollen and puffy hands and his overwhelming fatigue, he couldn't find the energy for the effort. Taking one of the blankets that had been provided he went over to the giant tree that had missed felling and collapsed onto one of the large roots, resting his head partially on it and partially on the dirt. Before he could even squiggle around to get comfortable he was asleep.

"You need some sleep," Edmund said as he entered the wooden hut that had been set up as a temporary hospital until there was time to build a real one. Daneh was at a bucket of steaming water, washing her hands as Rachel and another woman scrubbed at blood-covered tools.

"Don't start," she said tiredly. "I've had to do two amputations today, one major and one minor, while trying to get the heads of all the women in the camp around the fact that they're about to start bleeding."

"We need to talk about that," Edmund said. "You've requisitioned just about every scrap of cloth in the town for this and *all* the unspun cosilk. We have *other* needs, Daneh."

"I know, but this one is a *right now* need, Edmund," she snapped. "I'm running out of bandages. And the women are either going to have the material or they're going to run around bleeding all over the place. Which would you prefer?"

"Do you need so *much* is what I'm asking, as pleasantly as possible," Talbot replied, taking a deep breath. "We need the cloth in making tools. We need it to repair clothes; most of the people's clothes are getting to be in tatters."

"If we don't need it all, we'll turn it back in," she replied. "We won't be throwing any of it away; the women are being told to wash the material and reuse it. We'll only use as much as is needed. And this is for the benefit of the whole camp, Edmund."

"All right, Daneh," he said with a sigh. "You said that you've talked to the women in the town, what about out in the camps?"

"I hadn't even given it a thought," she said tiredly, looking out the open window to the darkness. "It's too late now . . ."

"And you're needed here," Edmund continued. "Rachel. You're doing it. Tomorrow. Go to each of the camps and all of the groups that are going through familiarization. If anyone gives you any trouble tell them to come see me. Talk to all the women, tell them what's going to happen and that we're getting materials ready."

"Yes, sir!" she said sarcastically.

"You're still young enough for me to turn over my knee, young lady," Edmund said with a smile. "Watch that tone."

"Oh, I wouldn't want *Daddy* mad at me," Rachel said, again snippily. "You realize *I'm* going to start any time, don't you?"

"Yes, I had thought about that," Talbot replied with another smile. "Take the appropriate precautions."

"Appropriate precautions," Daneh said with another sigh. "You realize that includes avoiding pregnancy?"

"Or terminating it after it starts," Talbot answered with a nod. "Sheep guts for the first and tansy for the second."

"You're serious," Daneh said with a shake of her head. "What do *sheep* guts have to do with preventing pregnancy?"

"Well, see, you rub them all over your body . . ." Edmund started and then laughed at her expression.

"Edmund . . ."

"Okay, seriously, you use the outer, hard, layer of sheep intestines as a prophylactic condom."

"A *what*?" Rachel asked. "What in the hell does that mean?"

"Prophylactic is a term for a preventative . . ." Daneh replied. "But . . ."

"You take a section of sheep intestine that is of appropriate length, cut it off and sew one end shut," Edmund said dryly. "The male slips the sheep intestine, which can be kept dry but has to be softened with water before use, over his penis. This prevents the ejacula from entering the woman's body."

"That's . . . obscene," Rachel said with a grimace.

"And of course some men have to use bigger animals than sheep," Edmund continued with a chuckle, shifting up his belt theatrically.

"That would probably work," Daneh said with a nod. "But the seam would tend to leak. And I'd have to find you a rabbit . . ."

"I think they probably waxed it," Edmund said thoughtfully, ignoring the jibe. "You'd test it by filling it with water and seeing if it held."

"I can't believe you're talking about this," Rachel said. "Come *on.*"

"Rachel, you've long wanted to be treated like an adult," Edmund replied without turning around. "Welcome to being treated like an adult. We could treat you like a child and tell you to leave if you wish."

Rachel opened her mouth to reply hotly then snapped it shut.

"Okay, I had that coming," she admitted. "But let me point out that you're my *mother and father.* Maybe I *am* too young to handle some conversations because discussions of my father's penis size is *definitely* one of them. Okay?"

"Okay," Edmund said with a laugh. "Sorry."

"What's 'tansy'?" Daneh asked.

"Oh, an herb," Edmund replied. "That's really all that I know about it. And that it's an abortifacient that's apparently pretty strong."

"There's so much I don't know," Daneh said with a sigh and a shake of her head. "Edmund, *please,* the next time you talk to Sheida, tell her that she will sustain a sister's curse if she doesn't figure out some way for me to get access to medical texts."

"I'll tell her," Edmund promised.

"It shouldn't be all that power intensive," Daneh argued.

"I'll tell her."

"And we really need it."

"I'll *tell* her," he said.

"Okay. And another thing, people are working themselves to death."

"*Some* people are working themselves to death," Edmund corrected. "What is your point."

"We need to start briefing people on safety. We've got people who have never held an axe before in their lives doing lumberjack work and people working with heavy machinery who have never done that. The major amputation was a person working in the mill who didn't have the sense to use some sort of lifting device to pick up one end of a huge beam. He's lost the bottom of his foot permanently; it was too crushed to even think about repairing. I know in the old days nobody really cared about safety except for 'try not to get yourself killed.' But I think we can do better than that, can't we?"

"I'll look into it," he said, pulling out a bundle of paper and a pencil. He held up his hand to forestall her outburst. "I'll *look into it*. You're right, in the old days nobody tried because nobody cared except the people getting hurt. And it might be possible to do better. But I *can't* guarantee it. Cutting down trees is inherently dangerous unless you have power systems and a cage. And even then accidents happen. So is farming. It never got much better the whole time men were doing it. So I don't know what exactly we can do. But we'll *try*. Okay?"

"Okay," she answered. "Last thing for you; we need to schedule a rest day."

"Daneh . . ."

"Every society in history had a rest day," she continued, ignoring the interruption. "Mostly they were religious in nature but they don't have to be. People working this hard *have* to have some time off. I'd suggest one day in seven since that was the old standard and it seemed to work."

"Sunday perhaps?" he said, amused.

"I don't care which day of the week you choose, as long as you choose one," she answered, firmly.

"All right, I'll figure out which one is the most prevalent. We do have a couple of Jews and at least one Muslim, I think they take Fridays off."

"Saturday," Rachel interjected. "For the Jews anyway. Friday night to Saturday night if I remember correctly."

"Saturday then," Edmund said with a shrug. "We'll want to think about holidays as well. Not many. But you're right, people need some time off."

"Kane's brought his herd in. Tomorrow get a horse from him or from Tom Raeburn," Daneh said to Rachel. "Take a bag with some bandages and go around to the camps. Brief the women on what's happening and check on everyone's over-all health. There's a lot of minor injuries here in town; I imagine there are out at the camps too."

"Yes, Mother," Rachel said, tiredly then looked up with a blush. "I'm sorry. You're right. And it's a responsibility. Thank you."

"You'll do well," Daneh said. "If there's anyone seriously hurt who hasn't been reported in, get them to me."

"I will."

"I think that's it," Daneh said.

"In that case, get some rest," Edmund replied. "Get up to the house. I don't want you getting up in the middle of the night unless it's a clear emergency."

"I'll stay here," Rachel interjected. "That way if there's something minor, I can take care of it."

"Good idea," Talbot said with a nod. "Now, milady?"

"I'm coming," Daneh replied. "Good night, Rachel."

"Good night Mother, Dad." She waited until they were gone, then finished cleaning up the infirmary and looked around. The only place to lie down was the rough wooden surgical table but it would have to do. Putting a couple of blankets on it, she made herself as comfortable as she could and then rolled over on her side. She knew there was no way she could get to sleep but even as she thought it she found her mind wandering into dream.

In the morning, Herzer felt like a basket case.

He woke up to a hand shaking him awake and groaned. He was curled in a fetal ball on his side and every muscle in his body protested movement.

"Come on," Jody said, not unkindly. "Breakfast is on and there's only thirty minutes to eat. You'd best get to it quick."

Herzer did not feel hungry in the slightest but his enforced starvation of the day before was vivid in his mind so he stumbled to his feet and made his way to the chowline.

The meal was cornmeal mush again with a side of some sort of herbal tea. But this time many of the people did not feel they could eat much. Many of them had only taken a half a bowl and some who had taken whole bowls, like Courtney, did not finish. There was enough left in the huge kettle that Herzer, Mike and a few others could have seconds and after the first bowl settled, Herzer felt drastically hungry. Not only did he get an additional bowl but by waiting by the pail for the used bowls he was able to cadge leftovers from several of the people, most of whom passed them over with every sign of bemusement. The exception was Nergui who when she saw his intention dumped her nearly full bowl out on the ground. This drew a furious reprimand from Dorsett.

"You don't waste food," he snarled, striding up behind her. "We don't have enough as it is. Do something like that again and you can skip the next meal!"

Herzer, at that point, was starting to feel as bloated as a tick so he reluctantly dumped his empty bowl in the bucket and went over to pick up his axe.

He looked at his hands doubtfully. Skin was already starting to spread across the ruined flesh of most of his hand, but much of it was still exposed and dirt had mixed in with a yellow goo that had appeared on the surface. It was an unappetizing sight and his stomach briefly regretted the hearty meal. Wielding an axe was going to be painful; even holding his bowl and using a spoon had been unpleasant—but there didn't seem to be much of a choice. He was contemplating a bleak day when he heard the clip-clop of horse hooves approaching.

"Hello, Herzer," Rachel said, dismounting and tying off the horse to a convenient branch. She took a set of saddlebags down and waved at Dorsett. "Jody, I'm here to see about any medical attention anyone needs and then I have to talk to the females you have here."

"How long is this going to take?" Jody asked. "We have a lot of ground to clear."

"That depends upon how much I have to do," she answered, snappily. "Do you have any major injuries?"

"No, but there's a few of them that have bad hands," Dorsett admitted, waving at Herzer. "Start with him and I'll get the others." Jody started gathering up the ones that he knew had blistered their hands the worst the day before.

"Hey!" Earnon yelled. "I can barely move and my back feels like it's on fire!"

"I'm not here to deal with sore muscles," Rachel said, looking at Herzer's hands. "Good God, Herzer, what were you *thinking*?"

"I was thinking we had a lot of trees to clear," Herzer answered, wincing as she probed his abused hands.

"Come down to the stream," she said, hoisting the saddlebags. "Jody, send the rest down with us."

"Have you seen Bast?" Herzer asked as they walked to the stream. It was muddy with dirt from the clearing but moving up into the uncleared portion brought them to water that was as clear as gin.

"She's been around. She's working with the hunters to bring in game." She held his hands in the cool water and gently wiped at the accumulated grime. "You need to keep stuff like this clean, Herzer. We're pretty resistant to disease but surface injuries like this can still get badly infected."

"I'll remember that," he said, grimacing in pain.

"The yellow stuff is suppuration, that's normal with a skin injury like this, or so Mom tells me. You're lucky really," she added.

"How?" he asked as she took the hand out and smeared on an ugly green ointment. There were bits of leaf to be seen in it.

"Unimproved humans would have been days recovering from damage like this," she replied, smearing on the ointment. "This is supposed to help healing. It's not much but it's something and it has stuff in it to keep the bacteria under control."

"Can I use my hands?" he asked, half hoping that the answer would be "no."

"I wish you wouldn't, but there's too much work to be done to have you idle." She took strips of cloth and leather out of the saddlebag and started wrapping his hands, first in the cosilk then with the leather. That she ended up tying off to hold the whole collection on.

"The leather will protect the base of your hands. Your fingers aren't bad, fortunately. Try to keep the damage to a minimum, okay?"

"Okay," he replied, flexing his hands. The bandages did reduce the pressure on the wounds.

"Your skin will probably regrow by tomorrow then start hardening. Like I said, in this at least we're lucky."

"Lucky, yeah," Herzer said grumpily then paused. "How's your mother?"

"She's doing okay," Rachel replied tartly. "She's keeping busy and I think that's good."

"Rachel, I . . ." he paused.

"I don't want to talk about it," she snapped, standing up. "You're good enough to get to work."

Herzer looked at her for a moment, then nodded and headed back to the encampment.

CHAPTER TWENTY

Rachel sighed as she finished the last of the badly blistered group. Most of them weren't as bad as Herzer but a few were close. Gathering up her gear she walked back to the camp and looked around for Jody. Fixing the hands had been the easy part.

"Jody, I need to talk to all the females, now," she said to the supervisor.

"What's this about?" he asked. "They're all working."

"Edmund told me to come up here, Jody, and I know they're busy. You really want me to have this conversation, though. Trust me."

"Okay," he said warily. "Courtney, Nergui, Shilan, Karlyn, Deann! Over here!"

He waited until the women had gathered around and turned to look at Rachel, folding his arms.

"And now *you* are going to take a walk," Rachel said.

"Why?"

"Because I said so, Jody," Rachel sighed. "Just go. Trust me, you don't want to be in on this."

He glared at her balefully for a moment and then strode off.

"Ladies, take a seat," Rachel said, gesturing at a couple of the fallen trees. We have to have a little girl talk."

She told them about the visit to Bethan and then about what had returned to visit the entire female species, then waited for the outbursts.

"You're *joking*," Nergui snapped. "That's just . . ."

"Disgusting," Rachel interjected. "Also true. And it's not going to go away."

"Ever?" Karlyn asked, eyes wide.

"When all the eggs are dumped it stops, say in fifty years. Maybe longer. But then, without the hormones, all sorts of other problems start. Or you can stay pregnant all the time."

"Fisk that!" Deann snapped.

"Been feeling a little testy lately?" Rachel said acidly.

"What about it?" Deann responded hotly. "All this . . ." she said, waving her arms around, "it's bound to make you a little angry."

"Angrier than normal?" Rachel replied taking a deep breath. "I can feel it coming on *me* and let me tell you *that* doesn't make me feel very damned happy at *all*. I'm *especially* looking forward to the cramps. Bethan said it's like a pulled muscle that just won't go away."

"Are we all going to be like that?" Shilan asked. "I'm not feeling . . . testy. Tired, yes, but not . . . unusually angry."

"I don't know," Rachel said. "Mom doesn't have any texts that cover it in detail. We'll just have to find out."

"This . . . this . . ." Courtney finally blurted out. "This just *sucks*."

"Yep, it does that," Rachel replied. "We're coming up with ways to . . . catch the flow. Like bandages to go on your . . . on your parts. And, remember, you're all *fertile* now. Get a little too friendly with your boyfriend and you're going to be carrying five or ten kilos of fetus and support structure around for *months*."

"I can't believe I'm hearing this," Nergui snapped.

"Believe it," Rachel replied angrily. "Believe it. Or don't and end up bleeding all over the ground! Or *pregnant*," she added with a tone of disgust.

"Hey, what's going on over here?" Jody said, walking over from the cutting.

"Jody, I don't want to say this again," Rachel snarled. "Butt the hell out!"

"Look, girl . . . !"

"No, you look!" she snapped right back. "This is a *female* conversation. Males are *not* invited. Now *go away!*"

"I don't care who your father is . . ."

"It's not who my *father* is that you have to worry about," Rachel said, standing up. "We're done anyway." She turned back to the women who were still sitting in positions of alternate bemusement and anger. "We'll try to get the supplies up to you by the end of the day. But be aware that this could start at any time."

"Oh, great," Karlyn replied, shaking her head in resignation. "Just fisking great." She stood up and walked over to an axe, looking for a likely tree branch. As soon as she spotted one she started hewing at it like it was the devil trying to climb out of a pit.

Rachel nodded shortly at the supervisor then went back to her horse, threw the saddlebags on, untied it, mounted and rode away at a canter.

"Is anyone going to tell me what just went on?" Jody asked angrily.

"Noooo," Deann answered carefully, getting to her feet and wiping her hands. "No, I don't really think you need to know. Not yet. And when you *need* to know you won't *want* to know."

"Nope," Courtney said, getting up and heading over to pick up her water bag.

"Uh, uh," Shilan added, walking away.

"Not in your dreams," Nergui replied, finally getting up.

"Just what in the hell is going on?" Jody asked the clearing, shaking his head.

"Strange days," Herzer replied.

The next two days continued much the same. With decent food—the second day there had even been a mess of venison stew with potatoes—and constant work Herzer could feel his already considerable muscles strengthening. His hands healed rapidly but he kept the wrappings of leather on nonetheless. He and Mike between them had felled the giant tree, an oak Jody told them, that had defeated the other teams, and the group had cleared a large area by the third day when they started cutting the wood to make buildings.

The day after Rachel's visit first Nergui, then Shilan had started to complain to Jody of diverse and mysterious maladies. They were quickly sent to town and returned later with bundles of cloth and odd cloth straps. Jody, after a visit from first Rachel and then Daneh, who looked drawn and tired, had passed the word to the males not to ask questions. But when Courtney had doubled over in the middle of the afternoon Mike wasn't willing to take "it's a girl thing" for an answer and the whole subject was brought out into the open. The reactions among the males ranged from bemusement to anger, especially since they were getting the details secondhand from

the women. That night when food was brought out, most of
the cooks were men from Raven's Mill, hastily conscripted from
various other jobs. Apparently what was happening in the
wood-cutting camp was also happening everywhere and from
the muttered comments of the males Raven's Mill was in an
uproar. The men, furthermore, were not well-trained cooks.
The mush was half burnt and an attempt to cook cornbread
in something called a "Dutch Oven" was a disaster.

Deann and Karlyn were apparently suffering from the same
maladies, but they had gone back to work almost immediately
on doing whatever the women were doing to manage it. Deann
mentioned that she was feeling cramps and a certain amount
of weakness, but in Karlyn's case there seemed to be no effect
other than the bleeding and not much of that. Courtney, as
soon as her cramps passed, was back at work as if nothing
had happened as was Shilan. Nergui continued to complain
of intense pain and while Jody tended to be unsympathetic,
without any way to judge the amount of pain involved there
was no way for him to order her back to work.

At the end of the fourth day at the site Herzer came over
with his food and sat down with Courtney and Mike. As he
did Cruz and Emory wandered over as well.

Courtney looked at him and gave him a wan smile.

"How you doing?" Herzer asked, spooning up a bite of beans.
The mixture this night was really good, some sort of meat
had been minced fine and added to the beans along with a
slightly hot spice.

"Better," Courtney answered. "The cramps are gone at least."

"So . . . this is going to go on for five days?" Herzer asked.
"I'm sorry, we're all pretty curious. If you really don't want
to talk about it . . ."

"No, it's okay. It just came as a shock at first. In a way
I'm glad we're out here; I don't want to think what it was
like down in the camps."

"Ugh," Mike said, spooning up another bite of the stew and
taking a bite of cornbread.

"Basically we bleed all the time, so we have to keep a pad
of rough cosilk on."

"That was those strap things they brought up?" Cruz asked.

"Yeah. We don't know exactly when it stops. And they say
it might get worse than it is this time. Karlyn is hardly bleeding
at all and Nergui is like a fountain."

"Yuck," Herzer said, looking at the rather red mixture in
his bowl doubtfully.

"I had the cramps for about twelve hours. Shilan and Karlyn didn't get them at all. Deann was just about put out by them. You couldn't tell by the way she was working but she was. Mine were . . . pretty bad. I couldn't work through them; I just wanted to curl up in a ball and put heat on them so they wouldn't hurt so much."

"Sorry," Herzer said.

"Why? There's nothing you could do," she replied with a smile. "I don't know how long it's going to last; Dr. Daneh says that five days is just an *average*."

Emory didn't talk very much, but he started chuckling now.

"What?" she asked.

"You won't want to hear it," he replied in a gravelly voice. "What I was thinking is 'never trust something that bleeds for five days and doesn't die.' "

"Oh, thank you very much!" Courtney snapped, fire in her eyes.

"Said you wouldn't like it," he chuckled.

Herzer and Cruz coughed in their hands while Mike just smiled.

"Thanks so very much," Courtney said with a frown then shook her head. "Men!"

"What about 'em?" Deann said, sitting down on one of the stumps.

"Can't live without 'em and there ought to be a bounty," Courtney replied.

"You'd better *think* about living without them," Deann replied. "Unless you want to be carrying around a baby."

"What's that mean?" Mike asked, sharply.

"I'm not trying to cut you off from your . . . friend," Deann replied just as sharply. "But bleeding means we're fertile again. Just like the other animals. So if you go making whoopie with Courtney, you're going to be looking at a baby in nine months."

"Well . . ." Mike looked at Courtney who blushed. "We'd . . . we've been thinking that having a child might make sense. But with the replicators gone . . ."

"That's the *point* lover boy," Deann said. "The replicators *ain't* gone. All us *women* are replicators now. We're *fertile*, Mike. We can have *babies*. That grow in our *bodies* like some sort of damn parasite!"

"It's not *that* bad!" Courtney replied. "I mean . . . I don't know. I'm sort of . . . looking forward to it. I want to see what it's like."

"How many times?" Deann asked. "You're talking about carrying around ten kilos of material in your belly."

"So? Deann, we're *designed* for it! That's what our bodies are *for*. Sure, if I had my choice I'd use a replicator. But I don't have that choice anymore. So . . ."

"So you're going to get pregnant?" Deann asked, aghast.

"If it's a choice of that or giving up guys, yeah," Courtney said with another blush.

"What a choice," Herzer said, shaking his head.

"Man, is this stupid war going to screw up everything in our lives?" Cruz snarled.

"Nice pun," Emory muttered.

"Wha . . . Oh, shit," Cruz said and laughed with the others.

Mike reached out with his boot and tapped Herzer on the foot.

"I think you've got a visitor," he said, gesturing over Herzer's shoulder.

"Hello, Herzer," Bast said, looking around at the group with a nod. She was carrying her usual panoply of weapons but also had a basket on her back.

"Bast," Herzer said, reaching towards her.

"Hello, lover boy," she repeated, swarming up him in a full-body hug. "Let's take a walk."

"If you'll excuse me," he said to the group.

"I'll carry your bowl back," Courtney said with a smile.

"Thanks," he said as Bast flipped off him and took his hand, leading him into the woods.

"Are you headed somewhere to take a bath?" Herzer asked. He knew full well that the clothes he was wearing reeked of days of sweat.

"Not yet," she replied as they passed out of the clearing into the woods. "There will be time later. There's a full moon tonight."

"And what does that mean?" he asked as she stopped to pull something from the ground.

"That we can see well enough to take a bath, silly," she smiled at him, stripping the dirt from the root she had dug up.

"What's that?"

"*Armoracia,*" she replied. "Horseradish. It's a hot spice to be added to food. It also can be used for poultices and to help clear the passages in bronchitis."

"This is *Rumex,*" she said touching another small, spreading plant. She tore off a small leaf and handed it to him. "It's best when cooked, especially with some pork as seasoning, but it can be eaten raw."

He nibbled at it and found it at tad bitter but overall quite tasty. He tore off a couple of more leaves and followed after her, feeling very much like a foraging horse.

"*Lindera*," she said, touching a small tree. "It can be used for spices or teas. The bark is the best but buds can be dried as well. *Betula*," another tree, this one tall and spreading at the top. "It's found along creek bottoms where you find willows and poplar. Its buds and twigs are pleasant to chew with a spicy taste and the under bark can be used as a sort of chewing gum."

They wandered on through the darkening woods as Bast pointed out plant after plant. She knew its growing habits, environment, medical and food uses as well as what animals fed upon it. Occasionally they saw small animals that crossed their paths, and she named each and gave its season of growing with barely a glance.

"Bast," he said finally, well stuffed with the various plants she had shown him were edible. "Is there anything you don't know?"

"I don't know why humans cannot leave these woods to their own life," she answered sadly.

He paused beside one of the small creeks that were everywhere along the mountains and looked at her. The sun was down but the moon had yet to crest the mountains across the valley to the east. The light from it was dimly visible over their shoulder but the valley was still in blackness. She was a barely visible shape in the tenebrous black under the spreading trees.

"Bast, have I hurt you by cutting down the trees?" he asked gently.

"Oh, no, I'm not upset with *you*, Herzer," she said, coming up to him and stroking his cheek. "Come, it is time to wash."

She led him to a spring-filled crack in the rocks, just big enough for two. They ended up washing not only themselves but Herzer's dirt encrusted clothes and spending half the time having water fights as the moon rose in the east. Finally they were both cleaned and Bast extracted the fur roll from the depths of the packbasket. There by the stream she lit a small fire and prepared a light salad of spring greens. By the light of the fire, with the water of the branch to wash it down, they ate the salad and then enjoyed each other until the moon was high in the sky.

Herzer awoke in the early dawn of the morning to a smell
of woodsmoke from the embers of the fire and reached to feel
for Bast, who was gone. Opening his eyes he looked around
but she was nowhere in sight. Only her basket and blanket
remained.

By the fire was a note, written on bark with one of the
coals.

*"Lover I have watched the trees of this valley grow since before
the cities were removed. I watched as the valley returned to
its natural state and have walked these woods since time
immemorial. I have known these trees, nut and branch, since
they were born. I can name them and tell you of their life,
each and every one.*

I can watch them die no longer.

*I shall walk far from the homes of men and visit the for-
ests and fields of my life. Perhaps I shall return some day and
perhaps not. I never say good bye, only "Esol." This means
"Tomorrow Again." Remember us as we were.*

Bast L'sol Tamel d'San."

Herzer set the note down after rubbing at the writing idly,
then looked around and sighed.

"Great, Bast. Very touching. But I don't know where I *am*."

For a change, Edmund and Daneh had an evening off at
the same time and could eat a simple but, and this was
significant, *peaceful* dinner. Not a snack snatched up between
critical operations or a meal supped with arguing council
members.

And it was clear to Edmund that they had no idea what
to talk about.

"So, how was your day, dear?" Edmund asked, realizing that
it was both prosaic and insufficient.

"The usual round of emergency surgeries without anesthetic.
I swear, I'm going to have to get all male nurses to hold down
the screamers."

Edmund wasn't sure if he should laugh or cringe so he
stayed silent.

"Jody Dorsett's going to have to relearn to use an axe," she
added after a moment. "He managed to cut off his left thumb."

"Ouch!"

"Even in the *old* days of medicine they would have been
able to reattach it. I've seen references to something called
a 'nerve graft' but I have no idea how you'd actually do it.
And practicing on someone who is twice your size and writhing

in pain is a trifle difficult." Everything was said in a light tone but he could feel the bitterness going bone deep. And she had barely touched her food.

"I'm sorry," he said. "Maybe when we have some poppies you can start working on anesthetics."

"What I really need is some decent medical reference works. I've been all through your library and everything else everyone had. But the only medical references are either first aid, very oblique and opaque statements or suited to a Middle Ages surgery. And I personally refuse to bring back bloodletting for common colds."

"Perhaps when Sheida . . ."

"Yes, 'when Sheida this,' 'when Sheida that.' I need this stuff *now*, Edmund! All I need is a smidgen of power, some nannites and the authority. Even a damned elementary *textbook*! But it has to *wait* doesn't it?"

Edmund finally realized that what she was saying was not what she was thinking. "Where are you at?" he asked after a moment. "And don't tell me about surgery."

"I'm in a very strange place, Edmund," she said after a long pause. "I'm thinking that it's time to go to bed with you. And part of me is saying 'Yes!' and part of me is screaming 'NO!' And I don't know which side is courage and which is cowardice. Or even which is right and which is wrong. And I'm tired of nightmares."

Edmund thought about that for a long time then sighed. "There is a part of me that says 'Say the *yes* is right!' And it's not even the part that's south of my expanding waistline." *If I can even remember how,* he added mentally. "It's the part of me that has missed my Daneh for many years. The Daneh that I fell madly in love with at first sight. The part that has missed you, all of you. That wants to hold you in the night and cuddle you and make you all better. But I also know that it's not going to be that easy. So I'm willing to wait. Be it until you find another or, if you can't decide, for the rest of your life. Because I love you, I always have loved you and I always will love you, no matter what road that takes us down."

On the afternoon of the sixth day in the woods, Herzer and the rest headed back to Raven's Mill. It took about two hours to walk to the Via Apallia, passing clearings being opened on both sides of the dirt track, and as they crossed the massive bridge over the Shenan, Herzer was surprised to see that Raven's Mill had changed even more.

Some of the original log shelters had been torn down, apparently to create an open area near town, and different structures had been put in. At the base of the hill to the east of the town a long, low building had been built and more work was taking place stretching up the hill. In addition, a wooden stockade was under construction. Based on the foundation that was being built it would eventually surround the entire "old town" and stretch up the hill near Talbot's house. Herzer, looking at it, realized that Edmund's house was precisely where a citadel or keep would be built and wondered how much of that was coincidence. He doubted that Edmund had designed the stockade to make his house the citadel but it would be very much like the old smith to choose the most defensible position to put in a house.

On reaching the edge of the town their group met two others coming in from the same general jobs. The three groups were stopped at the intersection and gestured to the side by a tall, thin gentleman with gray in his black hair.

"My name's Phil Sevetson. You didn't meet me before you set out on the first phase of your familiarization, but I'm in charge of the program. You've completed your first week successfully and the day after tomorrow you will start on the next phase. What that is depends upon which group you are in and the names and designations of the groups were *not* communicated before you set out," he added with a frown.

"Who is Herzer Herrick?"

"I am, sir," Herzer said raising his hand.

"The group that you are with is group A-5. Who is in the group with Herzer, that was just cutting in the west wood with Jody? Please raise a hand." He nodded as they raised their hands. "You are all group A-5, that is A for Anthony, Five. Any orders or information will be addressed to the group in that manner. That is, if there is a call for all groups to form in a certain area, you will gather with group A-5. Is that clear?" He waited until he got a nod from each then went on.

"Monique McBride? The group with Monique McBride, that was cutting in the west wood under the direction of Mislav Crnkovic, is group A-4. That is A as in Anthony, Four. All the members of A-4 please raise your hands."

He continued the process with group A-6 and ensured that, yes, they all knew that they were A-6 and would appropriately respond.

"Very well, now that you all know who you are. Much to everyone's surprise and massive damage to my training schedule, tomorrow has been designated as a day of rest. That means that you do not have to start your next phase tomorrow. Tomorrow you can rest. Just down the street from the town hall is the apprentice building," he said, pointing. "After we are done here, go there to draw your meal chits. Your overseers are there now making a report. You will be given sufficient meal chits for this evening, tomorrow and Sunday morning. After the morning meal on Sunday and before noon, report to the apprentice hall again for your next assignment. Is this all clear? Are there any questions?"

"They said we'd get money for doing this shit," Earnon said. "When do we get it?"

"Your supervisors are currently making their preliminary report to the apprentice hall," Sevetson replied, pursing his lips. "Additional funds above basic subsistence up to a certain maximum are their determination. The maximum is one additional meal chit per week and a bonus for quality and quantity of work of one chit."

"What?" Earnon growled. "That's *it*? A couple of *meals*?"

"Meal chits are now the de facto currency of Raven's Mill," Phil replied with a sniff. "They can, for example, be used to purchase a bath at the new bathhouse," he again gestured at the new buildings along the base of the hill. "They do not cost a full chit and there you can get change for whatever funds you are given."

"Change?" someone at the back of the crowd asked.

"Funds that do not equal a full meal chit," Sevetson replied. "You'll get used to the system after a bit; it is, after all, ancient and venerable. Questions?"

"Where do we sleep?"

"Many of the temporary shelters are still available. Be warned that there has been some robbery of materials and money. It is wise to remain at least in pairs."

"Can men and women sleep together now?" Earnon asked, sniggering.

"Not in the communal shelters," the supervisor replied, wrinkling his nose and sniffing again. "There are other places that can be rented and you can walk a short distance out of town and sleep in relative comfort in the woods."

"Great, we're right back where we started," Earnon grumbled.

"You are now familiarized with the tasks of woodcutting," Sevetson corrected. "This is one of the basic tasks of this level of technology. It is a skill that can earn you money, more if you parlay it into skill in charcoal making. Next week you will be familiarized with other skills. Eventually you will be complete and if you have performed well enough at one of the skills, the supervisors may consider taking you on as an apprentice. You are not 'right back where you started.' "

Earnon's only answer was a glare, so the supervisor shrugged.

"If there are no more questions, go down to the apprentice hall, draw your chits and then you are free to spend your time as you wish."

With that he strode off in the general direction of the apprentice hall and the rest followed.

In front of the hall under a wooden awning tables had been set up. Inside the hall, which was more of an elaborate log cabin, Herzer could see Jody, bandage on one hand, doggedly arguing with someone.

Earnon, Nergui and a few others from the other groups had pushed their way to the front so Herzer, Mike and Courtney hung back. When Earnon got his chits and counted them he let out a howl.

"I only got *one* chit for my work! I worked my tail off!"

The young woman parceling out the pay referred to her list again and shrugged.

"That's what it says," she replied.

"How much did Herzer get?" Nergui asked, nastily.

"I can't tell you how much others get. Next."

"Wait! I demand to see—"

"Me," Sevetson said, walking over to the argument. "You demand to see me." The man picked up the list then motioned Earnon to wait and walked into the room. He returned with a sheaf of paper bound together with string and opened it up.

"It says here, Earnon, that on the first day you caused an altercation, is that true?"

"No, it was Herzer that caused it, lying about me slacking off!"

"According to Mr. Dorsett, you *were* slacking off. Furthermore, you continued to contribute less than your fair share the entire week. As I said, you get, at most, one additional chit unless you get a bonus. Mr. Dorsett's recommendation was that you be given no additional chits because 'He's a loud-mouthed slacker who thinks the world owes him a living.' I can neither confirm nor deny the slacker portion but I did override his recommendation and ensure that you had at least some spending money. He further reports that you encouraged others in sloth. There is no place in this program for a person unwilling to work, Earnon. If you wish to earn more than this I would suggest that you apply yourself in the next phase of your training. Good day, Earnon. That is all."

Sevetson continued to stand by as others came up to receive their pay. On two more occasions there were disputes, one from Nergui who felt that she should have gotten a "bonus" and one from another camp who, like Earnon, had earned only a single additional chit. In both cases, Sevetson returned with their respective files and gave them a precise and unpleasant dressing down.

Herzer wasn't sure what he would get when it was his turn and when the girl handed him the chits, small pieces of a reddish metal stamped on one side with a raven and the other with a sheaf of grain, he just nodded his thanks and stepped away to wait for Mike and Courtney.

"How much did you get?" Courtney asked, counting hers. "I got five. Full pay anyway."

"Four, five . . . six," Herzer said, frowning.

"Me, too," Mike said, counting his. "I think we got a bonus."

"Why?" Herzer said, counting them again. "I got in a fight that first day."

"Hah! You have to ask?" Courtney said, taking both their arms. "You guys both worked your tail off. I was afraid I'd get docked for when I was out with the cramps. I guess they took pity on us womenfolk."

"Not on Nergui, apparently," Herzer replied, still frowning. "I didn't do more than my share."

"Yes, you did," Jody said, after walking up silently behind them. "You, Mike, Cruz, Emory, Karalyn and Deann all got bonuses. Karalyn and Deann didn't get as much done as you guys, but they worked like demons. Harder than you and Shilan, sorry Courtney."

"That's okay," she replied. "I don't think woodcutting is my niche!" she added with a smile.

"But you will find it," Jody said. "What are you guys doing now?"

"I don't know," Herzer replied, dropping the coins in his pocket.

"I was talking with some of the others," Jody said. "Some of the apprentice people who have been in town. There's

already a mini crime wave going on. Keep a close hold on
your money and watch for people trying to cheat you out of
it. If you want a suggestion, head up to the bathhouse and
get cleaned up. Dinner won't be for an hour or so yet."

"Sounds good to me," Mike said gruffly.

"Well, we do need a bath," Courtney chuckled.

"Let's go then," Herzer agreed.

CHAPTER TWENTY-ONE

The bathhouse was all the way across the encampment from the apprentice hall and it afforded them a look at the growing town. More buildings had gone up, mostly of logs but a few of cut planks with tile roofs. Most of the permanent structures seemed to have something to do with the burgeoning industries that had formed only in the last week. They displayed signs indicating potters and smiths, coopers and weavers. Most of them were only half finished and they allowed the three to see the people inside, hard at work.

"Rome wasn't built in a day," Herzer muttered.

"What?" Mike asked.

"They say that Rome wasn't built in a day," Herzer repeated. "But it looks like they're trying."

"Where'd all these crafts come from?" Courtney asked.

"Oh, the reenactors do all this stuff. It was their hobby before. Now, I suppose, it's more than a hobby."

"I guess these are going to be the people we'll be working with," the girl said. "I hope I'm better at this than woodcutting."

"I want a farm," Mike said. "I don't want to work in a shop all day."

"We'll get one," Courtney replied, soothingly.

"But which one?" Herzer asked. "I mean, do you just wander out and start one? Where do you get the tools you need?"

"I don't know," Courtney replied. "I'm not even sure what

sort of tools you have to have. Or how you plant and all the other stuff you have to do. Where do you get livestock?"

Mike didn't say anything, just grunted.

"Well, we'll find out in time," Herzer said. "I wonder if they've got a guard force?"

"Is that what you want to do?" Courtney asked.

"Something like it, yes," Herzer replied. He gestured with his chin at a person who was apparently a guard, standing by the entrance to a rather sturdy building. The man had on a surcoat with an embroidered Raven and carried a spear, but he was slouched under the awning of the building, apparently trying to keep out of the late afternoon sun. "But not like that. That's not a soldier, if you know what I mean."

"Are we going to need soldiers?" Courtney said. "Why?"

"Bandits," Herzer replied. "Eventually other towns will be causing us trouble, too. And then there's the war."

"Not much of a war," Mike said. "*We* haven't been attacked."

"Not yet," Herzer admitted. "But if we're going to oppose Paul, eventually we'll either be attacked or have to attack him."

"How can you attack a council member?" Courtney said, angrily. "They still have power!"

"So does Sheida and her group," Herzer replied with a shrug. "From here it looks like a stalemate. And I don't think Paul will let it stay that way even if Sheida is willing to."

This talk carried them through the encampment and up to the bathhouse where some people were hanging around the entrance.

"Wash your clothes for you, sir, ma'am?" a boy who looked as if he very much needed to use the bathhouse asked.

"Clothes?" Herzer asked, remembering Jody's advice. But the clothes did need work, not just washing but with a needle and thread. And he realized that they were the only thing, besides the basket and blanket Bast had left behind, that he now owned. No, he had a cloak that didn't fit, but he wasn't about to ask Daneh for it back.

"Oh, aye," the boy replied. "I'll take them and wash them when you're in getting your bath and bring them back for you."

"Dry?" Courtney asked.

"Well, I can't be promising *that*," the boy replied. "But dry*ish*, yes."

"Errr," Herzer said. "I think I'll try to figure something else out. Thanks just the same."

"Only a tenth chit, sir," the boy said earnestly, tugging at his sleeve. "And I know a lady that can mend them up for you, too."

"How do we know we'll get them back?" Courtney asked, pulling at her shirt which was, admittedly, filthy.

"Well, I'm here all the time, miss," the boy answered with a smile. "If I went stealing my customers' clothes, I wouldn't have many customers, would I?"

"Is that rapscallion digging at you?" a woman said, coming up behind them. "Darius, when are you going to get a real job?" she added with a smile.

"Ah, Mistress Lasker, I *have* a job," he said with a smile. "Would you be needing your clothes washed today?"

"Not today," the woman replied with another smile. "How is your mother?"

"Fine ma'am, thank you for asking."

"He's safe enough," the woman said. "I'm June Lasker. I'm sort of the town secretary. It's his mother who does the washing and mending."

"Is there a way to get some more clothes?" Herzer asked, pulling at his torn shirt. "These are getting raggedy. And I don't really want to be wandering around in wet clothes."

"There's a few clothes sellers," the woman said with a sigh. "But with no way to fab them they're terribly dear. Hardly anyone brought anything besides what was on their backs. They'll be fairly dry; there's a hot room that he can hang them in to dry out. It depends how long you're in there. If you wait an hour or so they'll be dry enough."

"All right, Darius is it?" Herzer asked.

"Darius Garsys," the boy said, touching his forelock.

"How do we pay you?"

"It's a tenth chit for a bath," the boy replied. "When they give you your change and you get a sheet, just come out with your clothes. You can pay me when they're done."

"Works for me," Herzer said. "I'll see you in a bit."

"I'll show you how this works," June said, stepping up into the first room of the bathhouse. There was a desk by the door and behind the desk were bundles of clothing and other gear. On the other side of the room were baskets with bundles of cloth and bricks of yellowish soap.

"Hello, Nick," June said to the man behind the desk.

"Hello, June," he replied looking them over. "Brought me some newbies have you?"

"And they've already been waylaid by Darius," she said with a smile. "I don't know you young people . . ." she temporized.

"I'm sorry," Courtney said. "How rude of me. I'm Courtney and this is Herzer and Mike. We're in apprentice group . . ."

"A-5," Herzer said.

"Been out in the woods have you?" Nick replied. "Okay, take off your clothes and put everything you're leaving in a bundle. Then I'll give you a receipt for it and when you're done come back and pick it up."

"Undress right here?" Courtney asked, wide-eyed.

"Unfortunately, dearie," June replied, suiting action to words. "You can use one of the sheets for modesty if you wish, but the baths are co-ed. They're working on another bathhouse that will have separate sections, but everyone's getting so used to bathing together I don't know why they bother."

Herzer hesitantly undressed then bundled his dirty clothes up. He quickly grabbed a bath sheet and wrapped it around himself. It was a thin piece of smooth material and he was pretty sure it wouldn't be very good for drying.

"I've got this basket . . ." he said, holding it up. "And what about our money."

"Well, I'm the one that sits on it all to make sure it stays where you left it," Nick said. He took the bundle and wrapped a strip of ribbon around it, tying it to a wooden marker. He handed a similar marker on a cord to Herzer.

"Put the bundle over by the others," he said. "Stuff your money well down in it so nobody can get it out without digging. I'll make sure it stays there."

"Okay," Herzer replied, doubtfully.

"Before you do, the cost of a bath is a tenth chit," the man said, holding out his hand. "That's for the soap, the water and the sheet. If you want anything more it's extra."

"What else is there?" Courtney asked digging out her money.

"Well, there's wine and snacks and body oils," June replied for him. "But, again, it's terribly expensive. I think once things get more established the costs will go down. But it's a full chit for a cup of wine and a few cuts of meat. Most people don't get it."

"It's not much more than my cost," Nick said defensively. "There's not much wine to be had. Nor the good meat that I serve. I have to buy it from McGibbon out of what he doesn't sell to the town. Prime wild boar isn't cheap."

"I know, Nick," she said with a shrug. "I'm just telling them the truth."

"Well, Nick, we'll pass for now," Herzer said. "We're not making much as apprentices." He handed over one of his chits then watched, fascinated, as the bath manager made change. The money he gave back was a mixture of small coins made of various types of metal and a few out of wood.

"This is a tenth piece," Nick said, holding up a small piece of what looked like steel. "The cost is a tenth and so I owe you nine tenths. But this is a half," he continued, holding up a small bit of the reddish metal. "It's made of copper like the chits but it's smaller and it's got a half inscribed on it. Another way of thinking of it is fifty hundredths. And this," he said, holding one of the pieces of wood, "is a hundredth. They're going to start making them of something else, but for now it's wood. The wood's no good, though, cause it cracks and you get in a fight and you end up with a pocket full of useless splinters. So that's nine tenths. I'd pay that rascal outside in the wood if I were you. Please pee *before* getting in the bath, not after."

Herzer took his clothes outside and dubiously handed them over to Darius then went back in and followed Nick's directions up the steps and into the first room. The walls were wood logs and the floor was made of sanded wood, logs that had been spit with their flat sides up. There were openings between the logs, apparently to let water through, and the surface was covered with a thin pattern of sand. On the left were pegs to hang their bath sheets and on the right there was a trough set well above head height. There were holes cut in the bottom of the trough, and steady streams of water flowed out of them. Under one of the streams June Lasker was already turning in place and rubbing a piece of the yellow soap between her hands.

"Don't rub the soap on your body," she said, stepping out from under the stream. "It will strip your skin right off."

Herzer noted in passing that her skin hadn't started to get the dry look that many older women's skin had and that she was pretty well set up. The thought triggered a memory of Bast bathing and he quickly turned away and willed himself to think about something, anything, else.

"This is one of the reasons that it's almost more embarrassing for men to take these communal showers than women," June noted with a chuckle. "That's what's called an involuntary vascular reaction."

"Well, Herzer's got nothing to be embarrassed about," Courtney said with a chuckle.

"Neither does Mike," June replied.

"Hey!" Mike growled.

"Mine," Courtney said, giving him a pat on the rump and getting under the water. "Yow! This is *cold!*"

"I can tell," Herzer replied, maliciously. Like Bast, Courtney had pink nipples but they were about twice the size. Or at least it appeared they normally would be; they currently were drawn up tight.

"Mine," Mike chuckled, but there was an edge to it.

"I'm putting my eyes back in my head," Herzer said. He stepped across the room and under one of the streams of water and gasped. It was as cold as any of the streams he and Bast had bathed in and after the warm afternoon it felt even more frigid.

"Well that took care of *his* involuntary vascular reaction." Courtney chuckled, picked up the soap and rubbed it in her hands. "Ow!"

"Rough, isn't it?" June sighed. She had soaped all over and now stepped back under the water to rinse off. "It's lye soap. Be careful in your private parts."

"What did you do when the . . . you know, the curse was hitting?" Courtney asked.

"Stayed home and washed as well as I could with a bucket," June admitted as she rinsed off.

Herzer soaped and rinsed without comment, hoping that the women would keep that line of conversation to a minimum.

"It was bad out in the woods but at least you could get some privacy to wash," was all the further comment Courtney made.

The far end of the shower room had a doorway covered with a leather flap. Stepping through it Herzer stopped and shook his head.

There was a catwalk down the middle, made of logs again, and on either side of it were six vats, three on the left and three on the right. Each of them was about two meters across and looked to be a meter and a half deep. And each was filled with steaming water.

"Down below there's an arrangement that lets hot air run through them in pipes," June said, lowering herself gingerly into the third tub along. "And they are *very* hot."

"Oh, this is wonderful," Courtney said, lowering herself into the tub next to the older woman. "Oh."

Herzer had to agree. The hot water immediately caused muscles he hadn't even noticed start to loosen. It also made him need to pee, badly.

"Uhmm . . ." Courtney said, before he could open his mouth.

"Far end, dear, left for the ladies, right for the gentlemen," June said, leaning back in the seat.

All three of the apprentices got out of the bath almost simultaneously, which caused a chuckle from Mike.

The latrine turned out to be a rather clean four seater and Herzer quickly dumped his bladder, heading back to the bath. He noticed as he did that the room was not particularly steamy, then saw that there were openings in the wall at the top and bottom.

"Whose idea was this? Nick's?"

"No," June said. "And he doesn't own it, although sometimes he acts like it. It was Edmund's idea and the town built it and maintains it. The construction up the hill is where we're building a larger one, more ornate. We need to get rid of the logs and get some tile in; people keep slipping on the wood."

"It's very nice," Courtney said, easing into the water as Mike walked back. "Whose idea did you say it was?"

"Mine," Edmund said, pushing aside the flap. "Hello, June, mind if I join you?"

"Not at all, Edmund, plenty of room."

All three of the apprentices were wide-eyed as the mayor lowered himself into the water. They were amazed to see the already semilegendary leader simply joining people in the bath.

Herzer was covert in his study but he had heard so much about Edmund Talbot that he knew he had a case of hero worship going. The smith's body was unusually hirsute; most people inhibited hair growth to a much greater degree. It also was immensely muscular, not like a bodybuilder but like a person who used a wide variety of his muscles every day for hard physical labor. He also had a full beard and mustache, which was unusual. Herzer had had all the hair on his face and most of his body inhibited except for a straggling mustache and he knew very few people who even had one of those.

"I'm surprised to see you," June said.

"Think I'm too good to hang out in the bath?" Edmund chuckled.

"Not that. I just thought you'd be too busy," June replied.

"I've got a couple of hours between meetings and for a wonder nothing was coming apart. So I thought I'd catch a quick bath. I can't stay long though."

"Sir, can I ask a question?" Herzer said.

"Ask away, I won't promise to answer," Edmund said, sliding down in the water and closing his eyes. "We haven't met by the way."

"I'm Herzer Herrick and this is Mike Boehlke and Courtney Deadwiler, sir."

"Herrick?" Talbot said, opening his eyes back up and peering at the boy. Herzer felt as if his brain was being probed but he just nodded.

"Heard a bit about you. Sorry, we *had* met before, hadn't we? Thanks for helping Daneh and Rachel on the trail."

"I . . . yes, sir," Herzer said in reply.

"Hmmm . . ." Edmund said and Herzer could tell that his evasive answer had been noted. "What was the question?"

"Err . . . is this a Roman bath? I was thinking about you being in here, too. It was said that the Roman senators would take the public baths because that way it proved that they did not think that they were not one of the people."

"You've studied history," Edmund replied after a long pause, staring at the boy again.

"More like dabbled in it, sir," Herzer replied. "Mostly military history but the Romans were such a major factor in preindustrial military thought that paying more attention to them than, say, the Egyptians just made sense."

"It's sort of a Roman bath," Edmund said after another pause. "Some aspects of Japanese also. The Romans would wipe their bodies with bent pieces of metal or wood and then take steam. Then they would swim or bathe in cooler water in the frigidarium. When the new baths are done we'll probably have a steam room as well as a sauna. But the hot soaking bath is a Japanese item as much as anyone's. And I prefer it to steam so I thought that would be the way to go."

"Some softer soap would be nice," June said acerbically.

"Working on it," Edmund said. "As soon as someone comes up with an industry making softer soap, we'll buy it. In the meantime, the apprentices are making lye soap and lye soap only."

"Because that way someone will start making better, sir?" Herzer asked, cautiously.

"Got it in one," Edmund said with a nod, lifting himself out of the water. "The town will keep people reasonably healthy and alive. As long as they work at it and as long as we can support them. But if I had my way all the town food would be nothing but gruel, and thin gruel at that."

"So people would find other work to get better food?" Courtney asked.

"Well, right now there's not much better than what people have been getting," Edmund admitted, drying himself off sketchily. "But there will be. And I don't want anyone permanently dependent upon the town. In a democracy that leads to bread and circuses and eventually to despotism. In a despotism it leads to bond labor. I won't have even the *beginnings* of either one as long as I'm mayor." He nodded at them and walked back out of the room.

"Wow," Courtney said.

"He's intense," June said with a nod.

"Actually, I think the term I was considering was 'charismatic,' " Courtney replied.

"Oh, that too," June chuckled. "Very charismatic. The one thing nobody has ever seemed to find a gene for."

When Edmund got back to his house it was nearing midnight, but as he entered the main hall he could see Daneh sitting by the fire, staring into it pensively.

"You're up late," he noted, walking over to the matching chair and sitting down in front of the fire. "And, frankly, you should be getting all the sleep you can."

"I've got a lot on my mind," Daneh replied. She stood up and bent over to poke the fire. "I guess I dimly realized how much I depended upon technology to do my job. But it's really gotten driven in lately. I've got a couple of cases . . . I don't think they're all going to live, Edmund."

He thought about getting up and giving her a hug but since . . . the encounter with Dionys she had never touched him. And he wasn't going to press her about it.

"Anything I can do?"

"Not unless you can cure gangrene," she sighed. "Or figure out how to repair an internal bleed with no dissolving sutures, no anesthetic and no sterile conditions to open somebody up."

Since he didn't have any of those things he kept his peace. But he knew that wasn't all that was on her mind. He had known her for a long time and her body language told him that there was more. Not what, but more.

"Anything else?" he finally asked.

"Yes," she said after a long pause. There was another as she poked at the fire again, this time with more vehemence. She finally set the poker down and sat back in the chair, still looking at the fire. "I haven't started bleeding."

He waited for more revelation than that, then shrugged. "Don't they . . . skip?" he asked.

"Sometimes, but almost all the women in the town have

had the 'curse.'" She paused and then closed her eyes and her face worked. "I asked some of the ones who didn't and they'd all . . . been engaged in sexual activity between the time of the Fall and now. Every. Single. One."

"Oh," Edmund said then thought for a moment. "Shit. Is there anything that we can do?" he asked.

"Like get rid of it?" she smiled, wanly. "Perhaps. But I'm not sure that I want to. Edmund, this will be the first child born of a woman's body in millennia. Surely such a wonderful miracle should be considered carefully before we decide to end it?"

CHAPTER TWENTY-TWO

"What is it now, Celine?" Chansa said, impatiently. He had given up running multiple avatars and had instead transferred to the lab.

"I thought you should see my newest toy," Celine said with a smile. "It's . . . right up your alley."

She led him down a corridor, then through a series of security screens until they were looking down into a metal-lined pit. Inside was a bipedal beast. It was nearly three meters in height, stoop shouldered and long of leg with massive biceps and thighs. The fingers were long and strong with hooked claws. The face was bestial but it looked up at them with a surprising degree of intelligence and Chansa could see it sizing up the walls trying to determine if it could reach the top. The eyes also burned with fury and it finally leapt into the air, striking a punitive force screen that threw it back to the floor. It screamed in pain and rage.

"Interesting," Chansa agreed. "This is, indeed, worth my time. If, of course, these things are controllable. And how hard are they to produce?"

"Well, this one is a prototype," Celine said with a feral grin. "Look closer. Do you see anything different?"

Chansa looked more closely and shrugged in irritation. "Don't play games with me, Celine. It's a Change."

"But not a *human* Change," Celine said with a laugh.

Chansa looked closer at the face and body and then blanched. "Elf?" he snapped. "Are you *mad*? If you bring the *elves* in on the Freedom side . . ."

"They don't know that I have him," Celine said imperturb-
ably. "And now that I'm done he can be eliminated. But
capturing elves and then converting them is so . . . intensive.
Follow me."

She led him deeper into the complex and down a series
of stairs deep under the lab. As they went downward the
composition of the walls changed from the smooth plastic of
the majority of the lab to rough masonry and then natural
rock.

"This facility is old," she said, waving around. "It was a
castle in the depths of time but later it was a military strong-
hold and research center. This portion is ancient, so old it
predates the known history. One wonders what mysteries were
plumbed since its construction."

There was cold breeze upon the stair that carried from the
depths a whiff of corruption, at first faint but then stronger
until they reached a stair above a large, deep cavern, apparently natural.

The passageway above had been lit by the cool, omnidi-
rectional light of glowpaint but the cavern was lit only by
torches placed at great distances. They gave off a faint, flickering light that barely relieved the gloom and weirdly lit the
eldritch scene. For the vast room was packed with life.

In the center was a pit filled with a black, nameless goo
that roiled with movement. Surrounding the pit were low
masses of nameless purple fungi that extended delicate
pseudpods to its edge and apparently drew sustenance from
it. Extending outward from these, others seem to draw from
them in turn until the entire room was packed with strange
growths, colored in noisome purple and leprous green. The
growths reached all the way to the walls and there pods
appeared, some still small but others the size of Chansa's torso.
The fungi were not still, but seemed to pulse in the odd light,
many of them shimmering with colors and giving off a faint
glow of their own. The overall impression was of a gigantic
organism driven to some malign purpose.

"Okay," he choked out after a moment, trying to conceal
how disgusted he was, "this is pretty . . . horrible."

"Oh, it is far more than that," Celine laughed lightly and
led him down the stairs and to one of the pods against the
wall.

"Here, look here," Celine said, excitedly, kneeling down to
rub the noisome black liquid off of the pouch. "Look."

Chansa, fighting his gorge, squatted down opposite her and

looked at the sack, moving the torch around to try to see through the translucent material of which it was made. As he moved the torch to the side and leaned forward for a better look, the sack gave a lurch from within and a face out of nightmare turned up to look at him.

It was the face of an elven child, perfect and pure, and it twisted and struggled against the enwrapping material, seeming to scream from within the liquid. It had an expression of absolute pain and total horror and its eyes were open and unseeing. After a brief, merciful, moment its writhings took it out of sight if not mind.

Chansa rocked back and looked across at the woman who had created this monstrosity.

"My *God*, Celine, even for you . . . !"

"It is perfect, no?" she replied, her eyes bright and her mouth moist in the torchlight. "Do you know the story of the elves?" she asked, snatching back the torch and standing up.

"No, I do not," Chansa said, considering translating out right now. For whatever reason they were brought to the conspiracy, this . . . infernal pit was beyond anything that could be allowed to exist.

"They were created by the North American Union as the perfect soldier," she said walking over to the main portion of the pit and turning to look at him with the pit as her backdrop. "But the spineless leaders of that weak and puling land wanted soldiers that could be trusted to bring as little harm as possible to the people that they fought. That . . . idiot society thought that they could take the sting, the horror, from war."

"That is a somewhat incorrect description . . ." Chansa said but was cut off.

"They created the elves as their supersoldiers, mostly from the genes of the chimpanzees. They had studied the best of their own soldiers and come to the conclusion that the primary strength of the greatest was, believe it or not, *calmness*. They wanted soldiers who would not, even in the greatest stress of battle, perform *atrocities*, so they made them *calm*. They bred a species that was so *calm* that after a time they would not fight at all. Indeed, many opted out from the beginning, preferring to spend all their time in games and, eventually, the Dream."

"Elves do not fight," Chansa said. "Well, hardly ever."

"Of course not," Celine snorted. "They're all living in a delightful world of perfect calmness; why should they *fight*? But the *basics* of the elves remain. Intense strength, incredible reflexes, superhuman intelligence and the ability to turn aside the stress of war and simply *be* in the most intense battle-field. And the weak scientists of Norau failed in only one particular. What they forgot was *anger*. These, *these* will never quit killing for all the rage and hatred for which they hold the world. And they are *fully* under our control, I have *ensured* that. Whosoever couples that to their side will surely defeat all of their opponents!"

"And . . . this?!" Chansa said, waving at the pit. "You breed *elves*?"

"I breed *demons*," Celine laughed happily. "The elves have not self bred for a thousand years; they are born of special trees under the dispensation of the Lady. I simply . . . tweaked the method a bit. There they are born in pain and that pain and anger remains with them all of their lives. The perfect monster. And they can grow with *anything*. Take a seed of the growing pit, put it in a dark place, feed it with fell meats, and . . . power! Just one specimen of the pit, fed with suffi-cient organic material, and this whole room will grow from it. And in time . . . warriors." She laughed delightedly and patted the pouch like a mother might pat her pregnant belly.

Chansa lowered the barriers of his horror and thought about that. "How long for them to grow?"

"Oh, some years," Celine admitted. "But they can grow on practically nothing, anywhere that conditions are appropriate in the caverns of the area. The cavern can't be too hot or too cold and there has to be no sunlight; the fungi are very susceptible to ultraviolet. But, within those constraints, we can grow them in job lots."

"We must keep this secret," Chansa said.

"Oh, yes," Celine replied. "We must surprise those weak fools who would stand in the way of my research."

"I wasn't thinking of them," Chansa snapped. "I'm still hoping beyond hope we can conceal it from Her Ladyship!"

"All it is is a bit of genetic manipulation," Celine smiled. "Everyone does that."

Azure woke up, stretched and sniffed the morning air. From the scent of the house it was obvious that the main human had gone and not much food was left around to scrounge. He walked to the back, nudged open the door and stalked outside.

Another quick sniff confirmed that there was nothing to eat, screw or fight in the immediate vicinity. How boring. There was a faint chittering of mice somewhere in the woodpile, but that was hardly worth his time. After contemplating the distressingly empty scene for a moment, he wandered down the hill to Raven's Mill.

It was immediately apparent that more of the humans were in town than normal. And the excess didn't seem to be doing anything except scratching fleas. He wandered through town, accepting the occasional pet on the head that was only his due, headed in the general direction of the kitchens. So there he was, peacefully minding his own business, when he spotted what he had been searching for; a new dog in town.

Perhaps apprised by an instinct for trouble, after a few moments the napping Rottweiler opened up his eyes and scanned the area. Much to his surprise, the first thing that he saw was the world's largest house cat. Glaring at him. Balefully.

Azure wasn't too sure what was going through the doggie's *simple* little mind, but it probably was something like this: Cat. Big cat, but cat. Must chase.

The Rottweiler began barking frantically, on his feet now and edging closer to the cat.

Azure cleaned one paw, sliding the five centimeter retractable claws out to carefully get underneath.

The dog got closer, barking harder, unable to believe that any cat, no matter *how* large, would be stupid enough to stand up to him.

Azure used the paw to clean his ear, rubbing hard to make sure he got it good, one eye closed in apparent ecstasy.

Finally, enraged beyond reason, the Rottweiler charged. With an apparently startled yowl, Azure leapt straight into the air, landing on the dog's back. The yelp that was emitted was more of a scream as sixty kilos of happy cat landed on the dog's back. The Rottweiler tried to roll and for a few moments there was nothing but dust, yelps and the furious yowling of an enraged tomcat.

Finally one side of the dust cloud spit out a badly mauled Rotweiler, which disappeared into the distance. As the dust settled Azure was revealed peacefully cleaning a spot of dirt off of one leg. After a moment he stood up, stretched, then wandered over to the patch of sunshine the Rottweiler had previously occupied.

Checking the area for signs of threat, he turned around a couple of times, dug at the ground to prepare it to properly accept his personage, and curled up in a ball. In a moment he was, apparently, sound asleep. But one ear was cocked vertically and twitched back and forth as if it were a doggie-search radar.

Herzer awoke with a feeling of disorientation and it took him a moment to remember that he was back in the dormitories in Raven's Mill. He had been sleeping out for so long, or so it felt, that the dimness of the interior was startling. He felt in his pockets for his chits and was relieved they were still there. After bathing the night before he had hung around with Courtney and Mike through dinner, then afterwards had wandered around the town. The entire population of the surrounding area seemed to have descended upon the town in anticipation of the free-day. The town was filled with groups of people, most of them sitting around talking. Almost no one had anything in the way of cash or trade available to them so while there were some merchants offering wares, there was very little in the way of buying.

Herzer ended up buying a small leather pouch to hold his coins and tossed a few more of those coins to a redheaded female fiddle player who had staked out a spot by the stream and was playing mostly traditional Celtic ballads. But the privations of the previous month had taught him the importance of always knowing where your next meal was coming from so he was careful not to run through his spare change too quickly.

After a moment he sat up, rolled up the fur blanket and stuffed it in the wicker basket, grateful for both of Bast's gifts. After the previous week he had become used to the relative comfort of a bed made of spruce boughs, especially compared to hard packed earth. But the blanket had enough cushion that it mitigated sleeping on the ground again. The part that annoyed him was that he had no place to *leave* anything; if he left the basket and blanket in the dormitories it was sure to disappear in an instant. That thought extended to the fact that except for his clothes, basket, blanket and now pouch, he had nothing of his *own*. Mike and Courtney didn't even have that. He had stepped in one moment from a life of wretched affluence to complete lack thereof. He realized that he wanted a place of his *own*, even if it was just a bed and . . . a place to store his blanket in relative security.

He walked out into the town wondering abstractedly if joining the apprenticeship program was really the best thing he could have done. He *had* skills related to this technology level. He *knew* he could fight, if he could get his hands on some weapons and equipment. There were things to be gathered in the wilderness; he remembered June's comments about clothing and how nobody had anything. There were deserted homes aplenty in the wilderness. He could find them, somehow, and pull out anything of value. Surely that would mean more than a couple of extra chits a week and bleeding hands from cutting trees.

On the other hand, some of the homes belonged to people who were right here in Raven's Mill. And how would *he* feel if someone went into his bungalow and took all of *his* clothes?

He thought about that for a little longer and contemplated, for the first time in his life, the whole subject of looting. All the games he had played had assumed an ethical indifference to it. Kill the orcs, take their gold. He suddenly realized the games never included hungry orc children when their crops had been burned.

Even a bow. He knew next to nothing about hunting but he knew that he could hit what he aimed at. He wondered for a moment if he should go look up the guard force and try to enlist. Did it make sense to waste another twelve weeks of his life learning things he would never have a need for? He knew he wasn't going to be a maker of charcoal or a woodcutter or a tanner. There had to be something more than this.

These gloomy thoughts carried him through his morning ablutions, peeing in the public jakes and washing his face in a font of water diverted from an uphill stream. He walked over to the community kitchens looking anxiously at the sky. The sun was well up. He had slept through the majority of the morning and he was afraid they might have already closed to prepare for the lunch meal. His stomach was rumbling and it would be unpleasant to wait.

They were open, however, and the smell from the kitchens made his mouth water. He handed over his chit to a pleasant-faced girl holding down the entrance and walked over to the serving line. To his amazement there was far more than a bubbling pot of mush. The mush was there but so were eggs to order, fried potatoes, rounds of a golden, rich-looking bread, jam, butter and piles of steaming sausage being kept warm in pans by the fire. Instead of the usual roughly formed wooden bowls there were slabs of wood.

"This is nice," he said to the server, giving her a warm smile.

"The council decided that a rest day should mean a day

of celebration," she replied, smiling back. "So they allotted extra food for today."

"And better," Herzer said. "What can I have?"

"Take anything you'd like," she said with a vixenish grin. "But eat everything that you take."

"Hmmm . . ." he replied.

"How would you like your eggs?" she asked, picking up a frying pan.

"Eggs . . ." Herzer said, shaking his head. "I have no idea."

"Fried? Scrambled? Over?"

"Over I guess. Uh . . . whites cooked."

"No problem," she said. "It'll take just a moment."

He picked up a piece of the bread. It was baked brown on the outside, not much bigger than his hand, and emitted a rich, buttery aroma. He broke it open and the interior, instead of being white, was a light golden brown. He took a sniff and a nibble, then ripped off a large piece and stuffed it in his mouth, chewing happily.

"Iff ig goob!" he muttered, his mouth full. "Iff ig erly goob!"

The two cooks laughed and the server who was doing his eggs flipped them over and winked at him.

"That's just about the oldest known recipe for bread in the world," the girl said. "We've just now been able to make enough flour for it."

"Wug ib it?" Herzer asked, then cleared his mouth. "I mean, 'what is it?'"

"That's the bread that built the pyramids," an older woman answered. "Egyptian bread. Heavy, doughy, chock full of vitamins and minerals."

"Bread and beer," he said with a nod. "I'd heard of it, but this was not what I expected as the 'bread.' This is a meal in itself."

"That's what they say," the server replied cheerily. "They built the pyramids on bread and beer with a little fish and, on a holiday like today, a bit of meat. And look what *they* did." She looked somber for a moment as she flipped his eggs out of the pan and onto his slab of a plate.

He leaned forward and laid a hand on hers.

"Someday they'll look back on us and say the same thing," he said with a nod.

She smiled back whimsically then leaned sideways and speared one of the link sausages.

"Sausage?" she asked, raising one eyebrow.

So how come it took the end of the world for women to start to notice me? Herzer thought. The term that came to Herzer's mind was "saucy wench." She was nicely, and unfashionably, rounded, and had somewhere dredged up a period dress that was just a tad too small for her up top; it showed a more than ample quantity of her limited bosom. Red curls peeked from under her cap but that was all that could be seen of her hair. Another memory floated to the surface and he smiled at her.

"No thanks," he said with a wink. "Sixteen's my limit."

He did grab a bowl of cornmeal mush—he didn't know what he'd do without a bowl of mush in the morning—another piece of the bread, and butter and jam for the mush. He took his heavily loaded tray over to one of the tables and sat down, looking out the open sides of the mess hall. More people were moving around but like the night before there wasn't any focus. Groups were gathering along the stream, talking, occasionally arguing. Looking around at all the people, he realized all the people he *didn't* know in the town. There must have been at least two or three thousand who had gathered to the town and he probably only knew fifteen or twenty of them. It was strange to feel alone with so many people around him. He also realized how . . . diverse and yet curiously constrained his life had been before the Fall.

He had never attended the Faires, and the largest gatherings he had ever been at before were parties like Marguerite's. His illness had tended to make him avoid groups where he didn't know the people and as it progressed he had become more and more of a loner. Right now he probably had more friends, counting some of the members of the class as friends, than he ever had in his life. And was around more people in one area than he had ever seen.

He thought about trying to run Mike and Courtney down or one of the other members of the class but he didn't have any idea how. The two of them had wandered off the night before to try to find someplace they could doss together rather than in the segregated dormitories and at this point they could be anywhere in the town. He considered going up to the baths. He could probably strike up a conversation there. But he reconsidered when he thought about his dwindling money supply. It was oddly depressing to realize how limiting it was to have an unavailability of funds. He'd been given two meal chits "over and above" his three squares a day. It was already so late in the day that it would be worth it to skip lunch, thus giving him that much more disposable funds. So that would give him three chits over and above food. He'd used a tenth for the bath and another tenth to have his clothes cleaned. A tenth for the singer and a quarter for the pouch. It seemed a lot for a little piece of sewn leather, but on the other hand he'd talked the vendor down from a half. He wasn't exactly burning through his money but there was tonight and tomorrow to think about. There was also next week; there was no guarantee that he'd get another bonus. When he got out of the apprenticeship program, whether he joined the guard or found another use for his skills, it would be good to have a little start-up money. So he intended to be very conservative.

While he was contemplating his money situation, his eyes unseeingly scanning the crowd outside the building, the server he had been talking to came over and plopped down on the bench across from him, breaking the view and bringing him back to the present with a jolt.

She fanned her hand theatrically at her face and sighed, smiling at him as she did so.

"Been working hard?" Herzer asked, stirring the last of the mush in his bowl.

"Ah! You missed it, it was a madhouse in here!" she said, waving at her face again although there was no apparent sweat. "But, I've got this afternoon and all of tomorrow off for working this morning. Morgen Kirby," she continued, extending her hand across the table.

"Herzer Herrick," Herzer replied, taking the hand. It was delightfully warm.

"*Herzer Her*rick," she said, rolling the sound on her tongue. "Her-zer Herrick! It's got a delightfully masculine sound to it!"

"Well you're the first person who ever said that." Herzer laughed, shaking his head.

"So what do you do for your meal chits, Herzer Herrick?"

"I'm in the apprenticeship program," he said, spooning up the last of the meal. The majority of the mob had apparently drifted off and they were close enough to the stream for the sound of chuckling water to reach them along with a pleasantly cool breeze. Herzer was pretty sure he could go on sitting here forever, especially if it meant not having to cut any more trees. And he really didn't even want to *think* about going back to work.

"Maybe I should go over there," she replied. "I am *not* going to stay working in a kitchen for the rest of my life. Will you *look* at these hands," she added, holding up the appendages in question.

Herzer's first thought was that they were quite shapely and altogether pleasant. But he was pretty sure she was referring to the fact that they were somewhat red and chapped. So saying "they look pretty good to me" was probably out.

"If I *never* wash *another* bowl in my *life* it will be too soon," she said, shaking her head.

Something, *something* . . . Herzer wracked his brains for a moment. Which plant was it? Bast had said something on their walk . . . It had broad leaves . . . and a purple flowerhead if he remembered correctly.

"I might know something that would help with that," he said, turning one of her hands over and running a finger across the palm, at which Morgen gave a delightful twitch.

"Really," she asked huskily then cleared her throat. "We had some oil that I rubbed on them, but it didn't help much."

"Well, I don't think it will cure anything *permanently*," Herzer pointed out thoughtfully. "But it should help *some*. It's a plant . . . and it will take some searching to find it. . . ."

"Where?"

"Out in the woods, along streambeds where it's dark and moist. I'll have to get up on the hills and out of the cleared areas."

"Out in the woods?" she asked dubiously, surprise evident on her face.

"Yeah," Herzer replied, raising an eyebrow. "Why?"

"Well . . . people don't go in the woods much these days. You know there are wild animals out there?"

"Yes."

"There are tigers and leopards and mountain lions?"

Herzer thought about it for a moment and shrugged.

"Haven't been eaten yet."

"Oh." Pause. "Well when are you planning on going?"

"I don't have anything better to do. I'll probably go now."

"Well, if you wait until we're done with the breakfast dishes, I could come along."

"Aren't you afraid of being eaten?" Herzer asked, then hastily added: "By a tiger?"

"Not if I'm with you," she replied.

"Well . . . I'll be back in a little bit."

She smiled and picked up his tray, carrying it back over to the serving area with a decided sway to her hips.

Okay, Herzer thought. *What* is *it about the end of the world?*

CHAPTER TWENTY-THREE

When Herzer walked back into town in the late afternoon his basket was half filled with slightly damp fur rug; the other half was filled with spring greens. He had found a large patch of asparagus as well as enough sweet leaf greens for a large salad. He had also found a patch of kudzi that had colonized a rock slip, and by the pool of water at the base of the rock slip they had invented numerous fascinating things that you could do with kudzi juice.

When they got back to town they could see that much of the town was deserted. Most of the people had gathered around the former Faire area near the line of hills north of town.

"Come on," Morgen said, taking his hand. "They've started the dancing."

"Oh." Pause. "Good."

"Oh, don't be a baby," she said with a laugh. "All you have to do is move your feet!"

One end of the field had been roped off and a stage set up. On it a group of minstrels, including the redheaded minstrel Herzer had seen the night before, were now belting out a fast jig. There was a large group of people dancing but most of the people in the area were gathered in small groups watching and talking. There were some logs left from clearing the area and a few trestle tables. But most of the people sat on the ground or the occasional uncleared stump. Herzer and Morgen, hand in hand, wandered into the crowd looking for a place to sit or, for that matter, anyone they knew.

Morgen, not too surprisingly, was the first to spot an acquaintance. She waved to two women who were standing side by side, their arms folded, and dragged Herzer over to meet them.

The slightly older looking one was sharp featured, short and well rounded with more womanly curves than had been fashionable. Her long dark hair was heavily curled and in the slightly humid atmosphere had started to frizz at the ends. She glanced at Morgen and Herzer with the calculating eye of a raptor looking over a likely meadow. The younger woman was a shade over normal height for a female but had the standard fashionable look: no hips, no breast, no butt. She looked at Herzer and Morgen without expression and then looked away.

"Hi," Morgen said with another wave. "Crystal," she said to the older woman, "this is Herzer Herrick. Herzer, Crystal Looney."

Herzer stuck his hand out and the woman just nodded at him, her arms still crossed. To the degree that there was any expression on her face it was disdain. Herzer took his hand and ostentatiously clasped it behind his back, nodding at the woman with a smile.

"A *pleasure* to meet you, Crystal was it?" he said.

"Shelly?" Morgen said after a moment, turning to the other woman. "This is Herzer. Herzer, Shelly Coleman."

Herzer didn't bother to stick out his hand that time. He just nodded his head at the woman who nodded briefly and then turned to watch the dancing again.

Morgen flushed at the apparent rebuff then smiled brittlely.

"So what are you guys doing?" she asked.

Crystal looked at her as if she couldn't believe the question.

"Watching The Dancing," the woman replied, slowly and distinctly.

Morgen flushed again as Herzer nodded his head. He took her by the arm and drew her against him.

"It has been a *pleasure* to *meet* you ladies," he said with patently false insincerity. "I hope we get to do this again *real* soon." He stuck his arm though Morgen's and walked away, at which Morgen was forced to follow.

"Bye," she said, waving. "I don't know what is with them," she continued when they were out of earshot. "They're normally friendly."

Herzer put his arm around Morgen's shoulders and gave her a half hug.

"Ah, I think the problem might be that you were with a *guy*," he said, carefully.

"What?"

"Never mind," Herzer said, rolling his eyes at the sky. "Let's go find some friends of mine. They're at least *somewhat* more likely to be friendly."

They walked along through the crowd until Herzer spotted first Shilan and then, sitting next to her, Cruz. They were parked along the stream at the edge of the crowd, leaning against some balks of timber.

"Hey, guys," Herzer said, wandering over with his arm around Morgen's waist. "How's it going?"

"To the dogs, Herzer, it's going to the dogs," Cruz replied. "Who's your friend?"

"Morgen, Cruz Foscue and Hsu Shilan, Shilan is like her first name. Cruz, Shilan, Morgen."

Herzer set the basket down and first lifted out the greens, which were bundled in some of the outer leaves, then took out the blanket and shook it out on the ground, hoping there wouldn't be any evident stains.

"Man, dude, you are always prepared," Cruz said. "Where'd you get the rabbit food?"

"We went for a walk in the woods," Morgen said and then blushed bright red.

"Bast showed me some of the stuff that's edible in the spring," Herzer replied. "You can eat all of this stuff raw, but some of it is better cooked." He pulled out a stick of asparagus and nibbled on it. "Umm . . . tasty. Just like the *deer* eat."

"It is good," Morgen said, finishing off another stalk of asparagus. "Am so'gif," she added, munching on a fern head.

"Oooo! Plums," Cruz said, snatching up the fruit.

"Nah, kudzi," Herzer corrected as Cruz's face twisted in surprise.

"It's good," Cruz said, taking another bite then handing the rest over to Shilan.

"Yeah, but you gotta watch that juice," Herzer said, straight-faced. But the comment still elicited a hysterical giggle from Morgen.

"I need to visit the little girl's room," Shilan suddenly said. "Care to come with me, Morgen?"

"Sounds like a fine idea," Morgen replied, dusting off her hands.

The two men watched the women leave and then Cruz shook his head.

"They do that just to make us nervous, you know that don't you?"

"Yeah," Herzer said. "But do they know that *we* know?"

"They're going to dissect us in the bathroom, you know that."

"Hey, they're latrines," Herzer pointed out. "Unless they smell *much* better than ours they're not going to stand *in* the latrine and dissect us."

"Huh. Good point," Cruz said with a shrug of his shoulders. "But that doesn't mean they won't stand *outside*. By the way, dude, I have *got* to ask you this."

"What?" Herzer said with a crease of his brow.

"Do you take a *pill* or something? I mean, give me a *break*. One day you're running around with a nymphomaniac *wood elf . . .*"

"She was *not* a nymphomaniac!" Herzer interjected.

"What*ever*. She's like three thousand years old and knows every position in the Kama Sutra!"

"Oh, *thousand . . . maybe . . .*" Herzer corrected. "And, okay, the Kama Sutra's like *primer!*"

"God almighty, man," Cruz laughed. "What? Is it a pill? Give *me* some."

"I *dunno*," Herzer said. "I was asking myself the same question. It's like: 'Hey, it's the end of the world. We can get Herzer laid now!' "

Cruz laughed so hard he rolled over on the ground, waving his hand in the air for Herzer to stop.

"It's not fair," he said, waving a finger at Herzer. "You're not the last man in the world! It's not supposed to work that way!"

"I dunno. End of the world, all of a sudden women find me interesting. Don't ask *me,* I just live here! If there was a pill I would have been taking it for the last five years. And, besides, hey, you, Shilan? Who are you to talk?"

"I've been working on Shilan for a *week,*" Cruz replied in exasperation. "Your wood elf takes off and the first time you come back to town it's *wham!*"

"I dunno," Herzer said with a shrug. "It's just my searing good looks."

"Oh, puh-leeeze," Cruz replied. Cruz was just a shade under two meters tall with long, wavy blond hair, green eyes and a chiseled face. Everyone in the society was good looking but even within that group, Cruz was on the high end.

"Look, Cruz, don't tell *me* that you have a lot of problems meeting girls," Herzer said. "When I was growing up I had . . . uh . . . a genetic problem. It made me act really weird. I twitched, I couldn't hold my hands steady, my head was always twitching. Nobody, and especially girls, wanted to get within ten meters of me in case it was catching. Even my damned parents 'gave me my adult freedom' at *fourteen*. By that time I hadn't seen either one of them in more than three years; all I had raising me was nannies."

"So what happened?" Cruz asked.

"Well, thank goodness just *before* the Fall it got fixed. By Dr. Daneh as a matter of fact."

"Edmund Talbot's wife?" Cruz asked.

"Uh . . . they're not . . . I don't think they're married but . . . yeah."

"So you know Edmund?"

"Except in passing, I'd never met Edmund until the other day in the bath. But I do know Dr. Daneh and I went to school with his daughter."

"Cool."

"Well, I mean that and a chit will get me a meal," Herzer said with a note of exasperation.

"Yeah," Cruz said, frowning. "But you *know* people. I don't know nobody here." For just a moment he looked haunted.

"Hey," Herzer said, leaning forward and punching him in the shoulder. "You know me, you know everybody in Class A-5 and you know Morgen. Before you know it you're going to know everybody in this town."

"Now there is a goal to strive for," Cruz smiled sadly. "But I had friends, you know? I never realized how scattered, but they were *friends*. Here . . . there's nobody for me. Nobody at my back."

"Yeah," Herzer admitted. But in truth, since he'd never *had* anyone at his back, he couldn't really empathize. "Speaking of which, have you seen Courtney and Mike?"

"Oh, yeah, Courtney drug Mike over to go dancing," Cruz said.

"With what?" Herzer laughed. "Oxen?"

"Pretty damned close, man," Cruz replied, smiling. "Actually, I think she just threatened to cut him off." He looked over Herzer's shoulder and chuckled. "Don't look now, the womenfolk are coming back."

"We gonna tell 'em we're on to their secret?" Herzer asked, raising one eyebrow.

"Nah," Cruz said. "Let 'em think they know something we don't."

✧   ✧   ✧

There were still some greens left when Mike and Courtney, streaming sweat in the cool spring air, came walking back from the dancing. Introductions were made and then Mike thumped to the ground with a theatrical groan.

"That's it, I'm done," he said, waving his hands in the air and lying back on the ground. "This is a *rest* day!"

"Wimp," Courtney said, her hands on her hips and obviously raring to go back to the dance floor. "How about you, Herzer?"

"Eh, nope, I have a prior engagement with Morgen here," he replied, standing up and holding out his hand. "Care to dance, milady?" he asked, sticking one leg out as he bowed with a flourish.

"Why certainly, sirrah," Morgen replied, snatching his hand and hoisting herself to her feet.

Herzer danced with Morgen for nearly an hour, jigs and reels and square dances, until he felt he was going to drop. Somewhere in there he had partnered off with Courtney and at one point even with Shilan but eventually came back to Morgen. After that dance the female minstrel held up her fiddle in apparent surrender.

"We're taking a little break now," she said to the crowd as she wiped sweat dramatically from her brow. "So should you!"

Herzer started to walk away then saw Edmund coming out of the edge of the crowd. He put his hand on Morgen's arm to stop her and both of them saw Edmund walk over to the stage and wiggle his finger at the female fiddler. She raised an eyebrow in return. Edmund's opinion of minstrels had become a standing joke in the town. So it was with an expression of obviously humorous trepidation that she stepped across the stage and leaned down to listen to what he had to say. Herzer wasn't close enough to hear but he saw both her eyebrows raise in surprise and then she nodded, at which Edmund nodded in return. He walked to the edge of the stage and motioned to someone in the crowd. The short, dark man stepped out carrying a set of bagpipes. The minstrel had gotten the rest of the band together. As the man carrying the pipes mounted the stage she stepped to the front and raised her hands.

"Excuse me, folks, we've been requested to do one more number, but it's nay a dance tune," she said with a rueful chuckle. She shook the piper's hand and waited for him to inflate the bellows, then nodded the beat.

Herzer's skin went cold at the shivery sound of the pipes. He'd heard pipe music before and in general could take them or leave them. But this was unlike any tune he had ever heard. It reached down into him and grabbed something in his soul, something old and wild and terrible. His skin flushed cold and goosebumps came out on his arms as the rest of the band joined in. Then the female began to sing and with the first lyric he was gone.

> "Axes flash, broadsword swing,
> Shining armour's piercing ring
> Horses run with polished shield,
> Fight Those Bastards till They Yield
> Midnight mare and blood red roan,
> Fight to Keep this Land Your Own
> Sound the horn and call the cry,
> *'How Many of Them Can We Make Die!'*"

Herzer could almost swear he heard the sound of sword on shield and the hoarse bellowing of battle in the distance. He stood there transfixed as the song ended and then looked at Morgen openmouthed. She returned it with an unreadable expression.

"That was amazing," he said finally.

"I liked it," she said, still looking at him with an odd expression in her eye. "But when *you* were listening to it, you looked *really* weird."

Herzer thought about that for a second then nodded, a muscle working in his jaw.

"Somebody told me once that we all wear masks," he said quietly. "I think that song just strips some of mine away."

Edmund had mounted the stage by then. He looked at the minstrel and nodded in approval then raised his hands above his head for quiet.

"OYEZ! OYEZ!" some of the people in the crowd shouted. Then in the back of the crowd there was a stentorian bellow of: "AT EASE!"

"Thank you, Gunny," Edmund said to some scattered chuckles. "I have some announcements to make, a couple of things to cover. And I'd like thank these, uhm . . . players here for getting everyone's attention for me." Over the scattered laughter Herzer considered not so much *what* Edmund was saying but *how*. The crowd was large and not entirely silent. Furthermore there were no acoustical effects to assist him. But he somehow pitched his voice to carry all the way to the rear of the crowd. Herzer wasn't sure how he had done it, but it was a darn good trick.

"Many of you are in the familiarization program also called the apprenticeship program," Talbot said. "The final schedules for that have been determined and posted. They cover all except for the last two weeks, which are going to be military training, including familiarization with longbow and other weapons. This will be in the last two weeks of training, at the end of which you will be given your final scores for the courses, and masters from some of the crafts will accept applications from those of you who they feel have some talent in the craft. Also at that time applications will be taken for the Raven's Mill Defense Force and persons who have shown aptitude in that area can apply.

"For everyone who is in the apprentice courses or not, you should be aware that the portion of the agreement that everyone made when arriving at Raven's Mill relating to defense of Raven's Mill was not just lip service. One of the things that the smiths are working on very hard right now is the production of defense weapons, primarily spears. Over the last two weeks the town council has been working on a charter for Raven's Mill and it will be presented next week. But one of the features of the charter that everyone should be aware of is a requirement that a person be skilled in one or more weapons of defense in order to be an eligible voter." At that there was a burst of surprised talking, although not as much as Herzer expected. It was pretty clear that many people either knew of the rule or expected it to be included. Edmund raised his hands to call for silence and waited until most of the talking had died down.

"The only exception to this are those who can show that they have clear philosophical or religious objections to violence. In which case they will be required to take training in the care of combat casualties. Everyone in this town *will* be prepared to defend it. Many of you had things taken from you by force when you were traveling here. Others still worse problems," he said, gazing from person to person in the crowd.

"Historically once bandits find that the pickings are slim on roads, they begin attacking towns. We *will* be prepared to defend this town. To emphasize this, Sheida Ghorbani is calling a constitutional convention with the intent to reconstitute the North American Union. It is my strongly held opinion, supported by Sheida and other council members, that this requirement, to be capable of defending one's self and the community, be a universal requirement within the North American Union."

"The fact is that we are in the midst of a civil war. It seems right now that we are not, but just as we are recovering and preparing, Paul and his faction are recovering and preparing. At the moment, the Council is fighting the Council, but that battle is effectively stalemated. So, in time, they will come for us. And we will be prepared. You have all gone through much hardship and these may seem somber thoughts for a day devoted to celebration. But they are important thoughts, things that we should all be thinking and talking about. And making our personal decisions. So that when the time comes for you to vote on these questions, you can vote with understanding and knowledge.

"And to tell you the truth I think that's enough to put on your plate for now. You should have plenty to talk about," he ended with a smile. "So as soon as these . . . uh . . . players get their breath back, you all go back to having a good time. Take care." He waved again and started to step down from the stage but turned back and raised his arms. "Oh, by the way, this requirement extends to minstrels!" At that there was a general laugh.

"Yeah? Well I swing a mean fiddle case," the redhead replied, swinging the case of her violin around her head.

"Well, we'll just see how you do with an axe," Edmund replied and stepped down from the stage.

A crowd had already gathered around Edmund so Herzer didn't feel it was the time to ask his questions. Instead he and Morgen wandered back to the patch by the stream that had been claimed by their group.

"He's right, that *is* a lot to talk about," Courtney said, flopping to the ground and leaning back against the balks of timber.

"Oof! North American Union!" was all Cruz said, shaking his head.

"Yeah, that's some deep stuff," Mike agreed.

"Well I don't think that it's right that everyone should have to use weapons," Morgen said angrily. "I don't have any interest in killing people. Or even hurting them."

"What if they are interested in hurting you?" Shilan asked quietly.

"Why would they hurt me?" Morgen challenged. "What have I done to them? If everyone starts getting ready for a fight, sooner or later you're going to have one!"

"People don't have to have a *reason* to hurt other people," Herzer said. "They just have to be the kind of people that enjoy it."

Shilan looked at him oddly for a moment then nodded.

"Listen to Herzer," she said.

"I take it you had trouble on the trip?" Courtney asked.

"Yeah," Shilan replied, sharply.

"What happened?" Morgen asked.

"I do not choose to discuss it," Shilan said. She wrapped her arms around her knees, pulling them tight to her and looking into the distance.

Cruz's face tightened as a muscle worked in his jaw. Then he looked off to the side.

"I'm sorry, Shilan," Morgen said. "I'm sorry for whatever happened to you. But I still don't agree. Violence never settles anything."

Herzer snorted and tried unsuccessfully to turn it into a laugh.

"What?" Morgen snapped.

"Sorry . . . sorry . . ." he said, still trying not to laugh. "I was just . . . thinking. Maybe you ought to ask the Melcon AI if violence ever settles anything. Or the Carthaginian Senate or the Islamic Jihad."

"What are you talking about?" Morgen asked.

"Have you ever heard of the Melcon AI?"

"Yes, I've heard of the Melcon AI."

"Does it still exist?" Herzer asked with a smile.

"No. It was destroyed in the AI wars," Morgen said, standing up and putting her hands on her hips. "But this is the forty-first century not the thirty-first! Surely we've risen above that, wrestling in wars like boys on a playground!"

"This we defend," Herzer said, shaking his head. "Or not, as the case may be," he continued, looking at Shilan.

"What he is trying to say is, people have always been violent," Courtney interjected. "There have always been wars and as long as we stay human beings there will always *be* wars. The period of the last thousand years was a golden age. And it would be nice to go back to that. But if the cost of going back to that is letting Paul decide what is right and wrong . . . You can try to limit it by diplomacy but the diplomacy has already broken down. It broke down in the Council hall. When Paul attacked Sheida."

"Well, we only have *her* word for that," Morgen pointed out.

"Oh, good God," Courtney replied, throwing her hands up in the air. "Herzer, you try."

"Nope ain't gonna do it," Herzer replied. "Morgen, you can say that you just want to sit this out. That's fine. But people aren't going to let you sit it out. You can choose to leave Raven's Mill. I'm sure that there are going to be communities that are not going to enforce the requirements. You can even say that you have strongly held philosophical objections and train to handle casualties. But if you go elsewhere, to a community that says they just want to be neutral or 'violence never settles anything' sooner or later Paul's forces will take you over and not ask your opinion. Or you'll be in the way of Sheida's forces and they'll take you over and not ask your opinion. I for one am not going to let Paul Bowman tell me how to run my life. I know enough history to understand what that road leads to. And I would rather sit here on the ground in the rain and eat maggoty bread than allow him to gain absolute power over Mother."

"But there's no way to fight him!" Morgen said. "He's a council member! They're all council members. Let *them* fight!"

"It's stalemated," Herzer said with a shrug. "And Bowman wants the entire world under his sway. He is going to come for you, Morgen. And for me and Shilan. Because he thinks it's the *right* thing to do. It's his mission in life. You can sit on one side or you can sit on the other. But if you sit in the middle, you're just going to get trampled."

"That's just . . . paranoia," Morgen said, stamping her foot. "You're all . . . warmongers! And you can just go to hell, Herzer Herrick!" With that she stomped away.

"Not bad, Romeo," Cruz said, leaning back. "Pick her up in the morning, have your way with her all afternoon and she's gone by evening. Not bad!"

Shilan took this opportunity to hit him in the shoulder as hard as she could with a week's worth of built up muscle.

"Ooow! Jeeze!"

"Less than you deserve," Courtney said.

"I was just *joking*," Cruz replied, rubbing his arm.

CHAPTER TWENTY-FOUR

After the argument Herzer hung out with the rest of the group as the afternoon descended into twilight. Two oxen had been roasting all afternoon and the evening meal was a communal barbecue. Reenactors who had either gotten quickly reestablished or who were permanent residents of Raven's Mill had contributed various side dishes. Herzer got his first taste of cream corn and collard greens and decided that he could live with them. But what mostly surprised him was the incredible diversity. Before the Fall, finding or inventing different food had been an almost universal pastime. For all that there was a sameness. Before the Fall, all dishes were blazingly *hot,* some to the point of insanity. The only difference seemed to be what type of acid was included, whether you got the delightful piquancy of sulfuric or the there and gone nuclear attack of fluoric.

These foods on the other hand had so much more diversity, not only in the secondary spices that they used but in the very fact that many of them didn't taste as if they were going to eat the insides off their containers. Some were *dreadfully* hot. He had a few bites of a cabbage dish and after a chewing on it for a moment he wondered why it hadn't eaten the spoon. But many of the others were not spicy at all. They were sweet or delicately flavored with subtle herbs.

He was spooning down mushrooms that had had simply been sautéed in butter, wine and just a hint of some herb, absolute ambrosia, when Shilan sat down next to him with two cups in her hand.

"Master Edmund has graciously agreed to let the town raid his wine cellar," she said, handing him a cup.

Herzer took a small sip and inhaled gratefully. The wine was heavy and sweet, with an almost earthy aftertaste and a decided kick.

"Ummm. This is good," Herzer said, setting down the cup and spearing more mushrooms.

"Are you referring to the mushrooms or are you being existentialist?" Shilan asked.

"Well the mushrooms, yes," Herzer replied, holding out some on the fork. "But what I really meant was this, here." He shrugged as she leaned forward and delicately pulled the mouthful off, nodding her head in agreement. "Better than being out in the woods."

"Not better than it was a month ago," Shilan said darkly.

"Yes, true," Herzer said, pushing the remaining mushrooms around. But there was an odd thoughtful frown on his face.

"Penny for your thoughts," Shilan said, cocking her head to the side with a smile. But then she laughed.

"What?"

" 'Penny for your thoughts,' " Shilan replied. "How old is that saying?"

"Yes," Herzer said, chuckling. "I mean, are you offering to pay a lot of money, or very little? It all depends on the value of the penny."

"I am willing to pay a lot for your thoughts, Herzer," she said, leaning forward again and looking him in the eye.

"Hmmm . . ." he replied with a frown. A muscle in his left cheek worked for a moment. "You said that it was better a month ago and I agreed."

"Sure," she said with a slight shrug. That reality was inarguable.

"Yes . . . and no," he said, the muscle working again. "This . . . this . . ." he said, waving his arms around at the groups talking and eating; in the distance was faint laughter.

"This is two things that were not a month ago," he continued. "One, it is *real*. It is not some Renn Faire where if the ground is too hard you can port in a pillow, and when it gets too late you can port home. This is real. If you want a pillow, you had better go out there and figure out a way to make a pillow. I don't know *why* that is important, but I can feel it in my soul." He held up his hand as Shilan started to say something.

"Hang on a second," he said. "Give me a little bit. The

second thing is that it has *soul*. Before, did you ever see so much passion? So much intensity out of people as you see today? No. Why? Because this is *real*. Before, before the Fall, no matter what you were discussing, no matter what you were arguing, you knew that the next day you would be getting up and going back and doing more or less the same thing all over again. But the point was, you *knew* you were getting up! You knew that you were going to be *alive* the next day.

"Now, the questions are not *trivial*. Not only lives but *generations* depend upon them. These people know that not only for themselves, but for their children and the children that they *will* have, they must work and succeed. And that Mother will not *catch* them when they fall. That brings a passion and intensity to things that I have never seen before.

"Now if I could press a button and turn it back to the way that it was before, would I? Yes. But that does not mean that I would not have regrets. There is a soul to this, to everything thing here. A soul that did not exist before the Fall. So, yes and . . . no," he concluded, picking out one last mushroom. "Damn, it's cold."

"Wow," Shilan said, frowning. "That was like . . . a chit's worth!"

"Nah," Herzer laughed, shaking his head. "You know like . . . maybe a tenth."

"I begin to understand why you seem to have a girl on your arm whenever I see you, Herzer," she said, smiling.

"Maybe you could explain it to me. It's been a very recent and very unexpected thing. If you're talking about that philosophical wandering: Bast hadn't said a word to me until she walked up, looked me over like a piece of meat and told me that I needed a bath but otherwise I'd do."

"Hmmm . . ." Shilan replied thoughtfully. She took a sip of her wine and cleared her throat. "Speaking of baths . . ."

"They're probably packed." Herzer shrugged, taking a sip from his own cup.

"Nope, most people are still eating and sitting around," Shilan said.

Herzer looked at the crowd and had to admit that it *was* the vast majority of the town.

"If we *hurry*?" Shilan continued in a questioning tone.

"Okay," Herzer replied, then paused. "Don't baths . . ." he started then cleared his throat. "Don't the baths make you feel uncomfortable?" he finally said in an absolutely neutral tone.

"Yes," she said. "But it would be less so if you were along."

Herzer started to smile, then an alarm bell went off in his head.

"Shilan, uhm . . . Cruz . . ."

"Cruz doesn't have me staked out," she replied, tartly. "I'm not planning on bedding you, Herzer. The operative term here is 'bath.'"

"I'm aware of that," Herzer said, not sure if he was aware of it or not. "And you're aware of that. That the operative term is 'bath,' I mean. But Cruz's feelings *are* going to be hurt if we go wandering off."

Herzer suddenly realized, by the expression on Shilan's face among other things, that he was in a situation where he *was* going to piss *someone* off, either Cruz or Shilan or, possibly, both. Shilan was not taking his careful hints and Cruz was not going to accept his explanation. *Look, buddy, it was either have her all pissed off at me or you all pissed off at me. All it was was a* bath. *Okay, so I saw your girlfriend nekkid and you haven't yet. Big deal!* Nope. Definitely wouldn't work. And this image of an axe or a mallet descending upon his sleeping head, wielded by either Cruz or Shilan, kept flashing through his mind. Eenie, meenie, minie, moe. He finally came to the conclusion that if he was going to get bludgeoned to death *anyway*, he might as well see Shilan, who after all was a comely wench, naked before he died.

All of this flashed through his brain in well under a half a second, hardly a pause. He had just opened his mouth to seal his fate when he saw Rachel coming through the crowd.

"Hang on a second, there's a friend of mine," he said to Shilan, waving his arm. "Hi, Rachel! How've you been doing?"

"Hello, Herzer," she said, walking over with a slightly abstracted frown. "How are the hands?"

"They're fine," Herzer said, holding them up, palms outward to show the heavy calluses. "I think you guys have met, but I don't think you've met, met," he continued. "Hsu Shilan, Rachel Ghorbani. Rachel, Shilan."

"We met when you came out to the camp and gave us a briefing on . . . uhm . . ." Shilan said then paused.

"Mother has dredged up the ancient term 'feminine hygiene,'" Rachel said with a smile.

"Oh, Lord, you're not going to start talking about that, are you?" Herzer chuckled.

"I certainly hope not," Rachel replied. "What are you guys doing?"

"We were just headed over to the baths," Herzer said then paused awkwardly.

Rachel looked at both of them in the pause until Shilan chuckled.

"I think what he is avoiding saying is 'would you like to come along?'" Shilan explained.

"Well, two's company and three's a crowd," Rachel replied dryly. "And if it's just more company, I'm *truly* not interested."

"It's not like that . . ." Herzer started to say.

"What Herzer would be saying if he could get his foot out of his mouth is that he would appreciate a chaperone," Shilan said, pursing her lips.

"It's not like that either!" Herzer said desperately.

"So, what *is* it like?" Rachel asked, putting her hands on her hips. "First you go trotting off with Bast, then you're rolling around in the woods with one of the serving girls and next you're going to the baths with *two* women!"

"Hmmm, since you put it that way," Shilan said, standing up and putting her hands on her own hips. She gave Herzer a mock scowl. "Would you care to explain yourself?"

"Oh for pity's sake!" Herzer said, throwing his hands in the air. "How did I get myself into this?"

"I lured you into it if you'll remember," Shilan finally relented. "Come on, Rachel, it will be fun. And Herzer really would prefer someone else along. He's got this weird *thing* about me and Cruz."

"Who's Cruz?" Rachel asked.

"I'll tell you when we're up to our necks in hot water," Shilan said.

"Oh, all right," Rachel replied. "And I'll tell you all of Herzer's dirty little secrets."

"Deal," Shilan said, sticking out her hand.

"And I'll buy," Herzer added, heaving himself to his feet. "That way I can brag about getting two women in the bath with me with a straight face."

"If you do you will rue the day," Rachel warned.

The baths, while not deserted, were not overrun either. Having stored their gear and collected their receipts, they worked their way through the stations. Herzer was as careful as possible about keeping his eyes in his head but he had to admit that both of the girls were extremely pretty, with or without clothes. Shilan was long and cool with high pert breasts and carefully sculpted hips and bottom. There was just enough rounding there to draw the male eye, but it was understated enough to be fashionable. Rachel on the other hand was very near his ideal of the female form: high, firm, well-rounded breasts with just enough sag to really accentuate their shape, lovely ribcage, narrow but not tiny waist, rounded hips, not wide but definitely flaring out from the waist and the most perfectly rounded bottom he had ever seen.

Not for the first time he wondered how much of his liking for the form was early canalization; he had had a crush on Rachel since before he knew what to do about it. Almost all of his "heroines" to be rescued had looked somewhat like Rachel, complete to the red hair and blue eyes.

He was very cautious not to let them catch him glancing and was even more cautious to control the natural male reaction to the situation. As he turned around to finish rinsing off he started to recite the names of all the Spartans at Thermopylae. When that, initially, was insufficient, he started at the end and worked his way back. The mental attention to details other than perky breasts, pertly rounded bottoms and mons venus worked and by the time he had a towel wrapped around him it wasn't clear that he was evincing any interest at all. Then, of course, the sight of Rachel in a nearly transparent bath sheet caused him to start reciting again. The fact that the towel barely made it to the top of her thighs while being tugged down far enough to show a tremendous amount of cleavage, required that he concentrate on doing so in the order and nature of their deaths.

"Herzer, what are you muttering," Rachel asked.

"Military history," he said in an only slightly strained voice. "You first."

Looking at anything but the two girls who preceded him, he followed Rachel to a tub that was unoccupied. There were about ten people in the room scattered around in groups and more than one of the males watched the two girls with a healthy amount of interest.

"This is why I hate coming in here," Rachel said, turning around to sweep the other bathers with a glare, "I hate to be ogled." She waited until she was sure no one was looking and shifted the skimpy towel around so that she could use it as a shield as she lowered herself into the bath.

Herzer thought it was quite the most erotic thing he had ever seen.

"Well I don't ogle you," he said, primly.

"Well, of course not," she snorted. She lowered herself until everything from the neck down was submerged in water and let out a sigh. "We've known each other since we were kids; of course you don't look."

"Well, yeah," Herzer said, taking a covert deep breath and willing himself to utter flaccidity. Once he was sure he was under control he flipped the towel off with becoming modesty and lowered himself into the bath quickly.

"What about me?" Shilan asked, raising one eyebrow and smiling in what could be taken as invitation.

"You're a friend," Herzer replied with a shrug. *Down boy! Down! Bad boy!*

Shilan wrinkled her eyebrows and peered at him as if attempting to divine what his real answer was.

"Shilan," Herzer sighed. "Do you *want* to go to bed? Or more precisely, do you want to go to bed to have sex?" When her face closed down he nodded. "Even if I *was* interested, it would take a real son of a bitch to press you right now, right?"

"Yes," she said quietly.

"I am many things. Well . . . I *can* be a son of a bitch. But in this, I'm not willing to be."

She wrinkled a brow again and then nodded, accepting the statement but still puzzled.

"Herzer," Rachel said dryly, but looking at him in a very searching way, "always the paladin."

"Not . . . always," Herzer corrected with a grin. "Paladins don't get laid much."

Shilan laughed delightedly and even Rachel had to smile.

"Can anyone join this party or are only young folk allowed?"

The man who addressed them was small and wiry with a graying beard and bright blue eyes.

"Hello, Augustus," Rachel said. "Of course you can join us."

The man whipped off his towel immodestly and hopped into the water like a frog.

"These were a grand idea," he said, ducking his head under the water and coming back up blowing. "I'd prefer a leathern tun, but we haven't enough leather to make a decent shoe!"

"And, Lord knows, we've got wood," Herzer said, shaking his head ruefully.

"Augustus, this is Herzer Herrick and . . . Hsu Shilan. They're in one of the apprenticeship programs. Herzer, Shilan, Augustus Scharpf. He's one of the reenactors who's started an industry since the Fall, in his case, tanning. You'll probably be working with him sometime soon."

"And you've been cutting wood, have you?" Augustus asked, peering at them dubiously. He seemed to like what he saw for after a moment he nodded at them approvingly. "It's good that you've gotten experience in the woods, you'll be needing it!"

"Why?" Shilan asked. "I mean, we don't have any idea what we're going to be doing. I might never go into the woods again. I understand most people who were in period didn't."

"Well, there's period and period," Augustus said. "We're more early industrial pioneer than High Middle Ages. And I meant for the Great Hunt, lassie."

"The Great Hunt?" Herzer asked.

"Gee, ye hadn't heard," Augustus replied with a wink. "It'll be grand bonny fun."

Herzer contemplated Augustus' appearing and disappearing brogue for a moment then shrugged. "Anyone going to tell us what it is?"

"My father's brilliant idea to give Mother and me more work," Rachel replied.

"Ah, you know better than that, lassie," Augustus corrected. "T'was not Edmund, t'was Myron that had the idea."

"Point," Rachel admitted. "Okay, *Myron's* great idea to give us more work!"

"I said before that we had no leather," the tanner said, ignoring the change. "The point is we've few enough slaughter animals as it is; the hunters have been bringing some in, but not enough. We need meat, bones, hooves, everything that you get from slaughter animals. And skin of course.

"Okay," he said, splashing water on his face and grimacing. "I was a huckster before the Fall, one of the people who could make things to sell at the Faire. I made leather goods, custom order, all very nice, hand stitched and tooled. A hobby, really, but they were all hobbies, weren't they, I pick up a few energy credits, who cares?" he added with a grimace. "But the point is, I can go from a raw skin to tooled leather. *If I've got the skins!* Do you know what the hunters brought in all of last week?"

"No," Herzer said, fascinated by the diatribe.

"Two feral cattle, we're eating them now, six boar, five deer, a mess of furs, three turkeys and an emu. That's not enough *meat* for three thousand people and it's definitely not enough leather."

"Not to mention the other things," Shilan added with a smile.

"Ack! Aye!" Augustus replied, winking at her. "The hooves

for the glue! The bones for the tools and the fertilizer! And a fine mess of brawn for a pretty lady?"

"Brawn?" Shilan asked.

"Pig brains," Herzer replied without thinking. "Usually served in gravy."

"Yuck!"

"So we need more animals," Herzer said. "The Great Hunt."

"Yes, and . . ." Rachel replied. "There are people who are already lining up to be farmers. One thing that makes farming easier is if you've got animals as part of your farm. There are ferals in the woods so the idea is to gather some of those at the same time."

"And as my former . . ." Herzer paused for a moment. "Ladyfriend pointed out there are also tigers in the woods."

"Aye!" Augustus said, winking madly. "Un thet's were it sta'ts to get *interestin'*!"

"Ooo," Shilan said. "Now I begin to understand the comment about work for the doctors."

"Oh forget the tigers," Rachel shrugged, sitting up so her breasts were just under the water. Herzer tried very hard not to notice the interesting ripple effect from the shrug. "They're out there, but there are feral pigs all over the place."

"Pigs?" Shilan asked, wrinkling her brow. "What's the problem with pigs?"

"Oh, sure," Rachel said acidly. "Squeak, squeak, see the funny little pig, ah-hah-hah. Pretty and pink and fluffy. Wait 'til you see these things."

"Oh, I haven't seen them but I've heard of them," Herzer laughed. "Four hundred kilos of bristle and tusk. This is gonna be *so* much fun. When are they planning this? I think I'm going to have a broken leg."

"If you've got a broken leg, they put you on *skinning* duty," Rachel said.

"Broken arm?"

"Carrying buckets of slop."

"Agh! I've seen videos of a skinning out. No thank you. Yuck!"

"You should have run away with your lady friend," Rachel said.

"Which one?" Shilan asked with a malicious grin.

"Begorum boy!" Augustus cried. "How many do you *have*?"

Herzer just groaned and slid down until his head was under the water.

✧　　✧　　✧

Daneh looked up from the sweating young man on the cot and nodded at Edmund and the woman accompanying him. Daneh hadn't seen this particular reenactor before but she knew the type of old. The woman was about twenty kilos overweight, which with the current conditions and medical conditions before the Fall had required conscious work, and was loaded down with silver jewelry. Most of it consisted of zodiac signs or other occult objects and the rest consisted of crystals.

"Daneh, this is Sharron, she's a herbalist," Edmund said.

"I don't think this is the time, Edmund," Daneh said sharply, lifting up a bandage from the young man's arm and wincing at the condition of the wound underneath. The young man had run afoul of an axe-head and the wound had almost immediately started to fester; modern human immune systems were strong but the skin was one of the hardest areas for the systems to access. Now the infected area had gone green-brown with gangrene and if she didn't figure out some way to stop the spread it was going to kill him. Quick.

"Gangrene," the woman said, leaning forward and sniffing with a disgusted shake of her head. "There's naught an herb on earth that can cure that, you need sulfanomide or one of the cillins."

Daneh turned and looked at the woman sharply at which the herbalist gave a grin. "Didn't expect me to be dredging up those terms, did you doctor? But penicillin's naught but a mold and sulfanomide, well that's just tar that's been worked over, hey?"

"Do you have any?" Daneh asked.

"No, but I just got here," the herbalist said with a nod. "And I don't think either would work here. Have you tried debriding?"

"Yes, but it's getting ahead of us," she said, waving at a fly. The damned things got in no matter what you did and they had an unpleasant tendency to land on open wounds.

"Leave it," Edmund said suddenly, as she waved at another that was trying to land on the mangled flesh.

"What?" both of the women asked, then looked at each other sheepishly.

"Let's take this outside," Edmund said, gesturing to the end of the infirmary.

It wasn't much of an infirmary, just an open bay with some cots and a "surgery" on one end that mostly consisted of a well-scrubbed table and some tools that made her think more of the inquisition than medicine. But it was getting better. And if this "herbalist" knew what she was doing they might get better still. Daneh was well aware that her knowledge of medicines, how they were made or administered, was barely theoretical. But between them, if the woman really knew anything, they might make one decent preindustrial doctor. She waved the fly away against his protestations and laid a fresh bandage on the wound, then followed Edmund out.

"What about flies is *good*, Edmund?" she snapped as they got outside. "They carry every imaginable sort of filth!"

"Yes, they do," he said. "And they lay eggs in rotting flesh which turn into maggots. And what do maggots eat?"

Daneh stopped and thought for a moment then shook her head. "You want me to let maggots eat his flesh?!"

"Dead flesh, yes," Edmund said uncomfortably. "Look, I know it sounds crazy. And, really, they're supposed to be *raised* maggots, you raise them on *clean* dead flesh, meat. But we don't have time for that, do we?"

"No," Daneh said simply. "We're going to lose him if we don't stop it. The traditional response is high amputation to get ahead of the infection."

"Can you make any of the stuff you were talking about, fast?" Edmund asked Sharron.

"No," she replied. "I have to *find* penicillin mold, out of . . . millions of molds. I need dishes to make cultures. You can often find . . . tetracycline molds in old graves, but we don't have any of those either."

"Graveyard dirt?" Edmund said then shook his head. "The point is, maggots *do* work. We just have to worry about secondary infections."

"What about . . ." Sharron said, creasing her brow. "What about finding a handful in . . . something and washing them?"

"Ugh!" Daneh replied. "I think I'd rather let the flies land."

"Gangrene is an anaerobic infection anyway," Edmund said. "Keeping the wound open would help more than hurt, I think."

"Is there any way to . . . get more oxygen to it?" Sharron asked.

"Not short of a hyperbaric chamber," Daneh replied. "Or some way to separate out oxygen, which is a high-pressure, supercold method. I'm not even sure it would get past the pressure protocols."

"Sheida?" Edmund asked.

"She's refused to give up *any* power so far," Daneh said exasperatedly. "She has enough to go gallivanting all over, but none for *medicine*!"

Edmund shook his head at her in a meaningful way then sighed. "I think the maggots are the only choice."

"That and some minor bacteriofacients I can come up with," Sharron said. "There are some herbs. I can make up a wash pretty quickly. It won't be as good as antibiotics but it will help some."

"Do it," Daneh said. "Please. And we need to get you a lab set up. Edmund?"

"I'll see the glassier about getting the appropriate materials," he grimaced. "He's gonna love this on top of everything else."

"Tell him that he might *need* it soon," Daneh replied sharply. "That should center his thoughts nicely."

"Sharron knows other herbs and medicines as well," Talbot noted, carefully. "Including tansy."

"Not something I recommend, short of absolute necessity," the woman interjected. "It's terribly dangerous from all I've heard. But there are others. I have some poppy seeds so as soon as we can get some poppies growing we'll have opiates. Strong and addicting, but there's few painkillers that equal it. And then there's willow bark."

"That one I know," Daneh said with a chuckle. "But, really, that's about as far as I can go. That and cherry bark."

"I think you two will get on just fine," Edmund said. "I've got . . ."

"Other things to do," Daneh said dryly. "That's okay. See you tonight?"

"Hopefully," he answered, glumly. "You're finally back and we never see each other." With a nod he strode briskly away in the general direction of the town hall.

"Well, you at least get to sleep together," Sharron said with a sly wink.

"No, we don't," Daneh replied.

"But . . . well . . ." Sharron stopped with a puzzled frown.

"Leave it," Daneh said then shook her head. "Let me put it this way, I may be the first candidate to try tansy."

Sharron looked at her for a moment until she realized the doctor was serious then blanched. "Oh, my Goddess."

CHAPTER TWENTY-FIVE

The next morning there was quite a row between Cruz and Shilan. The reason Cruz had disappeared were some friendly gents running a dice game. He ended up losing every chit he had and hadn't even had enough for breakfast. The burgeoning relationship between Cruz and Shilan was most definitely off, in her opinion. And Herzer had to wonder just what he had missed by playing the paladin.

He wasn't able to find out, though, because Class A-5 was told off immediately to the sawmill. There was a short briefing in which they were solemnly informed that cutting and forming wood was the basis of industry in preindustrial civilization. They were so informed by John Miller, the sawmill manager, who was a somber and unsmiling man. When asked about the *source* of the wood, and whether *it* might be the basis of industry he had unsmilingly told them that any idiot could *cut* wood, but it took a true master to form it.

After a number of warnings about how hands and feet no longer could be regrown if you cut them off, the class was put to work sawing and forming the endless stream of logs that was coming from the surrounding forests. For the first few days all they did was move the logs, roll the logs, position the logs and eventually run them through the band saw. It was again backbreaking work using many muscles that had not been developed while cutting and there was very little time for interaction.

The class stayed in barracks a group of which had been

set aside for members of the apprenticeship program who were in and around the town. The barracks were segregated by sex so Herzer was unable to determine if Shilan had actually been interested or if she had just been playing around with him. Or, as was just as likely, playing him off against Cruz. He invited her to the baths one night but she pled a rain check on the basis of extreme fatigue. Given how he was feeling, it could have been an honest answer.

The last two days they were introduced to woodworking tools, including lathing and drilling. There Miller proved that although he didn't appear to like apprentices too much, he truly loved wood. He was a master at lathing and carving and didn't laugh at their efforts. He simply commented that he'd been doing it for seventy-five years and couldn't expect them to master it in one session.

At the end of the week they were paid off and only Mike got a bonus. He had shown a remarkable aptitude for woodworking and Miller had even smiled at one of his efforts. Herzer, on the other hand, could best be described as "inept." He personally used the term "ham-handed." When he wanted a deep chip he got small, when he wanted a small chip he got deep and when he tried to plane, he gouged. He and wood simply didn't get along.

The first day they had been shown around the mill and seen the wooden turbine water wheel, the sprockets, the joins, and he had marveled that Miller and a few other similarly skilled craftsmen had been able to assemble it in a bare two weeks with nothing but hand tools. He didn't have any particular envy for their mastery, but it was impressive.

As they were being paid off, he touched Shilan's arm and raised an eyebrow. "Bath?"

"Oh, Herzer . . ." she said.

He held up a hand to forestall a reply. "It's okay. I just wanted to know where we were at. Last week you seemed to imply that you wanted something more than just waving in passing."

"Herzer, I'm kind of tired most evenings," she said, frowning sadly. "And right now I'm just not ready for any kind of relationship."

"Cool!" he replied with a nod. "Neither am I."

"What?!"

"You don't want just a casual roll in the hay and I don't particularly want a long-term relationship," he said with a shrug. "Cruz did, but I don't. It's not that I want to play the field, it's just that I like you as a *friend*."

"Oh," Shilan said.

"I was trying to tell you without hurting your feelings. This makes it a lot easier."

"Oh."

"Friends?" he asked, sticking out his hand.

Shilan looked at it for a moment as if confused and then shook it absentmindedly. "Friends."

"Hey, I plan on going to dinner with Mike and Courtney. Want to come along?"

"Uh, no," Shilan said. "I'm going to . . . I've got to . . ."

"Okay," Herzer said, waving. "See you when I see you. Bye."

He walked over to where Mike and Courtney were waiting for him.

"So, you gonna get lucky, *again?*" Mike asked.

"Nope," Herzer replied. Now that his back was turned to Shilan he smiled evilly. "I told her I just wanted to be friends."

Mike turned his own back and grimaced. "Ooo! Score one for *guydom!*"

Herzer kept walking, forcing Courtney, who had put the boiler on the fire and was busy screwing down the pressure relief valve, to catch up to him.

"You told her that you just want to be friends and you *don't* want to be friends?" she asked, furiously.

"No, no, I told her that I want to be friends and I *do* want to be friends. But I also want to screw her brains out!"

"Yes, yes, *YES!*" Mike said. "The shoe is on the other toe!"

"Why didn't you just *tell* her?" Courtney asked.

"What, and give her the opportunity to play me off against Cruz? That seemed to me to be where she was going. That or dangle me around like a little *marionette*. I don't know if that was what she was like before or if it's from what happened on her trip. But she was trying to play squeaky-toy with me already in the baths. No *thank* you."

"Wow, that's almost as bad as a *woman*," Mike said, only to be punched in the shoulder.

"Ah! You strike me to the quick, sirrah!" Herzer replied, grasping at his chest. "Tis not as wide as church door, nor deep as a well. But t'will do, t'will do!"

"You're both terrible," Courtney said.

"That's why you love us, right?" Herzer replied with a smile.

"HERRICK," a voice called from behind them. Herzer turned around and practically came to attention.

"Ah, Sir . . . uh . . . Edm . . . Mayor Talbot!"

"Rachel tells me that you played games in enhanced reality,

specifically the Quest for the Third Throne. True?" Edmund said
without preamble. But he did grace Courtney and Mike, who
were standing by open-mouthed, with a nod.

"Yes, Sir Edmund!"

"Just yes will do," Talbot said with a chuckle. "You played
it as a paladin. True?"

"Yes . . . Mayor Talbot."

"That requires riding. Did you use a horse?"

"Yes, Mayor Talbot."

"Specifically, that requires some pretty God-damned tricky
riding for a paladin character."

Herzer had a sudden clear flashback of falling into an endless
chasm, as he went right and his wildly flailing, and neighing, mount went left off of a narrow foot bridge.

"Yes, sir, I did."

"And you used your mount throughout the quest?"

"Yes, sir, I did."

"Just Edmund. Did you complete the quest?"

"Yes . . . Mayor Talbot, I did."

"*With* your mount?"

"Yes."

"And how many tries did it take for you to get across the
'who is the son of a bitch who put this bridge here' bridge?"

"I didn't know it had a name, sir," Herzer said with a laugh.

"Yeah, I know," Edmund replied. "How many times."

"Four."

"How did you get your mount across?"

"Made a sling out of the ropes. Winched it across the chasm,
kicking and squealing."

Edmund thought about it for a moment and then chuckled. "Jesus. What did you do, bring pack mules in with gear?"

"More or less, sir."

"Have you ever ridden a *real* horse? Or a mule for that
matter."

"Well, those were real horses, sir."

"I mean one that wasn't kenned. One that was born and
raised and broken to the saddle."

"Once, sir."

"Any problems?"

"Not particularly, sir. Can I ask why you're asking?"

"Okay," Edmund replied. "That will do it for me. We're doing
the big hunt next week. Monday morning you need to report
to Kane, the horse master, at the big corrals by the bridge
while everyone else is spreading out to start the drive."

"Oh, Lord," Herzer said. "I'm afraid that means I'm not going to be mucking out."

"Oh, I'm sure there will be some of that. But we need horsemen to help control the animals and run messages. And *you're* on that detail!"

"Yes, sir," was all Herzer could say.

Herzer was muttering something under his breath as Edmund walked away.

"Hey," said Courtney, kicking him on the ankle. "What are you saying?"

"'Shit, shit, shit I'm gonna *die*.'"

Rachel looked up from her stew as her mother came into the kitchen. "Stew's on."

"Thank you, Rachel," Daneh said, picking up a bowl and ladling some out.

"How are you doing?" Rachel asked.

"I've started throwing up in the morning," Daneh replied, sitting down. "But not all day, thank goodness."

"Are you sick?" Rachel asked, alarmed. She couldn't imagine a worse situation for the town to be in than for their only trained doctor to have something incurable.

"No," Daneh said, directly. "I'm pregnant."

Okay, that's worse.

"How? When?" Rachel asked then clapped her mouth shut. "Oh, *Mother*."

"It's not the end of the world," Daneh said, taking a bite of the stew and nodding. "Not too shabby."

"Mother!"

Daneh sighed and shrugged her shoulders. "Bad things happen. Bad things happened to *me* and they are still happening in a way."

"What are you going to do?" Rachel asked, finally moderating her tone. She suddenly realized that she was in a real, honest-to-God "adult" conversation. And it seemed she needed to start acting like one. She suddenly wished her father was a girl. He would know what to say. "Am I going to have a little sibling? Or are you going to . . . do something about it?"

"What?" Daneh snapped. "Do *you* know how to do an abortion? I certainly don't! And how, exactly, am I supposed to do it on myself? There's tansy, but from the sound of it it can kill you. So what am I supposed to do about this . . . thing that is growing inside of me?"

"I don't know, Mother," Rachel said, quietly. "But from what

I've been reading, childbirth is not a given thing. I mean, we've both got the . . . hips for it, unlike some. But . . . I mean, you're the *doctor*. If something goes wrong with you, what can *I* do?"

"What can *I* do?" Daneh asked in exasperation. "I don't have any proper tools! I've never *attended* a body birth! There hasn't been one in a thousand years! What in the hell do *I* know about it? Why do you expect miracles from *me*?!"

"Mom, I don't," Rachel said, choking a hot retort. "But you at least have some idea what is going *on*. I don't even know that."

"Well, in that case, it's time you started learning," Daneh said after a moment of controlling her temper. "That's your new research project. Whether it's me, if I can't get rid of it somehow, or someone else. You're going to be the *expert* on the theory of childbirth."

"Mom, I'm a *virgin*," she shouted, suddenly out of temper. "You want *me* to be a childbirth expert?"

"Who better," Daneh replied with an evil chuckle. "At least we don't have to worry about you being out of commission. For the time being. I notice you've been spending a lot of time around Herzer."

"Oh, Herzer," Rachel said, averting her eyes and picking up her spoon. "He's just a friend."

"Right," Daneh snorted. "So was Edmund. And look what resulted from that."

Everyone was calling it the "Big Roundup" and the familiarization groups had been co-opted, along with just about everyone else in Raven's Mill, to participate. The reason for it was simple; hunters had confirmed that there was quite a bit of feral stock in the woods and much of it would be useable for the planned farms. The stocks of food were also dwindling faster than anticipated. The intent of the "roundup" was to push animals out of the forest and onto some of the open areas. There domestic animals that were useable would be separated and pushed into pens. "Wild" animals would mostly be either pushed on or killed in the area and preserved.

To do this required a massive organization. The area that Herzer and Mike had worked on clearing, with the buildings that they had constructed, was intended as a giant slaughtering yard. Fences were being built, and more would be. When the time came groups of beaters would move through the forests pushing the game ahead of them. It was hoped that in this way sufficient farm animals could be gathered for all the farms that were planned. And since the protofarmers themselves would participate in the drive, there would be less of a stink about them getting the animals for "free."

Two reenactors, a husband and wife from down the valley, had moved most of their herd of horses up the valley to Raven's Mill. The reason was simple. Shortly after the Net dropped, all the controls on wild beasts had been released. Besides attacks on humans this had resulted in even more attacks on domestic herds. After losing a foal to what was probably a panther and having a horse badly clawed by a tiger, they had decided to relocate.

Horses were material and cost intensive. They needed either fodder or fairly large areas to graze. Although there had been nearly sufficient grazing at their home, it still would have been overgrazed by their large herds in the winter. But Edmund had agreed to cede a large pasture to them in return for using their horses as a base for the still nascent Raven's Mill cavalry. After thinking about it for quite some time—use as cavalry would mean some of their babies probably would not be coming home—they had agreed.

Before that, though, the horses would play an important part in the roundup. Although they would not be able to move in the trees, the area that the game was going to be pushed into was a recently cleared area across the river from Raven's Mill. It was hoped that between the horsemen and various half-trained reenactors it would be possible to sort the different species and then hold them in herds for further disposition.

The problem with that was there were not nearly enough trained horsemen.

And thus Herzer's detailing by Edmund.

As Herzer walked towards the corrals he looked the herd over. There were two distinct "types" of horses and he didn't know enough about them to know what breeds they were. One type was small and light-boned. When these trotted or reacted to the other horses they tended to trot with their legs held high, their necks and tails up. The trot looked like Bast dancing as the horses seemed to float across the ground.

The other breed was much larger and heavier bodied but it had some of the same grace as the smaller. When these trotted it wasn't quite as showy, but Herzer noticed that the trot itself looked . . . smoother. It wasn't as dancing as the first ones. And these were definitely fast. He saw one of the younger horses, a beautiful red one that he knew was called "chestnut" for some reason, dash from one side of the pasture to the other, apparently from sheer high spirits, and he was *very* glad he wasn't on its back.

There were two women and about ten men gathered by the fence to the pasture, looking at the herd and talking in low tones when Herzer walked up. The tallest of the men looked over at him and nodded. The man was wearing an outlandish period costume. From the feathered hat, topping graying brown hair that dropped halfway down his back, through the pointed mustache, and open, lace-front shirt to the thigh-high boots he was *clearly* a reenactor, but he also seemed to be in charge.

"Good day, sir," Herzer said, looking out at the horses. "I'm looking for the horse master."

The man grinned at that and laughed. "Well, I'm the *owner* of the horses," he replied. "And for my sins Talbot's put me in charge of rounding up whatever comes out of the woods. Now, I don't know if Edmund is aware of this but pigs don't herd worth a damn. Nor do deer. And I've only this dozen riders, none of whom has ever tried to herd with horses. But if you're looking for the 'horse master' I guess that's me. Kane," he said, sticking out his hand.

"Herzer Herrick," Herzer replied, sticking out his.

"This is Alyssa my wife," he said, touching the shoulder of the blond woman next to him. She was thin and wiry with a friendly, sun-weathered face. She too stuck out her hand.

"What can we do for you?" she asked in a furry voice.

"I've ridden before," Herzer replied. "I was training in reenactor combat before this happened," he added waving his arm around.

"Virtual reality?" Kane asked dubiously.

"Enhanced," Herzer corrected.

"Oh, so you *know* how to ride a *horse*," the man laughed broadly. "Not just think you do."

"Well, I've *ridden*," Herzer corrected. "A bit."

"Did you fight on horseback?" the horseman asked. "Or just ride a bit?"

"I was starting training in cavalry combat," Herzer admitted. "But it was . . . tough."

"Yeah, that it is," Alyssa said. "Everybody thinks it's easy until they try."

"Well, what's say we try you out on one of the boys," Kane said looking at his wife. "One of mine I think?"

"Oh, yes," the woman replied. "Mine could take him, but he's more suited to yours."

"What's this 'yours and mine' thing?" Herzer asked as Kane led him to a nearby shed.

"We brought both our herds down," the man explained. "Mine are Hanarahs and hers are Arabs. Do you know the difference?"

"I've seen them," Herzer said, gesturing at the herd.

"The Arabs are the little ones and the Hanarahs are the big ones," Kane said with a nod. "Do you want to know the rest?"

"How much?" Herzer said with a chuckle. "Lately I feel like my brain is getting overloaded!"

"Been in the familiarization program?" Kane asked, opening the door to the shed. Inside, saddles were hanging on boards that thrust out from the walls, and on the back wall was a series of pegs from which hung bridles and reins. Under the reins was a pile of blankets. The room had an odd, musty odor composed of old leather and horse sweat that was not unpleasant but definitely strong.

"Yes," Herzer said simply, taking the saddle that was thrust at him. He noticed that it had a high back and a low front. He had used similar saddles in his training, but with a higher front. He had no clue what the different parts were named except for the stirrups.

"Well Arabs are a very old breed. They've never been genengineered," Kane explained. "Nobody knows exactly where they came from but they were distinguished by being light of body, very human oriented, extremely fast and with great endurance. They also are missing one vertebrae which gives them less of a tendency to get 'swaybacked.'"

He grabbed a blanket and piled it and reins on Herzer's arms. "There, all set."

"Okay."

"There were originally basically two strains of horses, hotbloods and coldbloods, with me so far?"

"Yep."

"Hotbloods come down to Arabs. Coldbloods were found in Ropasa and were heavier bodied, relatively slow horses. They got bred up for size in the preindustrial period and worked well as cart horses and the like. But for a good cavalry horse you have to have speed and agility. So at some point, they started breeding Arabs into them and came up with a third strain called 'warmbloods.'"

"Hanarahs?" Herzer guessed as Kane led the way back outside.

"Hanarahs *are* warmbloods of a sort. But no matter how they worked, some of the qualities of Arabs just never took in warmbloods, notably the lack of that one vertebra. And they'd tend to get horses that were fast *or* had good stamina. Or if they were fast with good stamina, they were very delicate, had to have the right foods, that sort of thing."

"Hanarahs *are* genegineered," Herzer said definitely.

"Not quite from the ground up but pretty damned close," Kane admitted. "Incredible stamina, better than Arabs really, very friendly, damned protective, fierce to enemies and gentle as a lamb to a child. They're blindingly fast, can live on practically anything . . ."

"Superhorses," Herzer said, putting his saddle on the top of the corral fence.

"Not quite, but as close as the designers could get," Kane said. "I guess we'll find out how well they did."

"Are they sentient?" Herzer asked. They looked at least on the close order.

"Not hardly," Kane snorted. "What a dumb idea. As if any sentient being is going to let someone ride on their back day in and day out. And if they don't, and you coerce them, what's that?"

"Slavery?" Herzer guessed.

"Got it in one," Kane said. "Sentient horses. Give me a nice, not too dumb, nonsentient horse any day. So you can't talk with it, big deal. It also doesn't talk back. More than balances out, trust me."

"They look like the kind that I rode in my training," Herzer said.

"Probably were. Well written scenario if so." Kane put his fingers to his lips and whistled a complex arpeggio. At the sound the young chestnut that Herzer had seen tearing around the pasture came running in a broad canter, dodging through the herd like a gymnast.

"Oh, goody," Herzer said. "Now you're going to give the newbie the unrideable horse."

"Not at all," Kane said seriously. "That's a stupid trick; we can't afford any more injuries than we've already had. Diablo is gentle as a lamb."

"Diablo?"

"Look, we've got nearly sixty horses to name, you run *out*."

He leaned forward and stroked the horse on the muzzle, then gave it a small treat.

"They *like* people," Kane said. "But getting them to come

to you requires some incentive. Especially since this one's smart enough to see the saddle and know what's coming."

"He doesn't like to be ridden?"

"Would *you* like a hundred kilos or so thrown on your back?" Kane said, expertly slipping in the bridle. "You could probably ride him with a hackamore, but we'll start with the bridle."

He brought the horse out of the pasture, having to slap back two others that tried to bolt for it, and led it around to where the saddle sat.

"Go ahead and saddle him up while we get ready," Kane said. "There are a couple of other people who haven't had much recent experience and we were all going out for a trail ride to get broken in again."

"Uhmm . . ." Herzer temporized looking at the horse. It looked back at him with a decidedly intelligent expression that seemed to say *"Oh, My God. I've got a Newbie."*

"Yes?"

"I don't know how to saddle one," Herzer admitted.

"Let me guess," Kane said with a laugh. "They always appeared fully saddled and with their barding on?"

"Yep."

"Paladins. There ought to be a bounty on them. Okay, no problem. But watch so you'll know the next time."

CHAPTER TWENTY-SIX

Herzer returned to the corral tired and sore. The trail ride had turned out to be far more involved than simply riding along in a group chatting. They had started off that way and had taken the horses for a long tour of the area, including a ride through Raven's Mill. Then, apparently with Myron's permission, they had spent some time pushing his small herd of cattle around and attempting, with mostly laughable failure, something called "cutting out." Using only the horses, they were supposed to pick one member out of the herd and move it away from the rest. Supposedly, in the *really* old days, this had been so regular and common as to be without notice. Not so here. The cattle would hardly break up when the horses approached and when they did start running they tended to stay together. Trying to get into the herd and push a single individual out turned out to be nearly impossible for most of the riders. The exceptions were Kane, Alyssa and, strangely, Herzer.

The Arabs, which two of the men and one of the women were riding, seemed to take a strange delight in herding the cows. But with the exception of Alyssa, none of the others could get a single individual cut out. Alyssa was able to control her mount well enough, using mostly knee control and shifting weight, to manage the feat at least once. Kane, likewise, was able to control his mount to do the work.

In Herzer's case, he swore Diablo was prescient and, like the Arabs, the young stallion seemed to enjoy the herding.

All that Herzer had to do was get him pointed at the right cow and let him do the work.

After a sweat-soaked hour of running cows around—Myron came over while it was going on and remarked that they'd probably run a month's grazing off the herd—they headed back to the corrals. But the day wasn't over. They rode, mostly at a canter, back to the corrals and had a light lunch. Then Kane produced implements for a sport he called "Cowboy Polo" and broke them into two teams. The object of the game was using long mallets to strike an inflated rubber ball about a third of a meter across and drive it from one end of the massive pasture to the other, then through a small "goal" designated by two fence posts.

They played that for the rest of the day, changing horses twice although never people, and by the end of the day Herzer was exhausted but satisfied. He had played on Alyssa's team and while they had lost, four goals to Kane's team's six, he had scored three of the goals.

Again Diablo, who had played almost half the game, seemed to have a knack for running down the balls. It was like the chase game with the cows in a way. In the brief intervals between "chukkers" Kane had explained the genesis of the game. Supposedly it had been invented by the ancient Mongols and the original "balls" had been severed human heads. He also said that the usual "ball" used was about the size of a human fist. Having mis-hit the much larger ball any number of times, Herzer had as much disbelief in that as the human head story.

He had fallen off, been "unseated" as Kane put it, only once and had remembered to fall as "bonelessly" as possible. His prior combat training had come to the fore permitting him to turn the fall into a roll.

"You need to get right back up," Kane said, riding over. "If you fall off and you don't get right back up, you'll have one hell of a hard time riding again, ever."

Herzer shook his head to clear it and then nodded, "Get right back up. I'll remember," he said muzzily.

When he got back up the replacement for Diablo had been patiently waiting, cropping at some of the sparse grass on the recently cleared field. So he had remounted and gotten back in the game.

However, at the conclusion, he wasn't sure he ever wanted to see a horse again. Unfortunately, he desperately needed a bath and to have his clothes washed. And while riding over to the baths was an unpleasant prospect, walking over was about the only thing worse that he could imagine.

Kane had *told* them to go get a bath and to take a horse if they wanted to. Obviously the intent was not only to get the smelly, sweaty group cleaned up but to get them some more practice riding, so Herzer reluctantly walked over to the corral after the last chukker and whistled up Diablo.

The horse looked at least as uncertain about being ridden as Herzer felt about riding, but he soothed the animal with scratches and finally got the saddle on and adjusted. Riding over was very unpleasant but when he thought about walking he had to admit that riding was at least *shorter*.

There were at least six others headed over to the baths at about the same time. All the other riders, however, were reenactors who were old friends of Kane and Alyssa. While they didn't deliberately cut Herzer out of the conversation most of it was so "in" that he couldn't even keep up with the names so he just rode along in silence, nursing his various hurts.

At the baths he gladly handed his now dry but crusty clothes over to the ubiquitous Darius and headed for the baths. He had parked Diablo around the corner on a long enough lead that he could crop some grass and when they got back the horse was due for a good feed and a roll.

He scrubbed hard in the cold water of the showers and then nearly screamed when the hot water struck his raw spots. But the pain quickly subsided and as the heat penetrated all his abused muscles it induced a pleasant euphoria that lasted for some time. By the time he felt he could drag himself out of the bath it was dark and the kitchens were nearly closed. He got his clothes, trotted down on Diablo—sensibly riding high in the stirrups to protect his abused bottom—and got some of the last of the scraps. After that he rode back to the corrals, fed his horse, brushed it down, got it a good feed, put away his gear and staggered off to the building designated as a bunkhouse. He found his basket in the dark, rolled out his fur and was asleep practically before he could get his boots off.

"Edmund," Sheida said, appearing in his office as the town council filed in the door.

"Sheida, we're busy here," Edmund said. "Could you just *call* me or something? Maybe, just once, leave a message?"

The rest of the council stopped, shocked, at the sight of him chewing out a council member but Sheida just nodded in sympathy.

"I'm starting to forget that people *don't* split," she sighed, stroking the image of her flying lizard. "I'm sorry, Edmund."

"What is it this time?" he asked, still exasperated.

"I've freed up enough energy to have virtual meetings for the constitutional convention and more important, for the writing of the first draft. I want you to be on it."

"Great I'll slide that in my free time between figuring out how to feed three thousand people and defending them from raiders."

"Is it that bad out there?" she asked, frowning.

"McCanoc is back," he growled. "He burned Fredar."

"Oh," she said, shaking her head. "I don't know how that one passed me by. But it's not the first by a long stretch."

"Nor will it be the last," Edmund agreed. "And we may be next."

"Do you know his current location?" she asked. "He has come up . . . at a higher level lately."

"No, somewhere west of Fredar on the plains presumably," Edmund said. "When is this meeting?"

"When would be convenient?" she asked, looking around and nodding at the council members. "Sorry for taking your time."

"No problem." "Quite all right . . ."

"Tomorrow evening?" he asked.

"Eightish?" she said, glancing in the distance. "That will . . . work. See you then," she added and vanished.

"To have the power . . ." Deshurt said.

"I wouldn't want her headaches," Talbot responded. "Okay, if you'll all grab a seat, the first order of business is another crack at the banking code . . ."

"Rachel," Daneh called as her daughter was heading out the door of the infirmary. It had been a long day at the infirmary, it was late and Rachel was due some time off. But she had put this off long enough.

"Yes?" Rachel said.

"Could I talk to you for a minute?" Daneh asked, waving at her office. "It's not . . . I just need to ask you a question."

Rachel furrowed her brow quizzically but followed her mother into the office.

"You've been talking to more people than I have," Daneh said, when the door was closed. "One of the things that should be done about the women who were raped is they should talk about it."

"I wasn't, Mother," Rachel said, looking at her with a frown. "Or . . . do you want someone to talk to?" she said with a worried tone.

"Well, yes, but not you, dear," Daneh said with a chuckle. "I was wondering if you knew . . . anyone who might want to talk."

Rachel thought about it for a moment and shrugged. "Yes. That is, I know some girls who . . . had a bad time on the trip. I haven't tried to draw any of them out about it. Should I?"

It was Daneh's turn to frown in thought but then she shrugged. "Talking about it is very important for healing. But what I was wondering was, could you ask some of them to maybe meet *me* in the evenings? One of the important things I learned from Bast is that . . . there are odd thoughts and feelings that are lingering presences of the rape. I think it's about time that some of us who have had that experience share it with each other and start to try to . . . heal."

"Oh," Rachel said. "I'll . . . see what I can find out."

"Thank you," Daneh replied with a smile. "Do you have any idea how much you have changed . . . grown, since the Fall?"

"Sometimes I feel a thousand years old, if that's what you mean," Rachel sighed.

"You know," Daneh said, leaning back in her chair. "I'm your mother. We can talk about things other than work."

"It's okay, Mom, really," Rachel replied. "It's nothing as . . . big as what you have to work through. Just the same problem everybody has. I keep wishing that it would all go back the way it used to be, you know?"

"Yes, I do," Daneh said, sadly. "Do you ever whisper 'genie' to yourself? I know I do."

"Sometimes," Rachel replied with a nod. "Sometimes when I can't get to sleep I just imagine that we're all back the way we used to be." Her face worked for a moment and she shook her head. "I hate this world. Sometimes I wish I'd never been born!"

"Don't wish that," Daneh said, shaking her head. "I love you and the world would be a sadder place if you weren't in it. Know that. It's okay to grieve for what we've lost. But don't wish you hadn't existed. You have a long life to live and there is still joy to be found. Friends to cherish and love. Maybe even a boyfriend, hmmm? Edmund and I would like a grandchild some day."

"I'm a little young for that, Mother," Rachel said.

"Aren't we all," Daneh said, rubbing at her belly. "It's odd to know that there's something growing inside of me. I've been awfully tired lately, and I think that's part of it. But, even knowing that half of it is . . . from *them,* half of it is from *me.* And . . . I cannot find it in me to hate the child unborn."

"So . . . you're going to keep it?" Rachel asked.

"Well, even if there weren't some very serious dangers involved in getting rid of him or her," Daneh said, "I think the answer is: Yes. I'm going to keep him. Or her. I don't think I could do anything else. It's a child and I can't find it in me to kill a child."

"Okay," Rachel said. "If that's how you feel. I'm a little . . . intimidated by the whole idea. You know there are risks to *you,* right?"

"They're risks that women have faced for countless ages," Daneh shrugged. "Just because we were rid of them for a while, doesn't mean I should run away from them. And . . . neither should you."

"I have to find the right guy," Rachel replied with a frown. "That hasn't happened, yet."

"Herzer is . . . nice," Daneh said, carefully.

"Herzer is . . . Herzer," Rachel said with a frown. "And . . . he's not what I'm looking for. He's a good friend but . . . just a friend."

"So was your father," Daneh replied. "Until I got over thinking that I had to have something *besides* a friend. I'm not telling you to throw yourself at Herzer, but don't ignore an opportunity because the person is a 'friend.'"

"Okay, Mom," Rachel replied then paused. "Can I ask a question? And I know it's none of my business but . . ."

"Your father and I are . . . getting along," Daneh said, frowning slightly. "It has been . . . difficult. The first time . . . after was hard. Probably as hard on him as it was on me in a way."

"I'm not sure that I'm up to details about my parent's sex life, Mom," Rachel said in a choked voice. "I'm sorry. I was just wondering if you guys were okay?"

"We're okay, now," Daneh said with a chuckle. "And, I can see we're reaching the end of this little chat. Seriously, talk to me from time to time. I need a friend, too."

"I will, Mom," Rachel said, getting up and going around the desk to give her mother a hug. "I'll see you tomorrow, okay? And I'll always be your friend."

Edmund had just composed himself in his favorite chair when Sheida appeared.

"Ready?" she asked.

"Let's get to it," Edmund said and was immediately, apparently, transported to a large room filled with about ten other members. Some of them he recognized immediately; others were strangers.

"Thank you all for volunteering your time to this," Sheida said, waving her lizard away. The reptile took off from her shoulder and then apparently vanished as it left the zone she was broadcasting. "I think this first meeting should cover general principles of what we're trying to do. I think I'll let Edmund speak to that first. Edmund, please introduce yourself."

"I recognize some of you and others I don't know," Edmund said. "So I'll give my general background. I have what was once referred to as a doctorate in political science and another in military affairs. My specialty is preindustrial societies and militaries. In addition I have been a reenactor for much of my life. I'm currently the mayor of Raven's Mill, which is a growing survivor society in the Shenan Valley. Working under their aegis and agreement I'm here to propose that the original Constitution of Norau be enacted with minimal amendments and with all rights of the citizens kept intact. *All* rights."

The rest were introduced and most of them were from similar communities although two were working directly with the Council in projects. All agreed, in principle, that the original Constitution be enacted, but all had some reservations.

"Edmund," Sheida said, coming back to him again. "What changes would you enact?"

"The first that I would suggest is a stronger wording of the right to own weapons. That it be added that it is for self-defense, defense of the community and for protection from unconstitutional acts of the government. Furthermore it should be the *duty* of all citizens of military age to own and show capability of use of weapons."

"I have a strong objection to that," the delegate from Chitao town said, frowning. "We've had homesteads burned out by brigands already. I don't see why they should have weapons or the right to them."

"Are they citizens of the community?" Edmund replied. "Furthermore, it is not their ownership of the weapons that is at fault but the use to which they put them. In the codes section the first portion of the code should be a strong prohibition against illegal use of weapons with strong penalties. But in Raven's Mill we are arming our citizens. They are a strong proponent of the defense of the town. This particular position is what they used to call a 'litmus test' for us. We will not have our citizens disarmed by the government under any circumstances short of active rebellion and then only on an *individual* basis."

"I support Duke Edmund in this," Mike Spehar, the representative from Westphal said. He was a tall, fair man who had dressed for the meeting in armor. "The most important thing that a preindustrial republic must have is a well-distributed armed class. Failure to have such inevitably leads to the establishment of feudalism.

"I am not a duke anymore, Baron Longleaf," Edmund snapped.

"You are still listed on the Society rolls as such," Spehar said. "And it is that which I propose to amend. Many of the towns are developing from the skills of society members or those associated with them. Many of the towns have already reestablished a meritocratic aristocracy. And some that are holding out against the idea are doing so because of the existing rolls. My proposals fall into that area."

"Mike, you're nuts," Edmund replied. "First you rail against feudalism and then you want to bring in its trappings?"

"We're not just accepting society position gratis in Westphal," Spehar replied. "As I said, a *meritocratic*-based aristocracy. Instead of a Senate elected by the states or the state legislatures, a House of Lords, so to speak, that would have both hereditary aristocracy and members with lifetime appointments for particular merit. The latter, especially, would represent a true 'higher house' and the hereditary aristocracy could be used to woo those who are avoiding entry due to loss of privilege."

"You're talking about dictatorial warlords like that bastard down in Cartersville," the representative from Chitao snapped. "They're exactly what we want to *eliminate*!"

"And how would you eliminate them?" Spehar replied with a frown of contempt. "You're planning on disarming your citizens. Are you planning on winning them over by smiling a lot or by selling your daughters?"

"Gentlemen!" Sheida snapped. "Calm down. All right, that is two proposed modifications to the base document. I'm sure there will be more. We will all have a chance to present them and look them over, then we can get down to editing and arguing. For now, we'll just let them be presented. *Without* commentary."

This is going to be a long night, Edmund thought.

CHAPTER TWENTY-SEVEN

Kane woke Herzer well before dawn with the bad news that he was in charge of making breakfast. Herzer tried not to grumble and wandered out into the predawn darkness. He was presented with the materials and then Kane went back to bed.

Herzer had learned to use flint and steel to start a fire while woodcutting and it only took him ten or twenty tries to get the fire going. The first few that started went back out before he had a solid base and it took six or seven tries to get the tinder going each time. Finally he had a good roaring fire and it was time to start the mush. He lugged a bucket of water from the nearby stream and poured it in the kettle, then set the kettle on the fire while he went to get another bucket. Then he had to figure out how much of the cornmeal would make a good mush. He finally settled that question, by which time the water was starting to boil. He added the meal, which stopped the boil, then went to find more wood.

By the time he got back the concoction had boiled over and put the fire out.

There were a few coals left and he carefully nursed them to start a new fire, then went and got *more* wood and started all over again. He finally had a steady fire going, and the mush bubbling, by the time Kane reappeared.

"What'd you put in it besides meal?" Kane asked, taking a spoonful. "That's going to take a *long* time to cook down."

"I had some trouble," Herzer admitted, as if the wet ashes from the first fire weren't proof enough.

"I'll get some additions," Kane muttered, then wandered back to the building he and Alyssa shared.

When Kane came back he took over the fire and set Herzer to feeding the horses. It was a huge herd and like all horse herds extremely hierarchical. Kane had somewhere obtained a large quantity of hay and Herzer attempted to distribute it by spreading it around, one forkful at a time but that didn't work very well. The senior horses, a group of mares, had finished their share by the time he'd made his tenth trip and were driving the low-rank horses, including his own Diablo, off the piles. He was also getting worried about the health of the horses since the kicking and squealing was not only getting loud but vicious.

"Won't work like that," Alyssa said, walking over to him as he came back with another load. She was yawning and the squealing of the horses had clearly woken her but since he was sweating freely in the early morning cool he wasn't exactly heartbroken.

"With so many of them and all in a group, all you can do is pile it up in one place," she said. "It helps to move it to where they can get at it from every side."

She went into the corral with a halter and returned with one of the Hanarahs that she then hooked up to a small cart. Between the two of them they loaded the cart with hay, then Alyssa drove it into the corral while Herzer fended off the horses that tried to bolt through the gate. Once inside Herzer stood in the back of the cart and forked hay to the horses as Alyssa drove it through the paddock at a slow pace. Along the way she kept up a running commentary about the horses that showed that not only did she know them all by name but their individual quirks and their place in the hierarchy.

By the time they got back, the rest of the riders were up and the mush was done. It was the recipient of some comments.

"Damn, Kane," one of the riders muttered, taking a bite of the mush. "You're not only ugly you're a damned bad cook. Why'd Alyssa ever marry you?"

"Well I *am* a bad cook," Kane admitted, with a grin. "But this particular mess is all Herzer's fault. And the reason Alyssa married me had nothing to do with my kitchen skills."

"Wow, Herzer," Alyssa added. "If the way to a woman's heart is through her stomach, you're in big trouble."

Herzer took a bite of the mush and grimaced at the burned taste. "I guess," was all he said.

Hoping that the morning's fiascoes were past him, Herzer finished his food quickly and went looking for his horse.

Diablo seemed less than thrilled to see him and Herzer wondered if playing polo the day before had been a good idea. But he had held back a handful of the cornmeal and it was appreciated, so it was a horse in a much better mood that he led out of the paddock.

He saddled up himself this morning, remembering to get the horse to suck in its gut when he tightened the girth. Horses had a tendency to inhale and "blow themselves up" when the girth was being tightened. That way, as soon as the rider was done, they could let the air out and get some looseness in the girth. Diablo was just about as bad as a "normal" horse on that score but it sort of made sense; wearing a girth was a bit like a corset for a horse.

On the other hand, if the girth wasn't as tight as possible, the saddle would slip off and the rider would find himself lying face down in the dirt.

Herzer got all the straps in place and mounted creakily. All his "riding" muscles had stiffened up and it was positively painful to swing his leg over the horse's back. But once he was up there he started to loosen up and as he moved Diablo around so did the horse. He took him through a few of his paces to get the kinks out then rode back to the camp at an easy canter.

"Raring to go, huh?" Kane asked. He had emerged from the tack shed with some new gear and a long spear.

"Just warming up," Herzer said. "When are the beaters supposed to get here?"

"They started this morning but they have a few miles to beat and they're moving slow. So, say five hours from dawn. But there's going to be stuff running ahead of them. So we need to be in place in another hour or so. But Alyssa and I want to show you a few things and get with everybody to talk about responsibilities."

Herzer dismounted to wait and work on his horse. He pulled the saddle and bridle off, switching the latter for a halter, and gave the horse a thorough currying. The horses were losing their winter undercoat so Diablo especially appreciated that. Then he hunted up a feedbag and some feed; he knew he was going to be using the horse hard today and he didn't want it falling out from low blood sugar.

By the time he was done Kane had saddled his own horse and hooked the odd accoutrements to it. The tack turned out to be a holder for the spear, along with places to hook other weaponry. Kane also brought out a long battle axe and sword to go along with the spear. Herzer mentally changed the word "spear" to "lance" but he really couldn't see the difference.

In the meantime Alyssa had scared up one of the little Arabs and saddled it as well. Her saddle was much more ornate than Kane's but seemed just as functional. On the side of it she hung an odd, rectangular case. Just after Herzer recognized it, correctly, as a case for a recurve bow, she opened it up and removed the bow, which was unstrung. Stringing it turned out to be a major operation and actually took Kane doing most of the work. First she took out a long string, more of a rope, really, with two leather toggle and loop devices on either end and attached them to the opposite ends of the bow. Then as Kane lifted the bow in a curl, sweat almost immediately breaking out on his face, she carefully attached the actual string to the bow and ensured that the limbs were straight. That done Kane *slowly* let off pressure until the bow was fully strung. Herzer had to wonder, as she removed the stringer, how often she could actually *draw* the thing, which looked as if it must have a pull of sixty kilos or so.

A few of the older riders had been setting up targets and a few even brought out their own lances and holders. But Alyssa was the only one with a bow.

"Okay, cavalry means fighting from horseback," Kane said. "But most cavalry techniques derived from *hunting* on horseback and only got converted to killing people later."

"Well, the lance was probably the other way around," Denver Quilliam pointed out. The rider was one of Kane's coterie and while his horse work was only so-so he handled the lance with ease.

"Maybe, maybe not," Kane argued. "There's no clear archaeological record for it and admittedly it *seemed* to appear after the development of horse cavalry, but . . ."

"Kane," Alyssa said.

"Oh . . yeah . . . well we're going to show you a little about the lance and the horse-bow this morning while we're waiting for the first animal to arrive."

"Are we going to be *using* lances and bows?" Herzer asked.

"If anyone feels like they can handle them without falling off their horse they can try," Kane said with a laugh.

He started by demonstrating the two ways to hold the lance in a charge. The idea was to hold it lightly in the hand so that you could maintain targeting even on the horse, which was, of course, moving in three dimensions, then at the last moment "clamp down" and drive it into the target. Smaller lances could be used overhand with a throwing motion for similar effects. He drove one of each into the center of the target and then challenged others to copy his actions. Herzer and Denver probably got closest and Herzer had done his turn at a *gallop* like Kane; Denver had driven his home at a much more sedate canter.

Herzer had gotten very comfortable with riding Diablo. The massive chestnut was not unlike those in his enhanced reality training and was even a tad "smarter." But he still hadn't opened the horse "all the way up." He had seen that blazing gallop the first day and he was still a tad uncomfortable with seeing what it was like to be on his back under those conditions; a slower gallop was still like having a rocket between his legs.

After Kane was done and the lances recovered, Alyssa gave a demonstration with the horse-bow. She first demonstrated firing from a still horse at about seventy-five yards, putting three arrows into the center of the target just about as fast as she could draw and fire. After that she began to canter, putting an arrow into the central area of the target about every five or six seconds, then last she demonstrated the "Parthian shot," turning on her horse as it was galloping away and firing. These last were . . . more or less in the target area. But Herzer could see how it would be a nasty situation to deal with on a tactical level.

After the demonstrations Kane told them off to their duties. Herzer was going to be one of the "zone riders," in charge of managing a certain section of the main corral. He was supposed to move herd animals out of his sector and to the herding riders, break up dangerous activities, drag off any animals that were killed in his sector and otherwise handle any contingencies. Besides Diablo he would have two more animals to switch off to, an even larger bay gelding called Butch and a bad tempered palomino named Duchess. He'd have to lead them over himself but as long as Duchess was at the rear of the lead he wasn't worried.

Before they headed out to the slaughtering corral Herzer trotted over to Alyssa, who was in last minute consultation with Kane, and waited until she nodded in his direction.

"Ma'am, is there any way I could try out that bow for a moment?" he asked, diffidently.

"You've shot before?" she asked.

"Not from horseback and I know I can't shoot while riding. But I think I can hit the broad side of a barn from Diablo when he's still."

She looked at Kane and traded a look, then nodded and pulled out the bow. However, she then looked at his bulging forearms. Both of her own were guarded by bracers, but his were bare and the left would be turned into hamburger if he didn't have some protection. She paused and traded a look of consternation with the younger man; there was no way that her relatively dainty bracers would *ever* fit over his arms.

"Hang on a second," Kane said with a laugh and rode over to his hut. He went inside and emerged a moment later with a pair of metal bracers and another bow case.

"Really should be leather for bow work," he said. "But see if these fit."

Herzer tried them on and found that they fit fairly well. There was an internal leather strap arrangement that was somewhat adjustable and the bracers were, if anything, a tad large.

"Keep 'em," Kane said, remounting. "I won 'em off someone a while back and have just been carting them around. I don't use that kind of armor."

Herzer accepted the bow and a quiver of arrows with a nod and then trotted out to the range. He carefully checked to make sure no one was going to be riding across the way and then stopped Diablo with a gulp. He realized that if he missed he was going to look like an idiot but he had to try it anyway. He took a moment to check the inside of his bracer to ensure that there were no protruding bits of metal or sharp edges that would strike the bowstring, then drew out an arrow. He kneed Diablo to a stop, gave him a quiet word, then took a breath and nocked the arrow. The draw on the bow was, as he suspected, at least sixty kilos but he'd fired worse and the recent "exercise" he'd had helped in the strength department.

He drew it properly, pushing the bow away himself while "standing" with the string, then took aim. He'd forgotten how much a string could cut into your fingers and then recalled Alyssa was wearing bowman's gloves, very light gloves of thin leather. Nonetheless, despite the pain, he took a good aim and fired with a prayer to any watching gods. Diablo, bless him, didn't flinch in the slightest.

The arrow flew straight and true and dead into the center of the target, sinking to the fletching. He fired two more, just to ensure that that wasn't a fluke, and both were nearly as accurate. Then, despite the pain of his fingers and the fact that they appeared to have started bleeding again, he tried it at a walk, a trot and a canter.

At a walk he could get the arrows into more or less the center of the target at fifty yards. But he had to aim carefully and it was not a fast process. At a trot he was afraid that he'd lost a couple of Alyssa's arrows deep in the woods. At a canter he was a bit better, it was a smoother ride than a trot anyway, but the arrows still were only "near" the target; one hit in the center more or less by a fluke but the other two missed low.

"Where'd you learn to use a bow?" Alyssa asked as he rode back up after retrieving the arrows.

"The same place I learned to ride a horse," Herzer said with a rueful grin. "Stupid me, I kept all my stuff off-line rather than at my house or something. Or I'd be fully decked out. Lu, I had a beautiful bow," he added sadly.

"Did you do horse archery?" Kane asked. "And what kind of bow?"

"No, I didn't really fight from horseback at all; I'd dismount," Herzer replied. "And it was a long recurve, hundred kilo draw."

"A *hundred*?" Alyssa said, her jaw dropping.

"Well, I couldn't shoot it a lot," Herzer admitted. "But when I hit a fisking orc, it stayed dropped!"

"You weren't a reenactor, though," Kane said with a frown.

"I . . . no I wasn't," Herzer replied. "I had some physical problems up until recently. I was training to *start* being a reenactor. Then the Fall hit. And here we are."

"Well, if you'll help me string this thing, you can carry Alyssa's spare."

"I think I can do that," Herzer said. "And you'd better get me out one of those pig-stickers, too."

"You said you hadn't trained on horseback," Kane said with a frown.

"I haven't, but I'm thinking of the origin of the name," Herzer replied with a grin.

The capture corral had been established where the Little Shenan met the big Shenan, just to the side of the main bridge for the Via Apallia. In fact the "funnel" fences, split logs mostly tied to trees, extended *over* the road. Their own corrals were just to the south so it was a short ride up to where everyone had gathered. Buildings had been erected along the main road and there were now steel kettles being filled with water and A frames being erected in front of them.

"For the slaughtering," Kane said. "Get the water boiling hot, dip a pig in the water to loosen up the bristles. Other animals, too. And the frames are for slaughtering."

"Are they going to slaughter all the pigs?" Herzer asked. "They're important animals for a farmer."

"Wild pigs aren't anything for a new farmer to be handling," Kane pointed out. "We're not to kill any of the young ones. And the people along the fences are going to try to capture any that get through. But we're going to slaughter all the big ones and smoke them. We don't have enough salt to smoke them properly, but if you give them enough of a smoking they'll last a while. Unless there's a huge number of animals we're going to go through the food pretty quick. There's two types of deer that are going to be coming out, white tails and wapiti. The white tails will go right over the fences; kill any of them you can. But the wapiti can't cross them so we're going to collect them."

There were four smaller corrals off the main corral, planted so that herd animals could be driven in. Herzer, having seen how "easy" it was to drive animals the previous day thought them optimistic.

He tied off his two spare horses to the corral and took up his position, on the "outside" corner and waited for the first animals to come in. There were people starting to line the fences, many of them with spears made from saplings. He saw Shilan in his sector and waved at her, then spotted Rachel walking along the line, a bag slung over her back. That brought him back to the fact that many of the animals that were going to be coming in were not going to be exactly friendly. He thought about riding over and talking but stayed in his place instead, trying to figure out what his "good" lines of fire were. If he missed a shot the arrow would just keep going and eventually the entire line of fences were supposed to be manned. That was going to make shooting problematic. That being the case he left the bow and the spear where they were

Kane rode over with a coil of rope in his hands. "Can you tie a knot?" he asked.

"A few," Herzer admitted.

"There's a slip knot in the end," Kane said, handing over the rope. "If something gets killed, drag it off to the side; somebody will take care of it from there."

Herzer took the rope and found a place to tie it on the saddle. He wasn't sure about dragging something with Diablo, much less with Butch or Duchess. Butch and Duchess tended to wander away when he dismounted, among other things.

He didn't have much time to worry about it, though, because shortly afterwards, to a general cry, a deer jumped over one of the fences and into the open area. It was well outside his sector so he didn't bother to try to uncase his bow and get a shot and it quickly bounded across the open area. But when it saw the line of people along the fence it turned towards him.

He kneed Diablo towards it to get it turned, then saw it was ignoring the horses. He was just starting to get the bow out, not easy on a trotting horse, when an arrow from the side took it down. It still continued to run but then dropped as the message got through to its brain that it was dead. He trotted over to it, dropping the bow back in the case and dismounted, untying his rope. He got the slip knot around the rear legs then walked back to Diablo who unaccustomedly shied away.

"He doesn't like the smell of blood!" Kane called. "Talk to him."

"Shah, horse," Herzer crooned, letting out the rope. "Good horse. Stay. Whoa."

He finally got on its back, with the rope nearly at full extension, and kneed him toward the nearest fence. The weight of the deer nearly dragged him from the saddle but he wrapped it into the leather it had been tied on and started dragging. Unfortunately before he had gotten more than thirty meters the *second* animal appeared; a half mature tiger.

At the sight of the great cat, which was no more than fifty meters away, Diablo went nuts, rearing and trying to run away from the cat and the deer it was dragging simultaneously. Herzer somehow stayed in the saddle, his hand painfully caught in the leather and rope. He pointed the horse away from the tiger, which was just fine by it, and towards the fence. But the tiger, seeing something fleeing, started after the horse, then turned and leapt on the deer instead.

The combined weight of the deer and the tiger stopped the horse in its tracks, nearly throwing it on its side. This time Herzer managed to get his hand free in time but the rope burned through his hand painfully. He kicked Diablo into movement again and then turned to look at what was going on behind him.

The tiger had stopped on the carcass of the deer, looking around at the people and horse with a baleful glare. After a moment it crouched on top of the deer and let out a roar.

Despite his mount's rearing and shying Herzer managed to get it stopped and turned. Whispering to it he uncased the bow and pulled out an arrow. It was a clap shot if he could just get the horse to hold still for a moment; he wasn't about to dismount under the circumstances. He lined up the tiger and let fly just as Alyssa fired from the other vector.

His arrow flew into the tiger's chest just under the neck but one arrow, even driven from a compound bow, wasn't going to stop the beast and it turned around, snarling, wondering what had hit it. He fired again, before Alyssa and the second arrow drove into the tiger's ribcage.

It took three arrows from him, and more from Alyssa, before the cat finally stopped spinning and hissing. Herzer stayed where he was, though, and waited until a pair of hunters came out from the fences and prodded at the beast with their spears.

"Good shooting," Alyssa said, cantering by.

"Thanks," he responded, taking a moment to catch his breath and soothe his upset horse.

All things considered, he decided that it was best to keep his bow out.

While the excitement had been at his end of the corral, more animals had been filing into the area delineated by the fences. He saw some cattle and some absolutely gigantic deer that had to be the wapiti that Kane had talked about. They were nearly the size of the female cows and had antlers in velvet forming on their heads.

"Bull herd," Kane said. "Kill 'em or drive 'em to the corrals."

They were so magnificent he didn't want to have to kill them but when the first one entered his sector and he tried to drive it towards the pens it took extreme exception to the idea and reared on its hind legs, waving sharp hooves at the horse. Backing Diablo, who clearly wanted to show who was boss, he somehow drove three arrows into the deer's chest almost as fast as he could draw and fire, and the magnificent bull dropped to its knees then rolled over on the side.

He wasn't about to try to drag that monster so he waved to some of the men along the fence and went out looking for something that would actually drive.

The massive corral was starting to get crowded with animals by this time, all of them angry, bewildered and driven half mad by the smell of blood that was starting to permeate the area. But it didn't get really bad until the herd of pigs disgorged into the area.

The pigs had apparently stayed in their herd and Herzer had no idea that that many pigs were even *in* the forest, much less would stay together in a massive wave of tusks and smell. There must have been at least fifty of the larger ones and innumerable babies. Following them was a puma and then *another* tiger.

At the sight of the tidal wave of dangerous *and* deadly creatures most of the riders gave up any pretext of trying to herd cattle and wapiti and instead looked to their own defense. Many of them headed for the gates along the sides, abandoning the field altogether.

Herzer was well to the side of the mass and he started firing arrows for all he was worth. With a couple of exceptions he wasn't sure where they went except downward; he was being careful of the people on the far side of the fence. He saw more arrows coming from the few hunters with longbows along the sides of the fence but it wasn't stopping the pigs. The tiger had disappeared—he hoped nobody had been hurt when that happened—but the puma was chasing Kane for all it was worth.

Herzer took two shots at the running puma and saw one hit, turning it, then either Alyssa or one of the hunters got a killing shot in on it and it ran a few feet and dropped. But by that time the pig herd had scattered and there were at least a half a dozen big, nasty, angry "pigs" in his area.

He shot two and then saw one making a beeline for the fence and Shilan.

He dropped the bow in the case, pulled out his spear and decided to see if he could actually stay on Diablo's back at a full gallop. With a yell he dug his heels into the horse and pointed it at the charging pig.

It felt for a moment as if the world went sideways. The horse bunched its muscles and took off like lightning, so fast that he seemed to hear his own shouting doppler behind him. He realized he was screaming madly and trying to line up the pig with his spear but it was going to reach the fence first.

The six hundred kilos of enraged boar hit the rickety wooden fence at nearly thirty kilometers per hour and the fence didn't have a chance. The nearest posts snapped off even as the poles shivered to pieces. On the other hand, the encounter had seriously shaken the boar and it stopped for a moment to shake the blood out of its eyes. But when it had regained its senses the first thing it saw was Shilan, thrown backwards and onto the ground from the backlash of the fence.

Herzer shouted louder, hoping that the sound would turn the boar but there was no chance, it lowered its head and charged the stunned girl.

He never even realized that the lance was lined up when it slammed into the side of the boar, nearly unseating him from the impact.

Diablo was charging headlong and when the boar, caught by the spear driven through it and into the ground, stopped dead, there was nowhere to go but over.

Herzer somehow retained his hold on the spear but let it run through his hand as the horse went up and over. The combined fulcrum effect threw the mortally wounded boar over on its side and definitely prevented it from getting to the girl but the branch at the top of the jump could have cared less. With complete indignity it impacted on Herzer's forehead and flipped him back off of the horse in a welter of his own blood.

CHAPTER TWENTY-EIGHT

When Herzer came to, his mouth tasted like blood and leaf mold and he had the world's worst headache.

"Stay still," a female voice said. He ran it through a long, slow memory search and realized it was Dr. Daneh. He hadn't talked to her since he'd gotten to Raven's Mill, which seemed a couple of lifetimes ago.

"Mrwf," he managed to say.

"Can you move your legs?" she asked.

He complied, wincing when the concentration made him tense up his neck. His head was *really* starting to hurt.

"Good, fingers? Arms?"

He moved those then felt hands roll him over. He couldn't see at first and that terrified him, but then someone poured water on his face and his eyelids got unstuck. Dr. Daneh looked tired and worn, even worse than on the trip, even worse than after her encounter with Dionys. Well, maybe not *worse*.

"Uh ne' res'," Herzer said then worked his mouth and spit out some leaves.

"Yes, you do need some rest," she said and smiled. She used a small mirror to flash light in his eyes, which made him wince, but he noticed she nodded in satisfaction at whatever information she gleaned.

"Huh, uh," he said, injudiciously shaking his head. "*You* need some rest," he corrected.

At that she smiled again and t'chted. "I'm fine."

"No 'ur not," he said, trying to sit up.

355

"Wait," she said. "You're in pretty sorry shape yourself Herzer Herrick."

"Gotta get back on the horse," he said hoarsely. He pushed her hands to the side and sat up, wincing at the pain in his head and neck. He felt his forehead where a large patch was obviously bloody, and blinked his eyes, only then realizing that part of his vision problem was the blood and dirt encrusting them. He rubbed at them and got them mostly clear then started to stand, only to be hit by a wave of dizziness. He wasn't sure if he *could* get back on a horse, much less stay on one. And he was pretty sure he didn't want to, which only increased his determination.

"Help him up, Daneh," a male voice said. Strong hands lifted him from under his armpits and balanced him.

"Gotta get back on the horse," he said again. He looked around painfully and saw Diablo standing only a few feet away. His vision was going gray, in and out, and the horse looked as if it was at the end of a tunnel but it still appeared to have a sheepish expression on its face. His knees buckled for a moment as he thought he might faint but then the wave passed and he was still standing. Painfully, but standing.

"I need to get you to the infirmary," Daneh protested.

"He can get there on the horse," the voice said. "You can ride with him and balance."

"No, Rachel can go," Daneh said. "I'm needed here."

Herzer realized that the other voice was Sir Edmund but it didn't really matter. With Talbot steadying him he got a hand on Diablo's mane and a foot in the stirrup. With an effort that called forth another blinding flash of pain from his head he got up in the saddle and leaned forward, swaying.

"Got back up," he muttered, his eyes half closed against the pain. He was back up but he didn't know where to go or how to get there. He kneed the horse towards the corral and stopped when a hand clutched the horse's bridle, nearly unseating him again.

"Not back to work, hero," Edmund said humorously. "There's others to take over. You're for the infirmary."

Rachel was hoisted up behind him and with her pleasant anatomy pressed against his back the horse was led off to the infirmary. Distantly he heard some cheering.

"Was 'at," he muttered. He couldn't be bothered to lift his aching head.

"You don't know?" Rachel said with a note of humor in

her voice. "I guess you don't even realize what a spectacle you made of yourself."

"Whah specac . . . spec?" he asked.

"Later. Right now we have to get you into a bed and get your face cleaned up. Be glad you didn't impact your nose, it would be all over your face. As it is, I don't know why you don't have a damned skull fracture or subdural cerebral hematoma. And you just might."

Herzer wasn't sure what she was talking about. He wasn't even sure how he had ended up on the ground. The last thing he could remember was shooting his bow at a puma.

Somehow he managed to stay on the horse until they reached an open-sided building where willing hands helped him down from the horse. Diablo was starting to show some tendency to shy but Kane turned up and took control immediately.

"Need to . . . curry . . ." Herzer said. He really felt as if he was going to faint again.

"Get in *bed*, Herzer," Kane laughed. "You've done enough for one day."

Rachel led him into the building, which was blessedly dim, and set him down on a cot. It was, for a wonder, well padded with something. She didn't let him lie down, though, propping him up with pillows.

"Now, I'm going to get to work on this head wound," she said. "Don't pass out on me; that would be bad."

Fortunately she had a gentle touch. She washed the wound with warm water, eliciting a flow of blood, then wiped it clean and put on a wash that stung. But the sting was nothing to the pain in his head. Suddenly, he realized he was about to vomit.

"I'm going to . . ." he started to say then paused as his stomach flipped over.

She quickly picked up a bucket and held it for him as he emptied the entire contents of his last week of meals. Or so it seemed. The vomiting also increased his headache.

"Okay, that's normal," she said, setting the bucket to the side. "You've got a concussion. Just sit there and rest. You might be doing that for a few days."

He lay back on the pillows and closed his eyes against the limited light in the room as she brushed his clothes as clean as she could. He felt he really should be doing that himself but he was feeling *really* bad. All he wanted to do was *sleep*.

"Don't go to sleep on me," Rachel said, shaking his arm.

"Damn, I'm going to either have to sit here or get someone else to."

"Why?" he asked, tiredly.

"You've got a concussion," she repeated. "If you go to sleep you might not wake up again."

That was an unpleasant thought to say the least. And it managed to focus his mind on not sleeping. And other things.

"What were you talking about when we were riding over here?" he asked. "A spectacle." Then he started to remember where he'd gotten the head wound. "Oh, Mithras. That must have been a funny sight," he sighed.

"What?" she asked. She looked at his hand and tisked. "What did you do to your *fingers?*"

"I didn't have a bow-glove," he replied. He had been firing so fast he hadn't even noticed the pain in them.

"They're cut practically to the bone you idiot!" she said, starting to bandage those as well. "And I suppose you could say that it was funny, if everyone hadn't been watching all your other antics."

"Antics?" he asked.

"Herzer, you were all over the damned *field* on that great big war-horse of yours," she said acerbically, "killing things left and right. It was a bit more than spectacular. You save *Kane's* life at least twice, if not getting gored by an enraged bull counts as saving a life. Then to top it off was that *insane* gallop to save Shilan. I mean, you should have heard the *gasp* when you took off. You were halfway across the field before anyone else had even started to *react,* galloping so fast it looked like you were riding a jet-car, not a horse. It was pretty clear everybody who had a *moment* was watching to see what you'd do next. I heard people *betting* on you."

"Oh," he said, trying to cudgel his brain. Had he really been *that* noticeable?

"Everybody thought Shilan was dead with that boar coming down on her and then you go and not only *stick* the damned thing, you turn it over on its *side*. And then, as far as everyone could tell, get yourself killed. Nobody thought you were going to stand up after hitting that branch and you were out of most people's sight. The *applause* was because you came riding *out*."

"Oh."

"Do me a favor, okay? I've got enough problems as it is. Stop trying to be a *hero*."

"Okay," he said, puzzled.

"I'll go find somebody to keep you awake," she said, standing up and brushing off her skirt. "In fact, I think I know just the person."

Herzer closed his eyes and leaned back again but started when he realized he was half asleep. He wasn't sure if Rachel was serious about not waking up again, but he didn't want to find out. He also wondered how long the prohibition would last.

He opened up his eyes and looked around the dim room. There were a couple of other beds occupied but nobody close enough to talk to.

With the immediate problems settled and being at liberty for the moment, he started to catalogue his other hurts. His neck was killing him and from the description of what had happened he was surprised it wasn't broken. Really, *really,* glad. Being a quadriplegic in this society would suck. He might as well get some friend to cut his throat. For that matter, he wasn't sure if he *could* survive. Would he have been able to breathe?

After a few moments of such gloomy thoughts, he looked up to see Rachel and Shilan coming into the building. He started to smile and then noted that Shilan's arm was in a sling.

"Are you okay?" he asked with a wince from a sudden stab of pain in his head.

"Just a twisted elbow," she said with a smile, sitting down on the stool that Rachel had vacated. Rachel handed her a pottery jug and walked out with a backward wave.

"Are you supposed to keep me awake?" he asked.

"Awake but not active," Shilan said. "It sounds like a prescription for total boredom."

"Not with you here," he said then winced at another stab of pain.

"And she said you probably wouldn't want to talk," Shilan added, pulling out a book. "So you just lean back and rest while I read."

"Aloud?" he asked with another grimace. It felt like being a child again.

"I doubt you'd want me to," Shilan said with a chuckle. "It's a book on weaving techniques. I was watching one of the reenactors the other day and I got interested in it. I don't think I'm cut out to be a woodcutter."

"I think you'd be wasted as a weaver," Herzer said, leaning back and closing his eyes.

"I have to do something," she said. He could hear the worry in her voice.

"Mechanical looms aren't that hard to make," Herzer said. "They can be run on water-power. And there are plenty of things you can do. Doctor comes to mind."

"Thank you, no. I've seen too much of the strain that's on Dr. Daneh. Not having access to nannites is killing her."

"Is that what it is?" he asked.

"She lost a patient yesterday; one of the new apprentices working in the mill didn't heed the safety warnings."

"Shit."

"I don't want to face that, knowing that if I had the power I could save a life and then seeing it drift away."

"Somebody has to," Herzer said, shifting and then noticing he still had his bracers on. He opened his eyes and winced as he fumbled with the catches.

"Let me get that," Shilan said, setting down the book.

He leaned back and felt her cool hands on his arms and fought down a strange tide of lust. It wasn't the way he'd felt around her before and he wasn't in any shape to follow through. For that matter, it was making his headache worse. He tried to think of something to reduce it but his head was too muddled to think. Instead he put out one hand and ran it up her arm, cracking his eyes open to see her expression.

Shilan briefly froze and her face froze so he quickly removed his hand. "I'm sorry."

"So am I," she said sadly. "Maybe . . . maybe soon, Herzer."

"Not with me," he said. "I was serious earlier. I like you but I don't want . . . I don't think we're made for each other."

"You're in love with Rachel," Shilan said, looking at him.

"She's just a friend," he said, closing his eyes again, surprised that a tear leaked out.

"Oh, you poor dumb hero," she said quietly, stroking his face.

"A hero is somebody who does something they don't have to," Herzer replied, tightly. "A hero is somebody that is there when they're needed. I'm not a hero. Please don't call me one again. Please."

"What is with you?" she asked, confused.

"It's just . . . it's hard to explain. But . . . I'm not a hero."

"Sorry, Herzer, but I thought I was dead when that spear went through the boar. You're always going to be *my* hero."

Herzer shrugged and leaned back, unable to explain the welter of emotions that was running through his brain. The good news was that the wave of lust had receded, leaving him even tireder. "Mithras I wish I could sleep."

"Don't," Shilan said. "I'll be here if you need anything."

Herzer nearly corrected "*Almost* anything" but thought better of it and just let his mind wander instead.

The next two days passed in a fog. Herzer remembered Dr. Daneh coming in and Rachel being there. Others came by but he had no real memory of who they were. He remembered being moved to a wagon and the jolting as it moved him some-where, complaining querulously about the light. He remembered Shilan being there and one time when she was crying, quietly. He remembered trying to get her to stop crying, but couldn't remember anything else, what she was crying about or when she had stopped. It wasn't until the third day after the big roundup that he woke clear-headed. It was before dawn and Rachel was sitting on a more substantial, and more com-fortable, chair, fast asleep. He took a deep breath and looked around, more aware that his headache was gone than any-thing else.

He was definitely out of the shed and in a substantial house of stone. There was an oil lamp on the cupboard across the room and tapestries on three of the walls. The bed was incredibly soft; he identified the mattress as eiderdown from some deep memory. He also realized that he must have taken a harder blow than he'd thought; the last few days were such a blur he must have had some brain trauma. Rare as it was, that used to be fairly repairable. Given the current conditions he was just really glad he'd actually survived.

There was a table by the bed with a jug and a cup. Pick-ing up the cup he recognized water and gulped it down greedily; he was terribly parched. He sat up and fumbled for the jug, waking Rachel.

"I'll get that for you," she said, sleepily. "What are you doing awake?"

"Haven't I been sleeping enough?" he asked, pouring the water shakily. His hands were trembling so badly, he got some of it on the coverlet. He gave up the cup and jug to Rachel and leaned back, overcome with weariness.

"You nearly died, stupid," she said, pouring the water and holding the cup to his lips.

He had enough control to take the cup and drink from it again. "I had sort of figured that out."

"How long have you been awake?" she asked, putting her

hand on his forehead, gently. But the touch didn't elicit any pain.

"Not long," he replied. "Where am I?"

"In Dad's house. It was the only place Mom felt you'd get enough rest. I need to check something."

"Okay," he said as she pulled back the coverlet. Only then did he realize he was naked and snatched at the bedclothes.

"First of all, you weren't that modest in the baths," she said with a chuckle. "Second, I've seen it for the last three days."

"Oh," he said as she pulled back the covers again. She took what looked like a knitting needle and applied it to the end to his toes, painfully. "Ow!"

"Good," she said, working her way up his body. She checked all the extremities and various other apparently random spots. By the time she finished he was trembling in fatigue. Which really ticked him off. She covered him back up and put something in a notebook with a nod of satisfaction.

"Do I pass, Doctor?" he asked querulously.

"So far," she replied with a tired smile. "We were really worried about your responses. The second day some of your extremities were fairly numb. That's a bad sign. But it all has recovered. Try not to take too many more blows to the head, okay?"

"I will," he said. "What happened?"

"There's no way to tell for sure, but Mom thinks you developed a bruise on either the lining of the skull or the brain itself. It's called subdural cerebral hematoma. Just call it a brain bruise. Sometimes those can kill. In your case it looks like you just have a harder head than should be possible. No slurring of the voice, pain stimuli all good. The only thing left is to check your reflexes and I'll let Mom handle that."

"How is she?" Herzer asked. "She looked . . . awful out at the roundup. I heard she lost a patient."

"And you would have made two for two," Rachel said sadly. "Bob Towback. He fell into a couple of logs and they flailed his chest and abdomen. It took a while for him to go and there wasn't anything we could do. It hit Mom hard. Losing you would have hit her harder, I think."

"I don't know why," Herzer said quietly. "No, that's stupid. I understand."

"I know you do," Rachel replied, quietly.

"Where's Shilan?" he asked, to change the subject.

"Sleeping," Rachel said with a chuckle. "You'll have to wait to regain your strength anyway, Romeo."

"I wasn't thinking of that," he said, lying. "I was just worried about her."

"She was more worried about you," Rachel said. "She's been sitting in this chair most of the time. Mom sent her off to bed last night when it was pretty clear you were going to make it."

"I need to go to the bathroom," he said, suddenly. "Bad."

"I'll get a bedpan," she said, getting up.

"How far is it to . . ." he paused.

"Dad actually has indoor plumbing," Rachel said stepping out of the room. "But you're not getting up."

"The hell I'm not," Herzer replied, irritably. He sat up and worked his legs out of the covers awkwardly. Nothing would go the way he wanted and he briefly was afraid the brain bruise or whatever had damaged his motor circuits. But after a moment, as the room seemed to revolve around him, he got them under control. Just disuse. That was all. Disuse.

He hung onto that mantra as he slid out of bed.

"Oh you idiot," she said, grabbing him as he sagged. She had a strange and altogether unpleasant looking device in her hand which she tossed on the bed. "Damn, you're heavy."

"I can make it," he said, gritting his teeth as the room started spinning again. "Where is it?"

"Just down the hall," she said, getting her shoulder under his arm. "And go quiet. If you wake up Mother . . ."

"I'm already awake," Dr. Daneh said from the door. "And you should be in bed."

"I can make it to the jakes, Doctor," Herzer said, straightening up then swaying and grabbing at Rachel.

"Idiot," the doctor said, shaking her head. "But since I don't want to be wrestling with you while you pee, I'll help too."

Between the three of them they managed to stagger to the bathroom and Herzer relieved himself in relative peace. He even snagged a towel off a rack and got it around his waist before he staggered out the door.

"Back to bed, you," Dr. Daneh said, shaking her head. "The things people go through for privacy."

By the time Herzer was back in bed he was willing to admit that maybe the strange device, a white porcelain . . . jug, sort of, with a tube that did *not* look large enough, might have been a better idea.

"Get some rest," Dr. Daneh said, wiping a piece of hair out of her face. "You're going to need your strength."

"Why?" Herzer asked with a sigh as he lay back down.

"Fredar got raided," the doctor said. "That's what had me

up. Some brigands looted it and burned most of the buildings. We're going to be having more refugees. Edmund has
moved up the plan on building a real defense force. And he
wants *you* on it."

"Good," Herzer said. He could feel sleep pulling at him but
he felt that it was time for a good line. "Time to get back
on the horse."

"Idiot" was the last thing he heard.

CHAPTER TWENTY-NINE

On the fifth day after his accident, Herzer rebelled.

For two days after his head cleared up, Dr. Daneh had refused to let him get up and move around more than to the bathroom. But the fifth day he could make it that far just fine and felt more or less recovered. Rather less than more if pressed, he was still dreadfully weak, but that wasn't going to get better by lying in bed.

In the afternoon, after one of Daneh's "nurses" had left with his lunch, he was alone and apparently unguarded. Getting up he retrieved his mended clothes from the cupboard and went to find out what the repetitive banging sound was from behind the house.

He could hear clattering from the kitchen so he stepped out a side door and snuck around to the shed at the rear. He had expected to find one of the smith apprentices, even hopefully someone from his apprentice class, but it was Master Talbot himself standing at the anvil, hammering out a piece of bar-steel with a furious expression on his face.

Herzer started to step back but as he did Edmund looked up and nodded, distantly.

"I didn't think you were supposed to be out of bed," Talbot said, setting down the hammer and slipping the steel back into the coals in the forge.

"I suppose I'm AWOL," Herzer replied, stepping into the shed. It was less crowded than he expected, containing not much more than a table, some buckets, the forge and the anvil.

365

There were a few tools but not many. After a moment he took in bare patches on the floor and some recent wood work and realized that much of its contents had recently been removed. Down to the town and the growing smithies he supposed.

Despite the relative cool of the afternoon, it was hot as . . . well, as a forge inside. He could feel sweat beading on his brow immediately and Edmund was drenched.

The smith nodded in understanding and took a drink of water from a jug, handing it over to the boy. "Well, if you think you're recovered enough, you can work the bellows," he said, nodding to the apparatus. "Put on an apron, though, or you'll get sparks all in your clothes."

Herzer felt that was within his capability. He grabbed a leather apron and examined the bellows. There was a convenient stool so he sat down and started pumping.

"Not so hard," Edmund muttered, turning the steel. "You'll get the fire too hot."

Herzer slowed down the rhythm until he saw the smith nod, then stopped when Talbot pulled the steel, now glowing a low cherry-red, from the fire.

"Different types of steel form at different temperatures," Edmund explained. "Right now, I'm just working the surface carbon into the bar."

Herzer nodded as if he understood, wiping his face with his hands. Edmund wordlessly passed him a cloth and the jug.

"What are you making?" Herzer asked, drinking deeply. The water was cut with wine, very lightly, just enough to give it a bite. It felt refreshing after the plain water he'd been given for the last few days.

"Just a knife," Edmund replied, an irritable expression on his face again. "It was come out here and bang on some metal or take the hammer and bang heads."

Herzer watched in companionable silence as the smith hammered the metal out and then thrust it back in the fire.

"Pump," Edmund said, glancing at him, "Although you look as if you're already tiring out."

"I am," Herzer admitted. "But I don't know why. All I've been doing is lying around."

"A hard blow like that takes it right out of you," the smith replied, turning the metal in the coals. "Daneh thought you should lie abed for another three or four days. I disagreed, but I wasn't going to tell her."

"I think at this point I need exercise more than rest," Herzer gasped. The bellows were strongly sprung and his arm was already growing tired.

"Enough," Talbot grunted, pulling the steel back out. "Do you know why the apprentice pumps the bellows?"

"No."

"Pumping bellows is a very similar motion to hammering. It builds up the apprentice's strength in specific muscle groups. Besides just being weak from your injury, you're not used to using those muscles."

"Well, great, another group to work out," Herzer said with a wry grin, and took another sip of water. "So is the knife to stick in anyone in particular?"

"No," Edmund said with a chuckle. "Although I can think of a few I wouldn't mind handing it to point first."

Herzer recognized it as an oblique negative reference, but not anything specific.

"Although," Talbot said after a moment, banging on the steel a trifle harder, "most of them wouldn't get the hint."

Herzer nodded, not admitting that he didn't either.

"Pump," the smith said. "So, you heard we're speeding up the deployment of the guard force?"

"Dr. Daneh told me," Herzer said. He had caught his wind and in a way it was getting easier to pump than it had been at first. It was still hot as hell, though. "She said something about Fredar?"

"A group of brigands, I suppose you'd call them, hit it. I'd been out there just a couple of weeks ago. They had gotten the preliminary pronouncement of the Norau reformation and were making noises about the 'violent nature' of the proposals."

"The defense requirement?" Herzer asked, stopping the bellows as the smith drew the steel out.

"Aye," the smith admitted. "Their town council had taken a strictly nonviolent position; some of the reenactors who had stopped there moved when they did that and told me. I went over and tried to talk them out of it, the fools." He slammed the hammer down twice, hard then stopped, setting it down and putting the steel back in the fire. "Get some more charcoal, would you?" he said, gesturing with his chin at a bucket in the corner.

Herzer got the charcoal and then looked at his hands. Not only they but his arms were covered in soot. "Going to be hard to get past the doctor like this."

"We'll wash you up, don't worry," Edmund replied, taking

another drink. "Anyway, the . . . brigands killed most of the men, including the few skilled artisans, damnit, ran off with most of the women and left the children behind. Oh, and they burned everything down on their way out."

"Rape, loot, pillage and burn," Herzer said with a frown.

"Oh, yeah, they got it in the right order," Edmund said, sticking the steel back in the fire. "Pump. It's actually odd. Quite often raiders got the order out of sequence. Burning things down is quite fun under the circumstances; it's keeping people from burning that is tough."

Herzer looked at him sideways his brow furrowing. "That sounds like the voice of experience."

"So we've moved up the schedule for the guard force," Edmund said, ignoring the implied question. "You going to go for soldier?"

"Yes," Herzer replied.

"Which kind?" Edmund asked.

"I don't know what there's going to be," Herzer admitted. "I have sort of been out of the loop."

"It's going to be small," Talbot replied. "We don't need much right now. But I want it to be a good cadre for a larger force, so it's going to be brutal training."

"I'm up for it," Herzer said as the smith paused.

"That's what you think now," Edmund snorted. "The main force will be two groups, archers and line infantry. The archers will use longbows and the line infantry will be modeled, lightly, on the Roman infantry."

"Legions?" Herzer said, with a grin. "Now *that's* more like it!"

"Well, with your arm you'd make a hell of a bowman." Edmund frowned.

"Fine, if they tell me I have to be an archer, I'll be an archer," Herzer replied. "But if I have the choice I'll take the legions, thanks just the same."

"Why?" Edmund set down the steel and really looked at the young man for the first time

Herzer turned his face away from the regard and shrugged, his face hot. "I don't know," he temporized.

"Okay, tell me what you think."

Herzer hesitated for a moment then shrugged again. "Legions . . . well *archers*. Archers sit back and hit the enemy at a distance. They don't . . . close with them. They don't get a grip on them. I . . . I trained with a bow, and, yeah, I'm even pretty good, but I always preferred to close with cold steel. I call it 'iron hand.' It's just . . . my thing. Sometimes it was the wrong thing to do. But . . . it's what I preferred."

Edmund nodded again, an inscrutable expression on his face and picked up the steel. "Pump. The term you're groping for is 'shock infantry.' There's effectively two types, disciplined and undisciplined. Undisciplined is the Pict screaming forward with his axe raised overhead. That works, sometimes, against other undisciplined infantry. The other model is the phalanx, which advances in a steady force to take and hold ground. Iron hand . . . and I've heard the term before although you'd probably be surprised where it came from, iron hand is more about the screaming Pict. Can you grasp the difference?"

"Yes, sir," Herzer replied. "But I'd still prefer the legions. The legions . . . well . . ." He paused and shrugged.

Edmund smiled at him and nodded. "Again, I've got the advantage on you. I've had years of reading, consideration and studying to *define* what you're groping for. The legions are 'where the rubber meets the road,' another term that's hard to define. They are what will, ultimately, decide the tide of battle."

"Yeah," Herzer breathed, glad that *someone* could explain the . . . feeling that was in him. "I want to be where the rubber meets the road."

Edmund laughed at that and shook his head at the young man, who was looking embarrassed. "Don't worry, it's just . . . when you get *out* of basic, if you pass, I'm going to let you read a book. Hell, I'll *make* you read so many you'll hate me. Clausewitz, flawed as he is, Fusikawa, Keegan, Hanson. So you'll be able to define the terms. Knowing the lingo is half the battle in learning. But shock infantry isn't all that is needed. Long term I want a balanced combined arms force. Bow, ballista, legion, heavy and light cavalry."

"You're talking a big force," Herzer said, shaking his head. "Raven's Mill isn't going to support all that."

"Who's talking about just Raven's Mill?" Edmund chuckled. "That's what's getting me so upset with the council. They keep thinking just in terms of *here* and *now*."

"Do you *always* think about ten years down the road?" Herzer asked. "That's how long you have to be thinking. There's no way even to raise a full legion for . . . two years minimum."

"Why two?" Edmund asked, looking at him again.

"Stuff," Herzer shrugged. "Log . . . logistics?"

"You know some terms already."

"Just . . . I have no idea how many kilos of steel go into arming a legion of six thousand men . . ."

"Tons, go on."

"Tents, food. The tents were made from leather. We don't have enough *cows* to make the leather for that many tents!"

"And not enough men. Food."

"*Preserved* food," Herzer said, suddenly excited. "I mean . . . salt. It's what they paid the legions with . . ."

"Not strictly necessary as a payment method, but I get the point. It *is* necessary as a preservative, which is why we're having to eat this food so fast. It would have been better to wait until fall for a roundup, but we needed the food *now*. You remember what I said about 'cadre.' Do you know what it means?"

"The . . . core of a force?"

"We're at the tools to build the tools stage. The Raven's Mill defense force is designed to be the tools to build the tool. Can you get what that means?"

"Ouch," he said, looking at the hammer with a grin. "You want us to be a hammer?"

"And a hammer is heavier and harder than what it bangs," Edmund chuckled, nodding at the analogy. "You think you're heavy enough?"

"I don't know," Herzer admitted. "I hope I will be by the time you're finished. Are you the hammer that makes the hammer?"

"No," Edmund admitted. "I have someone better at it than I am. You'll find out. And I *guarantee* you'll hate it."

"Okay, what doesn't kill us makes us stronger, I guess," Herzer said. "I wish we had guns, though. Try to let some brigands get though a volley of rifle fire."

"Expansion rate protocols," Edmund said with a shrug. "Won't work."

"It doesn't make any sense to me," the younger man said, shaking his head. I mean, first of all *why* outlaw explosives and second how in the hell does it actually *work*? Expansion rate conversion never made any sense."

"You want an answer?" Talbot said, setting down the steel again and then sitting on the anvil. "I've about got my mad worked out, we'll let the forge cool off now that . . . Well, don't worry about pumping. So you want the answer?"

"Yes, I wouldn't have asked the question if I didn't."

"I know you went to day-school with Rachel," the smith

frowned. "And I know she knows this. So why do I have to explain it?"

"You don't if you don't want to," Herzer replied, standing up and stretching his legs. He felt better than he had all day. He really had needed some exercise. "But I took the preindustrial technologies track. I mean, it was covered in backgrounds to history, but that's all they said. And I never really cared before."

"Okay, but I'm not going to take fifty thousand words and if you don't understand it, you don't understand it. Got it?"

"Got it," Herzer said with a chuckle.

"The first thing is 'why?' " Talbot said. "The protocol got emplaced shortly after the AI war. You're up on that?"

"Somewhat. There was a class on it. I didn't sleep through it."

"So you know it was bad, bloody. Nearly as bad as this . . . shit we're in. There was a twenty-five percent die off in the first year of the war, some from fighting, most of it from starvation and other extermination programs of the AI's."

"Yes," Herzer said grimly. The Norau rump of the Council hadn't passed around current casualty estimates, but he'd seen the bodies by the tracks with his own eyes. If the human race had as little as a twenty-five percent die-off rate from this Dying Time he'd be very surprised.

"Anyway, the die-off and the war produced a great deal of pacifism in its wake. But at the same time it produced a lot of people who were pretty extreme. One group of them ambushed one of the members of the Council and wiped him and his bodyguards out. It wasn't easy. The 'assassins'— for want of a better word for a group of six hundred battle-armored infantry backed by AI tanks—were nearly wiped out by the bodyguards and the Council member, who for all his pacifism had gained it in the frontlines of the war.

"That really shook the Council. If Hollingsworth could be taken out, anyone could. The *only* thing that could prevent that was Mother."

"Ah."

"Now, no group of Council members had ever gotten large enough and unanimous enough to have Mother control crime or anything like that. That was so intrusive that they all recognized it would lead eventually to a revolt of one form or another. And most of them were against it in principle. On one level you know that Mother is always watching. But as long as you *know*, it doesn't matter . . . So, anyway, they

decided that they could either violate that long-held prohibition against using Mother for surveillance purposes, or they
could find some other way around it."

"Weapons controls?" Herzer asked. "But . . . But, I guess it
sort of makes sense . . ."

"Sure, if you have no understanding of *history*," Talbot
snarled. "Anything resembling universal suffrage is a
*post*industrial, *post*gunpowder concept. Gunpowder gave the
Everyman a way to kill the Lord on his horse. Industry,
by which I mean steam and internal combustion, removed
the need for day-in, day-out muscle use! As long as their
comfortable replication- and information-based society was
stable and stagnant, everything was fine. But take that away
and what do you have?"

"This," Herzer whispered, noticing how Edmund referred to
the pre-Fall society as "theirs." "Okay. So, no internal combustion, but why no steam?"

"Low power steam works," Talbot said. "But when you build
up really useable pressures it passes the point that Mother
is programmed to find dangerous and . . . the heat just . . . goes
away. Into the damned Net for Sheida to use, I suppose. It
even interferes with high temperature forges; forming steel is
a balancing act."

"Oh. Okay, that's the why. What's the 'how'?"

"Next you have to understand Mother."

"It's the central computer that runs the Web. So?"

"Oh, child," Edmund said with a grim chuckle. "Mother is
not a computer. Mother is a *program*. Actually, an OS/P, an
operating system/protocol. But Mother has become much more
than that. Mother is connected to every single outlet of the
Web. She sees through every nannite. She hears through every
ear. Her sensors detect every shift of the wind, every change
in kinetic energy, the potential of every raindrop, and have
a very good idea where the individual molecules are going
to end up. Have you ever heard that one about 'see every
sparrow fall'?"

"Yeah," Herzer said, caught in the odd spell of words that
Edmund seemed to be casting.

"Mother knows it before it starts to drop."

"So . . ." Herzer looked at the smith and shrugged. "Why
doesn't she stop this war?"

"Because Mother doesn't care," Edmund replied with a grin.
"She's not here to stop wars or start wars—wars are human
things and it's not her job to tell humans how to be human.

She just runs the Web and the various things that are attached to it. As long as the combatants don't do anything stupid to the actual information transfer architecture, Mother won't do anything to them."

"That is . . . weird."

"Mother was written by a guy who in retrospect turned out to be pretty damned weird. Name of Arthur King. Ever heard of him?"

"The name and that he was the founder of the Web."

"Not quite, he just wrote Mother. The Web existed before him, the only thing he really did was make the last major modification to its internal structure. And that was the last thing he did on this earth, apparently. Because he disappeared right afterwards. Vanished, without a trace."

"And this has what to do with the explosive protocols?"

"Remember, Mother knows all, Mother sees all. But the only time that Mother does things about it is if the Council tells her to. She's controlled by the Council members. They vote on what actions she should take *outside* of directly securing the Web. If enough of them told her to destroy the Earth, she would."

"What? How?" Herzer said.

"There are various ways that come to mind. It depends on if they just wanted the biosphere wiped out or really destroy the *Earth*. If they wanted the biosphere destroyed, she could probably just dump an enormous amount of power into the mantle and cause every volcano on Earth to erupt and keep erupting. That would wipe out everything but bacteria in time. She could wipe out any particular species simply by causing its chemical processes to stop. Are you feeling happier now?"

"That's *crazy!*" the boy said, shaking his head. "Since when?"

"Since looong before you were born, boy. Nobody talks about it and most people don't even think about it. Mother *owns* us, but we, in turn, own Mother, through the Council. There is a reason that I hate the Council, hated it long before this damned war, and thought that it needed far more oversight than it was getting."

"So you're saying that Mother stops explosions by knowing they are going to happen?"

"Partially. She also can sense that they have occurred. And while explosions propagate fast, they don't propagate faster than light or Mother's reactions. When one occurs, it gets surrounded by a force-field and 'damped' with the kinetic energy converted to electrical power then drained off into the

power net. All you get is a sort of wet 'thump' and a lump
of ash. I tried it with homemade gunpowder one time and
got a nasty note from the Council for my troubles."

"But . . . there are explosions that occur in nature all the
time. Lightning, volcanoes . . ."

"Like she can't tell the difference between a deliberately
detonated chemical explosive and lightning?" Edmund laughed.
"And chemical *explosions* don't happen in nature, at least not
much. There are a few species that come damned near to
having them, including plants. But Mother can filter for that.
Chemical explosions have a very distinct signature. As to
volcanoes, what makes you think she doesn't damp them?"

"Well, I've seen pictures . . ."

"Sure, plenty of pretty eruptions. Ever heard of Krakatoa?"

"No."

"Used to be an island. Then some salt water dropped into
a magma chamber and blew it up. *Big* explosion, killed a lot
of people, inundated islands, all the usual problems. With me?"

"Yeah."

"I mean *big* explosion. Ever heard of the Stone Lands?"

"I went there one time, it's . . . interesting. Geysers and hot
vents and stuff."

"Yeah. Did you know it once blew the hell up?"

"What?"

"Heh. Shortly after the AI war. Caused a hell of a stink
because there was a lot of suspicion that it had been done
deliberately; there are ways if you have access to power fields
and enough power. Anyway, it had always been really unstable
and the explosion had been sort of a background worry for
geologists for a long, *long* time, as long as they knew what
was going on down there. Similar to Krakatoa in that there
was a big hot spot and a lot of water in close proximity. If
it went, though, it was estimated that it would blow out not
only the Stone Lands but the area for several hundred kilometers in every direction. And I do mean 'blow out,' as in
blow it into the stratosphere."

"Wow."

"The hot spot had been heating the water for a few hundred thousand years and it was hoped that it would never
break down. Well, it did. Big time. Magma/steam explosion
estimated at something like one hundred megatons, that's a
really old expression to measure explosives."

"Okay."

"And what happened? Nada. Ground shook a bit, minor

earthquake. *That's* exactly how powerful Mother is. So forget making up a bunch of gunpowder and turning this into the New Model Army."

"Okay," Herzer said. "Damn. But one other thing?"

"Sure."

"Why *long*bows, crossbows are easier to train on and . . ."

"Oh not you *too!*"

CHAPTER THIRTY

Kane was checking one of the horse's shoes when Edmund entered the barn and he looked up in surprise at the mayor.

"When did they let you out of the cage?" he asked with a chuckle.

"I told my keepers to screw off and die," Talbot replied with a grin. "I was thinking about taking a ride if you'd loan me a horse and gear. And I thought you might like to ride along."

"Okay," Kane said, dropping the horse's hoof. "I don't suppose you remember much hot shoeing? I've been cold farriering these beasts but I'm about out of decent shoes."

"See Suwisa," Edmund said, pulling down a saddle and tack. "I'm pretty much out of the blacksmith business these days."

"I did," Kane said, following him out and whistling up a horse. "Hanarah or Arab?"

"Arab if Alyssa won't mind," Talbot replied. When the horse was called forward he caught it up and saddled it with ease. "We'll have to see if I remember how to ride."

"It's like sex," Kane replied, lifting himself into the saddle. "Once you've done it once you never forget."

"And, like sex," Talbot replied with a grunt as he hoisted himself upwards, "if you haven't done it for a while, the muscles lose their tone."

Despite his protests they trotted out of the corral and up towards Massan Mountain, taking a narrow trail up its woods covered sides. The day was clear and just turning to the summer heat but under the trees it was still cool from the morning and the horses were frisky. Suddenly, Edmund kicked his mount into a canter, then a full gallop, charging up the winding trail in a series of hair-raising turns.

Kane tried to keep up but the Hanarahs for all their speed were designed for the flats; the more nimble Arab easily left the larger horse behind.

Finally he debouched into a clearing on a shoulder of the mountain where Edmund was settling his prancing mount. As the Hanarah charged into the clearing the Arab reared, flailing its hooves at the apparent challenger.

Talbot easily kept his seat, grinning from the exhilarating ride and the antics of his mount. "I guess I *haven't* lost my touch," he said as the Arab got all four feet back on the ground.

"You were always a fine knight, King Edmund," Kane grinned.

"But no more," Edmund replied with a frown. "Mayor I am and mayor I'll stay if I have my way."

"What's that mean?" Kane said with a raised eyebrow.

"Those damned idiots in the constitutional committee . . ." Talbot said then shrugged. "We're going from a nice, clean constitution to something . . . They want to reinstitute an aristocracy and I can't stop the momentum."

"Well . . ." Kane temporized then shrugged. "I guess it depends on whether you're going to be the aristocrat or not. How are they going to 'choose' them?"

"They're going for a bicameral legislature; I got them that far," Edmund replied. "The lower house will be straight population representative, although broken up geographically. The 'upper' house, though, they want to be an aristocratic body. I *think* I'm going to get it to be partially representative. Probably with members chosen by district governments. But some of the representatives are insisting on an aristocratic addition. Give them their due, it's not all hereditary. But they also want 'notable persons' who will have lifetime appointments. I don't like lifetime appointments in general and I especially don't like the idea of hereditary appointees having a say in government."

"What's their argument?" Kane asked.

"Basically that there are some areas that already determined to have hereditary power transfer," Edmund sighed. "And we can't get them to join us unless we factor for it. There's also the fact that some of the members of the committee recognize that *they* are likely to be included. Their argument is that it gives a solid means of power transfer that people can identify with."

"Edmund, bear with me," Kane said carefully. "But . . . they have a point. As a society we have had one hell of a shock. People . . . people are looking for security as much as anything right now. Hereditary aristocracy . . . has a very *secure* feeling to it."

"Tell me something I don't know," Edmund replied. "But it's also a bad idea in the long term. You know how hard I've been working to avoid even de facto feudalism here. There are 'allies' that we're going to be forced to include that have *actual* feudalism brewing. And that is getting included as well, the *permission* for feudalistic society. Now, right *now* that is going to fly. But in time there are going to be areas that have serfs and areas that abhor the concept. That's a recipe for civil war if I've ever seen one."

"Ouch," Kane replied. "Good point."

In the meantime, I've a town to defend and that's what I really wanted to talk about."

"Oh?"

"I need two things and I think that you're the right person to handle both. The first is that we need some cavalry scouts and eventually we'll need some heavy cavalry. Good cavalry is as hard to come by as *good* archers and *good* legionnaires. In fact, I don't think you'll find it possible; it's the one arm I'm willing to admit will need at least a few generations to develop."

"Agreed," Kane said with a sigh. "And bow archers are even harder. I'd love to have a squadron of them. But this area will never develop the skills; too much woodland, not enough plains."

"True. But I want you to start working on it. They don't have to be full, professional quality cavalry, just the best that you can do. Start with the group that helped in the roundup. The main thing I need is cavalry scouts and those just need to be able to find their way around and stay on a horse."

"Okay, I'll start with Herzer," Kane said with a grin.

"Well, you'll have to discuss that with him," Talbot temporized and then chuckled. "He'd probably make a damned fine archer from evidence, Jody has been asking to have him back on his clearing crew, you want him for cavalry and from what I saw of him in my forge the other day he'd make a damned fine smith. The only person who's not asking for him is John Miller who called him 'a hack-handed idiot.'"

"So who gets him?" Kane asked with a smile; the sawmill manager was well known to the old re-enactors.

"He told me he wants to be a legionnaire," Edmund said with a shrug.

"Does he know about the cavalry?"

"No, but I doubt you'll change his mind," Talbot replied. "Actually, I think that once they're done training, we'll probably want some of the archers and infantry to get used to riding. But not as true 'cavalry.'"

"Okay, I'll work on it," Kane said with another grin. "Even without Herzer."

"The second item is like unto the first," Edmund said, starting to walk the horse sedately back down the hill. "I need someone to organize the militia. You can delegate that as you wish, but you're well known in the 'fighter' portion of the reenactors. And I just don't have time. I have Robert for the archers and Gunny for the legionnaires but I need someone to organize the disorganized militia."

"Fun, are you giving me the cavalry in compensation?"

"Something like that," Edmund chuckled. "Again, you can delegate it to others, but I want you to manage it in your munificent free time."

"Since the roundup I've actually *had* free time," Kane grumbled. "So much for that."

"We've all got our crosses to bear," Edmund said as they reached the flats. They were about a kilometer from the fences and that caused Edmund to grin. "Race you."

"Herzer, you have visitors," Rachel said, from the doorway of his bedroom.

Herzer looked up and smiled as Courtney and Mike came in the room and Rachel faded away. "Ah, visitors from far away lands," he said, setting down the book he had been reading. The visit to Edmund's forge had, not too unexpectedly, taken it out of him and he had suffered a small relapse. But he was feeling well again and getting tired of being confined. Fortunately, Master Talbot had a fine collection of old books so while the time was not passing pleasantly, it was passing.

"What is that supposed to mean?" Courtney asked.

"Never mind," Herzer chuckled. "I'd say 'pull up a chair' but it's more like 'pull up *the* chair.' I haven't been getting a lot of visitors," he continued. "So tell me all the news."

"How are you feeling?" Courtney asked, instead.

"Fine. I wish they'd let me out of here."

"You took a really bad hit," Mike said, leaning on the wall and crossing his arms. "You nearly punched out on us."

"Yeah, well, that was then, this is now," Herzer replied with a frustrated tone.

"Trust me, it's better than working," Courtney sighed, tossing her hair. "That's why you haven't been getting many visitors; we've all been running around like a chicken with its head cut off. And having seen a chicken with its head cut off, that now has a whole new meaning to me."

Herzer chuckled at the image and shook his head. "So, come on, what's been happening? I understand I missed quite a party at the big slaughter."

"Yeah, well, we did gorge ourselves for a couple of days there," Mike admitted.

"But we paid for it," Courtney said with a shudder.

"Pretty bad?" Herzer asked.

"You know that creek behind the slaughter buildings?" Courtney said and waited for a nod. "It was running red with blood. We ended up with about six hundred carcasses and it was like an assembly line. Hanging them, skinning them, cutting them up, separating out the guts . . ."

"Offal," Mike interjected. "It sounds better. Especially when you end up eating it."

"But we rounded up a lot of feral domestics," Courtney pointed out. "And tons of food that's being smoked. And that's part of what we wanted to talk to you about."

"Oh?"

"The class has been breaking up," Courtney said. "Emory ended up going to work with Jody clearing land and burning charcoal and Shilan has joined the weavers. We're in the farming portion of the class but . . . after that we're planning on quitting as well and we're nearly done. They're starting to parcel out the land for farms and there's a lottery for the domestics that were captured. Anyone can apply for land and everyone who was involved in the roundup gets tickets for the lottery."

"You see," Mike said. "They're going to take all the animals and parcel them out. There were a lot rounded up, but not enough for everyone to have what they want and everybody wants certain kinds."

"Am I in this lottery?" Herzer asked with a smile.

"Uh, yeah," Courtney replied with an embarrassed expression. "And we kind of wondered . . ."

"What I was planning on doing with whatever I got?" Herzer asked.

"Yeah."

"Well, I didn't even know it was going on, so this is all kind of new."

"You can apply for a land parcel, too," Mike said. "I don't know if it's a good idea or not. But if you apply for one that is next to ours, I can try to break and work both of them. You have to pay for the land in increasing size of payments. I don't know if I'd be able to work both of them, but I could try. And if it does work, I can split whatever profits we got off of it with you. And that would give you another source of income. Someday."

Herzer thought about it for a minute and then nodded his head. "Okay, hang on a second. Tell you what I'll do. Courtney, there's a pouch in the cupboard. Could you pull it out and toss it to me?"

She handed it to him and he dumped out the tokens that were in it onto the bed.

"I'm going to go for soldier," he said, sorting out the money that was in it into full tokens and change. "And from what I've been told, everything is going to be issued to me. But I got paid for the day before the roundup, the roundup and three days of convalescence. As a 'skilled rider,' no less. So I got a bonus on the roundup." He pulled out a full token and change and handed the rest to Courtney. "You guys can have whatever I get off of the lottery and I'll file a land grant alongside yours. That," he continued, pointing to the chits, "is a loan. There ought to be enough there to get you a few spare farm tools. And a few decent tools might a big difference."

"Thank you," Courtney said, looking at the money as if it was fairy gold.

"Aaah, I don't know about this," Mike said. "I was going to ask if you could do a loan on the lottery animals, but I don't know about this . . ."

"Oh, hush," Courtney snapped. "Just say 'thank you,' you dummy."

"Seriously," Herzer said, shaking his head. "You don't even have to say thank you. Like you said, you're going to try to work both farms. If you can do it, and I've got a feeling you're going to do well at it, then long term that means that not only is there, as you put it, a little extra income coming in, but in the old days soldiers used to dream of retiring and buying a farm. And I'll already have one!"

At that Mike laughed and shook his head but he obviously wasn't convinced.

"And on the cash I said it was a *loan*. You pay me back when you've got the money, but not until you're free and clear on everything else. I know you're good for it."

"Okay," Mike said, finally, shrugging his shoulders. "With that I can get some stuff that will help out. Woodworking tools, parts for a stump-jumping plow, spare rope. And if the lottery doesn't work out, we can put it all on a draft animal."

"So how's farm life suit you?" Herzer asked, changing the subject.

"Hard," Courtney replied. "I mean it's just constant. There's always something to get done. But . . ." she shrugged. "I agree with Mike; it's better than the other stuff we've done."

"I don't know," Mike said. "I could probably do woodworking or construction, something like that. But you do all of that with farming."

"Would you go back?" Herzer asked, crinkling his brow. "I mean, if everything suddenly turned back on? If you said 'genie' and your genie appeared?"

Mike thought about it for a moment, then nodded. "Yeah. There are days when I wake up and wonder where I am for a second 'cause it's all wrong, then it all comes back to me. And, man, those are some rotten days."

"Yeah, me too," Herzer said. But there was an odd note in his voice.

"Why am I unconvinced?" Courtney asked with a chuckle.

"Ah, it's hard to explain," Herzer admitted. "If I could just throw a switch and turn everything back on and have it go back to the way that it was, would I do it? Yeah." He sighed again and shrugged. "But. Hah! There'd be days I'd wake up and wonder where I was for a second; then it would all come back to me. And those would be some really bad days."

"That's weird," Mike said.

"Yeah, well, it's a long story."

"And one you're not telling today," Rachel said from the doorway.

"Oh, Rachel, come on!"

"The term is bed *rest*, not bed *activity*," Rachel said, then blushed. "That wasn't what I meant to say."

"I couldn't *tell*," Courtney laughed.

"I am resting, look!" Herzer said, leaning back in the bed. "See. Rest."

"Do you know what this idiot did the other day?" Rachel asked Courtney.

"I haven't a clue," the girl replied with a smile. "What *did* this idiot do?"

"He helped my father in the forge for four hours."

"Oh, now *that* was a good idea!" Courtney said.

"It wasn't that bad," Herzer complained. "So I got a little headache."

"I think you used the term 'blinding' at one point?" Rachel asked. "Something about purple spots? Bed rest. *Bed rest.*"

"Okay, we get the point," Mike said. "We're going."

"Herzer, I'll write up those agreements and get them over to you," Courtney said. "Thanks again. Get somebody else to look them over for you and make sure it's what you want before you sign them. Then I'll get them registered at the courthouse."

"Okay," Herzer replied. "I trust you guys. But if you *insist* on getting it written down . . ."

Herzer wasn't sure if it was by intent to make sure he was in the first class, but the day after Dr. Daneh stated that he was "fully recovered" the first call for recruits went out.

Herzer was at the recruiting station just after dawn the next day, walking up and looking around with interest in the predawn half-light. The recruiting station was a simple table in front of a group of tents, most of which had lanterns hanging in front of them. There were about a half dozen standing around who had beat him there. One of them was Deann.

"Decided to go for soldier?" he said, walking over and sticking out his hand, grinning.

"We were working in the tanneries," Deann admitted, taking it and shaking it hard. "I decided I had to find something else when the head tanner pointed out that once you lost your sense of smell things got a hundred percent better."

Herzer chuckled and looked around at the group, which was about half youngsters like himself and Deann and about half older. There wasn't much physical difference in the individuals, but it was noticeable in little ways, stance gestures. With modern technology, people didn't start to get "old" until they were well past two hundred. Herzer wondered how much of that was "built in" and would stick and how much was nannite generated and would go away with the Fall. For now, the "oldsters" seemed to be holding up.

They waited in companionable silence as others filtered up. Deann was the only one he knew by name, but several of the others nodded their heads at him as if they recognized him, which was odd. He was having a hard time adjusting to lots of people knowing him on sight.

"You're still the talk of the town," Deann said, chuckling quietly after one of the older arrivals had come by and tapped Herzer on the shoulder wordlessly.

"All I did was herd a few cattle," he muttered, shaking his head.

"Bull," she answered with a grin. "I made five chits off of you myself. Nobody thought you'd survive the first tiger. The way you were charging around, nobody thought you'd last half an hour."

Herzer's face worked but he didn't reply because about then the tent flap opened, revealing a figure in armor in the doorway.

"Step up to the table, give your true name, true age and answer the questions," the figure said brusquely. He stepped to the side as two women took up seats at the table.

Herzer waited for the line to form and took a place near Deann. The process was slow and he realized there was probably going to be a lot of waiting around today.

Finally it was his turn and he stepped up to the table. The sun was up by then and his belly rumbled, reminding him that he hadn't gotten any breakfast this morning.

"Herzer Herrick" he said. "Seventeen." Barely, he didn't add.

"Okay, I think I can put you down as experienced with horses and a bow." The woman chuckled.

"I'm not an expert . . ." he temporized.

"Not an expert, got it. Do you have any other skills you would like to list?"

"I am trained in individual swordsmanship," Herzer said. "Enhanced reality training. Some with a spear."

"And lance," the woman said.

"Not lance," the figure in armor said. "That was luck as much as anything. His seat was bloody awful."

Herzer cast a quick glance at the man. He was an oldster, he had white hair and wrinkles even, but he was a hard-ass, that was clear, wearing a loricated armor, armor made of curved plates that overlapped like the carapace of a centipede. Herzer wanted to dispute his statement, at least mentally, but he really couldn't. It *had* been lucky. The man was just being brutally honest. And astute.

"Do you know the fashioning of arms and armor?"

"No, I didn't even put it on myself in training," Herzer admitted. "And I don't know that much about caring for horses. I can ride, though."

"That is true," the armored figure said.

"Anything else?" the woman asked.

"No."

"Step into the tent and follow the directions you are given," she said, handing him a folder. "Hang onto that," the woman continued in a rote voice. "You've just become a record and that is it."

Herzer held onto his file and passed through the stations. There was a test of reading and writing, a simple test of strength involving mostly lifting various weights and then a physical examination. He submitted to this last with good grace; at this point he was so used to being poked and prodded that it just didn't seem his day was complete unless someone told him to stick out his tongue and say "aaaah." The examiner was one of the nurses being trained by Dr. Daneh who had turned up from time to time during his convalescence. She was a pretty enough brunette with the annoying habit of talking with her teeth clenched. She had been friendly enough during her visits but was professionally distant during the examination. Right up until the end when she chuckled.

"Given that Dr. Daneh did a complete exam a couple of days ago, this one seems pretty unnecessary," she said, making some notes on a piece of paper and slipping it into his file.

"I wasn't going to say anything," Herzer replied with a smile.

"Well, other than needing some exercise, you appear to be perfectly adequate sword fodder," she said with a frown in reply. "Do me a favor and don't get yourself killed. We've got a lot of work invested in you."

"Well, since you care so much, I'll try really hard not to."

"Okay," she smiled. "Through that door."

Herzer passed through the door into the outside, finally, and saw a small group of recruits milling around, one of whom was Deann. There was a man in mail, light helm and leather bracers who seemed to be in charge of the group and he nodded when Herzer appeared.

"That's twenty," the man said. "You lot, follow me."

The area behind the examination tents was a large, recently cleared, stump-covered field in the northeast quadrant of the Raven's Mill valley. One end of it had been set up with archery butts at various distances, each with a number at the top, and the man led them to a table where a series of bows were laid out. At one end of the table was a water bucket and a half barrel filled with arrows, the fletchings in multiple colors and patterns. To Herzer's eye something about the fletchings looked wrong.

"My name is Malcolm D'Erle," the man said when the group was gathered around. "Today I will be testing you on your ability to draw and fire bows. We're not really expecting anyone to be able to hit anything. We just want to see how much basic capability you have to draw and fire."

Herzer saw that, blessedly, there were some gloves and bracers laid out with the bows.

"This," Malcolm said, picking up one of the larger bows, "is called a longbow or a self-bow. It is so called because, as you can see, it is very long. The reason for its length is that the arrow has more distance that it can be driven by the spring of the bow. Shorter bows have less distance of travel and therefore can impart less energy to the arrow. This type of bow will, for the time being, be the basic bow of the Raven's Mill Defense Force archers. There are a couple of aspects to it. One is that it is a very strong bow, and difficult to draw. Especially repeatedly as is necessary in combat. The other is that it requires a person who is of normal male height or greater." He looked around the group and then at Deann. "You, young lady, for example, I don't think have much of a chance; you're just too short."

Deann grimaced at that and growled. "But you are going to *give* me a chance, right?"

"Of course. Now, does anyone here have any experience with bows?"

After a moment when no one else raised their hand, Herzer did so reluctantly.

"Oh, yeah. The guy on the horse. Where did you learn?"

"I was doing enhanced reality training before the Fall hit," Herzer replied.

"What do you normally use?"

"During training I used a one-hundred-kilo composite recurve, sir. But my muscles are out of shape and I don't think that I could handle that in my current condition."

"A hundred kilos? Well the good news is, I don't have one that strong so we won't be finding out if you could or not. I brought these other bows out just to show them to you," he continued, setting down the long bow. He picked up one of the smaller bows and bent it in his hands. "This is a short bow, which, as you can see, is shorter. It is otherwise similar to the longbow. The major difference is the distance an arrow can be thrown, the damage that it does and the amount and type of armor it can pierce. Mass fire of short bows are useful against groups of unarmored enemies. But unlike the longbow, just about any decent armor, including rivet mail, will shrug it off."

He picked up another bow that was about the same length but was broadly curved. "This, on the other hand, is a short, composite recurve bow. It is a much stronger bow and has a long draw. It uses sinew backing to give it extra strength. In the case of this one, it is made out of horn and sinew with a thin strip of wood in the middle. It is a very strong bow and quite as powerful as the longbow. However, they are extremely difficult to construct, require materials that we don't have available and tend to suffer from damp. They were used primarily by steppes horse archers for a reason. The steppes were dry, the bows could be used from horseback and they had the appropriate materials in abundance while lacking much wood."

"I'll let you take a look at the other bows as the tests progress. What we're going to do is take a shot at the target marked with the seventy-five. That is at seventy-five meters."

He took the longbow and drew an arrow from the barrel, nocking the bow and raising it.

"Note that I bring the arrow to my cheek and push the bow *away* from me," he said. "And also, notice that I'm aiming well *above* the target." He let fly with the arrow and it sunk deeply into the target on the right of the bullseye near the edge of the target.

"These arrows could be considered a test in themselves," he said grimly. "They're the first output of our apprentice fletchers and quite lousy. But all you have to do is *get* the arrow to the distance of the target. If you can do that, we'll do some more testing. Those that can't draw the bow, or even hold it off the ground, will be passed on to the next phase of testing."

"Can I ask a question?" Herzer said.

"Please.

"I take it that anyone who passes the test becomes an archer?"

"Both tests. This test and there will be a timed test. You have to draw and fire fifty arrows in ten minutes. If *no one* can do that, then we'll back off of the requirement."

"Can you?" Deann challenged.

In response Malcolm removed ten arrows and thrust them into the ground in a semicircle around him. Then he drew and fired all ten, driving each into the target, several close to or into the bullseye.

"I need to find out which ones were on," Malcolm commented dryly. "Those apprentices made decent arrows."

"What if you don't *want* to be an archer?" Herzer asked.

"We need archers," Malcolm answered. "Just about anyone can swing a sword. Archers are practically *born*, not *raised*. If you can be an archer, you're going to be an archer. You can *quit* but you can't choose *not* to be an archer."

Herzer opened his mouth to protest but then closed it with a clop.

"You start," Malcolm said, handing him the bow.

Herzer examined it for a moment and then took up a glove that more or less fit and a bracer.

"I used him as a demonstration for a reason," Malcolm noted. "If you don't use a glove at first, you'll turn your fingers into mush. And you'll *never* get over the need for a bracer. The bowstring slaps against the inside of your arm with each shot. In fact, metal bracers are arguably necessary for combat archery, although they should have something on the inner side to shield the bowstring."

"How many shots?" Herzer asked, pulling at the string to get a feel for the draw. He could feel his latissimus dorsae muscle protesting already; he was seriously out of shape. Despite that, he knew he could pass the initial test and probably the "combat shooting" test. But if he did, he'd be stuck as an archer.

"At least one," Malcolm said from behind him.

"I'd like five," Herzer replied. "And one ranging shot to get the feel of the bow."

"Okay."

Herzer could feel the eyes of the group on him as he drew the first arrow. He raised it to more or less the same angle as Malcolm and pushed the bow away from him, letting fly when the arrow was in-line to the target. It flew past and into the distance.

"Now we realize why I used apprentice arrows instead of good ones," Malcolm said, dryly. "We're going to lose a good few today."

Herzer didn't comment but simply picked up the next arrow and lowered the angle. He hadn't considered, before, that he was taller than Malcolm and, apparently, had a longer reach. He drew the bow and fired and the arrow, wobbling badly from poor manufacture, thumped into the lower left quadrant of the target. He drew and fired the next four in succession, if not as fast as Malcolm then with nearly the same success.

"The boy does know how to shoot," Malcolm said, accepting the bow from Herzer. "Take a break while I run the rest through."

Herzer got some water and watched the others fire for a bit and then picked up the composite bow and a couple of arrows and went down a ways to another lane. Malcolm's composite, not too surprisingly, had a slightly higher draw than Alyssa's but not too terrible. He drove a few of the horrible arrows into the butt and then actually examined one. They had been inexpertly fletched and the shafts were rarely straight. After a moment he realized that he had no idea how to make one, so he wasn't exactly the person to be criticizing.

He watched as Deann's turn came up and, sure enough, the bow was far too long for her. She tried to fire it but the bottom kept hitting the ground and one of the recoils from the strike nearly slapped her in the face. After a few aborted shots she gave it over to Malcolm with bad grace and stomped off.

Finally the whole group had finished shooting and Malcolm called a break.

"Okay, Herzer, Rosio, Ngan, Earnest and Maskell, you stay here. The rest fall back until we complete this test."

"I really don't want to be an archer," Herzer said quietly as the others were milling around.

"Why?" Malcolm asked, drawing him aside. "Herzer, damnit, we *need* archers! You're *trained*. And you've got the build for it. What do you want to be, cavalry?"

"No, I want to be line infantry," Herzer said just as quietly. "I can just fail the test. You *know* that."

"Is that what you're going to do?" D'Erle asked, furiously.

"No, I'm going to pass the damned thing. And then be a pain in the ass until you send me over to infantry."

"Do that and I'll boot you all the way out," D'Erle warned.

"No you won't," Herzer replied, stubbornly. "Because you're going to need good line infantry, too. Just let me walk."

"Take the test," Malcolm said after a moment. "Then we'll talk." He raised his head and looked over at the others. "Time to spread out."

A group of workers came out and laid out boxes with arrows along the lanes, and another archer came out with more bows.

"Rather than have each of you wait on the others, we're going to run all of you at once. You have to fire fifty arrows and you have to complete the course of fire in ten minutes. *Pace* yourself. You're going to get tired. Initially try for twelve arrows per minute. I'll call the minutes and you'll have a person handing you the arrows and doing the count. All that you have to do is manipulate the bow."

"Is that realistic?" Herzer asked. "I mean, in combat are we going to have someone handing us arrows?"

"Most of the time," Malcolm said with a nod. "An archer is simply the most important member of a *team*. He's just there to feed the bow. Others handle the logistics. Each archery team will have at least three people on it, one of whom is just there to feed the archer who in turn feeds the bow."

"Oh."

"This is a test of firing fifty arrows in ten minutes so that they at least make it to the ground at seventy-five meters. A fully trained archer will put out two hundred and fifty arrows in an *hour* at *two hundred* yards, hard enough to go through plate armor. This is *baby* steps, boys. Take your positions."

"I'll hand them to you steady, sir," the boy by the arrows said. "And I'll keep the count. There's fifty-three in here in case some get dropped or broken."

"Okay," Herzer said. "What's your name?"

"Trenton, sir," the boy said.

"Just feed me, Trenton," he said with a grin.

"Prepare to fire," Malcolm called, lifting a sand-glass.

Herzer took the first arrow and a deep breath.

"Fire!"

It was just a bit like feeding the bow. Herzer had assumed that he would be able to ace the timed fire but in short order he realized just what an incredible workout it was. He was drawing on a fifty-kilo bow so each draw was the equivalent of using his back and shoulder muscles to lift fifty kilos. It was brutal work and he was quickly sweating profusely. He had fired fifteen arrows on the first minute but only nine on the second and he felt himself falling progressively further and further behind. Digging deep down inside he let himself drift, searching for the "zone" and picked up the pace despite the fire that seemed to spread through his back with each additional draw. For that matter, the leather bracer was *not* enough and each additional slap against his forearm was spreading waves of pain up his arm. He was going to have one hell of a bruise when he was done.

"Last minute!" Malcolm called.

"Twenty, sir!" Trenton said.

Herzer was not about to fail at this point. Forgotten was any interest in line infantry, he was simply *not going to fail.* "FEED ME!"

From somewhere he got a second wind and began slamming arrow after arrow downrange. He forgot to even try to hit the target and just concentrated on getting them all over the range line. It was getting nearly impossible to do a full draw but he slammed one after another out nonetheless until Malcolm called "TIME!"

Herzer lowered the bow to rest on the ground and stood, breathing deeply, grimacing at the pain in his arm.

"You went two over, sir, sorry," Trenton said, taking the bow from him and getting a dipper of water.

"Well, one went short," Malcolm said, walking up to their station to survey the result with a grimace.

"So I passed," Herzer chuckled.

"Yeah," Malcolm said with another grimace. "You're the *only* one who passed. I *told* Edmund the test was too tough."

"And you were right," Talbot said, appearing behind them as if he had apported. "I thought you were going for line infantry, Herzer?"

"I was told I had to take the test, sir," Herzer replied.

"And you're the only one that passed," Edmund frowned. "How did the others do?"

Malcolm thought about it for a moment with a frown then shrugged. "The average is about thirty in ten minutes, taking Herzer out of the group."

"That's still better than crossbow," Edmund considered. "But not much."

"Their wind is awful," Malcolm commented. "I think they might be able to make archers, some day, but it will be a hell of a lot of work."

"Did all of them make at least thirty?" Talbot asked.

"All but one," Malcolm admitted.

"Drop the requirement to thirty and continue the testing," Edmund said. "And you're going to have to *drive* them."

"I will. What about Herzer?"

"I should make him one of your assistants," Talbot said, looking the still sweating boy up and down. "But I think we'll go ahead and pass him on to the next testing station."

CHAPTER THIRTY-ONE

After the archery test they were served a light lunch and ate it sitting on the ground. Herzer quickly downed the strips of salty pork, which were served on flat-bread, and chewed manfully on some large crackers that were just about as hard as rocks. It seemed that all of the testing groups had been gathered together and he looked around at the figures, wondering what would come next.

After lunch his group was approached by a young man, probably a few years older than he and Deann but it was hard to tell. He was inordinately tall, taller than Herzer, which was unusual, and muscular with legs that looked like tree trunks. The man was wearing a heavy, open-faced helmet, articulated body armor, a metal-plated leather kilt, greaves and heavy leather boots. He looked at the group and waved them to their feet.

"My name is Sergeant Greg Donahue," the man said. "You will address me as Sergeant Donahue. I do not respond to 'Hey, you' or 'Sarge.' I hope you're all fed and watered, because we've got a bit of work to do. Follow me."

He led them across the area, behind where more groups were preparing for the archery test, then westward towards the hills flanking the valley until he reached the base of a high hill that had to be near the river. On the ground were a large number of leather rucksacks arranged in a formation. On the side towards the hill was another sack, standing all alone. The young man walked to that sack and turned towards them.

"Everyone take a position by one of the sacks," he said, standing by his own sack with his feet spread and his hands locked behind his back. He waited until they were in position and cleared his throat.

"This town is called Raven's Mill. But since ravens are not native to this area, that begs the question: Why? Once upon a time a man lived in this area who was attempting to develop talking ravens, ones with nearly full human intelligence. In time he tired of the quest and released his ravens into the wild. Most of them died but a few of the hardier specimens survived. They tended to congregate around this hill and it, in time, was called Raven's Hill. Edmund Talbot, when he moved here, knew of the story and named the area for the ravens who had by that time died out completely.

"However, Master Edmund liked this hill for the same reason the ravens did, from the top of it you can see for miles. As such, for exercise, he had constructed a set of steps up the hill. Four hundred and twenty-three steps, to be precise. On the up side. There are three hundred and seventy-four on the down, which takes a slightly different path." He paused and nodded at someone behind the group.

Herzer turned involuntarily and saw the man who had been at the initial entry processing. He was easier to examine now and Herzer realized he must be about the same age as Edmund Talbot. He was tall and lean with gray, cold eyes and wearing the same outfit as Sergeant Donahue.

Herzer snapped his head around as the man snarled: "EYES FRONT!"

Sergeant Donahue nodded and continued. "We will be testing your ability to do the single most important function of the infantryman: Walking. You have been tested for adequate upper body strength and later we'll find out if you have the single-minded aggressiveness to be functional line infantry. And if you don't, we'll either weed you out or teach it to you. But for now, we have to know if you can keep up. If you can 'hang. He nodded grimly at the faces as the test sank in. "So now if you'll pick up the rucksacks and put them on your back, we can begin. Make sure they're comfortable. I will set the pace. Anyone who falls behind Gunnery Sergeant Rutherford is disqualified."

Herzer hoisted the ruck and settled it on his back, adjusting the leather straps as best he could. They had buckles but it was a pain to adjust them while they were on, so he unshipped his, changed the settings and then put it back on.

It was heavy as hell, probably sixty to eighty kilos. He looked up the hill and suddenly regretted even the skimpy meal they had been given.

Donahue nodded as the last pack was settled and then walked among the group checking their fit. He adjusted one or two, then walked back to his place.

"We'll start on the flats so that everyone can become accustomed to the weight and then we'll see if you can handle the Hill."

He settled them in a double file and marched them back towards the main encampment, keeping to some of the better leveled roads. They marched almost down to the creek that ran through the center of the encampment and then turned to a trail along the base of the northern hills. This led in a curve back to just before their starting point and Herzer got the first look at the steps. They appeared to go straight up.

"Single file, keep closed up, follow me," Donahue said, stepping onto the first step.

Herzer was about a third of the way back and as he reached the steps he looked up and got dizzy; the stairs seemed to be wavering and he had a moment of vertigo.

"Keep your eyes on the steps!" a voice from the rear called.

Afraid that he'd leave a gap, Herzer put his head down and started toiling upward.

The pace was brutal and it was a *long* way to the top of the hill. Before he was even a third of the way up Herzer was sweating and blowing again, pushing hard against the weight of his body and the pack. He barely noticed the first person to have stopped, but when another person blocked his way he blundered into them, nearly knocking them both down.

"Get out of the damned way," he snarled, stepping around them and hurrying to catch up to the group ahead of him. Suddenly the group stopped, just as he reached the trailing person and he nearly fell over again avoiding another collision, then the group started off again, faster than they had before and he perforce had to hurry to catch up. His legs felt as if they were on fire and when he looked around he realized that they had barely come half way.

This went on and on in starts and stops as more people fell by the wayside, panting and gasping and clutching their sides. Herzer could feel a sharp pain growing in his own side but he willed it down and concentrated on maintaining his breathing and keeping up with the person in front of him. Suddenly that person fell out as well and Herzer realized there was a gigantic gap ahead of him. He struggled to catch up to the leading figure but he could barely maintain an even pace. He didn't dare look back, knowing that somewhere behind him was that hard-faced, gray-eyed bastard, probably hoping that he'd fall out.

His vision was starting to gray and sweat was pouring down his face to such an extent that he never even noticed when there wasn't another step. As the wind blew across his face he stumbled forward, only to be caught and lowered to the ground.

"Take a rest," Donahue said in an even tone, clearly not even out of breath. Herzer looked up and him and the bastard was hardly *sweating*. "There's water in your rucksack. Drink it."

Herzer nodded and slipped his arms out of the pack, looking around as his vision started to clear. They were in a clearing at a lower summit of the hill with a clear view of the river on one side and Raven's Mill at the other. Besides the stairs they had come up, there was another set that went farther up the hill. Donahue and the man he'd identified as the gunnery sergeant were to one side of the clearing, talking. Other than them, there were only three others on the top of the hill. One of whom was Deann, who was bent over retching.

Herzer slipped his arms out of the rucksack and fumbled at the closures with fingers that felt like they were the size of watermelons. Finally he got it open and pulled out a waterbag. He sipped at the contents and then took a solid swig of the water that had been cut with wine.

"Keep your seats," the gunnery sergeant said, walking over to the group. "Quit trying to throw up and drink some water, girl. You all may be wondering why we're trying to kill you. It's very simple. Someday, your enemies *will* be trying to kill you. There is an old saying: The more you sweat, the less you bleed. We are going to sweat you like you've never been sweated before. Most of the people who signed up for this thought it would be a cakewalk, like the guards in town. Nothing but standing around and looking pretty for the girls. Plenty of them had been reenactors playing at being Vikings or Picts or medieval knights. But that word is: Playing. We're not going to play and we're not going to be any of those pansies for sure. We're designed to be the first line of defense for Raven's Mill; the line that nine times out of ten is the *only* line the enemy will face. The line that any enemy will break its teeth upon. A line that will die in place rather than give a foot of ground.

"This training is designed to produce cadre for legions. Each of you will see your fair share of fighting, but what we're really working to produce is the future *leaders* of the legions. Leaders that are harder and scarier than the hardest and scariest force on earth.

"So we're going to winnow you out. When we're done, we're going to have only those who *refuse* to quit, no matter what we throw at them. Soldiers that are so hard that they'd rather die than surrender or give any less than three hundred percent.

"And this is not the last test, or even the worst, that you will face. But only the strongest, the hardest, the most determined, will make it.

"There are two ways down from this hill. One is the way that you just came. The other is up another hill and down the far side. In just a moment, Sergeant Donahue and I will ascend the hill. From the time we reach the top, you will have seven minutes to join us. Those that join us in less than seven minutes will put their feet on the path to being Blood Lords. Those that do not may someday join the legions, but they will never be leaders and they will never be the elite.

"It's up to you."

With that he picked up his pack and started up the stairs at a lope.

Herzer watched the old man trotting up the stairs and shook his head. He looked around at the small group on the top of the hill, wondering who would be the first to struggle to their feet. As it happened, Deann was already there. She just kneeled down to get her arms in the straps and then, still retching, staggered towards the steps.

"Crap," he muttered, pushing himself up. He got the rucksack up, somehow, and followed her.

Around the turn of the first bend she was bent over, dry-heaving, but still managing to put one foot in front of the other.

"Come on," he said, taking her elbow.

"Leave me alone," she muttered between retches. "I can make it."

"If you're stupid enough to keep going, I'm stupid enough to help," he replied, hooking an arm under her rucksack.

Weaving back and forth, they both staggered upwards towards the summit and their future.

✧   ✧   ✧

Edmund chuckled as Gunny collapsed in the chair across from him. "You look like hell, Miles."

It was early evening and Edmund wondered how much longer he was going to be stuck behind the desk *today*. The supply situation had improved somewhat, between the influx from the roundup and a few caravans from nearby towns. But the demand had increased from the Resan refugees and a steady trickle of others. Getting farms into production was a top priority, but defending them, given the reputed size of the Resan raiders, was very close to the same. And spies had reported that Rowana was *definitely* getting some sort of support from the New Destiny Alliance. Which meant that sooner or later the two towns were going to come to blows.

"Thank you so much," Gunny growled, leaning back with a sigh. "I'm getting too old for this shit. Running up hills is a young man's game."

"Don't tell me you took the Hill?" Edmund said, startled. "I gave that up fifteen years ago; there's only so much medical science can do without a complete rebuild!"

"Well, I had to prove to them that I was tougher than they were," Gunny said. "I just dread having to do this with every class!"

"How'd it go?"

"Not bad, we're going to have sixty or seventy in the first group. The team I followed had young Herzer in it. I wanted to see if you were right."

"Was I?" Edmund asked, reaching into a drawer. "You look like you could use a belt."

"I never turn down free hooch." Gunny chuckled. "And, yeah, you were right; he can hang. He ended up dragging one of his friends all the way to the top. I think she would have made it on her own so I didn't jump his ass. But while he didn't exactly carry her, he was definitely a support. He'll do."

"He's acting like the devil is on his tail all the time," Edmund commented, pouring out two glasses. "There's more to whatever went on with him and Daneh than she'll tell me. But watch him; he's liable to do something stupid and heroic. We need all the trained troops we can get; losing that one to his own stupidity would . . . annoy me."

"Will do," Gunny said, downing the bourbon. "Not bad."

"I laid it down years ago," Edmund replied, taking a gulp himself. "How are the rest of the recruits?"

"They made it to the top of the hill which means they *really*

want to be here. We'll just have to see how they train up."
He paused and frowned. "I sometimes find it difficult to
remember that we were once as foolish as these young folks."

"Yep," Edmund admitted. "And the reality of it is that you
have to have people as foolish as this because we're no longer
dumb enough to do what has to be done."

"The scary part is that they look up to us," Gunny said,
chewing on his stogie. "We're like Gods to them. Some of them
know, intellectually, that we're just as human as they are. And
a few can even figure out that once upon a time we were Just
Like Them. The *better* of them, sure. But not even like the *best*."

"Yuh," Talbot grunted. "It seems like the best of our old
companions didn't make it this far."

"And when *we* were like them, somebody that *we* looked
up to kicked *our* ass into line. We are born in imperfection,
Edmund."

"We are that," Edmund grimaced. "And no matter how hard
I have tried, I think we're going for the simplicity of imperfection."

"Clarify?" Gunny said. "You're not talking about the training program, are you?"

"No," Edmund sighed. "The Constitution of the United Free
States has been drafted. It's got provisions for both aristocracy and de facto feudalism included. No matter what I did."

"Does it directly affect us?" Gunny said.

"Only in the aristocracy provisions," Talbot snarled. "I
managed to include a provision that local governments could
declare themselves 'serfdom free' within their local charters.
We're chartered in Overjay, a geographical area with Washan,
Warnan and a few others, including Rowana, which is not a
member."

"What about military forces?" Gunny asked, cutting to the
part that was important to him.

"Well, I got an amendment that full voters have to show
capability to use arms, but the feudal states got a provision
that 'secondary citizens' are to be *unarmed* and they count
towards their voters even if they can't vote. Local citizenry
raises its own weaponry and provides for its own defense.
Professional military forces swear oath to the United Free States.
And I'm pretty sure I'm going to get the Academy listed as
a part of the professional military force."

"What about the legions?" Gunny asked. "Is that going to be
the main force? Or are we going to have to take whatever comes
to a muster?"

"Well, the question is, who is going to be in charge?" Edmund replied with a chuckle. "The secret here is to have the best plan at the beginning and get the forces formed around yours. We'll have more than legions in the long term, but hopefully that will be the core force. On the other hand, the Kents have gone almost entirely towards cavalry. If we can get them to join the UFS, and they're balking badly, it would be stupid to put them on foot. On the other other hand, most of the city states are concentrating on infantry. And who's got the best infantry?"

"We do," Rutherford said, assuredly.

"That's right."

"So," Gunny said, changing the subject. "How's Daneh?"

"Getting weird on me."

When Edmund got home, his curtains had been replaced.

Indeed, on walking into his front room, he wasn't sure he was in the right house. The furniture had been rearranged, two of his favorite tapestries were gone and the big table that he was wont to pile stuff on until he figured out what to do with it had disappeared.

Daneh was in the middle of the room, on her hands and knees, measuring the floor with a piece of string.

"What are you doing?" he asked, carefully.

"Measuring for carpets," Daneh replied, making a note.

"I like tile," Edmund said.

"I know you do," Daneh replied, getting up off her knees with some effort. She had started to show lately and it was affecting her balance. "But, do you have any idea how uncomfortable tile is when your ankles are swelling and your feet feel like your arches are falling?"

"You're not that far along, yet," he temporized.

"No," she smiled. "That's why I'm measuring for carpets now."

"Is this a pregnant thing?" he asked, carefully. She had had a tendency to snap his head off lately if he asked searching questions about her "delicate condition."

"I don't know," she replied cheerfully. "But whether it is or not, you're getting carpet."

"And where is it coming from?"

"I met this nice girl named Shilan who is one of the apprentice weavers. And since the sheep dropped and we've got a bit of an excess of wool at the moment, and since the new powered mill is experimenting with different weaves, she thought she could get me some piled wool carpet. That's where the curtains came from, too."

"And my tapestries?" he asked cautiously.

"They're out in your workshop," she answered. "What do you want for supper?"

CHAPTER THIRTY-TWO

After a hearty dinner the recruits spent the night in bunk-houses that had been cleared out for them and were woken before dawn by one of the sergeants walking through, banging on a metal shield.

"Up and at 'em, rise and shine, it's another beautiful day in the legions," the sergeant said. "Ten minutes for the jakes then fall out in front of the barracks."

Herzer lined up for the latrines—there were only two seats available for the whole group—then washed sketchily in a rain barrel. Finally he joined the mob in front of the bunkhouse.

"We're not going to try to move you around in formations, yet," the sergeant said after doing a headcount, "because you'd just be falling over your own feet. So if you'd just follow me in your customary cluster fisk and try not to fall too far behind, we'll go get you in-processed.

The gaggle followed him to a series of buildings near the base of the western hills. These were more substantial than most of the "temporary" buildings that had been thrown up to handle the refugee influx and Herzer suspected they had supported the annual Faire. They gathered outside the first and then went in one by one.

The room inside had been separated into two by a series of rough tables. On one side were a few civilians and on the other were piles of rough cloth and more than twenty women hastily sewing uniforms from it.

"My, you're a big one," the man who seemed to be in charge

said. "Katie, I'm going to need an XXL for this one," the man called, pulling a string from around his neck. "What's your inseam, big-boy?"

"I have no idea," Herzer replied. "What's an inseam?"

"The length of the inside of your thigh," the man replied, squatting down and measuring it. He chuckled at Herzer's discomfort. "That's exactly why I told the silly gunnery sergeant you weren't to strip until *after* this bit! I need a forty-four inseam, Katie!"

"He'll have to do with a forty-six or so," the woman behind the counter said, handing over some gray clothing, a cloth bag and some sundry cloth strips.

"Take this and change behind that curtain," the man said, turning to the next recruit in line. "Put your civilian clothes in the bag. Keep your shoes on."

"What about the rest?" Herzer asked.

"Just hold onto it and go to the next room."

Herzer changed into the baggy clothes, noting as he did that there were two more sets just as badly made, and hitched the pants up as far as he could with his belt. After that, carrying his "civilian" clothes, money pouch and the other uniforms, he went into the next room.

"Put your old clothes and anything else you were carrying except money or valuables into the bag," a man said abruptly. "Didn't you listen?"

Herzer quickly complied and held the bag up. "What now?" The room had a large number of similar bags piled on one side, the table the officious man was at, a burning candle and a stack of badly constructed wooden chests. And that was it.

The man took out leather ties and a candle. "Tie this around it, seal the ties with the wax, put your fingerprint in the wax. When you're done with training it will be returned. Put your uniforms in the footlocker and carry it with you."

Herzer did as he was told. Then the man took the bag and handed him one of the chests. "Next room."

"Ah, very nice boots," the man in the next room said, kneeling to examine Herzer's footwear. "You probably would be better off keeping them but orders are orders. Take them off and let me measure your feet."

Herzer sat in a chair and looked around as he took them off. There were several recruits in the room being fitted for boots but he didn't see any boots in sight.

"Uhm, where *are* the boots?" he asked as the man pulled out string and started taking measurements.

"They'll have to be made, won't they?" the man chuckled. "It's not as if we have warehouses full. Big feet; you're going to use up most of a cow, boy."

"Sorry."

"Not a problem."

Herzer continued through room after room, occasionally moving to different buildings and being outfitted or, more often, measured. Helmet, cloak, blankets, underclothes and cloths to wrap to replace socks. They did have a helmet his size, although it wasn't fitted on the inside and rolled around on his head until he removed it and stowed it in the footlocker. The locker was getting heavy by the time he completed the circuit and emerged back into the sunlight. Some of the rest of the recruits he had spent the night with were waiting, most of them sitting on their footlockers, as well as the sergeant who had moved the "gaggle" over.

"What now, sir?" Herzer asked.

"We wait for the rest, of course."

Herzer took a seat and looked at the group that was there. He hadn't had much time to get to know them the night before and he wondered if they were all going to be in his training unit.

"Hi," he said to the person nearest him. "Herzer Herrick. Are you all line infantry?"

"Nope," the man said with a grin. "Lucky me, I passed the bow course."

"Oh," Herzer said, looking him over. The man wasn't nearly as heavily muscled as Herzer. "You did the fifty course? Congratulations."

"Oh, hell no," the man said with another grin. "Nobody passed that one, so they dropped it to thirty. I made that, no sweat."

"Oh."

"Well, I heard a *couple* of people passed it, but I'd have to see it to believe it. I mean, thirty nearly killed me. They told us they don't have many bows anyway, so the ones who did really well will be the archers at the beginning and the rest will be support."

"Ah."

"Didn't you pass? I mean, you're pretty big."

"He passed," Deann said, setting down her footlocker. "He passed the fifty course. Then he asked if he could go to line infantry."

"You're joking!" the man said, looking at Herzer askance. "What in the hell did you do that for?"

"I don't want to be stuck as an archer," Herzer replied with a shrug.

"He's a fisking lunatic," Deann added.

"And for our sins we followed him over," Cruz said from behind Herzer.

"Cruz!" Herzer said, getting to his feet to pump the young man's hand. "Where'd you come from?"

"The same place Deann did. After looking over what we were being offered I figured being a soldier *had* to be better! I mean, if I never see another hide or crosscut saw I'll be too happy. Even if it means being stuck with you guys!"

"You're all nuts! You guys are nothing but sword fodder; the archers are the elite."

"Yeah?" Herzer challenged. "Infantry is about movement. When you can do the Hill, I'll be impressed."

"Archers are going to have to keep up with us," Deann said smugly. "I think they'll face the Hill soon enough."

"On your feet you . . ." The sergeant looked around at the group as the last recruit joined them. He started to say more then shook his head. "Never mind. It's not even worth cussing." He started to call off a list of names, breaking them out into four groups. As he did, other sergeants drifted into the area.

Herzer's group was the smallest, with the archers being the most numerous, and two groups of women, presumably archer females and "line" females.

"I'm Drill Corporal Wilson," one of the NCO's said, coming over to Herzer's group. "I'll take you to meet your makers."

"Our what?" one of Herzer's group asked.

"You'll see," the corporal said with a chuckle.

He led the group, still carrying their footlockers, out of the area and along the base of the hills to a clearing where three figures in armor waited.

"WHAT THE FISK ARE YOU DOING JUST AMBLING ALONG LIKE A BUNCH OF GRANNIES?!" one of the figures shouted. "MOVE IT! MOVE IT! MOVE IT! YOU, THE BIG ONE, OVER HERE!"

Herzer looked to where he was pointing and trotted over to the spot as fast as he could carrying the box of materials.

"Footlocker on the ground behind you," the man said. He was nearly as tall as Herzer and just about as wide, with the articulated armor and helmet making him appear even larger. He pointed to the spot then chivvied the group with Herzer into a semicircle.

"I am Triari Sergeant Jeffcoat," the man said, walking along the line and looking at each of the recruits. "Triari is my rank, not my name. It is my sad duty to inform you that for the next couple of months I'm going to be your drill sergeant. The reason that it is my sad duty is that you are *not* going to like it! There are many things that I could be doing with my time *other* than training a group of such *useless* fisks as you yardbirds. But this is what I've been ordered to do and I will damned well do it, even if it kills you. Note, not if it kills *me* but if it kills you! This is Decurion Jones and Sergeant Paddy," he continued, pointing to the two persons in armor. "Along with Drill Corporal Wilson, they will be helping me in this unenviable task." He paused as one of the group raised his hand.

"Did I ask you to speak?" the sergeant said quietly.

"No, but I was wondering . . ."

"WHEN I TELL YOU TO WONDER YOU WILL WONDER, IS THAT UNDERSTOOD? DOWN, DOWN ON YOUR FACE. HANDS EXTENDED, LEGS EXTENDED AND LOCKED. FACE TO THE GROUND." He tapped the recruit into a push-up position and then nodded. "Now, on my count, you will do push-ups, is that clear?"

"Uh . . ."

"IF YOU UNDERSTAND THE ORDER YOU WILL SOUND OFF WITH A LOUD AND CLEAR 'CLEAR, SERGEANT!' YOU WILL ADDRESS ME AND THE OTHER SERGEANTS AS *SERGEANT* OR BY OUR RANK. IF YOU WISH TO ASK A QUESTION YOU WILL SAY 'PERMISSION TO SPEAK, SERGEANT.' IS THAT *CLEAR?*"

"Clear, sergeant!" the recruit said.

"ALL OF YOU, IS THAT CLEAR?"

"Clear, Sergeant." "Yes, Sergeant." "Uh, huh."

"THAT'S IT. ALL OF YOU, FRONT-LEANING-REST-POSITION, *MOVE!*"

Herzer, despite the fact that he had, in fact, sounded off nice and clear, joined the rest of the recruits and learned the proper way to count push-ups. After fifty, when most of the group was sweating and their arms buckling, the sergeant stopped and shook his head.

"I just don't know. This is the group that they want to defend our great town with. What a bunch of useless ragbags.

Look at this one," he continued, toeing one of the group. "What's your name, Fatty?"

"Cosgrove," the recruit replied.

"WHAT DO I HAVE TO DO TO GET YOU TO SOUND OFF?" the sergeant shouted. "THAT'S 'COSGROVE, SERGEANT'! IS THAT CLEAR!"

"Clear, Sergeant."

"LOUDER!"

"Clear, Sergeant!"

"LOU-DER!"

"CLEAR, SERGEANT!"

"Better. Almost there. Now, what is your name, Fatty?"

"COSGROVE, SERGEANT!"

"Well, we'll sweat that fat right off of you." He looked around again and shook his head. "On your feet. Now, the purpose of this little meeting is to get a few things straight. There will be no knives, other weapons, drugs, pornography or anything else that I feel unmilitary cluttering up my barracks. Is that clear?"

"CLEAR, SERGEANT!"

"So if you are carrying anything like that, Sergeant Paddy will now come around with a bag. Right now, you are on amnesty. Anything that goes in the bag is forgotten. If I catch anything unmilitary in my barracks, I will have your ass. Is that clear?"

"CLEAR, SERGEANT."

"If you have any money, you can keep it or turn it into the company safe. Decurion Jones will be following Sergeant Paddy with envelopes for money. He will give you a receipt. Now, this is an acceptable time for questions."

Herzer really didn't want to lose his money pouch so he raised his hand with a swallow of apprehension. "PERMISSION TO SPEAK, SERGEANT!"

"Speak, recruit asshole."

"TRIARI SERGEANT, I HAVE A PERSONAL POUCH. PERMISSION TO KEEP IT, SERGEANT!"

"Granted. Small personal items are acceptable as long as I do not look upon them with disfavor." He looked at Herzer and shook his head. "Recruit, that uniform looks like a fisking sack."

Herzer, not knowing how to reply, stayed mute.

Jeffcoat nodded after a moment and frowned. "There's a dusk retreat formation. Get it squared away before then."

Herzer had no idea how he could do that, but he fully

intended to try. He turned in his money, accepting the receipt, and held onto the pouch.

"When I say fall out you will fall into the temporary barracks. You will do so in a military fashion which means at a run. You will be assigned spots on the floor and gear for tonight. After you are squared away, there will be an inspection of your gear. FALL OUT!"

They barely had enough time to put their gear down on the ground before they were back outside being shouted at and began drilling. The group did not take well to drill. Some of them didn't seem to know their left feet from their right and before long the sergeants were hoarse with shouting. Despite his physique Herzer got to the point where he felt that he was going to die if he had to do one more push-up. After much instruction they could stand at attention and parade rest, march in step, stop and turn on command. That seemed to be the minimum necessary and the sergeants brought them back to the barracks and had them fall out.

"Now, we're going to assign some of you to temporary leadership positions. You're probably not going to keep them. Each of the leaders will be responsible for a certain group. One of you will be in charge of the rest. Herzer, fall in over here," he continued, pointing to a spot at the front. "You're the Recruit Triari. That means you're in charge of the whole group. When I take the triari you fall to the rear. Clear?"

"CLEAR, SERGEANT!" Herzer said, sweating. He realized he was just put in charge of the whole group and he wasn't even sure he wanted to be in charge of himself.

"Listen up you yardbirds! I'm going to be giving some of my orders through Herzer here. If he says jump, it's just like if I gave you the order. Clear?"

"CLEAR, SERGEANT."

"Cruz, stand here! Abrahamson, stand here!"

Jeffcoat continued laying out the decuris and maniples, chivvying each of them into place.

"There's sixty-two of you right now. By the time we're done, I'll be satisfied if there's forty. When I call for you to fall in you will fall in in this order. You will fall in and fall out at a run! Is that clear?"

"CLEAR, SERGEANT!"

"You have been formed in one triari or what we will call a triari. I am your triari sergeant. A triari normally consists of three decuri and the triari sergeant. A decuri is made up of two maniples and the decurion. A maniple consists of five legionaires including the maniple leader. For the time being, your recruit triari is Herzer Herrick. Your recruit decurions are Cruz, Abrahamson, Stahl and Pedersen. Now, I know that's not all clear, but you're going to be clear with it very shortly. By the tenth time you've fallen in on them, even you will have it figured out. Fall out and get into the barracks!"

Before the last person had gotten through the door he bellowed "FALL IN!"

Naturally, half the triari couldn't find their place. After much swearing and push-ups they were all in place at which point he had them fall out and fall in again and again until they were all finding their place without thought.

"When I give the order, fall in to the barracks. Lay your blanket down. Lay each of your items of equipment out in a neat and soldierly fashion. You will do this quickly. The sergeants and myself will then inspect your shit. I doubt that even you yardbirds could have screwed it up already, but we'll see. FALL OUT."

Naturally, nothing was to their satisfaction. Cloaks were improperly folded, helmets were tarnished, lockers were not neat. And they had a very direct method of expressing their displeasure at the quality of layout. Each of the recruit's bundles, with the exception of Herzer's, was tossed out the door of the barracks in a heap by the time they were done.

"Get you gear sorted out and laid out in a military fashion! Lay it out in the manner that Herzer has. We'll be back at dusk and all those ragbag uniforms had better be straight by then, too!"

Herzer found himself running from one recruit to the next, fielding their griping and cajoling or threatening them until most of the gear more or less ship-shape fashion. Along the way he rummaged up a set of needles and thread, and a couple of recruits who had some idea what they were doing with them, and got most of the uniforms more or less straight. They didn't have so much as a knife among them, so the extra fabric had to be tucked into the uniforms, but it was as good as it was going to get. Before he was done with the last person the three sergeants had charged into the barracks.

"Fall in at attention on your gear!" Decurion Jones shouted.

Herzer pounded to the far end of the barracks and waited in unhappy silence as the sergeants went through the gear. Fewer of the bundles went out the door but still more than half, and most of the triari, including Herzer, had been gigged on their uniforms. And it was starting to get dark; the barracks were darned near black.

"All of you get that gear back in here and laid out!" Jones said when they were done. "We're not stopping for chow until your shit is straight!"

The whole group fell out again, sorting out the piles and getting them laid out with more griping at the ones whose gear had not passed muster. The third time the sergeants came through it was to the light of torches that they passed to the recruits. Finally they were done and Jeffcoat nodded.

"That'll do for now," he said hoarsely. "All but those shitty-ass uniforms. But you can work on them in your free time. Fall out!"

The recruits were marched to dinner at a trot and lined up.

"The triari guide is the last one in," Jones said. "When he's done eating, you're all done. And he is going to eat *quickly*," the sergeant added, looking at Herzer significantly.

They passed through the line, getting wooden trays that the recruits heaped with slabs of meat, beans and cornbread.

Herzer, aware that he was going to be under scrutiny, got far less than he had intended and when he sat down he checked the rest of the group. Some of them, frankly, didn't seem to know what "eat quickly" meant. He dawdled over his own food as long as he could until he caught another significant look from Jones at which point he shoveled what was left into his mouth and stuffed in the last piece of cornbread on top of it.

"WHAT THE HELL ARE YOU DOING STILL EATING, YARDBIRD?" he heard behind him as he headed out of the mess building.

It didn't stop with dinner. The state of the barracks was not to their satisfaction and the recruits found themselves marching up and down, back and forth and finally halfway up the Hill before they were led back to the barracks. Herzer didn't know what time it was, but he realized that he'd gotten fully clocked into a dawn-to-dusk cycle and he was practically dropping on his feet by the time they got back to the barracks.

"Assign two-hour fire-guards among yourselves," Jones said, sticking a torch up outside the barracks. "The fire-guard will ensure that there is always a fresh torch and that said torch does not catch the barracks on fire." He held up an hourglass that was passed to him by Corporal Wilson. "This is a thirty-minute hourglass. The fire-guard will turn it each time

the sand runs out. Four turns and you're done. Twelve turns
to first call. One turn after first call to inspection. Good night,
yardbirds." With that he was gone.

"Holy LU!" Cruz said. "What the fisk have I gotten myself into?"

"A world of hurt," Herzer said. "Now who's got that damn
needle and thread? We've still got work to do."

"What the fisk do you mean?" one of the faces in the
dimness said. "Fisk that. I'm getting some sleep."

There was an unhappy mutter at that and Herzer glared
around angrily.

"You want to be running around singing about your shitty-
ass uniform?" he asked. "There's more than that. We're getting up one turn before first call and getting the barracks
straight. When they come through the door everything is going
to be shipshape, understand."

"Fisk you," one of the recruits said, turning around. "Who
made you God?"

Herzer grabbed him by the back of the collar and tossed
him more-or-less effortlessly against the nearest wall. "Sergeant
Jeffcoat did. And I'm not going to get my ass reamed because
your shit isn't squared away."

He glared around at the group as Cruz closed up on his
left side. "Are there any more questions?"

"Yeah, who's got first guard?" one of the group said.

"What's your name?" he asked the recruit who was slowly
getting up off the floor.

"Bryan," the guy said, shaking his head muzzily.

"You've got first watch, but none of us are going to sleep
any time soon. Watch the hourglass and turn it when the sand
runs out."

In the next hour he detailed the fire-guards, got the uniforms resewn, hopefully to the sergeant's satisfaction, and got
the triari laid out in lines on the floor instead of scattered
everywhere. He wasn't sure about going to sleep himself; some
of the troops were looking at him pretty blackly. But he figured he had to sleep some time.

"Remember, thirty minutes before first call," he said to the
troop that was supposed to be the last fire-guard.

"Got it," the recruit said sleepily.

He shook his head and looked around. Most of the triari
was already asleep but Stahl was nodding as well, seated
on the floor by the door where he could keep an eye on
the torch.

"Stand up," he said.

"Why?" the recruit said, but struggled to his feet anyway.

"You'll fall asleep. Pass it on to the fire-guard; I want to be awakened by each change of watch. If any of you fall asleep or sit down on watch I'll give you a pasting that makes getting thrown against the wall look like a love-tap."

"Think you're a big guy," Bryan muttered, but he leaned up against the wall as if he intended to stay that way.

"Damn straight, and a light sleeper," Herzer muttered and headed to his bundle on the floor. All there was was a blanket but he'd slept with worse and he was asleep practically before he lay down.

He vaguely remembered the rest of the night, as the fireguards woke him in turn. And it was way too early when the last shook his shoulder.

"One turn to first call," the guard said. "A little before, really. The guard before me told me he missed by a few minutes."

"Another great day in the legions," Herzer muttered, standing up. "On your feet!"

The triari got moving around, straightening out their gear and putting away their blankets. Some of them started to put on their uniforms but he waved that away and had them straighten out their footlockers instead. By the time the fireguard waved that the sergeants were coming the room was as straightened up as he could make it.

"Attention!" the fire-guard called and the triari stood at attention by their footlockers.

The first sergeant through the door was Jeffcoat, carrying a lantern. He looked around the room and grunted in dissatisfaction, walking down the lines of recruits, opening a footlocker here and there until he got to Herzer. He frowned at the recruit and then yelled, "Get your uniforms on and fall out you yardbirds." As Herzer bent to his footlocker he grabbed his arm. "Not you."

He led the recruit outside and pushed him up against the wall. "How long have you been up?"

"Sergeant, I had them get up thirty minutes before first call, Sergeant," Herzer admitted.

The sergeant stared at him in the light of the lantern, then shook his head. "Where'd you run across that trick?"

"I've read some books," Herzer said.

"You planning on doing this every morning?"

"As long as I'm the recruit triari," Herzer said then shrugged. "Or until somebody shoves a knife in my ribs."

The sergeant stared at him for a moment longer, then nodded. "Go get your shitty uniform on, Herzer."

The morning inspection was anything but a success, but Herzer could tell that it would have gone far worse if they'd waited until the "official" time to get ready. As soon as they had reassembled their gear the sergeants took them on a morning run that had half the unit falling out and the rest gasping for air by the time they got back. They were given thirty minutes to take a "bath" in rain barrels then had a fast breakfast. As they were coming out and getting in formation Herzer tapped Cruz on the arm.

"So, would you rather be here, or back in the apprentice program?"

"Oh, I don't know," Cruz said then chuckled. "At least we're not cutting trees."

When they were in formation, Jeffcoat looked them over and shook his head.

"You are, without a doubt, the sorriest group of individuals I've ever seen. But we will make men of you, oh, yes, we will. And the first thing you have to learn is what it means to be a soldier. Everyone thinks that it's all swinging a sword, but that is the *last* thing you learn. The *first* thing you learn is all the stuff that comes before swinging the sword. Now, who knows how to use a crosscut saw?"

Herzer stifled a chuckle as he raised a hand then saw Cruz do so after a moment's hesitation.

"Well, we're not going to be staying in these fine barracks forever. The first thing that a soldier learns is how to set up camp. And that is what we are going to do today."

The group was marched down the line of hills to a flat spot not far from the pathway up the Hill where they started building a "camp," really a small fort. There were piles of leather, and one decuri was put to work, under Decurion Jones' supervision, cutting them and forming them into tents. In the meantime the rest of the triari started clearing the ground.

CHAPTER THIRTY-THREE

It was similar to working for Jody and different at the same time. There were no oxen to haul the logs away so they were cut and split until a five-man maniple could get the resulting chunk up on their shoulders to be carried away. "In a soldierly fashion," which meant at a trot to a cadence of "ooga-chucka-ooga-chucka." Once the area was cleared, which took most of the first day, they started on stumping and digging a trench around the area. Tents were assembled in lines, latrines were dug and the camp was in every way made to be a permanent structure.

In their munificent free time there were regular inspections and intensive classes on field hygiene when, inevitably, somebody decided that a few minutes of free time was worth skipping their skimpy "baths."

But, finally, the camp was complete. The tents didn't leak, the gates could be gotten open and closed, the stump-holes were filled, the parapets and parade ground were to the sergeant's satisfaction and everything was shipshape. Small but functional. At which point more leather appeared.

Over the next few days the sergeants and a few artisans from the camp showed them how to cut and form the leather into rucksacks, jerkins and kilts. The boiled leather, when oiled, was nearly immune to the rain. At the same time they got their new issue of boots. The boots were heavy leather with hobnails on the soles and fit, in Herzer's opinion, poorly. The calluses that the triari had developed were in the wrong spots and there was a new round of blisters. These eventually passed and more equipment showed up for the maniples. Small mortars and pestles, kettles, axes and shovels.

When the full kit was issued to the triari the sergeants held classes on setting up field camps. How to cook for the maniple using nothing but field rations, parched corn, cornmeal, beans and a pressed and smoked meat compound that someone dredged up the name "monkey" for. Boiled until it was soft in the beans it wasn't bad. Added to a bannock in the "dutch ovens" that were part of the kit, it was survivable. Eaten straight, with the lightly salted parched corn, it was bloody awful. But they learned to choke it down, sometimes on the move. And once they did, the packs came out and drill began in earnest.

They marched and countermarched, learning complex opening drills and marching by squads and triari, all of it with the packs, filled with all their gear, three days' rations and, most of the time, filled sandbags for "good training." Every night they fell asleep with the sounds of orders in their ears, woke up before first call, got their shit straight and did it all over again. And when they didn't perform to the sergeant's satisfaction, they kept at it by the light of torches until it practically *was* first call.

Once they were marginally capable of maneuvering on the reasonably "flat" area of the parade ground, they headed out to the field and did it all over again. They marched up hills and down, up the Via Apallia as far as the edge of the Iron Hills and back. Generally they slept out two days and came back the third night but once they were gone for nearly a week, the last two days on half rations. They learned to cook their rations as a decuri and dig a new camp every night, with a full palisade and trench around it. They learned to choke down their monkey and parched corn while still moving. They learned the trick of using pegs and lines to lay out the camp and were instructed on how to expand it, how many latrines per however many men, where the different parts of the camp should be, how to set watches and how many to be on under what conditions, where the officers' tents would be set up.

They marched in rain and sun, through the tail end of the spring when a cold front came through with just above freezing temperatures and through the blazing heat that followed it. They learned to ford rivers and build temporary bridges. They slept out in the wet with nothing but their cloaks and woke before dawn to another day of marching.

The life was brutal and there was plenty of attrition. For the time being the positions were all voluntary and almost every morning there would be one or two who held up their hands and said: "Sorry, no more for me." The sergeants didn't berate them, just nodded and sent them over to be outprocessed. And there were plenty of days that Herzer considered it.

To his amazement he had managed to hold on to his position. He suspected that there were a few times that it should have been pulled, but he kept the triari's nose to the grindstone and it was pretty clear that at least half of the reason the group was doing as well as it was was his example. He was always the first one up and the last to bed. He dug into any unpleasant job and refused to quit until it was done *right*. There was some muttering about "brownnose" but it was pretty evident that he just was doing what needed to be done. And he never rubbed anyone's nose in it. When somebody was having trouble, and some of the jobs were more cerebral than it seemed from the outside, he was always there with a suggestion to make it easier. When a decuri was flagging at whatever physical feat was required of them, he was always there with a shoulder.

Occasionally he caught a glimpse of The Gunny. Generally it was a surprise. They'd be ten miles from camp, marching down another track and come around a corner to see him leaning against a tree. Or they'd be setting up a palisade and suddenly realize they'd just thrown dirt on somebody's shoes, only to have it be The Gunny.

He never said anything to the recruits; he just watched then wandered over to speak to the sergeants. Which generally meant some hellfire dropped on someone. Herzer began to wonder, after a while, what his function was.

Then they found out.

They came into camp from another long route march, lustily singing some song about "The Grand Trunk" road and saw The Gunny and Mayor Talbot in waiting on the far side of the parade ground. The sergeants dismissed them to barracks and told them to prepare for a retreat inspection. They piled into the barracks and began pulling out uniforms, looking for a clean one or at least one that wasn't awful; they hadn't had a wash day in nearly a week.

Nobody knew what was up so Herzer was pelted with questions.

"No idea," he said, grabbing one of the recruits and pulling at his uniform. "What the fisk did you do, put it away in a wad?"

The sergeants had shown them a method of ironing out the uniforms by heating up a steel rod, but there wasn't time and the best he could do with the recruit was pull the uniform tight and hope that the creases wouldn't be terribly evident.

"FALL OUT!"

He pounded out the door with the rest and fell in at the head of the formation, checking to see that everyone was in place. When they were he did a precise about face and saluted the drill sergeant, clenched right hand to left breast, the only time that sergeants were saluted.

"Triari Sergeant, all present or accounted for."

"Post."

Herzer did a precise right face and marched around the back of the triari. When he reached his position the sergeant called "OPEN RANKS, MARCH!"

Compared to some of the maneuvers they had practiced this one was simple. The front rank moved forward one pace, the second rank stayed in place and the rear ranks backed up so that there was sufficient gap for people to easily walk down the ranks.

It was, actually, toughest for the recruit triari; he had to back up six paces. But they had practiced backing over a hundred paces in training, so Herzer did it without thinking.

Gunny and Mayor Talbot walked the ranks and Herzer sighed. It was a "breeze" inspection; they were just glancing at the recruits rather than submitting them to a full inspection. He waited through it patiently, wondering like everyone what the inspection meant, then came to attention as they came to him.

"How are you, Herzer?" Mayor Edmund asked.

"Very well, sir!" Herzer barked.

Talbot smiled faintly and nodded his head. "I think you've gotten bigger, although that is hard to believe."

Not knowing what to reply Herzer stood mute as Edmund walked off, followed by the Gunnery Sergeant who gave him an unreadable look as he passed.

The Gunny took over the post from Triari Jeffcoat and then turned to face the triari.

"STAND-AT EASE!" he bellowed then waited until they had assumed the position of parade rest, looking at him.

"Class One of the Raven's Mill Legionnaire Training Center having successfully completed basic recruit training shall now move on to Advanced Legionnaire Training. What that means is that you've successfully shown that you can build, march and dig. Now, we'll teach you how to *fight*." He stared around at them and shook his head. "You may now cheer."

Herzer started the cheer and it was a lusty one; all of them had wondered when in the hell they were going to do more than march and dig.

"It doesn't get easier from here, but it does get different," the Gunny said. "Among other things, you'll be permitted some liberty to go into town. That does not mean that you can swagger down to Tarmac's tavern and get into a fight; anyone doing so will meet with *my* displeasure. And if you thought those packs were heavy, wait until *I* take you on a march in full kit. But you're on your way to being soldiers. You have a pass for the rest of the day and until lights out. First call as usual. Oh, and the females, the ones that are left, will be joining. They will be integrated into the squads. Now, don't get the impression that you're being issued your very own whores. They have been going through the identical training that you have and they are soldiers just like you. Furthermore, anyone found fisking on duty will face the full force of a court-martial, up to and including flogging and disrating. And you don't even want to think about *forcing* your attention on one of them. First of all, they'll probably hand you your balls on a spit. And if they don't, the penalty is *hanging*. We haven't had mixed groups up until now because you had to learn what discipline means.

"Tomorrow you'll be fitted for armor and issued training weapons. And then your *real* training starts. Fall out!"

When they fell into the barracks Herzer called at ease.

"We've got a pass for the evening," he said, looking around. "That doesn't mean you can just fisk off. Somebody's got to stay for fire-guard; that's by roster."

"Shit," the unlucky recruit said.

"Yeah. And if you're planning on going into town, you go in groups. At least one decurion is to be with each group and if anyone in the group fisks up he *and* the decurion will answer to me."

"What about *you*?" one of them asked.

"Well, I turned in all my money," he grinned. "So walking around town with nothing to spend doesn't appeal very much. And I'm not going to go ask Sergeant Jones if I can draw some cash. Are you?" He looked around and nodded. "Me? I'm going to get some *sleep*."

A few of the troops decided to go into town anyway and he assigned Pedersen from third decuri to accompany them, then headed for his spot on the floor.

"So you're just gonna flake out?" Cruz asked from his own spot.

"Damn straight," Herzer replied, plumping up the bundle of underwear he used as a pillow. "Tomorrow we start training with the Gunny. What do you wanna bet he's gonna bust our ass in the morning just to show us who's who?"

"What's he gonna do to us that they haven't done already?" Cruz asked. "Any problem if *I* go into town?"

"Not as long as you take somebody with you," Herzer replied, rolling over and trying to get comfortable. Normally he fell right to sleep but this was just too early. Nonetheless, he could hear Morpheus calling. He swore he was never going to pass up a chance to sleep again in his life. "But you'd better be back by lights out and ready to rock in the morning."

"Yes, sir!" Cruz snorted. "See you later, Herzer."

"Only if I'm still here and you can see."

Herzer, who was trailing the triari to round up stragglers, passed Cruz on the way up the Hill and patted him on the back.

"Thrown up all that rotgut, Cruz?" he asked cheerfully.

"You bastard, how did you know?" Cruz moaned.

"Just a lucky guess."

The Gunny had, indeed, decided to show who was boss. The triari was on its second ascent and the first hadn't been to the Gunny's satisfaction, which he had passed on in scathing tones.

"Cruz, if you wanna keep them recruit stripes, you'd better move on out," Decurion Jones said as he reached the two recruit leaders. "Move it out, Herzer."

"Yes, Sergeant," he said, grabbing Cruz's arm. "Let's go, party boy."

"Lu, I wanna die," Cruz moaned, struggling up the hill. Behind them the drill sergeants were chivvying the other recruits who had failed to keep up.

"How much did you drink?"

"I dunno, after the second mug of mead it was all sort of a blur," Cruz said and paused, briefly, to dry heave.

"Next time, listen to Papa Herzer, okay?" Herzer said with a laugh. "Even the gurrrls are doing better than you."

"You got it."

When they reached the top of the Hill, Gunny, who looked to have not even broken a sweat, the bastard, had assembled the triari. Herzer took his place at the back. There were seven women who had survived the Basic course and they had been integrated into the squads despite the fact that at least one of them had to be a Recruit Decurion. Herzer wasn't sure if Cruz was going to keep his place after this morning's showing, but Gunny didn't tell him to move down the decuri so apparently he was being lenient this morning.

"Well, I'd guess you're wondering why I called you here," Gunny said when the last sweating and panting recruit reached the formation. "There's a very fine book that says 'For everything there is a season' and you have just entered the season to put away childish games. And I'm the man to bag up the toys. Is *that* clear?"

"CLEAR, SERGEANT!"

"We're not going to have much time for fun and games over the next few weeks but I thought it was a good idea to remind you all that soldiers have to *move* when they are told to move. This valley has been battled over before and the general that *owned* it, in that day, depended upon his infantry. They moved so fast they were referred to as foot-cavalry. And that is the mark we *will* obtain. By the time you are done, you will be able to walk *any* cavalry into the ground and you will be able to move on tracks that a *goat* would find difficult. Or my name isn't Miles Arthur Rutherford. Is that *clear*?"

"CLEAR, SERGEANT."

"You will care for your personal gear before you care for yourself. If you are responsible for specialized gear, you will care for that before you care for your own gear. Your only goal is to perform the mission. Every day you can find something to enhance the mission and every day you *will* find something to enhance the mission!"

"So, what is the mission, Gunny?" Cruz asked, solemnly.

"Your mission is to die from an arrow or a sword blow or a halberd so that a civilian does *not*! It is the job of politicians to ensure that you do so! If you have a problem with that you can go join some rabble-snabble mercenary company or you can join the sloppy-ass milichee and go back and hide behind your momma's *skirts*! But in the meantime that is your mission! The civilians will not *know*, nor will they *care*. In time they will come to hate your *guts*. Nonetheless you *will* keep true to your salt and drive on to the mission everyday! Do I make myself CLEAR?!"

"CLEAR, GUNNY!"

"You are born in blood, in blood you shall live and in blood you shall die. From this day forward, you are not soldiers, you are not legionnaires, you are the Blood Lords. Bound by the blood, bound by the steel. Repeat after me: Blood to our blood . . ."

"Blood to our blood," Herzer repeated, cold chills running through his veins.

" . . . Steel to our steel . . ."

"Steel to our steel."

"In blood we live . . ."

"In blood we live . . ."

"In blood we shall die . . ."

"In blood we shall die . . ."

"Blood Lords . . ."

"Blood Lords . . ."

"LOUDER!"

"BLOOD LORDS!"

"LOUDER!"

"BLOOD LORDS!"

"Move back down the Hill and get chow. After that fall in and we'll see if any of you young idiots can figure out how to make armor."

The armor was waiting for them after lunch, a pile of boxes in the back of an ox cart.

Deann climbed into the cart and looked at the topmost box.

"Armor set, loricated, one each," she said, reading the label gummed to the top of the wooden box. "Size, small. That's me."

"Get them all off the cart," Gunny said. "Move them into the decuri bay and we'll show you how to assemble them."

The boxes, when opened, contained plates of steel, fittings, rivets, strips of leather and baffling instructions. Along with the boxes were some tools that Gunny added to their triari equipment.

Loricated armor was made by taking the plates of steel, bending them to the body and then overlapping them using the fittings and the leather strips. The plates had to be measured to the individual, however, so that they would fit snugly, but not too snugly, around the torso. The armor was then made in four sets. Two "torso" halves, one for the left side and one for the right, and two shoulder halves.

The triari worked for the next two days at the armor, cutting the plates to appropriate length, bending them around forms, punching holes for rivets, setting in the fittings and attaching the leather straps. In addition to the armor there was a thick "scarf" of cosilk that was wrapped in a tube then bent around the back of the neck and folded across the chest. This prevented chafing from the edges of the armor at the neck.

Herzer, as usual, had problems with "standard" sized anything and several of the pieces had to be form fitted for him. But after two days that encompassed much swearing as fumble-fingered recruits tried to get the pieces to go together, everyone in the triari was in armor.

After the armor finally passed Gunny's inspection, they were issued their new helmets, pilums, swords and large wooden shields. The helmet style was a "barbute," a solid helmet with a "T" opening at the front, instead of the Roman helmet. The barbute style had several things favoring it over the Roman. From a chance snippet of conversation Herzer overheard, he learned that the helmet was the hardest part of the armor to produce. And Roman helmets, with their several parts, rivets, fittings and hinges, were far more difficult to produce than barbute. But, despite this, the barbute was arguably a superior design. The open-faced Roman helmet, while light and permitting easy breathing, meant that a slash across the face or a point driven in was virtually guaranteed to drive home. The barbute covered much more of the surface area of the face and thus made injury less likely.

The downside to the barbute was that it permitted a lesser field of vision and was a pain to march with. On the whole, however, Herzer was glad they had chosen this design. He'd rather have a hard time seeing around than never see again.

The pilums were the spears of the Roman legions and it was another design that had been copied virtually intact. It consisted of a relatively short wooden shaft, no more than a meter and a bit, and an unusually long, thin spearhead with a wickedly sharp, barbed head. The weapon could be used as a spear and the triari trained extensively with it in that manner, marching in formation and then advancing with them lowered. But the primary use of the pilum was as a throwing weapon. The long, light-steel head was designed to penetrate a shield and then *bend*. With it stuck in a shield and bent over onto the ground, the enemy would be forced to stop and work it out, with their shield well out of line when they did so. Since the weapons were thrown at "point blank" range, the technique was to throw and then immediately charge. The front rank of the enemy would then be stuck, essentially shieldless and without a defense, open to a sword charge.

The swords they were issued were short and almost leaf-bladed, a Celtic design rather than the original Roman. They rode in a high scabbard tucked just forward of the armpit on the right side. Their primary method of employment was short, fast, chops and jabs, designed to wound the enemy as much as kill them. The ones that they were issued now were wooden with a heavy weight of lead down the center. Herzer hoped that the "real" ones would be a tad lighter.

The last of the new equipment was the shield, and Herzer found himself dissatisfied in the extreme with it. Instead of the shield being held at two points with the forearm going across the back, it was held at one point with the arm extended straight down. For formation fighting it was superb; the idea was to form a "shield wall" and the shield was difficult to hold any way but directly in front of the body. But for someone who had trained in a much more "open" style of combat, it was a pain to use and gave a feeling of being "trapped."

They began training immediately, primarily formation marching with the new weapons. Carrying the swords was simply an additional weight but the shield and pilum were another matter. When marching they did not "sling" their shields and simply holding onto the shields, which, like the swords, had been weighted with lead, was agony until the appropriate muscles strengthened.

The pilum wasn't as painful to carry, being lighter, but maneuvering with the things, until they got used to them, was difficult. More than once the armor was put to good use as a pilum head was jabbed into a back.

Each afternoon they were given one hour to prepare and then held a full dress inspection. The slightest hint of dirt on any of their equipment led to a harsh rebuke and rust was punished by the entire decuri being loaded with weights and forced to run the Hill. They quickly learned to take good care of the equipment they had been issued.

Finally, the Gunny pronounced himself marginally satisfied that they could march with the things. At which point, naturally, they went out on a long forced march.

If they thought the previous marches had been brutal, Gunny quickly disabused them of the notion. Instead of staying mostly to the Via and some of the better graded roads around it, the Gunny took them on long marches by tracks that only he seemed to know. At one point Herzer realized that they had never gotten more than twenty miles from the town, but it was impossible to recognize that from the terrain and the distances they had marched. They marched on traces along the ridgelines where hawks flew beneath their feet and narrow trails through marshes. They marched along the edges of cliffs where one slip would mean instant death and across rushing streams cold from spring water. And all of it at a clip that made the previous marches seem like nothing. Gunny wasn't as much into setting up camp; he seemed to think that movement was the key. They would awake in the morning and eat as they marched; for five days they ate nothing but parched corn and monkey washed down with water. For the last two days, before they met up with a packtrain in the middle of no-where, they were at half rations.

Every morning there was an inspection of their gear. Woe betide the person who had so much as a spot of rust on armor, pilum, shield, helmet or sword. If he did, the gunny loaded up the whole decuri's rucksacks with rocks until they could barely stagger. And then took off at full speed, fully expecting them to catch up.

After the second time that happened, people could be seen by the fires late at night, scrubbing at their gear.

When they did make a full camp, Herzer noticed that it was always in a tactically viable spot. The other sergeants seemed to just care about finding somewhere reasonably flat. Gunny always set up on a hill, generally one that commanded a view of the trail that they were using and generally at a chokepoint in the terrain. The Gunny never pointed that fact out and sometimes Herzer wondered if it was a subtle lesson or simply that the Gunny had been doing this for so long that he *always* chose a defensible spot.

Finally, after two weeks of marching, with a few limited tests of their pilum throwing ability but *no* training with sword or shield, they found themselves back in camp.

There was a new building among the tents and Corporal Wilson was set up outside it. Herzer noticed this as the gunny brought them into the parade ground and called them to a halt.

"TRIARI, LEFT, FACE!" he called, then "STAND-AT, EASE."

Herzer lowered his shield to rest against his left thigh, spread his feet shoulder width apart and placed both hands, overlapped, on top of the shield.

"By squads, on my command, fall out and turn your weapons in to the armory," the Gunny said, pointing at the new building. "Then fall back in on your positions."

They filed off and turned over their swords, still in the sheathes, and pilums, then fell back in on the Gunny.

"Tomorrow we're going to start training you to use that sword you just gave up as well as more training with the pilum. We're also going to show you that a shield is a weapon as well as something to keep weapons off of you. But that is tomorrow. Tonight, get a good solid meal and some rest. Because if you think the last couple of weeks have been tough, you've got another think coming. FALL OUT."

CHAPTER THIRTY-FOUR

Sheida looked at the document in front of her with a frown. She had used far too much power to assure a full "virtual" gathering of the various delegates of the proto-Free States because this was the last chance they would have to amend the document. Tomorrow copies would be made and circulated to the various states over long and in many cases dangerous paths. She was frowning because the final document, in her opinion, contained far too many compromises.

"I would like to make a comment before we go on," she said, raising the document. "I agree with Edmund that the long-term consequences of keeping the changes permitting local laws on bound service and the universal creation of an aristocratic class are severe. The only question I have is whether we will have an immediate civil war or one sometime in the future. I would like one more discussion on these points. The Honorable Representative from Chitao."

"The people I represent are unwilling to join if we do not have the provisions for bound service," he said, standing up. There had apparently been a bit of a power struggle in Chitao, because they had changed representatives twice, each time getting more and more determined to have the changes enacted. Chitao held a central trading location and it had already begun to expand its power base so that two other representatives from the area had joined it in its position as well as a smattering from throughout Norau. The split was not geographical but seemed to center around areas that had been major cities in the former North American Union. None of the representatives from "new" city-states, such as Raven's Mill and Warnan, were in favor. But the total population, still concentrated in the northeastern tier and the far west, favored permissive laws on bound service.

"When the Fall occurred, many people were unable or unwilling to recognize that work was a necessity. Those who did are quickly becoming prominent citizens. But they are attaining that prominence through their own hard work. Those who choose not to work as hard have been seeking to return to the days when the Net gave them all they needed to survive. But the Net is no more. They must learn to work under qualified overseers. Too often in our area they have worked only hard enough to fill their bellies, to the detriment of the whole society. They think nothing of the future, of the coming winter, when there will not be food in plenty but only what has been stored by the thrifty.

"Giving full vote to such people means that they can vote themselves bread and circuses, surely the greatest danger that any democratic society can face. Furthermore they will vote to take from the 'rich' during the lean times, the rich who have by their own hard work *prepared* for the lean times.

"By . . . filtering those votes through those who recognize the necessity for hard work and devotion to duty, the danger of social service voting is reduced. We of Chitao, and the societies of Mican, Io, Nawick and Boswash steadfastly refuse to join this union if we are to be placed at the mercy of those who think that charity is their right. If or when they learn the value of work, or if their children recognize it, provisions are in place for them to rise to the level of full citizen. But, until then, the ant, who prepares for the winter, is not going to be ordered about by the grasshopper who spends his time in frivolity." He nodded at the group and sat down in his virtual "seat."

Sheida nodded unhappily and then gestured to the representative from Westphal.

As always, the representative was dressed in armor and he rose to his feet with a creak of rivets.

"I have heard the debates on the subject of an aristocratic addition to the upper house. There are those who would argue against any such house, saying that all power should devolve to the people and the states. But I direct you to the history of democracies. Always, they have fallen in time to the passions of the mob. It is this moment-to-moment passion that

such a body seeks to mitigate. Further, simply having representatives from broad geographical regions who have a longer
term of service has been proven to be insufficient. Still, they
are playing to the cry of the mob. They must keep one eye
over their shoulder to its passions lest they be thrown from
office. But, often, such moment-to-moment passions are *not*
in the best interests of the society. Democracies seem to work
the best when they are well filtered. This is simply a very
strong filter, not a rejection of democracy.

"And this body that we propose is not just a body of aris-
tocrats. It will have, as full voting members, elected representatives from the states as well as members who have been
chosen for their history of civic works. Last but not least, the
aristocratic portion will be flexible. Familes . . . die. Members
will fall by the wayside and new members will be brought
in. Further, as the size of the body inevitably rises from
territorial increases, a like number will be brought in from
the civic and aristocratic side. It is a flexible body that can
change with the times but still act as a check upon those
moment-to-moment passions that so often have been the
downfall of democratic societies." He nodded at the group and
sat down.

"Edmund Talbot, Honorable Representative from Raven's Mill,
will now present the rebuttal," Sheida said, nodding at him.

Edmund rose to his feet with a sigh, knowing the futility
of what he was about to say.

"There is something within the human breast which seems
to love the slave chain," Edmund said, looking around at the
assemblage. "For this is what we debate, make no mistake
about it. Both the Honorable Representative from Chitao and
the Honorable Representative from Westphal speak truths. There
is a danger in any democratic society from the mindless
passions of the moment, whether they be for bread and circuses or for or against wars. And filtering those passions is
what a representative democracy is all about. But the filters
that they so passionately support are not filters, they are chains
upon us and upon our children. The Representative from Chitao
speaks of a permanent underclass and make no mistake. Once
debt bondage can be passed from generation to generation there
is no escape short of rebellion or death. And yet, which of
those permanent serfs, born in bondage and dying in bondage, is the next Washington, Tsukya or Assam? How will they
reach their potential if the only choice that they have, by
binding law upon which we now place our signature and our

honor, is to slave away day after day in their master's fields or factories?

"As to an hereditary aristocracy, there has never been an argument for it that stood the test of time. The Honorable Representative from Westphal speaks of 'standing against the mob,' but who was it but the Senate that opposed the actions of Scipio Africanus in the Punic Wars? And who but the mob supported him? Again and again you see such bodies acting not in the interests of the long-term good of the nation but because of the memes and beliefs of a tiny, self-selecting body that wishes to retain power to itself. The failings of the latter North American Union stemmed not from the 'mob' but from the fact that some of their political parties became fat and bloated by a de facto aristocracy of the rich. Rich that were so divorced from the reality of life that they could not see disaster looming on any number of fronts. The same can be said for the Ropasan Union that created a bureaucracy that became effectively hereditary and was always self-selecting. It started out divorced from reality and reached critical mass in short order.

"For myself, for my fellow representatives of Overjay and Kalinas, we will join this union. But know that within our borders, every one of the 'mob' is free, free to act, free to vote and grab whatever treasure and happiness they can under the law. If any 'serf' reaches our lands, they are *free* and you'll have to send an army to 'recover' them. Furthermore, while we will bear the mantle of 'aristocracy' if thrust upon us, we repudiate the *concept* utterly!"

Sheida nodded at him as he sat down, glaring at the representative from Chitao, and lifted her hand.

"The issues of aristocracy and debt peonage are the last that remain. We will now take a vote on the specific changes and determine which will remain and which will not. On the subject of allowing debt peonage in territories that support it, while disallowing it in those that do not, we will now take a vote."

As she had feared, the amendment stood. There were simply more representatives that supported it than those who rejected it. She wondered if she had made too many compromises in the towns she invited to this meeting. But she needed all the allies she could get. And, right now, that meant permitting a return to serfdom. If that was the cost, so be it.

"The measure passes," she said sadly, looking at Edmund who just shrugged.

"On the composition of the upper house to include both hereditary aristocracy and persons chosen to lifetime appointments for their civic virtues, we will now take a vote."

Again the vote was for aristocracy, by a wider margin than the debt peonage. She had to wonder if that was because most of the delegates knew they were shoo-ins for the first round of appointments.

"The draft constitution so stands," she said, gritting her teeth. "Copies of it will begin circulation immediately. When the copy reaches your locality, you should debate it as you see fit within your own charters and return it as soon as possible, either with or without approval. But this *is* the last draft; any society that chooses to reject it rejects it totally and is outside the support and succor of the Free States. Or myself," she added, looking at Edmund.

Edmund frowned at her but nodded his head and kept his peace.

"Thank you all for coming," she said with a nod and then dismissed the virtual figures except for Edmund. "Are you going to toss this overboard?" she asked.

"No," he answered after a moment. "But I'm serious about serfs who make it to Overjay. And I'll take my legions to damned Chitao if it takes that to make them get the point."

"How is the 'legion' coming?" she asked.

"It's not even a century," he admitted. "But it's going well."

"Well, as queen I'm going to have a say in the cabinet appointments," she said. "I want you for secretary of war."

"I don't," Edmund said. "I want a field command. I'm so sick and tired of being behind a desk you can't believe it."

"You were the one who told me to think strategic and not tactical," she reminded him.

"I am thinking strategic," he said. "I happen to know without a doubt that I'm the best general you have right now. Putting me in charge of forming the army is silly. That's a job for a military manager. As long as he knows to let the professionals do the job."

"Suggestions?" she asked.

"It's going to depend upon who is Prime Minister," he admitted. "But I'd suggest Spehar. He's not nearly as good a commander or a strategist as he thinks he is. But he'll accept insubordination from *me* or I'll damned well beat his head in with my hammer."

"I can believe it," she said. "Get going Edmund. And say hello to Daneh for me. How's she doing, by the way?"

"Better on the mental issues," Edmund said. "But the pregnancy is starting to slow her down."

"Pregnancy, yeck," Sheida said.

"Uhmm, my queen?" Edmund said with a smile. "You *do* know the primary duty of a monarch, don't you?"

"Yes, I do," she replied. "*That* is why I went *yeck.*"

"Are you planning on a body birth or a replicator?" Edmund said with a grin.

"We're far from that," Sheida pointed out. "Unless I clone myself, I have to find another genetic contributor. Got any plans for the weekend, Edmund?" She grinned.

"Try anything and Daneh will kill you," he replied with a grimace. "I've got to get back."

"Have fun with your army," Sheida said with a wave. "And keep the offer in mind."

There followed more weeks of training. Sword drill, pilum throwing, shield maneuvers marching in formation in the morning and engaging in sword and pilum training in the afternoon. The sword technique was simplicity in itself, consisting of nothing but a series of almost mechanical chops and jabs. They had set up wooden stakes wrapped in hay and they chopped and jabbed until they felt their arms would fall off.

The pilums, also, were used in a very disciplined manner. When used as spears in the advance, they were marched forward in time. The training method for this was a large construction of wooden shields on a sledge. Gunny would stand on the sledge, which was extremely heavy, and they would march into it, driving it back. Throwing was also "by the numbers," consisting of a two count "run" and then "hurl" command. By the end of the training period, they felt like military automatons, which Herzer guessed, correctly, was the point.

They learned to create complex formations based upon trumpet calls, waved flags and shouted orders. They formed lines and squares and triangles. They charged imaginary enemies and whacked at dummies. And still they worked the A-frame weights and lifted their rocks, which were made larger and larger as time went by. They got to the point that they preferred the long route marches when at least they had some "rest" while marching. But even on the route marches, when the camp was set up there was more drill. They fought, decuri against decuri and individual against individual. And when the time came, they were integrated with the bowmen.

They had seen the bowmen working out. From time to time on their innumerable road marches they would see some of the archers moving as well. There were about half the number of archers as line infantry, and most of them didn't seem to have bows. Herzer strongly suspected that they, too, had been doing quite a bit of weight work.

The archer camp was well away from the town, so that any errant arrow wouldn't cause injuries, and they had only gotten glimpses of them maneuvering. But when the bowmen showed up they proved that while they might not be able to handle long marches, they sure could maneuver pretty. The first exercise was simple; the line infantry was to take and hold a narrow gap that existed only in the imagination of the officers, while the archers were to set up and prepare to engage the enemy whenever they appeared.

The Blood Lords marched forward to their positions and assumed their open battle formation. Herzer knew that, technically, they should also have light armed skirmishers out in front. But since they didn't have enough bodies for them, they had to make play like they were out there. When the line forces were in place the archers were called forward and took up a position on a slight rise on their rear and to the right. They were permitted to watch the archers move into position and it was impressive. There was one archer to a team of three men. The archer carried his bow and a long stake. The two other men carried arrow barrels and large wooden "shields" that were taller than a man. The archer teams moved into position and dropped their stakes and shields. By the time the actual archer had his bow out of the case, the other two had set up the shield with the stake passed through it so that any enemy assaulting their position would run into a hedgehog of defenses. The archers then stepped to the side of the shield and prepared to fire.

The archers opened up first on the notional enemy and the air was filled with arrows. The first went out nearly two hundred meters and landed in a small patch that was the designated "enemy" force. Herzer was glad he didn't have to wade through the fire even armored as he was. But the Blood Lord's response would have been to form a "tortoise" with their shields over their heads. He wondered how effective that really would be with the rain of arrows crashing down. The archers were keeping up a steady fire and the other two members of their team existed just to feed the archer. When they took short breaks the assistant archers would provide water and even stools for the archer, meanwhile setting out arrows on the ground so that the archer only had to reach down to pick up his ammunition.

Finally the enemy was determined to be within pilum range and the Blood Lords rushed forward on command, one-two-hurl and cast them at the notional enemy. Then they took up their defensive positions and proceeded to hack at the imaginary enemy. Herzer felt a bit of a burke on the front lines, hacking at air, but as the time went on he realized that it was a test. From time to time the whole line would be given the command to bash and they would throw their shields forward into the imaginary enemy and step forward as if the enemy had fallen back. He wasn't sure it would work out that way, but what the hell, it was the drill.

The archers were still firing and, remembering how hard it was to fire one of those bows for even fifteen minutes, Herzer knew that they had been in some serious training. When he took the opportunity to look around, though, he saw that some of the archers had switched off with their assistants and were massaging their arms. A few of them were even *juggling*. After getting back to the business at hand he decided that it made sense; the continuous motion of firing had to be bad for their shoulders and another motion like that would reduce the likelihood of repetitive motion injuries.

Finally, after what seemed like all day, they were called to a halt and sent on the "chase" portion of the exercise. They recovered their packs and started marching.

The Blood Lords quickly left the archers behind. Somewhere back there was supposedly a pack train. That was left behind as well. In just their armor, with their standard three days of rations, they started off after a murthering great simulated battle on the march of their lives. Gunny had taken to a horse and led a string of others behind him. Late on the afternoon of the first day, Kane and a couple of riders turned up with a few more horses and a string of pack mules. And that was all they took as they headed out on what came to be called "The Long March."

Herzer wasn't too sure where they were going or what they were doing. There didn't seem to be any rhyme or reason to the march. They headed first down the valley to the head of Massan Mountain then across the base, up the east valley about half way, over the front ridge by one pass and back by another.

Half the time they were making the trails that they took and the crossing of the front ridge was especially hard. The trace they followed was apparently an old road bed but much of it had washed away into the stream that it followed. They cut down trees, reinforced turns, made temporary bridges and all of it with the Gunny driving them to go faster, faster, FASTER!

They finally made it across, though and headed back in the general direction of Raven's Mill only to cross *back* into the valley along an old railroad cut and then back down the east valley. They headed back up towards the top of Massan Mountain through the west valley but then turned and crossed it instead, another nightmarish march, nearly a thousand meters into the air on tracks the horses and mules nearly couldn't make and near the top of the mountain they ran into a tearing thunderstorm that had the horses going wild from sheets of lighting that rippled the trees around them. They then came down into the east valley and headed back *south* away from Raven's Mill.

The march had taken nearly three weeks. They had met up with pack trains twice. All the horses and mules had been switched out for ones that weren't broken down, but still they kept marching far into the night and generally were up before dawn. They marched up and down the west valley, into the Iron Hills, back towards and *past* Raven's Mill and then finally all the way down the valley to its base and ended up just short of the south end of Massan Mountain, exhausted, out of food, their leather clothes and heavy boots in tatters around them. They had marched through summer heat and pouring thunderstorms, through fields and forests as old as the fall of nations, sleeping in their cloaks and up to march the next day before the sun was up. Then, as the afternoon wore on, they came to a clearing in sight of the high mountain above them.

Everyone was there, though, with the exception of a few casualties they had had along the way who had been shipped back to Raven's Mill. Of the forty-four that had started on the trek from hell, forty made it to the clearing. And there, the Gunny had them fall out.

Herzer, at the word, simply collapsed on the ground. They were still tens of kilometers from Raven's Mill and he was sure they would be up in the morning and off on another march. For once he didn't even bother to post sentries. He would, before dark, but not right now. Right now, it was all he could do to keep his eyes open.

He saw the Gunny walk over to an old stone monument

on one side of the clearing and pick something up from the ground. After a moment he shook his head and walked back to where the triari was lying on the ground.

"Up, Herzer," he said, quietly.

Herzer thought for a moment he wasn't going to be able to but he got his arms out of his pack and used it to push himself to his feet.

"Yang, Locke, Stahl, first watch. Deann, you've got first sergeant of the guard."

"Ah, fisk," she said, staggering to her feet. "Up, you guys."

"Get up and moving around, the rest of you," Herzer said, walking over to the monument. "Dig in, Gunny?"

"No," the sergeant said. "Just rest your weary bones. Do your maintenance, get chow started; we're not going anywhere until tomorrow morning."

Herzer let the squads handle the drill as he walked over to the monument. It was so old and defaced by time and elements that nothing could be seen on its face except the vague outline of a couple of chemical fired rifles.

"Do you know what it is, Gunny?" he asked as Rutherford appeared at his side.

"No," he said. "Just that it's a tomb. But this was sitting in front of it." He held out a fresh lemon.

Herzer took it and looked at it quizzically. "There's nobody living around here, Gunny. Who put a lemon in front of it?"

"I don't know. This place has been used as a campground for people going to Faire and just hiking for . . . well practically forever. I don't think anybody knows who is in the tomb. But every day, there is a fresh lemon in front of it. Have it if you'd like; there will be another tomorrow."

Herzer shrugged and cut the lemon with his belt knife. It wasn't as sour as he expected; it was actually a bit sweet with a sharp bitter aftertaste.

"Want some?" he asked.

"Nope, not for me," the sergeant said with a nod. "I notice you're not taking charge of getting the camp set up."

"No, Gunny, I'm not," Herzer replied, sucking on the lemon. "The decurions know their jobs. I'll check up on them in a minute, but there won't be anything wrong; we can set up camp in our sleep."

"That you can," Rutherford chuckled.

"Permission to speak, Sergeant?" Herzer asked.

"Speak."

"Can we find out when we're going back to town? Please?

Or when we're going to meet up with a pack train? We're already on half rations and this meal will be it."

"Tomorrow," Rutherford replied. "There's a bullock train on its way down the valley. We'll march out tomorrow and meet it somewhere up the valley. So we'll only miss one meal."

"Thank you."

"For what? Get the fisk out of here, recruit," the Gunny growled, but he smiled as he did.

"Blood Lords," Herzer answered and went off to find out who had screwed up the perfectly simple process of making camp.

The bullock train was barely five kilometers north of their position and they reached it while the drivers were still barely stirring. They finally got a good, hot meal and to their amazement the Gunny had them mount up on the wagons and *ride* part of the way back.

They stayed with the bullock train for two days, riding in relative if very bumpy comfort, eating heavily to regain some of the weight they'd lost on the Death March and got off it when they were barely halfway back to Raven's Mill. By that time just about everyone was ready to move; the carts weren't all that comfortable and they could make much better time on foot.

They marched into Raven's Mill singing "March of Cambreath" in a light rain as the sun was setting over the Iron Mountains. When they arrived at the barracks area they were surprised to see a crowd awaiting them. Gunny dismounted stiffly then marched over to Mayor Talbot and gave him a crisp salute.

"My Lord, Class One of the Raven's Mill Academy has completed their training and are, in my opinion, fully qualified for service."

"Thank you, Gunnery Sergeant Rutherford," Edmund replied, saluting him in turn. "Post."

Instead of walking to the back of the formation, Rutherford stepped to the side as an armorer brought up a portable forge and anvil. The forge was already heated and Herzer looked at the glowing coals uneasily.

"Herzer Herrick," Edmund called. "Front and center."

Herzer walked from the back of the formation and made a series of rights and lefts until he was in front of Mayor Talbot.

"Raise your right hand and repeat after me. I, state your name . . ."

"I, Herzer Herrick."

"Do solemnly swear to uphold and defend the Constitution of the Kingdom of Free States . . ."

"Do solemnly swear . . ."

Talbot swore him in and then held out his hand. "Inspection, arms."

Herzer reached across his body and drew his hated training sword, holding it up and out, pommel first. Talbot took it and handed it to Gunny Rutherford who handed back a freshly forged sword. Talbot took it and held it up.

"May it never be drawn, but that it draw blood. Hold out your left arm, turned up."

Herzer did and Talbot drew the sword across his inner arm, drawing a line of blood.

"Blood to our blood . . ." he said, and paused.

"Steel to our steel," Herzer intoned.

Talbot handed him the sword and took a set of tongs the armorer held out. At the end of them was a metal symbol. "Hold out your arm."

Herzer did so and Talbot pressed it into the still bleeding wound.

Herzer gritted his teeth against the pain and thought for just a moment that he'd pass out. But he took a deep breath and refused to flinch away from the brand.

"In blood we are born . . ." Talbot said.

"In blood we live . . ." Gunny continued.

"And in blood we shall die," Herzer gasped as the brand was released. Talbot took a handful of ash and pressed it against the burn, then nodded at the armorer.

The armorer stepped forward and taking the still hot symbol, affixed it to the left breast of Herzer's armor.

"Take your place, Blood Lord Herrick. Welcome to the Brotherhood."

As each of the Blood Lords was brought forward to be sworn in, Herzer looked at the brand on his arm. It was an eagle with something clutched in either talon. In the center was a numeral one and over it were the words: Semper Fidelis.

He wasn't sure what they meant, but he knew he was going to have them burned into his brain, and his skin, for the rest of his life.

CHAPTER THIRTY-FIVE

"How goes it, Myron?" Edmund said, sitting down by his friend.

He hadn't been to Tarmac's tavern in a month or more and he was glad to see that the initial frenetic edge was wearing off. There were two other taverns in town at this point and Tarmac's had started to cater to the more established crowd. Edmund recognized most of the regulars as long-time Faire goers and there were surprisingly few "new" faces in the pub.

"Pretty good," Myron replied. "I got my first harvest of corn in, so we can quit worrying about stocks for the time being."

"That's good," Edmund replied, gesturing to Estrelle for a pint. "I'm worried about winter stores, though. There has to be some way to ensure that people don't starve. Other than 'owning' them that is," he added, blackly.

"I saw that provision in the constitution," Myron frowned. "I can't believe you let it stand."

"I was outvoted," Edmund said. "It was walk out of the whole thing or let it go. I think that once things settle down, though, it won't be as much of an issue as it seems. Debt peonage works best, economically, when the value of labor is low, that is, when labor has a minimal level of productivity. We're not dealing with straight medieval technology. The productivity of a person working with the power looms, for example, is much higher than a woman weaving in her home. And too many of the crafts require high degrees of training. Not to mention the economic effect of a competitive marketplace for labor and ideas. I think

439

that, long term, the areas that have gone for debt peonage are going to find they are falling behind economically and probably in population growth as well. It's then that the fecal matter is going to hit the fan."

"But in the meantime?" Myron asked.

"In the meantime the peons are guaranteed being fed over the winter," Edmund said. "Which is more than the casual laborers in this town can be sure of. Which worries me."

"Well, some of them are starting up new farms," Myron pointed out. "I think some of the ones who are out there are just insane if they think they're going to make farmers. But, on the other hand, a couple are probably going to do darn well. We'll just have to worry about it as it comes."

Mike smiled as they passed the rag marker tied to the tree. "This is it, Courtney, it's all ours."

"Ours and the township's," she said, looking around at the trees stretching in every direction. "We're . . . we've got a lot of work to do."

"But we'll do it," Mike said in a satisfied tone.

They had been incredibly lucky in the lottery, thanks mainly due to Herzer. His ticket had won one of the three jackasses the roundup had gathered. It was an incredibly valuable animal to someone who had mares to breed with it; the resulting mules would command high prices. But for Mike and Courtney it was more or less a dead end. However, the township had taken one fifth of all the beasts captured, and all of the slaughter meat, for itself and many of the animals were available to Myron Raeburn. His silos, intended to supply a surprising number of customers for the now defunct "Raven's Mill All Period Foods" had fed the community during the worst of the food crisis. He had not, however, given it away; it was provided to the community on credit.

Courtney had known this, because during their apprenticeship to Myron she had grown close to Bethan Raeburn. So when Mike was unsure what to do with the jackass, she had approached Bethan. Despite the fact that she looked upon Bethan as another mother, the dickering had been hard. The other jackasses had all gone to people who intended to use them for breeding and Myron's sole jack was getting old. The one that Mike and Courtney had won was young and surprisingly large and fit; it was a valuable animal.

In the end, Courtney had won from the Raeburns a young ox, a brace of chickens including a rooster, a sow that was believed to be pregnant and some old woodworking tools. Together with the young male shoat they had gotten as their other animal in the lottery and the plow, parts and rope they had been able to buy with a combination of their saved money and Herzer's "loan" they were better set up than virtually all of the other new "pioneers." In addition, Mike had befriended a badly beat up stray Rottweiller whose only fault seemed to be persistent friendliness and an odd fear of cats.

"I came out here with McGibbon the other day," Mike said, taking a faint track off the main road. "There's a good place for a farmhouse up in the trees."

They followed the trace for a couple of hundred meters to a small hill. Running along the trace was a brook that issued from a crevice on the hill. Courtney looked around and considered the country. With the trees cleared away, a major undertaking in itself, the land other than the hill would be flat and easily plowed. But the first order of the day was setting up camp.

Mike set to work on some of the smaller understory in the area, cutting saplings down to form a lean-to while Courtney tied off the ox and let out the chickens and pigs. She threw down a handful or so of their precious corn so that the animals would know they would be fed and then set to work clearing out the area that was to become their home.

Over the next few weeks they both worked from before sunrise until there was no light to see. Mike had the heaviest work to do, felling trees, leaving the tops where they were, cutting the trunks into manageable chunks and then using the ox to drag them into great piles to dry. He had formed a yoke for the ox on the second night, working late by the fire carving it and piercing it with the woodworking tools they had obtained from the Raeburns. Everything had to be made and if there was something that they could not make they had to do without. Without any help the work went slowly but steadily. To spare the corn that they had brought, Courtney wandered the woods finding the few plants that she knew were edible while Mike took occasions to set out snares and deadfalls. Between the two of them they kept food on the table, which they prepared over their open smoky fires.

Finally, they had enough of the area cleared away to plant and he fired the tops that had been left in place, filling the area with smoke but leaving behind nourishing ash to help the soil and killing the first sprout of weeds. On an auspicious silver moon Mike used the ox and the plow, only the share of which he had bought, the rest being made from the wood he had cut himself, to open the fertile ground and plant the corn that it was hoped would tide them over through the first year. Courtney started a truck garden with some tomato seedlings they had brought, cooking beans and other vegetables and legumes to supplement their diet. The first year was more about planting for survival than sale and they recognized that. But by the time the next planting season came around, Mike fully intended to have enough ground broken to produce a surplus.

Even with the corn in the ground there was much to do. He hesitated over which of the many farm buildings was the most important to build but finally came to a decision. He built a paddock out of split logs for the pigs, which had developed an unpleasant tendency to wander away in the woods if left out at night, and coops for the chickens. He had had to pick numerous rocks from the fields before plowing and he used these to construct a spring house, with a wooden roof, and a simple dam near the head of the spring. Without good mortar it leaked something fierce, but it was a place where meat could be kept cool for a day or two when they had the occasional excess. The sow was noticeably pregnant and they could hope for a good batch of piglets in the fall. All in all things were looking on track.

Then, in the midst of these preparations, they had a visitor; Jody Dorsett and his crew, including Emory, leading a team of oxen, stopped by.

"Good Lord, you've been working hard," Jody said as he walked up the narrow path to their farmstead. He looked around at the cleared land and the rows of newly sprouted corn laid among the stumps of the forest.

"It's the only way to do it," Mike replied, gruffly.

"It's the only way to do it *right*," Emory said with a laugh, shaking his hand. They hadn't been close in the apprenticeship program, but it was still good to see an old friend. "Earnon and Nergui have set up not too far off. He's got a couple of trees cleared away and already planted, with the sun only hitting the plants a couple of hours of the day."

"Won't work," Mike said, waving at the small field. "I didn't plant to the edges. Corn needs light. He was with Myron, he should know that."

"It's Earnon," Jody said, disgustedly. "And don't even talk to me about Karlyn. She's gone and joined a group of . . . well they're calling them the Crazy Coven. A bunch of women, no men allowed, thank you, and you wouldn't believe how *they're* set up. But that's not what I'm here about. Mike, I wanted your permission for something. I'm back to general woodcutting and charcoaling. Your land, but I'd like to cut some of your trees. You're right close to the road and we can either haul them back that way or, more likely, roll them into the river and pull them back with the oxen in a raft. It's a good setup and you'll get some cleared land out of it for the loss of the timber. Earnon's actually a bit closer but . . ."

"That would be—" Mike said.

"Would you and your crew like to eat lunch with us?" Courtney interjected. "I've found some fresh wild collards and one of Mike's deadfalls caught a shoat. It's really too much meat for us to eat before it spoils; we don't have a smokehouse yet and it'll only keep for a day or two in the springhouse."

"I'd be glad to," Jody replied. "I've brought hominy and some dried meat for meals while we're working, but some fresh greens and pork would be great."

"Well, we'll talk business after lunch," she said with a smile.

Mike didn't say anything or change his expression, but he knew that Jody was about to be shaken down until his teeth rattled.

Three weeks later Jody and his crew moved on. They left behind a swath of cleared land that led from the main road all the way to the farmyard, five good hickory and two chestnut trunks that had been split and stacked to dry. There were five bushels of charcoal as well. They'd left one in five of their haul but Mike had pitched in from time to time as well as offering his ox when it was available and Courtney had done most of the cooking for the whole camp. Jody had been able to make more of a haul than he'd expected and Mike and Courtney had a huge swath of cleared land ready to plant. Everyone was happy with the deal.

Mike wasn't sure what to do with the newly cleared land, however. It was already getting late in the season; the fast growing supercorn was already knee high and he didn't have much in the way of other seeds.

After much thought he planted some more corn, despite the fact that he wasn't sure if it would sprout in time, and then walked into town and looked up Myron Raeburn.

The farmer was working in his woodshop when Mike walked in and looked up in pleased surprise. "Mike, how's it going?"

Mike told him of their relative success and the good news of Jody's visit then went on to his problem. "The thing is,

I've got a couple of hectares of extra cleared land and I don't know what I should plant. And I don't have the seeds or, frankly, money to buy them."

"Bit of a problem," Myron admitted. "It's midsummer. Most of what you'd plant might not sprout unless you get a lucky thunderstorm for the water."

"I can probably run some irrigation in," Mike suggested. "I've got a good stream. But it'll erode it some."

"There's a way to plow around that," Myron said. "If the stream's well placed you can crosscut your plowing and run some water in that way, but it won't reach the full area. Corn might work. But . . . how much do you think you can water?"

"Of what's left I haven't planted, maybe a half a hectare," Mike suggested.

"I'll tell you what, this is a gamble," Myron said. "But you might be able to get a cosilk crop in. You'll have to keep it well watered and there'll have to be an Indian Summer to gather it in; you can't gather it wet. But if the weather holds good you could get in a good crop and the least you'll get is the seeds. I'll want a fifth of your crop and a fifth of the seeds for the seeds I'll give you."

Mike thought about it for a moment and frowned.

"Don't be thinking of siccing Courtney on me," Myron said with a grin. "I won't give her a better deal."

"Will do," Mike replied with a laugh.

"I'll throw in some good beans as well," Myron added, getting up from his seat. "They won't require as much water except for sprouting and you can water that by hand. And what you don't store you can sell in town."

So Mike returned with a basket full of seeds and went to work.

"Ishtar," Sheida said as she appeared in her friend's residence. "This is very nice."

The home was placed on a mountaintop in central Taurania and the style was distinctly Tauranian with an open plan that looked inward on a courtyard with a fountain in the center. The floors were tile while the walls were covered in frescoes made from semiprecious gems. Beyond the walls the view was of a continuous stretch of rugged, tree-covered mountains. Nowhere was there a sign of habitation but Sheida knew that literally millions lived under her friend's aegis.

Ishtar had been doing much the same thing as she had in the area of Taurania although the society she was creating was far more aristocratic than that in Norau. Ishtar's position was also much looser than Sheida's; she acted as a universal ombudsman to the various factions in the area rather than having a direct legal role. The people of the region were also much less legally attached, working in a very informal group of city-states.

Taurania had suffered less than many other areas because it had had a long tradition of maintaining "natural" society and because many of the homes in the area were traditional and centered on small towns rather than the broadly scattered societies in Norau and Ropasa. This had permitted the population to "fall in" on more or less stable societies. The entire region had once been environmentally devastated from millennia of overwork but even before the latter Council period aggressive reforestation and environmental rebuilding had refreshed the landscape. Sheida had seen pictures of the once denuded mountains and vast stretches of desert, but for the last few thousand years the region had been rebuilt until it was, once again, a virtual paradise.

Which had been fortunate for the residents of the region when the Fall occurred.

"Thank you," Ishtar replied. "Fortunately, Paul has seen fit to not attack my home, yet. I keep the defense up, nonetheless."

"Well, I hope he doesn't hit it," Sheida said. "We could barely spare the power. Which is what I'm here about." She extended a virtual simulacrum of what looked like a very large dragonfly. "Aikawa came up with this idea. We need power and we've tapped all the traditional methods. But one that we haven't tapped, because it is so diffuse, is solar."

"Setting up panels . . ." Ishtar frowned.

"Not panels," Sheida said. "What this does is spread nannites. It produces them in its body and then passes them on to other environmental enhancers like the pixies and hobs. It also is self-replicating; it's a totally natural biological. But the nannites will provide power only to those who have the appropriate protocols. So it can spread nannites which will gather solar power and pass them on to those who need it."

"It's a very diffuse form of power," Ishtar said, looking at the insect. "Then there's the fact that if we spread around nannites that draw solar power, they're bound to interfere with other solar processes, photosynthesis for example. And how does it fit in the environment? It will have to survive on its own."

"Well, it draws a bit of power for its own use," Sheida replied. "And it eats all the sorts of things that dragonflies eat. Naturally it will be a prey species as well. I've run some environmental models and it fits remarkably well, not too destabilizing at least."

"How do you propose to spread them?" Ishtar asked. "And what does your little friend think of them?" she added, gesturing at the lizard wrapped around Sheida's neck.

"He thinks they're a prey species," Sheida chuckled. "And they can be given a boost of energy and told to fly to specific places on earth. So they can be spread widely. But if you could start breeding them here, for example, and Ungphakorn in Soam, myself in Norau, etc."

"Can New Destiny use the power?" Ishtar asked.

"No, it doesn't dump in the Net," Sheida said. "It can be restricted from it. But they might copy us. At some point I could see battles for solar territory, but that's far off. We have to get the nannites spread first."

"Hmmm," Ishtar replied, closing her eyes. "Long term it might even be to Paul's advantage. He has more land area than we do and more of it in high solar regions. Do these interfere with photosynthesis?"

"No," Sheida assured her. "They absorb a completely different spectrum. And, of course, they cannot auto-replicate. So they'll spread slowly no matter what. The last thing is that they are self-repelling; they won't cover more than ten percent of any given square meter and that broadly distributed. I don't want the whole world to look like a dust bowl."

"Okay," Ishtar said. "I'll ken some of these creatures and get them distributed. I'll start in the Southern Marshes; they should like it there."

"Have you figured out who is supplying Paul with power?" Sheida asked.

"Not yet," Ishtar admitted. "I'm having to send out biological scouts similar to that one to try to find each of the Wolf 359 board members. That means going to their last known location and then trying to track them. It is going slowly. So far I have determined that six of them died either just prior to or just after the Fall. Others I haven't been able to find yet."

"Well, keep me posted," Sheida said. "I have the funny feeling it's going to bite us in the ass."

CHAPTER THIRTY-SIX

Herzer wasn't too sure what being in a permanent station would be like, but it turned out to be not too different from training. They still drilled intensively every day, worked their weights and took regular road marches, not to mention a daily stroll up the Hill. In addition, they were put to work building a more permanent camp, making wooden barracks with planked wood walls and floors instead of the tents they had been occupying and making furniture for them. Herzer was fine at the construction but his inability to handle fine woodwork followed him to the furniture making. After seeing his first few disastrous attempts, Jeffcoat set him to other tasks.

The physical area of the camp was expanded and workers from the town extended the ditch and palisades under Herzer's direction. He also found himself in charge of their maintenance and pay and discovered the horrors of paperwork. However, he turned out to be capable of that as well and Jeffcoat, who it turned out was on the near side of functionally illiterate, turned more and more of the administration of the camp over to him. Herzer soon found himself handling pay records, training plans, duty rosters and all the other minutiae that is necessary to a well run military operation. When he found himself *generating* paperwork he decided that he'd been at it too long and started working on expansion plans in his spare time.

At his suggestion, part of the triari's training was to begin regular "simulated" battles with the town militia. This did two things. The first was that it gave the troops and the militia good training, more realistic than either group fighting decuri to decuri. The second thing was that the militia quickly discovered, and passed along the message, that there was a big difference between the two forces. At the first encounter Herzer, who was acting in the position of triari commander, had been surprised how easily the militia, many of whom had been reenactors before the Fall, had been routed. Part of it was the bowmen, who had set up in record time and "counterfired" the crossbowmen and short bows of the militia before the two infantry forces had even come to blows. The second was the difference in the disciplined shield line and "open formation" of the Blood Lords versus the more-or-less mob approach of the militia.

The militia formed in two lines with a solid line of basically unarmed shield wielders followed by spear and polearm wielders. The "sawtoothed" formation of the Blood Lords, and their superior discipline, permitted them to break up the shield formation and then rout the lighter armed interior groups. And this was without a pilum cast or even engaging the militia with the longbowmen. It went a long way to quelling an incipient war that was developing between the "civilians" and the military forces.

There still was a terrific lack of luxuries or free time in Raven's Mill. Everyone was working nearly nonstop. So on the Saturday evenings when the "soldiers" were let free on pass, the fact that most of them had some money to spend, and the fact that the town so rarely saw the intensity of their daily drill, had caused a fair amount of resentment. There had been a few fights and one stabbing of a soldier, fortunately not fatal. But after the first militia battle, when the militia was so handily and speedily routed, and after it was pointed out that the Blood Lords would be the *first* to engage any enemy, and hopefully the last, some of the disturbance subsided. There were still a few hotheads, on both sides, but exercise had helped ease the tension. And the fact that it was Herzer's idea brought him, again, to Edmund Talbot's attention.

He was laying out the parameters for the next battle one evening when the door of the triari office opened to reveal Mayor Talbot.

"Herzer, it's Saturday night," Edmund said. "What the hell are you doing still working? When I saw the lamplight, I figured it was Gunny."

"I'm trying to tighten up the scenario for the next battle, Mayor Edmund," Herzer said defensively. "We've got a real problem with not being able to cover enough frontage and I think that the archers could be better employed. But that means making training arrows of some sort or coming up with a scoring system. And Kane's going to argue the scoring system unless I've got good data." He gestured to the books on the desk and shrugged. "I've been going over the accounts of Crecy, Poitiers and Agincourt to define how many arrows are going to do what damage to the opposing force."

"Good God, son," Edmund laughed. "You should have just asked me; I've got those numbers memorized. And the simple answer is that if the militia *really* fought your group, it would get slaughtered in the first couple of minutes. Even though, you're right, you can't cover enough frontage. Son, you need to take a break. Put down the quill, put away the sword and come on down to the tavern for a drink. I'll buy the first round."

"Well, sir," Herzer said uneasily. "I don't know. I don't actually have much cash at the moment."

"Come on," Talbot said, grabbing his arm and hoisting him to his feet. "You're leaving. All work and no play isn't conducive to good personal development. For that matter, why *don't* you have any cash? The big argument has been that you troops are overpaid."

"Well, I haven't been spending it," Herzer replied, blowing out the lantern as they went out the door. "Actually . . . I've been saving it or investing it. Robert Usawe is starting a dredging operation and he's taking investors. Given what the masons are paying for river sand and rock, it looks as if we can make back the investment on the dredges and barges in about five months. And the actual operations costs are relatively low. So I've poured most of my money lately into that. I also stood part value on a loan to John Miller for an expansion of the sawmill. So it's not that I don't have money, it's just tied up."

"And I heard about your deal with young Michael," Edmund said with another chuckle. "Haven't you ever heard 'live for today for tomorrow we die'? Grab what you can while you can, son. There's no guarantee that you'll wake up tomorrow. I mean, yes, doing some investing is all well and good. But you should keep some money for your expenses and some decent living."

The town was filled with people enjoying the pleasant late

summer evening and the two threaded their way through the crowds to Tarmac's tavern. The interior was crowded but Herzer saw that there was room at a table that had been taken over by First Decuri of the Blood Lords. Another section of the tavern was being held down by Kane, some of his cavalry troopers and a few of the militia/reenactors who were singing along to some song about barley. The redheaded minstrel was up on the stage—she seemed to have become a permanent fixture—and her band was leading the tune, with her singing loud enough to be heard over the off-key bellowing.

Herzer sat down by Pedersen as Edmund took the seat across from him and signaled to Estrelle for a round.

"What are you doing here?" Deann yelled over the noise. "I thought you'd still be burning the midnight oil!"

"I told him we don't have oil to burn!" Edmund called back, taking a brimming tankard and handing it to Herzer. "And that he needed to get out more!"

"Thass ri'!" Cruz shouted drunkenly. "Eat, drink and be merry, tomorrow we die!"

"And you're drinking on credit," Pedersen laughed. "Because you lost a week's pay to me at dice!"

"Tha' way you gonna make sure I li'!" Cruz said with a grin and a slap on the decurion's shoulder.

"What did you think of training?" Edmund asked.

"Bloody awful!" "Issh . . . ish shou'ln't happpppen er a dog!"

"It was . . . interesting," Herzer replied. "I think the death march at the end was a particularly nice touch."

"Thanks," Edmund replied. "That was all mine!"

"Was it you that had us stop at the clearing at the end?" Herzer asked. "What's with the grave."

"That's for you to find out," Edmund replied, somberly. "There's a great man buried there. A great man. One of the finest generals in the history of the world. And totally forgotten except for a few relics like myself."

"Do you put the lemons there?" Herzer asked.

"No," Talbot replied with a grin. "That was implemented before my time. I'm glad to know it's still happening."

"Well, they're not bad," Herzer said with a shrug. "Not as sour as most lemons."

"You didn't eat it, did you?" Edmund asked, askance.

"Uh, yeah," Herzer replied, worried. "Why?"

"Hmmm," Edmund muttered. "You're . . . not having any odd dreams, are you?" he asked, looking the boy up and down.

"No."

"You sit up straight already, is that something you've learned or . . ."

"I've always had good posture," Herzer said. "What the hell are you getting at, Baron Edmund?"

"Well," Talbot replied with a shrug and a chuckle. *"Probably* no harm done. But if you start lifting your left arm over your head when you're thinking, we'll have to perform an exorcism."

"What?!"

The band had completed their last song and Cruz looked up from his beer blearily and started banging the table rhythmically. "Cam-BREATH, Cam-BREATH, Cam-BREATH!"

The chant was taken up by others, including the cavalry in the corner and the minstrel shook her head.

"Fie on you soldiers!" she shouted with a laugh. "You're always calling for Cambreadth. I'll give you your Cambreadth!" With that she waved to the band and they started the song, but the lyrics were different than Herzer remembered. He knew the song well; it was practically the anthem of the Blood Lords and they sang it on every march. But this one was so different he began laughing and couldn't stop.

> "Rambo Frog travels by the moon,
> Meets with Mr Red Raccoon—
> Soon they're joined by Tortoise & Hare,
> To make sure the animals all play fair-
> A fight's broke out near the water hole,
> The natives have all lost control—
> Froggy's boys come from on high,
> 'HOW MANY OF YOU CAN CATCH A FLY?'"

When it got to the part where the frog was attacking the heron, Herzer was laughing so hard he had a hard time staying on the bench.

"Boy definitely needs to get out more," Deann laughed.

Herzer didn't realize that the first mug of beer was done until he was halfway through the second. And since the two beers had gotten together, they decided they needed some friends. As the evening went on it got a bit blurrier right up until both the groups were singing "Yellow Ribbon" and one of the cavalry troopers was suddenly shouting at Cruz.

"It's *cavalry* trooper you idiot!" the drunken trooper yelled, coming over to their table.

"It's legionnaire you pencil-necked horse-lover!" Cruz said, standing up.

"Yellow is the color of *cavalry,* you slope-browed moron!" the apparently suicidal trooper said. He was at least a head shorter than Cruz and at least twenty kilos lighter.

"Hey, hey, hey," Herzer said mildly, standing up and putting his hands on their chests to separate them. "Yel-low," he enunciated carefully, "is the col-or of the cav-al-ry, Cruj." Then he turned to the, yeah, pencil-necked cavalry trooper. "On the other han', the song is tradit . . . tradeee . . . of'en sung with udder symbo . . . udder stuff," he finished.

"Get away from me you cowardly fisk," the trooper said.

"What did you say?" Herzer asked, dangerously.

"You cut and *ran* on Doctor Ghorbani," the trooper sneered just before the fist crashed into his face.

Herzer didn't really remember most of the next minute or so. Later he had a clear view of Kane's face flashing past his eyes, apparently propelled through the air when trying to stop him and the cry of "BLOOD LORDS" from behind him. But the next thing he actually was aware of was a small, lithe body pressed into his back and holding his face to the floor with an absolutely unbreakable, and tremendously powerful, wrestling hold.

"No more drinks for *you,* Triari Herzer," Estrelle said calmly.

"Yes, ma'am," Herzer replied. The homunculus had his legs pinned in some sort of a scissors hold, his face braced into the floor and both of his arms twisted behind his back. And when he tried to writhe out she gave just enough of a twist for him to realize that she was only letting him have both shoulders stay together because she was programmed to reduce necessary harm. "I'll be good."

"Let him up, Estrelle," Herzer heard The Gunny say in his most Gunny voice.

Estrelle unwound herself and lifted his well-over-a-hundred-kilos weight as if he were a feather.

"What happened here?" Gunny asked.

"It was entirely my fault," Herzer said, miserably.

"There were words exchanged, Gunnery Sergeant Rutherford," Kane said, waving his hand as if to dismiss the incident. "One of my troopers made, quite loudly, a rather unfounded accusation. And Herzer took . . . violent exception to it."

"How is he?" the Gunny asked. "The trooper, that is."

"Well," Kane replied, rubbing a bruise that was starting to purple on his forehead, "we'll all live. But I think we might have to consider giving the cavalry and the Blood Lords different nights off."

"Herzer, did you lay hand on Cavalry Master Kane?" Gunny asked, coldly.

"I'm . . . not sure, Gunny," Herzer admitted.

"It was all a bit blurry to me as well," Kane said quickly. "I'd really suggest that bygones be bygones. Hot words, a few . . . clashes. They're soldiers, Gunny."

"No, my troops are *Blood Lords,* and they fight who I *tell* them to fight," Gunny said. "Herzer, return to the barracks. You are confined to quarters until I decide how this will be handled. You can consider yourself stripped of acting triari status. You are dismissed."

Herzer was lying in his bunk with his fingers interlaced behind his head when the other Blood Lords stumbled into the decuri bay.

"This is a fisking disgrace!" Deann said angrily. "That arrogant horse-fisker needed to be punched out. We can sing any damned thing we want!"

"I didn't hear what he said," Cruz said. "What the hell made you so angry; you practically punched him across the room. What a sweet sight, by the way."

"He said that I had cut and run on Doctor Ghorbani when she was raped," Herzer said, simply.

"WHAT?" Deann screamed. "When he gets out of the infirmary I'm going to kill him!"

"Deann," Herzer said quietly, "there's only one problem."

"What?!"

"It's true," he replied and rolled over on his side.

Kane came into Edmund's office when summoned and looked around at the others. Besides Edmund, who was behind the desk with a stony expression on his face, there were Gunny Rutherford and Daneh Ghorbani now swollen with child.

"Kane," Edmund said, gesturing at the couch next to Gunny. "Would you mind telling me, your side of the events last night. All of it, please."

"One of my troopers apparently tried to pick a fight with the Blood Lords over them changing the lyrics to a song," Kane said. "I was getting ready to drag him off when Herzer intervened and tried to separate them. The trooper, Trooper McIerran, then accused Herzer of having 'cut and run' when . . ."

"When I was raped," Daneh said, rubbing her stomach.

"Yes. At that point, Herzer punched him. Hard."

"His jaw is broken in multiple places," Daneh said. "I've tried to put it back together but he's never going to be much of a talker again. Fortunately, I might add," she said, spitefully.

Kane's face worked and he shrugged. "McIerran has . . . never been one of my best troops. The problem is that he was thrown across our table when Herzer hit him and a couple of my other troops took exception to the action, whether it was the blow or the drinks spilled everywhere. And then Herzer was going after McIerran as if to kill him. So we attempted to . . . intercede. Two of my other troopers and a couple of militiamen are . . ."

"Down for at least a few days," Daneh sighed and shifted positions. "Herzer is . . ."

"Herzer is the question we have to address," Edmund said pinching the bridge of his nose. "The problem is, according to Daneh, the accusation is true. Something she had so far failed to make clear," he added, stonily.

"True and . . . not how it sounds," Daneh sighed. "He was with McCanoc's band, but from what I have been able to glean they weren't doing anything wrong up until then. They were just . . . surviving. It was a confusing time. He was lost like most of the rest of us and he knew McCanoc and . . . Aggh!" she threw up her arms. "You *know* what that time was like! I shouldn't have to explain it!"

"Go on," Edmund said, quietly.

"Some of McCanoc's men caught me and brought the rest, including Herzer. He told McCanoc I was a friend of his and McCanoc's answer was, more or less, that that was good, he could go first."

"Ouch," Kane said, shaking his head.

"McCanoc had drawn his sword. Herzer was unarmed and outnumbered. If he'd tried to fight he would have died and it wouldn't have *changed* anything!" Daneh snarled then winced as the baby made a sudden motion. "This is *my* honor and *my* body that we are talking about and if anyone should be angry," she added, looking pointedly at Edmund, "it should be *me*."

"And you're not?" Kane asked, surprised.

"Herzer was my *patient*," she said with a sigh. "Before the Fall. I put a lot of work in him. I would prefer not to see it wasted." She paused and sighed again. "What other feelings I have beyond that are *mine*."

"Did Trooper McIerran actually have information about this?" Edmund asked.

"Well, he's not talking very well," Kane admitted. "But he indicated that, no, it was a shot in the dark. I've . . . heard the rumors too." He shook his head and shrugged. "Herzer has become popular in the community. He's well known to some of the major members of the community and his actions at the roundup are already legendary. Including his . . . somewhat intense heroism. That has caused a degree of envy. Some of the sequence of events are known about your . . . attack, doctor. Not *this* sequence but that Herzer was there even before any- one else."

"Rachel," Daneh said, pursing her lips.

"Probably, but not *generally*," Kane corrected. "Rachel to some friend to another friend all getting mixed into rumor. A nice juicy rumor to pull down somebody who just comes across as too Simon Pure to be true. A rumor which, unfor- tunately, now appears to be true."

"Gunny, effects on the Blood Lords," Edmund said with a sigh.

"Bad. Herzer's one of their natural leaders. They're not sure how to handle him now. Being a hero is what they're all about. 'Fight until you die and drop.' He ran. He's a coward in their eyes. They're very black and white about that. On the other hand, he's one of them. More now that he's not triari. They're rallying around him, but you can tell they're uneasy about doing it. We've had two more fights in the last two days."

"What's *your* take?" Edmund asked. "Where are you, Miles?"

Gunny thought about it for a moment then shook his head. "How many, Doctor?"

"Eight," she said neutrally.

"Armed?"

"One with a bow, McCanoc with a sword and a couple of other daggers."

"Maybe, *maybe* I could have fought my way out of that," Gunny said. "And kept you alive and unraped doing it. Herzer, no way. Not then. Probably not now. One day, sure even against McCanoc. He made the tactical decision to retreat and leave you behind. Sometimes, you have to cut your losses. When he came back, he was armed, wasn't he?"

"Yes," she said, softly, kneading her stomach.

"He was probably dreading coming back and finding you with your throat cut. If *he* has nightmares, that is probably them. And if he had, I don't think he'd be alive now, but most of them would be dead as well. He doesn't have an ounce of quit in him. He'll do. I can handle the Blood Lords. I'm not to sure how he's going to take it, though."

"He's liable to kill himself being the hero, is the answer," Edmund replied, gritting his teeth until the rest could hear them squeak.

"Edmund, forgive him," Daneh ordered sharply.

"I will," Edmund replied. "Just do me the favor to give me a little time. All right?"

"All right," she said, unhappily.

"People will be down on him, though," Edmund said. "That's natural. I'd watched people build him up even when he didn't mean it to happen. Now they're going to drag him down."

"I'll work on that," Daneh said determinedly. "I'll bring it up in the next session. And the Ladies will let it Be Known that coming down on Herzer doesn't work."

"Rachel," Edmund said.

"Family," Daneh said, nodding at the others.

"Okay, if that's it . . ."

"Not . . . quite," Kane said unhappily. "You know how you wanted me to send a patrol down valley?"

"Yes?" Edmund said. There had been a report from a pack trader that a "large force" was seen moving north near Rowana. The target could be either Raven's Mill or Washan. The patrol had been sent out to see if it was Washan and another was due to head down the valley to see what was happening there.

"Well, my 'patrol' is in the hospital. The rest of the riders are out patrolling south of Resan. I've only got three left hale, and myself. I'd rather be here for when the others get back. And I don't want to send three out by themselves. Besides, they're all . . . pretty inexperienced."

"Shit," Edmund said, shaking his head. He thought about it a moment longer then cursed. "Ah, hell."

"Yeah," Kane replied. "You just got to the part I got to a while ago."

"Herzer," Gunny grunted.

"He can stay on a horse better than most of my riders," Kane said. "Way better than the three I've got left. I mean, it's him, me or Edmund."

"I can ride," Gunny said. "I can even fight on horseback."

"No," Edmund said. "For the same reason Kane and I can't go. That pack trader said there were a bunch of them and he thought it was only part of the force. If this is the force that hit Resan, I don't want either of you off on a patrol, much less cut down on one."

"And you're thinking of sending *Herzer*?" Daneh asked.

"He's disposable," Edmund said brutally. "At least, more so than any of the three of us, or you for example."

"So you're thinking of sending him out on patrol with three cavalrymen when he's just put the rest of their squad in the hospital?" she asked. "You're out of your mind."

"Well, they won't give him any guff," Kane snorted. "Not to his face."

"Herzer's . . ." Daneh stopped and shook her head. "He's . . . more vulnerable to stuff behind his back than to his face. And how do you know one of them won't slip a knife in his ribs when he's asleep?"

"Oh, come on, Daneh," Kane said angrily. "They're not *that* mad. They're more contemptuous than mad. Getting him out of town is a benefit for that matter. It will let things settle down, give people something else to gossip about."

"How long?" Edmund asked.

"Two weeks," Kane replied. "Straight down the west valley then back up the east. Spare horse with fodder apiece."

"Do it," Talbot said.

"Edmund!"

"This discussion is over," he replied, coldly.

"I'll inform him," Gunny said, getting up. "Edmund, Kane, Mistress Ghorbani," he nodded then left the room followed by Kane.

"This discussion is *not* over," Daneh said, standing up and sweeping up her skirts.

"I'll see you tonight," Edmund sighed, picking up his glasses and turning back to his paperwork.

CHAPTER THIRTY-SEVEN

The "get his ass out of town" patrol, as Herzer thought of it, had not been a rousing success but at least it was nearly over. The three cavalrymen had not traded any more words with him than were necessary for the business of the patrol, but that was fine by him. He was in no mood to talk anyway, and the only subject that would come up he *really* didn't want to talk about. They had just done their job, riding in the long circuit down the west side of Massan Mountain then back up the east, finding nothing but birds and beasts of the field. Supposedly there was a large force out here somewhere, but if so they had seen no sign of it. One time they ran across signs of an encampment but the trail had disappeared when whoever used it had broken up. That had been on the southwest side of Massan Mountain and they had ridden carefully for a day but after seeing no more sign they had slipped back into simply riding.

The valley had started to slip into early fall and the nights were turning cool with the trees on the upper ridges already starting to change color. Down in the valley, though, it was still hot during the day and as they rode up the valley the air was slow and still.

Herzer took off his helmet and wiped his face, looking up at the sun to judge the time. If they rode hard and didn't stop for an afternoon break they could probably make it back to town that day, if late. The horses were doing fine; they had found plenty of forage on the patrol and they had hardly had to touch the grain they had carried with them except for a cup of it in the evenings to keep them happy. They were in good enough condition to make the town, tired but more than capable. He was pretty sure the cavalrymen were of the same mind but it didn't hurt to check. He turned to ask one of them what they thought of it when a mourning dove flew up out of the trees to the side of the trail and he suddenly dug his heels into Diablo.

"Ambush!" he yelled, spurring the horse hard as the air suddenly filled with arrows. They made an evil hiss in the air as they went overhead. He heard a scream from behind and him and looked back to see one of the cavalrymen swaying in his saddle with an arrow sticking out of his shoulder.

"Back to town," he yelled, then was yanked sideways as his pack horse went down with an arrow in its side.

"Loose the horses!" he said, cursing himself for not thinking of that himself. As he did so with his mount, and the other three charged past, he saw a group of six horsemen coming out of the woods on their tail.

"Keep moving!" he screamed. "One of us has to get back to town!"

He looked back and shook his head in resignation. The horses behind him were some breed that he didn't recognize but they were fast, as fast as Diablo when he was fresh. And their riders were in light armor whereas he was in his full Blood Lord plate. The cavalrymen were well clear, as long as there wasn't another ambush set up ahead of them. But he was lagging behind and the pursuers were catching up.

"Hi, Diablo! Run boy, run for your life," Herzer called. *And mine,* he added mentally.

This was an ignominious way to die, he thought. He had figured he'd die in battle, in the front lines, defending Raven's Mill. But, this was close. He was *in front* of the front lines. Chuckling, he spurred the flagging horse again as it ascended the Bellevue grade into a narrow defile. As he did he heard another yell from ahead of him and then a whole series of shouts.

As he crested the hill he saw one of the cavalrymen down and the other two fighting a group on the ground. Wishing he had a lance, Herzer drew his sword and charged into the group, slamming into one of them with Diablo and slashing downwards at another. He'd left his Blood Lord shield and sword behind, picking up a conventional kite shield and longsword from Baron Edmund before he left. He was glad he had; a short sword would be useless in this encounter as was his Blood Lord training. He'd have to depend on what he remembered of longsword work.

He reined the horse to a stop and looked at the narrow defile in which the skirmish was taking place. Well enough.

He pulled his shield off the side of the horse and hit it on the rump with the flat of his sword. "HI DIABLO," he called, "run for home!" With that he charged the group of infantry slashing from side to side. One of the group swung an axe at him but he blocked it with his shield without thinking and then slammed the steel boss into his opponent as he slashed another across the face.

"RUN YOU FOOLS!" he yelled as one of the remaining cavalrymen turned back to his aid. "Get to the town! That's an *order*!" He swung at another of the group, then backed up so that his back was to the wall of the cut. It was probably an old road-cut from the Norau days and it would do. If he could finish these three off he was well enough placed to face the cavalry. If.

Two had spears, one of which had apparently finished off the injured cavalryman since it was red-stained with blood, and the third had another crudely made axe. One of the spearmen charged him and Herzer caught the spear on the side of his shield and then cut at the shaft as if this were another drill. To his surprise the shaft snapped and he lunged forward to spit the spearman on his sword.

It was the first time that he had killed a man in earnest and intent and the man staggered backwards wailing as if in grief with blood pouring out of the wound and bits of intestine showing in the hole. He had black hair and a beard that was shot through with gray. His mouth was open in the beard and as Herzer watched he seemed to realize that his life was done. He opened and shut his mouth then slumped to the ground.

For a moment Herzer was shaken in hesitation but as the axeman swung he snapped back into drill, blocking the blow with his shield, then jumping forward in a bash at the axeman as the second spearman, the one with the blood of the cavalryman on his spear, tried to spit him from the side.

The point of the spear glanced off the plates of the armor but slipped up into the articulation on his side, barely piercing the cloth underneath.

Herzer grunted at the blow but slashed downward again, cutting the shaft off just below the spearhead. He then jumped back at the axeman who was still muzzy from the shield bash and finished him off with a slash across the throat. That left only the spearman who turned away to run.

Herzer picked up the axe and weighed it in his hand, then shrugged and as carefully as possible hurled it at the spearman. More by luck than training the weapon caught him between the shoulder blades and dropped him writhing in the dust.

Which would have been the end of it if the six cavalrymen hadn't crested the rise at almost the same moment.

Herzer sighed, tiredly, and took up a stance. This was just another drill. The cavalrymen didn't have lances, just swords. They would try to ride him down or cut him with the swords. He was heavily armored to a downward strike so the technique was to step to the left of one of the charging horses and slash it across the side, taking the blow of the sword on his armor and helmet.

The problem in this case was the six were crowding each other to get to him and there wasn't so much as a decimeter between them. For that matter the horses were either very well or very badly trained because instead of avoiding the injured spearman they pounded him into the ground. Which, Herzer figured, was what was just about to happen to him.

As they approached, therefore, he ran to the side of the defile and actually up onto the side, using the force of his run to lift himself into the air and up over the shoulder of the startled horse on the farthest left.

He didn't try anything fancy like staying on the horse or slashing at anything, he simply let a hundred plus kilos of body and another twenty of armor smash into the rider.

He couldn't tell if the rider was dead on the way down nor did he really care. But if he wasn't he assuredly was when Herzer landed on top of him and used the rider's body to break his own fall.

The landing, just about flat out on his face, still drove the air out of his lungs, and his helmet slammed face down quite painfully. But he stumbled to his feet, making sure of the enemy by lifting himself up on his swordpoint, which went through the cavalryman's chest and out the other side.

He got to his feet and took a deep breath, swishing the sword through the air and shaking his head at the last five riders. "Come on you bastards!" he called. "It's a long damned walk to town, I've got a headache and it's going to get dark soon! I want to be drinking ale before midnight."

The horsemen gathered together to charge forward again but

one of them held up his hand and reached down to open up the bow case at his knee.

Herzer went cold as the composite bow came out and the horseman reached down to flick out an arrow. The bow would go right through his armor and might just go through armor and shield. Furthermore, the bastard could keep out of range even if he charged.

It still was the only choice and he raised his shield up before his eyes and started running. "HOW MANY OF THEM CAN WE MAKE DIE!"

The other horsemen closed on him, hacking downward, but he was straitly concentrated on the bowman who was trying to settle his horse. At this range it was a clap shot and Herzer was looking right at the arrow pointed at his visor when there was a twang of a bowstring.

And the rider tumbled sideways out of his saddle.

The arrow went he knew not where and he turned to the side slashing at one of the other mounts as there was a rapid "Thwang, thwang, thwang" and the remaining riders tumbled to the ground, arrows in chest, neck, and eye.

He looked up at the rise above the defile as a light clad archer dropped to the ground and smiled at him naughtily.

"Hi there, lover boy," Bast said, hand on one outshot hip. "Sorry to ruin your fun, but I wasn't willing to break in a new boy-toy."

Herzer and Bast met Kane and a group of militia a kilometer short of the town border. The two were holding hands, Herzer riding a sorely lame and chagrined Diablo and Bast riding a bay Arab that had been one of the pack horses. They were trailing a string of horses, some of which had dead bodies thrown over their backs.

"I heard you were dead," Kane said with a grin.

"Not hardly," Herzer grinned back then sobered. "Barsten didn't make it, though. He's over his horse."

"Yeah," Kane said. "How many?"

"Six in the second ambush and six riders. I don't know how many in the first ambush, though. Lots. Bast saw more."

"As he said, lots," Bast said. "The rest I think should be shared with Edmund."

"Well, he will want to see you. I'll take the horses."

"Don't wait here, we don't know what's coming," Herzer said, looking up at the last of the light. "I doubt that it's going to come tonight, though."

"I'll follow you back, but you'd better hurry ahead," Kane said. "Move it, Triari."

"I lost that slot," Herzer said with a grimace.

"I don't think you'll be worrying about it for long," Kane said with an ambiguous expression.

Soon Diablo was up to a canter and Herzer didn't want to push him more than that. When they approached the town he could see torches moving into the stockaded area and somewhere a bell was ringing.

"I see the rest of the scouts made it back," Herzer said.

"Yes," Bast said, shaking her head. "And now the sheep huddle behind the walls of the paddock in fear of the wolves."

"These sheep have teeth," Herzer said as they cantered up to the gate. "And sheep dogs. Ho, Cruz, open the hell up. I've got the mother's own saddle sores and I want to get off this beast."

"HERZER!" Cruz yelled, jumping down off the stockade wall and shouting for help to open the gates.

As Herzer walked the horses through the gates he heard other people calling his name and suddenly the whole triari was gathered around him, crowding closely enough to make Diablo nervous.

"Back off!" He laughed, dismounting and then clutching at his shoulder. After the battle he had found that at least one of the horsemen had dented his armor hard enough to cause a bone bruise but other than that and the tag in his side he had come through his first battle well enough.

"You're alive," Cruz said, slapping him on the shoulder.

"Ow!" Herzer said. "Yes, I am. People keep saying that. And watch the shoulder."

"Your armor is a sight." Deann chuckled. It was, in fact, splashed over with blood. "You'd better not let Gunny see you."

"There wasn't much clean to wipe it with," Herzer admitted, swallowing as he remembered the remnants of the skirmish. "Kane's bringing the other horses and the bodies in. I'm supposed to report to Mayor Talbot."

"It's *Baron Edmund*," Deann said. "They passed the Constitution of the Free States while you were gone. And guess who one of the first nobles chosen by acclaim was?"

"Oh," Herzer said, working the name around. "I think . . . that fits. Somehow."

"Demoted to baron has he been?" Bast said with a laugh. "Fits him not, methinks. Duke, aye, King even, *Baron*? I think not."

"Well, time to report to the *baron* anyway," Herzer said, walking towards the town hall.

The guards at the doors were holding back a crowd but they passed him through with a nod of recognition and surprise. "I thought you was dead?" one of the guards said as Herzer heard his name muttered in the crowd. Something about that made his blood run cold.

"Close, but not yet."

Inside the council chamber was a strange sight. Most of the council had apparently been tossed out and it was only Gunny, Daneh, swollen with her pregnancy, Rachel and Baron Edmund gathered around something on the table. As Herzer approached he realized it was a rabbit. To be precise a flop-eared brown and white rabbit. It had a harness on, which was heavily hung with small weapons ranging from a knife the size of a fingernail all the way up to a pistol crossbow. He thought at first it was some sort of toy or joke until Bast hissed.

"Oh, By Wood and Water!" she snapped angrily. "What is *that* doing here?"

"Hya, Wood Bitch," the rabbit said in a high tenor, looking over his shoulder and nibbling at his back. "I could say the same of you."

"Herzer," Daneh said, rushing over and then stopping at the sight of his armor. "Good God, Herzer, what have you been doing?"

"Survivin'," Gunny said. "Welcome back, Triari."

"Glad to be here, Gunny," Herzer said with a nodded head at the un-demotion. "Doctor, Rachel, *Baron* Edmund."

"You heard," Edmund said with a nod. "What do you have to report?"

"We were approaching the Bellevue grade when we were ambushed by a large force of archers. They were obscured by trees so that I could not get an accurate count. We were pursued by a small group of six horsemen and ran into another group of infantry. Barsten had been hit by an arrow in the first ambush and was slain in the second. I dismounted and engaged the enemy there and slew those that remained. I then engaged the horsemen that had pursued us and was more or less saved by Bast."

"He says only the half of it," Bast laughed. " 'Slew those that remained' he says. Aye, all six against only him, then took down one of the horsemen by bounding off the cliff did he. Was well on his way to winning, bowmen and all, when I decided he'd simply had enough fun for one day."

"Well done, Triari," Gunny said with a nod.

"I haven't had opportunity to clean my armor, yet, Gunny, sorry," Herzer said, then looked at Rachel as she laughed.

"Just this once I'll let it pass," Gunny said with what looked suspiciously like a smile.

"It seems, Herzer, that we have a report from the enemy camp itself," Baron Edmund said dryly.

"The . . . rabbit?" Herzer asked.

"No rabbit that," Bast spat. "Demon of chaos. Bringer of discord."

"Thanks for all the compliments, sweet-cakes," the rabbit replied. "But, yeah, I came from those bozos that ambushed you. I watched 'em go and then got myself."

"Why?" Edmund asked.

"Look, it's a rabbit-eat-rabbit world, right?" the rabbit said, bending to scratch behind his ear. "So I hear there's some mighty army of evil forming, right? And I figure 'Hey, I'm evil. This could be fun.' But . . . lord they're screwed up. Evil is supposed to have its shit together. I mean, we're the bad guys, sure, but we don't have to be *stupid* about it. Not these bozos. They're violating every rule in the book. All the way up to the funky face-obscuring helmets and one-size-fits-all armor."

"Yes, and burning out towns and farms," Edmund said, grimly.

"No, that's just part of the *job,* you know? But these guys are like total idiots. I keep telling them, it's rape, loot, pillage and burn. Can they get the order right? No. Then they violated the Deal."

"What Deal?" Rachel asked, fascinated. "And . . . rape?" she added angrily.

"Well, not per se," the rabbit said. "I mean, I'm a rabbit. The best I can be is really affectionate, if you know what I mean," he sighed and looked positively dejected for a moment then brightened. "And, let me make this perfectly clear, at no time have I been with these guys when they have been doing any of that stuff. I wouldn't sully my good name with those idiots."

"What good name?" Bast scoffed. "Are a most hated bunny."

"Sure, but I'm *good* at being hated," the bunny replied. "I'm *made* that way. If I can let somebody fall in the soup by inaction it's my *priority*. And if I can push them that's even better. But I do it *smart*. Not *stupid*."

"So your job is to be evil?" Daneh said, carefully. "So you're a construct. AI?"

"Do I look like a nonsentient to you?" the bunny scoffed. "High-*end* AI, *thank* you."

"You must be old. A construct like you would be banned under current protocols."

"One of the first," Bast spat. "In the AI war was. *Both* sides."

"Hey, my *job* is causing discord. That and watching Baywatch. Okay, and killing telemarketers. Causing discord, watching *Baywatch* and killing telemarketers. That's my job. Oh, and trying to kill Santa Claus which is REALLY HARD WITH A MYTH," he shouted as if at the universe.

"What is *Baywatch*?" Herzer asked.

"What's a telemarketer?" Rachel asked in turn.

"Jeeze, kids these days," the rabbit sighed. "I swear, if I ever find a time machine I'm going back to the twentieth century and neutering some guy named Pete Abrams. With a spoon."

"So what was the Deal?" Edmund asked, again

"All the alfalfa hay I can eat and a big-titted blonde," the rabbit said immediately. "I'm willing to change sides since they went south on the Deal."

"No big-titted blonde?" Edmund asked, raising an eyebrow.

"They ran out of alfalfa," the rabbit said bitterly. "Wanted it for their *horses* can you believe it? And their damned smith was all the time following me around, trying to find out if I had a security hole that he could crack. The guy was a fisking idiot; I was made at the height of the most complex and paranoid period of the whole history of civilization. No modern bozo can crack *my* code!"

Bast looked at him for a long moment and then leaned forward. "*Burrow,*" she said.

The rabbit looked up at her in surprise and flinched. "Not good enough, Wood Bitch," he gasped.

"Burrow," she said again then leaned forward and whispered something in his ear.

"CURSES!" he shouted. "Damn you, Wood Bitch!"

"I take it you now are required to answer more precisely," Edmund said with a grin. "How many?"

"A bit over five hundred," the rabbit said with a glare at Bast.

"Five hundred?" Herzer gasped.

"Yeah, that camp of theirs you found was only the vanguard," the rabbit said. "They spotted you guys and set up the ambush. But you made it out. Incompetent, like I said."

"How are they armed?" Edmund said as if the news didn't

surprise him. "And where are they getting the materials to support a force that size?"

"They've got some smith from before the Fall. And they've got some heavy-duty power on their side. Among other things, most of their force are Changed. Really nasty Changed, too. Short, dark, broad, powerful and just as stupid as the day you were born. Light armor, though, mostly leather and not boiled at that. But there's a core of human fighters that are really heavily armed and armored. And their leader is some idiot named Dionys who thinks he's Satan's gift to evil."

"Do you know their plans?" Edmund asked.

"Everybody in the camp knows them," the rabbit said. "Stupid, like I said. They're planning on coming up the west bank of the east valley then fording the river somewhere south of the town. Then they'll approach along the east bank. Dionys has promised them that this is the richest town in the entire valley; they're planning on looting it and burning it when they're done, like Resan." The rabbit shrugged, difficult for a being that seemed to have no shoulders. "It's as good a plan as they can muster; anything more complex would have them so totally confused they'd end up attacking themselves."

"How truly good," Edmund said, musingly. "How truly wonderful."

"Yes," Gunny said in the same tone. "Let them come?"

"No, fire arrows," Edmund said. "Maneuver warfare."

"High disparity of force," Gunny pointed out.

"Reconnaissance, ground," Edmund replied.

"Hai, that would be me," Bast said with a smile. "A long time since we've fought together, my lord."

"With that size force they'll have a serious logistics problem," Edmund said.

"What are you talking about?" Daneh interjected. "For the militarily illiterate present?"

"They're talking about suicide if you want my opinion," the bunny said. "They're talking about taking their 'army' out and fighting them in the field."

"We can do without your comments, evil one," Bast growled.

"I answered the questions," the rabbit replied. "And my password *rotates* when used!"

"I can guess some of the others," Bast said silkily. "And I bet anything that you have an *override,* don't you."

"Curse you, Wood Bitch," the bunny snarled. "Stay away from me or you'll end up as a harem girl."

"Well, Mister Bunny," Edmund said. "I think that you've fulfilled the bargain."

"What about the Deal?" the rabbit asked. "The girl's a looker."

Edmund smiled tightly and stared at the rabbit until it, with apparent unconcern, nibbled at its back again. "I've been stared at by worse," the rabbit muttered.

"What do we get out of the Deal?" Edmund asked.

"Chaos!" Bast said. "Make no deals with the Devil, Edmund Talbot."

"I won't betray you to them," the rabbit replied, ignoring Bast. "I'll settle for just the alfalfa as long as it includes margaritas."

"We don't have any tequila."

"Damn I hate this fallen world. Okay, alfalfa and whatever you make in the way of hooch."

"I make a decent bourbon and there's some brandy," Edmund admitted. "How much?"

"Three shots a day and bottle of high test at New Year's eve. I'll find my own girls. And alfalfa. As much as I want."

"Alfalfa we have in quantity," Edmund said. "Deal. Shake on it."

"By my true name which no one may know," the rabbit said, sticking out a paw with a glance at the elf. "Right?"

"Fine by me," Bast replied with a shake of her head. "But I think you know not what you do, Edmund."

"I'm not going to trust him," Edmund said, shaking the small paw. "But now that I'm a baron, we need a court jester."

"Oh, very funny," the rabbit said, hopping off the table. "I'm going to go drink my ration. The rest of you can just blow me." With that he hopped out of the room, humming.

"Okay, what just happened?" Rachel asked.

"Your father made a most unsavory deal," Bast replied, shaking her head.

"I've heard of that rabbit," Edmund said with a grin. "Shall we say he is a small but doughty fighter."

"Aye, for both sides!"

"He won't fight for the side he is attached to unless he is tricked," Edmund said. "I'll just have to be tricky."

"When do we leave?" Herzer asked.

"And what is this about leaving?" Daneh added.

"We can't fight an army of that size at the walls," Edmund said, "even with every man and woman who can carry a blade. They'll just spread out and swarm the walls. So we're going to go out and fight them. We'll have to use some trickery, but it's better than just trying positional defense. If we had a real castle, maybe. I'll see if Sheida has any help to provide and send a rider to Angus as well. But I doubt the dwarves can arrive in time. So we'll go out and maneuver on them."

"That is why we have been training so much," Gunny added. "With the walls defended and us on their heels, they won't be able to attack the town."

"You'll be . . . badly outnumbered," Rachel said. "Worse than in the town."

"We'll try very hard not to let them surround us," Edmund chuckled. "Gunny, boots and saddles at one hour before dawn. Tomorrow, we march."

CHAPTER THIRTY-EIGHT

"Herzer," Edmund called to him as they were leaving. The baron walked up and put his hand on his shoulder. "Come up to the house. You haven't had any dinner, I think."

"I have to see to my armor, sir," Herzer protested, looking sideways at Daneh and Rachel. "And . . . I don't think I'd be welcome."

"You're quite welcome, son," Edmund said with a smile. "I'll admit I was a bit . . . put off about the news. But if anyone had any doubts about your courage, today has settled that well enough. Damn, twelve of them! I want a better report than that bald statement you made in the council chamber! And there's plenty of armor polish at the house."

"And you, too, Bast," Daneh said, linking arms with the wood elf. "From what Herzer said, I was afraid we'd never see you again in this lifetime."

"Well, when I heard tell of the army of McCanoc marching to the town, I knew I couldn't let Edmund and Herzer have all the fun," the elf replied with a smile and grabbed Rachel's arm to link into hers. "I could do with some supper. And I can't think of a better group than this!"

So the five of them proceeded up to Edmund's house. They moved slowly in deference to Daneh who was not as mobile as she had been. The night was busy with people and Herzer was glad to see that many of them were armed. He knew that the triari and the archers would do all that they could to stop the dark tide rolling towards the town but in the end it might just come down to these half-trained militia. And even if they were not proof against the Blood Lords, so many, and so armed, might be capable of holding the walls against whatever was left.

As they walked through the town, Edmund stopped from time to time to talk to one person or another. The rumor that the defenders were going to be marching out had spread in the town and there was a great deal of uncertainty, but wherever Edmund passed the uncertainty seemed to disappear. His simple answer that it was better to face them away from the town and fields was accepted, sometimes with reservation but always with at least reluctant agreement. And any time the subject of the difference in size of force was brought up, Edmund simply pointed to Herzer and his still blood-splattered armor and laughed. "If one Blood Lord can kill twelve of them, then what will the whole force do to them?" At each such explanation the people nodded at Herzer, many of them with wide eyes, and by the time they were halfway through the town there was a following of young boys who marched along in the most military manner they could manage.

Herzer started to realize that the invitation to dinner, honest though it might have been, had two purposes. And it also made him realize that most of Edmund's decisions were the same. He never took just one path to success but combined his actions for the maximum good. Herzer wasn't sure how he did it, but he intended to learn.

As they neared the house the crowds dwindled away and Edmund shook his head. "I need to leave someone behind to keep up the spirits of the town."

"Leave Herzer, then," Daneh said. "Surely he's done enough."

"My place is with the triari, Dr. Ghorbani," Herzer said quietly.

"That it is," Edmund said, shaking his head. "No, it will be Kane or Gunny. Of the two I think Kane. He won't like it but Alyssa's patrol is back and she can handle the cavalry well enough. And Kane has worked the most with the militia." He paused on the doorstep and smiled. "The good news is that I've hired a cook. Daneh is . . . a little encumbered and Rachel has many virtues but her cooking is not one of them."

He led them into the house and Herzer was oddly comforted. The house where he had convalesced was as much home as the barracks, more so. He realized, not for the first time but perhaps for the first time so forcefully, that he had not had a true home since his parents "gave him his freedom" at fourteen. Edmund's house was as close as it got.

"First, let's get you out of that armor," Edmund said. "Then you can have a cup of wine and a bath."

"I think there are some things around that might fit you," Daneh said, sitting down in one of the chairs and cradling her stomach. "Oh, I thought if I had to walk one more step I was just going to have the baby right then. I cannot *wait* to have this thing out of me!"

"I'll get the stuff for Herzer," Rachel said.

"I'm first for the bath," Bast said, starting to strip off her limited clothing as she walked towards the bathing room. "Saving boy-toys is sweaty work!"

Edmund helped Herzer out of his armor and then unstuck the leather and cloth from the wound on his side. "That's the problem of articulated armor; a well-placed thrust can get up under it."

"Why do we use it, then?" Herzer asked, grimacing as the baron applied a pungent and stinging salve to the wound.

"It's better for marching and digging forces," Edmund said. "Bending to do *anything* in plate or even just a full cuirass is a pain in the ass. This is armor for working infantry. And in battle most enemies don't get a chance for a measured upward thrust."

"What about putting mail underneath?" Herzer asked.

"Well, you can get some if you want the additional weight," Edmund nodded as he finished tying the bandage around Herzer's ribs. "That's up to you."

Herzer thought about all the weight the Blood Lords already carried and grimaced. "Good point."

"No armor is perfect," Edmund said. "It all involves compromise. All you can do is figure out which compromise is better or worse."

"A bit like life, then," Herzer chuckled.

"Well, I'm glad you find something funny," Rachel said as she entered the room, her arms full of clothes.

"Things could be worse," Herzer said.

"How?"

"I don't know," he replied with a grin. "But I'm sure we'll find out."

"Men," Rachel said with a shake of her head. "Next I suppose you'll go jump in the bath with Bast."

"Well, I've jumped in the bath with you before," Herzer pointed out.

"That's *different*," Rachel snapped, then left the room, her feet slapping the tile as she walked.

"What was that all about?" Edmund asked then shook his head. "Never mind. *Which* reason for her to be upset was that about?"

"All of them?" Herzer replied. "I think much of it is that you might have forgiven me for running out on Mistress Daneh, but Rachel will never forgive me for letting her mother be raped."

Edmund's jaw worked for a moment before he nodded acceptance. "Maybe not now, but in time. I know that you're . . . friends."

"Yes, that is exactly what we are," Herzer sighed, looking at the door through which the girl had retreated. "Friends." He shrugged his shoulders and then grinned. "But, on the other hand, she's such a good friend she made an excellent suggestion. So if you don't mind, sir, I'm going to go take a bath."

"Supper's in about thirty minutes," Edmund pointed out. "You'll have to be . . . quick."

"I'm far too tired for anything but a bath," Herzer replied with all the dignity he could muster.

"Sure," Edmund chuckled. "Like I don't remember being seventeen. And, you forget, I knew Bast before you were *born*."

Realizing he was defeated, Herzer shrugged his shoulders, picked up the pile of clothes and headed for the bath.

By unspoken consent the conversation at dinner avoided the topic of the impending battle. They talked about the increase to the sawmill, in which Herzer had a stake, and the expanding smithies and foundries. There were iron deposits on Massan Mountain still, despite its being heavily worked in the past, and some people were considering opening them, but Edward wasn't convinced it was worth it.

"Angus has access to already refined steel; all he has to do is rework it. And that mountain of his is shot through with ores. For that matter, the deposits in the valley are of an ore that is hard to form; it requires much higher heats and forging times than the western deposits. The trick is, we need a better system to access Angus' supplies."

"He lives near some rivers, doesn't he?" Herzer said, recalling a map he'd seen of the area.

"He does, but the river runs far to the north and into lands that are neutral at best and some of them are held by Paul's supporters. But there's an old road that contacts the Poma River. And that leads to the Shenan. I think getting that road up and running and a good system of boats is the better answer."

"There's not a town at the joining of the rivers," Herzer mused. "It would be worthwhile to start one there."

"I think we'll see what comes on its own," Edmund said as the cook brought out the desserts. "Oh, lovely."

"And thank you, mistress, for that delightful meal," Herzer said, nodding at the cook who was probably thrice his age but looked no more than twenty. "What was the meat? It was wonderful."

"Emu," the cook replied with a wink. "It's hard to cook because it's tough as nails. But if you put it in my special sauce and stew it well it's fine."

"And what is this?" Herzer asked. The small cakes were golden brown on the outside with a small white star on the top of each.

"Semolina," the cook replied. "Rough milled grain, that is. Cooked with honey and butter and mixed with pine nuts."

"Delicious," Bast said, her mouth full. "And I'm glad to see that you're eating well as well, Daneh."

"Oh, everything I can get," the doctor replied, taking one of the cakes and licking a drop of honey off her hand. "But it gives me some terrible indigestion sometimes. I swear, sometimes it feels like this kid's hair is in my stomach, I have no idea why."

"Thank you, mistress," Edmund added as the cook set out a pot of herbal tea. He sighed as she left and he filled a cup. "This is a damned poor substitute for real tea," he grumped. "I swear, if it's the last thing I do, I'm going to take ship to the far Indies and find a tea plantation. Or found one if I must."

"I think we need you too much here, dear," Daneh said with a chuckle. "Some day, maybe, someone else will take up the quest."

"Speaking of forlorn quests," Rachel said. "What are you planning?"

Edmund hesitated and took another sip of tea, then shook his head. "I generally don't talk about my plans, Rachel. Even to friends."

"Why?" Herzer asked.

Edmund paused again and then shrugged. "You'd be surprised how much intelligence plays a part in successful operations. I don't want there to be any chance for the enemy to know what I plan, or even how I plan it. Look at that rabbit coming in with their plans. The rest . . . I think you'll learn in time."

"You think there are spies in Raven's Mill?" Rachel asked.

"No, not yet," Edmund said. "And if there were, Dionys wouldn't know how to use them. But there are woodcutters and scavengers up in the hills that Dionys might capture and . . . question. I know that you will not be talking widely, but if I don't even tell my closest confidantes, nobody can get upset if I don't tell *them*. So I tell no one."

Later, after the wine had been served and cleared away Edmund stood up and looked around. "I give you the forces of the Kingdom of Free States," he said, raising his glass of brandy. "May they always side with the right."

"Hear, hear," Herzer replied, somewhat muzzily; he had had a bit too much of the wine.

"And with that, I think that we should all get some sleep," Edmund continued. "It's going to be an early day tomorrow."

"Herzer, you take Rachel's room," Daneh said. "She can take mine. I'll sleep with Edmund."

"Good," Bast said with a nod. "Glad I am to hear that. Come on, Herzer, I need to go tuck you in bed."

"I think you're a few letters of the alphabet away," Herzer said, chuckling.

"For *that* maybe I *will* just tuck you in bed!"

"Why am *I* getting kicked out?" Rachel asked.

"Because *my* bed is a single," Daneh chuckled. "Herzer, by himself, would have a hard time fitting in it. And I doubt he's going to be by himself!"

"Not if I have anything to do about it," Bast smiled. "Come on, lover boy, time to see how tired you are."

Edmund poured himself a small measure of brandy instead of leaving immediately and waved the bottle at Daneh.

"No more for me," she said, then thought better of it and held out her glass. "Herzer is starting to remind me a bit of Gunny."

"He's . . . a lot like Gunny when Miles was much younger," Edmund agreed. "Up to and including the lack of self-confidence."

"Now that, in Gunny, is hard to believe."

"Gunny is a character."

"Yeah, I'd sort of noticed."

"Noticed but not understood. There is a person called Miles Rutherford. And then there is the character Gunny. But Miles has done the character for so long that, like a good character actor, he's sort of assumed the role. I don't know if Gunny believes he's the reincarnation of a Marine Corps gunnery sergeant from world war two. But that is what he is. He lives every day as he envisions such a person would live. He has done that for nearly a hundred and fifty years. And before that he was a Roman centurion, doing the same thing. The only reason he switched was that he became convinced that the Marines had studied the centurions and *improved* upon them. He once talked about getting modified so that he could eat steel and shit nails. I have *no* idea why or what it means! For his period, Gunny is much more informed than I am."

"That would be . . . that would be a major mod," Daneh said, after contemplating the image with a grimace.

"Yeah I know."

"Steel teeth . . . ?" she mused.

"No, have to be diamond or something . . ." Edmund said with a smile.

"Tough mod . . . you could construct some gut nannites to . . . Oh, never mind!" she ended with a grin.

"Herzer can learn a lot from Gunny," Edmund said, looking off into the distance. "Gunny . . . well, he's been in situations that almost no one else in this world has and come back. On the other hand, if Herzer had learned a lot from Gunny before . . . your incident, Herzer would be dead and otherwise things would be the same."

"I was raped. You can say it, Edmund."

"No, *you* can say it. I still can't. In some ways you're stronger than me. You walked away from . . . from *us* when you knew it was right. I never could."

"And I walked back," she said, taking his hand, "when I knew it was right. It's late, Edmund. Come to bed."

"Are you sure?" he asked, looking at her in the torchlight. "The last time didn't go so well."

"I have never been so sure of anything in my life."

"Well, here we are again," Herzer said, stroking Bast's cheek.

"We've never done it in this bed," Bast replied with a grin. "I'm *sure* I'd remember!"

Herzer wrapped her in his arms and pulled her down on top of him, nibbling at her shoulder. "You know what I mean."

"And I also know that you'd rather Rachel were still in it."

He lifted her up to where he could see her face but she was still grinning. He ran his hand across her face and twined a bit of her hair into his fingers. "You know I love you . . ." he said.

"Sure," Bast said with an irrepressible smile. "Although, 'lust for you' is what you're really thinking. You *love* Rachel."

"Well . . ."

"Don't bother trying to lie to me," Bast said again, shaking her head. "Agggh, Ghorbani women! They'll be the death of me yet! First it was Sheida slipping away with Edmund and then Daneh . . ."

"*Sheida?* The council member?"

"Hai, she was a right vixen in her day," Bast frowned for a moment. "There I was, having my way with Sir Edmund, and suddenly he up and disappears. Over in the bushes with that tramp Sheida! And then she introduces him to her *sister* and it's like somebody hit him in the middle of the eyes with a mace! And now Rachel! May they all develop *spots*."

"Bast . . ."

"Tell me, Herzer," she said, smiling again. "If you had the choice of being in bed, tonight, with either me, Bast, the queen of all that is of the body, a thousand-year-old-lover who can squeeze the last dregs of pleasure from your body, or a callow youth who has, okay, decent hair and larger breasts, which would you choose?"

Herzer looked at her wide-eyed for a moment and then sighed. "Both?"

"Oh, you are a bastard!" Bast said with a chuckle as she struck him in the sternum.

"Bast . . ." he said.

"Don't whine." The elf smiled. "I do not intend leaving this bed before morning nor shall you be tossed from it. It is *fine* that you care for Rachel. She is a sweet and loving girl."

"Who looks right through me," Herzer said. "She hates me for not saving Daneh. *I* hate me for not saving Daneh, so I know how she feels."

"You *think* you know how she feels," Bast said. "But you've never *asked* her how she feels."

"It's pretty obvious."

"Maybe to you. I see a young woman who is terribly challenged by the life she's been thrust into and who looks upon you as a friend. One with faults, some of them aggravating faults, but I don't think she hates you."

"Really?" Herzer said, his face lighting up.

"Oh, great," Bast replied. "You're ready to go charging into her room right now!"

"Only to see if I could drag her back," he joked and raised his arms against blows that were surprisingly painful.

"Just for that I shall do the position of the Three Swans," Bast said, her eyes shooting lightning.

"Ah! No! Mercy!" Herzer chuckled.

"You laugh, but I shall have *no* mercy on you!" she replied, shifting lower. "And let me just see if I can get a red-haired young lady out of your mind!"

"Who?" Herzer laughed then involuntarily sucked in a breath of air. "This is gonna hurt, isn't it?"

The torchlit departure of the main guard force was surprisingly well attended; it seemed that everyone who was packed into the town had turned up.

"Myron, you and Daneh are in charge of the town while I'm gone," Edmund said, quietly. "At least the administrative side. Kane is charge of defense. And the administration is: give Kane whatever he needs to defend the town."

"Okay, Edmund," the farmer said unhappily.

"Kane knows his part of the plan. Just give him what he needs."

"Will do."

He turned to Daneh and smiled. "Off to the wars."

"Swaggerer," she said, handing him a small wooden box.

He opened it up and wrinkled his brow at the device within. It appeared to be a set of spectacles set in a metal frame that was padded by stitched cosilk to fit against the skin. "And what is this?"

"I took an old set of your glasses and had Suwisa make it," she replied. "It's designed to go under your helmet. You know you're blind as a bat beyond fifty feet without your glasses."

"Thank you," he said with a chuckle. "You were right, I should have had my eyes adjusted back when."

"I'm always right," she said. "Take care of yourself, Edmund Talbot."

"Will do, Mistress Ghorbani," he replied, holding out his arms. "Do I get a kiss?"

"How about half a kiss," she said, hugging him against her swollen belly and pecking him on the cheek. "You get the rest when you're back, safe and sound."

"Hi, Rachel," Herzer said. "I didn't expect to see you out here."

"My father's going off to war," she said with a shrug. "I thought I should say goodbye." She looked up at him in the lamplight and sighed. "And you too."

"Rachel . . ." Herzer said and then paused awkwardly. "Rachel . . . I'm sorry about what happened with Daneh. Really I am. I just . . ."

"Herzer," she said sharply, then seemed to shake herself. "Herzer, I had a lot of trouble with that. But . . . we've been friends for a long time. If Mother can forgive you and Dad can forgive you, so can I. Okay?"

"Okay," he said sadly.

"What?" she asked in exasperation.

"I . . . I love you, Rachel," Herzer said, desperately. "I have for years. I just . . . wanted you to know that, before."

She looked at him with a stunned expression that faded to anger. "So you just wanted me to know that before you go off and get yourself killed? Thanks very much, Herzer Herrick."

"It's not like that!"

"Oh," she breathed out, the anger going out with it. "I . . . I'm sorry. I know it's not. Herzer, you're a very good friend and you always will be my very good friend. Okay?"

"Okay," he said miserably.

"Let that be enough for now," she said, laying her hand on his arm. "Come back. Okay?"

"Okay," he said. "And . . . can we talk more then?"

"Yes," she said with a chuckle. "Always."

"Okay."

"Fall in," Gunny called quietly.

"I've got to go," Herzer said, desperately.

"Bye, Herzer," Rachel said, standing on tiptoe to kiss him on the cheek. "Don't do anything stupid. Again."

"I'll try," he said, hurrying to his place.

The small force still made a brave sight, marching out through the gates of the stockade. The cavalry, commanded by Alyssa, led the cavalcade with the Blood Lords marching behind and the archers, mounted on horses, following along with a small pack train of mules and horses. Edmund rode immediately in front of the Blood Lords, dressed in full armor with his long-handled hammer tossed casually over one shoulder; behind him marched Gunny with a piper by his side. Herzer carried the guidon of the troop, the silver screaming eagle with its bundle of arrows in one talon and olive branch in the other, on a field of blue.

As they passed the gates Gunny led off the song.

"Axes flash, broadsword swing,
Shining armour's piercing ring
Horses run with polished shield,
Fight Those Bastards till They Yield
Midnight mare and blood red roan,
Fight to Keep this Land Your Own
Sound the horn and call the cry,
'HOW MANY OF THEM CAN WE MAKE DIE!' "

CHAPTER THIRTY-NINE

They marched up to the Via Apallia, then passed over the Shenan bridge heading west.

"Where are we going?" Cruz muttered from the front rank. Everyone knew that the enemy was in the direction to the south. They seemed to be marching away from the oncoming force.

"Don't know," Deann replied as the same question was muttered among the others.

"Silence in the ranks," Gunny called.

They followed the Via on a fast march to the west, segueing from "March of Cambreadth" to "Yellow Ribbon," with the different parts of the force singing their particular versions, to "Grand Trunk Road" and "Drinking Bourbon." The cavalry tried to get them to sing Garryowen but since it was impossible to march to, and the archers didn't know the words, they had to sing it on their own. They continued on through the early morning rain, which required a song of its own, until they came to the Cryptopus Creek bridge.

At a wave to Alyssa from Edmund, the cavalry, less five troopers, broke into a trot and continued down the road as the rest of the band, crossed the river, broke into single file and turned south.

Their path was a narrow trail that followed the edge of the small river. It entered the tree-choked defile that led to the inner valley of Massan Mountain. The trail was narrow and bad and the troop was often forced to pause to shore it up

for the following horses or clear the way of deadfalls. Even
when they got into the valley itself the old track was barely
passable but they made decent time by marching hard. There
were brief breaks, mostly to rest the horses, but they didn't
even stop for a cooked lunch, eating parched corn and washing
it down with water from the now much reduced stream. But
by the time they reached the far end of the valley the sun
was long gone over the high mountains to their west and it
was starting to get dark.

"Camp," Edmund called. "Watches but no palisades."

The troop fell out into their well-practiced camp drill and
Gunny and McGibbon set the watches split between the Blood
Lords and the archers. The two groups didn't mingle much
but kept to their separate fires.

"So, what the hell is happening?" Cruz asked Herzer as they
bolted their evening meal. Herzer had drawn the slot of cook
and he had made up a simple bannock filled with monkey and
bits of salted pork. "Why the hell did the cavalry take off west?"

"Dunno," Herzer replied, thinking about the maps of the
area. They were about as far away from being able to directly
defend the town as it was possible to be.

'You were at the baron's last night," Cruz said. "He didn't
say anything?"

"No, he didn't," Herzer replied, not mentioning what Edmund
had said on the subject. "And if he did I wouldn't tell you."

"I think we're going to head up the mountain," Pedersen
said. The decurion looked up at the black mass above them
unhappily. "I hate that fisker."

"Me too," Deann said. "But if we are, we'd better get to
bed early." With that she strode out of the firelight and began
breaking out her bedroll.

"Agreed," Herzer said, getting up and grabbing the cooking gear. He washed it in the stream and then laid out his
bedding. He had retrieved his fur blanket and had added that
to his kit despite the additional weight. He laid down a leather
ground cloth, then the blanket, and pulled out a bundle of
clothes for a pillow. But before he lay down he took a stroll
around the sentries posted at the edge of the camp and made
sure everyone was alert and knew the duty roster. Then he
headed back, took off his armor and boots and lay down under
his cloak. It looked like it might rain sometime during the night
but he'd deal with that if and when. He, too, pondered the
possible intentions of their commander but before he came
to any conclusion he had already fallen asleep.

The next morning, after a hearty breakfast, they headed up the mountain.

The trail was as bad as the one on the way in, if not worse. It clearly followed an old roadbed, but the work of millennia had broken down many of the road cuts and embankments. The trail switched back and forth and most of the ends of the switchbacks were washed away. But the triari was familiar with such conditions from their continuous marching over the region and they fell to work on each obstacle, clearing the rock slides and shoring up the places where the road had washed away. Despite this, it took all day to ascend the summit of the mountain and Baron Edmund was clearly unhappy with the progress. They ate trail rations for lunch and supper and continued marching well into the night. The baron did not permit them torches and with the sky overcast the path along the summit of the mountain was a tree-choked nightmare. Herzer wasn't sure how late it was when Talbot finally called a halt, but when he did Herzer mustered the sentries and then crawled into his furs, without taking off his armor, and was asleep almost before he lay down.

They were up before dawn the next morning and continued on their way, catching brief glimpses through the trees of the valleys on either side. There was little to be seen— that part of the Shenan was almost entirely unpeopled—until late in the day as they neared the far end of the mountain. The ridge they had followed had sloped upwards and as they approached the summit they could see, far down in the valley and on the west side of the mountain, a large force moving slowly to the north.

They had passed the occasional ancient roadbed and it was on one of these, which was marked by the faint trace of a trail, that Edmund stopped and conferred with Gunny.

"Fall out," Gunny called. "Make full camp."

They stacked their weapons and started on the preparations for a fortified camp. First decuri and the archers started on the ditches and palisade while the other squads began cutting trees for a field of fire. The camp was at the top of the trail with the gate on the far side and a narrow passage available for movement up onto the summit.

Throughout the work Baron Edmund had been on a small hilltop to the south and as the afternoon wore on he suddenly nodded in satisfaction and raised a small mirror in his hand, catching the dying light of the sun. Then he trotted down to the nearly finished camp and looked around.

"Gunny, leave one decuri in the camp. The other three squads and the archers will follow me."

"Yes, my lord," the Gunny replied. "First, Third, Fourth, prepare to move out."

"Now what the fisk?" Cruz muttered as the tired and dirty soldiers began gathering their weapons. They had been able to see the enemy below moving northward for some time albeit only when they were down the slope.

"Just follow the orders, Cruz," Herzer said, picking up his spear and ruck.

"Take off your helmets and put on your cloaks," Edmund said as they prepared to move off. He had already done so. "I don't want the glitter of armor showing."

Herzer thought about that as they moved down the defile, and smiled. The mountain was very high and the line-of-sight distance to the enemy force was at least four miles. He had already noticed that the force in the valley was only viewable when there was a flash of metal, a view of an ox cart or from their afternoon fires. The group of bowmen and infantry filing down the mountain in their cloaks, which were a nondescript gray, would be nearly invisible to the enemy below.

They slithered and slipped down the mountain as the sun fell and the dusk faded to black. The clouds had cleared off after only dropping a smidgen of rain, and the gibbous moon gave just enough light to make their way. They followed the track almost to the base of the mountain where there was a small plateau about sixty meters wide, and paused. The baron called Herzer and McGibbon over to the edge of the plateau.

"Herzer, McGibbon, is there enough light for you to set up light defense works?" Edmund asked.

"Yes, sir," Herzer whispered. "But only a ditch; we can't see well enough to cut trees."

"You don't have to whisper, Herzer," Edmund chuckled. "McGibbon?"

"We can set up our shields and stakes," the archer said. "More than that I'm not sure."

"Set up a ditch across the defile with one opening," Edmund said after a moment. "We'll want some way to close it. Try to camouflage it as best you can. *Don't* set up the shields. Not yet. But have them ready to throw up in an instant."

"There's a big chestnut just there," Herzer said, pointing to the edge of the trail downslope. "If we fell it and tie lines to it, we can probably pull it up into the opening and block the trail. That's what you want, right?"

"Perfect," Edmund said, looking around. "Get to work."

Herzer set one maniple of third decuri to work on the tree while the rest dug a shallow trench along the edge of the plateau. When it was done he set them to cutting brush to mask the low wall and scouted for suitable saplings to make a better palisade. They had left their own stakes on the top of the ridge so they had to use local materials. He found that there *was* enough light and that there was a small grove of poplars, the result of a recent rock slide, that could provide the materials. When the trench was dug he sent the weary soldiers to work downing those and dragging the trunks over to improve the defenses until he was halted by Edmund.

"Well enough for now," Talbot said, nodding at the improving defenses. "Post sentries and get some sleep. We've got a murthering great battle in the morning."

Herzer called a halt to the preparations and then gave some thought to who should take watch. For most of them this would be their first battle and he knew that, despite their weariness, they would find it hard to sleep. He wasn't sure he could. He had already fought once, and survived, but this was his first experience of prebattle jitters. He called the three squads together and then tried to pick out those he figured weren't going to sleep anyway, giving them the duty of sentries, and sending the rest to their beds in the defenses.

When everything was settled, and the majority of the camp was either lying in wait, silently, or sleeping or standing watch, he moved around the defenses checking on the conditions. Halfway down the line, he found Baron Edmund doing the same.

"You need to get some sleep," the baron said with a nod.

"I could say the same for you, sir," Herzer replied. "It's to be an ambush, then?"

"We'll see," Edmund replied enigmatically. "Go get some rest, Herzer. First call before dawn. No fires. No one in armor is to show themselves above the parapet after dawn."

"I'll pass that on and then go to bed, sir," the triari replied. "Permission to carry on?" he asked, saluting.

"Right you are," Edmund said, returning the salute. As the boy passed into the darkness, Edmund shook his head and smiled, then went to bed.

Morning found them tired and sore and eating another cold breakfast of monkey and parched corn. But there was a bit of water cut with wine to wash it down at least. As dawn broke to the east with a limited dawn chorus in the cold of the morning, Edmund sent one of the cavalrymen down the defile with quietly whispered orders, then had the troops stand to in the defenses. The archers were arrayed at either end and the three squads of Blood Lords held the middle. There was a cut in the wall where the trail rose onto the plateau but ropes had been snugged around the butt of the large chestnut and they had determined that it could be moved with ease if everyone fell to the ropes.

A party out of armor and well wrapped in their cloaks to camouflage them against the gray of the trees had set to work improving the camouflage of the defenses when the lead of the enemy force came in view.

This time they were less than a mile away and the soldiers, having doffed their helmets lest the shine give away their positions, watched the force from Rowana straggle by. First came a spray of light cavalry, wandering down the valley pike as if they hadn't a care in the world, the men sitting silent and glum on their horses.

Then came the oddest sight any of them had ever seen. The force behind the cavalry was a motley group of infantry, but if they were human they had been horribly Changed. They were well below human height and stooped, with long powerful arms and bandy legs. They carried various weapons in their hands, axes both for fighting and wood felling, short swords, spears and clubs. They loped as much as walked, occasionally dropping to a knuckle walk when they had to speed up. Most of them were unarmored but they carried wooden shields across their backs and a few had a shirt of mail or a piece of plate stuck here and there. Despite the morning cold, many of them were virtually unclothed. Few of them wore shirts and many were naked save for a dirty loincloth.

"Orcs by God," Herzer muttered, rubbing at his eyes. "They're fisking orcs!"

"Chimp genes," Edmund said from behind him. The baron was peering at them carefully and he let out an angry sigh. "Sheida told me about this but I could hardly credit it!"

"Are they constructs?" Herzer asked, quietly.

"No, they're Change," Edmund growled. "Normal humans Changed by that bitch Celine's programs. This is . . . vile."

"Those poor *bastards*," Cruz said with a gulp. "So much for surrendering; I guarantee that those aren't guys who started *out* on his side."

"No, they're probably just poor damned refugees who got

caught in his vile net," Edmund replied, tightly. "And, yes, that's probably your fate if he gets his hands on you. But there's no way we can Change them back. They're not going to care if you care about them. They're beyond our help and as steeped in evil as he is. So the only thing we can do is *kill* them. Because if we don't, they're going to take the town and rape our women and burn it to the ground. Am I clear on this?"

"Yes, sir," Cruz replied.

"Baron, I've got a question," Herzer said.

"Shoot."

"Didn't the rabbit say that they were taking the *east* valley?"

"Of course he did," Edmund chuckled. "But he's *evil*. Or at least, extremely chaotic. So he, naturally, couldn't tell us the *whole* truth, even with Bast's geas. It would violate his nature."

"And you're letting him stick around?" Herzer asked, aghast.

"I've heard of him, as I said," Edmund replied. "Trust me, he's worth keeping on *your* side."

"Jesus, will you look at that horse?" Cruz gasped as the next group came into view.

The horse was monstrous, at least three times the size of the largest of Kane's Hanarahs, and it had to be to carry the massive figure in black plate on its back.

"Dionys?" Herzer asked.

"Oh, yeah," Edmund chuckled. "I wonder who he finally got to make his armor?"

"Pardon?"

"He wanted me to make that for him," Talbot replied with a sudden frown. "A good part of his . . . personal enmity is that I more or less told him to fisk himself."

Herzer thought of several replies, none of which were quite right. Finally he shrugged. "Well, I think we're going to do it for him this time, sir."

"We'll see," Edmund replied.

There was a large group of armed humans and a small group of cavalry in heavy plate following Dionys, and Herzer caught enough glimpses through upraised visors to recognize a few of his old cronies. He knew that each of them had participated in the rape of Daneh and it made his blood boil to watch them pass.

"Oh, for my old bow," he growled. "I could have picked most of them off as they rode past."

"Patience," Edmund replied. "Patience."

Following them was another group of Changed and then a ragtag of baggage carts and poorly dressed men and women. Among the baggage train were some strange sights, including a pony-sized unicorn that was being pulled behind one of the ox carts. Finally the last of the group had passed out of sight.

"We're just going to let them get away?" Herzer whispered.

"Patience," Edmund repeated, then chuckled as another group of cavalry came in sight. But this time, Alyssa could be glimpsed at their head and she was already uncasing her horse-bow.

The Raven's Mill cavalry passed by as well, and for a time there was nothing further to see. The sun had gotten up and was nearly over the mountain at their back when smoke could be seen from the direction the cavalcade had taken. Then they saw the cavalryman, who had been concealed in the woods at the base of the hill, ride out and wave to the north. Then more of the Raven's Mill cavalry appeared, one of them swaying in his saddle from an apparent arrow. They pounded up the defile, their horses blowing and sweating, until they reached the ledge, then spread across the back of the plateau as Alyssa and the rear guard came in sight.

"Three of you on the best horses head up the hill," Edmund called. "There are three places where there are rags tied on trees. Drop one horseman at each point. The rest of you rest for a bit."

Alyssa and the rear guard remained at the base of the hill until a group of enemy cavalry came pounding after them. Alyssa waited, an arrow nocked, until they got in short range, then fired at them and turned immediately up the hill, followed by the rest of the rear guard. One of the horseman tumbled back off his horse but the rest followed the Raven's Mill forces up the narrow defile.

"Wait for it," Edmund called. "Stay down. Archers, on command, I want *none* of them getting away!"

The enemy cavalry gave no indication that they realized they were running into an ambush, following the Raven's Mill riders up the narrow defile in single line.

"Wait for it," Edmund called as Alyssa and the rest ran through the defenses, carefully not looking to either side.

"NOW!"

At his call the archers stood up out of the trench and began firing, the shafts running nearly flat at the oncoming riders. Some of them missed but most were on target as the riders were having to slow to negotiate the poorly defined track. In moments all of them were out of their saddles, some of them still alive but most lying still on the ground. Some of the horses were hit as well and their shrill screams grated on Herzer's ears until the archers, mercifully, finished them off. A few of the horses continued up the trail, apparently following Alyssa's "herd" and they were caught by the Raven's Mill cavalry, which was now standing in plain sight. The rest milled around and then most of them began working their way down the hill to stand in a blown cluster at its base.

"Now to see . . . ah, hah," Edmund said as a straggling group of orcs, apparently led by one of the plate-armored riders, came in sight of the herd at the base of the mountain. The fate of the cavalry was also clear from where the rider stood but it wasn't clear if he knew there was a palisade blocking his way. He looked up the hill where the Raven's Mill cavalry was waiting and then waved the group of about fifty of the Changed up the hill.

"Now we're to it," Edmund said. "Alyssa," he continued, raising his voice. "Get over with a few bowmen. Let's see how long we can keep this a surprise."

Alyssa dismounted her whole troop, and three of her horse archers moved over to the gap. The orcs struggling up the steep slope were easy targets and Alyssa's archers began feathering them one after another as the others clearly prepared to defend the plateau. Some of the orcs, when hit, kept coming, pushing the arrows through their injured arms or sides, but others were killed and it quickly was apparent that the position was too well defended to be taken by the small force. The rider called them back and sent one of the uninjured Changed back in the direction of the main force.

"Come on, get a move on," Herzer muttered, looking through the vegetation that covered their trench.

"Oh, they will," Edmund said. "If they try to continue on, they know that Alyssa can sally out and attack them from behind again. They can block the defile at the base or chase her away up the mountain."

It was quickly apparent that "chase her away" was the plan as most of the enemy force began to appear in the valley.

"Okay, everyone down and get your helmets on," Edmund called. "Do not look up until I tell you or I'll have your decurions run a sword through you. Alyssa, you have to be our eyes," he added, putting on his own helmet.

"They're deploying. They have some archers too," Alyssa

said as a few arrows whistled up the slope and fell harmlessly on the plateau. "They don't have much of a chance from
there, though."

"Are they following the trail or spreading out?"

"Right up the trail," she said, nocking an arrow and firing. "They're coming up very dumb."

"Good, fire a few more arrows and then look as if you are
out," Edmund said. "Longbowmen, prepare to stand up."

"They're coming straight up the trail. Some of the archers
are stopping where they have shots." She fired again. "But
they're no problem. Two hundred meters . . . one fifty . . . They're
spread all down the trail, about a hundred of them. Fifty
meters . . ."

"ARCHERS UP!" Edmund called, standing up himself.

Herzer couldn't see what was happening but he could hear
and see the firing of the archers on either side and hear the
screams from down the trail. The archers had placed arrow
barrels all along the trench and he could see them pointing
out particular targets and laughing as the inhuman enemy fell
along the way. Finally Edmund shook his head.

"Stupid, stupid. I have to agree with the bunny."

"When do we stand up?" Herzer asked.

"When they have a chance of making it up the hill," Edmund
chuckled. "And right now they're clambering over bodies, which
is making it hard. Damn, they're retreating." He rubbed his
chin and shook his head. "And what are they doing elsewhere?"
he asked rhetorically. He turned around and looked at the sun,
which provoked a sneeze, then pulled out his small mirror.
Herzer could now see that there was a clear spot in the middle
and some sort of grid. Edmund lifted it and flashed up the
hill for a moment and then waited. After a moment, Herzer
could see a flag raised against the sun which twitched for a
moment then lowered and raised, twitching again.

"Thank the Lord for stupidity in our enemies," Edmund said,
twitching the mirror again. "They're turning their whole force
around and heading back this way."

It was noon before the full force was arrayed at the base of
the mountain and Herzer had ordered the troop to eat another
cold ration from their packs. They were running low on parched
corn but by the end of the day they should be able to dip into
their meal and have something cooked. Just after noon Dionys
put in his attack, sending his orc fighters straight up the trail
again as his archers tried to move up the steep hillside through
the trees to get a shot at their enemy archers.

The longbowmen began feathering the Changed again but this time the orcs were crouched behind their shields and some of them were making it up the trail. Finally Edmund nodded. "Herzer, get the tree in position."

"Triari! To the ropes!" Herzer called, scrambling up himself and getting a look at the battlefield for the first time since the early morning.

The first thing that he noticed was that the trail was choked with arrow-filled bodies, the horses and cavalrymen already starting to bloat in the sun. Farther down the trail there was a spray of orc bodies and a line of orcs, bent under their shields, scrambling over the bodies to try to reach the defenders. At the sight of the Blood Lords some of them stopped and screeched defiance, then came on under the weight of the fire, stumbling from time to time as an arrow found its way past their shields. As they got closer this became more common since the archers were firing from the sides, and even with their large round shields the orcs' bodies were in view to either side. Herzer could almost feel sorry for them as they came forward into the storm of arrows but he had other things to worry about as the triari took up the ropes and pulled.

The tree was a fully mature chestnut and very heavy. It took all their straining to get it moving up the hill but after a moment it slotted into position in the gap in the defenses, the trunk well up the hill and the branches pointed towards the oncoming enemy force, creating a well-nigh impassable tangle on the downhill side.

The Blood Lords fell in on their positions and took up their shields, standing in a silent, disciplined line along the wall. To either side the archers continued their fire, slower now as they began to weary from the continuous draw and fire. They were less accurate as well as they fatigued and some of them were switching out for their assistants, stepping to the side and massaging their weary shoulders.

"Swords," Edmund said as the first of the Changed approached the parapet. They had struggled around and through the branches of the felled tree and now clambered up the trunk, scrabbling at the stakes of the palisade. The first raised his head up in front of Cruz and fell back with a broad split in the side from the short, broad sword of the Blood Lord.

For a moment it was hot work all along the parapet as the Blood Lords hewed at the clutching arms of the orcs raising themselves up the parapet but there was no easy way for the Changed to force themselves past the soldiers. For the Blood

Lords it was like a drill. They simply hacked and jabbed at whatever target was presented to them, keeping their shields up and forward to prevent being hacked at in turn. In short order the attackers fell back down the trail leaving a line of their dead and wounded piled against the parapet and being feathered in the back by the archers at either end.

The battle had not been completely one sided. Several of the Blood Lords were living up to their names with slashes on arms, battered helmets, or shields. But their heavy armor had been proof against most of the thrusts of the enemy and no one was killed except one of the archer assistants who had been caught up by one of the powerful orcs and dragged over the parapet to be hacked to death.

"Well, that was interesting," Edmund said. "Consolidate your force, Triari. Post battle chores."

CHAPTER FORTY

Almost everyone was red-splashed by the battle and one of the first orders of business was to clean their armor and weapons. After that, Herzer got to work, setting some of the force to work on the wounded while others repaired the limited damage to the defenses. The orcs had tried to pull the stakes down from the parapet but they were well driven into the ground. A few had been hacked nearly through, but they were quickly replaced with spares that had been laid up before the battle. At the same time one decuri was given the duty to stand sentry and otherwise the remainder had been told to eat, rest and work on their gear.

All three squads had been given a chance to eat and rest before Edmund called them back to the parapet. The archers were back at work but this time the attacking force was led by some of the plate-clad figures, which didn't make Herzer happy at all.

"There's nothing you can do with a regular sword to plate," Edmund said to the Blood Lords. "But the arrows will go right through it at short range, as can your pilums if well driven. This is the place for the pilums, and lay your construction tools to hand; we'll show them how armored men-at-arms die."

The plate-clad men-at-arms were obviously making heavy work of climbing up the hill and as they closed, the primary archers took their positions, sending carefully aimed arrows into the joints at neck, elbow, knee and the vision gaps of the visors. The men-at-arms tried to keep their shields up but they could only cover one side, and the archers on the left flank were striking them hard. As the armored figures got closer, the arrows began to punch straight through their armor and they fell by the wayside. For that matter, the Blood Lords could get their pilums in play. The pilums couldn't penetrate the armor but they could penetrate the shields and when they did the soft steel heads bent down, adding their weight and leverage to the already unwieldy shields. The fighter then had to stop and try to extricate them, leaving them open to the archer fire, or try to come on with the spears stuck in their shields, which made them virtually useless. There had been only fourteen in the group, by the time they were at the top there were five.

"Let them cross the parapet," Edmund said in an amused tone as the first reached the top. "Step back," he added, stepping forward.

The armor-clad figure got a hand over the top of the parapet and hoisted itself up, almost falling into the interior and raising its shield and sword against the Blood Lords to the right.

By doing so he turned his back on Edmund who stepped forward and brought his great hammer down on the back of the figure's head. The thick steel of the helmet crumpled under the blow and the figure pitched forward on his face.

"That's the technique," Edmund said. "Get them separated, stop them with your shields in one direction and then bash them down with the axes and mallets." As another came up the parapet he smashed the hammer down upon the fighter's hand, eliciting a scream and a clanking sound as the fighter fell off the parapet and began to inexorably roll down the steep mountain's flank. "And, of course, don't fight fair."

There were only three of the fighters left and they were finished off in a similarly brutal fashion. The last caught sight of Herzer and raised his visor in desperation to reveal the visage of Galligan, one of Dionys' cronies,

"Herzer!" the man gasped, out of breath. "Please God . . ."

"See you in hell," Herzer ground out and drove his pilum into the man's face. He walked along the trench and flipped up visors.

"Benito's here as well," he said with satisfaction.

"Feel better?" Edmund asked as the first of the figures was tipped over the parapet to slide down the hill into the next wave of orcs.

"A bit," Herzer admitted. "I'll feel much better when *he's* dead," he continued, pointing down the hill to where McCanoc could be seen striding up and down.

"You're not supposed to enjoy this," Edmund pointed out.

"I don't *enjoy* killing people," Herzer said then shrugged. "Okay, there are a few that I get some satisfaction from. But I also don't get all wrapped up about it. Does that make me sick?"

"Not if you don't enjoy killing for its own sake," Edmund replied. "Some of the archers and your fellow soldiers are puking themselves sick. But that's just one end of the reaction to combat. Some people are like you, they just do it and go on. As long as you don't get to enjoying it *too* much."

"I like the competition," Herzer said. "I really like the winning. Even if it means the other guys die."

"Then if you survive for a while you'll make a pretty good soldier." Edmund smiled as McCanoc called back the last of his forces. "Hell, you're already making a pretty good soldier."

After a brief consultation between Dionys and a few of the armored riders, one of them rode towards the defense and stopped out of bowshot, waving a white rag on the end of his lance.

Edmund stood on the parapet and cupped his hands. "Come forward if you want to parley. Any tricks and you're going to look like a porcupine."

The rider worked his horse up the hill slowly as the half-trained horse shied constantly at the smell of the blood from the bodies. A few of the attackers were still alive but the rider didn't pay any attention to them, simply riding around their outstretched hands.

When he reached easy shouting distance of the Raven's Mill line he stopped again and raised his visor.

"Him I don't recognize," Herzer muttered.

"Sacrificial goat," Edmund guessed. "So, do you surrender?" he called.

"No," the man said with nary a flicker of humor in his grim visage. "But we call upon you to do so. If you do not we'll simply swarm your silly palisade and kill you all."

"You should have tried that at first," Talbot replied. "Now you're already down, what? Fifty? A hundred fighters? And the rest aren't going to be exactly ecstatic about attacking."

"Leave now and we'll permit you to live," the horseman called. "It's the best deal you'll get."

"Give us McCanoc and all of the survivors that participated

in the rape of my wife along with anyone who was in the sack of Resan and we'll let *you* live," Talbot replied contemptuously. "Oh, and head back to your hole. Then we'll let you get away alive."

"Is that your last word?" the armored figure asked.

"That's my final answer," Talbot replied with a grin. "Come on to it. We're just getting warmed up."

The horseman shook his head, then headed back down the hill. At the bottom he conferred with McCanoc who simply lifted his finger at the hill and gave a very ancient symbol of contempt.

"Now to see what they'll do," Edmund mused. "Tell the troops to get a bite to eat. I'll go talk with McGibbon and Alyssa."

Herzer passed the word and sat himself down to eat. The smell of the bodies was rising up over the palisade and between that and the cries of the wounded, for water among other things, it was not one of the best meals he'd ever had. But he managed to choke it down. Finally Edmund came back, chewing on a bar of monkey, and nodded at something down the hill. "He was serious."

The whole force had gathered at the base of the hill, with the armored figures in the center by the trail and the archers and Changed arrayed to either side. At a gesture from McCanoc, the whole force started up the hill.

"He's got some tactical sense," Edmund said. "He knows that with us in his rear he can't get to the town and that we can obviously outmaneuver him on the hills."

"So what are we going to do now?" Herzer asked nervously. The small force on the hill was outnumbered nearly a hundred to one.

"See how many of them we can make die," Edmund said with a chuckle. "And then, run away."

Herzer heard the horses start up the defile and looked around involuntarily.

"Eyes front," Edmund called. "They come up the hill and we kill them. Not much more to it."

The orcs moving among the trees were a poor target for the bowmen so they concentrated on the armored figures moving up the trail. Again the figures dropped, one by one, but behind them was a tide of orcs and as they ascended the trail the surviving enemy bowmen reached a position to start to fire back. Their bows were lighter than those of the Raven's Mill archers but they scored, mostly among the archers and their assistants. The archers shifted fire to get rid of them and in doing so gave the armored men-at-arms the chance to scramble up the hill unmolested.

The men-at-arms on the trail were making much better time than those on either side and they reached the palisade first. Again there was the desperate struggle around the giant tree as the armored figures burst over the palisade. Herzer waded in with a will, swinging a giant mallet used for driving in the stakes of the palisade, and his corded muscles brought it down with enormous force. But it required two hands to wield and one of the armored men-at-arms got past it, giving him a deep slash on his shield arm. However, in a brief flurry of battle all of the armored figures were down and it was time to deal with the orcs that followed them.

Herzer found himself in the thick of that battle as well. He picked up a dropped pilum and drove it down the hill into the shield of one of the orcs, then stooped to pick up his shield, drawing his short sword as he did so.

"BLOOD LORDS TO ME!" he called, slashing at the grotesquely Changed figures clambering over the parapet.

He found Cruz and Deann on either side of him and the three managed to get the shield wall reformed as the tide swept up the battlements. Then it was time to forget; all they did was hack and slash at the enemy in front of them, sweeping at exposed arms, dropping their shields just long enough to drive them into feet with an over-the-top jab at the face, covering their shield brethren.

In the midst of it, Herzer could sense Edmund moving to either side of him. Wherever the line needed bolstering, suddenly the hammer of the baron would crash down and an orc or two, or one time three, would be smashed back over the parapet in a welter of blood.

Herzer didn't know how long the battle went on; it was simply hack and hew, just like training, except for the screams of the orcs and the occasional grunt from either side of him. Finally the tide turned and the only people standing in the trench were the defenders from Raven's Mill.

The trench was filled with bodies, most of them orcs but a few of the Blood Lords, and more of the archers, were down. Ed Stalker was lying in the blood-filled trench, a sword driven all the way through his body, but his own sword in the throat of the orc that had killed him. Bue Pedersen had a nasty gash on his sword arm that was dripping blood from a hastily applied bandage and at least three of the archers were never going to see Raven's Mill again.

"Toss the bodies of the enemy over the side and start taking the parapet down," Edmund said. "Start moving the wounded up the hill. Bury our dead in the trench."

"Yes, sir," Herzer answered tiredly. "What about stripping the bodies?" he continued, looking at the corpses and a few that were wounded. The orcs were being finished off as he asked. "There's some good material here that the town could use."

"We can't carry it, though," Edmund pointed out. "I'd say leave it. McGibbon."

"My lord."

"Send half your archers up to the first retreat point," Talbot said. "There should be a rider waiting there."

Edmund stood on the plateau as the Blood Lords and the remaining archers went to work. "How long, Herzer?" he asked, shielding his eyes against the westering sun.

"Thirty minutes, Baron," Herzer gasped, lifting one of the palisade poles out of the ground with a wedge.

"Plenty of time," Edmund muttered, looking down the hill. "Look at them milling around. Archers, drop that and see if you can get a few arrows to reach that far."

With the covering fire of the archers, which did indeed make it to where the enemy was attempting to reassemble, the triari quickly took down their defensive position and buried the bodies of their fallen in the good earth. If they were in there with the blood of their enemies, so much the better, but all of the enemy was left on the ground for their "friends" to deal with. Or not. There were still ravens aplenty in the Shenan valley, and they had begun to gather already.

"Archers, move to the second defense point," Edmund said. "When you reach it, Mac, get the rest moving up the hill. Blood Lords, up to the camp. Move it."

Evening found them back in the palisades they had left the previous day. They had their first hot meal in a while and the bannocks and boiled salt pork had never tasted so good. The cavalry was gone before they got there but there were sufficient forces, between the archers and the Blood Lords, that they could go to minimal security and everyone could get a decent night's rest.

The fires of the enemy were twinkling in the valley and while they couldn't see many of them moving around, as long as the fires were there they could know that they hadn't moved.

Herzer quickly fell asleep when he went off watch but his sleep was filled with dreams to such an extent that he kept waking up. Around him when he woke the camp was filled with mutters and groans as others apparently relived the battle. Finally, before dawn, he gave up trying to get any more rest, put on his armor and wandered over to the fire at the center of the encampment. The baron was up as well and handed him a mug of sassafras tea.

"It's a damned poor substitute for real tea," Edmund growled, "but at least it's hot."

Herzer sipped it and warmed his hands, looking at the palisade. "Any news?"

"Not a sign. Which I think means they moved out in the middle of the night."

Herzer had taken a look at the valley before coming over and shook his head. "There are still fires."

"Sure, you leave a few people behind to keep them going and move the rest of your force out. It's an old trick."

"But we won't know where they've gone," Herzer said, worried. "They could be halfway down the valley!"

"So?" Edmund chuckled. "I don't care how fast they're moving. Now that you guys have gotten some rest, we can get ahead of them. We're *inside* their maneuver zone. Whichever way they go, we can cut them off. If they head north, we head north and either get ahead of them or move down to the bridge to cut them off. If they try to head back around the mountain, we can cross the river ahead of them and do the same. We're *inside* their arc."

"But how are we going to know which way to go?" Herzer asked then looked around. "The cavalry."

"I sent them out in two groups," Edmund replied. "They didn't get much sleep but I also sent the horses that the archers had been using. They can stay ahead of them and signal their intentions. They *might* have stayed in place, in which case they'll try to assault up the valley. Do you think they can take this fort? After what we did to them yesterday with less defenses?"

"No," Herzer admitted.

"Neither do I. We'll know where they are as soon as the sun rises. And on that note, it's about time to get everyone moving."

The camp was roused before dawn and by the time the sun

was up everyone had had a hot breakfast and was ready to face the day. The camp materials were packed and when the sun finally shone enough light they could get a good look at the valley.

As anticipated, the camp below was mostly empty. The news that it would be had gone around the camp so no one was perturbed by it. Edmund rode up to the summit to get a good look around. After about fifteen minutes he rode down to the camp, shaking his head.

"Don't bother breaking it down," Edmund said. "We'll probably make some sort of permanent structure up here in time. They're heading back down the valley and around to one of the fords on the east river. Time to move out."

The force moved out with the archers in the lead and the Blood Lords behind. The archers made good time but the Blood Lords were, quietly, unenthused by the rate of march.

"These guys need to work on marching more," Cruz muttered. "We can go twice this fast. In heavier armor."

"Hush," Deann chuckled. "I'd rather have them with us when we fight next, wouldn't you?"

"Silence in the ranks!" Gunny called.

They could catch occasional glimpses of the enemy force, now much reduced, as it made its way north. They also caught occasional glimpses of the cavalry screening force, which would signal with flags from time to time. Despite the slow speed of the archers they were clearly gaining on the enemy and passed ahead by noon. But Herzer was worried about the speed that they would be able to make down the valley, not to mention crossing the river. At this time of year it wasn't yet in spate, but it was a broad river and not to be crossed lightly. However, he had come to trust the baron and if Edmund said they could cut them off he was willing to believe it.

At the end of the main mountain, where it split into two ridges with the interior valley between, they took the right fork, continuing to follow an old hiking trail along the ridge. Herzer was glad they only had a few mules, now almost stripped of provisions, and Edmund's horses because the trail was very bad; with more horses they would have found it nearly impossible to negotiate. They followed it to the north, losing sight of the enemy force, which was attempting a crossing at some rapids, and continued into the afternoon until, just before dusk, they came upon a group of Raven's Mill townies at the head of a trail down the mountain.

"Hello, Herzer," one of them called. The men from the town had axes and spades and had apparently been hard at work improving the trail.

"Hello," Herzer replied, as the group headed down the mountain. Whatever the condition of the trail before, it was practically a road now. Where it was particularly steep it had either been given switchbacks or steps of rock and trunks. The spaces on the steps had been well filled with tamped earth and they held up under the pounding of the hobnailed force as it hurried down the hill.

"How long ago did you plan this, Baron Edmund?" Herzer asked as the baron came past, his horse delicately negotiating the steps.

"From the beginning," Edmund said. "I had Kane send them up yesterday to prepare this path and two others; I couldn't be sure which way he would hop."

Herzer just shook his head and wondered if he would ever get the knack of thinking that far ahead.

At the base of the mountain they followed the trail to the river where a ferry had been installed. It was a simple raft connected to heavy ropes but it was more than sufficient to permit the force to cross. By the time they were on the far side of the river it was solidly dark. But after removing the ferry and sending two men to pole the raft down stream they pushed on down the river to the Bellevue grade where he had made his stand against the original scouting force.

There, too, the men from the town had been hard at work. At that point the shoulder of the first ridge came down to a bend in the river and the only way across the shoulder was the cut of the old pike. Despite that fact, trees had been felled along the whole line from the river to the cliffs of the first ridge, forming an abatis, which had been reinforced with a pile of cross-logs to make a complicated breastwork. A ditch and parapet was under construction across the pike, and archer positions had been prepared on the east side of the pike, ranging up the shoulder of the ridge. With the Blood Lords in the parapet and along the west side and the archers above, able to fire down at anyone from their position to the river, the defenses were well nigh impregnable.

Herzer could still tell that it was going to be a hard fight.

A camp had been prepared on the far side of the defense and, after filing in through the small path that was the only way through the defenses, the group settled in and had a solid meal cooked by women from the town. There was a ration of wine for their supper and they had all they could eat, but best of all the baron gave them the night off; the militia could stand the watch for them.

Herzer fell asleep to the sight of the baron poring over maps by the light of a torch and his sleep, this time, was untroubled by dreams.

When Herzer awoke it was past noon and he blinked light from the sun that was up over the ridge out of his eyes. A few of the Blood Lords were already moving around but others were still asleep, curled up in limp balls. He wandered over to where Edmund was conferring with Alyssa and nodded at the two of them.

"They had a bad crossing," Alyssa said. She added, "He lost most of his carts and some of the infantry got washed away. The few men-at-arms he has with him are mostly on foot as well and I think at least one of them must have been lost since I saw only five. By my count, he's down to no more than three hundred. And they're moving slow."

"Two hundred and seventy-three under arms," Bast said, walking down the hill. "As of this morning when I lowered it from two hundred and seventy-seven. And now that they have flankers out, it's really slowed them down. Hi lover boy."

"Hi Bast," Herzer said with a grin and a surge of lust he hoped wasn't obvious on his face.

"I can tell you're glad to see me," the elf replied with a grin and a wink. "But there's a battle to be fought today and I don't do it with men in armor. It damned well pinches."

"So now we wait?" Herzer asked Talbot.

"More or less," Edmund replied. "But even with short of three hundred, he can swarm us if he hits the defenses in a wave." He nodded at the group and grabbed his horse, mounting easily despite the armor, and rode out of the defenses through the narrow, twisting path. He rode back and forth, then came back, nodding in satisfaction.

"Kane, I want a group of militia up here. Some archers and pikemen to man the defenses. McGibbon, Herzer, get your people down again. Let's see if we can fool him twice."

"I'll get some people to work on covered ways," Kane added. "That way if he stands off at night, the defense force can get off the parapet without being observed or at least get fed in the line."

"Good idea," Edmund said.

"Gunny, you need to head back to town, Herzer and I can handle it here. I want you to see if you can stiffen up the militia."

"Like using buckshot to stiffen up spit," Gunny muttered. "Permission to stay here, sir?"

"Permission denied," Edmund said with a grin. "With Kane here, I need you back there."

"Yes, sir," the NCO said, stolidly.

"Let's get to it."

CHAPTER FORTY-ONE

Sheida met Ishtar in alternate reality and with a projection rather than an avatar; Ishtar's summons had indicated that it was urgent. She hadn't bothered to adjust the reality of the space that was created and it was a formless gray plain that stretched, apparently, into infinity. Since it had no real existence, there was no infinity for it to reach.

"I have traced, as well as I can, all the members of the board of the terraforming group," Ishtar said as Sheida appeared. "The *only* survivor that I have been able to track down is Dionys McCanoc. As you suggested, several of them died shortly after the Fall, and none of them from 'accidents'; they had all been murdered."

"If you're playing for keeps you don't bother arranging 'accidents,'" Sheida said. "And if he dies, all the power reverts?"

"Until a quorum of the shareholders, or their heirs, can be contacted and a vote arranged," Ishtar nodded.

"And right now he's letting Chansa control his proxy?" Sheida mused. "Why?"

"Council members cannot have a membership on the board," Ishtar said with a wry grin. "But they can 'advise' as to power use. Chansa, or whoever controls him, cannot have the direct 'ownership' of it. He *has* to use a proxy."

"As would we," Sheida said. "Why isn't he using the power directly?"

"That I don't know," Ishtar admitted. "The only thing I can

imagine is that he's not aware he *can*. And why, if he has all this power, is he setting himself up as a bandit lord? He could *own* this war!"

"Not knowing would be like McCanoc," Sheida said. "He thinks he's brilliant but what he is is *cunning,* and he tends to only look at superficials. He knew he could distribute the power but not that he can draw upon it now. There's probably a very specific command he has to give to get it for his own use. And as to why he's set himself up as a bandit chief, that's what he *wants* to be. He's the sort of personality that revels in direct control over people, in forcing the people around him to live in fear and intimidation. It's his whole reason for being, to have people that he can *see be* afraid of him. He loves to *destroy,* not build. Having power that's beyond that level isn't the same for him. So probably the deal is that Chansa is letting him run around and be the evil conquering bastard he wants to be and 'oh, by the way, why don't you let me be your proxy for the terraforming system, otherwise Mother will be bothering you with updates all the time' or something."

"Yeah," Ishtar whispered. "But what do we do about it?"

"I'm not sure," Sheida admitted. "I need to find out where he is. The last I heard he was headed for . . . Oh, Shit!"

"What?"

"He was headed for Raven's Mill!" Sheida gasped. "Oh Fisk!"

"What's so bad? I mean, he may conquer it but, Sheida, I know you have friends there but . . ."

"Blow that," Sheida said, her mind racing. "He hasn't got a chance. He's up against *Edmund.* Edmund is going to put his head on a *pike*. After Daneh cuts off his *balls*!"

"I'm sure that Chansa gave him protection . . ."

"I don't care *what* Chansa did! He won't defeat Edmund, I guarantee it! I have to *go*." With that she vanished.

Daneh was tending to the last details of the preparations for the battle when Sheida appeared. Rachel and a few of the nurses had set up a forward aid station closer to the defenses but it had been decided to send the worst cases back to the town via horse carts and Daneh was determined to give them the best care possible. She was lifting her surgical tools from the vat of boiling water when Sheida appeared in the air over the cauldron.

"Daneh, where's Edmund?" her sister said abruptly. For once she didn't appear to have even a projection of her lizard with her.

"Out fighting McCanoc," Daneh said acerbically. "Without any help from you, I might add."

"He can't kill him!" Sheida said. "That's very important!"

"What do you *mean* he can't kill him?" Daneh asked angrily. "Do you know what he's been doing? What he did to *me*?" she said, gesturing at her stomach.

"Yes, I do," she replied, tautly. "I don't care. I'll explain later. Where is *Edmund*?"

"Up the road," Daneh said. "At the Bellevue grade."

"Get up there as soon as you can," Sheida said.

"Sheida, I'm *busy* here!"

"I *don't care!*" Sheida yelled, coming to a decision. She reached out and touched her sister and both of them suddenly appeared in the camp behind the defenses. The one part of her mind that she always kept attuned to power levels saw the slight drop and how it affected all the defenses that were arrayed against the continuous power of the enemy side. One of the shields on a fusion plant flickered at the abrupt power drain, slight as it was, but it held.

"Hello, Sheida," Edmund said, looking up from a schematic of the defenses. "Nice to see you, Daneh," he added with a nod.

"You can't kill McCanoc," Sheida said.

"Thank you for your input," Edmund said calmly. "But you'll forgive me if I pointedly ignore you."

"Listen to me!" the projection snarled. "It's *very* important. We've figured out where Paul is getting all this extra power and it's *McCanoc*." She then explained the problem and shook her head. "If we can *capture* him, we can get him to change his proxy. That gives *us* the power. We're holding them *despite* the power. They're not fighting *smart*. If we get it we can probably *end* this damned war!"

At that Edmund set down the sketch and rubbed his chin. "That, I'll admit, is a telling argument. But how are you going to get him to change his proxy? Or, for that matter, how are you going to do anything with him? At the first bit of danger Chansa will yank him out. I wonder that he lets him run around at all if he's that important."

"It's probably what Chansa offered him," Sheida said. "I can prevent him from calling on Chansa; Paul's side won't even know what's happening to him. I can wrap him in a teleport block and communications block."

"And what will that do to get him to change his proxy?" Daneh asked.

"Well, I'll offer him his life," Sheida said with a feral smile. "But that's *all*."

"Hmmm," Edmund muttered. "And you're asking that I not kill him. The man that raped my *wife*? Your *sister*?"

"Do you think *I* like it?" Sheida replied. "But it's necessary. Even if we can't win the war, this will give us spare power." She turned to Daneh. "Daneh, what would you give for enough power to summon nannites for healing?"

"Oh," Daneh said, struck by the thought. "I'd give much for just some damned medical texts and medicines. Nannites?!" She thought about it for a moment then sighed. "*God* I want him *dead*, though!"

"We all do," Sheida said. "Edmund, powered armor? Enhancements?"

"Don't really need them," he answered. "We've got a technique and a nice professional army that we're going to make larger. But, frankly, it's not up to me. I'm not the one who was directly affected." He turned to Daneh and nodded at her. "Milady, I know that this is a great burden to put on your shoulders, but as the one most affected, I leave it to you. Life? Or death?"

Daneh's jaw worked furiously and she shook her head. "Damn you, Sheida!"

"I'm sorry, Daneh," Sheida said, honestly. "But think, best case, we can destroy Paul's defenses and bring an end to this war. Worst case, we can have the power to aid all of us. Medical technology will be at the *top* of the list. I promise you."

Daneh rubbed her face and snarled. "Damn you, Sheida," she said again, then: "*Life*," she ground out through gritted teeth. "But it had better not be a life of *ease*!"

"I promise you, we'll find an interesting way for him to spend the rest of his miserable life. Although we might have to negotiate not to torture him, so chaining him to a rock to have his liver eaten out every day by a vulture might be out."

"I wouldn't ask for that," Daneh replied. "Just . . . confine him. Solitary confinement. For the rest of his life."

"Okay," Sheida replied. "He'll never see another human face for the rest of his life, nor hear a human voice except his own. You realize that solitary punishment like that is one of the cruelest tortures in the world? That it's going to drive him insane, more insane that is?"

"Yes," Daneh said coldly. "I do."

"Done," Sheida said, turning to Edmund. "Are you going to win this battle?"

"Probably," he replied. "If not here, then at the town. But he's probably got some power available for defense. Capturing him, or killing him for that matter, probably won't be easy."

"Just capture him," Sheida said. "I'm trying to get you some help. If it arrives it will have the means to make sure he doesn't escape. I've got to go but I'll keep a watch on things. If Paul or Chansa notice he's losing, I'll see what I can do to keep them from interfering directly. But I have to go." With that she disappeared.

"Oh, lovely," Daneh sighed. "Thanks for leaving me here, Sis."

"There are carts coming and going regularly from town," Edmund said. "Now that Sheida's gone I want to say something."

"What?"

"I'm glad that you agreed," Edmund sighed.

"What?" she gasped, angrily. "But . . ."

"Sheida is right," he said, holding up a hand to stop her angry retort. "We need the power. But there's more to it than that. I haven't discussed your rape and your therapy because I'm too close to you; I'm the wrong person to help. But that doesn't mean I haven't been . . . observing. And you've been wrapping yourself around hatred for McCanoc to a degree that's not healthy."

She looked at him for a long time and then sighed. "I know. But I don't know what to do about it."

"You just did most of it," Edmund replied. "By using your head instead of your heart, you've shown, to yourself, that you *can* get past it. That has probably done as much for you as Bast's little session. You've shown that even if McCanoc is at your mercy, you *can* let him live, for a good enough cause. If we *had* captured him, he would have been put to death. But only after a solid trial and by the rules. Emotion should have no play in it."

"Ask a question?" she said.

"Sure."

"If I'd said no, that is, that I wanted him *dead*, would you have done it? Even over Sheida's objections?"

"Yes," Edmund replied. "I don't think that getting his power will 'end the war.' Wars are rarely, effectively never, won through simple change points like that. They're far too complex. Killing him would have taken the power away from Paul's faction, which would have helped. But it wouldn't have ended the war. That said, the additional power would have been so helpful that *not* taking a chance at it would have been . . . not the best decision. But if it was the decision that you made, I would have stood by it."

"You are so . . . strange, Edmund Talbot," she sighed, smiling. "You always think of the future, don't you?"

"If you start living in the past you're already on the way to the grave," Edmund commented, then smiled. "You could stay for dinner; McCanoc won't be here tonight; he's been running into little traps we've set along the road."

"Unfortunately, I need to get back," she said, patting him on the cheek. "I'll stop by the aid station on my way back and check on Rachel. Do me a favor; don't come to my tender ministrations *tomorrow*. They won't be so tender." With that she waddled off to find one of the ox carts.

"Will do," Edmund replied, picking the sketch back up. As she walked away he set it back down and sighed. "HERZER!"

"Yes, Baron," the triari called from the far side of the camp.

"Find McGibbon, I've got to pass some supplementary orders."

When the two were there he told them of Sheida's request but not the reason. "I know why she's asking and I've agreed to abide by her wishes. He is *not* to be killed. Understood."

"Yes, sir," Herzer said, reluctantly.

"Why in the hell not?" McGibbon asked. "You *know* what he's done!"

"Yes, I do," Edmund said evenly. "And the reason is, I gave you an order. Are you going to abide by it and enforce it? Or am I going to have to ask Steinweggen to take over command?"

McGibbon's face worked but then he nodded. "You know I'll follow your orders, Edmund. But that doesn't mean I have to like it."

"None of us do," Edmund replied. "But it's necessary."

"Permission to speak, sir?" Herzer said.

"You're not a recruit anymore, Herzer," Talbot said with a smile.

"Does Dr. Daneh know about this?" Herzer asked.

"Yes," Edmund said.

"Uhmm . . ." Herzer tried to figure out a way to phrase it then shrugged. "Did she approve?"

"You'll have to ask her," Edmund replied. "When you get a chance."

"Yes, sir."

"Now, go spread the word."

"One last question; I know it will come up," McGibbon replied. "Can we at least *wound* him a little?"

"I doubt we'll be able to capture him if we don't," Edmund replied. "But the person who kills him will answer to me."

Herzer checked the guard posts after dinner then headed back to his packs. When he reached them he saw Bast laid out on his fur rug and he remembered that it was, in fact, hers.

"Come to reclaim your property?" he asked with a smile.

"Only if you want to call yourself that, lover," she replied with a light in her eyes.

"Bast . . . this is not a good idea," he said, squatting by the fur.

"One thing that you need to learn is that except when people are *actively* trying to kill you," she said, leaning up to kiss him, "*this* is always a good idea."

"I've got responsibilities," he temporized. "And I'm not going to do it right here in front of everyone."

"We'll cover up," she said with a grin, flipping his blanket over her legs. "It's getting cold anyway. Come over here and warm me up."

Herzer took off his armor and crawled in between the fur and the blanket, wrapping her in his arms. As he did he realized that they were not by any stretch of the imagination alone. There were couples among the militia and the archers and he was pretty sure he heard some murmurings from the direction of Deann's usual place. And Cruz wasn't next to him for that matter.

"I hope like Mithras the sentries are paying attention to their business," he muttered as between the two of them they got him out of his uniform.

"I'll go check on them when you're asleep," she murmured, pulling him down for another kiss.

"Thank you," he said, letting his hand wander down her side and watching the shiver it elicited. "I think I love you."

"And I love you as well," she murmured. "But love is not a single, perfect, emotion. You love Cruz as well."

"What?" he asked, sitting up. "I mean, he's a buddy, but . . ."

"But you are very het, my dear," she smiled, pulling him back down. "Don't let in so much cold air! But when you fight, you fight for your friends, for your comrades, to keep them alive as much as yourself. Yes?"

"Yes," he said, "but . . ."

"This, too, is *love*," she said, smiling. "Honor and courage are so often an expression of love. When I saw you, the first time, I saw in you a great capacity for love. Well, and, also, I thought: My that's a big boy, I wonder if he's to scale."

Herzer chuckled and butted her with his head. "And were you . . . pleased?"

"Ecstatic," she replied. "But love is what it's all about. Do you love the 'Kingdom of Free States'?"

"Well . . ."

"Okay, do you love Raven's Mill?"

He thought about that for a while. A group of strangers, survivors of disaster, thrown together in the wilderness. But . . .

"Yes," he said and then understood.

"So you could run away," she said. "It's possible that tomorrow you will die. But you do not. You stay. For your comrades, for your town, for your honor. This is *love*."

"If I desert, the penalty is death," Herzer pointed out.

"Does that bother you?" Bast chuckled. "Really?"

"No," he admitted.

"Love is what has driven soldiers into wars throughout the centuries. There are times when fear overcomes it, and then they have to be prodded into battle. And there are conscript armies driven forth by fear or for having nothing better in their lives. And there are those who simply like the killing; McCanoc is one such. But they make poor soldiers. It is the ones who love something, who go clear eyed into battle for it, who are the fiercest killers. Sometimes they have loved the wrong things. Jihads and pogroms and Holocausts. Hate mixed in with love. But to bring a soldier to the place of battle mostly requires a love of something. They may love something greater than themselves, but they must *love*. The greatest warriors *are* the greatest lovers. And I saw in you greatness."

"Thank you," he said, quietly.

"Now, no more talk," she whispered in his ear. "Let us *do*."

CHAPTER FORTY-TWO

Herzer was just getting out of his blankets in the predawn cold when Bast came striding back into the camp, obviously straight from a bath in the river; her hair was just starting to dry and her nipples were standing out so hard they were dimpling the leather of her halter-top.

"How come you were complaining about cold when you run around in a bikini all the time?" he asked, grumpily. He was sore in some very odd places; Bast had a grip like a vise and she sometimes forgot her own strength.

"I'm more or less immune to heat and cold," she admitted with a grin. "It doesn't mean I have to like it."

"So why do you run around in a bikini instead of something warmer?" he asked, perplexed.

"Do you know how many men I've killed who froze looking at my tits?" she asked, laughing merrily.

"Breakfast is on," Cruz said, walking past. "Bacon and eggs! New bread from town!"

"Sounds good," Herzer said, putting on his armor and checking that his sword was loose in its sheath. Their helmets were stacked on their crossed pilums and for the time being his could stay there.

Bast walked with him to the chow line and got only bread, then looked over at Edmund in the torchlight. "They're still where they stopped last night, about a kilometer and a half south," she said. "They weren't stirring yet when I left."

"Good," Edmund said, getting a full plate. "Thank you for checking."

515

"I thought someone should," she replied.

"There's a team of cavalry down the road," Edmund said.

"I know, I saw them as well," Bast chuckled, taking a bite of the bread and looking up at the stars in the clear sky. "It's a good day for battle. It will start cool but then get quite warm."

"You'll take a place with the archers?" Talbot asked, leading the group over to a large stump.

"Oh, yes, not for me the armored clash," she smiled. "I'll fill them so full they won't realize they're dead. I dislike these Changed intensely."

"I doubt it was their choice," Herzer said, sitting on the ground.

"No, but I still don't like them," she said fiercely. "They have slaves in the pack trains. You must rescue them, Edmund."

"First we have to *win*," Edmund pointed out. "We're sort of outnumbered."

"I'll take my quota," Bast said with a shrug. "Methinks I'll go find a good spot." With that she walked off into the darkness, whistling and occasionally spinning in place in dance.

"I'm glad she's so happy," Herzer said.

"She's like that," Edmund shrugged. "Battle is what she was bred for and she's just about as good at it as any elf I've ever met."

"We might have to retreat," Herzer said, looking at the defenses. "I hope not."

"I've got that covered," Edmund replied. "The militia is going to get to work today on fall-back positions for the archers. I've had extra pilums brought up as well and stashes placed along the way." He looked up at the sky and nodded. "Get your troops into position and down. It's getting on for dawn."

For much of the rest of the morning, Herzer and the Blood Lords remained crouched in the parapets. As Bast had predicted the morning cool had quickly been dispelled by the rising sun and by the time the mutters of the militia indicated that the enemy was in sight it was nearly noon and rising to a summer heat. He could see from his position the three horse scouts climb up the trail and then down, but he was out of sight of the enemy and vice versa.

Edmund walked over to his position and, without looking down, shielded his eyes and frowned. "What a gaggle."

"How's it look?" Herzer asked.

"They're all in a group. I think he's learning the term 'defeat in detail,' which means he'll try to rush us with the whole force. Ah, here he comes."

"As you can see, I'm waving a parley flag," McCanoc's ironic voice drifted up from beyond the low wall.

"I doubt you'd honor it in return," Edmund called. "But that's the difference between us. Are you surrendering this time? Tell you what, I'll guarantee that *you* are permitted to live and I'll even throw in not having you tortured every day for the rest of your miserable existence. All you have to do is disarm your force and have it stand down to be taken prisoner."

"You're so *funny*, Edmund Talbot!" McCanoc called. "I'll counter your offer. Send us out a shipment of tribute and we'll go back the way we came. Say, two tons of wheat and the same of corn and all the jewelry and other geegaws of the town."

"And you'd leave us alone from hence forward?" Edmund asked as if he was considering it.

"Well, not *exactly*," McCanoc replied. "Say, a quarterly payment. Oh, and we'd need some young ladies as well. Where you get them is up to you; remember you could always raid the other towns in your area for the tribute."

"Yes, very good point," Edmund said. "We could be sense-lessly destructive bastards just like you. But I think not. Last chance; surrender and I'll let *you* live. Your . . . *men* we'll have to consider."

"No, I don't think so," Dionys replied, venom in his voice. "Let me tell you what *I'm* going to do. First, I'm going to wipe out this pitiful militia. Your stupid *Blood Lords* and archers are still marching over here, aren't they? So all you have is this rabble militia, a bunch of has-been *reenactors* who can't handle reality so they hide in fantasy. Much good *they'll* do you against *my* army. And when *they* are gone, Edmund Talbot, I'm going to capture *you*. And the last thing that you'll see, before I have your eyes burned out, is me raping your daughter, the first of a *long* line of my men.

"Daneh, however, I will spare. I understand she is with *child*," he added delightedly. "I assuredly cannot kill my first-born. After it is birthed, though, it may be different. And I understand that women can continue to have sex during pregnancy. Especially if it's up the ass!"

Edmund had listened to the diatribe in perfect calm and his voice retained it. "Is that all?"

"Isn't that enough?"

"Only for an amateur," Edmund sighed loudly enough to be heard all along the line. "It's so *hard* to find qualified opponents these days," he added in a mutter. The baron lowered his visor and lifted his hammer to the figure in black plate. "Are you going to spend all day talking? Because I'm going to give you five minutes to get out of bowshot. That's part of this whole 'parley' thing, too."

"Does she dream of me?" McCanoc shouted angrily. "Does she dream of me on top of her, Edmund, when you are holding her in her nightmares?!"

"Not anymore," Edmund called in a bored tone. "Frankly, Dionys, she's pretty much gotten it out of her system. Other important things to do. Sorry. Four minutes."

Herzer couldn't see what McCanoc was doing but from the injured squeal of the horse he guessed that Dionys had reined it around sharply.

"It's so *hard* to get good opponents," Edmund sighed.

"I think this force is just about good enough, Baron," one of the militiamen said. "As opponents I mean."

"Really? You call that taunting? I've heard better taunting from children. I was half expecting him to say 'neener, neener, neener.' That's the quality of taunting you get these days."

"Great," Cruz muttered. "Somebody want to tell me what's happening?"

"He's gone back to his force and is exhorting them," Edmund said. "Probably about as well as he was taunting me, from the looks on their faces. They don't like this one bit. Now he's riding around behind them. That's where he's got his men-at-arms, too, probably to make sure the Changed keep going. And now, they're moving forward. Right down the road. Blood Lords, archers, stand by!"

"When are you going to have us stand up?" Herzer asked.

"When they're in pilum range," Edmund replied. "I can't believe he didn't put me together with you guys. For the stupidity of our foes, may we always be thankful."

"Probably thought you rode ahead," Herzer said, listening to the approaching force. Their feet could be felt pounding the ground and there was a deep-toned continuous wah-wah-wah from them. "I wouldn't have believed we could march that fast, either, especially with the archers."

"Keep those pilums down!" Edmund called.

"Squat in your positions," Herzer added as some of the militia archers started firing their short bows. He could hear the sharper notes of Bast's bow as well and was fairly sure that each of the hissing shafts had found its mark from the occasional scream in the distance. "Pilums across your knees, shields leaning against the wall."

"Wait for it!" Talbot called, swinging his hammer idly in one hand. "Wait for it . . ."

"So, where are you going on your holidays?" Cruz asked the air.

"UP AND AT 'EM!"

Herzer stood up and in one smooth motion drove the pilum outward into the first shield he saw. The missile penetrated the shield, and the orc that had been carrying it was suddenly burdened by an additional weight out on a long shaft. He stopped to struggle with the weapon and an arrow took him in the throat.

Herzer hadn't really seen the by-play since he stooped to pick up one of the additional pilums at his feet and drove it, in turn, into a shield, then drew his sword and settled down to the serious business of survival.

The orcs came in wave after wave, most of them shredded by arrow fire before they could ever reach the defenses. The militia had fallen back, leaving a double line of the Blood Lords across the narrow strip of road, and although the orcs crashed into the line again and again, they could neither push it back nor run it over. They first had to clamber up the parapet and then face the shields of the Blood Lords with their swords licking out to rend faces, arms, bodies. Even if they made it into or through the first line, the second was there to finish them off as the unfortunate orcs ran into a threshing machine of stabbing swords from the front, back and sides.

A few managed to make it all the way through that, only to face a wall of polearms wielded by the infantry. These weapons, most of them axelike halberds, quickly chopped any survivors into gobs.

Herzer hadn't been able to follow the ebb and flow of the fight, but he could tell when the orcs finally started to break. They had three times faced the Blood Lords and on each occasion they had been chopped to bits. Now, in the face of the defenses and the steady line of legionnaires and the air filled with arrows, they could face it no more. First singly, then in groups, then enmasse they streamed back down the hill. Those that survived.

As the last orc fell back from the parapet, Herzer was able to look around. There were dead Changed everywhere, on the parapet, in the trench and in piles in front of the wall. There were some familiar faces missing as well and he vaguely recalled someone filling in the gap next to him. He looked to his right and instead of the accustomed Deann it was Pedersen, the third decuri leader.

"Deann?" he gasped, lowering his sword and reaching for his hip flask for a drink of water.

"Hit bad," Pedersen replied. "They took her back to the aid station."

"Where's the baron?" he asked, looking around.

"Group of orcs are trying to flank us down by the river," Stahl replied. "He rode down there to cut them off."

"Shit," was all he said, looking down the hill. McCanoc was reining his horse back and forth furiously and then finally pointed it up the hill and started to charge.

"Look at that dumb bastard," Herzer muttered, finishing off his water and pulling out a rag to wipe his blood-covered sword. "I bet he doesn't make it five meters past the first range mark."

"I dunno," Cruz said from his left. "He's running pretty fast. What are you betting?"

"Never mind," Herzer said, dropping the cloth. He had heard the twang of Bast's arrow and had seen it fly straight and true. And bounce off something in mid air. "I think we're in trouble."

More arrows flew through the air and the massive horse first faltered and then fell on its side, legs kicking in agony as it squealed in pain. But the figure in black armor hit the ground lightly, as if supported, and leapt to his feet, charging forward and bellowing incoherently. As he did a mist seemed to form around him, a black cloud that reached out to the wounded on either side, and where he passed they twitched and groaned no more.

When McCanoc reached the parapet he leapt into the air, an impossible, obviously enhanced leap that carried him well above the parapet and onto the ground beyond. He was wielding a two-handed sword as if it was a feather, and as he swept it from side to side the blade clove through heavy wooden shields and steel armor as if they were cloth.

In a moment, Herzer saw a half a dozen of the second rank of the Blood Lords fall and he charged forward, screaming, to slam into the back of his much larger opponent.

Dionys wasn't even rocked by the blow, but he spun around as a power field cast Herzer back with a shower of sparks. Herzer found himself enmeshed in a black cloud and he could feel his strength slipping away from whatever program was running the nannite cloud.

"Well, if it isn't my old buddy, Herzer," Dionys said raising his sword. "Time to learn the penalty of betrayal."

Dionys stabbed downward but Herzer was already on his feet with a back roll he would forever afterwards find impossible. He had dropped his shield and as the blade swept down he parried it despairingly only to have his sword lopped off just above the guard. He backpedaled and picked up one of the spare pilums but Dionys leapt the distance between them and slashed downwards just as he was raising it. The power blade swept around, cleaving through the pilum and taking off most of Herzer's left hand with it.

Herzer stumbled backwards clutching at his wrist and snarling. "You're going down, Dionys," he said. But he could feel the black cloud sucking his strength away as he said it and his vision was going gray.

"What are you going to do, bleed on me?" Dionys asked, just as a white maelstrom landed on his back.

Azure had been watching the battle with interest. He didn't really feel he had a side in it, but his humans were certainly having fun and tearing big strips of fur off their opponents. But something about the black figure struck a cord and when the air brought the scent of him to the cat, he recognized someone with whom there was a score to settle.

The power field apparently didn't recognize that claws could kill and it had no effect upon the enraged feline. The sixty-kilo cat landed on the back of Dionys' armor and scrabbled at it, hissing and spitting.

Dionys spun around but the cat had hooked his top claws into the armor's chinks and was raking for all he was worth. And no matter how McCanoc writhed he could not dislodge the house lion.

Azure, however, did not like the black cloud one bit. It was making him think of going and lying in the sun to sleep it off. Finally, the cat gave up. The armor was proof against his claws and the cloud, ill-tuned as it was to the biology of a feline, was making inroads on his strength. Finally, with a yowl of disappointment, the cat disengaged.

Dionys took a swipe at the white figure as it ran off but missed and turned back to Herzer, just as the boy launched himself through the air. He had watched Azure's attack and recognized that the power field did not recognize a body within its reach. Despite the pain of his hand and the weakness caused by the cloud he threw himself on Dionys' shield arm, clasping McCanoc around the waist with his legs and trying to work a dagger into the chink between his cuirass and gorget.

Dionys let out a bellow of anger, shook himself again, stabbing with his sword and trying to rid himself of Herzer. But when he felt the dig of the dagger on the cloth under the armor he threw himself on the ground, slamming Herzer on his back and driving all the air from his lungs.

Herzer found himself on the ground, totally spent. The cloud had seeped the strength from his body and the impact of Dionys on him was the last straw. He felt ribs crack under his opponent's weight and his dagger flew out of nerveless fingers. As Dionys scrambled to his feet he tried to stand up, roll, anything, but all he could do was lie on the ground and await his fate.

"That's it," Dionys muttered, stumbling to his feet and lifting his sword. "I'm tired of you, Herzer." He raised the sword again, point downward and prepared to thrust just as a saber slashed out from the side and struck his armor in a shower of sparks.

Dionys spun in place and cut back, fast and hard, only to have Bast avoid the blow with a laugh. "You'll have to do better than that," she said, dancing backwards. "Nobody roughs up my pretty-boy and gets away with it."

"Will you people just *give up?*" Dionys shouted and leapt forward but wherever he slashed the elf was never there, dancing in with a merry chuckle and raking her sword along his armor. "Faster, Dionys McCanoc, faster," she said. "You need to learn the dance."

And, indeed, it was a dance she led him as McCanoc furiously chased her around the encampment. Occasionally someone else would attempt to intervene but none of their weapons could pierce the power shield around his armor and Bast laughingly waved them off as blow after blow fell upon his plate. But though she could pierce the power field, she could make not a dent in the armor and after a while there was nothing but the grunting of the giant plate-armored figure and the laughter of the elf. The militia had at first fallen back but now moved forward, watching the swordplay and commenting on it. They were careful, however, to stay far outside the range of the black cloud around McCanoc that seemed to have no effect on the elf.

Herzer found himself lifted to a sitting position by Rachel who frowned at his hand. "This is a right mess," she said, waving at some stretcher bearers.

Herzer shook his head as they approached. "I want to see," he said.

"Okay," she sighed, wrapping his mangled hand in a bandage. "We'll wait. But I think we're all doomed. Bast can't get through his armor and all he needs is one lucky blow. Oh, hell."

"Bast," Edmund said, stepping to the edge of the duel. "Feel like tagging out?"

Herzer didn't know where he'd come from; it was as if he'd just appeared. The boy wasn't sure what the old warrior was going to do against the nannite cloud and the much larger McCanoc, but having him there was comforting.

"Not . . . yet," she replied. The elf, for all her stamina, was slowing down and McCanoc seemed to have unlimited reserves of energy.

"I'm going to kill you," Dionys said, panting. "Then all the rest of you. Rape Daneh again, rape that bitch daughter, rape your still warm corpse."

"I don't think so," Bast gasped but as she said it her foot turned on a stone. She tried to turn the slip into a cartwheel but Dionys darted forward, his sword licking out, and caught her on the upper thigh. As the bright blue blood spilled out on the ground he raised the sword up, point downward, for a killing thrust.

"My turn," Edmund said, stepping forward to interpose his shield as Bast scrambled backwards. Some of the militia grabbed her and drew her back into their midst, shielding her from McCanoc's view.

"Now you, old man?" Dionys said, stepping back and laughing. "Don't you people give up? My orcs will be up here before long and your damned 'Blood Lord' pussies aren't going to be able to stop them with me in their midst."

"I see you kenned some armor," Talbot replied calmly, hefting his hammer.

"Kenned hell, Fukyama could see a good deal when it was presented to him," McCanoc replied, lifting his visor for a moment. He was far enough back that the cloud barely reached Talbot but he appeared puzzled that it didn't seem to have any effect. The cloud seemed to be hovering just a short distance from the baron's armor as if it was afraid to touch it. He looked at it questioningly for a moment and then dropped his visor, dropping into a guard position.

"You can't defeat me, either, 'Baron' Edmund," he said, stepping forward carefully and jabbing at Edmund with his sword. The hypersharp weapon struck Edmund's shield but the baron turned the blow aside, letting the point slither off the metal surface.

"No weapon is proof against my armor," McCanoc continued, circling his smaller opponent. "My blade will go right through your armor and my cloud will kill you even if my blade doesn't. Nice, isn't it? It's a medical protocol that Chansa gifted me with. Your wife will like it, I think. Perhaps I'll feed her to it, after our child is born. You are going to die, here, Edmund Talbot."

"I think not," the baron replied, sighing. "Taunting, taunting, taunting. I halfway expect you to say 'neener neener.' So far your cloud doesn't appear to be working." He turned aside another blow lightly and stepped to the side, holding his hammer at the ready. "And, you know, Dionys, you really aren't very good at taunting."

"D'you think you can do better?" Dionys snapped, leaping forward and driving a blow against Talbot's shield. This time, Talbot caught the blow full against it and the sword rang as it was stopped by the metal of the shield.

"Oh, yes," Edmund replied. "What? You don't think I'd have *standard* armor, do you? I'm a *master-smith*. Of *course* it's power-armor you twit! As to taunting . . . Try this." He thought for a moment then cleared his throat.

"Dionys, thou art a coward. Sooth doth thou send others before thee and refrain from the strife thyself. Thou strikest women yet shirk to strike a man, lest thy pustulent skin be cut by a blade fairer than thy own. Sooth, thou art a coward, McCanoc."

"What?" Dionys shouted, slamming another blow into the shield. Edmund turned it aside as if it was of no importance and continued.

"Dionys, thou art a braggart. Braggart thou art for nought, for in every contest thou art defeated. Fighter of weaklings and braggarts like thyself, whensoever a true knight face thee, thou runs away. Yet, in sooth, from this cowardly retreat doot thou make brag. McCanoc, thou art a braggart."

Herzer watched in amazement as the smith started to dance around his much larger opponent, taking blow after blow unfazed and practically singing his taunts as Dionys began slamming out blows in naked fury.

"Dionys, thou art smelly. Thy breath stinks of the rotten ejacula of horses, which, sooth, thou dost love as thy morning drink. Thy body reeks with the stench of fear, and the manure of asparagus-eating goats is better than the smell from thy mustache. McCanoc, thou art a stinker."

At this Dionys let out a bellow like none before and began chasing Edmund around the defile. Others got out of their way, laughing now at Edmund's taunts. Despite McCanoc's size he could never seem to catch the smith.

"Dionys, thou art ugly. Thy orcs doth not run forward to the fight, but away from thy countenance. Sooth, in the history of the ill-favored, thy name is held in high esteem. Thy whore mother screamed at first sight of thee as the replicator burst open of its own accord in horror. The ill-fortuned persons that were forced to care for thee had to put a pork chop around thy neck to get the dog to play with thee. Further, sooth, when it did, it mistook thy ass for thy face and preferred it to lick. McCanoc, thou art ugly.

"Dionys, thou art stupid. Thrice hast thou attacked us and thrice have we thrown thee back, though we be but, forsooth, a fraction of thy number. Thou art unlettered and hath never read of the term 'defeat in detail,' for, assuredly, but those few letters would require all day and the use of both of your pustulent forefingers. But the veriest simpleton canst understand that thine tactics are those of a school-yard bully held back until his tutors at last release him as a man full grown yet unable to manage fingerpainting. The very fact that thou canst breathe must be by the arts of some homunculi or hob, smarter than thou, who doth sit upon thy shoulder and whisper in thy ear, 'breathe in, breathe out' else surely thou wouldst cease in this vital activity for lack of thought. Canst thou walk and chew bubble gum at the same time it is asked and I cry 'Nay' for I have found you, face down, the bubble gum before you upon the ground as proof.

"McCanoc, thou art stupid."

"And *that*," he finished taking another blow on the shield and stopping his dance, "is how a professional insults someone! Now, go away, or I'll start in on Arabic you miserable mound of gelatinous pus!"

Herzer wished that he could see Dionys' face; he figured he was just about to have a stroke. His voice was hoarse and it sounded almost as if he was crying.

"You're going to pay for that Edmund Talbot!" McCanoc yelled, slamming his own shield into Edmund's and then striking with his sword. Edmund turned both attacks with almost contemptuous ease and slapped the sword blade aside with his hammer. Herzer noticed that while McCanoc was winded, Edmund appeared as fresh as when the contest had started.

"And that is such a comeback," Talbot sighed, hefting his hammer. "Do you know why it doesn't bother me when people taunt me with the name Edmund?"

"No," Dionys said, stepping forward until the black cloud enveloped the smith. "And I don't care. I'm going to *kill* you."

"It's because it's not my name," Talbot replied, softly. "It's the name of my brother, who died in Anarchia. He went there like a lot of young men used to go, to try to find some true competition in this world. And, like most, he fell victim to the anarchy that it is named after, killed in some pointless skirmish. I didn't know that at the time, so I followed him in. It took me years to determine his fate. Years in which, in searching for my brother, I found what I thought was my destiny."

His voice had gone cold and hard and even McCanoc had stopped, awed by some depth he couldn't understand, hidden in the simple tones of the smith.

"My name, is *Charles*," Talbot snarled at last, and as he did he was enwrapped in a blue glow that drove back the cloud in flashes of silver light. "And you, Dionys, are about to find out why I am called THE HAMMER!"

The hammer slashed forward faster than the eye could follow, faster even than Bast's lightning sword blows and Dionys was smashed backwards in a blast of sparks. His shield was shattered and he tossed it off with a cry, cradling his arm as the smith advanced.

"King of Anarchia you wished to be, right?" Talbot said, catching Dionys' wild swing on his shield and shedding the power blade as if it were a zephyr of wind. "Wanted to destroy all of *my* good work, did you?" he continued, slamming the hammer into Dionys' shoulder and casting him backwards in another blast of blue sparks. "Want to take over *my* town, do you?" he asked, hammering McCanoc's sword arm as his opponent took another wild swing. The sword sailed harmlessly away as Talbot stepped forward relentlessly, pressing the much larger fighter up against the edge of the road cut. "Raped my *wife*, did you?" Edmund said, fury in his voice as Dionys ducked his head and charged. "Kill her just like bastards like you killed my *brother*?"

Edmund stepped easily aside and laid the hammer across the back of McCanoc's helmet with another shower of sparks that made the hammer ring like a bell. The black-armored figure was left stretched in the dust and Edmund raised the hammer over his head for a killing blow. "I don't *think* so."

"Edmund!" Sheida called from above. The battlefield was suddenly shadowed as a flight of wyverns, each with a lance-wielding rider on its back, landed on the hills. "Don't!" She dismounted and scrambled to the ground, waving at him frantically as her lizard flew down ahead of her. "Damnit, even if we didn't need him, you can't kill him that way!"

Harry was on one of the wyverns as well and waved a sardonic salute at Edmund before the flight took off down the valley. The orcs had, indeed, been reforming for another assault but as the dragons swept down on them they scattered for the trees. The wyverns passed on and from down the valley came frantic neighing from the pack train as the beasts flew over.

Edmund flexed his hand on the hammer and looked up at the council member angrily. Finally, he nodded curtly, then raised the hammer over his head and brought it down on the small of Dionys' back instead of his head.

"Fine," he snarled. "I never said I'd let him walk again. Or use his dick."

Sheida shook her head angrily and climbed down from the heights, running to McCanoc. As she approached she lifted a hand and concentrated for a moment until the black cloud settled and dissipated into dust. She then ran her hand down McCanoc's back, looking inward and rocked back on her heels.

"That was a pretty precisely calculated blow," she said, looking up at Edmund.

"Yeah, wasn't it," he replied. "And if you *fix* it, all bets are *off*." He turned to Herzer and shook his head at his hand, and the downed Blood Lords scattered around the recumbent figure. "Sorry about that. I guess I should have sent you guys to deal with the orcs. Nobody's perfect."

Azure stalked over to the downed prey and sniffed at the body, yowling angrily. Then he turned around and kicked dirt onto the body, which was the only way to deal with a defeated enemy in *his* opinion. With a sniff, he wandered off. It was time to find some food and a good place to curl up in the sun.

CHAPTER FORTY-THREE

McCanoc pounded at the invisible walls of his prison and snarled at the two women.

"Fix me!" he demanded from his seat on the ground. All of his injuries had been healed, save one, and now he couldn't get higher than the perch afforded by propping himself up with his arms. He hammered at the force shield again and screamed. "FIX ME!"

"Tough job," Daneh said, maliciously. "Lots of damage there."

"I tell you what, Dionys," Sheida said with a smile. "If you turn over the proxy for the Wolf terraforming project, I'll think about it. Or, if you don't, I'll give you to Edmund."

"Oh, no," Daneh said, supporting the weight of her stomach, a glint in her eye. "Give him to *me*. I know just *exactly* where all the nerve endings are. And how to keep them alive for a *long* time, even after they've been . . . damaged."

"You wouldn't," McCanoc said, then gulped. "You're a *doctor*!"

"Or, if you give me some power, I'll change him into a woman," Daneh continued. "We captured a fair number of his orcs. And they're *awfully* bored."

"I've got an idea," Sheida said. "Why don't we go think about some other things we can do to him while Dionys thinks about what *we're* thinking about. And our offer. Which is, we'll let you live your full natural life. That's it."

"What about my *legs*?" Dionys snarled. "What about them?"

"I don't see why you'd need them in solitary confinement," Sheida answered as the two women walked out of the shed.

The building was on the far side of the Hill, far away from the prying eyes of the town. Most of the inhabitants of Raven's Mill, and the surrounding areas, had come into town for a serious party after being relieved of the threat of Dionys' attack. And the rumors of his capture, imprisonment, and the revelation that Baron Edmund was none other than Charles the Great of Anarchia had been swirling and being increased, if possible, in the retelling.

As the two women walked up and across the wall, nodding at the Council guards that kept prying eyes away, Daneh shook her head sadly.

"I didn't enjoy that as much as I thought I would," she said stopping to catch her breath.

"That's because you're a good person," Sheida agreed. "And no matter how much you hate him, torturing him, even mentally, goes against your grain."

"But if we can get the power, I can heal Bast," Daneh said, as much to herself as to the woman at her side. "And Herzer; he basically doesn't have a hand anymore. And it would be nice to have some medical backup when *this* happens," she added, rubbing her stomach.

"I know," Sheida replied. "The shield is tied into the power net and proof against just about anything Paul can throw at it. I hope. And, hopefully, Chansa won't even realize he's in trouble until we make him transfer the proxy, after which we'll just bury McCanoc somewhere deep, safe, and impossible to escape from. I'm thinking, the middle of a mountain. Maybe a magma bubble."

"But . . . I still don't like it."

"No, you wouldn't," Sheida said with a grim snort. "I think we should let him stew for a couple of hours and go enjoy the party in the meantime."

"That's one way to forget, I suppose," Daneh said, looking at her sister. "Tell you what, you play the beauty and I'll play the brains this time."

"Watch out. You know what happened the last time we did that!"

"Yep, I ended up marrying Edmund . . . Charles . . . Damn it, a woman should know the name of the man she's in love with!" She stopped dead in her tracks and cracked a grin. "Forget the damned party, let's go find Edmund. He's the best party in town."

"I'm with you."

❖   ❖   ❖

Rachel was wandering disconsolately through the crowds in the street when she heard her name called. The town was packed with revelers, many of them victors of the recent battles. There were militia in their motley armor and a spray of archers and Blood Lords. None of them needed to buy a drink as carefully hoarded liquor was dragged out and the entire town decided that *this* was a good time to do Faire.

For Rachel, though, there was no one. Her mother and father had just been acting . . . sotted all day and when she'd gone to visit Herzer in the hospital he'd moved himself, completely without authorization, over to the bed by Bast. The two of them were deep in conversation when she went in but they welcomed her and tried to get her to stay. Herzer's hand had had to be amputated, but her father had already offered to make a prosthetic that would work well enough to hold a shield. Deann, however, hadn't been as lucky; she had died on the horse cart back to town despite everything that Rachel could do to save her.

She wanted to stay and talk with the two of them, her best friends that she had in the town. However, she could tell when three was a crowd and finally wandered off to find someone else to be with.

She stopped and looked around and then saw a white, somewhat travel-stained unicorn, coming through the crowd.

"Barb?" she asked.

"Rachel!" the unicorn squeaked. "It *is* you! Oh, I'm so glad to find you, I've had such a terrible time!"

"Really?" Rachel asked. "How bad of a time could a unicorn have? I mean, you can browse, right?"

"I was captured by that horrible McCanoc person," the unicorn cried, her eyes brimming with tears. "And, oh! It was just terrible. The things he made me do!"

Rachel's brain shut down at that point and her mouth managed not to ask Barb to reiterate her experiences. But if she knew McCanoc her . . . friend had not had a good time.

"I'm sorry, Barb," Rachel finally managed to say. "Many people had a bad time with Dionys. But that's all done now."

"But he's still *alive*," Barb squeaked. "What if he gets away?"

"He won't," Rachel promised. "And if he tries anything, Dad will kill him."

"Okay," Barb replied. "But, at least I met a nice guy out of the whole thing."

"Oh?" Rachel squeaked back then cleared her throat. "Oh?"

"Yes, and I need a favor," Barb said. "Can you come help me with something?"

"Sure," Rachel said, weakly, following the unicorn through the crowds and out of the town.

They crossed the river and approached the horse corral, and Rachel grimaced as Diablo nickered and trotted over to the fence, whickering at Barb.

"I know what you're thinking, Rachel," Barb said sadly. "But he's kind to me and he doesn't try to take me out of season and he makes the other horses leave me alone. And, really, I just don't fit in anywhere else anymore."

"It's okay," Rachel said finally. "I understand."

"But . . . I can't work the latch on the gate," Barb pointed out. "And they threw me out this afternoon."

"I'll take care of it," Rachel replied, opening the gate just wide enough for her friend to slip through. "I'll make sure they know to . . . take care of you."

"Well, as long as Diablo is around, I'll be fine," Barb said. "Bye, now."

Rachel watched as the pair cantered to an out-of-the-way part of the field and stopped to graze. From time to time Diablo nibbled gently at his . . . mate and Barb would stop to run her horn along his neck. Finally, Rachel decided that love was where you found it.

"And where am I going to find it?" she asked herself sadly, walking back to the town in the darkness.

In the darkness McCanoc fumed and from time to time smashed a fist against the power screen, getting nothing for it but a bruise and a faint illumination.

Why were they after him for the terraforming proxy? Chansa had set that up before the Fall, but after the Fall he had assumed that the power had been dumped into the regular grid and locked out like all the rest. He certainly hadn't been able to summon so much as a genie.

But, maybe, the power *was* available. He hadn't tried to access it directly. And Chansa sure as hell wasn't answering his pages.

Finally he closed his eyes and held out his hands.

"Mother, as the sole surviving board member of the Wolf 359 terraforming project, I call upon the power stored for that project. Use all the power necessary to destroy this shield!"

Mother considered the call for a moment and then acquiesced.

❖   ❖   ❖

The fireball lifted a section of the hill into the air and dropped it in every direction. Most of the power had been shunted to destroying the shield and Mother only intended to use the minimum force necessary. But some of it, equivalent to about a two kiloton blast, escaped. Chunks of rock and bits of tree rained down on the town, killing many of the revelers and injuring scores.

At the shattering boom, Edmund, Daneh and Sheida hurried to the front of the house in time to see the last of the debris rain down.

"Damn it!" Sheida cursed. "Mother, this is Council Member Sheida Ghorbani. Is Dionys McCanoc alive or deceased?"

"Dionys McCanoc is deceased," a voice answered out of the air. Daneh forever after wondered if it was true that there was a note of satisfaction in the voice.

"What of the power for the Wolf 359 project?" Sheida demanded.

"The power has reverted to hold status," Mother replied. "Until a quorum of the stockholders or their heirs can be gathered to elect a new board or a vote of twelve can be held on the Council to shunt it to other purposes."

"Bloody hellfire!" Sheida shouted, slipping away to examine the damage. The shields had drained a significant portion of available power when they were attacked, but none of the shields had gone down. This was mostly because the power being pressed against them had gone down at the same instant. It was clear that Mother had cut Paul's available power the *instant* that McCanoc died. Her face worked in fury for a moment and then she sighed in disappointment.

"Hey, look on the bright side," Daneh said, shaking her head ruefully. "Now I don't have to hate you for the rest of my life for letting him live."

"Very funny, Daneh," Sheida replied with a rueful chuckle. "Very effing funny."

"Well, whatever," Daneh shrugged. "I need to get into town. There are people who are going to need my help."

"Are you sure you should?" Edmund said. "You're getting close to time."

"I worked on all the injured from the battle," Daneh said. "I can work on those who come in from this. I would appreciate some help getting to the hospital, though."

"I'll come with you," Talbot replied, pulling a cloak off the stand and wrapping it around her shoulders. "If for no other reason than to make sure you don't kill *yourself*. Or our baby. Sheida?"

"I have to go," the council member replied. "There's a lot of picking up to do on my end as well." She looked out at the hill, which was now black again in the moonlight and sighed. "We were so close."

"Don't sweat it," Edmund replied, pulling down his own cloak. "I guarantee it wouldn't have mattered; history *never* turns on small items. And anybody who tells you different is selling something."

EPILOGUE

Daneh let out a shriek and squeezed Edmund's hand harder.

"It's okay," he said, miserably. "You're doing fine." There was nothing he could do about it and it pained him to know that.

"It hurts!" she snarled, bearing down. "It *BLOODY* hurts!"

"You're doing fine, Mother," Rachel said, from somewhere down south. "I can see the crown of the baby's head. He's straight and you're dilating fine. You're in transition, which is why it hurts. Almost over. Just a few more pushes."

Sheida had brought more than dragon riders with her at the end. She had brought a crystalline device that used internal energies for power. The device had contained, among other things, a complete set of medical texts. And Rachel had been boning up for this exam.

"I'm tired," Daneh said, hating the whine in her voice and stepping on it ruthlessly. She took a few breaths and then felt the overwhelming urge to push sweep over her. "Aaaaaagh!"

"That's it," Rachel said. "Bear down. Bear down."

"Don't pant," Edmund said as the pain and pressure subsided. "Regular breaths. You need to get the air in your lungs."

"I'm NOT ENJOYING THIS!" she shouted, but slowed and steadied her breathing so that she could get the vital oxygen into her, for herself and the baby. "Oh, no," she said as the feeling swept over her again.

"That's it!" Rachel shouted. "PUSH! Dad, push on her stomach!"

Daneh bore down and felt a pulling and stretching that felt as if it would split her in two and then an overwhelming sense of relief. There was a moment's pause and then a wail split the air as the first baby born of woman in a thousand years protested the indignity of it all.

"It's a boy," Rachel said.

Rachel and one of the nurses clamped and cut the umbilical cord and wiped the baby, then handed it to Daneh. Daneh held her child and reached down to feel his tiny fingers. She touched the miniature nose and then looked at the ears. And blanched.

"Oh, no," she whispered.

"What?" Edmund asked then looked where she was pointing; the ears had a decided point to them. Edmund looked at them for a moment longer, then shrugged. "I don't care. So he's half that bastard. The other half is all you, my love. And I'll love all of him, as if he were my own."

"Thank you," she sighed, barely able to hold the child up. The baby's eyes were still closed but he lifted his head as if to look around and then grasped at her fingers. She shifted him over to her breast and he latched on as if he'd been doing it forever.

She lay back as her baby suckled, and looked at Edmund. "Are you sure? People . . . people would take him. And there's going to be talk."

"Yes, darling, I'm sure," Edmund said. "He's our future. He's *the* future. And we'll take that as it comes, one day at a time."

Chansa's avatar appeared outside the Council building and looked around. With the exception of a late spring snowfall it looked much as it had on the day of that last, fateful Council meeting. The other difference being the guards.

Outwardly they were human, but very large humans. And their eyes were absolutely dead, like those of sharks. They looked at Chansa and then looked away, cradling the rifles in their hands and scanning the area for threats.

The rifles were Paul's design, air rifles that compressed air to a pressure just under the level where Mother's protocols would start taking an interest. But while they had less range than an old style chemical rifle, much less the gauss rifles of the AI wars, their projectiles made them in a way even more deadly; each little dart that was loaded in the magazine had a drop of acid.

Anyone hit by a flail of the little bullets would not only have the damage that they made going through but would find their bodies riddled with acid.

Chansa wasn't worried about the guards per se. The avatar was a creature of energy fields, holograms and nannites, not a human being subject to the vagaries of flesh and blood. Furthermore, even the avatar was protected by a field more than proof against the darts of the guards. But something about them always made him shudder.

He entered the Council Chamber and stopped, looking at the new addition on the back wall.

"Do you like it?" Paul asked from over his left shoulder.

Chansa shook his head at the indoor waterfall and stream that now took up half the chamber.

"I don't know," he admitted. "It's *pretty*."

"I didn't summon it because it is *pretty*," Paul rasped.

Chansa turned to look at the head of the New Destiny Movement and tried not to let the shock show on his face; Paul looked like a skeleton. He was wearing nothing but rags and was shoeless. His hair had been allowed to grow out and now hung in his eyes in greasy strings. His fingernails had grown out as well, and there was a feral light in his eyes. He also stank as if he had not washed in days, not just the somewhat pleasant reek of body odor but a less pleasant undertone of funk.

"I walk the world, you know," Paul said, walking towards the water. "I visit my people and watch over them. I care for them and guard them in their sleep. But their life is so hard, so hard."

"Yes, Paul, but it's for the good of mankind," Chansa said uneasily.

"Of *course* it is," Paul snarled back. "But I cannot simply ignore their tragedy. I must *live* it. If it is good enough for the people then it is good enough for me."

Chansa looked at the falls and saw the pile of clothes by the side of the river. He began to get a sinking feeling about what they represented.

"As my avatars wander the world I come here to work," Paul said, dropping to his knees. "I work and I work and I work . . ."

Chansa watched him as the leader of half the world dipped the clothes in the swirling water and rubbed them on the rocks.

"I brought these back from a peasant woman who was

washing them by a river," Paul said. "I told her I would wash them for her. And I will."

"I see," Chansa replied. "Paul, have you been eating?"

"I eat what the people eat," Bowman responded. "Once a day I have a bowl of beans. On Sundays I add a little meat. I am one of the people. I will eat as the people do."

Chansa had spent enough time with his partisan groups that he knew that what Paul was saying had some truth. But only as an *average*. There were people who were starving, still. On the other hand, there were people who were eating very well indeed, especially the ones that he had promoted to positions of command. He had to say that what Paul was limiting himself to was even a *low-end* average daily food consumption.

If he starves himself to death, who gets the Key? Chansa wondered.

Only thirteen percent die-off, well under her estimates. Humans had, again, astounded her. And with the return of the terraforming power she again had sufficient energy to prevent non-human-induced catastrophe. The societies were reconstructing and many of them showed promise of tremendous growth. All in all an interesting outcome to the induced disaster.

It was going to be interesting to see how it all turned out. With that thought, Mother returned to her eternal vigil.